SARAH HARRIET BURNEY, THE ROMANCE OF PRIVATE LIFE (1839)

Chawton House Library Series: Women's Novels

Series Editors: *Stephen Bending*
Stephen Bygrave

Titles in this Series

The Histories of Some of the Penitents in the Magdalen-House
edited by Jennie Batchelor and Megan Hiatt

Stéphanie-Félicité de Genlis, *Adelaide and Theodore, or Letters on Education*
edited by Gillian Dow

E. M. Foster, *The Corinna of England*
edited by Sylvia Bordoni

Forthcoming Titles

Alicia LeFanu, *Strathallan*
edited by Anna M. Fitzer

Sarah Harriet Burney, *The Romance of Private Life* (1839)

Edited by

Lorna J. Clark

LONDON AND NEW YORK

First published 2008 by Pickering & Chatto (Publishers) Limited

Published 2016 by Routledge
2 Park Square, Milton Park, Abingdon, Oxfordshire OX14 4RN
711 Third Avenue, New York, NY 10017, USA

First issued in paperback 2016

Routledge is an imprint of the Taylor & Francis Group, an informa business

BRITISH LIBRARY CATALOGUING IN PUBLICATION DATA

Burney, Sarah Harriet, 1772–1844
The romance of private life
1. English – Italy – Fiction 2. Psychic trauma – Fiction 3. Gothic novels
I. Title II. Clark, Lorna J.
823.7[F]

ISBN 13: 978-1-138-23595-3 (pbk)
ISBN 13: 978-1-8519-6873-2 (hbk)

Typeset by Pickering & Chatto (Publishers) Limited

CONTENTS

To my mother and father

ACKNOWLEDGEMENTS

It takes a village to raise a child and a community to produce an edition. Many people have contributed along the way whom I would like to acknowledge.

I would first of all like to thank the series editors, Stephen Bending and Stephen Bygrave, who tracked me down in London where I had narrowly escaped the July 2005 transit-bombing to invite me to contribute. The project has seemed to me ever since bound up with the heightened feelings of that time. Both have been wonderfully supportive and helpful throughout and it has truly been a privilege to work with them. I would also like to thank Mark Pollard and his staff at Pickering & Chatto for their firm commitment to the project of bringing out the works of women writers, and for ensuring the quality of the product. I am grateful to Chawton House Library, and in particular to the librarian Helen Scott, for allowing the text to be copied and for giving me such a warm welcome when I visited.

Carleton University has provided me with a hospitable venue in which to work and knowledgeable and interested colleagues to draw upon. In particular, I would like to thank Robert Holton, Paul Keen, Donald Beecher and Andrew Wallace in the department of English; Sébastien Côté and Maud Revel in the Department of French; and Richard Smith in the Department of Earth Sciences, each of whom helped in specific ways. Christine Taylor of the Interlibrary Loans Department has been unfailingly helpful. The support and administrative staff at Carleton maintain a positive and constructive atmosphere: Karen MacKinnon, Mireille Fournier, Darlene Gilson, Mark Robinson and Jean-Charles Côté all facilitated my work in practical ways.

My student helpers Erica Leighton and Shyla Taylor were creative in their responses to the diverse demands on their ingenuity and showed an enthusiasm and energy above and beyond the call. Terry McIntyre helped at a late stage to catch any errors before going to press.

Like many a fictional heroine, I am indebted on my journey to the kindness of strangers. For specific problems, I sent out queries to the broader scholarly community, and am indebted to Carolyn D. Williams, Nancy Mayer, Dawn

Lewcock and Joel Berson for answering the call. On the FRANCOFIL list, I would like to thank Anne Freadman and Colin Connolly for their interest.

The community of Burney scholars and the Burney Society have become like an extended family to me, a never-failing source of support, encouragement and inspiration. Several in particular have given generously of their time and expertise for this project. I would like to express my sincere gratitude to Stewart Cooke, Hester Davenport, Isobel Grundy, Betty Rizzo, Peter Sabor, Geoffrey Sill, Gordon Turnbull and John Wiltshire for sustaining me with their friendship and sharing with me their knowledge.

For permission to quote from my articles published in *Lumen*, I would like to thank the co-editors, Claire Grogan and Ugo Dionne.

This project has been generously supported by the Social Sciences and Humanities Research Council of Canada.

Finally, my dearest and most faithful readers, long-time converts to the novels of Sarah Harriet Burney, did not live to see this project completed. I have dedicated this volume to their memory.

ABBREVIATIONS

Catalogue	*A Catalogue of the Miscellaneous Library of the late Charles Burney ... which will be sold by Auction by Leigh and Sotheby ... On Thursday, the 9th of June, 1814, and Eight following Days* ([London], [1814]).
Letters	*The Letters of Sarah Harriet Burney*, ed. L. J. Clark (Athens, GA: University of Georgia Press, 1997).
JL	*The Journals and Letters of Fanny Burney (Madame d'Arblay)*, ed. J. Hemlow et al., 12 vols (Oxford: Clarendon Press, 1972–84).
Larousse	*Grand Larousse de la Langue Francaise*, 7 vols (Paris: Larousse, 1971–8).
ODNB	*Oxford Dictionary of National Biography*, online edn, ed. L. Goldman, www.oup.com [accessed January 2008].
OED	*Oxford English Dictionary*, 2nd edn, 20 vols (Oxford: Clarendon Press, 1989).
Scholes	P. A. Scholes, *The Great Doctor Burney*, 2 vols (London: Oxford University Press, 1948).
SHB	Sarah Harriet Burney

INTRODUCTION

The Romance of Private Life (1839) represents a culmination of the literary career of Sarah Harriet Burney (1772–1844). Overshadowed in her lifetime and since by the reputation of her half-sister, she was a writer of talent whose novels were enjoyed by Jane Austen and preferred by some readers to those of Frances Burney. The two tales that make up her last work, published within a few years of her death, bring into focus the themes and ideas which preoccupied her throughout her lifetime.

Sarah Harriet Burney was born on 29 August 1772 in King's Lynn, Norfolk, the second of two children of Charles Burney and Elizabeth Allen. Her father was forty-six and her mother forty-four when she was born; the marriage was a second one for both parents after a first spouse had died. With one brother four years older, she had three half-siblings on her mother's side and six on her father's, the closest in age being more than ten years older. Born in the same year as her eldest niece, Sarah Harriet essentially grew up with the next generation. The large blended family remained an important network throughout her life but also a source of conflict which is reflected in her fiction.

Her earliest years were spent in Norfolk with her mother's family. In one of her novels, a shy child traumatized by the loss of a grandmother is introduced into a lively family, an incident which may be based on memories of arriving in London in 1775 to join her father's household. 'Little Sally is come home, & is one of the most innocent, artless, queer little things you ever saw',[1] wrote Frances Burney. Luxuriant hair was the best feature of her appearance which was not otherwise prepossessing, as she was ruefully aware.

The household in St Martin's Street was a busy one. Her father's career was blossoming, helped by the publication of his tours and *History of Music* (1776); a fashionable teacher of music, he entertained celebrities in his home with informal concerts that must have created a stir, even for a child in the nursery. Her half-brother, Captain James Burney, served in the navy, appearing at home on leave. Sarah Harriet was five in 1778 when Frances Burney's first novel, *Evelina*,

1 F. Burney, *The Early Journals and Letters of Fanny Burney*, ed. L. E. Troide et al., 6 vols (Oxford: Clarendon Press, 1988–), vol. 2, p. 163.

was published; witnessing her subsequent lionization may have inspired Sarah Harriet to try something similar when she grew up.

In 1781, Sarah Harriet was sent with her brother Richard to Switzerland for two years. Her tutelage under a French-speaking governess was her only formal education. She played the piano, though not very well (in her father's eyes), and showed prowess in drawing and languages. Like her sisters, she was left to range freely through her father's library and loved books, 'the dear mute companion[s]' of her life.[2] An awkward teenager, she disdained trying to improve her looks by attention to fashion. In 1786, when the last of her siblings left home, she remained alone with her parents: her mother, an assertive woman nicknamed 'the Lady' by her hostile stepchildren, and her father, who penned a poem to her on the day she turned a 'giddy, thoughtless, wild 14'.[3] The following year, Charles Burney moved into apartments at the Royal Hospital, Chelsea, which remained (with one decade's interruption) Burney's home-base from the age of fifteen to almost fifty.

In 1796, she published her first novel, *Clarentine*. Family connections probably paved the way with her father's friends and publishers. Advertised on 7 July, her novel appeared almost simultaneously with her sister's *Camilla*, a work which Charles Burney ardently promoted, while dismissing patronizingly his youngest daughter's effort.[4] It was left to her mother's relatives to try to ensure good reviews, an offer which Burney proudly refused; the reviewers were mildly complimentary and indicated that the authorship was an open secret.

An emotional watershed of a different kind occurred the same year with the loss of her mother. Her duties as nurse gave way to the care of her seventy-year-old father, who described her as a 'steady & prudent house-keeper'.[5] However, life alone with Charles Burney did not have the salutary effect on her character predicted by Frances Burney (ever-resentful of her stepmother and family); on the contrary, tensions developed and she complained of 'her Father's Severity and Coldness' towards her. On his part, Charles Burney had imbibed '*dreadful* Apprehensions' of her closeness to her half-brother James who was meanwhile separating from his wife and proposed boarding with his father, a suggestion which was refused. The next day, James and Sarah Harriet Burney left Chelsea together, forming an unconventional household for the next five years. While critics have jumped to the conclusion that the relationship was incestuous, such an allegation appears

2 *Letters*, p. 137.

3 Cited in 'Introduction' to *Letters*, p. xxxiv.

4 See my 'Jane Austen and Sarah Harriet Burney', *Persuasions*, 17 (1995), pp. 16–25, on p. 17; and 'Sarah Harriet Burney, Sister-Novelist', *Lumen*, 19 (2000), pp. 121–34, on pp. 121–2.

5 Charles Burney to Frances (Burney) d'Arblay, 2 December 1796, cited in 'Introduction' to *Letters*, p. xxxv.

unlikely.[6] Nevertheless, she seems to have had a special relationship with her half-brother, who provided the model for the hero in some of her works.

Life with James, begun with such high hopes, turned out to be somewhat disappointing (a pattern which recurs). After staying the first year near Bristol, they led an unsettled existence in London in a series of seedy lodgings, 'living in the most Grovling mean Style'. Although at first 'the Active life' agreed with her, eventually it grated, while the hastiness of James's temper added to the strain. Consciousness of her tenuous position as spinster begins at this time: 'I begin very devoutely to take the part of all old maiden Aunts', she wrote the year she turned thirty.[7] Her financial position certainly worsened; over the five years, she spent about one-third of her small capital. Finally, she adopted a new plan, taking a position as governess in the autumn of 1803.

Burney spent four years with the Wilbraham family who would remain lifelong friends and correspondents. Initially the luxurious surroundings and genteel pursuits came as a relief, although the tedium of her occupation would pall after a while. Mrs Wilbraham, a celebrated beauty in her day, was 'gentle, & elegant'; her two grown-up daughters were 'sweet-tempered, sociable, chearful' and accomplished.[8] The four lovely daughters (an eldest sister having died) may have inspired the Le Strange family in *The Renunciation*. The youngest was (like Bertha Strange) the least brilliant, even slow, but loyal and affectionate; she would also marry an older man who 'makes her very happy'.[9]

In 1807, the grand-daughter who had been keeping house for Charles Burney married. Expressing regret for 'her late rash & undutiful desertion' and her desire of making 'reparation',[10] Sarah Harriet moved back into her old apartments at Chelsea to care for the octogenarian. The first use she made of her increased leisure-time was to write a second novel, the epistolary *Geraldine Fauconberg*. Published in September 1808, it was praised by the reviewers as a 'faithful picture of genteel life'.[11]

This was not the only literary activity she pursued. As her father's amanuensis, Burney not only conducted his correspondence but transcribed his manuscripts, which may have encouraged her to dabble in writing 'little private reviews',[12] editing and translating to supplement her resources. She seems to have needed the

6 The possibility of incest was first raised by Joyce Hemlow in *The History of Fanny Burney* (Oxford: Clarendon Press, 1958), pp. 281–5, and is discussed in my 'Introduction' to *Letters*, pp. xxxvi–xl, with details in *Letters*, pp. 33–51, including passages from the letters of Maria (Allen) Rishton quoted here.

7 *Letters*, p. 43.

8 *Letters*, pp. 51–2.

9 *Letters*, p. 457.

10 Cited in *Letters*, p. 87, n. 1.

11 *Critical Review*, 16 (1809), pp. 104–5.

12 *Letters*, p. 116.

cash. 'Though there were no complaints of the old man's parsimony',[13] somehow both caregivers for the elderly Charles Burney managed to rack up debts. Sarah Harriet certainly spoke with relish of the profits she would make from a third work of fiction, this time offered to Henry Colburn, a more aggressive publisher, who paid her £50 a volume (a respectable figure) while insisting on her name on the title page. *Traits of Nature*, which came out on 25 April 1812, was the first of her works published under her name, the lustre of which Colburn exploited. His acumen certainly paid off; a commercial success, the first edition sold out within four months.[14]

Other than her literary ventures, Burney's life was 'dull, monotonous, and lonely',[15] confined to home by the care of a querulous invalid who expected her constant attendance. She rarely ventured out and found solace in books. The restrictions chafed, with heated exchanges described in her letters. When the end came on 12 April 1814, it was clear that Charles Burney had never forgiven her; in his will, he left her just £1,000 and £100 more 'if ever she marries' which brought her income up to £85.[16]

Deprived of her home, she moved to another apartment but found it difficult to make ends meet. She had recourse to various expedients, including sharing with a room-mate and tutoring, but also turned to her pen, and at the urging of her publisher undertook to write a series of tales. The first of her *Tales of Fancy*, entitled *The Shipwreck*, which shows the continuing influence of James, was published on 28 November 1815 (imprint date 1816), for which she received £100. After suffering from a possible breast cancer, she did not publish her second tale, *Country Neighbours; or The Secret*, until 30 December 1819 (imprint 1820).[17] The story is told by a spinster in her forties (like Burney herself) who watches the love affair of a beautiful niece; it inspired a sonnet by Charles Lamb.[18]

Later that year, tiring of her 'solitary paradise',[19] she decided on a new scheme to reduce her living expenses. Through the Wilbrahams, she was hired as companion to a wealthy young invalid. The post lasted just one year (1821–2) since her own ill-health and possible depression (following the death of her half-brother James) had interfered with the performance of her duties. However, the effect of having spent months living in Hamilton House, surrounded by casts of the Elgin marbles, had given her 'a taste for the antique'[20] and a strong desire to travel.

13 Hemlow, *The History of Fanny Burney*, p. 321.

14 *Letters*, p. 159, n. 9.

15 *Letters*, p. 284.

16 Scholes, vol. 2, p. 262; *Letters*, p. 185, n. 2.

17 *Letters*, p. 195, n. 1, pp. 197, 198, n. 7, p. 217, n. 2.

18 *Morning Chronicle*, 13 July 1820.

19 *Letters*, p. 221.

20 *Letters*, p. 235.

Another opportunity opened up almost immediately; a family friend, Lord Crewe, hired Burney to take charge of his grand-daughters at a generous salary of £300. Life at Crewe Hall was like 'being at a large Hotel' where visitors came and went, 'as in a Magic-Lanthorn'. Some discomfiture arose from contact with the 'superfines',[21] who ignored her, and with a widowed clergyman who flattered her with his attentions but then withdrew. At fifty-two, she may have received a proposal from the uncle of her charges, a gentleman twenty years her senior, the Revd James Greville.[22] To have turned down such an offer must have required courage; her dilemma was not unlike that of Miss Flemming in *The Hermitage* and the wooing must surely have been similar, countenanced by members of the family. When the Crewes had to retrench, however, Sarah Harriet was manoeuvred into resigning in 1829.

Set suddenly at liberty, she lost no time in fulfilling a long-held ambition. She set out from London with a Swiss voiturier in July 1829 and made her way to Lausanne whence after some months she 'crossed the Simplon, & repaired to beautiful Florence'.[23] By 25 November she was in Rome, where she met up with Henry Crabb Robinson, who, with several young travellers, squired her round the sights of Rome; their company and attention greatly enlivened her stay.

On 10 March 1830, she went to stay with the Wilbrahams in Florence, where she enjoyed 'easy access' to villas and gardens[24] and the society of English expatriates. For the summer, she joined her favourite niece Charlotte Barrett at the Baths of Lucca; however, friction developed between them leading to a coolness that lasted for years. The second winter in Florence was quieter, as she withdrew from the 'few English fine gents' she knew[25] and stopped attending formal parties where she felt ill at ease. She occupied herself by drawing, reading French and Italian, and writing a tale (the first in this volume) which allowed her to 'live in a little ideal world' of her own.[26] When Robinson arrived in May, he found her ensconced in his former lodgings with two Italian ladies who associated with the poet Niccolini. With the 'first fervour' towards Italy 'gradually abated' and her English friends leaving, she remained isolated, craving 'family intelligence'.[27] While appreciating the cheapness of living abroad, she was anxious to return to England but lacked courage to make the journey alone. After three years, she found safe conveyance, and arrived back in the autumn of 1833, 'all life & spirit'.[28]

21 *Letters*, p. 251.

22 See 'Introduction' to *Letters*, p. xlviii.

23 *Letters*, p. 457.

24 *Letters*, p. 304.

25 *Letters*, p. 328.

26 *Letters*, p. 227.

27 *Letters*, p. 348.

28 *JL*, vol. 12, p. 807.

Within a few months, she established herself at Bath in a ladies' boarding-house 'open at one end to the hills & fields',[29] with an odd assortment of spinsters and widows. Finding their society not 'intellectual' enough, she tried sharing an apartment with a 'friendly associate'[30] but quickly tired of her companion and moved back into her former quarters. She soon described herself as 'a Hermitess',[31] and was 'growing old very fast'.[32] When a series of illnesses depleted her resources, she was helped by Frances Burney, who left her an annuity of £200 when she died in 1840.[33] It was because she needed the money (she claimed) that she revised two tales and published them in 1839 as *The Romance of Private Life*. In 1841, she moved to Cheltenham where she enjoyed the company of men as well as women in her boarding-house and the animated scene on the promenade. With sight and hearing beginning to fail, she enjoyed a summer's convalescence with Charlotte Barrett. Her pupils were also faithful to the end, which came on 8 February 1844. In her will, she left momentoes to nieces and former pupils and divided the income of her estate (about £120) between a nephew and niece.[34]

II

Sarah Harriet Burney's literary career is remarkably consistent. The issues raised in her earlier fiction come to fruition in her last work, *The Romance of Private Life*. Aptly named, all of her writing deals with 'private life' as she explores the domestic circle and its function either as sanctuary or site of oppression. She also felt obligated to develop a romance, but only out of deference to her audience: 'I never insert love but to oblige my readers', she claimed;[35] she preferred aiming for wit and humour. It is remarkable how similar are the patterns and structures which can be traced through fifty years of writing; what changes is her developing skill in blending satire and romance and her power to convey her message successfully.

All of Burney's fiction involves some sort of loss or dislocation for the heroine, but *The Renunciation* begins with the most dramatic and violent of all – a kidnapping, which wrenches the heroine into an unknown and frightening world. Starting *in medias res* with a crowd pouring out of the theatre in Cheltenham, the whisper of 'Silence – or you die!' electrifies a stumbling child, and changes her life forever. In choosing a young heroine and following her progress, Burney shows the effect on character of early trauma and rupture of identity.

29 *Letters*, p. 385.

30 *Letters*, p. 400.

31 *Letters*, p. 432.

32 Henry Crabb Robinson, 6 June 1835, Diaries, cited in *Letters*, p. 396, n. 2.

33 *JL*, vol. 12, p. 978.

34 *Letters*, pp. 485–6.

35 *Letters*, p. 201.

Nor is this the only separation the heroine must undergo. The sense of bewilderment is multiplied in a series of removals. The most drastic is the separation from her early protectors but these are not (the reader learns) her actual parents, so her current bereavement builds on an earlier loss that makes her (not surprisingly for a Burney heroine) an orphan.[36] She also misses the countryside; transplanted to an urban landscape, she 'gazed through the little dingy window ... and sought to see the sky' (p. 16). She loses her companions, culture and language; she is 'without the means of making [herself] understood' (p. 14). After a long journey to Paris, 'she awoke late, and found herself alone' and gave way to 'a transport of grief' (p. 30). A final parting with her chaperone 'renewed many of those feelings of desolation she had experienced on being first torn from her early protectors' (p. 36).

Of all Burney's heroines, Agnes's sense of alienation is the most extreme; one grief cascades upon another as if she is condemned to repeat the original trauma. The striking opening to the tale has been remarked by critics; Isobel Grundy notes that 'it presents with convincing subjectivity'[37] the experience of the homesick child. The depth of resonance suggests a personal connection: the bewildering journey, shock of sudden immersion in French, and frightening awakening in a strange bed may draw on childhood memories (of her trip to Switzerland). Added to Agnes's sources of discomfiture are the imposition of a change of wardrobe, routine and occupation, even the novelty of schooling – all contribute to her sense of a loss of identity, and the need to construct a new one.

The name of the heroine caused problems from the start. Burney had trouble choosing one, so her name changes both prior to and during the story. First called Margaret, she was next named Emily[38] (which would have worked well in French) and finally emerges as Agnes, after the virgin saint whose name evokes Agnus Dei or 'Lamb of God'. The religious connotations of the name are exploited by Burney long before Dickens; Agnes is likened to 'a St. Cecilia' (p. 58) or 'a guardian angel' (p. 183).

Early on, Mr Wharton orders her to change her name to Lucy de Vere. Derived from the Latin for 'light' and 'vere' meaning 'true', the name signifies the heroine's integrity, 'of truth'. At one level, the name seems ironic, since its adoption implies her participation in a 'scheme of deception', but it is actually doubly ironic because the connotations are appropriate for her character, which displays the 'noblest disinterestedness' throughout (p. 78). The name 'de Vere'

36 None of Burney's seven heroines have both parents at story's end: three are orphans; two lose their mothers; just one mother survives. Fathers are more hardy; there are three, none of them sympathetic.

37 V. Blain, P. Clemens and I. Grundy (eds), *The Feminist Companion to Literature in English* (London: B.T. Batsford, 1990), p. 160.

38 *Letters*, pp. 355, 375.

could also be seen as a gentrified form of the plain surname it replaces, 'Danvers', which (with 'ver' and 'da') sounds like an anglicized version. The word-play raises deeper questions about the process of naming while implying that the heroine's character remains incorruptible. Agnes's dual identity but single-minded nature is suggested when she flees her luxurious surroundings for a humble dwelling; even in shabby clothing, her resemblance to the richly dressed heiress is recognized. Like layers of an onion being stripped away, Burney's text raises questions about the inscription of feminine identity.

The story follows a conventional pattern for 'feminocentric novels of social initiation', the basic plot being the heroine's quest for self-discovery and acceptance into patriarchal society. As an orphan, she needs to find a family to confirm a sense of belonging and construct a social persona. Agnes is seen at the moment of her coming out at that 'generative moment of narration', her entrance into the adult world.[39] She experiences the classic adolescent anxiety, rendered here as literal truth, of feeling alien to the parental figures in her life; she calls herself an 'impostor' (p. 48). The quest begins when she sees the name of lost kin and sets out in search. Her purpose, expressed in religious terms, suggests the importance of what she seeks. '"Heaven be praised! he lives, and I shall find him!"' (p. 50). In a sculpture depicting Oedipus, Agnes is fittingly identified with Antigone, the type of filial devotion, although it is not paternal but fraternal recognition that she seeks (brothers being of significance in Burney): 'Next to the authority of a father was that of a brother ... [who] was of all protectors the one she had most reason to desire' (p. 50). This desire will drive her across the face of Europe.

Dressed in disguise (signifying her adoption of a new role), the heroine leaves home in an escape that seems coded as an elopement but represents rather a quest for independence – not unlike the most dramatic moment of Burney's own life when she suddenly absconded from the family home. For the second time in her fiction, she visualizes the scene that unfolds when an absence is discovered: the unsuspecting father's arrival home, his discovery of the farewell note, and his mild reaction whose 'moderation and placability surprised and touched her' (p. 123). There is sympathy for the deserted though guilty father: '"Oh had I but been blessed," he cried, "with such a daughter!"' (p. 134), whose irony does not strike on first reading.

Like other heroines (including Clarentine and Adela of *Traits of Nature*), Agnes pursues 'the security of self-possession through a series of female alliances',[40] hence the importance of Lady Glenfeld and the Le Stranges in countenancing

39 N. K. Miller, *The Heroine's Text: Readings in the French and English Novel, 1722–1782* (New York: Columbia University Press, 1980), pp. 4–5. The argument also draws on my article 'The Family in the Novels of Sarah Harriet Burney', *Lumen* 20 (2001), pp. 71–81. I am grateful to co-editors Claire Grogan and Ugo Dionne for their permission to cite from my articles in *Lumen*.

40 Miller, *The Heroine's Text*, p. 150.

her departure. Like Clarissa, one of Agnes's first acts in her lodging is to set up the lifeline of correspondence; she orders in 'a quire of good writing paper, a small bottle of ink, half a dozen of pens, and a stick of sealing-wax' (p. 94). Soon she happily replicates the situation of an epistolary heroine, closeted in solitude, with hourly bulletins going back and forth; for a while, her correspondence constitutes the narrative with letters of commentary enclosing others that advance the plot. Agnes proves herself capable of managing her own life, apportioning her time rationally in her 'quiet and safe retreat' (p. 129), taking air and exercise, practising music and drawing; she is even able to support herself from the sale of her sketches.

The tale soon takes a swerve as the journey-motif intensifies and the heroine takes to the road on a pilgrimage to discover her origins. Travelling the same route followed by Burney herself in 1829, she sets off through France, crosses the Simplon and pauses in Milan and Florence on her way to Rome. While describing the journey, Burney stops short of providing a full travelogue, since 'so much has of late years been written on the subject of Italy' (pp. 160–1). At the end of her journey, Agnes sets up as a portrait-painter and (unlike *The Wanderer*) manages to become self-sufficient and proficient in her profession. Agnes shows none of the self-pity or squeamishiness that characterized Frances Burney's heroine; Sarah Harriet's protagonists tend to be practical, self-disciplined and unsentimental. Once her capacity for autonomy has been established, the quest for identity has in some sense been fulfilled. With a new self-confidence, the heroine is now prepared for a series of revelations.

True to the 'juste milieu' to which she must accommodate herself, Agnes finds what she is seeking but not in the way she expects: 'the favourite wish of her heart – that of finding herself possessed of a brother' (p. 176) is dashed. Like other Burney heroines, Agnes feels the crushing 'bitterness of sorrow', a Hardyesque moment of loneliness in the face of an uncaring universe: 'Once more she saw herself a lone being in creation ... she was without kindred – without a home – without even a name she could legally appropriate ... [which] filled her with grief, terror, and self-compassion' (pp. 178–9).

Her sense of self-worth is confirmed with the discovery that Mr St Hubert, an avuncular figure, proves to be her real uncle, which requires yet another change of name. Fortuitously, the love match she makes is with the rightful heir of the estate, so the fortune comes to her anyway (and with a dowry from her uncle, even her status as heiress is retained). Equally important are the sisterly ties she has formed with the Le Stranges. All converge on England to form a supportive family group within easy distance of each other. This use of overly 'ingenious incident' was mocked by the reviewers;[41] it is, however, in keeping

41 Review of *The Romance of Private Life*, by Sarah Harriet Burney, *Athenaeum*, 625 (19 October 1839), p. 793

with the upward trajectory of the orphan-heroine. The period of testing is over and she has learned how to integrate herself into society; her progress to maturity is symbolized when a new family group crystallizes around her that confirms her self-discovery and social success.

Rather than a tissue of coincidences, the machinery of the plot could be seen as a providential confirmation of the internal fitness of things that ironically bears witness to Mr Wharton's rationalization of restoring her 'to her proper station' (p. 48) or to the supposition that Agnes was his natural daughter. Trying the patience of the reviewers even further is the unexpected discovery that the little girl kidnapped at random turns out to be, unbeknownst to himself, Mr Wharton's long-lost daughter. With this final revelation, the layers of the onion are completely peeled away; after the multiple removals and the struggle to win acceptance, Agnes discovers that the web of kin-like relations she has built proves to be identical with her family of origin. She has in effect reconstructed her own kinship group. The point is surely that she has won their affection on her own merits, with family ties renewed and reinvigorated.

As ingenious as the plot sounds, the circular motion would become the norm for nineteenth-century domestic novels in which the heroine does not so much 'cross over to something new' but rather prolongs her stay 'in her family of origin'; marriage is simply a way of incorporating 'new life ... into the old'. Burney's work points forward to the novels of Dickens, another writer who codes romantic relationships as fraternal and charts a circuitous path for the heroine: 'the daughter's marriage is simply the means by which she can arrive at an improved relationship with her father'.[42]

Curiously, in Burney's tale, there will be no father-daughter reconciliation, although the way is prepared – in their mutual appreciation, in Agnes's instinctive sympathy, and in Mr St Hubert's offer of support. Yet Mr Wharton though admittedly 'neither demon nor angel' is left out of the charmed circle. His own narrative 'reads like the story of a hero of romance'; it ends happily when he marries a wealthy widow, an outcome he sees as 'the work of destiny' (p. 222). He too suffers from a form of repetition-compulsion; reading against the grain, one finds in his story a tragic pattern that replicates itself, with the loss of two wives and two daughters. As a potential narrative enclosed within Burney's, his tale might end fittingly with another family gathered around him in America to substitute for the one he has lost.

In Burney's fiction, the use of repetition often indicates 'important material is struggling to get through'.[43] The pattern of neglected children resonates

42 P. M. Cohen, *The Daughter's Dilemma: Family Process and the Nineteenth-Century Novel* (Ann Arbor, MI: University of Michigan Press, 1991), p. 26.

43 M. A. Doody, *Frances Burney: The Life in the Works* (New Brunswick, NJ: Rutgers University Press, 1988), p. 10 (about Frances Burney).

throughout the tale. Agnes's travails begin with a stepmother; she is eclipsed by a younger half-sister whom she later replaces. Walsingham's childhood is a mirror-image of her own; he too was overlooked after his mother remarried, which 'affected him deeply' (p. 221). Even Mr St Hubert tells of sibling conflicts and a petted 'darling' of the family (p. 174). The tale of the spoiled little sister reverses the usual message in Burney's fiction, that of protest against the favouring of boys; she makes up for its absence by openly advocating mixed-gender education, presenting Lady Glenfeld as the happy result of allowing girls the same freedom to develop as their brothers.

Besides sibling rivalry and parental rejection, another recurring motif is that of financial fraud. Mr Wharton's misdeeds are echoed in the inset tale told by Walsingham. At a deeper level, the duplication of certain constructs reflects the deep sense of insecurity caused by imperfectly blended families such as Burney's own, recalling how equivocal was her position. In her fiction, the family malfunctions; ruptured by multiple marriages, it fails to provide a 'safe place in the wider world'.[44] The significance of coupling Agnes and Walsingham, brought together by adversity as the products of poor parenting, each empowered to 'taunt the other on the subject of their relations' (p. 218), is open to question as an assertion of positive values. The concluding marriage hardly seems to offer sufficient shelter in the storm, nor does it solve the problem that created orphans in the first place.

In the resolution that embraces all characters, Mr Wharton is not the only omission. No mention is made of the lovely child of Walsingham's sister who had tragically lost both parents. When last mentioned, the four-year-old orphan (just Agnes's age when her aunt found her) had been entrusted 'to the care of a Swiss Lady' (p. 170) with whom she is presumably left at story's end when the others return to England to begin their future together. In the tying up of narrative threads, she is nowhere mentioned. The reader is not even told her name. Presumably, her uncle Walsingham harbours no benevolent intentions towards her, nor does Agnes, it seems, desire to play the part of loving guardian. In the little girl left out of the final pages of *The Renunciation*, another deserted orphan-heroine has been created, left to confront her fate in the next generation or narrative.

All of Sarah Harriet Burney's fiction focuses on the family, with various aspects refracted as in a kaleidoscope. For from offering a sanctuary of peace and safety, it is marked by absence, silence and dysfunction. Burney is a pivotal figure who builds on the conventions of the eighteenth-century novel and carries them forward; with echoes of Austen, her work points towards Hardy, Dickens and Eliot. These innovations are nowhere more evident than in the last tale she ever wrote, *The Hermitage*.

44 N. Ackerman, *The Psychodynamics of Family Life: Diagnosis and Treatment of Family Relationships* (New York: Basic Books, 1958), p. 112.

III

Sarah Harriet Burney's last tale represents a new departure, introducing a startling element (a murder) which would have portentous consequences for the development of the novel. *The Hermitage* may well be a hitherto unnoticed forerunner of a new kind of fiction.[45] Until now, Wilkie Collins's *The Moonstone* (1868) or one of Edgar Allan Poe's stories has usually been cited as the first detective story in English. But Burney's tale was published two years before Poe's and long before what is supposedly the first crime novel written by a woman.[46] Drawing on the female gothic and domestic novels of the late eighteenth century, Burney's tale challenges assumptions about the patriarchal origin of the genre and places it firmly in the female tradition of the novel.

The tale seems to change direction part way through. There are signs that it was written in stages, which would account for certain inconsistencies (e.g. in the accounts of Ernest's boyhood). The tale 'about one third finished' that Burney worked on and completed in 1837 may be the one abandoned in 1821 after eighty pages had been written[47] which would explain the atmosphere of an earlier era combined with the influence of later literary developments. In the 1830s, Burney was intrigued by books on the 'Manners & Customs' of Egypt (which add exotic touches to the tale) and appreciated the humour of Dickens's early work.[48]

The Hermitage starts out conventionally with a dialogue outlining the family group at the centre of the action: a young debutante with a wealthy suitor encouraged by her scheming mamma; a childless uncle with a fortune to bestow; a hospitable half-sister and cynical brother-in-law who provides commentary. Later a handsome brother and childhood friend are added to the mix, which promises nothing more problematic than the working out of matrimonial projects and testamentary intentions.

Some interest is added by shades of the Gothic, with passages reminiscent of Radcliffe when Ella rambles through her uncle's grounds, musing nostalgically upon the 'picturesque hermitage' with its 'mossy seat' and 'rustic bench' (p. 245). These touches serve to remind the reader that Burney began her career in the 1790s, and they extend the hints of her earlier novels (haughty tyrants, hidden portraits and gloomy castles).

Burney has other intentions for the hermitage, though. There is a subplot with a rustic beauty, Ruth, linked in gossip to the two young men. If the tale sounds familiar, it may be because it has been used since. George Eliot's *Adam*

45 Some of the argument is drawn from my article, 'The Hermitage: Late Gothic or Early Detective Fiction?', *Lumen*, 23 (2004), pp. 165–87.

46 Anna Katharine Green's *The Leavenworth Case* (1878).

47 *Letters*, pp. 419, 230.

48 *Letters*, pp. 424, 439–40.

Bede has striking parallels to Burney's work: a country lass who aspires above her station; a passionate young squire who seduces her in the open air; a feast that brings out class differences, and a plain-speaking farmer's wife. A hermitage also features in Eliot, set in a grove of trees which is the site of an altercation. Books are associated with both; the scarf that Arthur Donnithorne hides has its counterpart in the neck-cloth that Frederic Ormond has laid aside. The two stories then diverge, but the sense of underlying guilt that erodes the fabric of the community is the same. There is a moment of frozen horror in *Adam Bede* when a fight between the two men seems lethal; Arthur lies lifeless on the ground and Adam kneels before him 'like an image of despair gazing at an image of death'.[49]

A similar moment occurs in Burney's hermitage that is finely done. After overhearing a quarrel between her brother Frederic and Ernest de Gray, Ella returns to find her brother apparently asleep: 'she leant forward to imprint a kiss upon his forehead' but found it 'unnaturally chill':

> ... she took courage to feel for the beating of his heart. Its pulsation seemed to have entirely stopped ... what was her additional horror when, on, withdrawing her hand, she beheld it dyed in blood, and felt the warm stream dropping from her fingers upon her garments!
>
> A piercing shriek escaped her, at the same moment that a vivid flash of lightning revealed to her the *Egyptian dagger* ... its blade was reeking with fresh blood! (pp. 285–6)

The shriek that escapes Ella pierces the air and ushers in a new form of fiction. The unheard of event ('Not in my grounds, surely?' comments Sir Everard; p. 290) shatters the peace of this rural society, and transforms the narrative completely. As a transgressive crime, it exposes a hidden evil that severs the ties that bind. The victim of a murder mystery is often one who has violated social norms; this is certainly true of Frederic, who has betrayed Ruth's trust and would now abandon her. Ernest, in attempting to prevent the catastrophe, has incurred his wrath, and the quarrel between them has apparently ended fatally. The secret sin, like the blood that soaks Ella's garments, will spread its stain across the rural landscape, destroying the family at the farm. Ruth takes her own life and the others leave; within a year, the last survivor has died. With her image of the web, Eliot traces the consequences of an evil deed; Burney hints at repercussions but restricts her focus primarily to the heroine.

The reader, who is directed by Ella's consciousness, shares her belief in Ernest's guilt. Ella is discovered lying 'motionless and wholly insensible,' on the floor (p. 286), weltering in her brother's blood. Her first action on regaining consciousness is to re-enter the hermitage alone. There is clearly some kind of sexual content in Ella's eerie sojourn with her brother's corpse, beginning with a kiss,

49 G. Eliot, *Adam Bede*, ed. V. Cunningham (Oxford: Oxford University Press, 1996), p. 301.

the orgiastic 'paroxysm of tears', the secreting of the bloody dagger (that phallic symbol) 'beneath her dress' and her casting it into the waters of a 'well known stream' (pp. 287–8). Ella emerges from the hermitage bloodied, harrowed and changed forever, her innocence irretrievably lost.

She returns to her room, removes her blood-soaked clothing and collapses on her bed where 'with clasped hands and tearful eyes, [she] lay mournfully meditating' (p. 289). She does not rise from this position for months, victim of a nearly fatal illness which threatens her life and reason, in a form of post-traumatic depression. Throughout her debilitating fever, she resists falling into a delirium for fear of implicating her lover. Keeping a grim hold on her consciousness, unable to move, afraid to speak, she presents a powerful image of passive female suffering. Hiding her knowledge of guilt, she pays the price for this ruthless self-suppression with a breakdown that changes her looks and personality.

Ella enacts on her own body the kind of self-control exerted by other Burney heroines whose virtue is measured by their success in controlling their emotions. Clarentine, Geraldine and Adela all dissemble their love so well that its revelation comes as a surprise; in *The Shipwreck*, Viola successfully disguises her gender, as well as her affection. Burney's last heroine represents an extreme form of stasis, suggesting repressed sexuality. I have argued elsewhere that her frozen state is 'emblematic of the female condition' in Burney's fiction, 'the ultimate extension of the forces' shown at work.[50] The heroine's very name suggests her symbolic quality, derived from the French pronoun 'elle' meaning simply 'she'.[51] Ella's fate may be taken as a comment on female destiny.

Many of the elements in Burney's tale appear in *The Moonstone*: the exoticism of the East with an underlying threat of violence; the return of a childhood companion; the sexual symbolism of the crime (the nocturnal visit to Rachel's room, the stealing of her jewel and the stained nightgown, all suggesting a 'symbolic defloration').[52] Even more striking, however, is the similarity of the heroine's reaction. Both tales simply extend the pattern of secrecy which 'was basic to the lives of all respectable women of the mid-nineteenth century'.[53]

The question might well be asked of Burney (as it is of Collins), 'How could [she] who was necessarily ignorant of the genre [s]he was helping to create, have

50 See my 'Frances and Sarah Harriet: The Novels in the Family and the Family in the Novels', in L. J. Clark (ed.), *A Celebration of Frances Burney* (Cambridge: Cambridge Scholars Press, 2007), pp. 38–56, on p. 52.

51 Doody remarks that 'a multitude of [Frances] Burney's female characters have that hidden "elle" or "ella," that supportive "she" in their names' (p. 40).

52 C. Rycroft 'A Detective Story: Psychoanalytic Observations', *Psychoanalytic Quarterly*, 26 (1957), pp. 229–45.

53 E. Showalter, 'Desperate Remedies: Sensation Novels of the 1860s', *Victorian Newsletter*, 49 (1976), pp. 1–5, on p. 2.

adhered so closely to so many of its conventions?'[54] Other devices that she uses would later become conventional, for instance the splitting of hero and villain, implying self-division, which would be used by Collins as well as Dickens. The doublings in *The Hermitage* blur the question of guilt and innocence and implicate all four lovers in the central action of the murder.

The murderer and victim may be read as alter-egos of the two principals, acting out their subconscious impulses. A hidden connection links Ella and Ruth, marked by their physical resemblance. Ella seems like a younger sister, her kitten-like playfulness emphasizing her innocence. Ruth is more stately; enigmatic in her beauty, she seems already to have hidden depths. The connection between Ernest and Frederic is equally evident, brought up as brothers, 'their footing in the family so nearly equal' (p. 297). They seem to share some past involvement with Ruth; the suggestion of a love triangle is never fully repudiated. Moreover, there is a hint of attraction between Ella and Frederic (continuing a motif of fraternal incest in Burney). Her rapturous greeting when she 'embraced him over and over again', her 'gazing upon him' in admiration (p. 260), the demonstrative affection between them, all give an added dimension to the jealous accusations Frederic makes of de Gray. These hidden connections everywhere (characteristic of the Gothic) make hero and heroine complicit in the 'primal scene' enacted at the farm[55] and involve them in the fate of Frederic and Ruth, who die in expiation of their sins.

As well as the Freudian doubling of characters, other patterns are repeated. Ella is not the only one to suppress knowledge; Ernest, too, hides his discovery of guilt; he does not reveal the murderer whose identity he protects. Like Ella, he keeps silence, a vow that is voluntary and seems inadequately motivated. When Ella appeals to him to 'pronounce but this short sentence: "I am innocent"' (p. 316), he avoids it by leaving the room. Both Ella and Ernest, then, could be seen as scapegoat figures, taking sins upon themselves, enacting guilt on their own bodies. They undergo a period of suffering and self-alienation, Ella in her catatonic trance, Ernest in his homeless wanderings. When the period of expiation is over, their union will herald a reconstitution of the family group in a community cleansed of evil with disruptive elements (murderer and victim) cast out. *The Hermitage* sustains a reading which links it to the catharsis of Greek tragedy or a figuring of the Christian myth. Another possible interpretation is a rite of initiation, a ritualistic sacrifice in the rural groves and magical atmosphere of the Hermitage.

A last doubling introduces a new level of complexity, that of the hero and murderer. Ernest and Wilfred are foster-brothers raised by the same nurse. On the morning of the murder, Wilfred is in Ernest's closet; his urge to revenge

54 S. Lonoff, *Wilkie Collins and His Victorian Readers: A Study in the Rhetoric of Authorship* (New York: AMS Press, 1982), p. 175.

55 G. Pederson-Krag, 'Detective Stories and the Primal Scene', *Psychoanalytic Quarterly* 18 (1949), pp. 207–14.

is kindled partly by Frederic's taunting of Ernest which he overhears. In fact, Ernest could be said to provide the weapon (the dagger), the motive (jealousy), the occasion (the quarrel) and the opportunity (in the hermitage). He is present when Wilfred confesses and conceals the crime that he condones. His involvement gives resonance to his refusal to assert his own blamelessness. Ernest's sense of culpability expresses the generalized guilt and anxiety familiar from the Gothic. But it cannot be denied that the murder works out most fortunately for de Gray in removing the only barrier to a fortune and the woman he loves. With the heir disposed of, the estate is divided between Ernest and Ella with a clause to encourage their marriage. Ernest changes his surname, replacing Frederic both literally and figuratively as heir. Frederic's bitter accusation that de Gray is aiming to supplant him may not be far-fetched. The beneficial outcome sheds new light on the two 'secret sharers' in the mystery, in their suppression of crucial elements – she, the weapon, and he, the murderer.

The strong testamentary incentives are the only conditions powerful enough to persuade Ella's ambitious mother to sanction the union. Early on, while cherishing in secret her low-born lover, Ella 'had no plan for the future ... to time she trusted' (p. 252). Her trust is amply justified. In the fullness of time, the tragedy in the hermitage unfolds, removing all impediments; murder is the means to fulfilment of her desire. The transgressive crime, then, is contained within the structure of the comedy of manners and functions as no more than a blocking device. Within a year of the purging murder, the community comes together to celebrate a happy marriage and a brighter future. There is even a hint that, like Anne Elliot and Esther Summerson, Ella begins to recover her looks.

In reading Burney's *The Hermitage* as a forerunner of detective fiction, there is one notable omission, the presence of a detective (partly due to the fact that the force would not be organized in England until 1842). The 'detection' is carried out by Sir George Arundel, who gathers the facts and pieces them together into a coherent narrative which (in the psychoanalytic interpretation), is 'the characteristic action of all detective fiction: the restatement and restructuring in the present of a past event'. He cross-examines witnesses, seeks clues and transforms 'a fragmented and incomplete set of events into a more ordered and complete understanding'[56] which he then interprets in an incriminating way. Similar actions occur throughout Burney's fiction with the same spirit of malice. Several of her characters suffer from misrepresentation due to deluding appearances and are pursued by a malignant fiend who tries to turn others against them. The actions of Sir George differ only in degree: 'it *is* calumny ... but it is calumny to blast a man's reputation' (p. 337). Societal disapproval is all-powerful, as Ernest realizes when his friends turn away, he does not dare to venture outside and he expects to be arrested. The

56 A. D. Hutter, 'Dreams, Transformations, and Literature: The Implications of Detective Fiction', *Victorian Studies*, 19 (1975), pp. 181–209.

ultimate result of the defamation of his character may be the sacrifice of his life (the literal fulfilment of his function as scapegoat), an outcome that is evoked but avoided. The pressures of societal expectations and the insistence on conformity are often shown in Burney, but usually impact on the heroine.

There is one figure beside Sir George who is left out of the happily reconstituted society, Mrs Ormond. Her exclusion continues a trend in Burney's fiction: Adela's father in *Traits of Nature* was not worth conciliating; Mr Wharton was left in America. *The Hermitage* contains the only mother in all of Burney's fiction who survives to the end, but her presence is rather discomfiting. She is far from being gratified by the concluding marriage and blames herself for the disaster of her ill-managed son. Frederic Ormond is the last in the line of indulged sons whose upbringing spoils their characters and who never learn self-discipline, a lesson the heroines absorb all too well. The novel ends on this note of protest.

The last point underlines the significance of according to this tale its rightful place in the history of the detective novel which would then acquire a maternal rather than paternal ancestry. Reading *The Hermitage* as an early example of murder mystery helps to show how the genre developed in a direct line from the female Gothic, incorporating elements from feminocentric novels and domestic fiction. When placed in the context of the entire opus of Sarah Harriet Burney, the features that characterize it in incipient form seem the natural outcome of patterns that have been present in her fiction all along. Burney may be seen as a pivotal figure whose work spans almost fifty years from the late eighteenth century to the early Victorian period. The rediscovery of her last work of fiction, the two tales comprising *The Romance of Private Life*, helps us to understand this complex writer in the context of her family, her society and her time, and yields insight into the forms and genres she uses to express herself.

SELECT BIBLIOGRAPHY

Works by Sarah Harriet Burney

Clarentine: A Novel, 3 vols (London: G. G. and J. Robinson, 1796).

Geraldine Fauconberg, 3 vols (London: G. Wilkie and J. Robinson, 1808).

Traits of Nature, 5 vols (London: Henry Colburn, 1812).

Tales of Fancy, 3 vols (London: Henry Colburn, 1816–20).

The Romance of Private Life, 3 vols (London: Henry Colburn, 1839).

Primary Material

'Appendix', *Annual Register*, 97 (1855), p. 300.

Austen, J., *The Novels of Jane Austen*, ed. R. W. Chapman, 3rd edn (1932–4), rev. M. Lascelles, 5 vols (London: Oxford University Press, 1963–9; rpt 1973).

Beaumont, F., and J. Fletcher, *The Dramatic Works in the Beaumont and Fletcher Canon*, ed. F. Bowers, 3 vols (Cambridge: Cambridge University Press, 1966–76).

Burke, E., *A Philosophical Enquiry into the Origin of our Ideas of the Sublime and Beautiful* (London, 1757).

Burney, C., *The Present State of Music in France and Italy*, 2nd edn (London, 1773).

Burney, F., *The Complete Plays of Frances Burney*, ed. P. Sabor, 2 vols (London: William Pickering, 1995).

—, *The Early Journals and Letters of Fanny Burney*, ed. L. E. Troide et al., 6 vols (Oxford: Clarendon Press, 1988–).

Chaucer, G., *The Canterbury Tales of Chaucer, Modernis'd by Several Hands, Publish'd by Mr. Ogle*, 3 vols (London, 1741).

Collins, W., *Odes on Several Descriptive and Allegoric Subjects* (London, 1747).

Corneille, P., *Le Cid* (Paris, 1637).

Cowper, W., *Poems* (London, 1782).

—, *The Task* (London, 1785).

[Croker, J. W.], Review of *Memoirs of Doctor Burney*, by Madame d'Arblay, *Quarterly Review*, 49 (1833), pp. 97–125.

Dante Alighieri, *The Vision: or, Hell, Purgatory, and Paradise, of Dante Alighieri*, trans. H. F. Cary (London, 1814).

Davies, H., *The Stranger's Guide through Cheltenham*, 3rd edn (Cheltenham: H. Davies, [1842]).

Dodsley, R. (ed.), *A Collection of Poems. By Several Hands*, 6 vols (London, 1758).

Drayton, M., *Poems* (London, 1619).

Dryden, J., *Fables* (London, 1700).

—, *Absalom and Achitophel* (London, 1681).

Eliot, G., *Adam Bede*, ed. V. Cunningham (Oxford: Oxford University Press, 1996).

Frankland, T., *Cautions to Young Sportsmen*, 2nd edn (London, 1801).

Forsyth, J., *Remarks on Antiquities, Arts, and Letters, during an Excursion in Italy* (London, 1813).

Gentleman's Magazine, n.s. 12 (1839), p. 521.

Goldsmith, O., *The Traveller, or a Prospect of Society* (London, 1764).

Gray, T., *Ode for Music* (London, 1769).

—, *Elegy Written in a Country Churchyard* (London, 1751).

Hawker, P., *Instructions to Young Sportsmen*, 5th edn (London, 1826).

Johnson, S., *The Idler*, 2 vols (London, 1761).

—, *The Rambler*, 6 vols (London, 1752).

Knox, V., *Christian Philosophy*, 2 vols (London, 1795).

La Fontaine, J. de, *La Fontaine's Fables*, trans. E. Marsh (London: William Heinemann, 1933).

Mason, W., *Elegies* (London, 1763).

Massinger, P., *The Dramatick Works of Philip Massinger*, 4 vols (London, 1779).

Milton, J., *Complete Poems and Major Prose*, ed. M. Y. Hughes (Indianapolis, IN: Bobbs-Merrill Co., 1975).

—, *Paradise Lost: A Poem in Twelve Books*, 2nd rev. edn (London, 1674).

Monthly Review, 46 (1805).

Moore, T., *The Loves of the Angels* (London, 1823).

More, H., *Coelebs In Search of a Wife* (London, 1819).

Pope, A., *The Dunciad* (London, 1728).

—, *Windsor Forest* (London, 1713).

—, *An Essay on Criticism* (London, 1711).

Radcliffe, A., *The Mysteries of Udolpho*, ed. B. Dobrée (Oxford: Oxford University Press, 1998).

Review of *The Romance of Private Life*, by Sarah Harriet Burney, *Athenaeum*, 625 (19 October 1839), p. 793.

Review of *The Romance of Private Life*, by Sarah Harriet Burney, *New Monthly Magazine*, 2nd series, 57 (1839), pp. 276–7.

Seneca's Morals by way of Abstract, ed. R. l'Estrange, 12th edn (London, 1722).

Shakespeare, W., *The Complete Works*, ed. S. Wells and G. Taylor (Oxford: Clarendon Press, 1986).

Spencer, W. R., *Poems* (London, 1811).

Tasso, T., *Jerusalem Delivered: An Heroic Poem*, trans. J. Hoole, 3rd edn, 2 vols (London, 1767).

Voltaire (F.-M.-Arouet), *Nanine*, in *The Complete Works of Voltaire*, ed. M. de Labriolle and C. Duckworth (Oxford: Voltaire Foundation, 1994), Vol. 31B.

The Times, September–December 1839.

West, J., *An Elegy on the Death of the Right Honourable Edmund Burke* (London, 1797).

Secondary Material

Ackerman, N., *The Psychodynamics of Family Life: Diagnosis and Treatment of Family Relationships* (New York: Basic Books, 1958).

Blain, V., P. Clemens and I. Grundy (eds), *The Feminist Companion to Literature in English* (London: B.T. Batsford, 1990).

Clark, L. J., 'Jane Austen and Sarah Harriet Burney', *Persuasions*, 17 (1995), pp. 16–25.

—, 'A Contemporary's View of Jane Austen', *Notes and Queries*, 241 (1996), pp. 418–20.

—, 'Sarah Harriet Burney, Sister-Novelist', *Lumen*, 19 (2000), pp. 121–34.

—, 'The Family in the Novels of Sarah Harriet Burney', *Lumen*, 20 (2001), pp. 71–81.

—, 'From the Margins to the Centre: The Spinster as Author, Narrator and Actor', *Burney Journal*, 6 (2003), pp. 36–54.

—, 'The Hermitage: Late Gothic or Early Detective Fiction?', *Lumen*, 23 (2004), pp. 165–87.

—, 'Frances and Sarah Harriet Burney: The Novels in the Family and the Family in the Novels', in L. J. Clark (ed.), *A Celebration of Frances Burney* (Cambridge: Cambridge Scholars Press, 2007), pp. 38–56.

Cohen, P. M., *The Daughter's Dilemma: Family Process and the Nineteenth-Century Novel* (Ann Arbor, MI: University of Michigan Press, 1991).

Doody, M. A., *Frances Burney: The Life in the Works* (New Brunswick, NJ: Rutgers University Press, 1988).

Foster, S., *Across New Worlds: Nineteenth-Century Women Travellers and their Writings* (New York and London: Harvester Wheatsheaf, 1990).

Hemlow, J., *The History of Fanny Burney* (Oxford: Clarendon Press, 1958).

Hibbert, C., *The Grand Tour* (London: Weidenfeld& Nicolson, 1969).

Hutter, A. D., 'Dreams, Transformations, and Literature: The Implications of Detective Fiction', *Victorian Studies*, 19 (1975), pp. 181–209

Koss, S., *The Rise and Fall of the Political Press in Britain* (London: Hamish Hamilton, 1981).

Lonoff, S., *Wilkie Collins and His Victorian Readers: A Study in the Rhetoric of Authorship* (New York: AMS Press, 1982).

Lonsdale, R., *Dr. Charles Burney: A Literary Biography* (Oxford: Clarendon Press, 1965).

MacAlpine, I., and R. Hunter, *George III and the Mad-Business* (London: Allen Lane, 1969).

Miller, N. K., *The Heroine's Text: Readings in the French and English Novel, 1722–1782* (New York: Columbia University Press, 1980).

Pederson-Krag, G., 'Detective Stories and the Primal Scene', *Psychoanalytic Quarterly*, 18 (1949), pp. 207–14; rpt in G. W. Most and W. W. Stowe (eds), *The Poetics of Murder: Detective Fiction and Literary Theory* (San Diego, CA: Harcourt Brace Jovanovich, 1983).

Pescio, C., *Complete Guide for Visiting the Uffizi* (Firenze: Il Turismo, 1979).

—, *Complete Guide for Visiting Pitti Palace* (Firenze: Il Turismo, 1981).

Rycroft, C., 'A Detective Story: Psychoanalytic Observations', *Psychoanalytic Quarterly*, 26 (1957), pp. 229–45.

Showalter, E., 'Desperate Remedies: Sensation Novels of the 1860s', *Victorian Newsletter*, 49 (1976), pp. 1–5.

Weinreb, B., and C. Hibbert, *The London Encyclopedia* (Bethesda, MD: Adler & Adler, 1986).

NOTE ON THE TEXT

No manuscript is known to have survived for any of the novels of Sarah Harriet Burney; however, there are several references in her letters to *The Romance of Private Life* which help to date its composition.

The first tale, *The Renunciation*, in which the heroine journeys across Europe from France to Italy, was written soon after the author had made such a journey herself in 1829. Having worked on her story the first winter in Florence (1830), she took it to Pisa in April 1831 where she read it to her niece Charlotte Barrett, who found it 'very pretty & amusing'.[1] Burney revised it over the summer, 'retaining such parts as seem ... a little worth it, and altering what relates to the family & origin of the heroine'.[2] More than a year later, she 'put the finishing stroke' to it and was pleased with the result, 'singularly, clever, pithy, and agreeable'.[3]

She took the manuscript back to England with her in 1833 but did not try to publish it, since she had 'but a very so so-ish opinion of it' and dreaded 'the toil of copying, or rather, of remodelling it'.[4] A few years later, however, after a long and expensive illness, she had second thoughts about the 'long-dormant M.S.' which might help defray expenses. She took out again the 'little work quite ready, written at Florence' (*The Renunciation*) and a second which was 'about one third finished'.[5] *The Hermitage* may be the tale begun years before as a continuation of her *Tales of Fancy* (1816–20). She had written eighty pages by February 1821 when she abandoned it.[6] The lapse in time (of almost twenty years) before its completion would explain the atmosphere of an earlier era, a lack of continuity in some of the characters and other discrepancies.

The publisher of Burney's previous two novels had been Henry Colburn, the 'principal publisher of novels and light literature of his time',[7] who had a keen eye

1 Charlotte (Francis) Barrett to Henry Barrett, 28–30 April [1831], cited in *Letters*, p. 343, n. 4.

2 *Letters*, p. 355.

3 *Letters*, p. 375.

4 *Letters*, p. 409.

5 *Letters*, p. 419.

6 *Letters*, pp. 230.

7 'Appendix', *Annual Register*, 97 (1855), p. 300; see also *ODNB*.

for the market; somewhat 'unscrupulous' in his dealings,[8] he was nevertheless a generous paymaster. Lacking a male relative as go-between, Burney deputed her friend Henry Crabb Robinson, who submitted the manuscript to Colburn on 14 November 1837 and was pleased to be relieved of his 'troublesome commission' by a 'favourable answer'.[9] Five months later, the publication intended for March was again delayed until October. Complaining of the antics of 'That arch-rogue Colburn!' and confessing her need of the money, Burney asked for her manuscript back.[10] She may have been mollified by an advance in 1838, although it was not until February 1839 that she was finally preparing the work for the press.[11]

On 13 September 1839, Henry Colburn began to advertise in *The Times* 'Miss Burney's new novel' as 'Just ready' (though it probably was not quite); advertisements appeared throughout September and October. The date of actual publication was probably between 26 and 30 September;[12] it was sold at 31*s.* 6*d.* The book was certainly out by 17 October, when Henry Crabb Robinson recorded reading it in his diary. *The Renunciation* 'is an interesting story', he wrote, 'but the tale is left incomplete'. A month later, on 15 November, he ventured on *The Hermitage* and then wrote to Burney to tell her his 'opinion of her two tales' which was 'favourable'.[13]

Known for his puffery, Colburn did his best to trade on the fame of the family name. 'By itself alone the name of Burney must prove a passport to a work of fiction' read one advertisement (quoting from one of his own publications).[14] 'The influence of the name still exists, and the present volumes are worthy of the family and lustre' was another opinion quoted from a 'Dispatch', no doubt Colburn's own.[15]

8 *ODNB*, under Richard Bentley (1794–1871).

9 Henry Crabb Robinson, 14 and 17 November 1837, Diaries, cited in *Letters*, p. 425, n. 8.

10 *Letters*, p. 423.

11 Burney may have been paid in 1838, judging from the fact that she did not find it necessary to withdraw the usual funds from her bank account after 1 January 1839 (see *Letters*, p. 425, n. 8). In February 1839, she must have been preparing her work for the press when there was an exchange of letters between herself and her half-sister Frances about hunting for chapter epigraphs (*Letters*, p. 426).

12 On 26 September 1839, the words 'Orders received by all booksellers' were added to the advertisements, and on 30 September the wording was changed to 'Now ready'. Ten days later, distribution was further advanced; on 9 October, the work was said to be available 'at all the libraries' (*The Times*).

13 Henry Crabb Robinson noted his opinion of Burney's works and his writing to her on the subject in his diaries on 17 October and 15 November 1839, and 5 February 1840, cited in *Letters*, p. 442, n. 2.

14 Advertisement in *The Times*, 23 October 1839, quoting from the 'Court Journal'.

15 Advertisement in *The Times*, 22 November 1839.

The *Gentleman's Magazine* included *The Romance of Private Life* in a list of new publications in their November issue.[16] The *Athenaeum* reviewed it briefly, recalling the novels of Frances Burney nostalgically and remarking that 'The Miss Burney of to-day is ... quite as talkative, but by no means so well worth listening to'.[17] The *New Monthly Magazine* was much more complimentary, placing her work in 'the very first rank', praising the 'skilfully devised plot' and 'unity of effect' of *The Renunciation* and the 'well discriminated' characters and 'excitement' of *The Hermitage*.[18] The review reads like a puff, however, and it is no surprise to learn that the *New Monthly Magazine* was one of Colburn's concerns.

There was no second edition, but *The Renunciation* was published in 2 volumes in an American edition in Philadelphia by Lea & Blanchard in 1840.

The text in this volume is based on the Chawton House Library copy of the first and only English edition. We have retained the spelling, punctuation, capitalization and italicization of the original with all its inconsistencies. Regularization has been unavoidably introduced in features such as ellipses and dashes. Page endings in the original have been indicated by a marker '/'; where the page turns in the middle of a hyphenated word, the marker follows that word.

Words which ran over the line in the original and were broken by hyphens have been treated according to customary usage in the period or elsewhere in the volume. Compound words broken over the line by hyphens can be ambiguous; for these, the editor has tried to make the best choice possible.

Finally, the form used for quotations has been modernized to current British practice. Where errors in or the omission of punctuation in the original might lead to confusion, changes have been made to clarify meaning. All corrections are made sparingly and listed at the back of the volume.

16 *Gentleman's Magazine*, n.s. 12 (1839), p. 521.

17 Review of *The Romance of Private Life*, by Sarah Harriet Burney, *Athenaeum*, 625 (19 October 1839), p. 793.

18 Review of *The Romance of Private Life*, by Sarah Harriet Burney, *New Monthly Magazine*, 2nd ser., 57 (1839), pp. 276–7.

THE
ROMANCE
OF
PRIVATE LIFE.

BY
MISS BURNEY.

IN THREE VOLUMES.

VOL. I.

THE RENUNCIATION.

LONDON:

HENRY COLBURN, PUBLISHER,

GREAT MARLBOROUGH STREET.
1839. /

LONDON

SCHULZE AND CO. 13, POLAND STREET. /

THE RENUNCIATION.

CHAPTER I.

O night, who art so courteous unto all
Why should'st thou thus afflicting prove to me?
Let every creature else a friend thee call,
A bitter foe, alas! *I* find in thee.

MICHAEL DRAYTON.[1]

ON a wet, dark, and windy night, early in the month of April, a tradesman and his wife were returning home in high spirits from witnessing at the Cheltenham Theatre,[2] the first dramatic representation they had attended for upwards of five and twenty years. They were not inhabitants of the town, but accidental visitors, whom the news of the approaching marriage of their son had enticed from their / village shop to be present at the joyful ceremony. Every thing was new to them, and though far from young, every thing appeared delightful. The play, which had been full of rant, bustle, and shew, so engrossed their thoughts, and furnished them with so much to say, that for a while they seemed to have forgotten a poor little apprentice girl, who, half asleep, was with difficulty keeping pace with them. Dazzled by the occasional glare of the lamps, buffetted by the wind and rain, and sometimes involved in what, comparatively, might be called total obscurity, she at length stumbled and fell, uttering a plaintive cry, which, however, the sound of a passing carriage, and the turbulence of the blast, united in preventing her friends from hearing. They proceeded on their way, unconscious of what had happened to her; whilst she, frightened at the prospect of being deserted, made an effort to rise, and was preparing regardless of some trifling hurts she had received, to run after them as expeditiously as the darkness would permit; when her steps were arrested by the firm grasp of a / powerful hand, and her blood was almost frozen in her veins on hearing close to her ear the words – (uttered in a whisper, which though inaudible to others, to her was but too distinct). 'Silence – or you die!' She shook in every limb, but made no resistance, nor even moved except to shrink instinctively from the stranger's hold. He was aware of the involuntary movement, but relaxed not the force of his pressure, though as he made her walk beside him, he had all the appearance to those who met and might look at him, of one who was kindly up-holding and assisting a weary child. No remarks were made, nothing extraordinary was suspected, for so intimidated was the bewildered girl, and so irresistible appeared to her the coercive power of her resolute guide, that if she thought at all, she thought every effort to escape him would be vain. No traces of her former companions were any longer to be seen, for the stranger had early forsaken the main street; and after walking some time down a narrow and dark alley, had led his reluctant / charge towards the back entrance of a house of public resort; an inn, or rather, a respectable hotel. Few persons were about, and the stairs by which they ascended were obscurely lighted, and evidently destined for the use of the domestics. On the second floor, they came to a long passage, with doors opening into separate rooms on each side. One of the furthest of these, the stranger cautiously, but without knocking, opened, and instantly turning and locking it after him, advanced with his trembling companion towards a table, on which lights were burning, and at which sat a lady still young and rather pretty, reading. The room was carpetted, and having but momentarily raised her eyes on his approach, she neither heard nor saw the little stranger, till pointing towards her with one hand, whilst with the other he still securely held her, he said in a subdued voice – 'Mary look! – but hush!'

The lady hastily cast a glance as he directed, and starting forward in extreme agitation, exclaimed. /

'Oh Heaven! who is she? why have you brought her here? What purpose is she to answer?'

'Mary, Mary, be prudent! say nothing more now, but tell me, is your room ready? Has the chambermaid done all there is to do in it to-night?'

'Yes.'

'Then take this child thither, and let her sleep upon the sofa covered by my cloak.'

The lady hesitated – looked at him, then at the pale child, and seemed perplexed beyond expression. Observing this, he went round to her, led her to a distant part of the room, and held a whispering conference with her of some duration. Meanwhile the terrors of the little girl (whose name was Agnes), had abated, though they were by no means banished.

Simple, timid, and utterly ignorant of the world; unused to act, almost to think for herself, she was in a state of bewilderment partaking more of the nature of an agitating dream, than of waking, conscious reality. Who was / she with? Why had she been brought there? and why was she detained? She had an indistinct apprehension they were not of that description of persons whom she had been accustomed to call good. She thought of the worth and kind-heartedness of the protectors from whom she had been so inexplicably torn, and large drops fell from her eyes; whilst a gloom, an oppression weighed upon her spirits, that enfeebled alike her mental and bodily faculties. She could scarcely stand, and with difficulty refrained from throwing herself on the ground, and venting aloud in sobs and moans, the deep distress inflicted by so heavy and unlooked for a blow.

Suddenly an end was put to the mysterious dialogue of the lady and her companion, by a light, but smart tap at the room door. Agnes with the quickness of thought, was drawn, or rather snatched up, and carried by the stranger into the adjoining bed-chamber. A night lamp was dimly burning on the chimney-piece, by means of which he made her observe a sofa, on / which, she might if she chose, lie down and sleep: 'but,' added he, in a suppressed, yet peremptory tone, 'if you make the slightest noise, beware of the consequence! remember what I say, and for your own sake, be careful; – good night.'

The silent tears of Agnes gushed out afresh, and the stranger left her; but, not till he had examined the door leading into the passage, locked it, and taken away the key.

When alone, the harassed child sunk upon the resting-place appointed her, and burying her face in her hands, wept long and plenteously. She now and then heard voices in the adjoining room, as of persons speaking cheerfully, and even gaily; but she neither distinguished, nor sought to do so, the purport of their conversation; her heart was too full for idle curiosity, too sad for hope, too apprehensive even for sleep, late as was the hour, and wearied as she had long felt. One of her principal grievances was the sensation of abject fear, she was conscious of experiencing whenever / she was menaced by her stern oppressor.

'Oh what wickedness,' she mentally cried, 'he might make me commit!' The thought drew her from her seat to her knees, and she prayed fervently, though simply, that she might be preserved from *doing* as well as from *suffering* evil. The act composed and soothed her, and as she still knelt, her head dropt upon the sofa, and she insensibly fell asleep.

This interval of tranquillity, however, was not long. She was awakened by the voice she most dreaded, and heard herself addressed in these words:

'Get up, and follow me into the next room: – but first listen to me attentively. You are going a long journey, under the care of a person you must implicitly obey in every particular. She has authority to treat you with severity or indulgence according as your perverseness or docility may deserve. Before long you will see me again: meanwhile I have nothing further to add except this, – make / no complaints, nor, at your peril, even allude to the events of this night! – Do you understand me?'

A faint 'yes' escaped from her quivering lips, and he then drew back a few steps to give place to the lady, who at that moment entered. She made Agnes exchange her bonnet for one of black beaver, and her cotton shawl for a cloth cloak, both as exactly suited to her size as if they had originally been intended for her. This done, she was once more introduced into the sitting room, and there beheld another stranger; a female fashionably attired, with large dark eyes, very black but regular brows, a high colour, white teeth, and a small turned-up nose. She was standing as if on the point of departing: but on perceiving Agnes paused some moments, and then in a language wholly unintelligible to the child, spoke two or three sentences very fast, took her smilingly by the hand, made sundry graceful inclinations to the lady and gentleman, and quitted the room.

It was some relief to Agnes to leave her / lawless captor behind, and she conformed to the rapid movements of her new guide without requiring to be urged. They ascended another flight of stairs, and soon came to a room that presented a very curious spectacle. Every chair, every table, every part even of the floor was covered with band-boxes or packing-casses of different dimensions, some still open, and only half filled; others corded and ready for removal. The contents of such as were exposed to view, consisted of artificial flowers, feathers, gauzes, ribbons, blonde lace,[3] &c. and the remainder, probably held objects of a similar description. On the bed lay a very small white lap-dog, and, as being the only unoccupied space remaining, beside him was deposited a tray containing part of a loaf, plates, glasses, knives and forks, a decanter of water, and a half-empty bottle of wine. A young woman, dark, lank, plain and very untidy, yet with some attempt at smartness, was busily engaged in finishing the packing. /

The new comer, taking no further notice of Agnes flew to her dog, and caressed him most fondly; spoke with her accustomed volubility to the young assistant, whom she seemed to be reproving for her dilatoriness; and finally, casting off her gay bonnet and expensive shawl, and putting on a large apron, she applied herself with such dexterity and promptness to complete the labour, that in a very short time the room was nearly cleared, and what remained to be done it was evident might be left to the subordinate.

Unexhausted by her exertions, Madame then removed the tray from its unseemly station to the table, and drew forth from a covered basket some cold meat and a large plain cake. Agnes was beckoned forward, and invited to eat; the dog invited himself; the mistress, talking all the time, completed a very substantial repast; the maid, whilst still pursuing her occupation snatched a portion at intervals of what was intended for her; and when all was satisfied, the fragments were collected and replaced in the / basket, and Madame prepared herself to go to rest. It was evident that she had no intention to undress entirely, probably from being in expectation of an early summons to begin her journey; she merely tied a handkerchief round her head and substituted a wrapper for her upper garment. The maid, with somewhat less ceremony, accoutred herself also for the night, and was allowed to lie down beside her mistress; and Agnes had a pillow and some warm covering given to her, with signs to arrange for herself a bed upon chairs – sofa there was none.

It was yet profoundly dark, when the shrill barking of the dog, and the gruff voice of a man, accompanied by repeated raps at the chamber door, awoke the whole party. He provided them with a lighted candle, and made them understand that they must immediately send down their baggage, and lose no time in following it. The two Frenchwomen were ready in five minutes, and whilst the man who called them was assisting a porter to load himself / with some of the most cumbersome of the boxes, Madame hinted, in broken English, an ardent desire for a dish of coffee.

'Coffee?' repeated the fellow, with a grin, 'Lord love you, mistress! you had best go back to France, if you expect to find coffee at an inn at four o'clock in the morning.'

There was no redress; poor Madame arched her black brows, shrugged, muttered to herself, '*Quel chien d'homme!*'[4] and gave the matter up.

At length, the packing-cases and band-boxes, which though they occupied much space, were light, all found their proper station about the coach, and the three females entered the vehicle, upon condition, however, that as Madame had introduced a supernumerary passenger, the maid should repair to the outside, if her place should be wanted.

It was a cold, drizzling, gloomy morning, and Madame, shuddering and looking miserable, drew up both the glasses, wrapt herself round in her ample cloak, and taking '*le cher / petit Fanfan*' on her knees, put her feet upon the vacant seat opposite, and leant back in hopes of another nap. The maid, who whatever her exterior might promise, was splendidly distinguished by the classical elegance of her name – Athenaïs – sat sometime silent, and yet more miserable than her mistress, for the motion of the carriage affected her so disagreeably, that before they had proceeded two miles, she was forced to get upon the box beside the coachman, with what protection an umbrella could afford her, in addition to the various shawls and tippets, Madame good-naturedly handed out to her.

At different places on the road they took up two other travellers, much to the annoyance of the Frenchwoman, who had hoped for the permanent possession of the opposite seat as a resting-place for her feet. Such, however, was the easy hilarity of her nature, that finding the new passengers sociable persons, who spoke her own language fluently, she soon reconciled herself to their admission, and gaily entering / into conversation with them, became perfectly content.

Agnes it will be believed, was a mere nullity to the whole party. No longer under the influence of terror, she was somewhat in the state of one whom a heavy blow had stupified. She looked without seeing; she heard voices without knowing whence they came;[5] in short, she had so precisely the air that either deep distress, (so rare at her time of life) or natural imbecility would give, that one of the gentlemen, a middle-aged observant person, after regarding her attentively some time, became curious to ascertain to which of these two causes was to be ascribed the singularity of her aspect.

'Where do you come from, my dear?' inquired he.

She made no answer, for she was not aware that he had addressed her. He repeated the question, and gently touched her arm, to excite her attention. The whole countenance then / changed; a slight colour tinged her cheeks, and her eyes evinced intelligence. She said she came from Cheltenham: but at the moment she uttered this brief sentence, she felt her foot pressed by Madame, and looking towards her, saw a quick frown pass across her brow, that plainly indicated displeasure at her having spoken. The stranger, unconscious of what had passed, being so placed that he could not see the face of Madame, pursued his interrogations.

'And why do you look so sad, my poor child?' added he; 'have you left any friends you are regretting to part from?'

The enquiry came too near the truth, and Agnes would have been unable to answer it, even had the fear of Madame exerted no influence over her. She sighed from the bottom of her heart, her eyes filled with tears, and she put her head out of the window, to avoid being looked at or spoken to again.

The stranger forbore molesting her any further, / persuaded that he had discovered the source of her melancholy, for which, as he knew no remedy but time, he thought it best to leave her to its influence. /

CHAPTER II.

Well do'st thou hide from common sight
Thy close intrigues, too bad to bear the light.

DRYDEN.[6]

I do not think so fair an outward,
Such foul stuff within
Endows a man but him.

SHAKSPEARE.[7]

MEANWHILE, at Cheltenham, the distress occasioned by the disappearance of the child was extreme, and greatly aggravated to her recent protectors, Mr. and Mrs. Blake, by the reproaches they poured upon themselves for their neglect of the little creature in their way home from the theatre. Hour after hour during the night the good old man, sometimes alone, sometimes accompanied by his son, paced up and down the principal street, and occasionally through others leading into it, / watching eagerly to catch a glimpse of some form resembling little Agnes. As soon as the day was sufficiently advanced, he went, still attended by his son, and this time by his disconsolate wife also, to lay his complaint before the magistrate, and to solicit advice how to proceed. Hand-bills were immediately prepared, sent to the press, and posted up at every quarter of the town. In these, her person, age and dress were minutely described. The crier was employed to offer a reward, (large for a man in Blake's humble circumstances) to whoever would give information concerning her. In short, every measure was adopted, usual on such occasions, and deemed likely to produce a discovery. But so skilfully had the stranger conducted his nefarious plan, that not the slightest indication of the child's fate could be obtained. He showed himself in the streets and libraries as usual; and listened, with an air of interest, in common with others, to the hoarse voice of the crier proclaiming the extraordinary disappearance of Agnes Danvers, a / child of eleven years, with light brown hair, and dark eyes, slim and rather tall, and wearing a straw bonnet and flowered shawl.

Both these he well knew to have been securely disposed of in his drawing room fire; and no other traces remained by which he could possibly become implicated as an agent in the affair.

In a few days the shock and the wonder excited by so unusual an event subsided: but upon the spirits and the future happiness of Blake and his wife, it effected a very mournful and lasting change. They had known the poor girl from her earliest childhood, and though she had not always lived with them, they had uniformly felt anxious for her welfare and happiness. Her employment under their roof was light and easy; she assisted Mrs. Blake in plaiting straw for the bonnets with which it was her profession to supply the neighbourhood, or aided the husband in serving some of the minor customers, who, on market days, thronged around his counter. Her humility, / her sweet temper, and her anxious endeavours to render herself useful, had entirely won the hearts of the worthy pair; and no child of their own could have been treated with more kindness than they invariably manifested towards their 'good little Agnes.'

It was lamentable that the recent proof they had given of their affection, in bringing her so unnecessarily to Cheltenham should have turned out so fatally; and the play – that abominable play! How bitterly did they regret having taken her to it – nay, having even gone to it themselves. It was the intoxicating amusement they had derived from it that had occasioned their temporary forgetfulness of their helpless companion; and such was their own sorrow and contrition, that no possible inducement would ever have engaged them to enter a theatre again. Many persons, pitying their distress, went to see them, some with offers of pecuniary assistance, others merely to condole with them.

Amongst the rest, was a lady well known to the authors of poor Agnes's misfortune. On / her return from her charitable visit, having occasion to pass their hotel, she determined to take the present opportunity of calling upon them. She was received with the customary demonstrations of satisfaction, and a lively conversation ensued, in the course of which sundry local rumours, such as Cheltenham and all other watering places afford, were freely discussed. At last, some imperceptible link in the chain of her ideas, brought back to the visitor's mind the poor broken-hearted Blakes.

'I must tell you,' cried she, suddenly changing the subject of discourse, 'where I have been this morning. I was so sorry for those unhappy people who have lost their little girl, that I found out where they live, and went to see them.'

Mrs. Marchmont, the lady to whom this was addressed, felt her face in a glow which she judged it expedient to conceal by busying herself in looking for a glove on the floor. The countenance of her brother, Mr. Wharton, underwent no change. Their visitor thus went on:

'They seem very respectable and right-minded / people. The proposal that was made to them of raising a subscription to assist in defraying the expences they have been forced to incur, they thankfully but steadily declined. They spoke of the child in the most endearing terms, and in a manner that proves her to be singularly well disposed. Is it not dreadful to think she should have been thus infamously kidnapped? What ill-usage she may be exposed to! – what vicious habits she may contract! – At so tender an age what chance has she to resist the contagion of example, and the influence of bad associates?'

'It is impossible,' said Mr. Wharton, with his customary imperturbability, 'to conjecture what may be her fate.'

'I am exceedingly sorry,' added his sister, compelling herself to take some share in the conversation, 'for her poor friends.'

'You would have pitied them ten times more,' resumed the visitor, 'had you seen and heard them. The child is in no degree related to them, but circumstances early threw / her under the protection of one of their family, and for the last few years, under their own. "We always loved her," said poor Mrs. Blake, "even when we saw her but seldom; since she has lived with us, she has become as dear to us as one of our own children: yet, fond of her as I am, I think I would rather have followed her to her grave, than have had her taken from me in so suspicious and frightful a manner!"'

'She speaks,' said Mr. Wharton, 'like a good and sensible woman. Where do you say she and her husband reside? I have understood that they are only at Cheltenham on a visit to their son.'

'They live at the village of Meadwell, about five miles beyond Gloucester,[8] where Blake keeps what is commonly designated in every country place, THE SHOP, *par excellence*. He sells linen-drapery, grocery, pottery, in short, every thing except butcher's meat, and goods of a high price. His wife plaits and makes straw bonnets; and till this calamity overtook them, there is reason to think they / were the most prosperous and contented people in the world.'

The subject was now exhausted, and in a little while, the communicative visitor took leave.

When she was gone, Mr. Wharton wrote down the name of Meadwell in his pocket-book, while his sister, after having attended their friend to the room door, returned to her seat, and burst into tears:

'What is the matter?' cried her brother.

'Oh, Robert, can you ask me? Have we not been guilty of an action which, if known, would render us objects of universal reproach and detestation? and are we not meditating a fraud yet more unwarrantable, and a thousand degrees more dangerous?'

'Mary,' replied he, approaching nearer to her, and lowering his voice almost to a whisper – 'no other resource remains to me; – nothing else can save me – can save *either* of us – from the imminent ruin that threatens us. Let us however forbear these starts of useless compunction; / in you, they encourage weakness; in me, they would be the very mockery of virtue; for be assured, Mary, I shall steadily pursue my point!'

Mrs. Marchmont was silenced; – the 'small still voice,' the voice of conscience[9] – or rather, perhaps, the dread of detection, still spoke within; but she dared not let it be heard; and with a heavy heart obeyed the injunction of her brother to go and dress for the dinner-party to which they were engaged. /

CHAPTER III.

My friends, do they now and then send
A wish or a thought after me?
O tell me I yet have a friend,
Though a friend I am never to see!

COWPER.[10]

AGNES and her two foreign companions, Madame Leroux, and Mademoiselle Athenaïs, reached London in perfect safety about eight o'clock in the evening, and were conveyed in a hackney-coach from the inn at which they stopped, to the abode of Madame in Bury Street, St. James's.[11] Here, her husband, a flower-maker and *plumassier*,[12] who carried on his separate department of the business in another house, was very gallantly stationed to receive his *chère épouse*,[13] and welcome her return. There was, besides, a *demoiselle de / boutique*,[14] and a senior superintendant, or rather partner, who, with the female cook, all lined the passage as Madame alighted, and all joined in chorus to felicitate her and themselves on her fortunate arrival. After yielding first one cheek and then the other to the tender salute of her husband;[15] after courteously embracing the partner, Madame Morinval, and nodding and smiling to the rest of the establishment, she recommended her packages to their care, and pushed her way towards the stairs.

'*Mais qui est cette pauvre petite?*'[16] enquired Monsieur, looking, as well as the others, with great surprise at Agnes.

'*Laisse-la venir, mon ami. Je t'expliquerai tout cela tantôt.*'[17]

There was no more to be said: the child was suffered to follow her conductress, and in a very short time, found herself seated at a tempting little supper, which, under the direction of Monsieur, had been prepared to celebrate the *bien-heureux événement*[18] of the evening. Madame took joyful possession of an arm chair at the head of the table, declaring / it was the first inviting repast she had seen, and the first agreeable moment she had experienced since she quitted London. Her husband was enchanted; the ladies seemed highly flattered; the cook boasted of her *savoir faire*,[19] and recommended the dish which she thought her mistress ought to prefer; and the dog, who, very wisely, never allowed himself to be forgotten, was incessant in his demands for attention to his appetite.

The meal was cheerful to all but the little stranger, who, even had she been brought thither by her own consent, could not have derived much pleasure from the society of persons whose language was so utterly unknown to her. She regarded the whole party for a time with equal indifference; but by degrees, a slight interchange of more friendly looks, established itself between her and Madame Morinval, which promised to ripen into cordiality. Less flighty, and less inconsiderate than her principal, she felt for the poor desolate child; and whilst the others were only exclaiming at her *air triste*,[20] beheld in her dejected / countenance, a sweetness of expression, a modesty, and purity, that she had seldom seen surpassed. Madame Morinval was a mother herself; her children were grown up; but she could well imagine what would have been *their* unhappiness, at the same age, had they been thrown, like Agnes upon the mercy of foreigners, without the means of making themselves understood, and utterly bereft of every customary companion and protector. Touched by the thought, she determined, as far as it was in her power, to befriend and support her.

The two junior workwomen, Mademoiselle Eloise, and Mademoiselle Athenaïs, did not sleep in the house, and therefore, soon after supper, departed to their usual resting-place. It was then debated where to dispose of Agnes; and Madame Morinval offered to let her take a share of her own bed. This was objected to, on the plea of its being a tax upon her good-nature which she would find extremely incommodious: but she said it would not be the first time she had slept with a child; and / finally, upon certain conditions, her proposal was accepted. These conditions were, that Agnes except at night, was to live entirely in Madame Leroux's chamber; that she was never to be brought into the shew-rooms; never to be taken out till twilight; never to be talked of; and above all, never to be allowed access to any *English* person whatever.

'What the meaning,' she concluded, 'of these strange precautions may be, I am totally ignorant. I only know, that sleeping last night at the hotel from whence the stage was to set out, and hearing that one of my best customers was under the same roof, I went down at a late hour, to ask whether she had any commands to town. She gave me a very handsome order, without limiting me as to time; and then, after a short consultation with her brother, requested me to take charge of this child on the terms specified, and with the promise at the end of a few weeks, of a liberal recompence.' /

'It is an odd affair!' observed Monsieur Leroux.

'Very odd, indeed!' subjoined Madame Morinval, gravely.

'I agree with you both,' resumed Madame Leroux; 'but what could I do? I was not required to undertake any thing harsh or wicked. Nothing was asked of me but silence and discretion; and though I would rather have been without the trust, I could not find in my heart to refuse the request of persons so respectable, and who have long patronized me so generously.'

How Monsieur Leroux rested satisfied with his wife's apology, does not appear. To Madame Morinval its morality, to say the least of it, seemed exceedingly equivocal. She had no authority however, to contest the point, and no power to undo what had thus far been effected; for Madame Leroux having declined naming the parties by whom her services had been engaged, grew weary of the thoughtful / and perhaps disapproving looks of her auditors and complaining of sleepiness, rose to retire.

Madame Morinval immediately took possession of her new *protégée*,[21] and conducted her to her little bed-room. Neither its dimensions, nor the accommodations with which it was provided were such as could have induced any one but from motives of the truest kindness to admit into it an additional occupant. It was scarcely more than a closet; a small tent-bed pushed up against the wall, one chair, and a tottering chest of drawers, serving both for dressing-table and washing-stand, was all the furniture it contained – indeed, all that its limits *could* contain. Agnes had she been able to explain herself, would have told Madame Morinval how thankfully she felt the obligation she was conferring upon her; not that she considered the favour as enhanced by reflecting upon the smallness of the room, and the additional inconvenience her presence entailed upon its owner; she was neither of an age, nor of habits to pay any attention to such circumstances: / but what she wished to express was her gratitude for the compassionate attention of which she was the object. Her heart assured her she had at length fallen into benevolent and upright hands; and she became sensible of a feeling of security she had never for a moment experienced in the same unmixed degree since she had been separated from the Blakes. – Whilst undressing, she was upon the watch to observe whether there was any little service she could render her patroness; and if only allowed to untie a string, or unfasten a hook, her aspect brightened almost into a smile.

'*Comme elle est jolie!*'[22] thought Madame Morinval, as she looked at her on these occasions. The next moment, she sighed to think of her desolate situation, and wondered how any human being could have been found cruel enough to oppress so helpless and innocent a creature. The child, meanwhile, having knelt and prayed, crept into bed, and nestled so close to the wall, that the space she left, / scarcely seemed less than before she lay down. In five minutes, her mind being comparatively at ease, she was fast asleep.

The next morning, still under the auspices of her encouraging friend, she breakfasted at an early hour in a small, ill-lighted room, *under ground*, a specimen of architectural ingenuity wholly unknown in her beloved village, where they already found waiting for them the two young workwomen she had seen the night before. The house was not large, nor did Madame Leroux occupy the whole of it, having lodgers on the ground floor, and in two out of three of the attics. For this reason, as her best rooms were those in which her customers were received, and where her business was carried on, those that remained for domestic use, were the very refuse of the dwelling.

When Madame Morinval went upstairs, she supplied Agnes with some easy needle-work to employ her time till the mistress of the house, who often rose late, should think fit to send for her to her own apartment. /

The rain of the preceding day seemed to have cleared the air, and was followed by a fine bright spring morning. Agnes gazed through the little dingy window at which she sat and sought to see the sky; but the narrow yard into which it looked, was surrounded by high walls that entirely excluded it from her view. She heard, not the song, but the tuneless chirp, of innumerable, dusky, ragged looking sparrows, hopping pertly or voraciously about, in search of whatever provender they could find, and often assembling in large groups for the vilest and most disgusting prize. That the sun really shone she could only distinguish by seeing it illumine portions of the neighbouring houses. That any thing like a green leaf existed, she could only know from recollection, for, amongst the few garden pots standing out at different windows, she beheld none containing any plant that had yet been able to force itself into vegetation through all the smoke and fog to which it was exposed. She thought of Meadwell, and the contrast / between what she had there been accustomed to witness, and the scene before her was greater and far more dispiriting than if, born in a palace and accustomed to splendour, she had suddenly been removed to a prison!

The enjoyments derived from the loveliness of nature, from purity of air, from the freshness of early day, from the sight, sound, scent of ten thousand fragrant and reviving objects, not only far outweigh, in themselves, all the artificial advantages man can devise, but have the property of awakening a degree of attachment, which causes their loss to be deplored with nearly as much sorrow as the loss of a long-tried friend. Agnes did not reason upon the subject: but she felt – felt as a bird might have done freshly deprived of its liberty; and though she neither fluttered nor struggled to escape, she was just as miserable.

In due time Madame Leroux rose from her couch, got through the labours of the toilet, breakfasted, and when she was about to repair to her workwomen directed the cook, who was / also the housemaid, to shew the little English girl, as soon as the bed was made, the way up to her room: 'And tell her, Babet,' added she, 'you that can speak a little English, that my orders are, she does not go out of this apartment without my leave.'

Accordingly, when Babet's work was performed she went down to the child, grumbling at having so often to go up so many stairs, for she was neither very young nor very slender, and in broken English, said: 'Come den, my littel von – come vid me to de chambre of Madame; and remember dat I tell you, you be not to make von step out of de apartment, without de permission of Madame.'

Agnes silently folded her work, and followed her new guide.

The change was certainly an improvement. In the room to which she was now introduced there was more light, and somewhat more space: but it was in the back part of the house, and its prospect was the same, with the advantage only of being higher up, with that / she had thought so dismal below stairs. Its decorations, however, were much gayer; the walls being surrounded by innumerable coloured prints of ladies and children in the fashionable dresses of Paris during the two or three preceding years. Near the window, hung several cages, occupied by canaries, goldfinches, and linnets; and in the centre of the room was a tall stand, furnished with perches, on one of which a large grey parrot[23] sat solemnly looking about him, waiting for an audience to begin his daily and intolerable clamour. The moment he saw the well-known Babet, he screamed forth.

> 'Vilaine Cendrillon,
> 'Vite, vite, mon bouillon.'[24]

'*Tais-toi, impertinent!*'[25] cried the woman threatening him; – then addressing the child, she added: ''Tis vilain bird;[26] – always saying de insolences. Mademoiselle Athenaïs has learnt him dees pretty manners.'

The parrot, as if he understood her, laughed / at her anger, and then strenuously renewed his doggrel incivilities:

> 'Va t'en vite, vieille laidron,
> 'Va t'en vite à ton donjon.'[27]

Agnes understood not one word that was said either by the cook or the parrot, and was not a little surprised to see the former dash out of the room in a real fit of rage at what she called 'the bad nature of that pest of a beast!'

To the child its faculty of speaking so distinctly was marvellous; she had heard a magpie attempt to articulate, but never with the same success; and the beauty also of the creature charmed her. In a little while she and the bird became such friends, that he willingly permitted her to stroke his feathers, perched confidingly upon her hand; and had he not been chained to his stand, would have preferred her shoulder to any other station. /

With such associates, and the light employment that had been given her, Agnes's first morning in London passed away. When the hour of dinner arrived, she was called down by Mademoiselle Athenaïs, no longer the slovenly personage she had hitherto seen her, but a caricature of French fashion; a sort of walking doll, on whose well-dressed head, caps, hats, and bonnets might be tried, and whose body seemed intended for no other purpose than to serve as a machine on which might be exhibited to their purchasers, the effect of variously shaped gowns and trimmings. She conducted the little girl to the same room they had breakfasted in; and here she at length saw Madame Leroux, from whom she received a slight nod of recognition, and a signal to take her place at the end of the table.

Before the meal was half over, several thundering knocks at the door, compelled, first Madame Morinval, and afterwards her principal, to hasten up-stairs in order to receive persons, who, with whatever importance their / footmen announced them, came, perhaps only to walk through the rooms, look at their contents, enquire their prices, and drive away again.

Agnes meanwhile, returned to the other biped prisoners, by the chief of which, the parrot, she was hailed with pleasure, and with whom she spent the evening with as much concord as the morning.

At dusk, her good friend Madame Morinval, was permitted to take her out for a short walk. Her recent misadventure had rendered Agnes so extremely timid, that apprehensive of being, even for an instant, separated from her conductress whilst in the street, she contrived (not daring to take her arm) to keep tight hold during the whole way, of some part of her dress. They went into one or two shops, and Madame Morinval made several purchases: after which she afforded the poor child the advantage of breathing a somewhat fresher air in the Green Park.[28]

In the course of a few days, Agnes discovered / that the goods which had been bought were for her use. She was entirely re-equipped; her stuff frock was exchanged for the most delicate and fashionable white, or figured muslin; an ample supply of linen was provided for her; shoes, silk stockings, gloves, in short, whatever was necessary to contribute to her appearing as a gentleman's child, was unsparingly bestowed upon her. When thus habited, and with the advantage of having everything thoroughly well made, she struck both the French-women with delight at the credit she did to their taste and choice. She still looked humble and shy; but there was no awkward stiffness about her; her flexible form was by nature graceful; her fair skin gave her an air of delicacy, and the symmetry of her features an appearance of refinement, very remarkable in one accustomed to the most homely modes of life.

'Ah, how many duchesses and marchionesses,' exclaimed Madame Leroux, addressing / her partner in French, 'would give half they are worth, to see their daughters look as like ladies born as this poor child!'

'Luckily,' answered her friend, 'nature's gifts cannot be purchased; if they could, I fear there are many whom poverty would induce to part with its best compensations.'

From this day, even Madame Leroux began to regard her little inmate with something approaching to partiality; and with Madame Morinval, she increased in favour every hour. Could she have forgotten the words of the terrific stranger, 'you will soon see me again,' she would have been, comparatively, at ease. Every evening, when fair, she walked out with her kind protectress, and on their return, received from her a lesson in French; and with the facility that belongs to the organs of early youth, soon began to catch the right pronunciation, as well as to improve in the faculty of learning by heart. As yet, she was ignorant of the art of writing, but copies were given to her, and again Madame Morinval, with unwearied / patience, took upon herself the office of instructress. Monsieur Leroux, who prided himself upon the universality of his talents, (and well he might, since, in his time, he had exercised the profession of a soldier, of a dancing-master, of a hair-dresser, of a tailor, and now of a florist), captivated by the child's engaging exterior, undertook to teach her to dance. All the benefit she derived from his instructions, was that of acquiring a better carriage, and walking, perhaps, with more *aplomb*.[29] Upon the whole, the three months she spent in Bury Street could not be considered as very unhappy, or entirely without profit. Hearing nothing but French spoken, and having no occupation or interruption the whole day to prevent her applying to the lessons appointed for her, habit, and her own industry, spurred on by the desire of pleasing Madame Morinval, caused her to make a rapid progress. As she improved in the power of forming her letters, and putting them together, she often thought what a pleasure it would be / to write to her kind Mr. and Mrs. Blake. But against this danger, one, far more long-sighted than she was had already taken measures. In the first place, Mr. Wharton had directed that nothing should be taught her but French; and in the next, he had prepared for her in the name of Mr. Blake, and in characters resembling print, the following letter:

Meadwell, June 7.

Dear child,

My wife and I, as we know that you are no great scholar, have got a neighbour's son to write this for us, as like a book in print as he can, that you may the more easily read it. We are both well, but have been very unhappy about you, my poor dear Agnes, however, we have now seen the gentleman who sent you up to London, and he promises to do very handsomely by you; and says, that perhaps sooner than we think for, we may see you again. I pray to heaven we may! I am sorry to add, that he seems rather over-wilful and impatient, / and like one that will not very easily bear to be thwarted. His sister, I take it, is a kind and humane lady, and I advise you to make a friend of her, for she seems very well disposed towards you. We have taken a dislike to Meadwell now you are gone, and think of removing soon to some other place, as our son means to leave Cheltenham for Worcester, and we wish to be as near him as possible. I believe he has already found a house that will suit us. So, wishing you all prosperity, and that you may continue as honest and good as when you lived with us, no more at present, my dear child, from your loving friends,

A. AND M. BLAKE.

Whether or not this was the style of letter A. and M. Blake would have written, it passed unsuspected upon the unpracticed Agnes, and answered sundry purposes to its inventor. First, by asserting that he had had an interview with the Blakes, and had made known / her being in London, it must appear that they sanctioned her removal, or, at least, made no opposition to it. Secondly, by speaking of himself in such unmeasured terms, he kept up in her the awe upon which he so much depended for power to rule over her. Thirdly, he had described his sister in more favourable colours to avoid driving the friendless girl to absolute despair; and lastly, by suggesting that Meadwell was about to be abandoned, he took from her for an indefinite time, all hope of being able to address to them either message or letter. He now, therefore, considered her as absolutely in his power.

On the whole, the effect produced upon Agnes by this forgery, was most painful. She could not define to herself the deficiencies she found in it; the language was kind, the good wishes were precisely such as she would have expected from them; yet, there seemed a readiness to give her up, a calmness in their manner of speaking of her disappearance, that / pierced her to the heart, and awakened in her more melancholy regret than any, perhaps, that she had yet experienced.

After reading and re-reading the saddening scroll, and meditating long over it with almost as much surprise as grief, she was struck, on at length folding it up, to observe that it bore no other direction than this, 'For the little girl at Madame Leroux's, Bury Street, &c.' Had it, thus oddly addressed, arrived by the post? on first receiving it, so great was her impatience to know its contents, that she had paid no regard to its exterior. Mademoiselle Athenaïs had been sent up to her with it, and merely saying in French, 'here is a letter for you,' had immediately gone away again. Agnes kept the thought in her mind till dinner time, and when she was called down, took an opportunity of asking Madame Morinval, if she could tell how the letter had been brought?

'A countryman left it at the door, my dear,' / answered she, 'and walked on without stopping a moment.'

This had been planned by Mr. Wharton, to avoid the danger of letting her name (so well known at Cheltenham) be seen at the post office. The person who had delivered the letter, was a grazier's servant, sent up to London upon business, and employed by Mr. Wharton, who had accidentally heard of his journey, to execute for him this little commission.

Some weeks after, during a very hot evening early in July, whilst Agnes was strolling in the Green Park with Madame Morinval, the latter suddenly remarked, that the heat, great as it now was in England, would probably be of very short duration, compared with the time it generally lasted in France; 'And I fear,' continued she, 'I shall have much to suffer from it during my approaching journey.'

Agnes was thunderstruck; 'Your approaching / journey?' repeated she, 'What journey, dear madame? you are not,' she fearfully added, 'you are not going to France?'

'Yes, my child, I am; I have a son and daughter at Paris, whom I have not seen for four years; and Madame Leroux has consented to my paying them a visit this summer.'

Agnes was speechless, but not from insensibility. She was drowned in tears, and utterly incapable of articulating a word. Madame Morinval drew her towards an unoccupied bench, and when they were both seated, putting one arm kindly around her, she said:

'Do not thus afflict yourself, my dear little girl; remember that my absence will not be long.'

Still poor Agnes was either afraid or unable to give utterance to her feelings, but leaning her head upon her friend's shoulder, she wept in mute despondency. After a short pause, Madame Morinval, kissing her fair forehead, said in a tone more cheerful: – /

'My Agnes – would you like to go with me?'

The words had the effect of electricity! Starting up, and clasping her hands, the enraptured child exclaimed: –

'With *you*, dearest madam? – with *you* I would willingly go to the end of the world! You are my only friend on earth!' Her voice sunk as she said this, and her tearful eyes expressed at once, so much meekness, and so much sorrow that Madame Morinval snatched her to her heart, saying: 'Be comforted, my child, be comforted. If now I am your only earthly friend, there is a benignant Providence above who will raise up others to support you. Your life is but beginning, and though its outset may be cloudy, brighter days will succeed. You have qualities to gain you well-wishers wherever you are known; cultivate them assiduously; retain your native humility, your patience, your love of truth, your grateful disposition, and putting your trust in God, fear not what man can do unto you.' /

This was language that went straight to Agnes's heart – language which that heart was formed to understand. She embraced her kind monitress with mingled reverence and love, promising to remember her counsels to the latest hour of her life: 'But, dearest madam,' added she, 'are you – yes, yes, you *are* in earnest when you say you will take me abroad with you! Does Madame Leroux know it? Has she consented?'

'She has, my love; but we – that is, I – almost feared you would dislike to leave your country, and therefore I was cautious how I broke the news to you.'

'Ah, madam,' cried the desolate child, 'what is there in my country to make me regret it? I have no parents; the friends who once were so kind to me, seem now to have given me up. I know not in whose power I am – and, except yourself, I have no one to love, no one to trust.'

'Well, then, dear Agnes, as long as we are permitted, we will hold on our course together. / I am quite sure I shall continue to find you as tractable and good-tempered as you have hitherto always shown yourself; and whilst that is the case, you may depend upon the steadiness of my regard for you.'

Thanking her in the warmest terms, Agnes then ventured to say, though with hesitation, and changing colour, 'Do you know whether the person – the gentleman who put me under the care of Madame Leroux, will permit me to leave her?'

'All that has been arranged between them,' answered Madame Morinval. 'She has had a letter, or, I rather think an interview with that gentleman, and whatever she sanctions, it is with his authority.'

'Has he, then,' said Agnes, much agitated, 'been in London lately?'

'I believe he has. But make no further inquiries, my child, for I have no power to give you any further information. There are subjects upon which I have never sought your confidence; let the same prudence restrain / you from putting embarrassing questions to me.'

Madame Morinval was induced to say this in consequence of the persuasion which recent circumstances induced her to entertain that Agnes was the natural child of the person who had sent her to town; and that, after keeping her in seclusion during her infancy, he had determined to withdraw her gradually from obscurity, and at his own time, either to provide for her as his acknowledged daughter, or to secure to her a more humble maintenance under some other pretext. Such was very much the view of the subject also taken by Madame Leroux. Of the compulsion that had been used to gain possession of the poor little creature, neither of the Frenchwomen knew anything, but they both knew that he had liberally supplied the means of re-equipping her; that he had expressed an intention of sending her abroad for education; and that, for *family reasons*, he was extremely anxious, whilst she remained in England, to prevent her / being seen or talked of. Why so much mystery was to envelope her it was difficult to conjecture. Madame Morinval regretted that the advantages so long withheld from her young favourite, should, now they were conferred, be so totally unaccompanied by personal kindness. It was evident that Agnes had scarcely the smallest acquaintance with this supposed father; nor did it appear ever to have entered her imagination that it was in that capacity she ought to regard him. Madame Morinval, fearing to do wrong, forebore, though reluctantly, to suggest the idea. /

CHAPTER IV.

There's nothing that I cast my eyes upon
But shews both rich and admirable; all the rooms
Are hung as if a princess were to dwell here.

RULE A WIFE, AND HAVE A WIFE.[30]

ON the day appointed, no impediments having arisen, Agnes and her friend left London for Dover. Such was the child's kindness of disposition, that little as had been the notice or favour she had received from Madame Leroux, she could not quit her without some degree of concern; but perhaps, the object she parted from with the greatest regret was the friendly parrot, and the leave she took of him, was more affectionate than that which passed between her and any other member of the family. Monsieur Leroux, who was amongst those assembled at the door to / see her set off, exhorted her not to forget his dancing instructions, and evinced considerable regret at losing his scholar before he had had time to render her *parfaite*.

Their journey to Dover was without incidents; but great was the surprise of Madame Morinval, almost on arriving at the inn, to receive from the hands of a waiter, the following note written in French:

'You are entreated, madam, when you land at Calais, to secure a private lodging, and there to remain till you hear from me again. Your journey to Paris, though delayed, shall not be made the less convenient to you, it being my full intention to remunerate you amply for all expenses incurred through my means.

'Yours,
'R. W.'

That this application was made in reference to some affair connected with her young charge, Madame Morinval could not for an instant / doubt. She was sorry to be retarded on her way to her children, but for the sake of Agnes, she thought it right to submit; and her answer, therefore, was written in accordance with this determination, and given to the waiter who had brought her the note.

The first day or two spent at Calais, passed off lightly and cheerfully not only to Agnes, but even to Madame Morinval. She was on her native soil, she heard only her own language, and saw none but the faces of compatriots. The weather was fine, and she was consequently able to stroll about a great deal; and seeing Agnes in better spirits than she ever yet exhibited, she participated in her enjoyment, and considered the hours that were now elapsing, as portions, by no means irksome, of the holiday she had so long toiled to obtain. But when the third, fourth, fifth day closed – when, in short, above a week passed, and no fresh tidings of her correspondent reached her, she began to be at once perplexed and provoked. Agnes herself was full of inquiries / and wonder at their staying so long in the same place. No explanation of the circumstance could be prudently given her, but being told that there were indispensable reasons for the delay, she desisted from saying anything more; and could she have seen Madame Morinval perfectly at ease, would, under her protection, have been as well satisfied to remain at Calais as at any other place.

On the *tenth morning* of this wearisome detention, their room door was gently opened, whilst they sat at breakfast, and Mrs. Marchmont walked in. Agnes turned as pale as death at the sight, and her eyes seemed starting out of their sockets whilst gazing onwards to ascertain whether she was followed. Mrs. Marchmont understood the cause of this fearful scrutiny, and hastened to say: –

'I am alone, Agnes, you have no reason for apprehension of any sort.'

Then sitting down, and indeed she seemed to require it, for she looked weak, thin, and nervous, she bowed civilly to Madame Morinval, / addressed to her some obliging inquiries, and afterwards, calling to Agnes, and taking her by the hand with much kindness, she said: –

'You must try and conquer this extreme timidity, my good little girl. I am come on purpose to endeavour to encourage you, and to prepare you for the probability there is, that you and I before long may become inhabitants of the same house.'

Agnes cast her streaming eyes towards Madame Morinval, and then buried her face in her hands. Mrs. Marchmont herself was not unmoved; she sighed, and after a short silence, added:

'These tears, in my presence, Agnes, may be shed with impunity; I can only behold them with compassion: but you must be more on your guard before another person, whose resentment I would not have you on any account regard lightly. If you are placid and submissive, however, you will have nothing to fear even from *that* quarter; and from me, you / may rely upon always meeting with indulgence. Compose your spirits whilst you remain here, and let me hope that when I see you again, I shall find you less disturbed.'

She then arose, thanked Madame Morinval for delaying her departure, and requesting her, in a low voice, to represent to the child the necessity of exerting more command over herself, she took her leave.

The poor little girl remained after she was gone, in a state of such overwhelming distress, that Madame Morinval, not knowing how to soothe her, sent her into the adjoining bed-chamber, and bade her kneel, and pray to God to give her greater courage and resignation. She did so; she knelt, but it was long before she could pray – before she could do anything but weep and wring her hands. The dread she felt of seeing again Mr. Wharton – of being condemned to live under the same roof with him, was indescribable. His figure, his voice, his countenance, the remembrance of the first terrific words he had addressed to her, of / the iron grasp of his hand, of his subsequent menaces, all, – all recurred to her imagination, and affected it even to agony. When Madame Morinval joined her, though she found her apparently less agitated, it was evident that she was ill. Her hands were hot and dry, her cheeks flushed, and her eyes heavy and languid. With the tenderest care she made the harmless sufferer lie down, and administered to her such simple and cooling remedies as she thought the case required. During the remainder of the day she sat by her, sometimes addressing to her a few cheering and consolatory words; oftener endeavouring to detach her thoughts from her own concerns, by reading to her, or telling her some amusing anecdote.

But, alas! it would not do, for so intimate is the connection between body and mind, that whatever strongly affects the latter, operates upon the former, and contributes as much to derange the health, as peace and contentment tend to its establishment. Agnes had not / firmness of nerves sufficient to withstand the shock to which she had been exposed, or to struggle effectually against her own terrors, and before morning, in defiance of the judicious treatment and unceasing assiduity of her kind attendant, she was not only in a high fever, but delirious and unconscious of everything passing around her. Her plaintive broken sentences, half French, half English, denoted plainly the leading impression on her mind.

Alarmed at the height to which the disorder had arisen, Madame Morinval saw that no time was to be lost in sending for a physician; yet she was reluctant to expose the little girl during these ravings to the observations of a stranger: but there was no alternative, and as she did not know where to send to Mrs. Marchmont for authority to act, she took upon herself the whole responsibility, and requested to speak with her landlord, a respectable tradesman, whose shop adjoined her lodging. On his appearing, she told him that the child under her care had been taken ill in the night, / and begged him to recommend to her some skilful medical man. He gave the information she required, and it was not long before the practitioner he advised her to apply to, arrived. On examining the sick child, he said that though at this early stage of the illness, it was not easy to conjecture how it would terminate, he saw no reason to speak with despondency since there was every thing to hope from the youth of the patient and her apparently good constitution. He advised Madame to procure some assistant in the task of nursing her, wrote a prescription, and promised to call again in the evening.

Scarcely had he been gone ten minutes, when a slip of paper was passed under the bed-room door, on which, with a pencil, these words were written: –

'Can you leave your invalid a moment, and come to us in the next room?'

She went, though with regret, for the delirium of Agnes made her unwilling to lose sight of her, lest she should attempt to get / out of bed during her absence; and as a measure of precaution, she left the door a little ajar that she might hear her in case she stirred.

She found in the front room, Mrs. Marchmont, accompanied by her brother.

In a suppressed voice the latter said: 'What is this, Madame, that we are told by your landlord and his wife concerning your little charge? Is she indeed so seriously ill as the physician has represented?'

Madame Morinval described some of the symptoms of the case, and professed her belief that the attack would be a very severe one.

Mr. Wharton was beginning some further inquiry, when, in one of her worst paroxysms, the child's voice was distinctly heard, crying out: –

'Oh, don't murder me! – Have mercy, have mercy! – I won't struggle – I won't complain – but don't hold me so hard! – Don't be so cruel to me – let me go, let me go!' /

Mrs. Marchmont, trembling, and utterly confounded, looked anxiously at her brother, as if seeking to ascertain what effect was produced upon *him* by these unconscious, but not causeless lamentations. His long-exercised power of self-command, baffled, however, the scrutiny even of one accustomed to study his countenance for years. Agnes had expressed herself in English; for though now she scarcely found any difficulty in speaking French, yet, in moments of perturbation and strong emotion, it was natural that she should recur to her native language – the language in which she still *thought*, even when giving utterance to those thoughts in a foreign tongue. Mr. Wharton was convinced Madame Morinval had not understood the tenour of the child's ravings, and therefore, calmly, though with an air of concern, said: –

'You are perfectly right, madam – her illness is by no means trifling. Pray avail yourself of every possible means of diminishing the fatigue of attending upon her. My sister, / I am sure, will gladly lend you her maid as an assistant. She is a young Swiss woman, and may prove more useful from understanding your language. I am much interested for this poor child, and it is with sincere regret that I find myself compelled by business to hasten on to Paris before the result of her malady can be known. Mrs. Marchmont, however, will remain at Calais, at the — Hotel, till all uncertainty is at an end. When she joins me, should the little girl recover, it would be a real charity in you, madam, to accept a place in my sister's carriage, and assist her in taking care of the convalescent during the journey.'

The fact is, he found that he had carried his rigour and threats too far, and that the little girl's delicate temperament was not proof against such harshness. He judged that the best way to tranquillize her, if a rational interval occurred, would be to assure her that he had left her vicinity, and that the time when she might perhaps be under the same roof / with him, was distant and uncertain. He left to his sister and Madame Morinval the care of giving her this (no doubt) welcome information; and after supplying the latter with money to defray the various expences this illness must occasion, he retired, expressing a hope that all would end well.

Thus almost unavoidably driven to remain at her post, Madame Morinval resigning herself for the sake of her young charge to the disappointment of the personal views that had brought her to France, persevered most zealously in the performance of every kind office in the sick room. Mrs Marchmont, with less judgment, displayed nearly equal solicitude, and was frequent in her attendance. For many days, Agnes was wholly insensible of her presence; but as the fever abated, and glimmerings of reason began to appear, Madame Morinval ventured to suggest that it might be better, while the child was in so feeble and confused a state, that *one* person / only should be seen by her, and that one, a person to whom she was accustomed. This hint was effectual, and Mrs. Marchmont was careful not to show herself till Agnes had been prepared to expect her, and Madame Morinval had been permitted to tell her that Mr. Wharton had preceded his sister to Paris alone.

Illness tames every passion, even those of fear and hatred. In Agnes mild and placable as was her nature, it required much injustice, much ill treatment to awaken the latter feeling, but such had been the conduct of Mr. Wharton, that even in *her* gentle and generous heart, a detestation of him so intense had implanted itself, that she never thought of him without a shudder. She arose from her sick bed with sentiments more chastised, her nerves became gradually less irritable, her spirit was no longer so bitterly resentful, and when she was able to receive and speak to Mrs. Marchmont, it was with comparative serenity, and an endeavour, / at least to appear thankful for the attentions which that lady, as she had heard from Madame Morinval, had shewn her.

Recovery once begun, at Agnes' age, is rapid in its progress, and some step was made daily towards returning health, till at the end of three weeks she was declared sufficiently restored to be able to travel.

The prospect of being still accompanied by Madame Morinval was most consolatory to her; for whatever sobriety her vindictive feelings might have attained, those of gratitude and love for that almost maternal friend were more fervent than ever.

Attended by an experienced courier, the four females, Mrs. Marchmont, her maid, Madame Morinval and Agnes, in an English travelling carriage, proceeded post from Calais to Boulogne, where, in consideration of the child's remaining weakness, they rested the first night. The subsequent part of the route was traversed with more rapidity; but at every town of any consequence Mrs. Marchmont always sent to / the post-office to enquire for letters. She received several, and at night wrote many herself. Other employment she had none; for though an educated and fashionable woman, a love of reading was not amongst her most shining qualifications. She had a few volumes in the carriage, but they were chiefly road-books; and it amused her infinitely more to make Madame Morinval describe the court or bridal dresses of the preceding London season, than to peruse their dry pages. Upon the whole, the opinion which the sagacious Frenchwoman formed of her was, that she was free from pride, was good-natured, and not devoid of feeling, but that she was frivolous to a childish degree, weak in understanding, and but partially well principled. On various occasions Madame Morinval was aware she deviated from the truth, and that even in matters of indifference and almost without consciousness. A habit of this description, attached to poverty of intellect, leads insensibly to many and many a deed of baseness, for he who is guilty of falsehood / when no purpose is to be answered by it will hardly break through the dangerous custom when self-interest instigates its continuance.

The dejection, and the look of ill health she had worn on her first appearance at Calais, diminished day by day and before the end of the journey, she was scarcely recognizable. Her spirits seemed lightened of some heavy load, she recovered her bloom, became talkative; joked with her Swiss maid; encouraged Agnes to be familiar with her; and instead of dwelling with Madame Morinval upon the fashion of gowns and caps, she sought to make her tell anecdotes of their wearers. Unfortunately, she applied to one who was extremely averse to such subjects, and gleaned from her but little information. Madame Leroux might perhaps have satisfied her better.

As they approached Paris, and soon after the delivery of one of the long letters she almost daily received, she ventured for the first time to talk, though in measured terms, of Mr. Wharton. /

'It is wonderful,' she said, addressing Madame Morinval, 'how much more cheerful his letters have become. I am sure we shall find him in high good humour, and it is impossible to describe how different a man he is, when at ease and in spirits. The society, the amusements, and I believe the air of Paris, always do him good.'

As Agnes bore this beginning tolerably well, Mrs. Marchmont allowed herself to go a little further.

'In the letter I had from him this morning, he gives me a little piece of information respecting you, my dear Agnes, that I was entirely unacquainted with.'

The child opened her eyes wide, and looked anxious for an explanation. Mrs. Marchmont smiled: 'Do not be frightened, my good girl,' she resumed, 'all I meant is this; he says (and his authority is not to be disputed) that you have *two* Christian names; Agnes and Lucy.[31] Now, as Lucy appears to me much the prettiest, I shall substitute it for that of / Agnes which, as Madame Morinval can tell you, is given in France to almost every *Soubrette*[32] or shop-girl one meets with.'

The little girl was surprised, but not caring enough about the matter to object to the change, the affair was considered as settled.

They at length reached Paris, and drove up to the house which Agnes was henceforth to consider as her home. Still languid from recent indisposition, her spirits failed her as the carriage stopped. She turned very pale, seemed to gasp for breath, and was seized with a universal tremor. Mrs. Marchmont observed it, and hastened to say: 'I have engaged Madame Morinval, my dear little girl, to sleep here to-night, and you must take care of each other, and go to bed early to recover from the fatigue of your journey. I shall do the same, for I dare say Mr. Wharton is out, and will not return till one or two o'clock in the morning.'

She was then assisted to alight, and conducted, without seeing any thing alarming by / the way, to one of the prettiest apartments she had ever entered. It consisted of a dressing-room, bed-chamber, and light closet adjoining for a maid. That maid soon appeared, with (as in England) a tea-tray in her hands, followed by a footman bearing a kettle and lamp. She congratulated the young lady on her safe arrival; and informed her with much civility, that she had been appointed to have the honour of serving her, and hoped her zeal to give satisfaction would be successful. She spoke excellent French, and was a neat and pleasing looking person of about five and thirty.

The astonished girl unused to such honours, neither knew how to look, nor what to say to her. Madame Morinval, however, to whom it all appeared very natural and proper, spoke for her; she assured Mademoiselle Adrienne that she would find her young mistress *bien douce et bien raisonnable*,[33] and would soon become exceedingly attached to her. Mademoiselle Adrienne replied that she did not doubt it *le moins du monde*[34] for the young lady had an air *on ne / peut pas plus aimable quoiqu'encore un peu abattue*.[35]

These civil speeches passed while tea was preparing, and as soon as it was poured out, the new attendant went into Agnes' bed-room, to unpack her clothes, and get every thing ready for her going to rest.

When they were by themselves, Madame Morinval was anxious to induce the child to look around her with some pleasure, hoping that an air of thankfulness and content would recommend her to those who had provided for her so many accommodations.

'You must not,' she gently observed, 'appear too indifferent, my dear Agnes, when your protectors are doing so much to gratify you.'

'But will they let me go and see you, dear madame?' cried the little creature, 'after tonight, shall I not be separated from you, and left entirely with all these strangers?'

'You cannot now, my dear child, consider Mrs. Marchmont as a stranger, and your new / maid seems to me a very prepossessing young woman. But at all events, I shall be permitted, without a doubt, to come and visit you.'

This was a most welcome assurance, since whatever time might effect, Agnes was as yet in no frame of mind to take an interest in the luxuries that had been brought together for her, all of which appeared as nothing in her eyes, compared with one benevolent look or word from Madame Morinval.

They slept together as usual; in the morning the shutters having been kept closed, and the most perfect silence reigning around her, she awoke late, and found herself alone. Her heart misgave her, she pronounced aloud the name of Madame Morinval and instead of her, saw Mademoiselle Adrienne advance from the adjoining room.

The whole truth flashed upon her mind; she was certain that her kind friend had left her, and equally unable and unwilling to speak, threw herself back upon her pillow in a transport / of grief. Adrienne appeared prepared for this burst of sorrow; she immediately admitted light into the room, and presented to the sobbing Agnes the following note, telling her that Madame Morinval had commissioned her to deliver it the moment her young lady awoke. After some delay, the afflicted girl opened it, and as well as her tears would allow her, read these words:

'I steal away from you, dearest Agnes, to spare both your feelings and my own. I hope I have not judged amiss in seeking to avoid a deliberate leave-taking; forgive me, if you think I have. Mrs. Marchmont has authorized your Adrienne to inform me that I shall be welcome to visit you; depend therefore on seeing me very soon, and meanwhile, exert yourself dear child, to avoid giving a check to the favourable impression it is so desirable that you should make upon your present friends. Heaven bless you, and in every situation of life enable you / to preserve your present artlessness and integrity; this is the hearty prayer of yours

FRANÇOISE MORINVAL.'

The pains taken by Adrienne to sooth and cheer the poor little mourner, and the patience and good feeling she evinced were not without their effect. Desolate and helpless as she was, the child caught at every twig for support, and the compassionate looks and voice of her new comforter were of greater value at that moment than they ever could have been at any other.

When dressed, Adrienne engaged her to enter the sitting-room, where at an open window looking into a small but well arranged flower garden, her solitary breakfast table had been placed. Various amusing objects, such as prints, a small *Camera Oscura*,[36] a magnet, &c., had been sent up stairs, which were to be examined and explained when her meal was over. With singular attention also to what might be supposed most adapted to the taste / of one so long accustomed to the country, her room had been decorated with a variety of fresh and fragrant plants; in addition to which several live pets, amongst which a squirrel and a beautiful little Blenheim spaniel,[37] failed not to attract her notice even at that moment of unaffected sorrow. Thus surrounded, and still attended by the assiduous Adrienne, who contrived a thousand pretexts for not leaving her to brood over her melancholy alone, she insensibly became more composed, and when her breakfast was concluded, found some pleasure in attending to the various novelties that were exhibited to her.

Thus passed the time till noon, when Mrs. Marchmont *en robe de chambre*,[38] came to see her. After sundry kind enquiries, some general chat and many caresses bestowed upon the lively little dog Azor, she told Agnes that at two o'clock her carriage would be at the door to take her to a multitude of shops, and that if she liked it, she should accompany her. Agnes with her wonted humility, said: 'I will, if / you please, ma'am,' and Adrienne was told to get her ready at the time appointed.

Accordingly when summoned, she followed the footman to the landing place on the drawing-room floor, where Mrs. Marchmont stood expecting her, and whence she was about to descend with her to the carriage, when a door suddenly opened and Mr. Wharton appeared! Agnes had hardly time to feel her heart beat, and her knees knock against each other, before he approached her almost with a smile, and in an accent wholly dissimilar to the terrific one in which she had heretofore heard him speak, in an accent, in short of goodnature and cordiality he said:

'Ah, my poor little girl, is it you? I am glad to see you so much better. You do not, however look very strong yet. Take care of her Mrs. Marchmont and when you have done your shopping, give her the refreshment of an airing.'

He then passed on, leaving Agnes so overwhelmed with amazement, that she remained / transfixed to the spot where he had quitted her, and Mrs. Marchmont was obliged to call her two or three times before she heard her, or could recover sufficient recollection to understand what she was expected to do.

The traces of astonishment were still too visible in her face for some time after she entered the carriage, to be overlooked by her companion, who forbearing however to make any remark upon it, only said: 'Did I not foretell very truly Lucy, that this dear Paris would make quite another creature of my brother? He is as lively now as in his earliest youth, and nothing seems to put him out of humour a moment.'

Agnes had she dared, could very sincerely have answered that she had more reason to rejoice at this than any one else; but she was silent though her thoughts were all at work, since unable to account for what had passed and ignorant that Mr. Wharton had overheard her delirious lamentations, and was acting a part politically determined upon, she felt no / dependance upon the durability of his good humour, and it lessened but little her fear of him to find that he was subject to such extraordinary mutations of temper. A more gradual change would have had a better effect, but it would have cost him more trouble, and he was desirous at once to place himself upon the footing with her which it best suited his views to establish.

The purchases Mrs. Marchmont made, and the orders she gave, were almost as numerous for Agnes as for herself, and the day was far spent before she had terminated these, to her, most agreeable avocations. There was no time for the airing her brother had recommended; Agnes was told that amends should be made her the next day: and they drove home.

Unused to such late hours, and faint from want of nourishment, the forethought of Adrienne was never better directed than in providing that everything should be in readiness for her to dine the instant she came in. / She waited upon her during the repast; induced her to give some account of the different places to which she had been, and of some of the gay things she had seen; admired the new purchases; promised to work hard to get them ready for her to wear; and contrived so well, that she kept melancholy aloof, and almost beguiled the little creature of a smile.

The remainder of the day was equally tranquil. Mrs. Marchmont had her own engagements, and appeared no more; nor did Mr. Wharton again show himself. Adrienne, in the cool of the evening, took her young lady down into the flower garden, where she amused herself in tying up the straggling plants, and still more in watering such as required it. On their return to the dressing-room, the ingenious French woman proposed teaching her any easy sort of fancy-work she might wish to learn. Agnes fixed upon what she thought it would least try the patience of her instructress to show her, and it was determined her first attempts should be to weave, with straw and ribbon, a little basket. When / tired of applying to this occupation, Adrienne found a new method of entertaining her – one that never, at any future time, lost its power to charm. She offered to read to her a story in French; and if there were parts of it she did not sufficiently know the language to understand, she said she would stop and explain them. They sat down close to each other, that the child's eye might follow the reader's, and Adrienne began one of Berquin's many beautiful tales.[39]

Agnes' hour of rest struck from the gilt chimney clock, and neither mistress nor maid had been sensible of the progress of time. To the latter, it was most gratifying to witness the interest with which she was heard; to the former, an evening so spent had all the charm of novelty, of vivid and unalloyed delight. True, she was uncultivated; but the soil was good, and ready to receive and to fertilize whatever wholesome seed was thrown into it.

Agnes had lived with those whose minds, like her own, were illiterate; but not therefore / senseless or coarse. Young as she was, the time she had lost might easily be recovered; – there was nothing bad to eradicate, no perverse feelings, no vulgar cunning, no indolent unaptness. All that was to be wished was, that she might be preserved from contracting evil impressions; there was no fear of her neglecting, when placed within its reach, to acquire useful instruction. She went to bed with her mind full of the incidents of the story to which she had been listening – scarcely remembered, for a moment anything relating to herself, or to her own extraordinary situation, collected her thoughts with some difficulty to repeat her customary prayers; and when her head was upon the pillow, probably retraced in her dreams a large portion of what she had been hearing.

Much in the same manner were spent the three or four following days. At the end of that time, she had, at length, the so often longed-for gratification of seeing her dear Madame Morinval. Their meeting was most / affectionate. Agnes made her immediately consent to spend the whole evening with her; took off her bonnet and shawl herself; and asked as many questions about her friend's children, and showed as much interest about them, and everything connected with their mother's happiness, as if she had herself been a member of the same family. Madame Morinval was delighted with her reception, and above all, with the animation her young favourite exhibited, and the evident improvement she saw both in her looks and spirits. She made acquaintance with her two pets, Azor and the squirrel; explored the little museum of curiosities, to which almost daily additions had been made, and when, at a late hour, she was suffered to depart, upon giving a formal promise of speedily renewing her visit, carried away with her a firm conviction that the innocent child had at length been admitted to her most natural and secure asylum – the house of her father.

In her way down stairs, Madame Morinval / was seen and civilly spoken to by Mr. Wharton; who, however, took the earliest opportunity of cautioning his sister not to let her have quite such free access to the house.

'She knows, or at least must suspect too much,' he said, 'to make it safe that she should have such free communication either with the child, or the servants.'

'On the contrary,' answered Mrs. Marchmont, smiling, 'she thinks all that you are doing a mere matter of justice; and if she says anything to the little girl, it will only be to instil into her, ideas of duty, obedience, and gratitude. Her opinion is – for she almost in plain words owned it during our journey – that Agnes is your natural daughter; that you have hitherto had important reasons for keeping her out of sight, but that being now at liberty to take her under your immediate care, you have determined upon educating her conformably to the station in life she is hereafter to fill.'

'A most happy delusion!' exclaimed Mr. / Wharton, much relieved. 'A most fortunate instance of the fertility of Gallic imaginations! But, Mary,' added he, more seriously, 'you must endeavour to put this good woman's harmless powers of invention to a still further use. It is indispensable that the child should change not only her baptismal but her family name. I wish it to be done without contention or compulsion. Perhaps, by representing the case properly to Morinval, the thing might be managed through her agency, with ease and plausibility.'

'Undoubtedly; and you may depend upon its being effected as soon as possible, after I have had a conference with her on her next visit.'

Such commissions, of which fiction, and a certain species of address were to be the indispensable moving springs, suited exactly the talents of Mrs. Marchmont, and rendered her occasionally an invaluable assistant to her brother.

Adrienne, though she was deemed for the / present fully competent to give her young mistress a good French pronunciation, was not thought adequate to supplying the place of instructors in any other branch of education. Masters, therefore, of various descriptions, were engaged, who, in a very little while, scarcely left Agnes more leisure than was requisite for taking daily air and exercise. Her residence was in the neighbourhood of a large public garden, and thither she was sent to walk with Adrienne morning and evening, whenever the weather permitted it. She was also allowed, with the same companion, who was herself a protestant, to attend the service performed at a Lutheran chapel; and occasionally Mrs. Marchmont joined in the same duty.

The assurance she had given her brother of being easily able to induce Madame Morinval to obtain Agnes' consent to the change of name they wished to effect, was fully made good by the event. After speaking in private to the Frenchwoman, and representing Mr. Wharton's motives in the light which she / thought would set them in the fairest point of view, she requested her to go up and speak to the child, and apprize her it was desirable she should henceforth only be known by the name of Lucy de Vere.[40]

Madame Morinval succeeded not in executing this commission without some difficulty. Agnes cared not what she was called; but she could not reconcile herself to the idea of telling what was not true; and she debated the point long and vigorously; more especially as Madame Morinval, not being authorized to mention the near affinity she believed her to bear to Mr. Wharton, could not bring forward that circumstance in support of her advice. However, she urged upon her the propriety of conceding to the wishes of her protectors, in proof of gratitude for all they were doing for her; said it was possible they might have reasons for what they proposed, which, if known, would satisfy every scruple; and, finally, when she found that the honest little creature still resisted, she told her, that whatever opposition / she might make, time would convince her that it was not in her power to prevent the accomplishment of their purpose. 'Therefore, my dearest child,' concluded she, 'submit to what you cannot help with a good grace.'

'To what I cannot help, I suppose I must,' said Agnes, looking much dissatisfied: 'but I cannot imagine why such deceit should be necessary, or why, at least, they should not explain to us the reason of its being required. Every time I hear myself called by these false names, my cheeks will tingle with shame.'

'In all probability, very causelessly, dear Agnes. I cannot for a moment believe that this lady and gentleman have any improper motive for what they have asked; and you must endeavour to entertain of them more respectful thoughts.'

Agnes mentally exclaimed, 'Ah, madame, if you knew all!'

She however refrained, though with difficulty from breaking through the promise that had been extorted from her never to complain, nor / to allude to the events of the memorable night at Cheltenham; and Madame Morinval left her, to inform Mrs. Marchmont of the result of her negociation. That lady and her brother, as if to testify their approbation of Agnes' submission, vied with each other in lavishing indulgences upon her. She was presented with a beautiful pony; and after taking some lessons at a riding school, was frequently sent with a steady old groom, to enjoy a canter in the Bois de Boulogne.[41] Fresh nicknacks were continually placed in her apartment, many of which were exceedingly costly; and she had, her age considered, a large allowance of pocket money assigned her; and there was scarcely an exhibition in Paris which, notwithstanding the frequent interruption thereby given to her lessons, she was not taken to see.

So many excitements, it will readily be believed, were not wholly without their influence. Agnes grew accustomed to the inmates she was with, and though unable to love them, ceased to feel unhappy in their presence. Over Mrs. / Marchmont she imperceptibly and unconsciously gained so much ascendancy, that she became, in fact, the ruler rather than the ruled. Of Mr. Wharton she still continued to stand in awe; but more from her own unconquerable aversion to him, than from any remaining severity exhibited on his part towards her.

Of the comfort of associating with Madame Morinval she was deprived, to her deep regret, at the end of two months, when that true friend came to bid her farewell, previous to leaving France. Agnes made her write down the name and address of her daughter, that she might, through that channel, gain authentic information of her health and welfare; and with some difficulty prevailed upon the disinterested Frenchwoman to accept, as keepsakes, a variety of little presents she had been for some time collecting against this melancholy occasion. They parted with mutual reluctance, and with repeated as well as sincere assurances of lasting attachment.

This separation, for awhile, again depressed / the spirits of Agnes and renewed many of those feelings of desolation she had experienced on being first torn from her early protectors. As these gradually subsided, she was able to attend once more to the instructions of her several masters; and under their tuition, aided by excellent natural abilities and an hourly-increasing passion for reading, she gave the fairest promise of future talent and distinction. She lost however, no part of the modest diffidence she had carried with her to Madame Leroux's. Having no other young person to compare herself with, she was insensible of her own unusual progress; the love of employment was natural to her, and she considered it but as a thing of course that what she was skilfully taught she should be successful in learning. – Her self constituted guardians regarded not the matter with equal *sang-froid*;[42] to Mrs. Marchmont, she soon shone forth as an absolute prodigy; and Mr. Wharton, contemptuously as he viewed female acquirements in general, found it impossible to withhold from hers the / meed of approbation to which they were justly entitled. Discerning as he was, he failed not, ere long, to discover also, that superadded to her capacity of attaining accomplishments, she possessed a vigour of understanding, a clearness of judgment, and a soundness of practical good sense rarely to be met with[43] even in the most intelligent of his own sex. Though involuntarily impressed with a certain species of consideration for one so favorably endowed, it is by no means clear that he would not greatly have preferred having to deal with a girl of considerably more shallow intellect, such a one as in her early youth he remembered Mrs. Marchmont to have been, the flexibility of whose character still rendered her the easiest of creatures to be governed, and the most useful of tools in the hands of a designing man. From Agnes he plainly saw that nothing was to be hoped by admitting her to a participation of his schemes, however artfully coloured; she must be made to work in ignorance, for hers was not a mind that could be seduced by false / representations, or motives of expediency, to call evil good, and good evil. With her it would ever be necessary to hold himself as much upon his guard as with the world at large; and he could not but lament his ill-luck in having selected an instrument which he feared would often prove so troublesome.

With little variation, save of residence, – being taken for a few months to Nice every winter – four years elapsed. The most remarkable occurrence during that period was the establishment in the family of an English governess, who, after Agnes had acquired perfect facility in speaking French, was engaged to supply the numerous deficiencies which, of course, were to be found in Adrienne. She was a respectable and well-principled woman; her manners were unexceptionable, and her temper was mild: but she was dull and phlegmatic; incapable of taking an animated interest in anything: and satisfied, when the routine of the day was over, to sit down to her needle-work and remain silent for hours together. To poor / Agnes, such a companion was a heavy grievance. With a mind active, and overflowing with new and lively impressions, it was indeed hard to be condemned to live with one insensible alike to the inexhaustible pleasures of literature, or the fascination of the fine arts. – There was but one point on which they perfectly agreed. They were both charitable, Mrs. Dawson from duty, and Agnes in addition to these motives, from the impulse of a warm and generous heart. Hers was the purse, and hers was the enjoyment of purchasing the materials with which her governess employed herself indefatigably in making garments for the poor. When one set was finished, she calmly prepared to begin another; resigning to her young pupil, with an apathy at which the latter could never sufficiently wonder, the delight of conveying, (attended by Adrienne) and of presenting in person, to the indigent beings for whom they were designed, these useful and welcome succours. In addition to such gifts, she urged the poor people who had children to send them to / school; promising on that condition to bestow upon the parents a specified weekly allowance. That many complied, was proved by the little specimens of infantine industry which, in a few weeks, were tendered to her, as offerings. These were moments of exquisite gratification to her – of honest pride to the poor children and of heart-felt thankfulness on the part of the parents. Adrienne stood by, half-smiling, half tearful, and in such true admiration of her lovely mistress, that she thought no creature 'of earth's mould,'[44] worthy to be compared with her. /

CHAPTER V.

> He's sick with self-love, and so well persuaded of himself, so crammed as he thinks with excellencies, that it is his ground of faith that all who look on him, love him.
>
> SHAKESPEARE.[45]

ONE of the many indulgences granted to Agnes was the frequent permission of giving juvenile balls at home, or of attending those to which she was invited. With the gay cotemporaries thus brought together it is true she was sedulously restricted from forming any intimacy: but at least it was pleasant to mix with them for a few hours; it gave her manners more polish, taught her the usages of society, and prevented her contracting that old-fashioned / preciseness so often observed in girls who live entirely with grown-up persons.

Mr. Wharton was in the habit of making frequent trips to England, and on his return from one of these, he brought back with him a very handsome youth, whom he introduced to Mrs. Marchmont and Agnes by the name of Harry Cowley. It was during the most animated period of one of the above mentioned youthful balls. The new comer was presented as a partner to the mistress of the revels, and danced with an ease and vivacity not often seen in an English school boy; for such was still Harry Cowley. Agnes was caught by his expressive and ever-varying countenance and the careless sprightliness of his conversation. He told her, that he was a ward of Mr. Wharton's, a distant relation, a sort of cousin, fifty times removed! – 'He came to bid me good bye' added the communicative lad, 'the day before our midsummer holidays were to begin, and I assailed him with such irresistable importunity for permission to accompany him abroad, that / I gained my point almost whether he would or no. Now I am here, I intend to see every thing that is to be seen in Paris, and I promise myself more amusement than I ever yet enjoyed in my life.'

'Do you speak French?' enquired Agnes. 'Very vilely, as most English boys do, who are taught it at school: but I understand it tolerably. You must correct and assist me, for I suppose it is a language as familiar to you as your own. We are to be in the same house, so you will have plenty of opportunity to lend me a helping hand.'

Then, after a brief pause – 'I have often,' he continued, 'heard of you, but you are not the least like what I expected.'

'Heard of *me!*' cried Agnes, in amazement – 'How is it possible?'

'Nothing more easy,' answered he, laughing – 'I had only to listen, and the thing was done! You are to know, that having no father's house to go to, I have spent all my holidays with one of Mr. Wharton's friends, / who frequently heard from him. Well – what I gathered concerning you through his means, induced me to believe that I should find you a sort of invalid, very grave, and very prim, and looking as pale and as good as a little nun!'

'And pray do you now think I look otherwise than good?' enquired Agnes, half in surprise, half in playfulness.

'Oh, good as gold! But, not in the sort of way I expected. When you left England, you were supposed to be in such a precarious state, that it was thought very likely you would never recover; and though Mr. Wharton has been constantly writing over improved accounts of your health, the annual journeys you have been obliged to make to Nice,[46] have kept up the impression that you are not, even yet, thoroughly recovered. Now in my eyes, you look as if nothing ever ailed you; as if you had excellent spirits; and as if, though you may not be a rattle yourself, you would tolerate / my noise and nonsense with all the patience and good-nature in the world.'

Agnes was much amused by this boyish and abrupt familiarity: but she took great care to assure him that the journeys to Nice had not the slightest inference to her health, which had never known interruption from the time she had been so ill at Calais.

'Well, so much the better,' cried he: 'but people who have staid so long out of their own country, must expect that a plentiful quantity of fabrications will be circulated at their expence.'

During this dialogue, Mr. Wharton, at no very remote part of the room, kept a guarded but attentive eye upon them, and, from what his penetration enabled him to conjecture, felt satisfied that nothing passed which could lead to any untoward discoveries. Their first conversation, if at all animated, and sociable, was that from which he thought it probable there was most to fear: afterwards, their subjects / would be those of the passing moment, – and England, and English people, and allusions to gone-by times, would be far less likely to occur.

The youth he had thus unexpectedly introduced to the acquaintance of Agnes and Mrs. Marchmont, was his natural son, promoted by him, within the last two or three years, to become the unconscious aider and abettor of his future projects. Harry, as he advanced in growth, exhibited great personal beauty; and his father discerned in him also the seeds of much sagacity, and every promise he could desire of those qualities which would best fit him for the destiny he meant him to fulfil. In consequence of these observations, the lad was taken from the obscure private seminary at which he had hitherto been educated, and sent to a public school upon the footing of a gentleman's son. The self-distrust, and *mauvaise honte*[47] with which he, at first, was overcome on being suddenly placed in a situation, and amongst associates differing so much from / all that he had hitherto been accustomed to, soon wore off; he became the boldest of the bold; displayed considerable talent, not always unseasoned with presumption; was full of energy; and sanguine in his expectations of attaining to celebrity in whatever career he pursued.

Agnes with her plain, straightforward good sense, was not blinded by the shewiness of his parts to overlook his self-sufficiency: – but he was the first companion of an age approximating to her own, with whom she had been permitted to form anything resembling a domestic intimacy, and his society was a most enlivening episode in the uniformity of her school-room life. Like herself, he was fond of reading – but chiefly poetry, or high-sounding specimens of oratorical eloquence. A fine *tirade*[48] in a Parliamentary debate, in an harangue at the bar, or a discourse in the pulpit, were equally enchanting to him. Possessed of a memory almost miraculous, the immense store he had acquired of these fragments of / 'the sublime and beautiful'[49] was scarcely credible. He declaimed with pompous dignity, with vehemence, or with indignant sarcasm, according to the different themes he took in hand. Agnes listened to him, often with admiration, sometimes with a lurking smile, and not always without weariness. Quick-sighted, where his vanity was concerned, he challenged her, on these latter occasions, to explain the symptoms he had detected:

'Do you not feel the beauties of our English oratory, my dear Lucy?' said he – 'Have you lived so much abroad that your taste has become vitiated and Frenchified?'

'I do not know,' answered she, good humouredly, 'whether my long residence abroad has anything to do with it: but certainly, I have no taste for bombast either in diction or in subject.'

'Do you call these fine passages, bombastic?'

'Not all; but many are; and to tell you the truth, your manner of reciting them does / not by any means contribute to make them less so.'

'Would you have them delivered with tameness and insipidity?'

'Is there no medium? – Must you either tear a passion to rags,[50] or set us all to sleep?'

The youth was silenced for a moment; but, speedily recovering his wonted confidence, exclaimed: – 'Come, dear girl, let us end this useless discussion, and talk of something else. When you have seen and heard a little more, you will be a better judge of these sort of matters.'

Agnes, who had no wish to hurt his pride, dropped the subject, though not insensible of the absurdity of hearing a boy, only a twelve-month older than herself, cast reflections upon her want of experience. At his request, she played and sung to him; which, as he had a genuine love for music, and a correct ear, was an entertainment they could participate together without so much danger of differing in opinion. /

In many things, indeed, (as would have been the case with most other young people) their tastes coincided. They both loved riding, and often made excursions together, attended by the old groom. With Mr. Wharton or Mrs. Marchmont they frequently visited the public galleries, or some one of the thousand interesting sights with which Paris abounds. Their evenings were generally spent at the theatre; and thus furnished with amusement for every successive hour, the six weeks allotted to Harry for his stay in France, rapidly and insensibly glided away. He was to visit them again the following year, a prospect which however distant it appeared to him, somewhat diminished the reluctance with which he now departed. Agnes frankly testified her regret on taking leave of him; and for many days after he was gone, found the silence of the school-room, and the torpidity of Mrs. Dawson, almost intolerable. Soon recovering her wonted cheerfulness, however, and resuming with fresh diligence the studies with her several / masters which had of late been so continually interrupted, a week had not passed, ere every trace of concern had vanished from her mind.

The days of education, though sometimes looked back to with pleasure, are monotonous whilst in progress, and admit of little description. In the present instance they differed not from the general rule.

True they were enlivened by an annual visit from Harry Cowley, and by journeys either into Switzerland, to Spa,[51] or whatever other watering-place was in fashion for the season. These, though they checked for awhile the progress Agnes was making with her masters, neither inured her to habits of idleness, nor were otherwise than useful in contributing to confirm her health, and enlarge her understanding. Observant and intelligent, few objects worth remark passed by her unnoticed; and whilst filling her sketch book with striking views, and picturesque figures or groups, she was far from being inattentive to the diversity of customs and manners, or the characteristic / singularities amongst the different classes of people she was able to have communication with.

Amusing as these travelling parties always proved, they succeeded not however in detaching her memory from the early friend to whom she owed so deep a debt of gratitude. Her first care, invariably on returning to Paris, was to despatch Adrienne to enquire after Madame Morinval at the residence of her daughter; or, if possible, to hasten thither herself. She wrote to her frequently, and seized every opportunity of forwarding to her some fresh token of affectionate remembrance. The daughter, who was now married, and pursued the same business as the mother, she constantly employed herself, and recommended successfully to her young friends. The son she had less ability to serve: but fortunately, he little required it; he was the head clerk at a wine merchant's, and by his good character and conduct, gave promise of attaining to future ease and independence.

Harry Cowley, now converted from a flippant / school-boy, to a self-sufficient and somewhat dogmatical collegian, had usually been one of the party during the summer excursions of Mr. Wharton and his family, receiving from that gentleman every possible encouragement to pay his court to Agnes. Nor would the indulgent guardian have even scrupled to sanction their immediate union, although the oldest of the two was yet little more than nineteen. At all events, he was desirous that they should engage themselves to each other; and Harry, thus privileged, and tormented by no diffidence of success, sought 'once a pliant hour,'[52] whilst they were travelling in Switzerland, to draw from her a confession of her regard, after volubly and fervently declaring his own. Agnes could not be much surprised at this language, for it required little sagacity to anticipate that the intimacy she was permitted to form exclusively with young Cowley, was intended by Mr. Wharton to lead to their marriage: but she was pained by it, though prepared, long since, to decline the engagement. /

The character of Harry had not improved upon her; she wished him well, and as an acquaintance, she had no dislike to him; – as a husband, the case was far different. To the presumption and conceit he had very early manifested, she had since seen superadded an abundant share of egotism and petulance. Disdainful of others, consequential and sarcastic, the expression of his countenance, handsome as it was, had often offended her, – and the mistrust she had imbibed of the goodness of his temper, confirmed the prepossession she entertained against him. With all the delicacy, however, and gentleness that the subject would admit, she proceeded to answer his declaration, and put an end to his hopes; but so deeply did he resent what he deemed her insulting rejection, that it seemed at first as if he would scarcely deign to take the trouble of soliciting a more favourable sentence. It was evident that he had not harboured the slightest apprehension of failure; and one of the exclamations he the oftenest repeated was: /

'This repulse utterly confounds me! It is in every respect incomprehensible!'

Agnes bit her lips, but said nothing, and turned to rejoin Mrs. Marchmont who was walking with her brother at some distance behind them.

In a few seconds, Harry started forward and overtook her:

'Give me, at least,' cried he, struggling to controul his anger – 'give me some reason for this extraordinary refusal! Have I done anything to displease you? Have any busy tongues been at work to convey to you reports to my disadvantage? Tell me, in short, what has led to a decision which your whole preceding conduct had given me so little cause to anticipate?'

'Has any part of my preceding conduct, Harry, given you cause to think I was in love with you? Ask yourself honestly what has been the amount of the partiality I have ever shewn you? Has it extended beyond the bounds of good-will and regard such as a residence / under the same roof, and an intercourse so habitual as ours would naturally awaken? You cannot, with justice, accuse me of having played the coquette; neither can you, with justice, object to my exercising the right I possess of maintaining my own independence.'

Never had the young man received such a lesson, and never till this moment had he been so sensible of the high value he attached to Agnes's favour! Had she unhesitatingly accepted him, as he concluded would be the case, he might not have known how absolutely she reigned in his heart; – advantages too easily obtained are apt to lose their importance: – but now, in danger of utterly losing her, every attraction she possessed, every emotion of tenderness she had ever inspired, assumed a stronger colouring; in short, the man who had proposed himself with the easy security of a coxcomb, quitted her, when repulsed with the impassioned feelings of a lover.[53]

It was immediately apparent to the keen eye of Mr. Wharton on seeing them again, / that something conclusive had occurred. Agnes had overcome the servile fear of him which she had felt as a child; yet it was not without some acceleration of pulse, that she stood before him, after having dared to decide for herself, in a matter proposed to her by his authority. Great, then, was her relief, when, addressing her with an open and almost smiling aspect he said: 'I see, my dear Lucy, how the business stands; Harry has offered himself to your acceptance, and you have refused him. So much the worse, poor fellow, for him! His disappointment, I am aware, must be severe, but never suppose, my good girl, that I wish to play the tyrannical guardian, and to fetter your free choice; it is true, Harry, had my permission, to address you, and my best wishes, I will not deny, for his success; further, I neither promised, nor ever meant to go.'

Then, turning to the crest-fallen youth: 'My poor boy,' said he, 'I feel for the distress you are suffering, bear up against it, however, / like a man. Lucy I am persuaded, will never become indifferent to the welfare and happiness of her early friend; and though she may not admit you to a dearer title, she will not when you are in England, deny you the consolation of becoming her correspondent, nor withdraw from you the sisterly interest she has hitherto shewn you. I never could understand why a woman should refuse a man's friendship, because she has refused him her love.'

Agnes was too young and inexperienced to see through the wiliness of this speech. She stretched forth her hand to the deeply-mortified youth; assured him of her lasting regard; consented to receive his letters, and promised to answer them.

To Harry this appeared a miserable recompense for what he was losing. Mr. Wharton, however, in a private conference with him, undertook to demonstrate, that it was calculated to secure the attainment of all he could desire. 'Who knows,' said he, 'whether / your letters may not have more influence over her, than any personal assiduities? You must season them with ardent professions of attachment, with much adroit flattery, with scraps of impassioned poetry, with appeals to her compassion for the wretchedness to which she has doomed you, with complaints, incidently and artfully thrown out, of the debilitated state of your health, and the unconquerable depression of your spirits. Follow up this plan with perseverance; get Mr. Gage, (the friend whose house was Harry's home during every vacation,) to write to me occasionally such letters as may confirm these insinuations, and, my life for it, in less than a twelvemonth, Lucy will be brought round; her coldness will vanish, and she will be ready to yield to your wishes. Meanwhile, *my* plan must be, to act the indulgent and undesigning guardian; to harass her neither by remonstrances nor persuasion, but, effectually to secure her from holding intercourse with any other marriageable man, and cautiously to / disseminate the opinion that she is already engaged.'

Here was perhaps more subtlety than Harry, uninfluenced by self-interest might have deemed honourable, or, differently circumstanced, might have been prevailed upon to adopt; but as the case now stood, the temptation was too strong for him, and he determined to follow the advice of his crafty counseller.

He deferred not long, after this, his departure from Switzerland, and return to England. Agnes seeing him look subdued and unhappy, treated him with great kindness on his bidding her farewell; and fondly anticipated the pleasure of seeing him revisit Paris at no very distant period, an altered man, – that is, a man no longer in love – at least, with her.

Time glided on, and she attained her eighteenth year.[54] Every prospect before her, was bright and cheering; she was caressed at home, and courted abroad; she lived in the enjoyment of all that youth, health, and affluence / could bestow; yet, at that very period, she first began to experience the pangs of secret self-condemnation; to wonder at, and to regard as almost criminal, the thoughtless quiescence in which she had so long existed; and to awaken, as from deep sleep to the full consciousness of having been the passive instrument employed to carry on a scheme of mystery – of deception – perhaps of the darkest guilt!

The circumstance to which this view of her situation was owing, though simple, was in its effects immediate and decisive.

Mrs. Marchmont, always eager to forestall her wishes, had volunteered to lend her a beautiful little writing-desk, whilst her own was undergoing some alteration, saying at the same time,

'I would give it you, my dear, with pleasure, were it not too small to be of any real use. However, it may preserve you, during the few days you will want it, from stooping so much over your writing.' /

Agnes accepted the temporary substitute with thanks; and in the evening, having occasion to answer a note, had recourse to the desk, remembering to have seen in it a quire or two of ornamented blank paper. On taking out one of these, there dropped from between its leaves, an unfolded letter in a child's hand, which, being full of blots and erasures, was probably only the rough draft of the one actually sent. This letter was signed, *Lucy de Vere!* – Agnes started as if an adder had stung her, and with difficulty repressed a scream of astonishment. Fearful, however, of attracting the observation of Mrs. Dawson, who was sitting with her, she arose as calmly as she could, and taking up a candle went into her own room. There, with breathless agitation, she read the following lines,

'My dear papa,

'This is my birthday – and I am writing to you upon a beautiful new desk, Mrs. Marchmont has made me a present of this morning. / I am very well, dear papa, but I wish you would come home, for I want you to see how nicely the flower-roots you sent me, have blown. I have put eight in glasses, and the rest in garden-pots. My bullfinch pipes better than ever, and eats seeds out of my hand. I cannot think of anything more to say, so good bye, dear papa, love your little girl, and she will always be your dutiful and affectionate

LUCY DE VERE.'

Agnes could not read this letter to the end without the deepest emotion. 'Poor innocent!' she cried – 'where art thou now? Why hast thou been spirited away? Why has a stranger been substituted in thy place? Wretch that I am! how I hate myself for having been so long the unresisting usurper of all thy rights! How many indications ought ere this, to have pointed out to me that Lucy de Vere was no imaginary personage! But I shut my eyes against conviction, and have been living contentedly upon the reward earned / by my silent and base acquiescence! Oh, forgive me, gracious heaven, and vouchsafe to aid me in the task of extricating myself from this guilty path!'

As her eye rested again upon the letter of the injured child, and she again repeated – 'What has become of you?' her blood ran cold whilst the image of Mr. Wharton crossed her mind. In defiance of every effort he had made to ingratiate himself in her favour, he had never succeeded in thoroughly effacing the first evil impression he had stamped upon her mind. There was a something in his countenance from which her nature had always recoiled – a lurking duplicity, a covert look of suspicion – an almost superhuman keenness of penetration, that at once denoted his own distrust, and awakened it in others. She never for a moment, if she could avoid it, remained alone with him, for his eye when fixed upon her (as it often was) was as fearful to her as would have been the gaze of the basilisk.

'And this man,' she mentally cried, 'this / dark and unfathomable being, has had the disposal, it appears, of the unhappy child, I am assisting to despoil! She mentions Mrs. Marchmont in her letter as if residing with her; – probably, the brother and sister were inmates, as now. What have they done with their charge? Have they destroyed her by ill-treatment? Is she really dead, or living in want and obscurity? Oh that I could, if such has been her fate, get justice done her, and obtain for her the restoration of all her rights! With what joy would I surrender the place I am so illegally holding!'

Lost in these reflections she forgot the progress of time till, at length, hearing Mrs. Dawson move in the next room, she became aware of the necessity of putting more command upon herself; and securing the letter, to her so every way interesting, returned to her former post. From her unobservant governess she well knew she had nothing to fear however silently she might spend the remainder of the evening. Provided she was under her own / eye, appeared well, and seemed engaged in any of her customary pursuits, Mrs. Dawson was satisfied, and took it for granted that all was right. Adrienne was more discerning; and at a later hour, whilst assisting her to undress, could not forbear saying, with a look of anxiety,

'Something has vexed you, my dear young lady; you are not like yourself this evening.'

'True, Adrienne,' answered Agnes, turning towards her with much kindness, 'but do not ask me any questions. If I could confide in any body, it should be in you. At present, however, I am obliged to remain silent. Make no remarks in the house that may draw attention upon me. Time will set everything right; and meanwhile be assured I am truly grateful for the concern you show for me.'

Adrienne, though superior to many of her class, was not superior to the weakness common amongst all female domestics, of shedding tears abundantly upon every little untoward / occurrence. Agnes implored her to refrain, but ineffectually. She then recommended her not to go down stairs again that night; and the poor creature, yielding to her wishes, retired supperless to bed, and cried herself to sleep.

Agnes lay awake half the night, trying to form some plan for the future, and vainly wishing that she had any disinterested and efficient friend, whose wisdom might guide, and whose authority might protect her. But so vigilantly had she been watched, that in the midst of a crowded city, and living much in society, she never had had an opportunity of establishing a confidential intercourse with any one. Thrown therefore, entirely upon the resources of her own mind, the difficulties attending almost every expedient that suggested itself seemed so various and so insuperable, as nearly to drive her to despair. Should she seek to withdraw herself privately from Mr. Wharton's house, whither could she go? Who would countenance, who would employ / her? And without employment, how was she to subsist?

She sometimes thought, though with trepidation, of referring to Mr. Wharton himself for the elucidation of all the mysteries with which he had surrounded her? She could have told him that she had no projects of hostility – no desire to bring disgrace upon him; but the firmest resolution to lend herself no longer to his schemes, and the most ardent desire to see justice done, if she yet survived, to the unfortunate Lucy. With a man like Wharton, however, she justly feared that such an appeal would prove but a vain and romantic experiment. She had once, in a moment of impatience, hazarded saying to Mrs. Marchmont, who was pleading the cause of Harry Cowley:

'Why, if you are his friend, madam, should you wish him to marry an impostor? You know, as well as I do, that I am not what I seem! – my very name is a forgery. Where then is the man whose wife I could lawfully become?' /

Mrs. Marchmont, struck and abashed by this warm and unwonted remonstrance, flew, in great alarm, to her brother, to whom she repeated the whole. He was not a man to be so easily disconcerted:

'Go back to her, Mary,' said he, calmly, 'tell her that you have related to me what has passed; and tell her, at the same time, that though her scruples do her honour, they are perfectly unfounded, and originate only in her ignorance of the real class of life in which she was born, and the circumstances that led to her being rescued from obscurity, and restored to her proper station. Add, that the day is not far distant, when the whole affair will be cleared up to her – Something,' he muttered indistinctly, 'must be held forth to quiet her confounded suspicions! Would she were of weaker intellects and more ductile materials!'

He thought of his sister, and lamented that the same description of mind had not animated the person of his ward. /

Silenced by an answer so positive and so plausible, Agnes had once more suffered her conscience to slumber, till so effectually roused by the discovery of Lucy de Vere's letter. This, no doubt, deprived Mr. Wharton's assertions of all credibility; but it did not therefore follow that he would acknowledge his fraud. Some new subterfuge would be devised; or, such might be his rage at being detected, that she might fall a sacrifice to his revenge. Who was there to protect her? who was interested to enquire after her fate? She stood alone in the world; she had neither friends, kindred, nor fortune; and she was removed from all possibility of throwing herself for protection upon the laws of her country.

Had Mrs. Dawson, whom she knew to be a really good and well principled woman, been of a more energetic character, she might have opened to her her heart, and sought from her counsel and assistance; but tame and unenterprizing as she was, there was every reason / to fear she would shrink affrighted from taking any active part, and merely mourn and lament over her in helpless despondency.

Exhausted by long wakefulness and meditations, ending as they had begun, in perplexity and indecision, Agnes, towards morning, dropt asleep, after recommending herself for future guidance to the mercy of Providence.

The following day, if it opened to her as its predecessor had closed, in sadness and disquietude, speedily shone forth the brightest of her life. She breakfasted so much earlier than Mrs. Marchmont, that she was permitted to take that meal up stairs with her governess; and Adrienne, knowing the newspapers were always acceptable to her, and were not wanted below till a much later hour, brought two into the room whilst they were pouring out their coffee. Mrs. Dawson took up one, and Agnes, with profound indifference, cast her eyes over the other, which was English. A name at the bottom of a long paragraph awakened her attention; she turned back to the beginning of / the column, and read with sensations impossible to describe the following article:

'An admirable group from the chisel of an English artist, now residing in Rome, was lately landed at Dover, and conveyed to the seat of Lord — in Gloucestershire. His Lordship permitted it to be viewed at his house in town for several days before it was sent off; and we were amongst the fortunate few apprized of its arrival and admitted to behold it. The subject is truly classical, and represents Antigone guiding the steps of her blind father, the ill-fated Œdipus.[55] The contrast of age and of sex, is one of its least striking merits; what the artist has most excelled in is the singular propriety with which he has preserved the respective characters of his two personages. Œdipus, fallen from his high estate, blind, persecuted both by gods and men, a wanderer, and a predestined victim, yet retains an air of dignity the most majestic – a countenance which though clouded / by affliction and no longer young, is eminently handsome, and a figure, slightly bent, but of heroic proportions, and the finest symmetry. Of Antigone, the sweet Antigone – the most touching female character in fabulous or historic times – we can find no words to describe the purity, the loveliness, the grace and sensibility. Whilst gazing upwards at the noble old man, every tender feeling that pity and filial reverence can engender, is visible in her soft and mournful aspect; its expression indeed is so truly pathetic, that it may be almost said of itself to tell the story of her father's woes, and to be alone sufficient to fill the beholder's eyes with sympathizing tears. Altogether, it is a work that does the highest honour as well to the artist, as to the country that gave him birth. We understand that his name is Danvers, and that he is a native of the West of England.'

How did the heart of Agnes beat! – how did her cheeks glow when she came to the last line / of this paragraph! She sat in silent ecstacy, fearing to move lest she should be looked at, but full of mental thankfulness for this ray of comfort, this gleam of hope! She remembered having in her childhood heard continual allusions made to her brother William Danvers. She had never seen him, or at least she had no recollection of him, for he had left home before she was old enough to pay any attention to the circumstance; but she was persuaded that her memory was correct in reminding her that it had been said he was established as an artist in some foreign country. The impression also struck her that his extraordinary cleverness had been often alluded to; and once again she seemed to behold in 'her mind's eye,'[56] the model in clay of a favourite dog which used to stand upon her mother's chimney, and was always spoken of as the work of her brother William, when a boy.

This last particular was in her estimation conclusive, and rendered his identity with the sculptor at Rome unquestionable. So enchanted / was she at the moment this newly remembered model recurred to her thoughts, that, forgetting Mrs. Dawson was present, she unconsciously clasped her hands, and ejaculated half aloud:

'Heaven be praised! he lives, and I shall find him!'

Surprised out of her usual apathy, Mrs. Dawson looked up, and with some approach to quickness, said:

'What are you talking of, my dear? What *him* do you mean?'

Agnes laughed, but evading the question, only answered:

'Make haste, dear Mrs. Dawson, and finish the paper you are reading, or you will have no time to look at the other; for Adrienne, you know, always comes for them at ten o'clock.'

The hint was effectual; Mrs. Dawson read for her life; and Agnes was left to her joyful meditations.

Desolate, unfriended, unconnected as she had believed herself but a quarter of an hour / before, what a change was there now in all her feelings! How thankful to Providence was her heart! how gladdened by the belief that through its merciful interposition her eye had been guided to the consolatory paragraph! Next to the authority of a father was that of a brother. A brother, therefore, in her orphan state, was of all protectors the one she had most reason to desire.

'He does not know me,' she thought, 'but he will be kind to me, for our mother's sake, perhaps he will even rejoice to gain a sister, and to find that he is no longer without a tie upon earth; that nature has provided him a friend who will take a deeper interest in his happiness than all the world beside. Oh, that I had wings to fly to him like a bird! That forsaking all the unhallowed profusion showered upon me here, I could find myself in peace and innocence seated by his side, watching the progress of his honest employment!'

The result of these and similar meditations, was, at the end of a few days a determination / to address a letter to him, *poste-restante*,[57] Rome. Its purport was as follows:

'A person, deeply interested in the enquiry, entreats to be informed whether Mr. Danvers, whose name lately appeared, coupled with so much commendation in the English newspapers, is a native of the village of Meadwell in Gloucestershire, and the son of William and Elizabeth Danvers, long resident in that parish? His answer will be most anxiously expected, as it will either confirm or destroy a hope unspeakably dear to the present writer.

'Mr. Danvers is requested to address to A. Z. under cover to Mademoiselle Adrienne la Roche, chez Jean Dupuis, Rue du Colombier, No. 29, Paris.'[58]

The direction given above was one previously agreed upon with Adrienne, in whom Agnes had been compelled to place a partial confidence, with the firmest reliance, however, / upon her most perfect discretion. In the street referred to, the maid had a kinsman who was a printer, and who would, after receiving due notice from her, take the letter in, and keep it in safe custody till called for.

Whether Mr. Wharton remarked the paragraph, so important to Agnes, she had no means of verifying. His was not a countenance by which any judgment of what was passing in his mind could be formed. He had it under such perfect command that it was scarcely possible to trace in it anything he wished to conceal. /

CHAPTER VI.

> Every man has not a soul of crystal, for all men to read their thoughts through; men's hearts and faces are so far asunder that they hold no intelligence.
>
> BEAUMONT AND FLETCHER.[59]

CAUTIOUS as Mr. Wharton had ever been with regard to the persons, English more especially, whom Agnes was suffered to become acquainted with, he was compelled, about this time, to relax somewhat from the severity of his system.

A family party from England, the leader of which, Mrs. Le Strange,[60] was the sister of Mrs. Marchmont's late husband, was hourly expected at Paris. A handsome hotel had been taken for one of her daughters, just married; whilst the other three were to accompany their mother to the residence of Mr. Wharton, whose guests they were for a / time invited to become. The youngest girl, however, a great favourite with the bride, and with her new brother-in-law, it was finally settled should remain with them; and consequently Mrs. Le Strange, with only two of her flock, made her appearance at Mr. Wharton's.

Between Mrs. Le Strange and Mrs. Marchmont, there was no other affinity than that resulting from family connexion; in disposition they were essentially different. The latter was vain, silly, good-natured, easily intimidated, and perhaps from that very circumstance dangerous, since fear could have rendered her capable of almost any excess. Fortunately she was, if dealt with by one who understood her, just as easily reassured.

Mrs. Le Strange was completely a woman of the world, intent upon forwarding the interests of her family; remarkable for self-possession, skilful in practising upon the foibles of others, yet incapable of meanness, except upon a large scale. She descended to no petty tricks, but formed schemes that had / magnificence in them; decided that her daughters should all attain to high rank; that her eldest son should rise to the first dignities in the state, (he was a member of parliament,) and that the younger, (a Woolwich cadet,)[61] should hereafter surpass his cotemporaries in valour, abilities, and success.

A tacit convention seemed to have been agreed upon between her and Mr. Wharton. They never interfered one with the other; but, equally clear sighted, each party appeared to appreciate properly the qualities of the other; and no two people were ever more smiling, amiable, and well-bred than they were whenever they met. It was certain, however, that in his heart he hated and feared her; whilst she, knowing him to be a yet more expert dissembler than herself, despaired of gaining any thing by watching him, and was studious to imitate, if she could not rival, the vigilant guard he kept over his looks and language. She little imagined how insignificant were the artifices *she* sought to conceal, compared with / those it was his ceaseless endeavour to render impenetrable!

The two daughters by whom she came accompanied to his house, united to pre-eminent attractions of person, very superior accomplishments, and an air of distinguished fashion. The eldest was three-and-twenty, the other a year younger. Their third sister was the one lately married; and the fourth, Isabel, equalled both the eldest in beauty, was their superior in natural endowments, and in no respect fell short of them in acquired talents. She had not yet been brought out in London, but was to make her first appearance in the fashionable world the ensuing season, and had long been speculated upon by her mother as the sister likely to form the most brilliant establishment. They all, Louisa, Caroline, and Isabel, excelled in whatever could contribute to the amusement of the circle – the little world within the world – to which they belonged.

As guests in a country house they were invaluable. They could act, and act well, whether / in serious or comic parts; they were incomparable mimics; could give specimens of the national dances of almost every country in Europe; and dressed better for the representation of tableaux, combined the groups, and placed the lights and shadows with more skill than any young ladies unassisted by professed artists, had ever been known to do. They were also good musicians, and drew, not merely as copyists, but from imagination and from nature. Their sketches, whether slightly shadowed, or mere outlines, were almost quarrelled for, and could money have obtained them, would have been bought up with avidity. In addition to these qualifications, and the knowledge of several languages, their conversation was lively, and sometimes gave evidence of a reasonable share of good sense. They were not often arrogant, they had not bad tempers, and showed but little want of feeling.[62]

The third sister – the one 'dim star' in this resplendent constellation,[63] had early exhibited / deficiencies, too hopeless and too glaring to be viewed without unutterable mortification by her disappointed mother. From her thirteenth year, when the fatal discovery was made, that she had neither ear nor voice; that she danced ungracefully and out of time; that her memory was slow; that she would always be short; that her teeth, though white, insisted upon growing uneven in defiance of the ablest dentists; and that she had often a hesitation in her speech, – when all these enormities were ascertained, nearly every chance of future success seemed at an end, and when she was mentioned, it became the habit of the house to call her 'poor Bertha.'

This humiliating comparison, and the disparaging remarks she was continually obliged to hear, failed however to depress her in the degree that might have been expected. She was willing to admit her inferiority to her sisters, but firmly determined not to consider herself either as a fool or a monster of ugliness. She thought that she might do very well in despite / of her imperfections. She had good health, good spirits. She knew that even if she never married, she was secure of a competency; she had many resources, though devoid of accomplishments. She delighted in gardening; she was fond of reading, of riding, and of walking; she was expert in all sorts of fancy-work, and felt persuaded, as she often told her governess, that there were quantities of people not at all better looking than herself, who, though they had no chance of being admired, passed uncensured, and were contented and happy.

Meanwhile, sweet tempered and unenvious, she was perhaps herself the most enviable member of the family. So moderate were her expectations, that whatever notice was bestowed upon her was received as an obligation; and neglect, if she experienced it, was overlooked, or considered as a thing of course. Thus roughly, but usefully disciplined, she pursued her unoffending way, often enchanted by the simplest pleasures, and never depressed by mortified ambition. /

Who would believe that this slighted, this untalented, this despaired of Bertha, could become the subject of the following letter? It had been written to her mother, by Mrs. Marchmont not very long before the arrival of the former in Paris.

'My dear Mrs. Le Strange,

'My brother has just communicated to me a report so universally prevalent amongst our English friends, and apparently so well authenticated, that nothing but your silence makes me hesitate in believing it. Is it true that Lord Glenfeld has made proposals for Bertha? I am all impatience for your answer. I long to write to the dear girl; but till I hear how the case really stands, it may be more prudent to abstain. Pray how has she grown up in point of looks? I did not used to think that she gave such flattering promise as might have been expected from the beauty of her sisters.

'Be that as it may, it seems clear that I / may congratulate you on the approaching marriage of *one* of your daughters; and I have such a true regard for them all, that whichever it may be, it gives me the sincerest pleasure.

'Adieu, my dear sister; Robert unites in every kind wish with yours affectionately,

'MARY MARCHMONT.'

'Well said, my dear affectionate Mary;' cried Mrs. Le Strange, after reading this epistle, 'or rather, well said, my politic friend Robert Wharton: for this has been penned under his dictation, I am fully persuaded. Not caring three straws for any of my girls, or for any girl in the world, except his marvellous heiress; yet thinking it may prove of use to be upon a good footing with the future Lady Glenfeld, he recommends to his half-witted sister a form of felicitation which will equally suit any one of the damsels, and which I am left to fill up as circumstances may require. Well, I have a spare quarter of an hour, and / will e'en employ it in relieving their perplexity.

Thus soliloquizing, Mrs. Le Strange took up a pen – deliberated for a moment, and then wrote in these terms:

'My dear sister,

'Report has been a little premature, for when the information you mention reached your side of the water, Lord Glenfeld's proposal had not been made. Yesterday, however, decided the affair, and this morning I should probably have written to you, even had your kind letter given no spur to my activity, for I well know the pleasure you will receive from the confirmation of the rumour.[64] The marriage will take place in about a month, and it would gratify me extremely were you and Mr. Wharton able to be present at the ceremony. What is it that so bewitches you to Paris? Your ward, I hear, is in perfect health now, and requires no longer those annual migrations to Nice which formerly were recommended. / Bring her amongst us then, and let her at length learn, to consider herself as an Englishwoman.

'Adieu, my dear Mary. Give my best compliments to Mr. Wharton, and believe me, ever very truly yours,

'AUGUSTA LE STRANGE.'

P.S. I was closing my letter, when it occurred to me, I had omitted to state that *Bertha* is indeed the object to whom your congratulations may be addressed. Further let me add, that should you prove deaf to our wishes of seeing you in England, there is every chance of your having an early opportunity of judging for yourself of the personal appearance of the young bride. There is great talk amongst us of an intended trip to Paris shortly after the marriage. Once more, dear MARY, ADIEU.'

Mrs. Marchmont, alas! was not permitted to accept this invitation, though dying to make one in the pleasurable bustle of a fashionable / wedding; and well convinced she could never have enjoyed a more favourable opportunity of shining forth with effect in all her Parisian elegance. But Mr. Wharton was inexorable:

'I cannot accompany you,' he said, 'for so public an exposure to the observation of my creditors, would ruin me. Whenever necessity takes me to England, you are aware of the disguises to which I am compelled to have recourse. That Agnes should go with you is equally impracticable. Every thing depends upon keeping her out of the way of officious intermeddlers, till her marriage with Harry is concluded. It would not however, be easy to give a reason for leaving her behind on so gay an occasion – and perhaps, some disapprobation might be excited by her being left here exclusively under my protection.'

There was no controverting the justice of this representation, and Mrs. Marchmont, with a sigh, submitted; but as total inaction in such a case was not to be borne, she wrote two pages of felicitation to Bertha, pressing / her in the most urgent manner to undertake the projected excursion to which Mrs. Le Strange had alluded; making a thousand offers of service, and assuring her that nobody was better qualified to be of use, either in selecting for her, a suitable residence before she came, or in directing her after her arrival to the tradespeople most in vogue.

Bertha, new to such amiable attentions, for this was the first letter Mrs. Marchmont had ever addressed to her, carried it immediately to her mother, to consult with her how it ought to be answered.

'Leave the whole business to me, my dear,' said Mrs. Le Strange, smiling, 'it cannot be supposed that you, at present, have time to reply to all the complimentary epistles that may be poured down upon your devoted head. This, though from so near a connexion, is much of the same class as the others. I must necessarily write to her again soon, concerning the arrangements she must make for your sisters, and myself preparatory to our entering Paris; / and when the pen is in my hand, I will say all that is right and proper for you.'

Had the arrival of the Le Stranges preceded the despatch of Agnes's letter to Rome, had she met them with the degrading consciousness of being the usurper in society of a place that was not her due, the introduction to them would have been painful and embarrassing. As it was, regarding herself as a merely temporary intruder, it amused her to have an opportunity of observing the difference between English and French people of *ton*.[65] There was not quite the dissimilarity of appearance she had expected to see. But there were points of distinction that gradually became more and more perceptible. The English women wanted that conciliating, and almost benign amenity of expression a French woman of high breeding knows so well how to throw into her voice and countenance, and which, duly modified, is so welcome an encouragement on a first introduction, to the young and the diffident. Neither Mrs. Le Strange nor her daughters had the / slightest intention of being deficient in courtesy towards Agnes; nor was she in the least annoyed by any display of haughtiness; yet she went to bed impressed with the idea that they were in fact extremely fine ladies. They had *examined* rather than simply *looked* at her; almost every word they had spoken, had been in the form of a question; and such had altogether been their demeanour, that it convinced her she could never, under any possible circumstances have liked them. Their estimate of *her* was more favourable. After she had retired, Mrs. Marchmont asked them how they liked her?

'Even more,' answered Mrs. Le Strange, 'than I had expected, though from various quarters I had heard much in her praise. She has a very charming character of countenance, and her manners are extremely lady-like, and graceful.'

'And what beautiful eyes she has!' cried one of the girls, 'they put me in mind of a / St. Cecilia,[66] or of some seraphic being too good for this world!'

Mr. Wharton, during these remarks, seemed to be intently engaged in looking over a pamphlet; but he lost not one word that was said.

'I will tell you who she brought to *my* recollection,' said Caroline, the second sister, 'do you remember, mamma, the interesting and sweet little girl we used to see at the village where our straw bonnets were made when we lived at Willerton Manor?'

'Oh, I remember her perfectly,' interrupted Louisa. 'That was the little creature our drawing master once saw at church, and made from memory, such a beautiful sketch of, as a praying cherub.'

'That sketch,' resumed Caroline, 'hangs in my room now, and might pass for the portrait of Miss de Vere when a child. The features are the same in every respect, only grown to womanhood, and the expression is almost as angelic.' /

'I have some idea you once pointed her out to me,' said the mother, 'but I do not clearly remember her. You young artists have more tenacious memories than we have, of countenances that have once struck you. Is it not so, Mr Wharton?'

'I beg your pardon,' said he, looking up, 'I did not hear what you were talking of.'

'Well, never mind now,' cried his sister, not liking the subject of the conversation, 'it is getting very late, and I am sure you must all want rest.'

'I can answer for its being my case,' said Mrs. Le Strange; 'come, girls, light one of those candles for me, and let us bid Mr. Wharton good night.'

'Stop one moment, mamma,' cried Caroline, 'I just want to ask my aunt whether she was not at Cheltenham the year a poor child disappeared so mysteriously, and was advertised in all the county newspapers, and rewards offered for her discovery?' /

Mrs. Marchmont was wholly unable to speak, which her brother not failing to observe, quietly answered for her:

'I remember the whole circumstances, though I do not think that Mary can, as she was at that period almost entirely shut up in the sick room of Lucy. But what made you ask, Miss Caroline?'

'The wish to know whether my aunt, who afterwards staid a good while at Cheltenham, ever heard anything more about that child, for she was the very same of whom we have been speaking.'

'How do you know that, my dear?' enquired Mrs. Le Strange.

'By seeing her name Agnes Danvers, inserted in all the newspapers, and hearing the horrid adventure confirmed by the people she lived with.'

'I am not aware,' said Mr. Wharton, 'that any success ever attended the means that were taken to discover her.'

'What a pity!' exclaimed the two young / ladies; whilst their mother tired of standing, took leave of Mr. Wharton, and conducted by his sister, proceeded with her daughters to the chambers severally allotted to them.

As they retired, their host looked after them with a contemptuous sneer; closed the door, and pacing up and down the room, thus communed with his own thoughts:

'I fear ye not, ye idle praters, though ye *seem* to touch the clue, which, if unwound, would lead to my destruction! It is but seeming. She who could alone, exclusive of my sister, have made any fatal revelations, is now no more; and Agnes,' he exultingly continued, 'Agnes saint-like as they say she looks, will not I trust, be proof against two such powerful enticements, as wealth and flattery. What the one began, the other will accomplish. She was first secured to me by the allurements of elegance and luxury; the romantic protestations, and devoted homage of Harry Cowley will do the rest. She is mine, there can be no / fear of her – she is irrevocably mine. These girls then, and their would-be subtle mother, may harmlessly descant on they know not what. They are unprovided with the faintest initiatory knowledge to guide them to any fatal detection! and the only weak part in the machinery I have been forced to employ, is the character of poor Mary. She has neither nerves nor sense to be a safe confederate; the sister-in-law, much as I detest her, the sister-in-law, it must be owned, would have been an auxiliary far better assorted to me. Mrs. Marchmont can tamper with the truth, and give to her fictions much of the colouring of probability; but in all other respects she is useless, she is even perilous. Fear might make her do anything, however treacherous. The only way to manage her, is to instil into her an implicit belief in the security of our position; arguments or reproaches are of no avail with one whose paralysed lips, glazed eye, and tottering frame, on the slightest appearance / of danger, are precisely calculated to infuse suspicion into minds that never had harboured it before.'

At that moment Mrs. Marchmont entered the room, illustrating with singular truth the accuracy of this description. Her looks were almost ghastly; and after carefully shutting the door, she approached her brother with stealthy steps, and laying her hand upon his arm, whispered: 'Oh, Robert! What will become of us? the way in which they talk frightens me to death! I am sure they mean something most extraordinary!'

'Would you then, think it less extraordinary if they meant nothing?'

This was uttered in a tone of good humoured raillery that absolutely electrified the timorous woman, who, after gazing at him some moments with distended eyes, ventured, at length a gentle remonstrance on his choosing such a time for jesting.

'My dear Mary,' said he, sitting down, and inducing her to do the same, 'perhaps under / our circumstances, no time can be very fit for jesting; but certainly the present is not worse adapted to it than the past has been during many years. Your apprehensions at this minute have no foundation. The Le Stranges, I am convinced have not the remotest idea that what they said could affect us at all more than themselves. It is our consciousness only that makes us wince. We must fortify our courage, and steady our nerves by reflecting, that hitherto all is safe, and that the only way to continue so, is to listen to them without apparent agitation.'

'But, my dear brother, they positively, whilst we were going up stairs, expressed their wonder, that *Miss de Vere* who, when a child, had not the least resemblance to Agnes Danvers, should as a woman, be so remarkably like her! Can you believe that such an observation was made at random?'

'I believe that it was made in consequence of its being an undeniable fact! In their place, we should have made it ourselves. But, even / if it was spoken in malice, what can such a speech, or five hundred of the same nature prove against us? who is there to accuse us? Old Hannah is safe in her grave. The Blakes know not of our existence; Harry Cowley never heard of such a being as Agnes Danvers; and the two French women, Morinval and Leroux, believe that in all I have done for her, I have been influenced by parental affection. Rest assured then, Mary, that if we know how to keep our own counsel, we are now in less danger, than we have ever been since the girl first came under our roof.'

The steady look, and firm voice, with which this was spoken, communicated to Mrs. Marchmont some portion of the confidence they displayed; and she at length went to rest, tolerably recovered from her panic.

The next was to be a busy day. Mrs. Le Strange and her daughters had a thousand places to call at, a thousand commissions to execute, and notes to write, and trades-people to receive; and every instant of their time was / fully employed the whole morning. This exceedingly annoyed Mrs. Marchmont, who wished to have paid her first visit to Lady Glenfeld without delay, but did not like going alone, as it was very possible she might make a mistake between the sisters, and address to Isabel the civil speeches meant for Bertha. But about an hour before dinner, whilst pouring forth her lamentations in the patient ears of Agnes, Lady Glenfeld and Miss Isabel Le Strange were announced.

Whether it was that rank and wealth had the privilege of supplying in the eyes of Mrs. Marchmont the place of beauty, or whether her newly-married niece really appeared to her much better looking than she had expected, she was quite enchanted with her. Yet assuredly the personal attractions of Bertha were far from constituting her strongest claims to approbation. It was the kindness of disposition evident in her feminine and engaging countenance, and the inartificial sweetness of her manners, that gave her power / to please. No longer apprehensive of rebuke, or subject to sarcasm, she had already acquired an air of modest ease and contentment, it did the beholder good to look upon. Every thing she said was natural and simple, but indicated sense and observation, and her good breeding, without being strictly either of the English or Parisian school, was that of a benevolent heart, and would have endeared her equally, in whatever country she had visited.

Isabel was more brilliant, her figure was strikingly graceful, and well proportioned; her face sparkling with animation; her features were beautifully formed, and her complexion was the purest emblem of health, of freshness, and of all that in the spring tide of their bloom, gives to flowers their lustre, and to youth its charm.

To Agnes, these attractive, though very different sisters, were objects of such unusual interest, that whilst listening to, and gazing delightedly at them, she was insensible of the / impression she made upon them herself. They both surveyed her with unqualified admiration. Bertha's was not a nature formed for envy; and Isabel knew too well her own fascinations, to dread anything from those of a competitor. To do her justice, Mrs. Le Strange had not infused into the mind of her 'Three Graces,'[67] any littleness of mind respecting the merit of their young cotemporaries. She left them in no doubt of their own superiority, and early, and frankly represented to them, that it not only would be becoming, but was their duty to spare something from the praise due to themselves in behalf of those, who, without being so handsome, were yet entitled to rank amongst the beauties of the day. Thus schooled, they possessed a large fund of specious liberality, from which, as occasion offered, they could draw for an adequate supply of conventional candour, and mechanical good nature.

On taking leave, Lady Glenfeld, with more than the usual cordiality of a new acquaintance, / pressed the hand of Agnes, and said: 'I hope we may meet often; I hope we shall soon be friends as well as neighbours.'

A soft and grateful smile answered for Agnes, better than words could have done; and Isabel, seeing her so well disposed to meet their advances, whispered to her sister; 'Ask her to dine with us to-morrow; I am sure she would consent.'

'Are you?' cried Bertha, half-laughing, but without lowering her voice. 'Suppose we refer the matter to Miss de Vere herself.'

She repeated to Agnes the purport of the whisper, adding, in the most persuasive voice, 'Let me have the pleasure of finding that my sister is a good interpreter of looks, and has not deceived herself in fancying that you would (not unwillingly) comply with our wishes.'

Agnes internally delighted, directed her eyes towards Mrs. Marchmont for permission to accept this most tempting invitation, and receiving a nod of assent, ingratiated herself / still further with the two sisters, by the alacrity of her compliance.

Mrs. Marchmont during the rest of the day, talked incessantly, and in terms of the highest commendation of Lady Glenfeld. Her brother however, was but little pleased at the engagement Agnes had been suffered to form, and felt much inclined to compel his sister to find some excuse for breaking through it. Had he known her less, he might have wondered, that timid as she was, she could so easily forget the urgency with which he had invariably represented to her the imprudence of suffering Agnes to visit by herself; but he had little difficulty in recollecting, that Mrs. Marchmont was one who never thought of consequences, till by her own fault they actually came upon her, and was then ever one of the last to know how to support them.

That Agnes should be led, in the absence of himself and his sister, to betray what she probably considered it as much for her own interest as theirs to conceal, he had no apprehension. / But it was uncertain what new acquaintance she might form when removed from under their eye; and though he deemed the eventual success of Harry highly probable, he was aware she entertained no passion for him, and felt, that if another candidate should start forward with even very moderate recommendations, there was much reason to fear he might be preferred. As one means to obviate this peril, Mr. Wharton lost no time in promulgating – openly in her absence, and by hints and inuendoes in her presence – the attachment for her which long intimacy had nourished in Harry, and the correspondence she indulged him with as a solace during their separation. Mrs. Le Strange and her two daughters, being made acquainted with this circumstance, would not fail, he was convinced, to communicate it to Lady Glenfeld; and thus an opinion would be established that Agnes was already engaged. /

CHAPTER VII.

> She is not fair
> Nor beautiful; those words express her not;
> Her gentle looks have something excellent,
> That wants a name.
>
> BEAUMONT AND FLETCHER.[68]

MEANWHILE, Mrs. Marchmont, still inexhaustible on the subject of Lady Glenfeld's merits, yet, in her secret heart, somewhat surprised, after beholding the splendid beauty of Isabel that her sister should have forestalled her at the 'connubial altar,' accompanied Mrs. Le Strange to her apartment when she retired at night, and dismissing the maid till she was rung for, sat down near the toilette, and thus abruptly began: /

'My dear Augusta, you *must* tell me how you brought about this charming marriage! Where did Lord Glenfeld first become acquainted with Bertha? And how was he induced to select her in preference to any of the others? Tell me – how did you manage it?'

'I did not manage it at all, Mary: from first to last the affair was wholly of his own doing.'

'But where did the courtship begin? At whose house did they meet? Did he never see her sisters till after he had proposed? Was he caught by her without being influenced by you, or any other friend?'

'I again repeat, that I exerted no influence whatever. He never saw her but under my roof; her sisters were always in the house with her; and yet, as you find, she carried off the prize!'

'Well, – I thought that in these days – especially in England – so much manœuvring was necessary to get a girl well married, unless resplendently beautiful, or immensely rich – / that I was curious to know how the case had stood in the present instance.'

After a little further trifling with the patience of her auditress, Mrs. Le Strange was at length induced to enter into some detail.

'I do not know,' she began, 'whether you saw, about three months ago an account in the English newspapers of the overturn of Mr. Stanmore whilst travelling rapidly along the northern road on the way towards his own place in Yorkshire. Lord Glenfeld was in the carriage with him, being engaged to pass a fortnight at his house. When the accident occurred they were within a stone's throw of my gate; and Lord Glenfeld extremely hurt, was brought, bleeding and speechless, into my house. It was utterly impossible that he should proceed on his journey; Mr. Stanmore, who had, comparatively, escaped uninjured, thankfully accepted the offer I immediately made of assigning to his friend an apartment, and also remained himself at Westwood till the surgeons were able to hold out a hope that / their patient would eventually do well. In the mean time, his lordship's carriage which followed that of Mr. Stanmore, brought his own servants, and whilst he continued a prisoner in his bed-room, they were his only attendants. When sufficiently recovered to venture for a few hours to change the scene, I put him in possession of what we call the small picture-room, and thither he had all the books and papers brought with which it appears his carriage had been loaded. Observing frequently when I went in to see him, that he was lying upon his sofa with his eyes fixed in a melancholy manner upon those same papers and books, it struck me to be owing to his long incapacity to look into them without pain to his sight. I asked whether that was the case, and he owned I had guessed right: "I have before me," he added, "all the means of pursuing an employment the most interesting to me, – one that I had set my heart upon bringing to a prosperous termination, and in connexion with which I had collected many / curious facts which it was desirable to put into shape in conjunction with such remarks as the subject seemed to demand: – but this wretched accident deprives me of all power to prosecute my purpose; – and who can tell how much longer I may remain in this helpless state?"'

'I really felt for the poor man, and expressing a hope that we might be able to render ourselves of some use to him, I begged to know the subject of the papers in question. Great was my consternation when told they related to the construction, upon a plan of his own, of a certain number of light and portable fire-engines, to be established for the use of the farmers and cottagers, in every parish in his own country over which he had any influence. This was not a text, I well knew, upon which either Louisa or Caroline could be prevailed on to offer him their services; and Isabel was still in the hands of a governess who found her ample employment in the school-room. Even Bertha, I was almost afraid would prove a little restive: but I resolved to reduce her / to obedience by a *coup de main*;[69] since, having raised an expectation that I had some aid to offer, I was bound in honour not to retract. Accordingly, I sent immediately for her; informed her of her nomination to be Lord Glenfeld's secretary, and charged her to follow the directions of her noble employer with all possible diligence and docility. She was not in the habit of disputing my commands; and though she looked, I must confess, somewhat astounded, she silently drew a chair to the table at the spot his Lordship pointed out, and I left her, pen in hand, ready to begin her task.'

'But meanwhile,' interrupted Mrs. Marchmont, 'had your other girls entirely kept aloof from him?'

'Why nearly so, for he still seemed so languid, and so disinclined to talk, that their visits could afford neither to him nor to themselves the smallest satisfaction.'

'And how did Bertha endure the penance you had imposed upon her?' /

'Why, to speak the truth, with admirable good humour, poor child! She was soon struck with what she was pleased to call the benevolence of Lord Glenfeld's views, and conceived for him the highest respect. I own I was not quite so charitable towards him. Lord Glenfeld, like many other wealthy men, with much leisure, much speculative usefulness, a good deal of activity of imagination, and some vanity, is never so happy as when engaged in any project that has the appearance of originality, and may call forth complimentary observations in one or two reviews, and the honour of being applauded and drank to at a public dinner. I am not aware that he has ever accomplished any really important undertaking, though for years, he has constantly had some scheme or other in hand. However, *I* have no reason to censure his turn for experiments, since Bertha clearly owes her conquest of his heart to this fortunate one of the fire-engines. She was so sincerely interested by his representation of the wonderful advantage / that would be derived to the poor from these machines; – he described to her so energetically the calamities that *might*, rather than *had* attended the want of them – (reminding her, at the same time, how often she must have heard briefs read in country churches, setting forth the ravages occasioned by fires in remote districts unprovided with engines) that she regarded his plan not only as one of the most meritorious that had ever been invented, but as one that was of the highest national importance. This unaffected enthusiasm in favour of the hobby of the moment, could not but at once flatter and touch him. She thought no time too much, no pains too great to devote to so laudable an undertaking. Day, after day, she cheerfully gave up her rides, her walks, every favourite pursuit to dedicate her whole attention to him; – and the matter ended, as at last I began to foresee it probably would, by her winning his heart, and losing her own.'

'She really then, married for love?' /

'I am firmly convinced of it. She looked up to him as one born to be the benefactor of the human race. She saw merit in everything he did. His perseverance, amidst pain and weakness, in his design; his disinterested solicitude, as she termed it, to ameliorate the condition of the peasantry; the liberal assistance he offered towards the furtherance of his views – all these enchanted her; and though now a wife of five weeks' standing, she is still in as happy a fool's paradise, as any young lady of nineteen could desire.'

'You think then that the delusion will not last?'

'What delusion ever does? However, she will have little reason to complain of her lot, even after its tinge of romance is removed. She will find, indeed, that she has not married a man all made up of unalloyed philanthropy; that his character is not wholly without imperfection, nor his temper without infirmities; but she will find also that she has married a man of honour; a man of reasonably generous / sentiments, and, as the world goes, of considerable feeling; and if she is wise, she will rest content, and own herself a fortunate woman.'

'And with good cause,' observed Mrs. Marchmont, who would have pursued her enquiries for another hour; but Mrs. Le Strange had already been more communicative than she had set out with any intention of being; and declaring herself tired and sleepy, she summoned her maid, and declined prolonging the conversation. /

CHAPTER VIII.

I will resign what I usurp, or have
Unjustly held.
And now, my friend,
Thou know'st no less than all; I have unclasp'd
To thee the book even of my secret soul.

SHAKESPEARE.[70]

AGNES' anticipations of an agreeable day at Lady Glenfeld's were not disappointed – they were surpassed. She was received with more than politeness – with warmth and cordiality; and Lord Glenfeld, when she was introduced to him, assisted by his good breeding in making her feel at ease. He appeared to be about four or five-and-thirty; had in all respects the air of a gentleman; was grave and calm, but looked happy, particularly when speaking to or listening to his wife.

Agnes was their only guest; but with the / variety of resources which her talents and Isabel's afforded, time could not pass languidly, even in so small a party. In the evening they had music; and the rich and highly cultivated voice of Agnes perhaps put the generosity of Isabel to a severer trial than even a greater degree of personal beauty might have done. She struggled successfully, however, against the momentary sensation of envy she had experienced; and though perfectly conscious that she was vying with one who far excelled her, hesitated not when Agnes quitted the instrument, to take her place and sing after her. The Glenfelds were neither of them qualified to institute comparisons between the young performers; they thought them equally admirable.

But what delighted both the husband and wife infinitely more than the finished recitative and fine Italian expression of their opera music, were the lively and amusing French songs of which Agnes had an endless variety in her memory; to these she gave a grace and / playfulness that were so exhilarating to her little auditory, that even Lord Glenfeld's white teeth became visible whilst he stood smiling beside the instrument; and the two sisters were most animated in their plaudits.

Agnes' heart softened a little towards Mr. Wharton, as she this evening felt the value of the accomplishments he had enabled her to acquire. She had often sung to, and been admired by persons it was a matter of indifference to her whether she was approved by or not. This was the first time she had ever enjoyed the gratification of giving pleasure to those she was inclined to love.

At a late hour, and just as she was concluding her last song, two gentlemen were announced, whose names however her own performance prevented her hearing, but whom she perceived were greeted with smiles, though in silence, till her final chord was struck, and she rose from her seat. Lady Glenfeld then, addressing herself good humouredly to one of them, said: /

'You deserve what has happened to you for coming so late. You might have heard some charming music, and have obtained the honour of making acquaintance with the performer.'

'But why should it be too late, Lady Glenfeld,' cried the stranger with some eagerness, 'to allow me that honour even now?'

Before this question could be answered, a servant entered, and, addressing Agnes, announced Mr. Wharton's carriage.

'Oh then,' cried Bertha, 'it is positively past the time for an introduction to-night. When I have anything very good to bestow upon my friends, I never like to hurry over its presentation as though it were of no value; and besides this will teach you to prize more highly my future invitations.'

'You know neither mercy nor measure in your chastisements, but punish even for involuntary faults. I should have been here an hour and half ago, had not Aubrey, (looking towards his companion) compelled me to accompany / him on a visit of condolence to a gentle youth suffering from the perfidy – not of a favourite fair one – but of certain wines, to which he was tempted last night to entrust somewhat too confidently the safe keeping of his brains. A monitory fall down half-a-dozen stairs has laid him on his sofa with a sprained knee, and sundry contusions on the forehead, of hues more various than beautiful.'

Entertained by this little dialogue, Agnes was reluctant to go away; but afraid of detaining the carriage, she compelled herself to take leave of Lady Glenfeld, and then approached Isabel for the same purpose. When she was at some distance,

'Who is she?' cried the stranger, in an eager but subdued voice.

'She is one,' answered Bertha, smiling, '"who," to quote your own words, "is the last woman in the world you would seek to be acquainted with!" for which very reason, as I like to break through irrational prejudices, I asked you here this evening. Now spare your / reproaches till I have said a few more parting words to her; and when I come back, you may pour out all your resentment upon me.'

She then hastened to Agnes, who was still talking with Isabel, to settle at what hour she might call for her the next day to go to some exhibition; and then returning to her male visitor,

'Well,' cried she, 'have you thought of any thing bitter enough to say to me?'

With an air of well assumed solemnity, he answered:

'Words would be too weak to express my indignation! I leave you to your own remorse.'

Saying this, he stalked away, and took a seat beside her husband.

But here he was no safer from attack than with the wife:

'I hope, my good friend,' said his Lordship, 'the sight of Miss de Vere has brought you a little to your senses. Are you quite as / much bent upon shunning her as when we last had the pleasure of hearing you talk on the subject?'

'More than ever, my Lord; for what I have now seen proves to me that I might admire her too much.'

'And what would be the harm of admiring her as much as she merits?'

'Would you have a poor devil like me, not worth as many hundreds as she has thousands, run into temptation of falling in love with her?'

'I cannot perceive where the disgrace would be.'

The stranger, whose name was Walsingham, laughed, and said:

'No, no, I must not think of it! I have always hated heiresses, perhaps for no better reason than because it is an heiress who stands in the way of my being an heir! If Miss de Vere, you know, had never existed, I should have succeeded to her mother's fortune. Here / then is one most laudable excuse for hating *her* beyond all other heiresses that ever lived!'

'So then, you are afraid of falling in love with her because you hate her? The case is truly singular!'

To this Mr. Walsingham made some laughing answer, and the subject was dropped.

Dating from this day, the intercourse between Lady Glenfeld and Agnes became progressively more and more frequent – more and more intimate. There were many traits in their dispositions not dissimilar; and under whatever circumstances they might have met, it is probable they would have been attracted towards each other. But Agnes sometimes feared she was taking unfair advantage of her new friend's ignorance of her real position.

'Am I doing right,' she mentally said, 'in imposing myself upon her for what I am not? How will she endure me when she knows the truth? It had been better for me, perhaps, had I never become acquainted with / her – for soon I may be called upon to resign her society for ever! With her sisters, with her mother, I can carry on this transient intercourse without a pang; they entertain and often please me. But when I lose sight of them, how little will be my regret compared with that which I shall suffer on parting from this charming Lady Glenfeld!'

These reflections, in addition to other sources of inquietude, induced Agnes to decline as often as she could, without exciting suspicion, the frequent and pressing invitations of Bertha. To her utter surprise, she found that Louisa and Caroline Le Strange were impressed with an idea that her approaching marriage with Harry Cowley was an event that admitted not a doubt. They harassed her with questions about him; and what was worse, she detected in Harry's own letters an encreasing confidence in her regard – an importunate eagerness in pleading his cause, which she had never remarked in them before. Mr. Wharton also she fancied, watched her with more than usual / vigilance; and her early dread of him seemed to revive. At the sound of his voice she involuntarily sought to avoid him; if he spoke to her, she endeavoured not to let him read her looks; – and to escape from him more completely, she entered eagerly into every scheme of amusement proposed by the Le Stranges.

Happily, these precautions were effectual. Mr. Wharton's intrepid reliance upon the prudence of his own machinations, facilitated her success; past security blinded him to the chance of future danger; and the arguments he had used only to tranquillize his sister, had produced the effect of strengthening his own confidence.

Lord and Lady Glenfeld and Isabel had called one morning at Mrs. Marchmont's to induce Agnes to accompany them on an excursion to St. Cloud,[71] and afterwards to dine and spend the day with them. She was already equipped however to set out with Mrs. Marchmont and the two Le Stranges on some other / expedition, and therefore had the less difficulty in excusing herself. But Lady Glenfeld though too reasonable to object to her present plea, expressed a little mortification at the frequent refusals she had recently received: and gently, yet half reproachfully said:

'Am I, dear Lucy, to undergo the severe disappointment of finding you inclined to be rather capricious?'

'Oh no! do not suspect it! If you knew but the tenth part of the grateful attachment I bear you, you could never harbour such an idea!'

'Why then, dear girl, have you of late so unkindly avoided me? You look embarrassed – ah, my friend, you have no good reason to give! But if you repent, and mean henceforward to behave better, begin your reformation to-morrow. Isabel is going to a splendid fete with a party of French ladies who are friends of Lord Glenfeld. I have declined accompanying them, because such engagements give me more fatigue than pleasure: consequently, / I shall be alone the whole evening, and it will be a serious grievance to me if you refuse to join me.'

What could Agnes say? How could she forbear listening to the suggestions of her own heart, all urging her to comply? She gave the consent required, and Bertha departed appeased, and even thankful.

Instead of Agnes, Mrs. Le Strange had consented to occupy the fourth seat in her daughter's carriage; and as it drove from Mr. Wharton's door, she casually remarked that Miss de Vere seemed forcing herself to appear in better spirits than she really felt.

'The same thing has struck me, mamma,' cried Isabel. 'How pale she was this morning when we first went up, and how faint, how almost sad was every smile we succeeded in drawing from her.'

'I fear,' resumed Mrs. Le Strange, 'the match talked of for her, is less of her own choice than of Mr. Wharton's.'

'Surely, surely,' cried Isabel, indignantly, / 'they might have done better for her than connect her with the obscure *protégé* of that insufferable old Gage, who used to haunt us whenever we dined last winter at my uncle's, and talked louder than any body else, and told tiresome stories full of oaths, and called us *fair damsels*[72] – and once actually had the impertinence to squeeze Caroline's hand! Perhaps the *protégé* resembles his protector; and in that case, what a prospect for poor Lucy with all her refinement and in-born delicacy, to be condemned to spend her life with the vulgar son of such a vulgar father!'

'Gently, gently, dear girl,' said Mrs. Le Strange; 'I am not prone, you will allow, to lecture either you or your sisters, – the fact is, few young persons ever required it less; but on this occasion I must put you on your guard. Vulgarity is not a term we should be too lavish in using, for I have often heard the remark made, that the less we know about it ourselves, the less apt we are to / attribute it to others. Besides, Harry Cowley, whatever his protector may be, is himself any thing but vulgar; on the contrary, he is (for I have seen him once or twice) a very fine young man, a little coxcombical, but deficient neither in talents nor in good manners. One word more, my Isabel, and I have done. Vulgarity, we should remember, is a conventional word, the exact meaning of which has never yet been defined.[73] What in one society is regarded as the exclusive standard of propriety, in the next, is thought preposterous and absurd.'

'So true is your observation,' said Lord Glenfeld, smiling, 'that it recalls to my mind a warm dispute I heard lately in an English family on the pretended vulgarity of saying a *dish of tea* instead of a *cup of tea*. One half of the party maintained that in all good company the word in use was *cup*; the other half averred that *cup* was horrid, and only to be heard in the very lowest class. They referred to me, and I really was puzzled; for / I perfectly remember that a schism which proved interminable, had subsisted in my father's house on this very subject. My mother, who deemed herself at the summit of all fashion, could not forbear remonstrating with my father, at least once a month, on the impropriety of talking of a dish of tea; whilst my father, equally jealous of his pre-eminence in the fine world, protested that nothing could be more plebeian than to speak of a cup! The dispute was never settled, and I confess that my own opinion still remains undecided.'

Isabel laughed at this little anecdote, and called it an excellent appendix to her mother's text; and Mrs. Le Strange was gratified by the support her son-in-law had thus given to her maternal advice.

The next day, at an earlier hour than she had expected, the carriage of Lady Glenfeld called for Agnes, who found that it was a dinner as well as an evening engagement she was supposed to have formed. 'Well, be / it so,' she thought: 'I shall have few opportunities of spending so many hours with her again; and some time hence, the recollection of this day will be very dear to me.'

The party that sat down to table was nearly as small as on the former occasion; there was only one additional guest, and that was Mr. Walsingham. He had heard the evening before that Miss De Vere had promised to dine with Lady Glenfeld the following day, and asked permission to do so likewise. 'Would you really venture to encounter her?' said Bertha; 'is she not still the same hateful heiress you were so determined to shun?'

'By no means. I hear she is engaged to be married; her French songs, therefore, may now be listened to in all safety.'

'Oh, you remember then that she can sing?'

'Hitherto, I have heard nothing else from her to remember; her speaking voice I am / yet unacquainted with. But, dear Lady Glenfeld, pray let me dine with her, and the day after, I will frankly tell you, whether she has left me with any wish ever to do so again.'

His request was granted, and it cannot be denied that he contributed much to render the repast agreeable, by the mingled sense and gaiety of his conversation. He was prompt in detecting, and loved to point out whatever was ridiculous in the fashions and opinions of the day; but there was no asperity, no gall in his strictures, which were aimed rather against things than persons, and confined themselves to subjects so general, that it would have been unjust to interpret them into invidious personalities. On matters connected with literature and the fine arts, he spoke with equal taste and feeling, and incidentally discovered opinions that bore testimony to the humanity of a warm and upright heart. In all he said – in the expression of his countenance – in his manners – even in his dress, / might be traced the most absolute exemption from every species of affection. Young, well-born, independent, and favoured by nature with the most prepossessing exterior, he hated display and exaggeration. His pursuits were manly, his habits simple, but not inelegant; in a word, he was one who, producing little sensation on a slight acquaintance, was formed to win his way to the very inmost heart when intimately known. Lady Glenfeld had been one of the number who had thus known him for many years, and the regard she felt for him was that of the most affectionate sister.

His acquaintance with Agnes on this first meeting (for the previous glimpse they had had of each other could hardly be called a meeting) made but small progress. She talked less than usual, though she listened with pleasure, and he rarely addressed himself directly to her. Bertha, and occasionally her lord, chiefly contributed to support the conversation, and prevent its turning wholly on / the subject of the expected *fête*, of which Isabel was forming such brilliant anticipations, that she could talk of nothing else.

A little fatigued, perhaps, by her perseverance in dwelling upon these visionary delights, Walsingham at length, turning to her with a smile, said: 'If I were the churl that many people think me, I should almost regret that I were not dining with you to-morrow instead of to-day; but I have more good-nature than I obtain credit for, and really *try* to take pleasure in listening to the gay hopes on which you are exercising your fancy.'

'But suppose,' said Isabel, half conscious of the veiled reproof; 'suppose this were tomorrow, what difference would there be in my way of feeling and expressing myself?'

'The difference there always is between expectation and reality. You would feel, and if honest, would confess, that there were present at this ball some who almost equalled you in beauty; that your partner, fascinated / as he had appeared, allowed his eyes to wander to another, even whilst you were talking to him; that many had succeeded in dressing as becomingly as yourself; and that all, young and old, male and female, united in attributing to their own countrywomen the merit of dancing incomparably better than any *Anglaise* who ever breathed. Will not these things disenchant you, and compel you to-morrow, to speak of this entertainment with more sobriety than you do to-day?'

'Certainly, if I only went for the gratification of my vanity; but I go – you may believe me – as much to see as to be seen; and say what you please, I am determined not to convert an expected pleasure into a self-inflicted mortification.'

'You have disarmed me; – may so wise and good-humoured a resolution be rewarded by the accomplishment of all your pleasantest anticipations!'

Agnes was struck by the sweetness of expression that accompanied these words, and / felt that a reproof made amends for in so open and friendly a manner, was almost preferable to the most flattering praise.

When the hour came for Isabel to begin her toilette, the whole female part of the establishment was thrown, more or less, into a bustle. She was to appear in a fancy-dress, the novelty and elegance of which was as great a source of admiration to the French maids, as the personal beauty of its wearer was to the English ones. Lady Glenfeld and Agnes were repeatedly sent for and consulted on the distribution of various parts of the attire, so new to the uninitiated girl, (dressing for her first great ball) that she was continually wishing the milliner could herself have presided over the arrangement of her own decorations. However, the 'pleasing, anxious'[74] labour was at length concluded, and Isabel, fatigued, but glowing with conscious success, was conducted to the carriage by Lord Glenfeld, who ascended it after her, and they drove off. Mr. Walsingham had quietly departed soon after Bertha / left the drawing-room to comply with her sister's first summons.

When the doors were closed, and all was tranquil: – 'Now then, my dear Lucy,' said the sober young wife, 'let us enjoy what remains of the evening with true English comfort. We will have tea in my boudoir, where we shall be more snug than in this great *salon*, and we will dismiss all recollection of fancy-balls, and fancy-dresses.'

To the boudoir they repaired, and after having had tea, seated side by side on a sofa, each with some light work in her hand, they entered into a connected conversation. Lady Glenfeld began with a little hesitation, by saying:–

'Shall I pain you, dearest Lucy, if I venture to speak to you of your well known engagement?'

'No, my kind Lady Glenfeld; it is a subject that can cause me neither pain nor pleasure, being a mere idle rumour, without the slightest foundation in fact.' /

'You astonish me! – Are you aware that it is Mr. Wharton himself who spreads the report?'

'Of course it can come from no other quarter; but I again most solemnly assure you, there is no reality in it whatever.'

'But why then does he so boldly assert it?'

'Perhaps, because what he wishes to be true, he has taught himself to believe may become so.'

'Well, you really take the matter with wonderful coolness!' resumed Bertha, smiling. 'But shall I own to you, dear girl, that my mother – and even the less observant Isabel – fancied that of late some distress weighed upon your mind? And when I found – pardon me, Lucy – that you seemed to avoid me, I began to think you were afraid I should torment you with questions it might not be either wise or useful to answer?'

Agnes was somewhat embarrassed by this speech, and for a few seconds remained wholly / silent; but soon recovering her steadiness, she answered:

'I never was apprehensive that so indulgent a friend as you are, would ask anything you would not have forgiven me for declining to answer if prudence required it.'

'Come, I see you understand me, and that being the case, I may venture to observe, with regard to your asserted engagement, that although you may no longer wish to ratify it, the time surely has been when you freely acceded to it?'

'What induces you to think so, dear Lady Glenfeld?'

'The frequent and regular correspondence established between you and Mr. Cowley. My sisters have told me, that during the whole time they have known you, Mr. Wharton has never delivered to you fewer than two letters a week from him.'

'But what does this prove?'

'It indicates at least, if it does not prove, that there can be no very vehement antipathy / subsisting in your breast against a correspondent so partially favoured. Young ladies,' she added, archly, 'do not employ so many precious hours in reading and answering the letters of an avowed lover, if they have irrevocably made up their minds to refuse him! so long therefore, my sweet Lucy, as this epistolary intercourse continues, you must suffer me and all others who hear of it, to conclude that your present rejection of him is meant, but as a sort of expiatory probation for some offence, which, in the end, will be rewarded by a full restoration to your good graces.'

'And unless such is the case, shall I have been doing wrong to correspond with him?'

Agnes said this with an air of such *naive* and genuine simplicity, that Lady Glenfeld could not without some difficulty, preserve her gravity.

'I will not go so far,' she gently answered, 'as to talk of your having done *wrong*, my dearest; but you have gone a little beyond / the line prescribed by custom: you have been induced to listen to the prayers of this young man with more condescension than seems perfectly consistent with the indifference you profess, or with your declared resolution of finally rejecting his suit.'

Abashed and humbled, Agnes hung her head for some moments in mute self-condemnation, and then exclaimed:

'My eyes are opened, and I see, I see my own folly! But in justice to myself, let me explain how I fell into this error.'

She then gave a succinct account of the beginning and progress of her acquaintance with Harry; spoke of the sisterly regard she had conceived for him, and the regret with which she heard his avowal of a warmer sentiment. 'But I immediately,' she continued, 'and distinctly declared that I had no encouragement to give him, in short, I most positively refused his proposal. Mr. Wharton I had feared, would have resented this exertion of independence; to my great relief however / he bore it temperately, and was the first to suggest, in mitigation of Harry's disappointment, the correspondence which, *as friends*, we might engage in.'

'And tell me, Lucy, has Mr. Cowley always written as a mere *friend?*'

'I wish I could say he had! the truth is, his letters have constantly been more impassioned than I liked. At first, I made allowance for this by reflecting on the sort of flighty enthusiasm that forms a part of his character; and latterly, I have borne with his irksome ravings in consideration of the melancholy state of health he is represented to be reduced to by his friend, Mr. Gage, and which he occasionally alludes to himself.'

'I am sorry for his indisposition, if it is real,' said Lady Glenfeld; 'but I am still more sorry, my Lucy, that you have had to deal with persons so much too designing for your artless, and unsuspecting nature! Mr. Wharton most particularly, has ill fulfilled, in this affair, the duties of a guardian. He, who, / knowing your inexperience, ought to have been the first to preserve you from committing any imprudence, he it is, rather than either Harry or yourself, to whom the fault of this correspondence must be attributed. Break it off, dearest, whilst it is yet time; unless indeed, you think it probable that the tried fidelity of your lover, aided by your own compassion for him, may eventually, soften your feelings in his favour.'

'No, Lady Glenfeld; such a change, I am convinced, will never take place. Harry's temper is unpleasing to me, from the circumstance of its being so lamentably deficient in consideration for others; he has talents and acquirements, I allow, but they are deformed by self-sufficiency; his mirth fails to exhilarate by being mingled with sneers and superciliousness; and his bursts of romantic sentiment, appear to me rather like dramatic ebullitions, than symptoms of true feeling, such as might contribute to domestic happiness.'

'Come, come, your affections I see,' cried / Bertha, playfully, 'are in no danger of being enslaved by the merits of Harry Cowley! Mercy upon him, poor youth! how clear-sighted you are to all his failings! But if thus at heart's ease concerning him, what is it, dearest Lucy, that has rendered you of late, so different to what you were when I first saw you? Of course, on observing the change, I connected it with the idea of this supposed marriage; but now that I am undeceived, some other anxiety I fear, must be sought for as its cause. Open to me your heart, dear girl, I will not betray the trust, and perhaps I may be happy enough to suggest some means of alleviating your disquiet.'

Observing that Agnes now dropt her employment, and tried to avert her conscious face, Lady Glenfeld took one of her hands, and added, with the kindest earnestness:

'Speak to me, my Lucy; it is no idle curiosity that induces me to seek your confidence, but a sincere and warm affection; speak to me, consider me as a sister, you could / never have had one who would have loved you better!'

Agnes's agitation shook her whole frame, and covering her face with the only hand she had at liberty, she faintly murmured:

'Do not, do not, dearest Lady Glenfeld, pursue this conversation! If I dared.... but it must not be! and yet, how often have I wished for a friend!'

'What *must not be?*' cried Bertha, 'what is it you do not *dare?* why, if you have wished for a friend, will you not accept me?'

And as she rapidly uttered these interrogations, she drew the hand of Agnes from her face, and saw that it was bathed in tears.

'Oh, this is too much, dear Lucy! here lurks, I am sure, some most painful secret! Why are you so reluctant to trust me? no look, no word of mine shall ever betray your confidence to any human being. Tell me then, my Lucy, what is it that thus grieves you?'

Agnes letting her head fall upon Lady / Glenfeld's shoulder, said, nearly in a whisper –

'Do not call me Lucy! you know not the pain you give me!'

Lady Glenfeld thought her almost delirious, and with the extremest amazement, exclaimed:

'What can you possibly mean?'

Agnes more and more agitated, with difficulty arose, and began slowly – pensively – and in unbroken silence, to pace backwards and forwards across the room. Bertha in fearful suspense, sat gazing at her without having courage to pronounce a word. What to expect she knew not; but that the secret labouring in her friend's mind, was of momentous import, she could no longer doubt; and she began now to dread almost as much as she had hitherto wished to learn its nature.

At length Agnes returned to her seat, her face was as colourless as marble, but speaking with tolerable firmness, she said:

'Hear me with patience, with indulgence, / Lady Glenfeld, and do not interrupt me.' Then, after a momentary pause, she thus went on – 'I have hesitated – I have debated the point within myself long enough to become convinced, that the mystery I still meant to observe, may cruelly prejudice me in your opinion, without essentially availing the person whose character will be ruined by my disclosure. Such is the nature of the transaction I am about to communicate, that it cannot be concealed without culpability on my part, nor made public without infamy to its contriver. Yet a little while however, and its notoriety must become general. In anticipating that moment, I give way to the feelings of gratitude the warm interest you have expressed for me calls forth, and I venture to flatter myself, that, betide me what may, I shall ever retain some portion of your esteem.'

The seriousness almost amounting to solemnity of this exordium, took from Bertha all desire, and nearly all power to break through the / silence imposed upon her, at the same time that it heightened her impatience to know what was to follow. Without further circumlocution Agnes then entered upon the detail of what passed on her first meeting with the stranger at Cheltenham. She sought not to give dramatic effect to her narration, but, at once, announced that stranger's name, and declared her own, as well as the humble station in which he had found her. The menaces he had employed; the arbitrary sternness of his looks and voice, she described minutely, and Lady Glenfeld, listening with intense eagerness, scarcely allowed herself to breathe, lest she should lose a syllable of the strange recital. Agnes next proceeded to give an account of her being transferred to the care of Madame Leroux, – of her journey from Cheltenham to London, – of her residence during three months in Bury Street. She spoke of Madame Morinval with just and earnest praise; dwelt upon the innumerable proofs she had given of her good principles, and feeling heart, / – and, in a manner that sensibly affected her auditress, recounted the conversation she and Madame Morinval had held together in the park, the evening that worthy woman had announced to her that she was going to Paris.

'How melancholy was the sense of desolation,' continued Agnes, 'with which I heard that this only friend remaining to me in the wide world, was about to leave me! With what rapturous gratitude did I afterwards hear that she meant to make me the companion of her journey! We sailed, dear Lady Glenfeld, – we landed in France, – and from that hour, my foot has never trod on English ground; – from that hour, the imposition I was to be trained to countenance, was systematically begun.'

Thus, step by step, she told all that bore upon that part of her history which was connected with the scheme of deception Mr. Wharton had so pertinaciously held in view; and concluded, by recounting the accidental discovery she had recently made of the real / existence of HER to whom belonged, of right, the name and fortune she had so long usurped, and the paragraph relating to William Danvers, which, in a moment so grievously perplexing, had given to her despondency such a welcome and joyous reprieve.

When her tale was finished – a tale which had almost petrified Lady Glenfeld, and left her, at its conclusion, panting and aghast – she thus proceeded:

'I have now recapitulated, as fully and as clearly as I am able, every particular of my past life. I have stated the hope I entertain that the blessing yet remains to me of having a brother; and that I have ventured to write to him: – but his answer does not arrive, and, alas! I want courage to bid open defiance to Mr. Wharton, and to publish, whilst under his roof, a secret, the disclosure of which might goad him to madness! I have meditated intently upon a plan that would obviate this evil: but I fear, it may appear too romantic.'

Shaking off the nearly overwhelming emotion / to which Agnes's narrative had given rise, Lady Glenfeld now fervently exclaimed:

'Meditate no other plan, incomparable girl! than that of throwing yourself, from this moment, upon Lord Glenfeld's protection and mine! To espouse such a cause as yours – to assist, to guard, to honour such a being as you are, will reflect honour upon ourselves! You bade me not interrupt you when you began, and, in truth, I should hardly have had the power: but now that I have voice, and you have leisure to listen to me, you must let me say, that the voluntary resignation you have determined upon, is a proof of the noblest disinterestedness and most inflexible integrity, I ever heard of. Your name – your *real* name, dear girl, is not new to me; – I have often heard it pronounced by my sisters, who, in your childhood, saw you at Meadwell, within a few miles of which my mother then had a house. How far was I from thinking that the interesting little Agnes Danvers, whose melancholy disappearance was so often talked of and / lamented in our school-room, would hereafter become personally known to me, and the chosen friend of my heart!'

Saying this, she tenderly embraced the half-smiling, half-weeping girl, and was proceeding to descant on the happiness it would give her to retain such a companion in her house, when, mildly but steadily interrupting her, Agnes said:

'No, my generous and dear Lady Glenfeld, – no, the proposal you make must not be thought of! There is now a family connexion between your husband and Mr. Wharton; Mrs. Marchmont is the sister-in-law of your mother, who is her guest, and who, with her two beautiful daughters, would be covered with shame were any public exposure to take place whilst they were residing with him. I have confided in you, – but not that you might become a party in my cause. It is for my brother (if I really am so happy as to have one) to secure me from future violence, as the protector appointed for me by nature. I will / involve no one else in the affair, least of all, any member of your family. What may ensue from the desperation to which Mr. Wharton will be driven when the certainty of detection breaks upon him, I scarcely dare venture to surmise! The shock will be tremendous to him! He will have to account for the fate of the hapless Lucy de Vere; – he will have to account, I imagine, for the large sums which, under false pretences, he has been drawing for; – and heavy, heavy will be the day of reckoning that awaits him! No – his own connexions must have nothing to do with his punishment; nor will *I* take any step that shall suddenly, and without preparation inflict it upon him; for I now feel, that the time is drawing near, when I shall pity more than hate him. My plan is, to withdraw privately from his house, and to seek a temporary shelter in some poor but honest family, where I may await, with what patience I can muster, the tidings I still hope for from Rome; – if no such tidings arrive....' /

'I cannot,' interrupted Lady Glenfeld, 'listen to so wild a project! My dearest creature, what should you do in this poor family? What do you know of them? How can you rely upon them? No, no; come privately to us; we will conceal you with all imaginary precaution till your letters from Rome arrive; and not even to my mother will I betray the place of your retreat.'

Agnes warmly thanked her, but renewed, and supported by stronger reasons than before, her objections to this offer: – 'Yours,' she said, 'is one of the first houses in which I should be sought for. You might, indeed, hide me, but how many odious falsehoods would you be obliged to utter – how many must you instruct your servants to utter – and still, how easily by the slightest even unintentional imprudence of theirs, might I be detected. Mine, be assured, Lady Glenfeld, though not the most alluring is by far the safest plan, and principally on account of the small number of persons it will compel me to admit into my / confidence. You ask me what I know of the poor family I mentioned, and what reliance I can place upon them? Personally I have no knowledge of any but the youngest child, who being the god-daughter of my maid Adrienne, has sometimes been brought to our house to offer a *bouquet* on a *jour de fête*,[75] or to exhibit some little prize gained at her school. The father is an industrious and sober man who works at a printer's; he has four sons, two nearly grown up, who are employed by various tradesmen and manufactures in the neighborhood, and two who are still at home, except during the hours they spend at a day-school. The mother has wretched health, but does what she can towards the support of her family by taking in needlework. Adrienne has known them from her childhood, and has the greatest affection and esteem for them. These are the persons with whom I mean to take refuge. They have lately contrived by hard savings, and a little help afforded by a friend, to hire an additional room in the house where / they reside, and to fit it up decently for a lodger. Adrienne has already engaged it at my desire, but without having the most distant suspicion that it is for *me!* – that, I dare not at present let her know, for she will, of course, be more strictly examined, when I am first missed, than any one else, and I am desirous that she should be able honestly and truly to say, that she knows not whither I am gone. In a few days, or, at least, as soon as the confusion occasioned by my flight is abated, I entrust to you, dearest Lady Glenfeld the benevolent task of relieving her apprehensions, by informing her where I am: but caution her earnestly not to come to me till *you* give her leave. Mr. Wharton will be very likely to set spies upon her, and therefore tell her, that she must, as a proof of her affection, controul her impatience, and implicitly obey your directions.'

'When I look at you,' said Lady Glenfeld, her eyes swimming in tears – 'when I reflect how young you are – how unused to act for / yourself – how long accustomed to every indulgence, I can scarcely conceive how the energy, the forethought, the spirit of helpfulness you now display, can really belong to you! But tell me, dearest, what is to be the end of this adventure? If no answer, or, an unfavourable one, (which heaven forbid) arrives from Italy, how shall you act?'

'I have yet scarcely carried my thoughts so far into the future,' answered Agnes; 'but in the case you mention, I believe the best thing I could do, would be to go to England, and to endeavour, through the friendship of Madame Morinval, to procure some sort of reputable employment.'

'What! Become a shop-woman! My dear creature, it is madness to think of it!'

'Have I any choice?' enquired Agnes, smiling at Lady Glenfeld's unwonted vehemence – 'Rather than be without protection, without a home, I would, at least for a time, most thankfully take up my abode where, when a child, I was known, and am still, I / firmly believe, remembered with affection. Moreover, it is by no means indispensable that I should become a *shop-woman*; Madame Morinval, I learn from her daughter, is now at the head of the establishment she formerly carried on in partnership with the Leroux's; her business flourishes, she is in great vogue, and much respected by many of the principal families in town. May she not be able to obtain scholars for me? I have no pride that would revolt against such an exercise of the talents I may have acquired; – on the contrary, a maintainance thus earned would re-animate and cheer me; and I should still be in possession, and applying to honourable use the only advantage resulting from Mr. Wharton's profusion which it would not be disgraceful to retain.'

'All this,' thought Lady Glenfeld, 'is very pretty talking: but we shall allow you, my fair Agnes, to undertake no such drudgery!' However, seeing how sincerely she was in earnest, and how ill-timed at that moment would / have been any jesting remonstrance, she made no remark upon her friend's last words, but proceeded to another subject:

'Have you yet, dearest,' she said, 'arranged your plans sufficiently to be able to decide how and when you are to leave Mr. Wharton's house?'

'That must depend entirely upon my success in finding a fit opportunity of doing so unperceived. The day before yesterday I went with Mrs. Marchmont, who is sitting for her portrait, to a painter's. He has two rooms opening into each other, and both have a door leading to the staircase. It struck me, that if I accompanied her there again, I might whilst she was engaged with the artist, saunter into the adjoining room as if to look at the pictures hanging round it, and thence, quietly creep down into the street.'

'Good heavens! – And when there, how would you know which way to turn, or what would become of you?'

'Oh, no harm. I should be very plainly / dressed, it would be broad daylight, and probably I should soon procure a *fiacre*[76] in which to proceed, by the direction I have engraven on my memory, to the house of the poor printer. The circumstance that would make it so desirable to seize that moment for the enterprise is, that neither carriage nor servants would be in waiting, as Mrs. Marchmont, knowing exactly the time she is to sit, dismisses them when she alights, and tells them when to return.'

'If she had participated less in her brother's guilt,' said Lady Glenfeld, sighing, 'I should pity her from my very soul for the shock – the agony she will suffer when it is known that you have positively absconded!'

Agnes was silent; she also felt some compassion for the misguided woman, but it was not of a nature sufficiently powerful to turn her from her purpose.

Much further conversation passed upon this inexhaustible subject. Lady Glenfeld was urgent with Agnes to promise that on / whatever day she again accompanied Mrs. Marchmont to the painter's, she would write one line before getting into the carriage, and immediately send it off to her by Adrienne. Agnes inquired the motive of this request.

'Its motive is very simple, and I hope you will think very rational. If we knew the precise time when you would be at the artist's, Lord Glenfeld can – and I am sure he readily will – station himself out of reach of observation, but near at hand, to afford you his protection till you are provided with a *fiacre*. Consent to this request, dearest Agnes, if not for your own sake, at least for mine. I have so little of your spirit of enterprise, that the idea of your being alone in the streets, quite frightens me!'

'Ah, dear Lady Glenfeld,' said Agnes, half laughing, 'I look forward to undertakings so much more adventurous, that this seems nothing. However, if you think Lord Glenfeld will condescend to be employed on such a mission, and if you are kind enough / to make a point of it, I accept the offer with gratitude. This,' added she, 'is taking it for granted that I mean to allow you to communicate to him the substance of what I have been revealing to you; and the truth is, I am so intimately persuaded of his prudence and honour, that I had already, in my heart, given you the permission before it was asked for.'

'Thanks – thanks!' cried Bertha, pressing her hand, 'you have heightened the value of your compliance by the grace with which you have accorded it. Poor Lord Glenfeld, it is true, will have a heavy tax to pay for the honour of being admitted to share with me your confidence. The sight of Mr. Wharton will become odious to him, and were he left at liberty to follow his own impulse, I have no doubt that he would turn his back upon him wherever he met him. But I shall make it clearly understood, that it was upon the express condition he made no outward change in his behaviour to that gentleman, you consented / to my recapitulating to him the narrative I have drawn from you. And now, my noble Agnes, suffer me to descend to a more vulgar subject; tell me, shall you want money for your removal?'

'No, dear Lady Glenfeld; of that I have always had an abundant supply, and for some time past I have been economizing from a vague idea that the moment was approaching when I might want it. The trinkets and valuable ornaments that have been accumulated upon me, I shall of course leave behind me; but I cannot be so self-denying as to go away utterly pennyless.'

'I only wish the money had come to you from a worthier quarter! It pains me, methinks, that a creature whose motives are so pure, should sully the brightest action of her life, by availing herself for its accomplishment, of pelf which she knows to have been so lawlessly obtained! My own Agnes! leave that horrid money, as well as the jewels, to him whose defiled conscience will have to / answer for its appropriation! You will prosper much better by borrowing a little untainted gold from me.'

Agnes saw the reasonableness of this representation, and ingenuously confessed it.

'You are right, my most dear Lady Glenfeld,' she earnestly exclaimed, 'you are perfectly right! This! as you say, would be seeking to bring about a lawful end by the use of unlawful means. I had not sufficiently considered the matter: for, alas! it is but too true, I am yet a mere novice in the practice of real integrity.'

'Well, well, for a new beginner,' said Lady Glenfeld, playfully, 'you are not doing so much amiss!'

Then rising, and unlocking a writing-table drawer, she took from it two or three *rouleaux*,[77] insisting upon Agnes's accepting a loan of nearly double the amount she had intended to receive.

'You can give it me back if you do not want it,' said the generous Bertha; 'here it / lies, doing nothing, for I have not a want to gratify, and have yet been too short a time in this great city to have found out for myself such deserving objects of charity as I have been accustomed to relieve at home. Take it then, my friend, and say no more about it, but let me know how I must direct to you at your printer's?'

Agnes gave her precisely the same address she had sent to Mr. Danvers at Rome.

When, at a late hour, the carriage was announced that had been sent for her friend, and Lady Glenfeld was obliged to let her depart, she could not repress her emotion. She threw her arms around her, and straining her to her heart, called down blessings upon her head; pledged to her unchangeable affection; charged her to remember that in every difficulty she had a devoted friend to recur to; thanked her for the trust she had reposed in her, and to the last moment that she remained in sight, persevered in fervently repeating – /

'Heaven bless and prosper you! Heaven bless and protect you!'

This touching farewell, though it sent Agnes home weeping, was not to be reflected upon without feelings the most soothing and grateful. She regarded the tender affection of Lady Glenfeld as another proof that Providence was not unmindful of her fate; since, just at the moment she most required such a support, just as her expectations from the brother she had hoped to have found, began to fade, this new, and gentle, and endearing friend started up, and held forth to her a prospect of lasting and zealous attachment.

On alighting at Mr. Wharton's, it was a very acceptable relief to her to hear from Adrienne, who met her on the stairs, that the ladies had not long been returned from some great evening party; had all complained of fatigue, and were gone to bed. The redness of her eyes might have called forth enquiries, which, from her hatred of equivocation, she would have found it difficult to / answer. Adrienne saw at once, that something had been the matter, but, taught by experience, asked no questions, merely shedding, as she seemed to think herself in duty bound, a few silent tears for company. /

CHAPTER IX.

So prayed the maid, and peace, a wonted guest
Sought the known mansion of her spotless breast;
'Gainst every peril arm'd, to care resigned,
Cheer in her looks, and patience in her mind.

OGLE'S CHAUCER.[78]

As every day might now be the last of her residence in that house, Agnes, as soon as she was left to herself, instead of getting into bed, wrapt her dressing-gown round her, re-lit at her night lamp, the candle Adrienne had extinguished, and sat down to write a short, but significant letter to Mr. Wharton. She then collected and arranged in their cases, all her trinkets; folded in paper, and deposited amongst them, whatever money she had by / her, and locked up the whole in the bureau. The key she inserted in the cover of her billet to Mr. Wharton, including also within the same envelop the childish, but to her most important letter, of Lucy de Vere. This little packet she intended to consign to the care of Mr. Wharton's valet, should her hopes be answered of speedily receiving a second invitation to accompany Mrs. Marchmont to the painter's.

These painful, but indispensable preparations completed, Agnes threw herself on her knees, and recommended herself, with more than her wonted fervour, to the guidance and protection of heaven; after which, she at length sought her pillow, and was visited by the unbroken and refreshing sleep enjoyed by those whose conscience is at peace.

Before going down to breakfast the next morning, she told Adrienne, it was probable the person for whom the printer's lodging had been engaged, would wish to take possession / of it in a very few days; 'I therefore should be glad,' added she, 'that you would write a little note to serve this person as an introduction to your friend Madame Dupuis. Say that your mistress knows the new tenant, and will be answerable for her; that at present she only wishes to be called Agnes – Mademoiselle Agnes – and has particular reasons, but not disgraceful ones, for desiring to be as little talked of as possible. It will oblige me very much, Adrienne, if you will get this note ready by the time I come up from breakfast.'

Adrienne promised to comply, and Agnes left her.

On entering the room in which the family was assembled, she found that a rather warm contest was going on between Mrs. Marchmont and her brother, which appeared to afford singular amusement to Louisa and Caroline Le Strange, though they did their best to conceal their risibility. The debate / was on the subject of Mrs. Marchmont's portrait, which Mr. Wharton had heard of for the first time that morning.

He had expressed considerable surprise at her choosing to undergo the penance of sitting for a picture which had no peculiar destination, and which, as a mere piece of ornamental furniture, would have answered its purpose so much better had it been painted ten or fifteen years earlier. Mrs. Marchmont affected to laugh at this sarcastic insinuation; she protested, it was not from a desire of seeing her own likeness hanging up in the drawing-room, that she had consented to be painted, but from a wish to serve a deserving and diligent young artist, whose talents appeared to her to merit encouragement. She mentioned the names of several persons of respectability who had recommended him to her notice; and ended, as she had begun, by asserting, that it was solely with a view to his benefit she had employed him.

'And how many sittings has he had?' /

'*You* can answer that question Miss de Vere,' cried Louisa, unable to remain either grave or silent any longer. 'You, I think, have been the only one amongst us whose patience has outstood the tediousness of these endless visits! Come, tell us how often you have accompanied my aunt to this man's dull habitation?'

'I never had the least objection to going,' said Agnes, frightened to death, lest Mr. Wharton should throw any impediment in the way of his sister's attending the painter again.

'Thank you, dear Lucy,' cried Mrs. Marchmont, casting a glance of reproach towards her nieces. '*You* are always obliging – always good-natured!'

'That I do not deny,' resumed Mr. Wharton; 'but shall I tell you how her good-nature might be beneficial to us all, as well as to you, Mary? By prevailing upon the painter to substitute her face for yours on his canvass.' /

Though this was apparently spoken in jest, there was an expression in his eye that gave it more than point enough to annoy Mrs. Marchmont, and to renew the involuntary smiles of her nieces. Agnes however, had the satisfaction of rising from breakfast with the hope that the artist would be allowed to finish what he had begun.

But the day passed, and she heard no more of the matter. Great part of the morning, she drove about with the Le Stranges, paying visits, shopping, or seeing sights; and at a later hour, repaired to one of the most fashionable drives, where, having for some time formed part of the string of carriages moving at a foot's pace, they got out and walked, till the approach of dusk obliged them to return home. In this gay scene, as Agnes looked round, and reflected that she was now in all probability, sharing for the last time its splendour; when she beheld numbers of smiling and familiar faces directing towards her their courteous salutations; when she contemplated the brilliant equipages, and elegant / dresses of persons all accustomed to consider her as their equal, she could not but remember with a sigh! the contrast in her circumstances that was so soon to take place! Yet this sigh was less given to the pageantry before her, than to the melancholy recollection that she was henceforth to be estranged from the society of the educated and refined.

Fortunately, the consideration soon occurred to her, that the privation would be but temporary; or, at all events, that the indigence and obscurity to which she was consigning herself, would cease to be so painful, as the frugal habits and simple tastes of her childhood gradually revived.

The hour for making the experiment was at hand. Before she left her room the next morning, Mrs. Marchmont sent to beg that she would come and speak to her; and as soon as she entered that lady's apartment, she was thus addressed:

'My dear Lucy, I want to know whether you have made any particular engagement with my nieces this morning? If you have / not, will you oblige me by driving to the painter's with me at two o'clock?'

With a fluttering heart, Agnes said she would be ready to attend her.

'You are a dear girl! I knew I might depend upon you. But Lucy, I do not wish that any thing should be said about it at breakfast. My brother is not kind about this picture; and the two Le Stranges are positively impertinent! Surely at seven and thirty, a woman is not yet so old as to make it preposterous that she should sit for her portrait! Why, Mrs. Le Strange, who is considerably my senior, sat for her miniature very lately; she told me so herself.'

Agnes knew that she had, but it was to please Bertha, who had asked for it as a wedding present. It was not her business however to say so; and as soon as she could get away, she flew back to her own apartment. Adrienne was still there; and Agnes desired her to wait whilst she hastily wrote these words to Lady Glenfeld: /

'I have agreed to accompany her to-day at two o'clock to Monsieur Lefevre's. You know where he lives.

'Adieu, adieu! Fear nothing for me; my spirits are good, and my resolution is unshaken.'

She delivered this to Adrienne, charging her to carry it immediately to Lady Glenfeld's, to whose maid she was to consign it, with directions to give it to her lady as soon as possible.

This done, nothing remained but to find a fit opportunity of speaking to Mr. Wharton's valet. Such a one occurred about half an hour before Mrs. Marchmont's carriage came to the door. She was alone in the drawing-room, when the man was sent by his master to look for a direction on the chimney.

'Is Mr. Wharton going out soon, Larue?' enquired Agnes.

'Immediately, ma'am, I believe.' /

'Then, when he is gone, come up again; I want to speak to you.'

There was nothing in her voice that excited Larue's particular attention, and only answering,

'Yes ma'am,' he left the room, without either feeling or expressing any surprise. He had been accustomed to undertake little commissions at the watch-maker's or jeweller's, and it is probable he imagined, that such was her present business.

In about five minutes he returned. Agnes met him near the door, and with all the composure she could assume, said:

'Be so good as to put this little packet upon your master's dressing table. I wish him to see it before he sits down to dinner. That is all I had to say, Larue.'

The man took the packet, promised to obey her orders, and went away.

'The die is cast!'[79] thought Agnes, 'and who can tell what may be its consequence.' /

It was to her a solemn moment. The reputation, perhaps the existence of Mr. Wharton, seemed inseparably connected with its result. Her gentle and compassionate nature was affected with emotions she almost wondered at herself for experiencing. She had never been attached to Mr. Wharton; how was it, then, that she thus keenly felt for him? She could find no answer to this enquiry; but certain it is, that had her interest only been at stake, she would even yet, have gladly renounced her purpose. It was a case however that admitted not of temporizing. Her path was plain before her, and come what might, it was her duty to proceed.

The carriage was soon after announced, and whilst waiting for Mrs. Marchmont, she looked round at every well known decoration in the room with that species of dejection so commonly felt when aware that we are never again to behold even an inanimate object we have been accustomed to view from childhood. All things connected with the habits of the six / preceding years of her life were now to be considered not only as having passed away, but as having never been. Yet, what was she leaving that deserved really to be valued? who had she ever, exclusive of Adrienne, been attached to in that house? were the scenes of revelry she had witnessed, and participated in within its walls, worthy to call forth her regret? No, no! She felt ashamed of her own weakness, and struggled successfully to shake it off.

Mrs. Marchmont now made her appearance, and Agnes effectually self-tutored, firmly and bravely followed her down stairs, entered the carriage, and was driven from that door through which she was no more to pass.

They had not proceeded far, when Mrs. Marchmont's attention was arrested by the extreme plainness of her dress:

'My dearest Lucy,' cried she, 'why have you made such a dowdy figure of yourself? That bonnet is only fit for a quaker.[80] Pray love, do not wear it again. And why wrap / yourself in the middle of summer, in such a dark and dismal-looking shawl? Believe me,' added she, half laughing, 'I shall not be very anxious to exhibit myself with you at *Long-Champs*,[81] when the sitting is over! How differently you were attired yesterday! Do not come out any more, dear girl, in such a ridiculous costume, I entreat!'

Agnes made the best defence she could for herself, and on arriving at the artist's, Mrs. Marchmont's discomposure immediately passed away at sight of the progress he had made, since the last sitting, in the accessories of the picture. The back ground, and the drapery were nearly finished, and she was enchanted by the effect they produced. She was represented in a character, for which, assuredly, few persons would have perceived her requisites; the selection had originated in her having an oval face, and a profusion of dark hair, which, floating over her shoulders, was to entitle her to pass for *Melpomene*.[82] Neither dagger nor bowl had been forgotten; but, as / the face, unfortunately, was extremely like, these tragic emblems contrasted so singularly with its tameness and inanity, that Melpomene seemed to be disguised in the mask of Pope's Goddess of Dullness.[83]

The artist was facetious and complimentary, talked incessantly, laughed a great deal, and kept alive all Agnes' hopes, that after remaining stationary a reasonable time, she might from the next room get down stairs unheard, and probably find her way into the adjoining street before she was missed. While indulging these ideas, and thinking every minute an age of delay, a band of itinerant musicians began performing almost opposite the house. This was an opportunity of quitting her post not to be neglected; she started up, and hastened to the open window of the unoccupied room, Mrs. Marchmont calling after her, to desire she would give the people something to make it worth their while to play their prettiest airs. Agnes scarcely heard her, for at that instant, she descried at the door of a bookseller's shop, / nearly facing her, Lord Glenfeld, looking up at the window where she stood. She inly breathed a fervent ejaculation of thanks to her charming Bertha, and then, availing herself of a moment when the din of hautbois,[84] clarinets, French horns, and drums was at its height, she glided from the window, stept lightly across the room, opened the door leading to the stairs, and the next moment found herself in the street, supported by the arm, and reassured by the friendly voice of Lord Glenfeld. He hurried her forward till they came to a turning that secured them from being seen from the house she had quitted. Here he had stationed a *fiacre*, into which he assisted her to ascend, saying at the same time:

'I am not a man accustomed to utter many professions; but I cannot leave you, dear madam, without confirming the assurances your friend Bertha tells me she has given you, that there is nothing in my power, I would not joyfully undertake to serve you. I honour and respect your conduct, more than I have / words to express! Farewell; I must not at this critical moment, detain you any longer; let me only add, that Bertha bade me say, you would hear from her very shortly.'

He then bowed and left her. The coachman asked whither he was to go, which Agnes, as soon as she could collect her thoughts, having told him, he mounted his box, and, at the usual pace of a hackney-coach, drove off.

It took some time after the vehicle was in motion, to still the beatings of her heart, and to enable her to recover from the trepidation which the last eventful five minutes had given birth to. As she became more calm, it struck her, that to enter the house of Dupuis as a permanent lodger, without the customary appendage of a trunk, or baggage of any kind, would give them a very equivocal opinion of her. She therefore let down the front glass, and told the coachman to stop at the first ready-made linen warehouse he came to. Here she bought whatever was of most indispensable necessity for present use; and fearing to / alight at other shops, lest her ill-fortune should bring Mr. Wharton in her way, she prevailed upon the people she was now dealing with, to let her have a moderate sized wooden box, in which her purchases were deposited, and which, being paid for and conveyed to the carriage, she re-entered it, and resumed her slow progress towards the house of Dupuis.

On arriving at the door, she asked a little boy who was standing on the threshold, whether he would be kind enough to go and tell Madame Dupuis there was a person below wished to speak with her?

'Ah, oui, mademoiselle, bien volontiers,' answered the boy, briskly, 'C'est ma mère.'[85]

He was off in a moment, and the mother very soon appeared. Agnes was sorry to see that she looked pitiably weak and pale; but she was extremely clean, and still bore traces of having once been a remarkably pretty woman. /

Pretty women, be it observed, are from habit, always more attentive to personal neatness than others who are more homely. Why this should be, let those decide who may think it worth considering.

'This letter,' said Agnes, holding forth the introductory epistle she had made Adrienne provide her with, 'will explain to you who I am. Pray read it, and let me know whether I may alight.'

Madame Dupuis hastily glanced her eye over it, and then exclaimed: 'Ah, qu'oui, mademoiselle. Tout est prêt; donnez-vous la peine d'entrer.'[86]

Agnes on hearing this, directed her wooden box (of which she felt almost proud, as being the first property that for so long a time, she owed not to imposture), to be taken into the house; paid the coachman, and complimented him on his civility, jumped from the vehicle, and without permitting the mother to touch it, insisted upon helping the little boy to carry the box up stairs. /

Here was much popularity gained on easy terms. Agnes had not acted upon calculation, but if she had, what wiser policy could she have adopted?

'Voilà un commencement,' thought Madame Dupuis, 'de bien bonne augure! Comme elle est gentille et aimable, cette chère demoiselle! Et belle comme le jour!'[87]

Jeannot, the little boy, the youngest but one of Madame Dupuis' sons, was all activity, and eagerness to be of use. He led the way, notwithstanding the weight he helped to support, quicker than his poor mother could follow, to the new lodger's room, and triumphantly throwing open the door:

'There, mademoiselle,' cried he, 'there's your chamber, and a beautiful one I am sure you will think it! Look what a nice bed here is, with calico curtains; and see, here's a curtain to the window too; and here's a quite new table, and a fine looking-glass, and a chest of drawers. And then, here's a press full of shelves, with a lock and key; and a / nice set of pretty chairs, all new; and every thing in the world that even a queen could desire! I hope you like it, mademoiselle? I hope you are content?'

'I like it very much indeed, my good little boy; and I like you too, for being so alert and willing to assist me. What is your name?'

'Jeannot, Mademoiselle, at your service.'

'Well, Jeannot, if your mother permits it, you shall every morning, before you go to school, or in the afternoon when you return from it, be my little *commissionnaire*.[88] When I want to send out for any thing, you shall go and buy it for me.'

The mother had by this time, breathing short from the exertion, reached the door of the room, and asked leave to come in.

'Oh yes, by all means,' cried Agnes; and taking her by the hand, she drew her to a chair, saying: 'Pray sit down; I wish I could see you looking a little stronger. But you are better than you have been, are you not? With / good care, who knows whether you may not still recover your former health.'

'Ah! no, mademoiselle, I must not hope it: – but I am thankful for the amendment I *have* obtained; and every day of my life I pray for a blessing on the head of the kind lady to whom, under Providence, I am indebted for being spared a little longer to my poor children. The lady I mean, is the mistress of our good friend Adrienne, who tells me in the note you brought, that you are acquainted with her. Ah, mademoiselle – is she not an angel?'

'I am sure,' answered Agnes, 'nothing would make her happier than to know that she had been the means of doing you good.'

'Never fear, mademoiselle; our kind Adrienne has taken care of that, I'll answer for it! Last winter, you are to know, whilst her lady was at Nice, I kept my bed three months. My poor husband did what he could for me, and sometimes got me a little advice from a physician, and a few medecines; but I fancy the young doctor was not very clever, – / for he did me no good, and I gave myself up for lost. At last, Adrienne's mistress came back, and Adrienne soon after called here. Poor soul! she cried like a child when she saw what a state I was in; and out of her own pocket, before she went away, she gave her god-daughter, my little Agathe, a *pièce de vingt francs!*[89] The very next day another physician came, a sensible and skilful person, and he attended me regularly four or five times a week for nearly two months. It was Mademoiselle de Vere who sent him, and paid for all my medecines, and furnished me with money to procure lighter and better food than I had been able to provide before; and ordered for me an easy chair, to sit up in when I first left my bed, and a large supply of fire-wood; and used to send me such kind messages and good wishes by Adrienne, that I never could listen to them with dry eyes!'

Agnes had hitherto been withheld from interrupting this detail, partly by embarrassment / and partly by the apprehension of being thought to take no interest in the poor woman's sufferings; but she had now heard quite as much as she could bear in her own praise; and, to change the subject without appearing to depart from it too abruptly, she availed herself of the present pause to say:

'Adrienne seems to be a very true and excellent friend.'

'Indeed she is, mademoiselle; and if it had not been for her kind interference, her lady would never have known of our distress – and by this time, most likely, my children would have been motherless. I have two younger than that boy, mademoiselle, and he is only eight years old; and two others who are lads, one of fourteen, and the other of sixteen. They, to be sure, do not want me so much as these young ones; but they love me, and it would have gone to their heart had they lost me.'

'But, mother,' cried Jeannot, 'may I tell / mademoiselle a little more about the lady? May I tell her who gave us all the pretty furniture of this room?'

'You shall keep that information for tomorrow,' said Agnes, smiling good-humouredly upon him; – 'I want to talk to your mother now about my dinner. Perhaps she will allow you to go to some good *traiteur's*[90] in the neighborhood, and desire him to call here, that I may make some arrangement with him by the week for all my meals.'

Madame Dupuis instantly consented; directed the child where to go, and charged him not to loiter a moment on the way.

'That I won't, mother,' cried the boy, 'for I am sure if poor mademoiselle has not dined yet, she must be terribly hungry!'

Whilst he was gone, Madame Dupuis shewed Agnes a press in the wall, containing what even the poorest French family possesses, an ample supply of table-linen, towels, and sheets, all looking beautifully white, though coarse. / She gave into her care also, two silver forks, and an equal number of large and small spoons.

'Whatever else you want, *ma chère demoiselle*,' said the good woman, 'we shall be too happy to procure for you, as far as our means will permit.'

'Thank you, Madame Dupuis; you will not, I hope, find me encroaching, or difficult to please. But while we are on the subject of these domestic concerns, let me warn you that I am determined you shall incur no additional fatigue by my being in the house. You must have quite enough to do in attending to your own family. Find me, therefore, some trusty tidy person, who can come every morning and put my room in order, and whatever you think proper, I will pay her.'

Madame Dupuis tried to convince Agnes that she should want no such assistant; that she and her little girl could do all that would be required, without putting mademoiselle to / any fresh expense, assuring her that Agatha, though still such a mere child, was as handy and notable as many a full-grown woman.

Agnes gently interrupted her: 'Let Agatha,' cried she, 'rest satisfied to work at her needle till she comes to her strength, and attend regularly at her school; – I will accept none of her services; and as for *you*, Madame Dupuis, I would sooner undertake to wait entirely upon myself, than suffer you to attempt it! So try whether you cannot recommend to me such a person as I want.'

'Since you *will* have it so, mademoiselle, I need not go far to find poor people enough who would be glad of the employment. There is in this very house a widow-woman in very indifferent circumstances, but as honest as the day, who would be too thankful to earn a few *sous*[91] on such easy terms.'

'Well, then, speak to her this evening, and let her come to me about nine o'clock to-morrow morning.'

The arrival of the *traiteur*, conducted by / Jeannot, broke up this little conference. Agnes, though new to the practical part of business of every description, had not been so inattentive to what she had casually heard in conversation, as to be totally incapable of entering into its details. She made the *traiteur* agree to serve her upon reasonable terms; told him what dishes she should in general prefer, and requested that as a sample of his skill, he would let her have that day's dinner as hot, and as speedily as possible.

There was an unassuming – an unconscious superiority about her, softened by a manner so gentle and gracious, that she excited at once good-will and respect. The *traiteur* bowed as low as if his fortune had depended upon her custom, assured her she should be punctually obeyed, and retired.

Whilst Madame Dupuis was laying the cloth, Agnes asked Jeannot whether he went to school any more that day?

'No, mademoiselle; our master has given us a half-holiday, because it is the *jour de fête* of his little girl.' /

'Then you have time this afternoon, to do two or three more errands for me?'

'Oh yes, mademoiselle, as many as you please.'

She patted his cheek, which instantly dimpled and glowed with pleasure, and then told him he must consult his mother what shop to go to for a quire[92] of good writing paper, a small bottle of ink, half a dozen of pens, and a stick of sealing-wax. 'When I have all these things,' added she, 'I shall be able to write down my next commissions, without loading your memory with so long a list.'

'I assure you, mademoiselle,' said the mother, 'he will not forget a single article; I often send him to two or three different shops, to buy one thing at one, and another at another, and he comes back bringing them all as exactly as possible.'

'He is a good boy,' said Agnes, 'and you, Madame Dupuis, have been a good mother to bring him up so well.'

To both parent and child, this was most / grateful praise; and each thought that for *such* a lady, they could never do too much. Jeannot was furnished with money for his commissions; and soon after he had set out to execute them, Agnes's dinner arrived. Madame Dupuis placed a little bell upon the table in case she should want any thing, and left the room.

The provisions with which she had been furnished, satisfied Agnes so perfectly, that she only wanted an associate to partake of the repast with her, to think it one of the best she had ever eaten. As nearly half what had been sent, would amply have sufficed her, she longed for the return of Jeannot, to give him a portion of what remained. But he came not, and she at last gently touched the bell. Fortunately for Madame Dupuis as well as for her lodger, she lived upon the same floor, and could attend to such an occasional summons without difficulty. On her entrance, Agnes asked what had become of her little messenger?

'He has been come back some time, mademoiselle, / and has brought every thing you ordered quite right, I believe.'

'Then why did he not come and show me his purchases?'

'I would not let him enter whilst you were at dinner, mademoiselle; – it would have made him appear so rude and greedy!'

'I cannot but commend your delicacy, my good Madame Dupuis, though it disappointed me of the pleasure of seeing him finish with a hearty appetite, after so much running about, a part of what I have left. Take it all away, however, and do whatever you please with it. I never eat supper, and shall want nothing more before I go to bed, except the coffee I have desired the *traiteur* to send me at eight o'clock.'

Madame Dupuis was in amazement! To her, trifling as it appears, this was a trait of liberality more striking than any other could have been. She had received money from the rich, and services from the poor; but she had never lived with one capable of thus gratuitously / disposing of the overplus of a meal. Those who have often been in fear of wanting bread, – who have saved every remaining morsel of a scanty dinner to eke out its hard-earned fellow of the morrow, those only can form an idea of the admiration with which a poor artizan's wife would look up to a person, in a rank apparently not much more elevated than her own, for a donation so rare and unexpected.

While taking the things away, after gratefully expressing her thanks, Madame Dupuis said: 'Be sure, mademoiselle, Jeannot shall not go without his share, for I see you have been good enough to take a fancy to him: but I hope you will also like *ma petite Agathe*; she is an excellent child, and our only girl, and we are all very fond of her.'

Agnes said she wished to see her very much, and asked where she was?

'She is not yet come home from school, mademoiselle, but I expect her now every moment.' /

'Then pray bring her to me when she returns. I hope, by degrees to know all your family.'

'Ah, mademoiselle, my two elder boys would die with shame, were you to see them in their dirty labouring dresses; one works at an ironmonger's, and the other at a bricklayer's, and it is impossible they should keep themselves neat at such employments. But *Dimanche*,[93] when they have time to clean themselves, and put on their best clothes, I shall be proud to present them to you. They are, at least in my eyes, as fine lads as any you can meet with.'

When Jeannot was allowed to enter with the purchases he had made, and an eager request to know what he was to do next, Agnes said she had one more errand for him, if he was not tired, and then he might go and amuse himself.

'Tired, ma'm'selle? No, that I am not! Why the *traiteur*, and the stationer live close by, and I have been no where else.' /

After writing a few words on a slip of paper which she gave him, Agnes said: 'This is a list, my little friend of materials for work; show it to the person at the shop, and they will give you what you are to bring.'

Away he flew; and Agnes, whose time, it appeared, was not to hang heavy upon her hands that day by being spent in solitude, was presently visited again by Madame Dupuis, leading in Agathe with face and hands newly washed, and bright hair smoothly brushed, and turned up and fastened with a comb at the top of her head. She was more bashful than her brother, who had what the French call *un air éveillé*,[94] that announced quick parts and a gay disposition; but she was much prettier, although her countenance was less open, and its expression seemed to denote a greater tendency to fretfulness. Agnes well remembered, the moment she saw her, her down-cast little face, and shrinking manner; and thought it by no means unlikely she should be recognized herself; but the probability disturbed her not; / for *Mademoiselle Agnes* arriving alone in a hackney coach, as the lodger of Madame Dupuis, was so unlike any idea they could have formed of *Miss de Vere*, the rich heiress, living in splendour at her guardian's, that let the child say what she would, there was not the slightest danger her remarks would be attended to.

When, by dint of the kindest encouragement, the little girl at last became sufficiently at her ease in the presence of a stranger to raise her eyes, they remained fixed upon Agnes' face with an air of doubt, surprise, and perplexity impossible to describe. She who was thus gazed at bore the scrutiny unshrinkingly; and, amused by the feelings she was exciting, said with a smile:

'Now that you *do* look at me, Agathe, you appear to see something that half frightens you. What, or who do I put you in mind of?'

It was some time before Agathe gained courage to make any reply; but urged equally by / her mother, and the new lodger, she at length ventured to say, in a very low voice:

'I looked at you, ma'am, because you are so like......'

'Who, my dear?' enquired Agnes, finding she had come to a dead pause – 'Who am I so like? – Nobody who ever did you any harm, I hope?'

'O no, ma'am! – I meant the lady my godmother lives with.'

'What, Mademoiselle de Vere?' cried the mother. 'Is this good young lady like *her?* Then heaven has written angel in *both* their faces, and, if they had equal means, I do believe, they would both prove themselves angels by their own actions!'

Ah, why, thought Agnes, should we accuse the poor of wanting gratitude? This woman's thankful heart makes her almost eloquent!

The rest of the day, she spent quietly at work, her thoughts, whilst thus employed, wandering continually to the habitation she had / left. – How had Mr. Wharton borne her flight? How had Mrs. Marchmont exculpated herself from the charge of negligence and want of discernment? In what light was her escape regarded by the Le Stranges? And how had it affected poor Adrienne? – It was next to certain that faithful attendant would undergo a close and severe examination: but if they had a spark of judgment left, they *must* see she knew as little of the matter as themselves. Perhaps Lady Glenfeld might have some tidings to send in the morning; and if she had, Agnes well knew she would not for a moment defer forwarding them. /

CHAPTER X.

> I've made some trial of my strength in this
> My solitary life; and yet I find not
> A faintness coming on me.
> Do you inhabit here?
> 'Tis my own free choice;
> I live here poorly but contentedly.
>
> BEAUMONT AND FLETCHER.[95]

BUT how, in reality, had Mr. Wharton supported the tremendous blow inflicted upon him?

On his return home to dress for dinner, an air of consternation visible amongst the domestics instantly caught his notice. He asked no questions till he reached his own room, and was attended by Larue:

'Has any thing unusual happened this morning?' said he.

'I know nothing with any certainty, Monsieur. Mademoiselle de Vere before she went / out, desired me to give you this packet as soon as you returned. Perhaps that may explain every thing.'

He put Agnes' letter into his master's hand, and quitted the room.[96]

Mr. Wharton bolted himself in. He had not a nerve that did not quiver with fear; his face was livid; his eye-sight was confused; – some horrible revelation was about to be made to him; and, loaded as was his conscience, he knew not that anything was too awful to expect. All, – all was at stake – character – personal freedom; the means of existence, all and each were in peril. – If this girl had betrayed him, – if she had sought other protection, what remained for him but flight, or – death! –

Becoming gradually somewhat calmer, and reflecting how little foundation he yet had for his fearful anticipations, he steadied his hand sufficiently to break the letter open.

It was in these terms: /

'When you read this, I shall have left your house, I trust, for ever. My motive for doing so may be explained in two words: it is, that I may free myself from the necessity of longer performing a part which my whole soul has learnt, though late, to abhor. It may surprise you, that having during so may years lent myself to be the instrument of a fraud almost without a parallel, these scruples should so suddenly have come upon me. Terror and compulsion, as you well know, began what habit, and want of reflection, continued: the accidental discovery of the letter I enclose aroused me to better feelings. – Read it – you can need no other explanation.

'As it is next to impossible you should trace my retreat, you will attribute to no interested motive my declaring, at this parting moment, that I quit you with a just sense of what I owe you, not so much for the means of instruction you have afforded me – for in that respect you probably only considered what was due to the opinion of the world – but for the / far greater benefit of having placed around me none but uncorrupt and well-intentioned persons.

'I have only to add, that in taking the step this letter announces, I have studiously avoided seeking to gain accomplices amongst any of your domestics. – Adrienne is as profoundly ignorant on the subject as all the others.

'And now, with joy, not unmixed with commiseration for the pang you will suffer on beholding it, I resume the humble name I ought never to have relinquished,

'Agnes Danvers.'

The name did, indeed, flash across his eyes with the dazzling effect of a sheet of lightning! So long, and so scrupulously had it been avoided, that he believed time had almost obliterated it from her memory: but here was proof – terrible proof that he had deceived himself! – The letter dropt from his nerveless hand, and, in unutterable consternation, he sat without motion, apparently without sensibility, / in deep and gloomy abstraction. – At last, slowly recovering from this species of stupor, his fixed eyes regained their expression, his powers of perception returned, and seeing the letter still lying on the floor, he took it up, and once more perused it. – 'This is no idle threat!' cried he, when he came to its conclusion. 'Her purpose is fixed; – she deals in no flights – in no girlish extravagance! – All she has written denotes the coolness and deliberation of a heart and head equally resolved! – Well may she say, she has had no advisers or assistants in this house! it contains not a mind capable of directing so noble a spirit; her own sense, her own courage effected the whole. – In truth, she has proved herself a magnanimous creature!'

A deep sigh burst from him as he uttered these words, and his eye, for a moment, was moistened with a tear: – 'Oh had I but been blessed,' he cried, 'with such a daughter!' No man is wholly evil, – and what was undepraved in the unhappy being now writhing / under the sense of his own misdeeds, derived some consolation from meditating upon the allusion made by Agnes to the vigilance with which she had been guarded from perversion in his family, and suffered to grow up as pure, as unambitious, and as disinterested as when he first bore her from her obscure home.

But these milder emotions – circumstanced as he was – tottering on the verge of an abyss – aware that no reparation was in his power, and that no compromise would be listened to, soon gave place to more turbulent feelings. The letter of poor Lucy de Vere still remained unread, and lay upon the table beside him. He seemed to regard it with fear and hesitation, as if repugnant to touch it: but seizing it at length with an almost angry vehemence, and giving it an hurried perusal, he tore it, gnashing his teeth, into a thousand atoms, exclaiming:

'Why was the infernal memorial preserved? – How came it into Agnes' hands? – Has my / sister – my besotted sister, been so brainless as to hoard up such perilous fragments......'

Just then he heard approaching footsteps, and some one knocked at the door. With such composure as he could summon, he opened it, and Mrs. Marchmont's maid delivered to him a note and retired.

'I hear you are in the house, but I dare not seek an interview! – You are aware that she has disappeared. She went with me this morning to the painter's; a band of musicians in the street, attracted her to the open window of the room adjoining that in which I was sitting. I have never seen her since! – We suspected nothing till the performers were gone, I then called her – the whole house was put in motion – no traces of her were to be discovered. – I was brought home in strong hysterics, and even now my hand shakes so dreadfully, I can hardly hold my pen. – Can any thing be done, or are we ruined past redemption.' /

'*To the painter's!*' mentally repeated Mr. Wharton with ineffable contempt. – 'Vain fool!'

He paused – he meditated profoundly – he looked at the key which Agnes had enclosed to him, and labelled, 'Key of the bureau in my dressing-room, containing trinket-box and money.' Again he became rapt in intense thought; – at last, a scornful smile stole over his disordered features; he seemed to have come to a decision, and forcibly smoothing his contracted brow, drank a large glass of water, shook off all evidences of the agitation that had almost convulsed him, and quietly opening his door, walked, with his usual step and gait, past some of the servants who were loitering about the hall, and went up to his sister's apartment.

Her own maid, and Adrienne (whose facility in weeping, it may well be believed, was not inactive on the present occasion) were both in the room; and Mrs. Marchmont, her hair dishevelled, and her eyes swollen, lay half reclined / on the sofa, affording, at that moment, a far better model for the *Tragic Muse*,[97] than it had ever been the good fortune of the painter to see her exhibit. She looked up as her brother entered, prepared already to shriek at the angry expression she expected him to wear. What then was her astonishment, when she saw him standing at the door regarding her with a tranquil and natural smile!

'Good Heaven!' exclaimed she, starting up; 'have you read my note?'

'Yes,' answered he, in French, that the two women might understand him. 'Yes, I *have* read your note, and I have comfort to give you; for I also have received one from Miss de Vere; I know where she is; and though I do not approve of the fright she has occasioned you, I am satisfied she is in proper company, and will be restored to us either tomorrow, or the day after.'

This was uttered with an apparent freedom from effort – the words, the tone of the voice, and the look of sincerity that accompanied / them, were all so inimitably true to nature, that Mrs. Marchmont, long as she had known him, gave implicit credit to the whole fabrication. The maids were enchanted, Adrienne especially: but her terrors being calmed, she next began, in the true spirit of her vocation, to bemoan the inconvenience her mistress would suffer from having no change of apparel.

'Could I not send some of her things, sir?' inquired she, addressing Mr. Wharton. 'Where is she gone?'

'She has been carried off by Madame Monbar and her two daughters to the house of one of their friends at Neuilly,[98] where, this evening, some private theatricals are to be performed. They were driving through the street in which Monsieur Lefevre lives, when they saw Miss de Vere at his window. One of the girls ran up to ask her to go and speak to her mother in the carriage, and when once they had her in their power, they refused to part with her in despite of all her entreaties to be allowed / to return and inform Mrs. Marchmont of their invitation. I suppose,' he continued, speaking to his sister, 'the noise in the street prevented your hearing the entrance of Sophie Monbar, and she took care not to let you see her, lest you should oppose her *espièglerie*.[99] The young ladies, Adrienne, will lend your mistress whatever she may want; and, for so short an absence, it is hardly worth while to send a messenger on purpose; moreover, I do not exactly know what direction to give him.'

'Upon my word,' cried Mrs. Marchmont, in whom fear had entirely given place to pique, 'I never knew a more unpardonable trick! – I always thought Sophie Monbar a giddy, hare-brained girl, but I had no idea she would have ventured upon such a flight as this! The mother, however, is quite as much to blame; she ought not to suffer her daughters to conduct themselves so wildly. Whenever I see them again, how I will scold them!'

'*Que voulez-vous!*'[100] said her brother, shrugging / his shoulders. 'Young people's little vagaries must not be censured too severely. The worst is over now; you know that Lucy is in safe hands, and the wisest thing you can do, is to take the matter quietly. Where is Mrs. Le Strange? Is she informed of the panic you have been in?'

'I have not seen her; I believe she is still out with her girls.'

'You all dine at Lady Glenfeld's to-day, I think?'

'Yes, – and you dine there also, do you not?'

'I may join you there in the evening; but I am forced to meet a man on business, who sets off early to-morrow morning for England, and I shall probably dine at a restaurateur's.'

He then begged her to apologize for him to Lord Glenfeld, and went back to his room.

Larue was there in attendance, waiting to dress him. Without alluding to Agnes's packet, his master told him, Miss de Vere / was gone for a day or two with Madame Monbar to Neuilly; and desired that a footman might be sent to Monsieur Lefevre's to inform him that Mrs. Marchmont was perfectly recovered, and that all anxiety respecting Miss de Vere was at an end.

But the re-assuring message reached Monsieur Lefevre too late to prevent the report of Agnes's disappearance from getting abroad. One of his warmest patrons, a young Frenchman of fortune, named de Verneuil, had been amongst the first to whom the intelligence was communicated. He was a passionate admirer of Agnes, whom he had occasionally met in the family of Monbar. So serious, indeed, had been the impression she had made on him, that he had ventured to declare his sentiments to Mr. Wharton, soliciting his permission to address her. The proposal was civilly negatived, the lover being told that Miss de Vere's hand was already engaged to one of her own countrymen. It happened, that just after hearing from Lefevre the scarcely-credible / story of her flight, he met his supposed rival, Harry Cowley, in the street. Harry had arrived in Paris within the last hour, and was proceeding towards Mr. Wharton's from the hotel where he meant to take up his quarters, when the agitated Frenchman, whom he slightly knew, and bowed to, passed him with an air of marked and violent rudeness. Harry as fiery as himself, followed him with his eyes a moment, and then sent after him an audible and contemptuous laugh. A quarrel ensued, and a challenge, as precipitately accepted as given, immediately took place. After this insane *fracas*,[101] de Verneuil encountering again the loquacious painter, was informed by him, that Mrs. Marchmont had ascertained Miss de Vere was only gone to Neuilly, whither she had been enticed for a few days by Mesdemoiselles Monbar. More than ever suspicious of some lurking iniquity (being assured beyond all doubt those ladies were actually paying a visit at the distance of upwards of fifty miles from the capital) he hastened to / secure a second for his approaching encounter; and accidentally at the turning of a corner, came suddenly upon Walsingham. They had known each other some time, and were become intimate, Verneuil not being *always* so devoid of good sense as he was now showing himself. Having briefly stated the predicament in which he stood, he asked Walsingham whether he would accompany him on the morrow to the scene of action?

'Who is your antagonist?' enquired the Englishman – 'and what's your cause of quarrel?'

'He is a countryman of yours, and for that reason I am best pleased to be provided, if possible, with a second of his own nation. There will be less opportunity given for objections to be made to the want of form and regularity in the conduct of the business.'

'True; – but why do you fight at all?'

'I have every reason in the world to believe, that the man in question, who is said to be engaged to a lady I ardently admire, has had / the indelicacy to avail himself of the authority of her guardian, in order to be forced upon her choice. He is just come over from England, with the view, no doubt of solemnizing the marriage; – but this very morning, the lady, probably apprized of his approach, has disappeared, nobody knows whither, undoubtedly driven to extremities by aversion to the pretender imposed upon her.'

Walsingham could not wholly suppress a smile: –

'All this, my dear Verneuil, is but conjectural; would you really blow out a man's brains because you *believe*, and you *suppose*, and you think it *probable* he may have done something you do not like?'

Verneuil, a little disconcerted, answered with more moderation:

'You will allow, my friend, that mine is a hard case! I have been rejected by the guardian without his having even deigned to apprize the lady of my application. She has now made an effort to emancipate herself from his / controul; whilst he, for some villanous purpose, tries to impose upon the world by asserting that he knows where she is – and even naming the family he pretends she is on a visit to at Neuilly. This, to my certain knowledge is an absolute – an infamous falsehood!'

'If ever a falsehood can be otherwise than infamous, I think this is a case when it may be so regarded. Should the lady, as is very possible, return after a while, to her guardian's house, it may preserve her reputation from the blemish her rashness might otherwise cast upon it. Come, come, Verneuil, shake off your captious feelings against my poor countryman; tell me who he is, and be reasonable enough to consent to my endeavouring to accommodate this unreasonable quarrel. He and you ought to be the best friends in the world, for as lovers you seem to be equally unsuccessful.'

After some further debate, Verneuil withdrew his opposition to his friend's rational proposal; made him acquainted with the name / of his adversary, and suffered him to depart on his errand of pacification.

The mind of Walsingham as he went, was busy in conjecturing what extraordinary inducement could have engaged Miss de Vere to take the questionable step he had heard ascribed to her. She was one whose demeanor delicate and modest, had prepared him for anything rather than the temerity of thus braving the opinion of the world. Full of perplexity, and deeply ruminating on the ungrateful subject, he determined to see Lady Glenfeld as speedily as possible, hoping to elicit from her some explanation of this most incomprehensible affair. Meanwhile, he arrived at Mr. Wharton's door.

That gentleman was still at home, notwithstanding the engagement he had pleaded to his sister in excuse for declining to accompany her to the Glenfeld dinner-party. The unexpected sight of Harry Cowley at the moment he was in fact sallying forth, had detained / him: – and, on sending in his name, Mr. Walsingham was immediately admitted.

Wharton knew him by sight only, – and to Harry he was an entire stranger.

As concisely, and as simply as he could, he made known the object of his visit. He attributed to his friend Verneuil a character in the highest degree honourable and generous, but allowed it to be liable to occasional starts of impetuosity no less inconvenient to himself than to others. Something had occurred that morning to disturb and irritate him beyond his wont. A more temperate and rational spirit, Mr. Walsingham was happy to add, now possessed him; and he was authorized to say, that unless Mr. Cowley insisted upon more sanguinary satisfaction, his friend was fully disposed to apologize for what had passed.

To Mr. Wharton the whole affair had hitherto been a mystery. During the brief interval they had been together, Harry had dropped no hint of what had taken place: – / but his eyes now flashed with passion, and his whole aspect shewed him disposed to persevere in hostile measures. The alarmed father, struck by the manly interference of Walsingham, and quick in observing the flushed brow of his son, hastened to interpose both authority and argument in opposition of the intended contest.

Cowley was hard to appease, and complained, perhaps not without reason, of having had to pay the penalty, due by another, for putting Monsieur de Verneuil into an ill-humour!

Walsingham could have replied that it was the sudden appearance of Cowley himself that had kindled the lurking resentment of de Verneuil into a flame: but desiring only to conciliate, he, of course, forebore; and assisted by the father, at length brought the young man though not without considerable difficulty, to reason.

But the trials Harry was that day to undergo, were not yet at end. So multiplied were / his enquiries respecting Agnes, and so great the impatience he evinced to see her, and judge by her looks of her actual feelings towards him, that his father became painfully aware of the necessity of preparing him for the overthrow of those hopes he had himself so prematurely contributed to encourage.

'Harry,' said he, 'we must attempt to deceive ourselves no longer; Lucy de Vere will never realize the expectations we had formed; her affection for you has not made the slightest progress since you parted.'

'Her letters,' replied Harry, dejectedly, 'gave me no reason to flatter myself it had! But I trust, sir, she has formed no other attachment?'

'Of that I am entirely ignorant; there is reason, however, to believe, no such circumstance has taken place. At all events, my dear Cowley, you must arm yourself with resolution to bear up against disappointment as well on this account, as on others that are perhaps awaiting you. Lucy is at present from / home. Let me recommend to you to make your stay in Paris as short as possible; to renew with increased energy the prosecution of those studies which may best fit you for an honourable profession; and no longer to place the smallest reliance upon the golden visions which the prospect of this marriage once set before you. Your education has been liberal, and your future prosperity must depend entirely upon your own exertions. Mr. Gage, I am persuaded, will always be a friend to you; but he has many claimants in his own family, and you must not forget, my dear lad, that exclusive of the limited assistance he may be able to afford you, the utmost you have to depend upon, is the slender pittance of two hundred a year: – It is all your father had power to do for you.'

'And I neither require nor wish for more!' cried the sanguine youth. 'With such abilities as nature may have given me – with an intense desire to surpass the common herd – with powers of application that never vary / – with memory – some clearness of apprehension – some vigour, I trust, of mind as well as body – what have I to fear? The career leading to fortune and eminence is open before me; and I nothing distrust my own success in attaining the goal.'

'May your happiest prognostics be verified!' said Mr. Wharton, with a smile not unmixed with sadness; – 'and now, dear Harry, let us go forth and seek a dinner. Afterwards, you will do well to repair for amusement to one of the theatres, whilst I return hither to write letters.'

Accordingly, they went together to a restaurateur's, and their repast over, separated till the following morning. /

CHAPTER XI.

Je trouve en elle une femme indulgente
Dont l'humeur douce et compatissante,
A mes désirs facile à se plier,
Daigne avec moi me réconcilier:
Me gouverner sans être tyrannique,
Me corriger sans prendre un ton caustique;
Et dans mon cœur pénétrer pas-à-pas
Comme un jour doux dans des yeux délicats.

VOLTAIRE'S NANINE, *Comédie.*[102]

IT was with no little astonishment, Lady Glenfeld, amongst the foremost guests at her dinner party, saw Mrs. Marchmont enter, arm in arm with one of the Le Stranges. She was as gaily dressed, and her mind seemed to be as much at ease as usual. The only perceptible difference was an unwonted degree of paleness, the inevitable result of the alarm she had undergone. 'What can be the meaning,' thought Bertha, 'of her going / about with so unconcerned an appearance whilst such a sword is hanging over her head? *He* comes not, I perceive, but that *she* should have the resolution to do so, exceeds – utterly exceeds, my powers of comprehension!'

Mrs. Marchmont, however, unsuspicious of the strictures she was exciting, after having repeated to Lord Glenfeld the apology sent by her brother, proceeded to give a full detail of the events of the morning. She told of her having gone to Monsieur Lefevre for her eighth sitting; of the musicians who had drawn Agnes to the window; of the unspeakable consternation she had been thrown into when she first missed her; of the violent nervous attack she had suffered; and of the pitiable state in which she had been conveyed home.

'And what relieved you, Madam, from your alarm?' gravely enquired Lord Glenfeld.

'Why, a note sent by Lucy to Mr. Wharton, informing him she had been carried off, almost by compulsion, to Neuilly by Madame / Monbar, and her freakish daughters, to see a play represented this evening by some amateurs, at the house of one of their neighbours. Poor Lucy was not at all prepared for a frolic of that kind; she was worse dressed, as it happened, than I ever saw her;

she had no time to send for any change of clothes; was without a maid; and very likely without money to repay the services she must accept from the *femme de chambre*[103] of Madame Monbar.'

'Mamma,' cried Isabel, 'will you allow me to call *this* a vulgar joke? I know you are very loath to permit the use of that word; but surely here is an occasion when it may be applied with all safety of conscience!'

'It is so unlike the usual style of French *badinage*,'[104] said Lord Glenfeld, expressively, 'that if I had not heard Mrs. Marchmont assert it as a fact, I should have been tempted to call it a clumsy fabrication.'

Bertha attentively observed her aunt to see how she bore this speech, and perceiving that / she blenched not, but seemed to assent to it as a very just observation, she remained satisfied that the falsehood originated with Mr. Wharton, and had been suggested to his credulous sister, that she might put it in circulation.

'Who are these Monbars?' enquired Mrs. Le Strange. 'Have we ever seen them at your house, Mary?'

'I don't know,' answered Mrs. Marchmont, 'but I rather think not. They are the wife and daughters of an eminent banker, and often give delightful balls, to many of which Lucy has gone. In fact, she has known the girls ever since she first came to Paris, and a certain degree of intimacy may be said to subsist between them; but I never suffered her to become their guest for more than an evening; and after this affair, I shall be less inclined to do so than ever.'

Other company now came in, and more general subjects of conversation were started.

Bertha, it was remarked by her mother, / was less cheerful than usual, and, at intervals, appeared absent, and lost in thought. Lord Glenfeld was habitually grave, and seldom exerted himself much to talk; but on this day, it was more than gravity – it was a cloudiness of aspect that denoted internal anger; a preoccupation of mind so great, that it was rarely he could prevail upon himself to speak at all. Here was ample field for those infallible powers of penetration on which Mrs. Le Strange so highly prided herself. She looked from the husband to the wife – from the wife to the husband – and mentally settled the whole matter.

'Humph! a first quarrel!' thought she, 'they are always the worst! The critical time for every married pair is the first half year; *that* once passed, things settle into their right place, and it becomes understood which of the parties is to keep the reins in hand. I had fancied, however, that Bertha's pliant temper would have yielded without a struggle to the supremacy of her lord; but I / suppose we are all alike, all willing to secure a little power if we can. I shall take no notice of what I see; preserve me, common sense, from interfering between man and wife! I am sorry the breeze has sprung up to-day, however, because it makes the party dull, and may induce young Ross to invent some excuse for not staying the evening.'

Mr. Ross, though at present a mere commoner, was next in succession to a peerage, and possessed already of a large fortune. He had frequently met the Le Stranges since their arrival in Paris; had paid particular attention to Louisa, and was just such a suitor as her mother approved. Caroline, amongst her own countrymen, was also much admired; but it gave Mrs. Le Strange no small disturbance to find, that Isabel, on whose attractions she had always rested her most ambitious hopes, openly professed her preference of the conversation and assiduities of foreigners. At that very moment, there sat next to her a young, animated Frenchman, / whom Isabel, to judge by the exclusive attention she bestowed upon him, was not very far from thinking much more agreeable than her mother wished. But Isabel was playing a not very generous game. The truth is, she had been extremely struck, at various parties where she had seen him, with the manners, and spirited deportment of Monsieur de Verneuil; and her present courtesy to the youth beside her, owed its origin entirely to his being one of de Verneuil's most frequent companions. She had the art, without directly introducing his name, to draw forth continual allusions to him; to learn what houses he frequented the oftenest; what his favorite pursuits were; what style of beauty he most admired, and innumerable other details, which though trivial in themselves, were interesting to her, and not displeasing to her neighbour; since the mention of de Verneuil seemed only incidental, and the present speaker believed himself, in fact, the principal personage in whatever he related. /

So ominous of evil appeared to Lord and Lady Glenfeld the unnatural calm that had followed the flight of Agnes, that they both sought with anxiety an opportunity of holding together a moment's conference. There was no difficulty in effecting this after they entered the drawing-room: some of the party sat down to cards, and others gathered round the instrument to listen to the singing of her sisters. Bertha then asked her husband what he thought of Mr. Wharton's present conduct? 'It seems to me,' she said, 'to teem with undefined mischief. I tremble for Agnes, since there can scarcely be a doubt that he is assiduously employing the interval in trying to trace her steps. Can we give her no protection?'

Lord Glenfeld considered for a moment, and then kindly pressing her hand, said: 'You shall before long, be relieved from this suspense, my dear Bertha. If I am missed, make some excuse for me. I go myself to obtain for you that information, which we / must trust no other agent to procure for us. I cannot endure to see you so uneasy; and to speak the truth, I think you have cause.'

He then left the room, and soon after the house.

His purpose was, to proceed in a *fiacre* to the end of the street, in which Agnes now resided, there to get out, and find his way on foot to the printer's house. If any light still appeared at the windows, he meant to enquire for one of the Dupuis', and send up to Agnes a single line, which he had prepared before he left home, waiting below for her answer. He had written only these words:

'Is all well? Have you been unmolested? Write to Bertha to-morrow by the *petite poste*.'[105]

The Dupuis were all in bed. It was eleven o'clock; the father and sons were obliged to rise early, the wife had weak health, and consequently they never deferred going to rest till the night was so far advanced; but a faint ray of light glimmered from an upper window, and / Lord Glenfeld saw a woman take in a bird-cage which had been hanging against the wall. He spoke to her, and begged she would come down and receive a letter for a person in that house. It was the poor widow, whom Madame Dupuis had mentioned to Agnes, and who already knew the functions she was to enter upon on the morrow, and the name of the new lodger. She made no difficulty in complying with Lord Glenfeld's request; and when she joined him, he further begged her, if possible, to procure for him an answer to his note.

'I will do what I can, Monsieur,' said the civil widow; and accordingly, leaving the stranger in the passage, she went up to Agnes' door, at which she gently knocked.

'Who is there?' enquired the solitary girl.

'I have a letter for you, mademoiselle,' said the messenger, 'and a gentleman below waits for an answer.'

Agnes, in her night-cap and dressing-gown, instantly unlocked the door, and with some / trepidation, held out her hand for this unexpected missive; its contents drew from her a smile of tender gratitude; she flew to her table, and wrote thus:

'I have been perfectly tranquil; and my heart is overflowing with thankfulness for the generous interest you and Lady Glenfeld feel for me. I will despatch a longer letter to-morrow.'

Lord Glenfeld read these lines by the feeble light of the widow's candle, and was fully reassured. He recompensed the poor woman for her trouble, bade her good night, and returned to his *fiacre*.

But his efforts to give entire contentment to his wife, terminated not here. Mr. Wharton's house was at a short distance from his own, and when he drew near it, he alighted from and dismissed his conveyance. It was his wish to ascertain whether that gentleman really was at home. He strongly suspected him of being actively employed in finding / agents, and in setting them to recover his lost prey. Under this impression, he was crossing over to the porter's lodge to apply for admission into the house, when a side gate being opened to let out one of the servants, he distinctly saw Mr. Wharton, with a candle in his hand, pass one of the upper windows. Glad to have his apprehensions put an end to, he immediately directed his steps homewards.

He re-entered his own drawing-room just as the party was beginning to disperse. Bertha's eye sought his the moment he appeared, and a nod and a half smile, were earnest sufficient of favourable news, to enable her to await patiently the departure of her remaining guests. As soon as the last carriage had driven away, she entreated to hear what he had been doing.

He told her, and at the same time, put Agnes' note into her hand.

'How good and kind you have been!' cried Bertha, 'and how glad I should be, if, / in addition to *my* acknowledgments, Agnes were here to reward you with one of her gayest French songs.'

'Agnes' French songs have their merit,' answered he, 'but I am quite satisfied with your English smiles.'

Lord Glenfeld was beginning to find, that instead of having, as he supposed, merely married Bertha *for* love, he had, in fact, rather married her *to* love. As the sense of his own improved happiness directed him to her as its cause, her sweetness of disposition, her affectionate and disinterested spirit, gained hourly upon his tenderness. The dormant virtues of his character were warmed into life; and mere speculations no longer satisfied one, who was thrown into such constant communication with a being whose good qualities were all so practical and active. Few men find they have drawn a richer prize than they had imagined, in the matrimonial lottery; but such had been the enviable case of Lord Glenfeld. /

After a conversation of some length on the subject of Agnes, her present obscure asylum, and her apparent cheerfulness under the extraordinary reverse of fortune, to which she had condemned herself, Bertha said: 'The fable my aunt was furnished with to-day, and sent hither to repeat, is, I think more formidable than any out-break of rage could be. It fills me with a mysterious dread, of I know not what. That Wharton's object is to gain time, cannot be doubted; but why does he want this time?'

'My dear Bertha, we must have patience; such characters as Wharton's must ever be unfathomable to people of honourable minds. Let us keep watch over Agnes, and for the rest, we must await for its development hereafter. Here, on foreign ground, where he is only amenable to the laws for offences committed on the spot, it would avail but little towards forwarding the ends of justice, to proclaim his guilt: but manœuvre how he may, it / will be absolutely out of his power long to ward off its discovery, or the consequent dishonour it will bring upon him.'

Agnes' expected letter to Lady Glenfeld arrived on the morrow, according to her promise. Its beginning was but an out-pouring of gratitude for the protecting kindness extended over her. Sincere and fervent as this was, it would be but of little interest to the general reader, and therefore it may be best to come at once to what more immediately related to herself.

'But now to speak of my humble self, and my present humble mode of life. You will think me as plebeian in taste as I am once more in condition, when I tell you, that I by no means dislike my new home. The room I inhabit is clean and airy, its prospect is not picturesque, it is that of a stone-mason's yard, but I infinitely prefer it to a front view, looking towards the street. The people I am with, impress me more and more, with a persuasion / they are good. They bring up their children in habits of truth and honesty; and the whole family is remarkable for its civil and unobtrusive demeanour. My chief intercourse is with the mother, and a dear little boy, whose very countenance is a letter of recommendation, and whose ready services are always at my command. Through him, I have procured almost every thing I want; materials for writing, for drawing and for work; and this evening when he comes from school, I shall by his means get a catalogue from the nearest library, and hire books. Meanwhile, I have made a discovery that may answer the double end of amusing me, and of being useful to one in great want of aid. There lodges in a garret of this house, an old Italian, who whilst I was at breakfast, was playing at an open window upon his guitar. His taste, and the rich tone of his instrument, and the neatness of his execution delighted me; but now and then, he spoilt all, by chusing to sing as well as play; and his poor broken tremulous / voice was at once pitiable and ridiculous. I asked Madame Dupuis who he was? And she told me he had been formerly a guitar master in great repute; but an accident he met with two years ago, (which confined him for many months to his bed) has rendered him lame for life, and deprived him of nearly all his scholars. Those even, who are still willing to employ him, he is unable to attend without incurring the expense of coach hire; and there are few who choose to let him raise his terms in consideration of this unavoidable diminution of his gains. To shorten my story, finding he was in great indigence, I determined to invite him to my room, with his guitar two or three times a week, and in exchange for what I may perhaps learn from him, to give him some of the best of my drawings to sell for whatever they will produce. I dare say, dear Lady Glenfeld, you will scold me for not paying him in ready money; but do not envy me the pleasure of requiting him by my own exertions. I cannot bear to expend what I have allowed you to advance / to me for *necessaries*, on a mere whim; and after all, as I should draw whether this poor man were here or not, it will give much more interest to the occupation, if I pursue it with his advantage in view.

'When you have any thing to tell me, I know you will let me hear from you, and I must own, I shall soon become a little impatient. I often think of Adrienne; set her mind at ease about me, dear Lady Glenfeld, as soon as you prudently can.

'Adieu, my best friend. Were I forsaken by all the rest of the world, you and Lord Glenfeld, I am confident, would still adhere to me. Imagine the comfort such a persuasion must give me.

'Yours, ever, ever,
AGNES DANVERS.'

To this letter, Agnes received an answer that evening after dark, brought again, as cautiously as the night before, by Lord Glenfeld, who waited below till she wrote (as desired by Bertha / on the outside of her letter) these words on a slip of paper – 'All's well.'

'You will think it most extraordinary, dearest Agnes,' wrote Lady Glenfeld; 'that up to this moment nothing has transpired of what is passing at Mr. Wharton's. He yesterday set a report about, through my aunt, that you had been carried off for some days, by a lady and her daughters into the country. What the story is at present, I have had no means of hearing; for though I have been twice to the house, I had the ill fortune each time, to call when mamma and my sisters as well as Mrs. Marchmont, were out. This evening, I heard from my maid, that Adrienne was here in renewed perplexity about you, and very impatient for your return. I sent for her, and she came up to my dressing-room. She looked pitifully dejected, and as unlike a French *femme-de-chambre*, such as we usually describe, as any thing you can well imagine. I said what I could to cheer her, bidding her rest assured / that you were in perfect safety, and adding: "Can you suppose that if there were the least reason to think otherwise, I should not be as unhappy as you are?"

'"I dare say you would, Miladi," answered the good creature, "but it is natural you should not take alarm so readily as I do, because you have not known Mademoiselle de Vere so long, and cannot be aware so well as I am, how unlike her it is, to have joined in such a strange frolic. She, who never once, during all the years I have lived with her, accepted any invitation without the permission of madame; she, who never, during that whole time, has slept anywhere but at home, that she should in this thoughtless manner, dash off with a family she has so little intimacy with, without leave, without clothes, (great stress was laid upon these last words), is to me perfectly *incroyable*."[106]

'"But you find Ma'm'selle Adrienne, that Monsieur Wharton and his sister, are quite easy about her."

'"And so was I at first, Miladi, at least, tolerably / so, when I first heard where she was gone, but Monsieur said then, that she would be back, most likely to-day, yet here is the second evening come, and she is not returned!"

'I renewed my endeavours to comfort her, and after some time, she appeared a little revived, and told me Mr. Cowley was returned to Paris, looking, poor young gentleman! quite melancholy. He and her master had dined out, but where, she could not tell, as none of the ladies had gone with them.

'"Well, ma'm'selle," said I, to terminate the dialogue, "try to keep up your spirits, and if you have any better news to bring me to-morrow, let me see you early; but whether you have or not, come hither, and perhaps I may have something good to communicate to you."

'I said this with a smile that seemed exceedingly to puzzle her, but which at the same time it was evident, infused into her a more cheerful feeling. She made her civil curt'sy, and retired. /

'I would have told her more, had I not been afraid her countenance might betray her, if she were seen by Mr. Wharton after she got home, and might lead to interrogations she would find it no easy matter to evade. The danger of speaking out every hour will diminish, and tomorrow I may with safety communicate what to-day I thought it more prudent to keep back.

'No, dearest Agnes, I do not think your taste plebeian; I rather envy you the happy disposition, that enables you to accommodate yourself so well to the great and sudden change your circumstances have undergone. Many persons in your place would be wretched;[107] many, though they might try to be philosophical, would feel so bewildered and unsettled, that they would be incapable of all exertion. You have had the resolution, and the good sense to seek immediately for occupation; – nay, what is more, to look out for such simple means of amusement as are within your reach. Pray send me the name, and the terms of your / poor old guitar player; I mean those that on account of his lameness he ought now to charge. If I can procure him any scholars, I shall be very glad. I fear it would be vain to ask you to change your intended mode of paying him. Proud girl!

'But, adieu, my most dear Agnes. Till we meet, we must send each other a few lines every day. Heaven bless you,

'B. GLENFELD.'

Agnes still held this letter in her hand, and was lingering with fond affection over every kind expression it contained, when once more, she heard the widow, Madame Bernard, approach her room, saying as she did so to some one who seemed to be following her:

'Montez, montez, monsieur, c'est ici.'[108]

Quick as thought, as if impelled by an irresistible impulse, the apprehensive girl instinctively sprang to the door, bolted, and double locked it, and then stood leaning against the / panel of the wainscot, anxiously listening for what was to follow.

Madame Bernard gave her usual gentle tap, which not being immediately attended to, she repeated, at the same time raising her voice and saying:

'On vous demande, mademoiselle, ouvrez s'il vous plait.'[109]

Agnes remained immoveable, confirming herself more and more in her determination not to speak.

A few words were now uttered in a whisper on the landing place, after which the widow said aloud:

'It is a messenger, mademoiselle, from the same person who was here just now with the letter I brought up to you.'

Still she maintained an inflexible silence, and presently Madame Dupuis, who was at supper with her husband and sons in the opposite room, came forth, and asked the widow why she was teazing mademoiselle to admit any one she did not wish to receive? /

'Je demande bien pardon à la chère demoiselle,'[110] answered the humble creature, 'but I did not know when I brought the gentleman up, that she would object to see him; I am sure if I had, I would not have given her this trouble for the world.'

Again there was a little whispered parley without, during which Agnes felt her courage revive, conscious that while the Dupuis were at hand, she was secure of protection. Every moment she expected to hear the intruder depart; but she soon found she had been too sanguine. The whispering ceased, indeed, and appeared to have produced very little effect, since Madame Dupuis, as if to cut the matter short, was finally heard to say:

'Tout ce que vous dites, monsieur est peut-être, bel et bon, mais ne servira à rien! Donnez-vous la peine de descendre, et Madame Bernard vous éclairera.'[111]

'Have patience one moment, madame,' at last said a voice, which though not quite so alarming to Agnes as the one she had anticipated, / was sufficiently unwelcome. – 'Let me, from the place where I stand, speak a few words to your young lodger, and I am gone. Lucy,' he continued in English, 'dearest Lucy, why have you so inexplicably renounced your friends? Why have you sought concealment in this most strange retreat? Am I unhappy enough to have contributed, by my return, to so desperate a step? What could you apprehend from my reappearance? Who has the power, who has even the wish, to put any constraint upon your inclinations? Come back to us, beloved Lucy! The duration of my abode in Paris shall be regulated entirely by your will, and not one hour shall it be prolonged beyond what you prescribe. Admit me only to a brief conference, and consent to listen to the voice of an old friend whose arguments and persuasions may not appear to you, perhaps to be without some weight.'

Here he paused as if awaiting her reply, but finding she still continued silent:

'You are too impracticable, Lucy,' cried / he reproachfully. 'This disdainful silence is unkind, and unmerited! – I come not as the agent of another; neither has it been by any deliberate pursuit that I have traced you. Chance alone conducted me hither. I had occasion to visit this neighborhood in search of a poor Englishman who once lived in my service a few months, and sent me this morning a most deplorable account of sickness and want. At the moment I was leaving his miserable lodging, I saw Lord Glenfeld, much muffled up, alight from a hackney coach, and walk hastily down the street till he reached this house. It was not to be supposed that any common motive could have brought him to such a spot; and having learnt in the course of the day that the report of your being with Madame Monbar was unfounded, and knowing also, your intimacy with Lady Glenfeld, the truth instantly flashed upon me. I waited till he returned to his *fiacre*, and then gained admission myself. The woman who admitted me, acknowledged that such a young person as / I described, had very lately come to reside here. You must be convinced, therefore, Lucy, that I cannot doubt there is only this door between us, however you may chose to wound and mortify me by refusing to open it!'

Agnes was, at intervals, almost worked upon during this long speech, to yield to his entreaties; but she considered in the first place, that circumstanced as she was, the doing so might not be thought wholly exempt from impropriety; – and she reflected next, that some little security from Mr. Wharton's machinations might be gained by compelling Harry to go away without having acquired any occular demonstration of her being the person he sought.

These reasons induced her steadily to persist in continuing mute. His arguments, his remonstrances, his intercessions were all equally vain. He kept his temper, however, as far as speech was concerned, though it grew evident to Madame Dupuis that his internal vexation was becoming extreme. Her husband, and / her elder boys had now also assembled round the pertinacious stranger, whose expression of countenance, increasing every moment in exasperation, induced them – as well as the singularity of his choosing to soliloquize so long at a door obstinately closed against him – to suspect that he was either mad or intoxicated. The husband, therefore, at last, thought it best to interfere, and plainly, yet in civil terms, told him, that as it was getting very late, it might be more adviseable Monsieur should go home. Rage, long suppressed, darted from Harry's eyes; – he saw mockery in those of the lads who encircled him, and overwhelmed with confusion and disappointment, rushed vehemently down stairs, and out of the house. Madame Dupuis instantly despatched one of the young men to fasten the street door, whilst her husband and the others returned to their own room.

Agnes, in the joy of her heart was congratulating herself on the happy termination of this singular scene, when Madame Dupuis, / accompanied by the widow, modestly petitioned for leave to enter. They were immediately admitted, and the sincerest acknowledgements were poured upon the former for the friendly part she had acted. Poor Madame Bernard was frightened at what she imagined might be the consequence of her imprudent officiousness: but Agnes kindly reassured her, merely entreating that she would hereafter be more cautious, and never bring any one up without her express permission. This was solemnly promised, and the humble dame, much comforted, bade her good night, and went away. Madame Dupuis prepared to follow, but lingered one moment to say:

'It was not for the sake of being thanked, dear mademoiselle, I asked to come in, but simply to tell you, that if you have any reason to fear the person who is just gone may repeat his visits, I will detain my eldest son at home for a few days, and set him to be your guard. He works with a very good-natured / master who is our distant relation, and who, I am sure, will not refuse me this little favour.'

'Thanks, thanks – a thousand thanks, my worthy Madame Dupuis!' answered Agnes, deeply touched by this provident kindness. 'I would accept your offer with as much frankness as it is made, were there the least occasion for it. But the result of this attempt convinces me that I have, in fact, nothing to apprehend. No force can be employed against me, and no legal authority can be pretended; neither can any harm overtake me in an honest house like this; and besides, with a good lock and key,' added she, smiling, 'nothing can come upon me by surprise, for henceforward, I shall, when alone, invariably fasten my door.'

Madame Dupuis commended the precaution, and hoping what had occurred would not prevent mademoiselle from having a good night, she took leave, and went back to her family. /

It was clear to Agnes from all that Harry had said, that he was still completely ignorant of the real state of her affairs. She was glad to find that one, for whom she continued to feel considerable regard, remained still uninitiated in Mr. Wharton's dark secrets. Faults he had, which Agnes was any thing but blind to; but she had never believed him to be deficient in sentiments of probity – and was now well satisfied to find her opinion confirmed.

END OF VOL. I.

LONDON:
SCHULZE AND CO. 13, POLAND STREET.

THE
ROMANCE
OF
PRIVATE LIFE.

BY
MISS BURNEY.

IN THREE VOLUMES.

VOL II.

THE RENUNCIATION.

LONDON:

HENRY COLBURN, PUBLISHER

GREAT MARLBOROUGH STREET.
1839. /

LONDON

SCHULZE AND CO 13, POLAND STREET. /

THE RENUNCIATION.

CHAPTER I.

I do partly think
A due sincerity governed his deeds,
Till he did look on me.

MEASURE FOR MEASURE.[1]

THE succeeding morning, whilst Agnes was diligently employed at her drawing-table, she heard, with a mixture of pleasure and surprise, not wholly unalloyed by apprehension, the well known voice of Adrienne, disputing on the landing place with Madame Dupuis, and half gaily, and half angrily, asserting her right to see mademoiselle without delay. /

'It does not depend upon me, Adrienne,' said the good landlady, 'to procure you admission. She keeps her door locked, and will not open it to any one she does not know.'

'Et elle ne me connaitrait pas, *moi*, par example?' cried the impatient Abigail. 'Allez, ma chère, vous ne savez ce que vous dites. Je vais frapper à sa porte, et vous verrez si elle me connait!'[2]

Agnes at that moment stepped forth, but whilst kindly holding out one hand to her overjoyed attendant, she placed the fore-finger of the other upon her lips to enjoin circumspection. Madame Dupuis, on observing this signal, immediately retired, and Agnes introduced Adrienne into her humble apartment.

Her first inquiry was, how Lady Glenfeld, who alone knew the place of her concealment, had been induced to permit this incautious visit in the very face of day?

'Read that, dear mademoiselle,' answered / Adrienne, presenting to her a letter. 'But, *mon Dieu*,' added she, gazing round her, 'who would ever have supposed it was for your own habitation you made me hire this poor, shabby bit of a room! What a place for *you* to live in!'

'A very good place,' cried Agnes cheerfully. 'I never slept better, nor was more easy in mind any where; I won't have it abused.'

She then opened the letter, within which a second was inclosed, directed to Lord Glenfeld, on the outside of which Bertha had written; 'Read this first.' – She hastily ran her eye over it, and saw that it was signed Robt. Wharton. It was dated from his own house on the preceding evening, and ran thus:

'My Lord,

'I have forborn soliciting any personal communication with your Lordship, from being well assured that to neither party it / would have been desirable. Do me the favour however, to peruse this document with patience and impartiality. You will find in it no endeavour to vindicate the past, or to defy its consequences; nor any effort attempted, by degrading solicitations, to awaken commiseration for what is to come. I do myself justice, and hesitate not to acknowledge, that whatever ills await me, I must submit to bear, as the deserved penalty my conduct has incurred.

'But let me hasten, my Lord, to explain the cause of this address.

'I find on inspecting her apartment, that the young person lately domesticated in my family, has absconded without furnishing herself with any means of subsistence; jewels, clothes, money – she has left every thing behind her. Such a circumstance has naturally led me to the conclusion, that in this business she must have secured some powerful and willing assistant. I have inquired who the / persons are she has associated with of late on the most intimate terms, and I am told Lady Glenfeld stands foremost on the list. Can I then doubt who the friend is that protects her? Or hesitate to believe that the fugitive has acquainted her with the particulars of her story, and given permission to extend its revelation to your Lordship? If I am mistaken, my present application must appear to you, my Lord, most extraordinary, and most unintelligible; and cannot but have the effect of awakening conjectures and suspicions concerning me, which for a short time, might still have remained dormant. But I am willing to abide the hazard. The difference between giving an immediate or somewhat more remote clue to detection, is not of sufficient importance to merit attention; and two inducements urge me to venture on the step I am taking, both of which are of a nature less personal, and less interested than have been / for many years the usual motives of my actions.

'I begin by that, which, to you, my Lord, will appear most material.

'Mr. Walsingham, for whom I know you entertain a warm regard, has always been considered as the indisputable heir of my late wife in failure of the daughter she had by her first marriage. That daughter, your Lordship need not be told, was committed on her mother's decease, to my guardianship. She was a beautiful and a promising child; and till her tenth year, never gave me, either personally or mentally, the slightest cause for inquietude. At that age, she fell into bad health. All that the most skilful medical advice, – the most assiduous and unremitting attention could do to restore her, was had recourse to in vain. I saw her gradually declining, and foreboded the inevitably-fatal termination of her short career. I loved her, my Lord; but let me own, that / was not the sole reason of the anguish her perilous state occasioned me. Deeply involved in debt, without profession, and seeing before me no prospect of future amelioration of circumstances, my whole fate seemed involved in that of the young creature whose life, at every breath, was threatened with extinction. My acceptance in society, in fact my very existence in the station of a gentleman, depended upon the permanency of the advantages I derived from the large allowance appointed for her maintenance and education. She was, at length, sent abroad by her physicians, and died *at Calais*, where she was privately buried as the child of the woman who had lived with her as her Nurse, and had been gained over by me to consent to the imposition. You will turn with abhorrence from this part of my story: but think you, my Lord, I recount it with no struggle? Think you my feelings, at this moment, are in an enviable state? No – veteran as I am in evil, / this cool recapitulation of former deeds, is a mental torture I would not willingly condemn my worst enemy to endure. But what to you can be these feelings and reflections? It is fit I should spare you their description, and proceed as briefly and as calmly as I can with my tale.

'During several months prior to the departure for the continent of my despaired-of ward, Mrs. Marchmont and I resided with her at Cheltenham. One evening, in the course of that melancholy period, I had sauntered, scarcely knowing whither I went, in the direction of the play-house. A little girl I overtook on the way, caught my attention; her age, height, figure and complexion, were so similar to those of poor Lucy in her day of health, that had she been in a higher condition, and better dressed, few persons who had not intimately and daily associated with the young heiress, could have perceived any difference. This child was in company with a man and woman, who / appeared to be what they proved, petty shop-keepers in the country. With no fixed plan, but indescribably struck, I followed them into the theatre, and placed myself in the same humble part of the house immediately behind them. I found from their conversation, that they were strangers at Cheltenham, that the little girl was not their own, but lived with them, and that, perhaps on the morrow, they would be returning to their village. Many, many wishes, but which all seemed chimerical, darted across my mind as I listened to them, and the longer and the more I looked at the child, the more convinced I became that had I the power of making her pass for my ward, no eye on a cursory view, would detect the fallacy. Under this impression, I followed them when they left the theatre, but merely with the view of ascertaining where they would go. An evil genius at that moment interposed, and threw in my way such facilities towards the accomplishment of my incipient design, that I / had not firmness to resist the temptation. Aided by the darkness of the night, the rolling of the carriages, and the bewildered faculties of the ill-guarded child, (left to find her way how she could in the rear of her companions), I was enabled to effect her noiseless though forcible seizure, without attracting the attention of a single human being. I bore her off safely to the hotel in which we resided, and a fortunate opportunity offered itself that very night of getting her removed to London, under the care of Mrs. Marchmont's milliner. In that person's family she remained, till I gave directions for having her conveyed to France. The moment I saw was fast approaching, when poor Lucy at least could be no sufferer by the substitution of another into her rights. Three days only, after landing at Calais, she expired; and inconsistent with other parts of my conduct as it may appear, I can most truly aver, that never parent felt deeper distress than I did, on the loss of that beloved child. She was surrounded / to the last with every comfort and accommodation that could alleviate her sufferings; but when finally gone, it became time to exert myself for the secure execution of my project. I had brought no servants with me from England except a foreign courier; a young Swiss waiting-maid, who only joined us the day we sailed, and the nurse, who in the eyes of the foreigners now around us, was to personate the mother of the deceased. After the funeral, it had been my intention immediately to proceed to Paris with my sister, and our new charge, the young Agnes, under the name of Lucy de Vere. But a violent and alarming illness attacked her, and discovering that her terror-struck imagination dwelt, during the ravings of fever, upon the compulsion I had used in separating her from her friends, I thought it best to depart alone, and leave to time and returning health the task of enabling her to bear my presence.

'You are aware, my Lord, in what manner she has been educated, and what mode of / treatment has been adopted towards her. On those two points, I have nothing to reproach myself with. That she has never loved me, has always been manifest; but it cannot be said, that subsequent to her first rough detention, my conduct has, at any time merited her hatred. The feeling she frequently excited in me, (strange to tell!) was a sort of cowering embarrassment, I was always unable entirely to overcome. I could have loved, but I feared her, and if she was my bondmaid she was, at the same time my scourge. No interchange of sentiments could subsist between us, and it ended in my regarding her as a necessary, but dangerous instrument, by means of which, even without her participation, I was to effect the purposes I had in view. May she be happy, as I know she is deserving!

'What remains to be said, is little.

'The rough copy of a note, signed Lucy de Vere, which was afterwards transcribed by the affectionate writer, and addressed to me, then / absent on a short tour to Holland and the Netherlands, fell into the hands of Agnes, and led to the momentous step she has taken. I had as I believed, though not without some regret, destroyed every vestige of her existence that remained. Mrs. Marchmont it appears, was less prudent, and a scheme which had been successful for nearly seven years, was defeated in a moment.

'You will of course, my Lord, apprise Mr. Walsingham of a disclosure which, I trust, will put him in immediate uncontested possession of the property, from which he has so long been withheld. On a recent occasion, the part he acted in behalf of one of the few beings I still take an interest in, gives him a claim upon my gratitude, which I should rejoice to be in circumstances to repay by more than words; but that is impossible, since the sums for which I am in arrears to him, I could no more replace than I could take upon myself the government of the universe. In penury and exile I must / wear out the remainder of my existence in another hemisphere; and when this letter reaches you, my Lord my pilgrimage will already have begun.

'Perhaps Lady Glenfeld and her family may be induced to extend a supporting hand to my unhappy sister. She has been, I allow, no stranger to my proceedings; it is but justice, however, to add, that she never approved, and combatted them often. I forsake her with concern, though aware, that with her habits, and her helplessness of character, such an enterprize as I am about to undertake, would appear worse almost than death itself. In retirement and humble mediocrity, she may yet contrive to subsist.

'And now my Lord, for the last, as this has been the first time of my addressing you, allow me to subscribe myself with great respect, your Lordship's most obedient humble servant,

'Robert Wharton.'

Agnes' hand, with the letter it held, dropt / upon her lap as she came to its conclusion, and she unconsciously heaved a deep sigh. A mixture of emotions assailed her, amongst which, sorrow for the writer was the most predominant. There were passages also in what she had been reading, that filled her with shame and self-reproach; she was shocked to find how cruelly she had wronged him by her injurious suspicions respecting the death of Lucy. The affection with which he spoke of her, bore all the appearance of sincerity, and for ever put an end to the most distant idea of foul dealing. Where she was mentioned herself, it was done with so much temper, that considering the catastrophe she had brought upon him, his moderation and placability surprised and touched her. She *had* hated him, no doubt; but less at the moment when by her flight, she effected his ruin, than at most other periods of her life; the knowledge of what he would suffer, had then mollified her aversion, and it had been with true regret she came to the conclusion, that his prosperity and / her sense of right could never be made compatible.

The letter in which Mr. Wharton's had been inclosed, still remained to be read. Agnes now turned to it:

'You are feeling, I am convinced, dearest Agnes,' said Lady Glenfeld, 'exactly as we are on the subject of poor Wharton; we blame (who can do otherwise?) but we also compassionate him. He was meant, I cannot help thinking, for better things. The style of his letter, though perfectly well-bred, manifests a certain degree of pride somewhat extraordinary in his present circumstances; but it seems to me a pride more nearly akin to manliness, and far more becoming, than a parade of abasement, the sincerity of which might so easily be called in question. He is not addressing Lord Glenfeld as a father confessor, from whom he is supplicating absolution after the avowal of his sins; but he is writing a plain, unvarnished statement of / facts (degrading, no doubt) but demanding from us neither censure nor applause, and evidently with no other aim than to give us useful information.

'It is provoking that Walsingham, who is so deeply interested in the result of this affair, should have left Paris yesterday at an hour's notice, without informing the people with whom he lodged whither he was going. However, a brief delay will throw no serious obstacle in the way of his ultimate success; and the noble resignation of my Agnes will not have been made in vain.

'Adrienne will be your best informant as to what passed this morning at my aunt's. She brought us Mr. Wharton's letter, and after reading it, I naturally told her where she might find you, and made her its bearer. There can now, my dearest, be no danger in shewing yourself, and therefore Lord Glenfeld unites with me most urgently in entreating you to come to us immediately. Your apartment is fixed upon, / and already prepared for your reception, and we only defer sending the carriage, till we know at what hour you would like to have it.

'Adieu, then my own Agnes, till we meet.

Yours ever,
'BERTHA GLENFELD.'

On being interrogated, Adrienne readily communicated all the information for which Agnes had been referred to her.

Monsieur Wharton, she said, had scarcely been at home two hours together from the moment mademoiselle left his house; however, the first night he slept in his own bed; but the second he went out at nearly midnight, and had never returned! Larue sat up for him, and at break of day, still momentarily expecting him, entered his apartment to prepare everything for his arrival. He soon discovered, and was awakened to suspicion by the circumstance, that whatever valuables monsieur possessed, of a portable nature, had disappeared. On the dressing table lay two letters sealed and directed, / one to Lord Glenfeld, and the other to Mrs. Marchmont. These, Larue gave to that lady's maid. She carried them up without delay to her mistress's room, who no sooner read the lines addressed to herself, than losing sight of all prudence, she gave vent to screams, sobs, and exclamations that soon made known to the whole house the purport of what her brother had written, and put all the servants in the establishment on the alert respecting the arrears of wages due to them. Many also were uneasy on account of various sums owing to tradesmen who were their friends; in short, a respectful, well-regulated set of dependents were suddenly converted into mistrustful, discontented, and almost clamerous mutineers.

Mrs. Le Strange and her daughters were speedily made acquainted by their own personal attendants with the confusion that reigned throughout the household. The former hastily repaired to Mrs. Marchmont to know what such extraordinary disturbance meant. All she could / clearly gather from her was, that her brother had entirely deserted her; that he had invented the story of Miss de Vere's visit to Neuilly, and that, that young lady was gone, like himself, no one knew whither. She further declared, that she was left with scarcely ten pounds in the house, and bills innumerable to pay, and ended by asserting, that she saw herself condemned to live and die a pauper!

Shocked and astonished, Mrs. Le Strange instantly struck off a few lines to Lady Glenfeld, and despatched them by Adrienne in addition to the letter Mr. Wharton had left for her son-in-law.

Thus far only was Adrienne able to relate the occurrences of the morning; what remained to be told was recounted to Agnes, at a later period, by Lady Glenfeld herself.

The summons from her mother was speedily obeyed, and the disorder still prevailing amongst the domestics was so obvious as she entered, that she scarcely thought the females of / her family in safety amongst so enraged a crew. Mrs. Le Strange met her with anger and disgust painted on her brow:

'Bertha,' cried she, 'we are all the dupes of a consummate swindler, and a well-trained cheat! Mrs. Marchmont whose feeble intellects seem quite to have abandoned her, has suffered me to see her brother's letter. It plainly refers to the irreparable failure of their long-successful imposition; bids her prepare for a complete discovery, and recommends to her (for her own sake) sincerity of dealing with those who have a right to interrogate her. He further tells her, that *Agnes Danvers*, discarding for ever the assumed name she has borne, will appear no more in the character of *Lucy de Vere*. And adding a few faintly-expressed professions of brotherly affection, concludes by informing her, that he is about to depart from Europe never to re-visit it again. Wretched man!' continued Mrs. Le Strange, 'what a system of fraud and villany do these few lines lay / open! I have not patience to reflect upon it! nor capacity to understand how it can all have been effected. Where is the real Lucy, if the creature who passed for her is an imposter?'

'My dear mother,' interrupted Bertha, too much pained by such language to let it proceed, 'this is not the moment to enter upon a full explanation; but I solemnly protest to you, that I can on my own knowledge, completely justify the dear girl you so hastily accuse! You did not, however, send for me to hear her vindication. Let me know, dear mamma, what would you wish me to do.'

'I wish you,' answered the mother, gradually softening; 'I wish you, my dear, whilst the house is in such confusion, to take charge of Louisa and Caroline. I shall stay with poor, weak Mary till some arrangement can be made for her. She may, perhaps, be induced to return with young Cowley to England. He is just come in, and is gone up to her room. / As we passed each other on the stairs, I suggested to him the propriety of recommending to her this plan, and begged him to let me know her determination. Should she agree to it, they might depart as soon as their passports could be made out; and during the interval, my maid and hers would have leisure to pack up.'

Lady Glenfeld most readily and kindly consented to take her sisters home with her; and on alighting, hastened to her husband to tell him what she had ventured to do, and to inform him of the state of insurrection in which she had found the chief part of her aunt's household. On hearing this account, Lord Glenfeld immediately said:

'I will go and see what can be done to pacify them. Poor people! they have some excuse for their murmurs. Probably, they have not been more provident than their master in laying by for what is called "a rainy day,"[3] and the wages they are so clamorous for, may be / all they have now to depend upon. Besides, if no measures are taken to content them, they may join in a body to prevent Mrs. Marchmont's departure.'

Nothing could be better timed than his appearance, and unexpected interposition amongst the insurgents. His high character gained him respect wherever he was known, and his present generosity silenced all complaints, and restored every thing to order. He afterwards desired to see young Cowley, with whom he held a conference of some length. It was obvious that hitherto Harry had neither known nor suspected the nature of those transactions Mr Wharton had for so many years been engaged in. Personal regard for him still survived in the young man's bosom; but of the dishonourable portion of his conduct he seemed to shrink from speaking, as if struck by it with a sense of shame to which he was loath to give utterance. One of the most peculiar characteristics of Mr. Wharton, was the uniform propriety of conversation / and manners he had maintained in the presence of his young associates, blinding them thereby to his own want of principle, and scrupulously abstaining from seeking to weaken theirs. Never had either Agnes or Harry heard him utter an immoral sentiment, so that of him it might most justly be said, according to Lord Glenfeld, that if individually, somewhat too subservient to the devil, he at least had the merit of not seeking to gain for him any other proselytes: 'A rare case!' added his Lordship; 'for bad men, generally speaking, seem to have nothing more at heart, than to go to the infernal regions with the largest possible number of recruits raised from amongst their *particular friends*.'

The result of the Earl's conversation with Harry, was a cordial assurance of his readiness to serve him if ever the occasion should present itself; and a request, that on his (Lord Glenfeld's) return to London, Mr. Cowley would call upon him. /

CHAPTER II.

With her no earthly thing is ever right;
T' expect to alter to her taste were vain,
For who could mend so fast as she complain?

Dodsley's Collection.[4]

In her reply to Lady Glenfeld's affectionate invitation, Agnes after dwelling at considerable length upon what related to Mr. Wharton, proceeded to speak of herself:

'Ask me not, kindest of friends, to remove to your house. I am not in a state of mind, (whilst still held in suspense as to the success of my application to Mr. Danvers), that fits me either for general society, or for a large family circle. You will perhaps say, that I / may live under your roof in retirement, and see only yourself and Lord Glenfeld. True, but to my pride, or my delicacy, or perhaps a mixture of both, this plan is repugnant. It would look as if I were ashamed of shewing myself; ashamed of the reverse in my circumstances, ashamed of my new, and *honest* name, ashamed of the humble rank to which I now belong – none of these things, you will do me the justice to believe are true; yet to prove this to others, I must force myself into company, and undergo a species of scrutiny resulting from the singularity of my story, that, to say the least of it, would be far from agreeable. Whoever experiences any extraordinary change, whether for better or worse, becomes an object of curiosity even to their most intimate associates. I have experienced the idle feeling myself; but have not the courage to be exposed to it in my own person. Let me then, remain in my obscure, but quiet and safe retreat; and when I have the happiness of seeing you, let / it only be as a visitor for a few hours, not as a permanent guest.

'Adrienne, my faithfully attached Adrienne, has just left me, and has insisted upon having a room found for her in some other part of the premises, being determined to return to night with all her wardrobe, and establish herself in the house as long as I occupy any place under its roof. Madame Dupuis has known her too long, and loves her too well to start unnecessary difficulties, but I really believe she is much puzzled to know how to comply with her wishes. I leave them to settle the point how they can; for after all, I am certain Adrienne is hardly more desirous to come, than Madame Dupuis is to receive her. It is an arrangement, however, I suffer but *provisionally* (to speak in the diplomatic style), and chiefly to give myself time gradually to prepare Adrienne for our separation. I am well assured she will take it grievously to heart; and I myself shall feel it severely. She has lived with me so / long, has so many excellent qualities, and – with some trifling exceptions, more to be attributed to her station than to herself – I am aware she has so much good sense, that I confess she would be a great support and comfort to me. But in my actual circumstances, to keep a regular waiting-maid would be preposterous; and, to be frank with you, dear Lady Glenfeld, I never will consent to *your* keeping one for me. I speak in time, because I already anticipate the thousand and one good reasons (compassion for Adrienne's feelings – regard for my past habits, &c.) that your warm heart will induce you to urge in opposition to what I have declared. All I can promise is, that till I hear from Rome, I will leave matters as they are. If no tidings arrive, or if they are unfavourable, then will be indeed the trying moment to act.'

This letter brought Lady Glenfeld, in the course of the evening, to visit her too-scrupulous / friend. With a delicacy, however, that was due to Agnes's feelings, she forbore to combat a resolution so deliberately taken; yet anxious not to be deprived entirely of the society of one she loved so well, she had stolen from the family party assembled at her house; and enjoyed a two hours' interview with unfeigned delight.

Little had occurred since the morning worthy being mentioned. The only novelty was, that Mrs. Marchmont, after much hesitation, and with undisguised reluctance, had agreed to return to England escorted by Harry Cowley.

'Lord Glenfeld,' said Bertha, 'was pleased with this young man. He asked him what profession he had fixed upon, and heard that he wished to dedicate himself to the law. He encouraged the project, and says, that of all the youthful aspirants for forensic honours he ever saw, this Harry of yours seems the most likely to succeed. He has a gentleman-like / address, a fine voice, a penetrating eye, great fluency of speech, and no excess of timidity to hold him back, and paralyse his efforts.'

'No, truly!' said the half-laughing Agnes, 'Harry Cowley can never be taxed with *that* defect.'

She then, with some humour, recounted to Lady Glenfeld his attempt and failure of the preceding night, and the whole absurd scene at the head of the stairs.

'Poor fellow!' cried Bertha, diverted in spite of herself, but trying to look compassionate. 'You treated him very barbarously. But do you really mean to let him leave Paris without seeing you? He and my aunt set off at an early hour the day after to-morrow.'

'Heaven prosper them on their way!' replied Agnes. 'I have no wish, however, to see either of them, as we are now respectively situated.'

'I have not told you,' resumed her Ladyship, / 'that my aunt, silencing her selfish outcries against Mr. Wharton, has made to mamma something that resembles an unreserved confession of the share she bore in the deception your uncompromising integrity has brought to light. But as you will easily believe, her narrative abounded so much more in personal justification than in coherency or frankness, that but for Wharton's letter, and the commentary with which I was able to illustrate it, it would have been almost unintelligible. I have the pleasure, dearest Agnes, to add, that mamma and my sister, when at last they *did* understand your story, were struck by it with enthusiastic admiration, and are longing to obtain your permission to come and embrace you.'

'I shall rejoice to see them,' answered Agnes; 'of course, they know what to expect when they visit so humble a residence; but if they are willing to encounter steep and narrow stairs, an ill-lighted passage and diminutive / room, I have no false shame to make me reluctant to receive them.'

'Shame!' repeated Bertha, energetically – 'might you not rather set proudly in this little asylum, and say with Constance:

> "Here is my throne; bid kings come bow to it!"[5]

Who that has any heart – any sense of honour – could see you now, and remember what you were and what you might *still* have been, without wishing to do homage to the virtue that impelled you voluntarily to renounce advantages in general so highly prized?'

Gently placing her hand over Lady Glenfeld's mouth, Agnes now gaily said – 'Come, come, my dear friend, you must not try to make me believe, that honesty is of so very heroic a character. Rather look at these two little drawings, and tell me what you think of them.'

They were small whole-length figures, touched / with much spirit, and slightly coloured, representing, the one, a boy attentively reading by candle light, his arms resting on a table, supporting his cheek; the other, a little girl threading her needle, while a kitten was pulling the work out of her lap. There was so much nature, ease, and grace in the attitudes of the two children – they were both so pretty, the girl especially, and they seemed to have been struck off with such admirable facility, that Lady Glenfeld protested, she had scarcely ever seen any drawings that had given her so much pleasure.

'They were done from living subjects,' said Agnes, 'and exactly in the positions in which, at different times, I happened to see them. You guess, no doubt, that they are the portraits of Madame Dupuis's two youngest children. Jeannot, the boy, was here last night, eagerly reading a little book of stories I had made him buy for himself in the course of the day. At an earlier hour, Agathe, at my desire / had brought her work to show me, and staid some time to finish a part of it, whilst I sketched her lovely little figure. The kitten I put in from fancy. Such models are invaluable; no attitude in which they can place themselves, that has not its merit; and the rather, as they do not know what I am about, and fall into no stiffness or affectation.'

'And are these charming drawings to be given to the old guitar master for sale?'

'Even so, and he assures me they will be very *marketable*.'

'*There needs no ghost to tell us this!*[6] But ask the old man, my Agnes, at what shop he means to dispose of them, for I am determined they shall be mine.'

Soon after having obtained from her friend the promise she required, Lady Glenfeld reluctantly departed.

In the mean time, Adrienne maintaining her purpose, had effectually installed herself at the / Dupuis's, and was laughing and talking with them at their frugal supper, with even more than her wonted animation. To be once again under the same roof with her beloved young lady, seemed to intoxicate her with happiness – every word was a jest, – and every jest was followed by a burst of general gaity that reached to Agnes's room, and almost incited her to join in their mirth, though ignorant of its cause. Neither did the revelation made to her the following day of the heads of her mistress's story, produce any change in her spirits, she listened to it indeed with intense interest – one moment pitying the terrors of Agnes's unprotected childhood – the next, inveighing against the cruelty of Mr. Wharton – or bewailing the anguish inflicted upon the early friends from whom she had been torn; but that her dismission was to be the consequence of the disappointment of his fraud, never entered her imagination. Agnes had decided not to go too / far on this first disclosure, and therefore, said nothing to destroy a delusion she well knew it would be so painful to her to renounce.

A fortnight now elapsed, during which the daily visits of Lady Glenfeld, and the variety of occupations Agnes found for herself, made the hours pass like minutes. The Le Stranges failed not to avail themselves of her consent to receive them, and behaved with much good feeling and propriety. Lord Glenfeld supplied her with the newest books; and through the interest of these various friends, she had the gratification of procuring for the poor guitar-player, several new scholars, and sundry subscribers to a set of Easy Lessons he was about to publish. Added to this, she now enjoyed the advantage, having the attendance of Adrienne, of taking air and exercise in a neighbouring public garden, which, from being in a district so remote from the fashionable world, was generally very private, and at no time likely to attract any of her former associates. / These resources, joined to the delight she took in varying the sketches she was continually making, either of the two children – of their faded but interesting mother – or of the picturesque figures she often saw in the stone-mason's yard beneath her windows, filled up most pleasantly every moment of her time. Her little designs sold so well, (probably from a general order given to their purchaser to preserve them all for Lady Glenfeld,) that after awhile, the honest old Italian refused to accept the whole amount of their produce; and Agnes had the triumph of being able to begin forming a little purse for future contingencies from the fruits of her own industry.

A break in this even and placid mode of life was now to take place, and Agnes with a shaking hand, received the letter she had so long been expecting from Rome. It informed her, that Mr. Danvers to whom she had written, was, in reality (as had been surmised) the son of George and Elizabeth Danvers, / residing at the time of his birth, not in Gloucestershire, but at Evesham in Somersetshire; he remembered, however, that his mother, after his departure from England, had established herself at Meadwell, whence she had often written to him. Then followed a most earnest request to know what had drawn forth the inquiry; and an extremely civil apology for having, apparently, neglected to send an earlier answer. The reason assigned was, that Mr. Danvers had been some weeks absent from home, and had left no orders to have his letters sent after him.

Transported by the tenour of what she had read, Agnes foresook all other employment to communicate to Lady Glenfeld the joyful news. After briefly recapitulating the satisfactory contents of the despatch, she thus went on:

'I could not wait to give you this intelligence, dearest Lady Glenfeld, till our usual / hour of meeting; – besides, you seemed not very certain when you went away last night, that you should have it in your power to come to-day; and my heart is so full, that if not by speech, it must relieve itself by writing.

'I have a natural protector then? A friend by kindred? A guide who will make my interest his own? in one word – *a brother*, oh Lady Glenfeld – you who have never experienced the desolate and forlorn feelings of an orphan estranged from every early connection – you who have been surrounded all your life by family ties – you can form no conception of the happiness of my present feelings! I am a new being; I seem to have gained importance in my own eyes; and at this moment, there is not one amongst the children of men whose fate I would exchange for my own.

'The only draw-back from so much felicity is the thought of being so soon separated from you, my most admirable and true friend – I must set out for Rome as expeditiously as possible, / for I can now bear the thought of existing no where else: but with what regret I shall leave you, I have not words to express – you will give me credit for sincerity, I well know; nor can I doubt your participating in my concern.

'Before I close this incoherent letter, may I, dearest Lady Glenfeld, solicit you to make some inquiries amongst your friends as to the best and properest mode of undertaking the long journey I have in view? – Here there is of course, no one I can consult, except my poor guitar-master; and when I was talking with him lately on the subject, he advised the diligence. I will, however, go in no way that you and Lord Glenfeld do not recommend.'

In her answer to this letter, Bertha, who was indeed prevented by company at home from seeing Agnes that day, expressed herself thus:

'We congratulate you, dearest, most heartily / and cordially on the arrival of your brother's letter. You are proud of being able to talk of *a brother;* but depend upon it, he will be just as proud to be able to talk and think of such a *sister*. – I would give much to be present at your first meeting. Lord Glenfeld who has often seen him at Rome, says he appears to be about two or three and thirty; has an open manly countenance: a remarkably finely-shaped head, already beginning to be a little bald; – a good every day sort of figure; and altogether, a very prepossessing gentleman-like appearance. I think I should have no objection to such a brother myself.

'Now, my Agnes, let me talk about your journey. Lord Glenfeld has had in contemplation a scheme which, if it could have been brought to bear, would have been enchanting to me, and highly advantageous to you. – This scheme was no other, than that we should conduct you to Italy ourselves. He knew that such an expedition would delight me at *any* time; but on / no possible occasion could it have been half so interesting as the present. How I adored him for his indulgence! – and how from my heart did I assure him that, if I could help it, I would not let his kindness spoil me – he said I was a good girl, and even if I *did* become a little spoilt, he would not mind it, I suppose, because it would be his own doing. – Well, he wrote to England, to know if his speedy return could be dispensed with. Not that he has any urgent business to transact, either public or private: but he has an uncle who is much attached to him, whose health has become very precarious, and whom it would grieve him to be at a distance from, were his illness to increase. No motives of interest suggest these scruples, for the affectionate and benevolent old man has little beside his benediction to bequeath. He is a general officer on half-pay, with the slenderest remnant of hereditary fortune that ever well-born gentleman was reduced to live upon. Such as it is, however, / he has always found his income sufficient to befriend the destitute, and to shew kindness to the younger members of his family; and many a time, when Lord Glenfeld, at school or at college, got into difficulties, and was afraid of applying to his father, his generous uncle, out of his small revenue, has relieved him without a word or a look of reproach! these are not services – these are not proofs of love that can ever be forgotten. We therefore wait to hear from the general's physician, and with still greater anxiety from his attached old servant, their sincere opinion of the invalid's case. If the answer is alarming, we return immediately to England; if they write encouragingly, we depart for Italy three days after the receipt of the letter. For my sake, then, dearest Agnes, bridle your impatience, and consent to wait the arrival of the next post from England before you seek to make any positive arrangement for your journey. If we fail you, I know several families on the point of setting out, and shall have no difficulty / in procuring for you, from amongst them, the protection you require. At all events, Lord Glenfeld says you must have nothing to do with the *diligence*.[7] For a lady and her husband, or for an elderly woman it may do very well: but not for unaccompanied young damsels. If nothing better offers, you might without impropriety join a well-recommended party, travelling with a swiss *voiturier*.[8] It is a tedious, but secure and respectable mode of making the journey; and the only one connected with any thing like a public conveyance, that we could bear to let you think of.

'Adieu, till to-morrow.'

It may well be supposed that after the perusal of this letter, Agnes hesitated not to renounce her intention of immediately commencing her journey alone. She was indeed too happy in the prospect of travelling with such companions to regret very deeply the short delay to which she was urged to consent. So brief / was the term of her suspense, that on the third morning after receiving the above, Lady Glenfeld called upon her to announce that the expected letters had arrived, and were alas! wholly unfavourable to the plan she had in view. – She felt the disappointment acutely, and more even on Agnes's account than her own. But she was too sensible of all she owed to the kind intentions of her husband, to let him perceive in its full extent the mortification she experienced. They had consulted together on the best arrangement that could be made for the young traveller, now destined to undertake her long journey without them; and the result of their deliberations was this:

'There is now at Paris,' said Bertha, 'an English lady, named Temple, who, with her daughter, is on the point of setting out for Italy. Lord Glenfeld was formerly well acquainted with her husband, and knows them to be persons of the highest respectability. They are not rich, however, and instead of travelling / post, with a courier and lady's maid they go with a *voiturier*, and only take with them one man servant. A third traveller, a handsome venerable old gentleman, whose name is St. Hubert, has engaged one of the two remaining places; and we heard from Miss Temple this morning, that they now only defer their departure till the fourth vacancy is filled up. Lord Glenfeld then informed them, that there is a young lady who, he believes, would be glad to belong to their party; and he has promised to send them her definite answer this evening. Now, my Agnes, tell me whether you feel inclined to profit by this opportunity? I scarcely think we shall hear of a better. It is no small advantage, when obliged to associate with those who are personally strangers to us, to know from good authority, who and what they are; and the Temples have always classed amongst the best informed and most polished gentry in Lord Glenfeld's neighbourhood. Your going with / them will be attended also with this advantage namely, that as there is only one outside traveller, (the Temple's servant,) there will be room of Adrienne, and we *insist* upon your taking her.'

'My dearest friend,' Agnes began, shaking her head.

But Lady Glenfeld, interpreting her meaning, hastily interrupted her, saying: 'We have yielded to your delicacies and refinements, Agnes as no other people *would* have yielded;[9] and now there is an end of the matter; for, at this point of the business, we will listen to you no longer. On the contrary, Lord Glenfeld, I can assure you, would be highly disobliged were you still to persevere in rejecting his advice. He says, that with regard to the pecuniary part of the affair, you must leave him to settle it with your brother at some future time. At present, you are to consider yourself as under *his* immediate protection. He found this mode of conveyance / for you; he means to arrange every thing relative to your travelling expenses with the *voiturier;* he undertakes to procure your passport; and, in short, he chooses to act, and requires you to confide in him as your guardian. Do not, dear girl, mortify him by a refusal of his services.'

To urgency such as this, what could Agnes oppose? She found herself not only compelled to submit, but to love and admire, more and more, the generous spirits with which she had been contending. It was now, therefore, speedily determined, that the journey should take place under the auspices proposed, and with the attendance of her devoted Adrienne.

When at length all opposition had been overcome, Lady Glenfeld found herself under the painful necessity of rising to depart, and that without any hope of being able to see Agnes again. /

'We set off to-morrow,' said she; 'and between this and then, as much of my time must be devoted to mamma, and some to the ceremony of farewell visits, I fear there will be no possibility of coming to you any more. But perhaps it may be better for me not to have the pain of bidding you a second time adieu. Mamma is herself engaged in all "the horrors of the last,"[10] for she and my sisters are preparing for a little trip to Spa. They purpose, however, before they go, to have the pleasure of calling upon you once more. And, now, my own Agnes, I must tear myself away: but I leave you with some courage, because Lord Glenfeld has given me his word of honour that if we are in circumstances next year to travel so far, he will repay me for what he calls my present sacrifice, by taking me to Italy to join you. In the interval,' added she, trying to smile, 'if you will have the good-nature to marry the first creditable Englishman who asks you, it will be shortening the term of our / separation, and conferring upon me an essential obligation!'

'I will not fail,' answered the laughing Agnes, 'to attend to so timely and useful a recommendation!'

The two friends, then, after a long and most affectionate embrace, not daring to trust to their voices, parted with silent and mutual sorrow.

As soon as Agnes could sufficiently recover herself to speak with any composure, she summoned Adrienne to inform her of her approaching journey, and to ask whether she was willing to accompany her?

'Wherever you please, mademoiselle,' answered she cheerfully; 'I love Paris, it is true; but, if I may say so, I love you still better; and in your service, one place will be the same to me as another.'

'Thank you, dear Adrienne! – I was sure you would not wish to leave me, and I hope we may long, long be able to remain together. / But you must accustom yourself to call me by my real name; I have no right, as I told you, to that of *de Vere*, and if you continue to use it, you may sometimes occasion me much embarrassment.'

'I comprehend, mademoiselle; and I will do *mon possible*[11] not to disobey you.'

When the news of their inmate's impending departure reached the ears of Madame Dupuis' younger children, they were inconsolable; Jeannot in particular; and the sight of anything resembling sadness on that frank and sprightly face, was painful to behold. The little girl had not excited an equal degree of interest; she was *a favourite*, and the indulgence she was ever secure of finding, often rendered her captious and exacting. Symptoms of this had sometimes shown themselves even in Agnes's presence; and the admirable good temper and forbearance with which Jeannot had borne them, contributed not a little to increase the prepossession he had awakened. / She allowed him to hover round her during nearly the whole of the last day she spent in the house, and talked to him, as a friend, of his future prospects. She had observed that he was an extraordinarily ready arithmetician for his age, and was fond of long and difficult calculations; and she had heard him frequently declare there was nothing in the world he wished so much as to be apprenticed to a mathematical instrument maker. There was one in the neighbourhood who had shown him great good-will, and pronounced that he had a decided turn for mathematics and geometry. This man had often lent him books, over which he pored with indefatigable perseverance, and gave him free access to his shop. With such predilections, Agnes thought it a thousand pities the boy should be devoted to the coarse labours of a mere mechanic. She urged him to be as diligent as possible in acquiring all that was to be learnt at his school, to take especial pains with his orthography and / hand writing, (which, to say the truth, were still very bad;) 'and when,' continued she, 'you are able to send me a long, well spelt, and legibly written letter to Rome, (I will give you the proper direction), I promise to answer you immediately; and if I have the power, and you continue to wish it, I will help you to become an instrument-maker.'

The intelligent and grateful boy, was deeply touched by these exhortations and promises, the impression of which was never effaced from his memory, and materially contributed to stimulate him to the attainment of whatever minor branches of knowledge he had hitherto neglected.

But Agnes, partial as she was to Jeannot, omitted not to extend to his mother all the kindness she had the means of showing. Lady Glenfeld's loan she forebore to touch except on occasions connected with her own personal and indispensable wants; deeming it wrong to appropriate to acts of apparent beneficence, money / which, in fact, was not her own. But the overplus of this little sum obtained by her drawings, and so honourably resigned by the poor musician, she felt at liberty to dispose of as she pleased; and only regretting that its amount was so small, presented it to the grateful Madame Dupuis, in addition to what was due for the hire of her apartment.

Loaded with blessings, not unaccompanied with tears, it was on a bright morning towards the end of August that Agnes departed from the worthy woman's house, and found herself seated in the *voiturier's* slow-paced, lumbering, but not otherwise incommodious vehicle. Opposite to her were her two female fellow-travellers, Mrs. and Miss Temple; and beside her sat Mr. St. Hubert. On her entrance into the carriage, she was most courteously greeted by the whole party; but more especially by Miss Temple, who seemed amply disposed on that, and all other occasions, to be spokeswoman in chief for every person present. / At first, Agnes had attributed her abundant civility to the desire of doing honour to Lord Glenfeld's friendly recommendation; but she soon found that Miss Temple had yet a stronger inducement for putting herself so forward; the love of being paramount on every possible occasion. There was an unfortunate superfluity of briskness about her, that never suffered her to be at rest; she would have had spirits and energy sufficient, had she been married, to have ruled a family of any amount – husband included. As it was, her lawful jurisdiction extending only over her mother and her maid, this limited empire left her with so much unemployed power of exertion, that she was ready to take the affairs of every chance associate into her hands, and never so happy as when she could dictate to a new *protégée* how to act – to speak – to look – and even to think. The expression of the countenance corresponded perfectly with her disposition; it was restless, busy, and inquisitive; nothing escaped / the vigilance of her eye, and she seemed to have the faculty, even while appearing to look in one direction, of seeing every thing that was passing in another. Agnes at the end of the second day, thought her insufferable. The first display of graciousness with which she had been welcomed having subsided, she found that she was by no means to be exempted from enduring her full share of the infliction such a temper can impose; she quietly therefore, availed herself of the same resource Mr. St. Hubert had adopted, and to avoid being dogmatically set right every time she ventured a remark, borrowed from him a volume of travels, and whenever the scenery failed to amuse her, turned without scruple to her book.

Mrs. Temple was a lady-like, well-bred person, always gentle, always complacent; surrendering herself to the sovereignty of her daughter without a thought of resistance; submitting to be contradicted, often silenced – with only a smile of placid resignation. But / even slavery has its privileges; and Mrs. Temple, generally so yielding and quiescent, was not to be interfered with on one momentous point, – and that was, dress! Dress was her ruling passion; and aware that her taste was exquisite, she assumed the right of exercising on such matters, 'absolute rule.' Her whole stock of ideas, and every power of observation was directed towards that subject. She looked at no female but to see what she wore, and how she had put the garment on; and she sought only in the countenances of men to discover the effect produced by a fashionable bonnet, or a well-chosen ornament. In her own attire she was an unerring model of all that was most graceful and becoming in the mode of the day. She retained a beautiful figure, and when conscious that it was set off to advantage by the ability with which she had adorned it – empires might fall, and governors perish in their ruins, – 'the great globe itself,'[12] might go to wreck – nothing was / capable of deranging the equanimity of her soul! She sat the image of benignant vanity, pitying the bad taste of others, and gratefully enjoying the superiority of her own.

Of Mr. St. Hubert it was difficult to form any distinct opinion. He either was deaf in reality, or often affected to be so, taking little part in the conversation, and continually leaving it doubtful whether he heard what was addressed to him. Agnes had her suspicions that much of this was put on; for till he had been nearly two days in the carriage, his deafness had not been observable; and even since he had been afflicted with it, if Miss Temple, at the inns, happened to leave the room, it was wonderful what an improvement in his auricular powers immediately took place. There was also an occasional expression in his eye, and in the lurking smile playing about his mouth, that struck Agnes as being full of comic humour; but which the danger of being betrayed into a laugh, made her always afraid / to look at when Miss Temple said any thing more than usually pragmatical. By degrees, he and his young companion, without having any verbal communication, came mutually to understand each other's thoughts respecting their fellow-traveller; and from the mere consciousness of this sympathy, a sort of tacit confidence established itself between them, that gave Agnes the pleasant hope of having acquired a new friend.

One day, on re-entering the carriage after their customary two hours' bait, Miss Temple observing that Mr. St. Hubert was composing himself for a nap, whilst Agnes was preparing to resume her book, said with some asperity:

'Our little party does not appear to me to improve in sociality! The only gentleman with us, goes to sleep every day after our early dinner; and you, Miss Danvers, are never happy but when poring over a book. I wonder what entertainment you can find in the stupid work you are reading! I looked / into it last night, and I think it a complete farrago of nonsense and falsehood.'

'I am not so difficult to please,' answered Agnes; 'it has amused me exceedingly.'

'Have you read Foresyth?'[13]

'No, ma'am; but Mr. St. Hubert has promised that I shall do so, as soon as I have finished what I am now about.'

'It is a pity Mr. St. Hubert lets you lose your time over such trumpery as you have at present in hand. Why does he not give you Foresyth's work at once, if he has it with him?'

'Because,' said Agnes, smiling, 'I have bad taste enough to wish to read the whole of this.'

'Well – you are your own mistress, and if you choose to bestow your leisure upon trash so little worth it, I have nothing further to say. But it always gives me pain to see very young persons fall into the habit of reading indiscriminately every paltry book they can get hold / of. Much more might be learnt by conversation, when they have the opportunity of profitting from the experience and remarks of better-informed companions.'

To this, no answer was necessary; and Agnes after gazing a little while through the window at the flat uninteresting country they were traversing, lent back, and resolutely opened her volume.

'My dear Miss Danvers,' said Mrs. Temple, gently, after a short pause, 'you will ruin your bonnet by letting it rub against the lining of the carriage! At the next good town we come to, do buy a travelling cap, and let your maid take care of that pretty Leghorn.'[14]

'Why, my dear madam,' interposed her daughter, 'one would think you were ignorant that Leghorn is in Italy, and that we are going there ourselves, and shall find bonnets of this sort, cheaper and more common than the coarsest Dunstable in England!'[15] /

This was precisely the ground upon which Mrs. Temple was always ready to combat – and that, with some vigour.

'My dear,' replied she, 'you must allow me to be a better judge of what we are now talking of than any person you could meet with. I know perfectly that Leghorn bonnets, unless extremely fine, are sold for next to nothing in Italy. I therefore did not exhort Miss Danvers to take care of hers on account of its intrinsic value, but its shape is remarkably pretty, and highly becoming to her.'

'Since you think so, ma'am,' said Agnes, 'I will begin to treat it with more respect; and it shall travel upon my knees when I lean back, and if I can procure any tolerable substitute for it, I will take your advice, and give it in charge to Adrienne during the remainder of the journey.'

How cheaply as has been already observed may a little popularity be purchased! This good-humoured tractability was so new to Mrs. / Temple, and at the same time was exercised on a subject which in her estimation was of such vital importance, that Agnes was ever after one of her most distinguished favourites.

Pursuing the discourse with real *effusion de cœur:*[16] 'You will not repent your compliance, my dear young lady' resumed she; 'for there are two things to be considered in regard to dress: the richness of the materials, and the beauty of the form. The last is perhaps, the most essential, since a very exquisite substance may be spoilt by being ill shaped, and a very ordinary one rendered valuable by the taste with which it is made up.' –

'If this important disquisition is ended' said Miss Temple, contemptuously – 'I should be obliged to Miss Danvers (before she returns to her book) if she would answer one or two questions I wish to put to her.'

Agnes keeping her finger within the leaves of the volume that she might not lose her place, and letting it rest upon her lap, fixed her eyes / upon Miss Temple, and silently awaited the inquisition she was to undergo. –

'Pray, if it is not impertinent,' the lady began, 'what is the strange story in circulation at Paris respecting an aunt of Lady Glenfeld's, who, assisted by her brother, has cheated half the tradespeople she employed, and has now run away with a young gallant?'

'My intimacy with Lady Glenfeld,' answered Agnes gravely, 'gives me no right to speak of her family affairs. I can only say, that the latter part of your charge against her aunt, is utterly unfounded.' –

Miss Temple was disconcerted for a moment, and Agnes flattered herself the examination was over: but soon recovering herself:

'My dear,' resumed she, 'I do not ask you to betray any *private* concerns: the names of Mrs. Marchmont, and Mr. Wharton, coupled with infamy, are in every body's mouth. You could probably tell nothing half so bad of them / as public report has already disseminated. Do you know where they are gone?'

'Not exactly.' –

'Lord Glenfeld has been rather unfortunate in connecting himself with such a family.' –

'Unfortunate!' repeated Agnes, colouring with anger – 'Unfortunate, in having married the sweetest creature that ever existed!' –

'Ah, I see you are very partial to her, and I allow that she is a pleasing person enough, and seems good-natured, and unaffected: but Lord Glenfeld, you must permit me to observe, might have done better for himself in fifty ways. She is badly allied; her mother is an ambitious, manœuvring, hollow-hearted fine lady; her sisters are arrogant, supercilious would be prodigies; – and though she herself may be a very harmless little creature, she had scarcely a common gentlewoman's fortune; has no talents; very little beauty, and is the niece of persons stained with every kind of dishonour.' /

'With all these disadvantages,' cried Agnes warmly, 'and ten thousand others, if she had them, she has the merit of having made Lord Glenfeld (naturally a serious and reserved character) the happiest and most cheerful man I know!' –

Miss Temple contented herself with replying to this by an emphatical hem! – and then, dismissing Lady Glenfeld from the scene, she introduced a new personage:

'Were you acquainted,' said she, 'with Miss de Vere, the ward of Mr. Wharton?'

Taken a little by surprise, Agnes hesitated a moment, and, then, deeming it better to treat such an inquirer with levity than to make her curiosity a matter of too much importance, she laughingly answered:

'Yes, I know her very well; pray say no harm of her, for she is my particular friend!' –

'She was engaged to be married, was she not?' /

'I rather think you have been misinformed.'

'I heard it however, from one who had been told so by Mr. Wharton himself. But whether it is true or not, which very little matters, the general belief is, that she and her guardian have eloped together.'

'Oh now,' cried Agnes, 'I am really puzzled how to answer a charge that so far exceeds any thing I could have anticipated. All I know is, that when I left Paris, Lord and Lady Glenfeld, Mrs. Le Strange, her daughters, and every domestic in the family, were equally well acquainted with the present intentions, and future prospects of the poor girl you are speaking of; and I assure you they had nothing in them of the nature of an elopement either with Mr. Wharton, or any younger lover.'

So saying without waiting for an answer, she opened the volume in her hand, and resumed her lecture.

Miss Temple was unaccustomed to being / foiled in this cool sort of manner. She had often provoked anger, and drawn upon herself vehement abuse; these she could endure with magnanimous composure, and, perhaps, rather enjoy as tests of her power; but the quiet firmness of Agnes, and the indifference with which she seemed always ready to give up the contest, inflexibly retaining however her own opinion, set persecution at defiance, and blunted the force of every stroke directed against her. Whether to hate or admire her, Miss Temple scarcely knew. In her heart she could not but be sensible Agnes had dealt with her (on an attack so unsparing against those she professed to call her friends), temperately and mildly; yet her pride was hurt at the discomfiture she had received, and during many hours she meditated upon it with unabated chagrin.

Mr. St. Hubert who had so happily exempted himself from suffering in his own person / any annoyance by the pugnacity of their indefatigable companion, yet felt for Agnes, and in the course of the evening found an opportunity, without being overheard, of saying to her:

'My good young lady, I am afraid you are going through a very tedious probation, but you seem to bear it more patiently than most persons would do at your age. Methinks our associate held forth this afternoon with greater volubility than usual, for I heard the sharp tones of her disagreeable voice even through my nap. She is a premature old maid in the worst sense of the term,[17] and I would sooner condemn myself to perpetual silence, not only during this journey to Italy, but during my whole remaining journey through life, than incur the risk of being drawn in to defend and prove, argue and discuss every sentence I happened to utter in her presence. She is too young yet (though no chicken!) to have the right of being such a pest. But I will tell / you what you shall do to alleviate the evil. Whenever she starts any subject which you foresee may become painful to you, give me a cautious jog (never mind whether I am asleep or awake), and I will immediately begin discoursing with our coachman, (who is almost always walking by the side of the carriage) in so loud a voice, that her shrill treble will be completely set at defiance.'

Agnes laughed heartily at this proposal, and while she was thanking him, Miss Temple entered the room. She looked not a little surprised at the facility with which Agnes was able to converse with the 'poor deaf old soul;' and asked her some time after, in a low voice, how she contrived to make him hear her?

'I can hardly ever,' she added, 'get an answer to the purpose from him; and yet I speak as distinctly as most people, from having been accustomed to adapt my voice to those who are afflicted with his infirmity. Mamma has an old cousin who has lived with us a good deal, / and who is dreadfully deaf, yet she always said she could hear me when she could hear nobody else, and sometimes, if I happened to say any thing she did not like, she used to complain that she heard me *too* well.'

Agnes' eye met Mr. St. Hubert's at this part of Miss Temple's speech, and the meaning with which it was fraught, forced her to turn hastily away, and busy herself with the ornaments on the chimney-piece.

There being so little to do in her own party, one member of which was thrown *hors de combat*[18] by his deafness; whilst another was too perverse to avail herself of the opportunity of being trained to wisdom, and a third was already completely broken in, Miss Temple turned her active powers in another direction. There was an English family on the road, travelling post, and consequently moving at a much quicker rate than the *voiturier*, but they gained little in point of time, since, by setting out later in the morning, they almost every / evening slept at the same inn. These strangers, Miss Temple determined to take under her protection; and she began by the maid, who in addition to her mistress, a lady in delicate health, had the charge of a beautiful little girl of about four years old. Miss Temple was all anxiety for the accommodation of these interesting persons. She followed the maid into the bed-rooms; advised her – assisted her – cautioned her; formed an intimacy with the child, recommended sundry reformations in her dress, her diet, her mode of sleeping; ran up and down stairs to make the chambermaid use despatch in her attendance; called for more water, and larger basons; was in terror lest the sheets should be damp; in short, was busy to her heart's content, and so bewildered the poor maid, that though obliged to seem thankful, she often wished the good lady a thousand miles off. At supper she could not forbear pouring forth to Adrienne a torrent of lamentations, saying that kindly as she supposed / it was all meant, this new counsellor had made her so much more forgetful than she had ever been before, that if they continued to travel in company, she would be very likely to make her lose her place.

Adrienne asked her why she submitted to such persecution?

'What would you do in my place?' enquired the other, 'how would you prevent it?'

'I would lock the door as soon as I got into a bed-room that suited me.'

'That would do no good; I must let the coach-seats, and the dressing-cases be brought in; and this lady would be sure to take the opportunity of entering at the same time. I see no remedy, and so I suppose I must bear it as well as I can; but it makes me dread to arrive at a sleeping-place, and the sight of her as soon as I get into the inn, takes away my breath, and puts me into a fluster from head to foot!'

'Well,' resumed Adrienne, 'there is one / resource open to you still, and since you wish to keep your place, it may be worth trying. Tell your mistress how you are beset, and ask her to come this evening into the child's room whilst you are unpacking, and if Miss Temple joins you, beg your lady will be good enough to speak to her.'

This straight forward mode of proceeding had not occurred to the stranger's attendant, but when recommended to her by another, struck her as the perfection of wisdom, and she very joyfully declared she would follow the suggestion.

Accordingly, the succeeding evening, when Miss Temple had selected for herself and her mother the room she chose to have, and had made a hasty toilette, she left Mrs. Temple seated at the looking-glass, deliberately arranging her head-dress; and impatient to be in action, enquired out the little girl's apartment, and hastened towards it. On opening the door, which she did without the ceremony of knocking, the usual / aspect of affairs was totally changed. The room was quiet, and already in tolerable order; at one end of it, the maid was diligently sorting the things she had been unpacking, and at the other, sat a lady opposite a small table at which a child was eating her simple supper.

Miss Temple paused at the door, curt'sied to the stranger, nodded to the child, and as she put her hand again upon the lock, preparing to retire, said protectingly to the maid:

'You see I had not forgotten you; but I will come a little later.'

'Pardon me, madam,' said the lady, with great civility, but some seriousness, 'pardon me for detaining you a moment; but I have to entreat you will give yourself no further trouble about the arrangements this young woman has my orders to make. She understands how I wish to be served, and how my little girl is to be managed, and not having a very good memory, it confuses her to receive directions / from two different persons. Accept my best thanks for your kind intentions, and allow me to beg you will think of us no more.'

Extremely affronted, Miss Temple left the room, even more abruptly than she had entered it; and muttering to herself that she was sorry for the poor maid, though after all, the lady would be the greatest sufferer, she repaired to the *salon*[19] where the cloth was laying for supper.

Agnes was alone, walking up and down the room, to exercise her limbs, crampt by so many hours' confinement in the carriage.

'What have you done with the amusing Mr. St. Hubert?' said Miss Temple, trying to look unruffled, but still evidently far from serene.

'He is gone out to take a walk.'

'Without you? How came that about? You have of late been his invariable companion.' /

'He has found somebody else to go with.'

'Has he? Who is it? A traveller, or an inhabitant of this place?'

'A traveller, I believe.'

'I wonder who it can be? Is this the first time they have met?'

'I really do not know,' and Agnes continued her walk.

After a short silence: 'You have one habit, Miss Danvers,' resumed her companion, 'that would have suited you admirably for a sailor.'

'Have I ma'am? What is it?'

'That practice of pacing backwards and forwards as if you were walking the quarter-deck.'

'Sailors have recourse to it for the same reason that I have, they have no other means of taking exercise.'

'It may be extremely wholesome, but / I must say, it is very tiresome to other people.'

Agnes was willing to allow that might be possible, and immediately sat down.

Soon after Mr. St. Hubert returned, Mrs. Temple, as delicately attired as if she had been going to a party, also made her appearance. Supper was brought in, and they all took their seats at table.

'I hope, sir, you had a pleasant walk?' said Miss Temple to their male companion, screaming as loud as her strength would permit her.

He looked up with the most innocent air imaginable, as if uncertain what she had said, and turning to Agnes regarded her with an enquiring face that seemed to ask; 'was she speaking to me?'

'How horribly deaf he is! I think he gets worse and worse every day! My dear, as you are sitting next him, do ask why he does not use a trumpet?'[20] /

Agnes, preserving her gravity as well as she could, repeated to him the question in Miss Temple's name:

'Because,' answered he, 'for some time past, I have heard more than I like, even without a trumpet.'

'How supremely gallant!' cried Miss Temple, in a tone of pique, 'we really are all too much obliged to him! I hope, my dear madam,' she added, turning to her mother, 'you are fully aware how highly the result of your labours at the dressing-table must be appreciated by such an associate. I do not wonder that to please so partial an admirer of our sex, you should think nothing of the fatigue of unpacking so many things; nothing of giving the grumbling *voiturier* the trouble of loading and unloading, night and morning so much luggage, and nothing of the torment it is to me, to have it all to pack again before I can get into bed.' /

'My dear, if you would let me, I would pack it myself.'

'But how my dear mother? you know very well you have not a cap nor a gown you would think fit ever to put on again, if I were to allow you to attempt replacing them in their boxes.'

'It is very true, my dear, you manage these matters much better than I should.'

'I have had a long apprenticeship. But it is hard to give me the employment every night, so unnecessarily.'

'It is never unnecessary, my dear, to make oneself fit to be seen.'

'Seen by whom, ma'am? By Mr. St. Hubert? by the *voiturier*? by the waiters?'

'I should change my dress for dinner, even if I dined alone.'

'I dare believe you would! And even if you were dining in a dungeon!' /

Mrs. Temple bore all this with patience, asked for the salad, and went on eating her supper with undiminished appetite.

That night Agnes went to bed more indisposed against this harsh daughter than she had ever yet felt. Such taunts from a child to a parent were shocking to her, and she firmly determined that the acquaintance should terminate with the journey.

The early hour at which the *voiturier* obliged them to start every morning, had now habituated her to wake uncalled, and she was at a little before five, completely dressed, and assisting Adrienne to tie up some of the packages, when she heard a gentle tap at her door. She concluded it was the coachman come to take the things down to the carriage, and Adrienne, proud of their diligence, called out that they were ready, and bade the person come in. It was not the *voiturier* however, but Miss Temple, who, in her dressing-gown / and night-cap, and looking extremely pale, stept hastily forward, and taking Agnes' hand, said:

'O my dear Miss Danvers, I am sure you will be very sorry to hear that my poor mother is most severely indisposed. I trust there is no real danger to be apprehended, because I have known her suffer these attacks before; but she will not be able to travel to-day, nor even to quit her bed. Will you have the charity to consent to this delay?'

'Most assuredly; but I grieve for the occasion.'

'I sincerely believe it! No one can know my dear mother without loving her. There never was a sweeter, nor a more amiable nature. Be kind enough to speak for me to Mr. St. Hubert, and try to prevail upon him to remain here this one day. I have seen the *voiturier*, and he declares himself perfectly willing to stay, if the whole party / agrees in wishing it, and will pay him for the expenses he must incur here.'

'There can be no doubt of Mr. St. Hubert's consent; it would be inhuman to hesitate in such a case. But is there nothing Miss Temple, that Adrienne or I could do to be of use? – command either of us in any way you please.'

'I am truly grateful for your kindness, and if I want assistance I will freely ask for it: but at present, all that the poor invalid requires, is perfect quiet. She has had a wretched night, – however, she is easier now, and I am not without hopes that if left undisturbed, she may get a little sleep. – I must now go back to her.' –

She then went away, leaving Agnes full of wonder at the sudden transformation she had undergone. There was now no asperity – no dogmatising – no causticity; – her voice was softened, her countenance subdued, and her language kind and grateful. /

'And she really loves the mother whom she treats with such irreverence!' thought Agnes, 'poor thing! her faults then are more of temper than of heart![21] I had been unjust enough to suspect that they proceeded from both.'

In the room where they had supped, she found Mr. St. Hubert, as yet unapprised of the projected change in their plans, and ready equipped for the prosecution of their journey. She informed him of Mrs. Temple's illness, and of the delay requested by the daughter: 'I ventured,' added she, 'to answer for your consent. Did I do wrong?'

'By no means. I am quite willing to grant this little favour to the poor mother; how I might have felt inclined had it been asked for the daughter, is another part of speech!'

'Even the daughter,' resumed Agnes, 'such has been the salutary effect of fear, would now excite in you some interest. She is entirely changed; her bustling, important manner has disappeared; she speaks of her mother in the / most affectionate terms, and seems to have no thought but how to contribute to her relief and comfort.' –

'Humph! – "sweet are the uses of adversity," says my dear Shakespear:[22] but in Miss Temple's case, will these good effects last beyond the cause that gave them rise? – Is she not one, who like stagnant air over a morass, is never safe to approach but when a hurricane has arisen, and dispersed for awhile, the noxious vapours that surrounded it?'

'The comparison may be just, but it is not charitable!'

'Why that is true; but she has worn out all my charity. After I had escaped myself, by a stratagem, from the torment of her tongue, she fell upon you: *passe pour cela;*[23] you are young and good-humoured, and endured the persecution with constancy, knowing it could not be of long duration, and perhaps thinking that a little penance for past peccadillos might not be amiss! but when she at last directed / her shafts against the mild, unresisting mother, so deserving of a kinder daughter, – I gave her up!' –

He then consulted with Agnes as to the best method of spending the long day they had before them, and asked her whether she could ride.

'Yes,' answered she, 'but I prefer making use of the opportunity to write a letter.' –

'Well, then, if I can procure a decent courser, I will, to translate a Frenchman's idiom, *take a walk on horseback*[24] by myself. The country hereabouts (they were in the neighbourhood of Dole) is pleasant, and the day promises to be fine. Meanwhile, as it is too early to call for a regular breakfast, come out with me, my young friend, for a little stroll.'

Agnes consented, after desiring Adrienne to keep in the way, lest Miss Temple should want her.

As they were returning from their ramble, Adrienne met them near the house, to tell her / Mistress that Miss Temple had been enquiring for her with some anxiety, and desired to be informed the moment she came in.

The motive for this was soon explained.

'I have always,' said Miss Temple, 'after any of these seizures, been in the habit of making my mother take small doses of James' Powders.[25] We brought a packet with us from England; but I fear it has been left at Paris, or lost on the road; for after the most minute search, I have been forced to give up all hopes of finding it. The English lady who slept here last night, is still in the house, and does not set out till eight o'clock. She has a little medecine chest with her, which I once saw in her maid's room. It probably contains some of these powders. You would do me the greatest favour in the world, my dear Miss Danvers, and I should be inexpressibly obliged to you, if you would send to her for permission to see her a moment – would state to her the case, and / solicit the grant of two or three grains of this medecine. I should have made the application myself; but to own the truth, a little misunderstanding occurred between us last night, and I should find it awkward to present myself to her as a petitioner this morning.'

Agnes readily undertook the embassy, and said she would immediately despatch Adrienne to enquire when the lady would be visible.

Miss Temple was most cordial in her acknowledgments, and hurried back to her charge; whilst Adrienne was deputed to the English maid, with directions what message to carry to her mistress.

The answer returned was, that the stranger would be happy to receive the young lady a little before eight o'clock. It was now only half past six.

'We have time then,' said Mr. St. Hubert, 'to breakfast in comfort. I intend to do great honour to their coffee and eggs, for I always find my appetite improves in proportion to the / leisure I have to indulge it. When we are whisked off at five, I can rest content with a scanty breakfast, eaten in haste; and I think no more of food till we arrive at our baiting-place: but this morning, it will be a different affair, as I speedily mean to demonstrate.'

The appointed time being come, Agnes guided by Adrienne, who knew the way, proceeded to the traveller's apartment to execute her commission. She was received with great courtesy by a lady who was still seated at the breakfast table, and appeared to be about one or two and twenty. Her countenance was prepossessing though dejected, and she exhibited evident symptoms of declining health. When apprized of the motive of Agnes's visit, she consented with the greatest alacrity to comply with her wishes, and hastened into the next room in search of the medecine required. The door had scarcely been closed two minutes, when it opened again, and a gentleman entered whom / Agnes immediately recognized to be Mr. Walsingham. Their surprise was reciprocal, but in no other respect did their feelings seem to assimilate. Hers were of unmixed satisfaction at seeing again a friend of Lady Glenfeld – a man she had thought particularly agreeable, and one whom she might have it in her power to serve by giving him immediate information of the recent events in Mr. Wharton's family. On his part, though a momentary flash of pleasure had darted from his eye on first perceiving her, his mode of addressing her was so distant and so grave, that not only his manner, but his whole countenance – his very voice, appeared to have undergone an entire change.

'I hope,' he said, slowly advancing, 'I have the pleasure of seeing Miss de Vere quite well?'

Agnes bowed, and would have given the world for courage to set him right respecting her appellation; but intimidated by his formality, she continued silent, till, conscious of / the awkwardness of their mutual situation, he once more forced himself to speak, and directed to her some question concerning her journey.

'You are travelling towards Italy, I imagine?' said he.

'Yes; I am going to Rome.'

'I congratulate you on having got over the most tedious part of the journey. The road from Paris hither, through what the natives call their *belle France*, has appeared to me insupportably barren of interest and of beauty.'

Unable to pursue the conversation on such general topics, whilst her mind was engrossed by thoughts so different, Agnes without replying to his last observation, said;

'You left Paris rather suddenly, did you not?'

'Unexpectedly so, even to myself. Who did you hear of my departure from?'

'From Lady Glenfeld.' /

'Indeed!' and (brightening up,) he added, 'you have then seen her since – I mean, you have seen her – rather recently?'

Agnes was a little perplexed by this broken and hesitating mode of expressing himself, but simply answered:

'Yes; she was kind enough to call and take leave of me the very day before she set off for England.'

'She is in England, then? How long has she been gone?'

'About ten or twelve days. She regretted much the impossibility of writing to you, having news to communicate which she was anxious you should immediately become acquainted with: but you had left no direction at your lodgings; and therefore Lord Glenfeld suggested the plan of writing to you under cover to your banker, with directions to forward the letter wherever you might be.'

'And do you at all know what were the / news they were both so desirous of transmitting to me? Something very pleasant I hope?'

Agnes smiled, but had no time to answer him, as, at that moment, the lady returned. She bore in her hand two or three little packets of the powders, which she said she had been weighing, from an apprehension Miss Temple might not be provided with scales. 'I have written upon each paper,' added she, 'the exact number of grains it contains, though I sincerely hope that only one dose may be required.'

Thanking her in the warmest terms for all the trouble she had taken, and making many excuses for having interrupted her breakfast, Agnes then retired, and hastened to the door of Miss Temple's room to announce the success of her mission. She was hailed with great delight: the powders were received as a boon scarcely to have been hoped for; and / the happiest anticipations were entertained from their well-remembered good effect on former occasions.

Agnes spent nearly the whole day alone, and had ample leisure to write to Lady Glenfeld one of the longest letters she had ever penned. After a detailed account of all the little incidents of her journey; a description of her fellow travellers, and a few characteristic traits of their peculiarities, she proceeded to speak of the unexpected meeting she had just had with Mr. Walsingham: 'I am afraid,' she said, 'that he has no longer a good opinion of me. Perhaps the fact of seeing me, (whom he still supposes to be the affluent heiress, Miss de Vere,) travelling, or rather, (as it must appear to him,) *strolling* over the world,[26] without attendants, without protectors, without, in short, any of the pomp and circumstance, that ought to accompany her, may account for, and be sufficient to excuse whatever distrust of me his behaviour may have betrayed. Let / me add, however, that before our short interview terminated, he seemed to be in better humour with me, particularly after I had spoken of *you*, and he saw reason to believe I was still in some credit with you. I should be truly sorry were his prejudice against me to be lasting, for he is one whom you taught me to think well of, and whose manners and conversation must always recommend him. Should an opportunity occur of speaking to him again, I will avail myself of it to tell him, at least, a part of the truth. There will be no necessity to enter into particulars; but I might let him know that it has been proved I have no title to the name or inheritance of de Vere, and am, in consequence, proceeding to Rome to put myself under the protection of a brother, my only surviving relation. This plain statement, I should hope, might re-establish me in his esteem, and put an end to the mortifying feelings inflicted by his misconception of my character. /

'The lady in whose apartment I saw him is, I fancy, in some way related to him, for they seem to be travelling together, and I saw by the appearance of the breakfast-table, that he had been sharing that meal with her, though when I entered, he was absent; probably, from imagining that what I had to say to her might be of a private nature. Whither they are bound, I have not the remotest idea. During my short dialogue with him, he dropped not a word concerning his own destination. The name of his fellow-traveller is also a mystery to me. I might attempt to learn it through Adrienne, who has become acquainted with the lady's maid; but it would be merely an *attempt*; for she mis-pronounces all English names so abominably, that I should gain no certainty by it. It is possible she may be Mr. Walsingham's wife.'

Having finished this long epistle, and ascertained that neither she nor Adrienne could / make themselves of any use in Mrs. Temple's room, she took the former by the arm, and set forth on a pleasant and refreshing ramble. They avoided going out of sight of houses; but entered several dwellings of the poor, particularly those in which they saw any tokens of industry; and in the midst of privations, often amounting to wretchedness, met with good-humour and civility, – an ever ready impulse to talk, (in accents rather louder and more nasal than Agnes quite liked), great admiration of the materials of which their clothes were made, and no little curiosity as to whence they came, and whither they were going. Agnes distributed a few *sous* amongst the children; and then proceeded to a little shop further on, curious to look at some books which she thought she could discern exhibited for sale at the window. Books, indeed, they were – but of a sort ill calculated to excite her interest; they consisted wholly of legends of saints, and details of martyrdom too horrible / to be endured. On turning away, she was accosted by a good woman, who, seeing her enter so many habitations, persuaded herself she was looking for a lodging; and having had, for a much longer period than was convenient, such an accommodation to dispose of she invited the two strangers to walk in and look at it. They endeavoured to excuse themselves, but in vain; the voluble and eager dame would take no denial. She said she was sure they never had seen a neater or more convenient apartment; it looked upon the prettiest garden in the world; had a superb view beyond; was not more than three steps from the parish church, &c. &c. Agnes to pacify her, at length consented to look, not at the house, but at the garden. So late in the year, it, of course, exhibited but few remaining flowers; but it *had* been profusely stored with them; was of some extent, and provided with numberless arbours, each containing a long narrow table, and a bench on / the other side. Agnes asked the meaning of these:

'Why, mademoiselle,' answered Adrienne half angrily, 'don't you see that you have been invited to become a lodger in a place fitted up for a *guinguette?*'[27]

Agnes laughed, and asked no more questions; but after remaining a reasonable time to hear the praises lavished upon her premises by their owner, accepted the *bouquet* she presented to her at parting, made her some little compensation both for her flowers and her failure in securing an occupant for her vacant rooms, and returned to the inn.

Mr. St. Hubert, tired and hungry, was waiting for her with some impatience, and allowed the people of the house no rest till dinner was served. Miss Temple was waited upon in her mother's room by the active and good-natured Adrienne.

Having somewhat appeased the first cravings of his appetite, Mr. St. Hubert asked how the poor lady did? And whether there was any / prospect of her being able to re-commence her journey the next day?

'I have not heard,' replied Agnes, 'nor is it probable Miss Temple herself could answer that question till she sees how her mother does to-morrow morning.'

'For my own part,' resumed he, 'I am not impatient: when there is good riding weather, and tolerable scenery to be looked at, I can always find amusement. But this is dull work for you, my poor young lady.'

'I certainly should not wish it to last: but I could bear it very well another day.'

Their repast being finished, Mr. St. Hubert, with the consent of Agnes, ordered a little fire, the evenings beginning to be chill, and establishing himself beside it in a comfortable arm chair, was asleep in less than five minutes. He had given her full authority to call for candles whenever she pleased: 'because,' said he, 'when once I am in a sound slumber, and have been previously somewhat fatigued, / all the light you could bring before me could not wake me.'

Agnes availed herself of this permission, as soon as it grew too dusk to read; and found that, as he had said, the entrance of candles made no difference in the calmness with which he reposed. Whilst looking at him, thus profoundly tranquil, the wish occurred to her of making a slight sketch of him. She could scarcely have chosen a handsomer subject. His finely arched brow; his noble forehead; his hair, 'a sable silvered,'[28] waving round his face, – his Grecian nose, and beautifully shaped mouth, rendered him, even without the advantage of seeing his dark eyes open, a model fit for a statuary. As she advanced in her employment, she grew more and more interested in it; the likeness became apparent: the outline, at length was completed, and she was impatiently rolling up a slip of paper to use as a stump for the shadows, when, to her infinite surprise she heard him exclaim: /

'Hold, hold! Not so fast; let me first see how you have put your work together.'

'Dear sir,' cried Agnes, 'have you been long awake?'

'I don't know; I have been too much amused in watching your proceedings, to remember any thing about the matter. Come, show me your sketch, and I will tell you honestly whether it is worth going on with.'

She handed it to him.

'Very well!' cried he, after an attentive examination. 'Very well, indeed; this does you credit; it is in perfect drawing, and there is a sharpness and freedom in the touch that I like exceedingly. You have been under a very clever master.'

'I had one of the best in Paris, and learnt five years. But you are yourself a designer, I perceive.'

'I have been a little of every thing, my dear; much to the annoyance of my excellent father. / He was himself a military man, and at the age of eighteen, I would go into the army also. There, as at school, I was always sketching as I called it, – that is to say, scrawling figures on walls and wainscots, and blotching them with paint. My father flattered himself I had real genius for the fine arts, – advised me to sell my commission, of which I was heartily tired, – and placed me in the study of an eminent painter. The sight of brush and pallet then became odious to me, and I never rested till I got my father's consent to go to sea. On board of ship, the mania for drawing perversely came upon me again; and I painted all the portraits of all my brother officers, and studied from the finest living models among the common men. Moreover, I seized every opportunity when we were on shore of taking views, or making designs from the various objects I saw, whether in the East Indies, in America, on the coast of Africa, or in the Baltic. Little by little, I acquired real ability; and giving up / the navy, I established myself at Rome, where I practised as a regular artist for several years.

At last, I was recalled to England on the demise of a distant relation I had never seen nor heard of, whose property amounting to forty thousand pounds, I was discovered to be entitled to as heir at law. All this wealth, however, has come too late to induce me to change my accustomed mode of life. I can, it is true, assist others more essentially: but I cannot give up my own frugal and simple habits. It would be an intollerable slavery to me to be at the head of a great establishment, and to be obliged to aim at the manners, and ape the importance of a *Grand Seigneur*.[29] I have of course, given up painting as a profession: but it is an art I still love: and that love it is which, in some measure, carries me again into Italy. But, moreover, I have the additional motive of wishing to visit a nephew of mine, risen into celebrity by his talents as a sculptor. I want to see his works, only one of which, of / any consequence, has found its way into England. I was much struck by it last spring in London, and it immediately decided me to begin this journey.'

'May I ask,' said Agnes in a voice trembling between hope and fear, 'what your nephew's name is?'

'His name, like your own, is Danvers. He is the son of my eldest sister, whose husband, an architect, died young, and left her in somewhat embarrassed circumstances. Her boy gave early indications of talent, and she sent him to London to study under an able statuary. At a later period, my father who was very anxious for the poor lad's advancement, assisted the mother in furnishing him with the means of residing some time in Italy. He was so taken with the country, and with all its treasures of art, that he has never returned from it. He is making, not a rapid, but an honourable and handsome fortune, is surrounded by friends and well-wishers, / and is very generally patronized by most of the wealthy Englishmen who visit Rome.'

Agnes had listened to these details with the deepest interest, and when Mr. St. Hubert came to a pause, her eyes still remained fixed upon him, as if desirous to hear more. He observed it, and said smiling:

'I have nothing to add, my dear; so, if you like to go on with your drawing, I will sit as still as a mouse.'

But Agnes could not so easily comply with this invitation; endeavouring however, to controul her agitated feeling, she ventured in an accent almost as unsteady as her hand, to say:

'Is your nephew, sir, an only child? Has he no brother? no – sister?'

'Neither, that I ever heard of; but I was a wanderer over the face of the earth so many years, that it is possible other sons and daughters may have been born without my knowing / it. If such was ever the case, there cannot now be any of them living, or I must have heard of it.'

Tears rushed into Agnes's eyes on receiving this discouraging answer, and the wish she had for a moment indulged of making herself known to him whom she believed to be her uncle, vanished entirely. She had no proof to bring forward in attestation of her right to claim kindred with him, and the dread of being regarded as an artful adventurer, (stimulated by hearing of his wealth to fabricate such a tale) was so insurmountable, that she determined to let the matter rest in silence till she saw her brother, and was able to consult with him how to act. *He*, she was persuaded, must possess some document declaratory of her affinity to him, well remembering to have heard from the Blakes, that at her mother's decease, all her papers had been forwarded to her son.

These thoughts passed rapidly through her mind, and when her resolution was taken, she / dashed away unobserved, the tears that dimmed her sight, placed the drawing before her, and as composedly as she could, proceeded with the occupation it afforded her.

After silently observing her progress for some time, Mr. St. Hubert said:

'Do you know, my dear young friend, that I am convinced from your expertness of hand, and correctness of eye, you could, with some further study and practice, become a very excellent artist? Now, at Rome you will be in the very centre of all that may best contribute to your improvement; and I really think it pity, however independent you may be, that you should not profit from the opportunities that will be continually presenting themselves. What harm will it do you, albeit a lady, to paint better than other ladies?'

'Certainly none at all, sir; and it is very possible I may hereafter require such a resource, / although hitherto accustomed to draw only for amusement.'

'Say you so, my dear? Why then, depend upon my most zealous endeavours to serve you. I may be able at once, to give you some useful hints in your art, to guide you to the best subjects to copy from, and to make you known amongst those who may most essentially patronize you. Have you ever painted in oils?'

'Less than I now wish I had. My most finished performances, (such as they are) have all been in miniature.'

'Who was your master?'

She named one of the most eminent in Paris.[30]

'Well, my dear, and what more fortunate choice could have been made for you? He is at the head of his particular branch of the profession, and French artists are universally allowed to surpass those of every other nation / as painters in miniature. Go on then in that style; for after all, it is the best adapted to the love of cleanliness, the taste and delicacy of your sex. Oil painting is dirty and cumbrous work; and for one whom you might equal or outvie on canvass, you may excel a hundred on ivory.'

He then enquired whether she had any of her pictures with her? She produced two or three portraits taken from nature with which he expressed himself in the highest degree satisfied.

'I should like,' said he, 'before we go to Rome, to accompany you for a month to Venice. It would be a great advantage to you to study the colouring of that school; I do not mean to depreciate your own; but, perhaps it is a little too vivid, a little too like the brilliancy of flowers, instead of those clear, yet blended tints, those soft and imperceptible gradations of hue which ought to distinguish the human complexion. Would it be very / indecorous to travel, you and your maid, with a gay bachelor of sixty-five?'

'No,' replied the smiling Agnes, 'but perhaps, the whole future aspect of my life depends upon the result of the affair that carries me to Rome; and I confess, I am most impatient to arrive there.'

'I am sorry for it, my dear lady, because, be as impatient as you please, you must per force make some delay, after entering Italy, before you attempt to go on to Rome. It is now the very beginning of September, and no one in their senses ever thinks of braving the *mal aria*[31] of Rome at that early season. Now be guided by me, an old traveller, and an experienced. At Milan, I am intimate with an Italian lady who goes annually to Venice to visit her married daughter. This is about the time when she usually sets out. Let us join her, and make the journey as she does, with a *vetturino*. You will find her a very agreeable companion, and a thoroughly respectable chaperon. / What say you to my scheme? if you agree to it, we shall get rid of terrible Miss Temple; you will have leisure to contemplate the Venetian school; and I can ensure you all manner of courteous treatment from the family of my friend.'

This proposal was too tempting to be resisted, and Agnes, knowing that she had more than money sufficient to defray its expenses, immediately assented to it. She was now for the first time aware that it was impracticable (or at least hazardous) to go straight to Rome, and considered that it would cost her nearly as much to stay at Milan or Pavia, as to spend the interval at Venice.

Before she and Mr. St. Hubert separated for the night, they had the pleasure of hearing that Mrs. Temple was considerably better, and would probably be well enough to resume her journey the succeeding day, though at a somewhat later hour than that at which they usually started. /

These hopes were not disappointed. When the morning came, Mrs. Temple's amendment was so confirmed, that before eight o'clock, she was able to ascend the carriage, and with her usual gentleness and good breeding, to express to Agnes and Mr. St. Hubert her gratitude for the consideration they had shown her, and the patience they had exerted.

The improvement effected in her daughter by the alarm she had endured, was still very perceptible, and her manners towards both her fellow-travellers were so much softened, that Mr. St. Hubert was almost betrayed into forgetting his *deafness*. It is not to be supposed however, that habits of long standing can be on a sudden, and permanently overcome. The same meddling and fidgetty spirit that usually dictated her interference in the affairs of others now set itself to work nearer home; and she speedily made herself as troublesome as ever by the excessive anxiety with which she was tormented on every little change in her mother's / countenance, on every surmise that she was growing tired, that she sat uncomfortably, that she found the carriage too hot or too cold – that she wanted more room for her feet – or more support for her back; and so on. Three or four times she compelled the poor lady to change her seat, either with herself or Agnes. She had her eye incessantly fixed upon her; was drawing up, or letting down the windows every five minutes, and forced her during the first stage to smell to her salts, or take lavender drops, as often as the suspicion struck her, that she was growing languid and exhausted.

All this proceeded no doubt, from a better motive than her antecedent restlessness; but it was of the same family, a little differently modified, and it was evident to Agnes, that Mr. St. Hubert had some difficulty in refraining to express his annoyance:

'I was afraid,' he told her afterwards, 'of *bringing an old house about my ears*,[32] or I / would have told her a little bit of my mind! With half an eye she might have seen that she was wearisome even to the poor convalescent herself; who, if she had not the temper of a saint, or the insensibility of an automaton, would have started up and shaken her! I shall not have kept holiday more rejoicingly since I was a school-boy, than I shall the day we are delivered from her company!'

'You might even now, sir, escape from her many hours,' said Agnes, 'if you took Adrienne's place in the *coupé*,[33] and sent her to occupy yours in the inside.'

'But my dear, maid servants are always sick in a carriage, especially, if they have a smart fellow to converse with on the outside; and I dare say Adrienne will find it suits her health much better to stay with Miss Temple's footman, than to be admitted to the honour of sitting mum-chance, opposite Miss Temple herself.'

'Adrienne,' said Agnes, laughing, 'is exempt / from the first infirmity you mention; and as to the second, the love of flirting, she can enjoy it but little, since Monsieur Thomas can speak no French, and she can speak no English.'

'Oh, well, well – since that is the case, I frankly agree to your offer.'

Accordingly, after dinner, this new distribution of the personages of their little company took place, and seemed to give Miss Temple infinite satisfaction. She availed herself of Adrienne's humane readiness to serve any one who was indisposed, in order to make her support Mrs. Temple's feet upon her lap, and rub her ankles. Sometimes, she contrived to crowd Agnes, Adrienne and herself upon the same seat, to obtain room for her mother to recline upon the other. In vain did poor Mrs. Temple plead for respite both in favour of herself and others; her daughter begged her to let herself be managed in the way that was best / for her; paid Agnes some compliments on the good nature she was willing to attribute to her, and persevered in tormenting all around her, in order to kill her patient with kindness.[34] /

CHAPTER III.

O Italy! – where science loves to rove,
Where Genius feels his noblest powers expand,
Where Sculpture steals Promethean fire from Jove,
And Painting wields her lovely magic wand. –

Elegy, by Mrs. West.[35]

In modern times, at least when war is not raging, adventures rarely occur to travellers in Europe. Agnes' journey was attended by no circumstances worthy of record; and even to herself, had few of the charms of novelty, till after she had passed through Switzerland, having, the preceding year, visited that country in the greatest detail with Mr. Wharton, Mrs. Marchmont, and Harry Cowley.

At length the scenery began to excite in her / the most animated interest. They were approaching the Simplon,[36] too often spoken of to admit of any fresh description, but always inexpressibly striking to every new beholder. It was four o'clock in the morning when they began their slow ascent; and they had the advantage of a magnificent moon-light, and the most perfectly calm weather. The gradual changes in the tinge of the surrounding mountains, first seen in the silvery radiance of the moon; then in the thousand glowing colours of sun-rise; and finally, in the full fervour of his meridian blaze, called forth all the enthusiasm and admiration of which Agnes' unhackneyed feelings were susceptible. Throughout the day, a succession of the most diversified prospects rivetted her attention, and left her nothing to wish for, but more congenial companions. The first night spent at an Italian inn, was to her full of amusement. The walls decorated with fresco paintings, roughly executed, but producing a gay and pleasing / effect, she infinitely preferred to the unmeaning patterns of the papers with which most rooms are covered in France and England. The *brick floors* did not quite so much invite her approbation; but, in a hot climate, she allowed they might be desirable, however unsightly. The loftiness of the ceilings, which, if left, as was often the case, unplastered, exhibited sundry fantastic devices painted on the rafters; the sort of Eastern elegance as well as utility of the light musquito curtains, all attracted her notice, and diverted her imagination. At the charming inn at Baveno, where they dined the next day, she was enchanted with the view of Lago Maggiore,[37] and above all, by the indescribably-softening effect of the atmosphere upon even the most prominent objects; it left every outline distinct, and yet mellowed; it was, as if the landscape had been seen through some medium differing from common air, some exquisitely transparent veil, that subdued its brilliancy without / injuring its clearness; and over all, seemed to float every tint of the opal, – lilac, amber, pink, and the purest pale blue. The lake, a sheet of crystal, partook of the same beautiful rainbow hues, and with the same mildness, the same exemption from glare. 'Ah,' thought Agnes, 'if it were given to human intellects to possess so much brightness, combined with so much meekness, how near to the excellency of angelic natures would mortals approach.'

On their arrival at Milan, Mr. St. Hubert's first care was to call upon his friend la Signora Romanelli, who, ere an hour had elapsed came with him to the hotel, for the express purpose of inviting Agnes to accompany him immediately to her house, there to take up her abode till they all set out together for Venice. This hospitable proposal was made with so much grace and cordiality, and Mr. St. Hubert so strongly urged her to accept it, that the affair was settled in five minutes; and, to her own / surprise, Agnes from being a mere bird of passage through the country, found herself transplanted, all at once, into the interior of an Italian family, and welcomed into it as an old friend.

Mrs. and Miss Temple, not well understanding the language in which la Signora's invitation had been made, saw Agnes depart with equal wonder and curiosity. The mother, however, stept forward before she went, and kindly taking her hand, said with unusual feeling: 'I am very, very sorry, my dear Miss Danvers, we are going to part. You have invariably shown so much good nature and sweetness during the journey, that it will be long before I cease to regret the loss of so charming a companion.'

Agnes, who had always felt well-disposed towards the poor lady, was touched by the benignity of this address, and bade her farewell with many grateful acknowledgments for the favourable opinion she had expressed of / her, and the sincerest good wishes for the prosperous termination of her journey. The leave taking ceremonial between her and Miss Temple, (silent from astonishment, and forming a thousand different conjectures,) was slighter though civil; they shook hands for form-sake, and separated with no desire, at least in one of the parties, ever to meet again.

During Agnes's short stay at Milan, she was accompanied by her aimable hostess, or conducted by Mr. St. Hubert to see every thing that was worthy of attention in the city or its environs. To trace her steps, day by day, would be but rehearsing what every guide book, or volume of travels contains, and is far from being the object of these pages. Peculiarities, beneath the notice of more important works, – or the impressions made upon the mind of Agnes, by what to her was strange, may occasionally come under review; but so much has of late years been written on the subject of Italy – and so well, that it would be / a vain attempt to add any thing new to the picture.[38] Amongst the deviations from what she had been accustomed to, that principally struck her, were the domestic habits she found established at la Signora Romanelli's. That lady, though an early riser, was never supposed to be visible till one or two o'clock. There was no general re-union of the company at breakfast, but each person took coffee in his own apartment. The magnificent drawing-room, except in the evening, was useless; morning visitors, if there ever came any, were received, Agnes could not tell where, for the truth is, she never saw any place properly adapted to such a purpose; neither was the attire of the lady of the house, till the moment of going out, at all better suited to admit company. She often wandered from room to room in a loose wrapping gown,[39] with her hair in papers, or wholly concealed under a silk handkerchief, seeming entirely unemployed, yet looking lively and good humoured, – a circumstance / at which Agnes, so abhorrent of idleness, could never sufficiently marvel! In the evening, there was generally a numerous circle assembled, and cards, conversation, or music furnished amusements for the guests. Refreshments there were none, except *eau sucrée*,[40] not even fruit; and tea was never thought of but as a *tisane*[41] for a fever. Agnes read and understood Italian perfectly, but want of practice prevented her speaking it with fluency. She found that almost every body knew French, and was favoured, from motives of politeness, with so much of that language, ill-pronounced, that she would have rejoiced to meet with any one who spoke only Italian. One of the things that disappointed her most in this 'land of music,'[42] was the harsh, discordant, and loud voices of a large proportion of the Italian ladies she conversed with;[43] the very children rasped her ears, and when she compared these accents with the sweet tones of Lady Glenfeld, and even with those of / Isabel and her sisters, she could not but lament that custom and example should give to the organs of one set of people, inflections so dissimilar to those of another.

In about a week after her friend's arrival, Signora Romanelli was fully prepared to set out for Venice. Their journey was attended with no novelty of incident; they stopped where every body else stops; they saw all that was most remarkable on their way, and continued to be in such perfect harmony with each other, that they reached their destination more amicably disposed even than when they had set out. The fact is, notwithstanding that when two or three Italian friends get together, they scream so loud at each other as to give an idea that they are quarrelling,[44] they either are, or to foreigners appear to be, particularly good-tempered. Their first address is calm, natural, and conciliating; they evince much desire to oblige, – and on a superficial view, which is nearly all that strangers can / obtain, create a very favourable opinion of their urbanity, and kindness of disposition.[45]

Mr. St. Hubert, though he declined it for himself, preferring the freedom of an hotel, persuaded Agnes, from a truly paternal attention to propriety in all that related to her, to accept the invitation soon made to her by Signora Romanelli's daughter, of removing to her Palazzo. He promised to call for her every morning that they might visit together the principal churches, and finest collections of pictures. He advised her also to study as much as the time would permit, from the best paintings he or his friends might be able to borrow for her; and commending her to the care of the kind Signora, left her in the sumptuous mansion of that lady's son-in-law.

The same attention with which she had hitherto been treated by the mother, was now extended towards her by the daughter. Nothing / could exceed their unwearied complacency. They regarded her as the child of their old friend, and would have loved her for his sake had she not possessed half the attaching qualities a closer intimacy enabled them to discover in her. They were proud also of her beauty, and solicitous to exhibit her as their guest, wherever there was a prospect of securing for her the admiration which they thought her due. She speedily became, though with less newspaper *éclat*[46] than a foreign beauty in London, the reigning idol and fashion at Venice, where she was not merely styled *la bella*, but *la bellissima Inglese*,[47] and attracted all eyes whenever she appeared at the theatre, or entered a *conversazione*.[48] Mr. St. Hubert was pleased with her success on a double account, first, as seeing that it was borne with modesty and good sense; and next, as helping to repay, by the gratification it afforded them, the hospitality, and disinterested kindness of their Italian friends. /

The hour of separation at length arrived, and it was an hour of severe trial to the whole party. So many proofs of favour and benignity heaped upon her for an entire month, could not but make a deep impression upon Agnes's grateful nature. She had likewise learnt to love the spot where she had been regarded with so much partiality; and truly asserted, at parting, that Venice would ever retain the foremost place in her affection and remembrance.

From Venice to Florence, still travelling with a *vetturino*, they were accompanied by a lady and gentleman, both English; but full of antiquated prejudices; positive, credulous, and vulgarly national. Why they came to a country they seemed to take such pleasure in depreciating, it was not easy to divine. They undervalued, in detail and in the gross, whatever was Italian; recounted a thousand extravagant and outrageous stories of the deliberate *custom* amongst servants of poisoning / their masters for every trivial provocation; declared they had never been engaged in any pecuniary transaction with an Italian, of whatever rank, without being infamously cheated; abused their houses, their soil, their productions, – their very climate! and exempted nothing from this sweeping censure but their oil and their ortolans![49] Mr. St. Hubert, aware of the uselessness of entering into argument with such personages, took not the trouble of attempting it; he sometimes heard them with a laugh: and at others, withdrew from them all attention, and composed himself to sleep. Agnes recurred to her old resource – reading.

At Florence, they bade these pleasant companions adieu; and Mr. St. Hubert conducted his young *protégée* to a respectable boarding-house, where there were two or three other ladies, and where he took up his quarters himself.

How were all these attentions to her comfort / and credit enhanced in value to Agnes, by reflecting that she was perhaps receiving them (though without his knowing it), from an uncle!

As their stay in Florence was not to exceed a week, their time was principally divided between the so justly celebrated gallery, and the Palazzo Pitti.[50] Churches, and private collections they deferred inspecting till some future opportunity. On the third morning of their arrival, whilst they were intently engaged in surveying the beautiful statues of Niobe and her children;[51] and Mr. St. Hubert was commenting upon the admirable diversity of attitude and expression observable in each figure – upon the pathetic dignity of the mother – the drooping sorrow of the daughters – the vain attempt at resistance of the sons, – Agnes's attention to his discourse was somewhat enfeebled by seeing Mr. Walsingham enter the room. He did not immediately perceive them, but as he advanced / to the spot where they stood, his eye suddenly rested upon her, and he hastily approached:

'This,' cried he, addressing her, – 'this is a pleasure I no longer hoped for! Where have you been since I last saw you?' Then, observing Mr. St. Hubert, with whom he had become slightly acquainted at the inn where Mrs. Temple's illness had occurred, 'And have I also the satisfaction of again meeting you, sir? This is the most fortunate day I have known since we parted.'

He spoke with a mixture of cheerfulness and dejection, that showed he had undergone some deep and recent anxiety.

'I hope,' said Mr. St. Hubert, 'neither your fellow traveller, nor her little girl, have been ill on the road?'

'The former,' answered he, 'has been most alarmingly ill. We reached this place with difficulty, about three weeks ago, and yesterday, for the first time, she was able for a few hours to leave her bed.' /

'This is a sad account! But I trust, since, some little amendment has began to show itself, she will ere long, recruit her strength, and afford you the gratification of gradually seeing her entirely recover. How are her spirits?'

'Better in the midst of all her sufferings, than mine have been in witnessing them.'

'I am afraid it is too usually the case with men to be desponding in matters relating to illness, whether of our friends, or of ourselves. Women make better patients, as well as better nurses. Has your invalid any friends in Florence?'

'None at all, I believe; but she has been so little in a state to bear society, that I have entirely foreborn making inquiries concerning any of the English who might now be here.'

Then looking round at the noble statues by which they were encircled:

'I am glad,' cried he, 'especially glad, to have met you in this room! It is the spot / that most exclusively attracts me, and many a day I have entered the gallery and departed, without casting a glance towards any of its other treasures.'

'Perhaps the saddened mood of your mind had some share in exciting this peculiar preference. These are, in truth, most appropriate objects of contemplation to a melancholy man; but, believe me, – as your friend revives, you will acquire a taste for something less mournful, and the Venus de' Medici[52] will obtain her due portion of homage.'

'On such terms, may your augury soon be verified,' cried Walsingham.

And again addressing Agnes; 'You have not,' said he, 'answered my inquiry, and told me where you have been?'

'I am just arrived from Venice.'

'And what impression did that singular city make upon you?'

'I saw it under so many advantages, that I am perhaps scarcely a disinterested judge of / it. Everything contributed to make my residence there delightful, and, of course, to make me love both the people and the place.'

'A native inhabitant could scarcely say more.'

'A native inhabitant,' cried Mr. St. Hubert, 'would say a great deal more! He would tell you, there is no other city fit to live in. What we regard as inconveniences, to him are recommendations. Our paved streets, and the noise of horses and carriages, to him are odious. Riding and walking are efforts he hates as much as the Turks; and his dismal black gondolas, and muddy canals, (represented by Canaletti as being so translucent),[53] are as dear to him as are mists, and precipices and barren mountains to the Swiss or Highlander.'

'The gayest description of Venice I have any where met with,' said Walsingham, 'is in Goldoni's Memoirs:[54] but although, even in *his* time it had fallen considerably from its / "high estate," how infinitely lower must it now be sunk! The sight of its decaying and empty palaces, and all its vestiges of past magnificence, would sadden the most indifferent observer, were it not for the remembrance that the government of Venice, in her day of power, was the most systematically atrocious on the face of the earth!'

'Bad enough! – bad enough!' cried Mr. St. Hubert. 'But even the devil, you know, is not quite so black as he is painted. For my own part, I confess, I am but imperfectly acquainted with Venetian history. I have a strong impression, however, that the despotism exercised by their rulers, fell, not upon the people, but upon the nobles; and I console myself by reflecting, that "amongst all those potent grave, and reverend Signors,"[55] not one would have exchanged his perilous rank for the security of a humble station. But we will discuss the point more at length another time; for here comes the *custode*, to warn us that it / is near three o'clock, and to invite us to march off.'

Walsingham accompanied them to the door of their boarding house, and asked permission to call upon them in the evening. The request was readily granted, and they parted.

'And now, my dear,' said Mr. St. Hubert when he was gone, 'tell me who this new friend of mine is, for to you he seems to be well known, though I am ignorant even of his name. I met him strolling about one evening near our memorable inn at Dole,[56] and we walked and talked an hour or two together, but I had never seen him before, and hardly expected to have seen him again.'

Agnes readily gave him all the information in her power.

'I am glad,' said the old gentleman, 'your acquaintance with him began under such favourable auspices. The guest and associate of Lord Glenfeld cannot but be a man of character and respectability. But who is / the sick lady he travels with? Is he married?'

'I do not know,' answered Agnes, 'and I am a little surprised at the sort of mystery he seems to make of the nature of his connexion with her.'

'Were it not for that same mystery – which, after all, may be purely accidental – I would have recommended to you, to make an offer of going to see the poor desolate soul. It might be acceptable now she seems recovering a little.'

'I would have proposed it most gladly,' cried Agnes, 'had I not been apprehensive of causing him more embarrassment than pleasure. But you, dear sir, might insinuate, when I am not by, such a wish on my part, and that would leave him more at liberty to decline or accept it, than if the offer were made directly by myself.'

Mr. St. Hubert agreed with her, that this would be the most delicate way of proceeding, / and without hesitation undertook to be her spokesman.

Walsingham neglected not to profit by the permission he had received, and re-appeared in the evening with an aspect somewhat less over-cast. The conversation for a considerable time, turned on general subjects, and was kept up with a certain degree of animation; but during a pause, Agnes who had been arguing herself into courage for the purpose, ventured to say:

'Have you yet, Mr. Walsingham, received any letters from your friends in Paris?'

With a singular expression, partaking, as it appeared, both of pity and admiration, he answered; 'From Paris I have not, – but from my agent in London, I found tidings awaiting me at Bologna that overwhelmed me with astonishment! From the moment I read his extraordinary communication, till I fortunately encountered you this morning, my thoughts have been incessantly dwelling, with / shame and self-reproach, upon the remembrance of the brief interview

I had with you at the inn in France. Misguided by injurious surmises, instead of accosting you with the respect and deference due to your noble – your exalted firmness, under a reverse so trying, – I am painfully conscious that the reserve and distance of my behaviour must have wounded and shocked you!'

'For a few moments,' answered Agnes, blushing, yet gently smiling, 'perhaps it did: but I had been taught to think too well of you, to imagine it possible that the change could originate from anything but misconception. Let me not talk of myself, however; rather give me leave to ask whether you are doing quite wisely to remain here in Italy when you ought to be actively attending to your affairs in England?'

'They can suffer no detriment by my absence. There is no one to dispute with me the claim Mr. Wharton's own attestation / has invested me with: – but – were it otherwise – were I in danger of losing all by my delay, I cannot forsake the charge I have undertaken.'

To this, Agnes could hazard no reply: but she would have given much to know in what exact light to regard that charge.

When Walsingham took leave, Mr. St. Hubert accompanied him down stairs, and at the door, said: 'Miss Danvers, I have reason to think, would be most happy to relieve, as far as might be in her power, the solitude of your friend's sick chamber: but, without some encouragement, she is too modest to venture on what would, perhaps, be deemed an intrusion.'

'If my poor Georgiana could prevail on herself to admit any body, Miss Danvers is the person she would in preference to all others select. She was charmed with her during their transient meeting on the road. But, Mr. St. Hubert – she is now a different creature; ill, – / very ill, both in body and mind! Her nature is gentle and patient; but disease sometimes overmasters her; her discourse is rambling and incoherent; and knowing how little she can command herself, she dreads being seen, lest she should suffer any words to escape her that might betray the subjects of sorrow she regards as sacred. State all this to Miss Danvers, dear sir, and bid her pity and forgive us!'

Mr. St. Hubert could find no words to answer this mournful representation, but pressing the young man's hand with affectionate sympathy, he returned to the impatient Agnes.

She eagerly enquired how the application she had authorized him to make, had been received, and heard with sincere compassion the answer it had drawn forth. They speculated upon the affair in sundry ways, agreeing that there now seemed little reason to imagine the invalid was Walsingham's wife, since the sorrows he had spoken of seemed to be exclusively / her own, and only participated in by him from kindness and commiseration: 'At all events,' said Mr. St. Hubert: 'I firmly believe this young man is devoting himself to some office of charity, that if well understood, would do honour to the goodness of his heart. I have lived many years in the world, and have seen and heard of much vice and iniquity; but I have not yet learnt to distrust the existence of real virtue, and am always willing to hail its unostentatious appearance whenever I meet with it. And who is there amongst us, who has not encountered more good than evil in the course of his career? The fact unfortunately is, the latter makes more impression upon us than the former; but I deny that it is more frequent. For one thoroughly depraved scoundrel, we might reckon up, (besides the truly excellent) fifty tolerably honest men, and fifty others of negative worth, who, if they do no good, may be said to do no harm.' /

'I love,' said Agnes, 'to hear you profess, dear sir, these kind and liberal sentiments! They are often asserted to belong only to youth, but in you they still glow as warmly as ever, and are, I really believe, the cause of your being so gay and happy, and so acceptable to persons of all ages.'

'You have made me a very pretty speech, my fair friend, for which I should like vastly, in return, to ask you a few impertinent questions!'

'As many as you please,' said Agnes, amused by this result of her compliment.

'Well then, will you tell me what Walsingham was alluding to when he spoke of your *trying reverse*, and his own *injurious surmises?* In short, will you explain to me, what was the general meaning of the long speech, that with so contrite a visage, he addressed to you?'

'It meant, dear sir, that when he first knew me, I was supposed to be a great heiress, and / was living in luxury and splendour. A little later it was discovered, that there was a mighty flaw in my title; that I had no right even to the name I bore, much less to the fortune that had been ascribed to me; and later still, it has been ascertained that Mr. Walsingham himself is the legal heir whom I had been unconsciously defrauding. When we met near Dole, he knew nothing of his own newly-acquired affluence, nor of my recent downfall; but he considered me, I imagine, as a fugitive from my guardian and friends, and a young damsel, who, not very respectably, was seeking adventures on the King's highway. Accordingly, he treated me rather coolly; but, on the whole, quite as well as he was justified in thinking I deserved.'

'*Cospetto!*[67] what a history! and have you, my good child, been able to preserve so much unaffected serenity in the midst of so woeful a change in all your prospects, in all your former habits? I honour you, from my soul, for / such dignity of mind! The fatherly regard for you which has been creeping on in my heart more and more warmly every day, is, from this hour, secured to you for life!'

He extended his hand to her, with moistened eyes as he ceased speaking, and Agnes weeping and smiling at the same moment, eagerly seized and carried it to her lips. After this little effusion of reciprocal kindness, he made her give him a more minute account of her past life. She told every thing except what related to the supposed consanguinity between them; and ended by saying, she believed, or rather hoped, she had a near relation at Rome, on whose protection she depended; and added, that it was to seek him she had determined upon visiting Italy.

With increased interest in her behalf, Mr. St. Hubert, when she paused, earnestly said: 'Should he however, disappoint your expectations, rely upon me, my child; I will never abandon you.' /

What balm to her heart was this assurance! She thought of his recent words: 'Who is there amongst us who has not encountered more good than evil in his career?' The circumstance of meeting with so many disinterested spirits, willing to befriend her in her portionless state, illustrated most strikingly, (in her case, at least) the justice of his observation.

'It is strange,' resumed he, after a few moments' silent meditation, 'that from so many different quarters I should so continually hear the name of Wharton sounded in my ears! Miss Temple – the meek and quiet – began the strain; Mr. Walsingham next took it up, and now it is pursued by you. The name is not very uncommon, and had I heard it but once or twice it would have made no impression upon me; but haunted by it as I have been, it recalls to my mind times long since gone by, and throws me into some perplexity. Whilst I was practising my profession / at Rome, I heard from my father that the youngest of my two sisters had married a Mr. Wharton. He spoke of him with warm affection, and the highest esteem, and whatever he may have turned out afterwards, there is reason to think he was at that time an honourable and deserving man. Subsequent letters informed me that my sister was the happiest of wives, and Wharton daily giving stronger proofs of undiminished attachment to her. Ere the first year of their marriage had elapsed, she died, alas! in giving birth to a daughter, and terrible was the desolation throughout her whole family. She was the general darling – the pride – the gem of our race. My poor father never entirely recovered the shock, and all his later letters were tinctured with melancholy regrets. Mr. Wharton, I was afterwards informed, in terms most indignant, by my eldest sister Mrs. Danvers, had at the end of three years married again. To say the truth, / this did not appear to me an act that merited such severe reprehension; he was young, had shewn himself fond of domestic life, and of female society, and I saw nothing in his making a second choice but what was naturally to be expected. Mrs. Danvers however, was always a little eccentric, her feelings were enthusiastic, and her temper, though generous, was hasty and impetuous. She had adored her lost sister, and thought it a sort of insult to her memory to give her (*so soon*, as she was pleased to term it) a successor. She never saw him I believe, after the heinous deed she so much reprobated; his little girl I understood, followed her mother to an early grave, and I ceased to hear any thing further of my unknown brother-in-law till I began this journey. Now, do you think my dear child, that *my* Wharton, distinguished for probity and honour, can be the same as your plotting and deceitful guardian?' /

'Do you know sir, whether *your* Wharton had a sister? A widow, named Marchmont?'

'No – of that circumstance I know nothing. She either was too insignificant to be mentioned by my family correspondents, or they were themselves unacquainted with her.'

'Then,' resumed Agnes, 'I am totally unable to assist you in ascertaining his identity with the person you have been speaking of. During the seven years I lived with him, I never heard any allusion made to his having been twice married. The only wife that was ever spoken of, had been, when he was united to her, an extremely wealthy widow with one daughter, who was left to his sole guardianship at her mother's death. That daughter, as I have informed you, expired at Calais in her eleventh year, and I was immediately compelled to become her substitute.'

'It seems impossible, at this distance of / time, to clear up the point in question; and therefore, we will let the subject drop. It would do me no great honour, nor to my nephew either, to be able to prove our connexion with such a personage; and it was only as a matter of curiosity I sought any information about it.'

He then bade her good night, and they proceeded to their several chambers.

The next morning, Mr. Walsingham called upon them at an early hour, and accompanied them to one of their usual haunts, the Palazzo Pitti. In their way thither, he said to Agnes with an air of deep feeling:

'You will not, I hope, hesitate to believe, that it was with the warmest gratitude I listened last night to the benevolent offer made in your name! On every account, I grieve that it cannot be accepted. When you saw my poor Georgina in France, though already a shaken and nervous valetudinarian, she was very far from being reduced to the deplorable / state she is in now. The letters she has since received from England, have nearly demolished her; and to confess to you the sad truth, I am become almost hopeless of ever seeing her recover!'

'Are you not,' said Agnes compassionately, 'too easily alarming yourself? Does her physician countenance these gloomy forebodings?'

'He is an honest and a sensible man, and when I have urged him to exert his utmost skill in this pitiable case, has answered in the poet's words, and answered wisely, and truly: Her malady, alas! is beyond my reach; I have not the art to

> Erase the written troubles of the brain.[58]

Medicine can do nothing for her. Yet,' continued Walsingham, 'it is not her spirit that has rebelled against misfortune, but her fragile constitution, that has sunk under it. A more humble and submissive / temper was never given to a human being. Perhaps she was always destined to be early snatched away, and the grief to which her loss will be attributed, may have been but the auxiliary, not the principal agent in her destruction.'

To give a little relief to the sadness of this conversation, Mr. St. Hubert now asked, how the child who accompanied them, had been disposed of during her mother's illness?

'I have entrusted her to the care of a Swiss lady, who takes in a few scholars of about the same age, and appears to make them happy, which is nearly all that at four years old can be required.'

On entering the long suite of rooms in the Palazzo, so splendidly adorned with the *chefs-d'œuvre*[59] of almost every school, Mr. St. Hubert, as was his wont, made Agnes pause before each picture he deemed particularly deserving attention, delivering at the same time, an instructive and amusing little / lecture upon its distinguishing merits, or partial defects. Walsingham, standing beside them, and listening to these comments, almost forgot his anxieties in the pleasure of hearing the one talk, and seeing the other intently hearken. Her countenance was so intelligent, her occasional remarks were so apt and spirited, her deference to her instructor was so affectionately respectful, and she herself, when the old man described the essential characteristics of beauty, both as relates to expression and form, presented so perfect an illustration of his text, that Walsingham felt he had but to look at Agnes, to understand the whole dissertation. Whilst in the rooms, he spoke but little; as they afterwards proceeded homeward, however, he said: 'I never before experienced so forcibly, the advantage of being admitted to survey works of art, under the guidance of a really enlightened connoisseur. My eyes have been opened this morning to behold innumerable excellencies, I had hitherto / been utterly blind to; to estimate difficulties overcome, and premeditated effects produced, which, till now, I had never dreamt of. I should not despair, could I promise myself the benefit of a longer association with such an instructor, of becoming in time more worthy to contemplate, and more capable of enjoying the master-pieces of this country.'

'It is very true,' said Mr. St. Hubert, disdaining all false modesty, 'that an experienced old guide, such as I am, may be of infinite use to one who has never made a regular study of the arts. The eye requires to be gradually exercised and educated before it can appreciate the attainments of real genius of any description. In poetry, for instance, an ignorant man, or a child (which is nearly synonymous) will delight in a familiar ballad, and turn from a sublime ode, or a classical epic with indifference; a wax figure, coloured, and gaudily decked out, will please a peasant / more than the noblest marble statue; and where has there ever been a servant, or an uninformed mechanic, that has not found more amusement at a shewy pantomime, or a vulgar farce, than at a regular dramatic production, however admirable? It is the same with painting and music, and every other talent, the produce of a high degree of civilization and refinement; and I fear there are many who class themselves amongst the really well-educated, who, if they were honest, would own that the portrait of a favourite horse, or fox-hound, or the minute finish of a Dutch green-stall,[60] gave them a thousand times more gratification, than the works of all the Italian masters put together.'

'I beg you, however, to believe,' said Walsingham, with the first smile which had that morning escaped him, 'my ignorance, though great and acknowledged, does not extend quite so far!' /

'I never supposed it did,' returned Mr. St. Hubert, laughing at his own superfluous oratory; 'but when a man begins riding a darling hobby, he seldom knows how to stop.'

Whilst thus discoursing, the trio arrived in sight of the post office, and Agnes entreated permission to stop and enquire whether there were any letters for her. In a few minutes, she was put in possession, with true delight, of a thick despatch from Lady Glenfeld, to whom she had written early on her arrival at Venice, and requested that her answer might be directed, *Poste Restante*,[61] Florence. Walsingham, at the door of their temporary home, solicited leave to linger with them a little longer, that he might, when Miss Danvers had perused her letter, hear what news their mutual friend had sent from England.

Nearly half the first page of her large paper, / was devoted by the kind Bertha, to thanking Agnes, for her two long letters; and to the most affectionate expressions of regret at their separation. She then proceeded to talk of family affairs; told her that Lord Glenfeld's uncle was with them in the country, and a shade better, though too evidently declining. Mrs. Le Strange and her daughters were returned from Spa; the two eldest engaged, and on the point of being well married; but Isabel was come back thin, spiritless, and quite unlike her former self. 'I greatly fear,' continued Bertha, 'she has left her heart behind her, or rather, that its present possessor has followed her to England, has been rejected by mamma, and is deeply regretted by my poor sister. Should you meet with Walsingham again, I wish you could ask him from me, what he knows and thinks of a young Frenchman, Monsieur de Verneuil, whom he used to be much with, and appeared to have a friendship for, at Paris. He was once, I / have heard, a fervent admirer of yours, but though it has been said that

> "Love will hope where reason would despair,"[62]

it does not appear that *his* love has been able to survive the complete annihilation of hope, which your departure has effected. Isabel, who knew something of him at Paris, met him again at Spa, and in despite of all mamma's watchfulness, an attachment arose between them, which, I must own, does not seem to be either of a slight or transient nature.

'Harry Cowley, another of your quondam lovers, is up to the ears in the study of the law, and Lord Glenfeld thinks he will force himself forward, and hereafter make a figure in the profession. He called once or twice during the short stay we made in town, and my Lord encouraged him to come to us often when we return. My aunt Marchmont is doing penance, but not rigorously, as boarder / in the family of a country apothecary, one hundred and twenty miles from London. She has one maid, a village girl; visits, if condescendingly inclined, the wife of the curate or attorney; gets a drive occasionally, in the one horse chaise of a neighbouring farmer, and thinks it a great event when the squire of the parish and his daughters, in their old fashioned chariot, pass her window in their way to the nearest town.[63] What a life, after seven years past in all the gaiety and dissipation of Paris! But she will, by degrees, become perfectly reconciled to it, for as mamma says, (to whom she has already repeatedly written, to know what the latest fashions are for bonnets, &c.) "these little things please little men,"[64] and it is only pursuing upon a smaller scale, the same interests that engrossed her abroad.

'I fancy, my dearest, the lady who is travelling with Walsingham, is not unknown to me. I am not at liberty however, to enter into any details respecting her; but I may / safely recommend to you, if you see him any more, to speak gently to him, my Agnes; you know not how well he merits it! I am afraid our letter to him has miscarried; but no matter, it was very short, and wholly on business, and the probability is, he has, ere this, learnt through some other channel, the change in his fortune. Just at present, the news will but little affect him. Remember me to him most affectionately, if ever you have the opportunity, and tell him, that neither of my brothers are more truly dear to me than he is.'

The rest of the letter contained little that would be interesting to repeat, though to Agnes every word in it was precious.

Walsingham had silently observed her, as she stood reading it at the window, and traced every change it produced in her expressive face; sometimes he saw a half smile escape her; then a look more serious, followed by a / gentle sigh, and at last, he caught a momentary glance directed towards himself, so full of softness, that it drew him involuntarily to her side:

'Has our friend,' said he, with some diffidence, 'communicated to you any thing that I may be permitted to hear?'

Agnes without hesitation read to him, in a voice that gave full effect to the words, Lady Glenfeld's tender and sisterly greeting. He was sensibly affected by it, and with much emotion, cried:

'Sweet, and ever-amiable Bertha! Where was there ever a heart more warm and friendly than hers? I will go home, and write to her this very day.'

'You must first give yourself time,' said Agnes, 'to hear another passage in her letter, which you only can answer.' She then read aloud the enquiry concerning Monsieur de Verneuil, which she had been requested to address to him. /

'I shall be glad,' said Walsingham, 'of an opportunity of doing de Verneuil justice. I both esteem and love him.'

He then bade Agnes and Mr. St. Hubert good morning, and was leaving the room, when the latter called after him:

'We shall see you this evening?'

'Thank you a thousand times for your patient endurance of my *maussade*[65] company! I must not, however, permit myself to play truant too often, or too long from my poor charge. She is able sometimes to listen to a little reading, though her sight is so weakened by constant head-aches, she is forbidden to open a book herself. To-morrow, if you will allow me, I shall be most happy to accompany you again on your perambulations.'

'To-morrow, then, be it; we shall expect you at half past ten.'

Accordingly, the next morning he came at the hour appointed.

As one of the effects of Lady Glenfeld's / newly-received letter, was to bring up the frequent mention of her name between Agnes and Mr. Walsingham, she availed herself of the circumstance, in the course of the many hours they were together, to ask whether he was related to her?

'Not at all,' he answered, 'but I have known her from her very infancy. Her eldest brother and I, were school-fellows and intimate friends. I had lost my father, and my home was not a happy one. Le Strange knew it, and prevailed upon his mother, to let him invite me to spend with him many of my holidays at her country house. Bertha was then a mere child, but always the most amiable of children, and, of the four sisters, the only one I was ever permitted to be sociable, and at my ease with. Mrs. Le Strange would have been frightened, stripling as I was, to have seen me presume to pay any attention to the other daughters. Isabel however, / would gladly have broken from the restraints imposed upon her, to join with her brothers and myself in our minor sports; but a vigilant governess, and a lynx-eyed mother, were over-matches for her, and she was forced to look on at a distance, whilst Bertha, neither being so pretty, nor so nearly approaching to womanhood, was suffered to ride with us, to learn archery, to row, or to steer the pleasure-boat, in short, to become expert in most of the pastimes usual amongst boys.[66] The consequence as you can testify, has not been to render her manners boisterous and unfeminine, or to harden her heart; on the contrary, she in many instances inspired us with humanity, but never was seduced herself to be guilty of the smallest want of feeling.'

'That I can well believe,' said Agnes, 'and also, that upon the whole, the intercourse she was allowed to hold with you or her brothers, was beneficial to both parties. / It must have made her more helpful and courageous, and you more considerate and gentle.'

'I am persuaded,' said Mr. St. Hubert, 'that it is always an advantage to boys to have sisters. I hope you see a proof of it in my own amiable person! I had two; one who plagued and domineered over me without mercy, and was allowed to do so in right of primogeniture, but who loved me in the main, and would have put her hand into the fire to serve me; the other, much the junior of both, was a little pet lamb, all innocence and softness, whom it was a pleasure to protect, and a privilege to amuse. I have lost them both; but I still look back with affection to the days of childhood, when she who tyrannised over me, and I, who so often rebelled, agreed only in being the voluntary slaves of our mutual darling.'

'In how few strokes, Mr. St. Hubert,' / said Walsingham, 'have you drawn a family picture, that sets you all in full view before us!'

'Help it out with a little imagination, and you might indeed make of it what the French call a good *tableau de genre*.[67] Represent a mutinous and sulky boy, repelling one sister, and detaining the other on his knee; a tall, angry miss looking haughtily at him, and holding forth a bunch of grapes to bribe the little one away. Add to the picture a kitten and puppy quarrelling; an old nurse scolding as she enters; and above all, give interest to the scene, by the delineation of the loveliest smiling child that ever was beheld.'

'What a pity, dear sir,' cried Agnes, 'you should never have painted upon canvass, a picture you know so well how to paint in words.'

'It would have been thrown away, at Rome – who would have cared for such a domestic / representation there? To my father it would, no doubt, have been valuable, but the idea never occurred to me in his life time; and the individual exists not at the present day, whom it would interest, either in England or elsewhere.'

The period appointed for Agnes' residence in Florence passed rapidly away, and her newly-awakened misgivings as to the reception she might meet with from Mr. Danvers, made it natural that she should feel impatient to be at a certainty respecting her future fate, and eager to avoid all unnecessary delays in the prosecution of the journey. Yet, it grieved her to leave Walsingham a prey to still greater melancholy than he had experienced before their arrival. He had for many days tasted the pleasure of familiar intercourse; he had evidently attached himself to their society, and found relief from their conversation. Whenever the subject of their departure was touched upon, the whole expression / of his countenance became saddened; but he forbore giving utterance to his regrets, and two days before they went, took leave of them, after a long visit, with the same calmness apparently as usual. On the next, they every moment expected to see him again; but he appeared no more; and they at last decided, that he purposely held aloof to avoid the misery of saying farewell. They both drew a sigh of pity for the desolate state in which they left him; and Agnes never thought of, or heard him mentioned, but with an aching heart.

They travelled by the Perugia[68] road, and spent at that place one very interesting day, pursuing on the next, their way to Rome without again stopping, (as the weather was bad,) except to dine and sleep.

It is hard to speak of a first entrance into ROME with the same indifference we should speak of a first entrance into an English market town! But so diffusely has the subject / been already treated, that nothing remains to be said. Classical tourists, romantic tourists, political tourists, tourists for pleasure, for health, or for fashion, have been so numerous and so recent, that no readers remain who would have patience to endure the threadbare topic. If the present writer has the misfortune to be found tedious, it shall not be by the common-places of shallow learning, and affected enthusiasm.

Before their journey terminated, Agnes' plan of proceeding had been fully arranged in her own mind. When asked by Mr. St. Hubert, (after they had passed their examination at the Custom House), where she desired to be set down? Her answer was, that she had no choice at present but to go to an hotel, not being yet certain that the home she had looked forward to, would be open to receive her.

The good old man seemed pained by this reply. – 'Would to heaven,' he exclaimed, / 'the home you speak of were beneath my roof! It vexes me, my dear child, to leave you at an inn in this unprotected state, unknown to, and unknowing a single individual in the place; it seems like an unmanly desertion of you; and methinks I should feel happier to stay with you, than to expose myself to the reproaches of my own conscience by losing sight of you.'

'You are too – too good, dearest sir!' cried Agnes, affected almost to tears by his kindness, – 'but fear nothing for me: have I not got my faithful Adrienne with me? And do I not rely upon you to recommend me to a respectable house? Besides – it will probably be but for one night that I shall require such an abode. Meanwhile,' she added, presenting to him a sealed letter, 'may I request you to take charge of this, and to give it into your nephew's hands? I might have sent it,' she smilingly continued, 'by a common messenger, and spared you the surprise / I see painted in your looks! But I prefer avoiding, as much as I am able, the very appearance of mystery; and though I cannot immediately explain to you the purport of this letter, – I wish to make no secret of having business with your nephew, which, if he calls upon me, (as I request), to-morrow morning, requires me to be alone with him during his visit. Therefore, dear sir, come not near me till after two o'clock. When you have seen me properly disposed of, you can tell him where to find me.'

'You are a most singular being!' cried her astonished auditor, 'open and guarded at the same moment! But though you somewhat puzzle me, my child, I have no suspicion in the remotest degree to your disadvantage. Your letter shall be punctually delivered, and you may depend upon not seeing me till the hour you appoint.'

He then gave orders to their driver to conduct them to an hotel he named; saw her / installed in a suitable apartment – recommended her strongly to the mistress of the house; and bade her adieu.

Agnes' sleep was broken and uneasy. The crisis of her fate was at hand, and she felt herself called upon, whatever might ensue from the conference of the next day, to bear it with courage and calmness. To lose the favourite wish of her heart – that of finding herself possessed of a brother – seemed to her, now, but too probable. In compensation, she had acquired not only a warm friend in Mr. St. Hubert, but an active protector, able to guide her labours, and to secure for her the patronage, without which they must be unavailing. Should she – thus aided – succeed in obtaining for herself the little independence she coveted, she determined, if possible, not to think herself unhappy.

The hour arrived – to her so important – that brought Mr. Danvers to the hotel. She trembled as she heard him announced, and in / defiance of all her efforts to maintain a composed demeanour, could with difficulty, on his entrance motion to him to be seated, or find voice to utter a word. On his part, there was of course none of the same agitation; but much, and very obvious impatience, to know the cause for which he had been summoned, After a short silence:

'I have obeyed your directions, madam,' said he, 'and brought with me the papers you wished me to refer to in your presence. May I be permitted to ask from what motive you have expressed such a desire?'

Agnes summoning all her firmness, answered (at first, in an ill-assured and tremulous accent, but as she proceeded, with more steadiness,)

'I can only reply to your question, sir, by troubling you with a long and a strange recital, personally regarding myself. If you can arm yourself with patience to hear it, you will clearly understand both the reason of my / writing to you from Paris, and of my seeking this conference with you here.'

'You are then, as I suspected, the lady who addressed to me some months ago, an inquiry concerning my birth-place, and the name of my parents?'

Agnes bowed assent, and then began her 'round unvarnished tale,'[69] bringing it down to the present moment. Except his astonishment, nothing could exceed the fixed and earnest attention with which Mr. Danvers heard her. Of the genuineness of her story he entertained not a moment's doubt. She spoke of his mother with such perfect knowledge of her temper and habits; she recorded so many little anecdotes of himself which she could only have gathered from that mother's lips; and in stating her removal after the death of Mrs. Danvers, to the habitation of the Blakes, she so completely confirmed what they themselves had written to him, that he hesitated not one moment to give implicit credit to all she said. / Yet – promising as was this circumstance, he found himself under the painful necessity of telling her, that notwithstanding the perfect credibility of her narrative, the conclusion she had naturally drawn from it of being the daughter of Mrs. Danvers was utterly erroneous.

'The proof of this is, my dear young lady,' added he, with an air of unaffected concern, 'that my father has been dead five and twenty years, and left me, an only child, under the care of my mother and grandfather, when I was just entering my eighth year. At that age, I could not have remained in ignorance of it, had she married again; – and I am positively convinced she never did. Her own letters all attest it; they bear her usual signature, and so does her last will. That something extraordinary – inexplicable, was attached to her connexion with you, struck me from the very first. In writing to me, you will believe, she never sought to represent you as her daughter; but / she occasionally alluded to having taken charge of a motherless child, though without specifying whence she came, or to whom she owed her birth. There was indeed, a sort of wildness and incoherency in her manner of touching upon the subject, that often surprised me. It was as if she was harassed one moment, by starts of compunction, counteracted the next, by anger and hatred. I often applied to her for the solution of these inconsistencies; but always in vain. In this posthumous document,' continued he, selecting a particular paper from the packet he had brought, 'you will see the most remarkable illustration of what I mean. It bears no date, and is neither signed nor directed; but Mr. Blake, who was left her executor, found it amongst her effects, and forwarded it to me exactly in the state in which you see it.'

He then handed to Agnes the following unintelligible rhapsody: – /

'Man without a heart! Oh, that I could but hope I had found at last the means to make thee feel! That I could but know thou wert mourning in bitterness and sorrow thy irrevocable loss! Yes – it *shall* be irrevocable, unless I should one day hear thou hast begun to show symptoms of surviving humanity and affection. Hard, hard of nature hast thou hitherto been! – without memory – without gratitude for past felicity – without concern for the living or reverence for the dead! Was it not monstrous to seclude from sight – to neglect – to treat as a base-born intruder, the treasure Providence still entrusted to thy love? How did I find her situated in her father's splendid mansion? She was consigned to the worst room it contained; she was as meanly clad as she was lodged; she was committed to the sole care of a young and inexperienced peasant girl; and if ever she was remembered by her unnatural parent – if ever she beheld him, it was as it were by *stealth* – he was / *ashamed* of his little Agnes! Wretch! wretch! What are the pangs that can ever sufficiently expiate such a dereliction from all virtue – from all sense of justice – all remains of honour? Poor babe! She is here at least beloved; here, in obscurity and almost indigence, she is happier than in the chilling atmosphere of her father's dwelling. Yet – I sometimes tremble lest in seeking to punish *thee*, I should have brought down evil upon *her* innocent head! When I am gone, who is there to protect?....'

Here the blotted and scarcely-decipherable scroll suddenly broke off, and Agnes letting it drop despondingly from her hands, exclaimed: –

'Alas! who shall venture to give meaning to such an enigma as this? I can scarcely even hope that time will clear it up, since, pardon me, sir, it appears to me more like / the ravings of delirium, than the language of one in full possession of her reason.'

'Such,' cried Mr. Danvers, 'I must confess, has ever been my own opinion. Let me, however, observe, that the remonstrance – acrimonious and flighty as it is – was mentally addressed, there can be no doubt, to a real person, and that person I believe to have been your father. Whether culpable or innocent, whether altogether the victim of my mother's misconceptions, or suffering in consequence of his own aggressions, there is nothing here to explain. These letters,' he added, putting the packet on the table, 'you may take your own time to peruse. I am sorry to say, they contain not any thing that can tend to render the affair less impenetrable. Amongst them is the one addressed to me by Mr. Blake, after my mother's death. In it he speaks of you in all simplicity of heart, as her daughter; but knowing so well how mistaken was his belief, I never gave his / words any serious attention, and it is probable he thinks me, of all brothers, the most unnatural. Meanwhile, dear madam, your case appears to me so peculiarly cruel, that I cannot but feel for you from my very soul! If there is any method by which I can serve you, name it, I entreat, and be assured there is nothing I will not gladly undertake to prove to you how sincerely interested I am in your behalf.'

Poor Agnes, who had had time to overcome the first bitterness of sorrow that accompanied the total discomfiture of the feeble hope she had till now involuntarily entertained – answered his friendly offers with the gratitude they deserved, and the frankness natural to her disposition: –

'You are probably aware, sir,' she said, 'that Mr. St. Hubert, your excellent uncle, has been the companion of my journey from the day I left Paris. He has been kind enough, after having seen some of my attempts, to encourage me to pursue miniature painting as a / profession, and should I find employment, I shall ever regard the counsels and directions he has given me, as the main foundations of my success. You, sir, who are obliging enough to express a wish to be useful to me, can in no way contribute more to my advantage, than by uniting your good offices to his, if after examining what I have done, you are not afraid that I shall disgrace your recommendation.'

And so saying, renouncing all further recurrence to the subject on which their conversation had begun, she put before him the few miniatures she had brought from France, and some of the studies she had made at Venice, awaiting his decision in silent and timid anxiety. The opinion he gave was gratifying and consolatory; and he readily promised to exert himself to the utmost to obtain for her the encouragement her talents so well merited. They parted soon after, and Agnes left to herself, yielded to nature, and gave relief to her oppressed heart, by the indulgence of an abundant / flood of tears. Once more she saw herself a lone being in creation; at eighteen years of age, with the probability of a long life before her, she was without kindred – without a home – without even a name she could legally appropriate – without other means of existence than such as depended upon the precarious favour of the public! It was a perspective that at once filled her with grief, terror, and self-compassion, and her tears long continued to flow with undiminished bitterness. By degrees, the elasticity of spirit natural to youth, and constitutionally so to her, began to regain its ascendancy, and the brighter side of the picture became visible. The fond friendship of Lady Glenfeld – the paternal kindness of Mr. St. Hubert; the good-will manifested for her by his nephew; the faithful attachment of Adrienne, – one by one, each of these blessings presented itself to her remembrance, in addition to the inestimable advantage of possessing perfect health / and talents that might at once contribute to her independence and her amusement. She offered up to heaven a silent prayer for submission to its decrees, and thankfulness for what she still possessed, bathed her swollen and aching eyes, and pacing some time up and down the room, was almost restored, when Mr. St. Hubert arrived, to her customary state of spirits.

'Well, my dear child,' said he, on entering, 'I hope I am not come too soon? I have had my watch in my hand this half hour, and did not set out for your hotel till ten minutes after the time you had appointed. So, you see, I was willing to give you law, and to show you also how well you might trust to my discretion.'

Agnes assured him, with great truth, that at no moment could his presence have been more welcome to her. 'I have much need, dear sir,' she added, 'of your advice and assistance, and I feel so well convinced that I / may securely depend upon both, that I shall make no scruple of laying such a tax upon your good nature.'

'That's right – that's right; without further preface, come to the point – I am at your disposal; only remember, that I hate suspense.'

She then told him (what indeed he knew already, though he had been too delicate to allude to it) that her interview with his nephew had convinced her she had nothing henceforward to rely upon but her own exertions. 'I am, therefore,' she continued, 'resolved to devote myself immediately, with all the diligence of which I am capable, to the art of painting, and to make it my exclusive employment. To put such a plan in execution, it will be necessary I should be provided with a fixed home, and what I wish to consult you about, is the choice of such a home. Were it practicable, I should like to be received as a boarder in some quiet, respectable, family; but if that is attended with any difficulty, it would / be a great comfort to me to procure a lodging as near you as possible.'

Mr. St. Hubert rubbed his hands, and with an air of glee, answered: 'You will never do for the heroine of a novel, my dear, for you seem to have no taste for self-incurred difficulties, and no pleasure in throwing yourself in the way of needless adventures! you have most of the other attributes for such a personage; but to destroy the interest of your story, you have common sense (a terrible dead weight in a romance) and you have forethought, and a strong propensity, to prefer what is proper, to what is striking. Well such being your straight forward dullness of character, I have an arrangement to propose, which I think may exactly suit you. The enormous size of many of the Italian houses you are well acquainted with. That which I inhabit is an ancient Palazzo, big enough to contain a troop of cavalry, horses and all. The family to which it belongs, is much reduced in circumstances, / but consists of persons well-mannered and well-born. They give up to me the number of rooms I want for myself and my servant, and, on the same floor, there are three or four others, still unoccupied, which I looked at this morning, and which on every account, would be the most desirable you could meet with. The light for painting is good in the room which you might make your *studio;* the situation is healthy and airy; the price is moderate, and though we should be living in separate apartments, and in perfect independence of each other, we should in fact, be inmates. – Now, tell me, my dear child, whether this is a plan you approve?'

So infinitely did its advantages surpass whatever Agnes could have hoped for, that it seemed no longer an effort to her to be resigned and contented; – she recovered her spirits completely; thanked her zealous friend with the brightest smiles, and instantly consented to go with him, and survey the rooms in question. / Adrienne accompanied her, and saw so much to recommend the apartment as it already was, and so much which she might do to improve it, that she rejoiced when the affair was settled, and when she was told that they were to take possession of their new quarters that very evening.

The worst was now over; of Agnes it might be said, that she had definitively *pris son parti*,[70] and the various softening circumstances attending her decision, soon produced their full effect. To spare her feelings on first entering upon her professional career Mr. St. Hubert and his nephew, instead of trying to induce fastidious employers to sit to her for likenesses, sought out the most beautiful originals they could find amongst the peasantry, and encouraged her to paint on ivory, in their picturesque costume, the half-length portraits of young females or the heads of strikingly handsome children. These highly finished, correctly drawn, and admirably coloured, were shown as / fast as they were ready, in attestation of the young artist's abilities; and not only sold well, but drew forth commissions for fresh works. Thus prospering in her new undertaking, and gaining courage by degrees to receive regular sitters, Agnes was at the summit of her wishes. She saw her little property gradually accumulating, and with honest pride, exulted in the idea that she was to no one an incumbrance; that as long as Providence spared her health, she was not merely secure of necessaries, but in a fair way of acquiring a competent provision for life. To aid in the preservation of that health so infinitely valuable to her, Mr. St. Hubert never permitted her to spend an entire day in her painting room; he insisted upon her taking regular exercise, either on foot or in a carriage, according to the weather; he collected in the evening agreeable people in his apartment, and appointed her to do the honours of his *soirées*. Thus, if she no longer, as at Paris, ranked high on the list of fashion, as an heiress and a / beauty, she was courted in societies where none could gain admittance, who had not recommendations far superior to any, that mere wealth or personal attractions could bestow. She was here introduced to individuals rendered eminent either by genius – by conversational powers of a high order, by brilliant accomplishments or by some other distinguished endowment, calculated to give a charm and interest to their presence. Sometimes to vary her amusements, Mr. St. Hubert took her to the theatre, or persuaded her to accept the invitations that appeared most promising, to dancing or music parties; and the general admiration and respect her beauty, her talents, and her faultless conduct excited, went straight to his heart, and filled him with cordial and generous delight. It cannot be supposed, that amidst all these engagements, the homage due to the usual objects of veneration abounding in Rome, was with gothic barbarism, omitted. Most assiduously, on the contrary, / and most profitably (under such an escort) did Agnes visit every celebrated gallery, every noble relique of antiquity, and every splendid monument of more modern times. /

CHAPTER IV.

Let us about it; it is admirable pleasures, and very honest knaveries.

SIR HUGH EVANS, IN MERRY WIVES OF WINDSOR.

Vouchsafe me for my meed but one fair look;
A smaller boon than this I cannot crave,
And less than this, I'm sure you cannot give.

SHAKESPEAR.[71]

WHILST thus usefully and agreeably, Agnes' first winter at Rome passed away, the correspondence which Walsingham, before she had left France, had opened with Lady Glenfeld, was punctually and regularly kept up. In his first letter he had spoken of her friend in terms too gratifying to Bertha, to let her easily permit the subject to die away. After dwelling upon many other far less pleasing topics, he had, in a sort of postscript, introduced the following panegyric, affording abundant proof, that his / past prejudices against *heiresses,* were not of so insurmountable a nature, as necessarily to outlive the destruction of their prosperity.

'Your Agnes's sweet countenance, whilst I could behold it, soothed my feelings, and did me more good than any thing, I can again hope to contemplate. – It seems formed to give comfort to the unhappy, and expresses more genuine indulgence of temper, more kindness of heart, and more true delicacy of character, than I have ever yet witnessed in any other human creature: – nay, there is something even beyond this in her irresistible face; there is in it an approach, to what in my visionary moments, I have often imagined must be the aspect of a guardian angel; – it seems as if no evil passion could harbour in that pure bosom; as if truth and meekness, and holy innocence had fixed their abode in the mind that animates those symmetrical and lovely features.'

In answer to this warm burst of admiration, Lady Glenfeld wrote thus: 'He whose *beau / ideal,*[72] my dear Gerald, comprises so much intellectual perfection, merits that the image created by his own brain, should, as far as is compatible with humanity, be substantiated. No man whose own mind was not full of delicacy and refinement, could delight in such a spiritualized representation. Roses and lilies, coral lips, pearly teeth, and "wreathed smiles,"[73] constitute the usual themes of lovers rhapsodies. Who thinks of a beautiful girl's temper, or general disposition? To reward you for doing more justice to my dear Agnes, I will now entrust you with some of the particulars relating to her. She appears to you simply in the light of a courageous young creature, who has calmly submitted to an inevitable reverse of fortune; – you are far from imagining how very short from what is due to her is such an impression. Her declension is entirely her own doing; she did not merely yield unmurmuringly on the discovery of her guardian's imposture / – she outran that discovery; she fled from the unlawful advantages she was enjoying, and by so doing, compelled the unwilling Wharton to make confession of his long successful fraud, and to seek safety in another quarter of the globe.' After this little preface, she detailed to him the whole of her friend's history, and ended by saying, 'So free from parade, so modest and simple is her character, that I believe even Mr. St. Hubert, her devoted and almost paternal protector, knows not yet any of the particulars that do her so much credit. Like you, he probably thinks that to accident alone is to be ascribed the guardian's downfall, and the ruin of the ward. The day I trust, is not very distant when he may, from some other quarter, obtain more accurate and circumstantial information.

'Write to me, dear Gerald, as often as your spirits will permit; the exertion will do you good, and I shall be grateful for such a proof / of your confidence in my friendship: remember our Shakespeare's exhortation –

> Give sorrow words: the grief that does not speak
> "Whispers the o'er frought heart, and bids it break".'[74] –

To a man already so much disposed to admire and love the subject of this letter, it may easily be imagined to what a height of enthusiasm its contents would elevate him. Chained down however, by principle and compassion to the spot where Agnes had left him, his *thoughts* only flew to Rome, and not for one moment did he harbour the cruel idea of *personally* forsaking his hapless charge. That her life drew towards its close, was daily more apparent, and daily did he feel, that to have embittered its short remainder by any remission of assiduity, would have subjected him to eternal self-reproach. The first green leaves of an Italian spring began to shoot forth; the temperature of the air softened, and grew delicious; the blue and cloudless firmament, clear / as the most faultless sapphire, shone radiant over head; myriads of happy birds fluttered from tree to tree, and filled the air with notes of gladness, cheering to the convalescent, and echoed spontaneously by the blithe and healthy hearer. But on her, these sights and sounds, and animating sensations were lost; one by one, every faculty declined; every perception but of increasing languour forsook her; the acuteness of pain itself seemed out-worn: and when, after five months' struggle, her final hour arrived, her drooping head sought support on the shoulder of Walsingham, and one long, quivering sigh, terminated without agony all her earthly sufferings.

The news of this event reached Mr. St. Hubert at Rome, speedily after its occurrence, through the medium of an English acquaintance, settled at Florence, and always one of the first to hear, and to communicate the passing intelligence of the day. 'I am told,' he / wrote, 'that on Monday will be buried, a young countrywoman of ours, lately dead of a decline, over whose history, and even name, a most extraordinary veil of mystery has been thrown. It is reported, that in writing his prescriptions, her physician himself was forced to designate her merely by her initials; and that on her coffin and grave-stone, these same initials are all that are to be inscribed. I shall make a point of ascertaining these strange rumours, by asking to look at the prescriptions at the chemist's, and by going to the funeral; of course the pall will be withdrawn from the coffin when it is lowered, and then one may see what has been written upon it. I am not sure it is quite right to let a person receive christian burial under such suspicious circumstances! Who can tell what she may have done, or who she may have been? However, I shall not interfere in the matter, in consideration of her friend, or her relation, or her husband, or whatever he may / have been, Mr. Walsingham. I have seen him sometimes in his solitary rambles out in the country. He is a fine young man, and I feel a sort of interest for him.'

Mr. St. Hubert brought this letter to Agnes, saying as he gave it her:

'You cannot but be prepared, my dear, for the catastrophe herein announced; but I was not prepared, I must own, for the egregious folly of my precious correspondent! His sanctimonious scruples, and impertinent curiosity, if they did not excite too much contempt, would almost make me indignant.'

'To me,' said Agnes, 'they appear something worse than folly, they are really inhuman and shocking!'

'The fellow who wrote this, is not of the metal of which *shocking* and *inhuman* men are made; nothing so dignified belongs to him; he is only of the stuff that forms prying and idle blockheads. But I wonder what our / friend Walsingham will now do with himself, and which way he will direct his steps?'

'I hope I shall hear,' said Agnes, 'when Lady Glenfeld next writes. He surely will have little desire to prolong his residence at Florence, now his melancholy duty there is at an end.'

Whilst she was speaking, Adrienne, just returned from the post office, entered the room with a large, square, and singularly-shaped letter in her hand, directed in what she termed *une écriture superbe*[75] to Mademoiselle Danvers. Agnes opened it with some eagerness, and smilingly read at the bottom of the page, in great and well-flourished characters, the name of her intelligent little friend, Jeannot Dupuis. He began by telling her, that he had never forgotten the good advice she had given him at parting, and had laboured incessantly to be able to write to her, as she had desired, *a well-spelt and legible letter*. He now hoped that mademoiselle would hardly find one mistake. / He then proceeded to say, that neither he nor any of his family, had ceased to regret her departure, and to love her for all her goodness.

The old guitar master, he told her, was in better health, and had as many scholars as he could teach. Finally, he ventured to say, that his kind friend the instrument-maker, continued to lend him books, and to encourage his visits to the shop, and he believed, would not refuse to take him as an apprentice, if it was ever proposed to him.

Agnes immediately felt, that in this last sentence was conveyed the principal motive the poor boy had in writing it. She remembered the conditional promise she had made him, and gladly reflected on the power she now possessed of fulfilling it. When alone with Adrienne, she consulted with her on the best means, at such a distance from Paris, of giving effect to her design; and after some demur, the following easy and simple plan was adopted. Adrienne, who knew the instrument-maker / (she was the friend or acquaintance of almost all Dupuis' neighbours) undertook to write to him, desiring to know whether he would take Jeannot as an apprentice, and on what terms? If his demands were moderate, she told him she had authority, in the name of Miss Danvers, to answer for their being complied with, whenever a safe opportunity should occur, of remitting the money from Italy. Another letter was prepared to sound the inclinations of the father, and to engage him, for the sake of his son, not to oppose the anxious desire he felt to embrace a profession, it was probable he would so steadily and willingly pursue.

On her part, Agnes set aside every other occupation, to write immediately, and that in the kindest manner, to the boy himself. She highly applauded the proficiency his letter proved him to have made, and gratified him by allowing that she had not been able to detect in it 'one mistake.' To increase the / pleasure which she hoped her answer would give him, she entered into some details concerning the places she had seen, but particularly Venice, which she described in a manner perfectly suited to his comprehension, and at the same time, well calculated to surprise and amuse him. The concluding paragraph was filled with good wishes to himself, and cordial remembrances to his mother; and just before she signed her name, these words were inserted, which she well knew would be to him the most interesting in the whole letter. 'If your father approves the plan, I trust you will soon find every thing arranged, concerning your apprenticeship, entirely to your satisfaction. Farewell, my dear Jeannot.'

About a week after this little transaction, Mr. St. Hubert returning one evening from a dinner party, told Agnes, he had promised for her, knowing she had an hour at her disposal the next morning, that she would receive / a young French lady, desirous of sitting for her miniature. Accordingly, at the time appointed, the stranger came, accompanied by a friend. She entered with many mincing and superannuated *minauderies*[76] that surprised Agnes, in one whose appearance, was otherwise so juvenile. Her deep veil being thrown up displayed a well-formed face, loaded with an extravagant quantity of the most brilliant *rouge*,[77] eye-brows black as jet, and clusters of ringlets half covering her cheeks, of an equally raven dye. Her walk was affected, and made up of short, tottering steps, as if she were propt upon very high heels, (and such, in fact, was the case); she spoke little, and her voice was husky and indistinct; but to make amends, she rolled her black eyes, and bent her graceful neck in so languishing a manner, and now and then smiled with such ineffable sweetness, that Agnes not only found great difficulty in tracing her features, but still greater in forbearing to laugh. The companion was a complete / contrast to her sentimental friend. Her hair and eye-brows were of the palest flaxen. She was immensely tall, and though her features were fine, had altogether an air the most masculine and unprepossessing. On first arriving, she was tolerably quiet; but probably thinking it her duty to enliven her friend, during the dull process she was going through, she soon burst forth into a torrent of words, uttered with such volubility, and in an accent so provincial, that Agnes entertained not a doubt of her being fresh from the banks of the Garonne.[78] She paid the young artist many compliments on the distinguished reputation to which she had attained; attributing with much pride of country, her eminent success to the instructions it was understood she had received at Paris. From time to time, she arose to examine the progress of the outline, and without ceremony, pointed out the improvements it might undergo.

'You have caught the *contour* of those / charming eyes,' she cried; 'but beware of not losing their expression!'

Agnes looking up to see how she might best obey this injunction, beheld those *charming eyes* fixed on vacancy, spiritless, dull, and totally without meaning! The brush almost dropt from her hand in despair; but the tall friend, disregarding her evident perplexity, proceeded to expatiate on the beautiful mouth of her model.

'Alas!' she exclaimed, 'how will you ever be able to do justice to the soft, and almost imperceptible smile that plays around that "cupid's bow"?[79] Where, indeed, is the mortal hand that could succeed in rendering its fascinating loveliness?'

Once more, Agnes ventured to gaze at the lady with the black ringlets. The *soft smile*, if it had ever existed, was fled; the lips were firmly compressed together, and the whole countenance was so motionless, it looked like a coloured mask! /

Utterly disconcerted, and almost frightened, she pushed back her chair, and in a supplicating voice, cried: 'I beseech you to forgive me, ladies! but I am really quite incapable of executing this portrait. The subject, though undoubtedly worthy of all praise, is too difficult for me, and requires the skill of an abler, and more experienced artist.'

'No, no,' said the *belle blonde*, 'you will succeed exceedingly well, if you do but shake off this unnecessary diffidence. Give a little touch to that left brow, and observe, how even and regular an arch it forms.'

Thus urged, she again, though reluctantly, resumed her post, and directed her eyes towards the *regular arch* that had been described. It was contracted into a frown so tremendous, that she almost screamed at the sight, and resolutely starting up, exclaimed: 'Indeed, indeed you must excuse me! Not for the world would I *attempt* to add another stroke to this unsuccessful attempt!' /

Both ladies arose; she of the dark ringlets hastily let down her veil, and moved towards the door; her tall friend, with a look of solemn admonition, said: 'Some allowance, we are sensible, must be made for your youth, and want of self-confidence; but you have certainly carried your timidity too far. However, I trust that to-morrow we shall find you with nerves better fortified, and....

'Believe me, madam,' interrupted Agnes, 'you will be giving yourselves unavailing trouble. I am convinced it will never be in my power, to acquit myself of the task I had undertaken.'

'We are too much your well-wishers to listen to this disclaiming language. Expect us to-morrow at the same hour, and let not your too great modesty stand in the way of your own advantage.' So saying, with an inclination of her person, that was neither bow nor curt'sy, but partook a little of both, she joined her friend at the door, and they went away. /

'They are mad!' thought Agnes, 'or their sole purpose in coming, was to divert themselves by tormenting me. Was ever any thing more absurd, than their rage to ascribe to extraordinary diffidence my unwillingness to proceed?'

Firmly determined not to admit them again, and rejoicing at their departure, she put away the unfortunate rough sketch she had been tracing; and to re-compose her spirits, applied herself to finish the accessories of a more agreeable picture.

Meanwhile, Mr. St. Hubert paid her his customary morning visit.

'Well, my dear,' said he, 'was the French lady true to her time? Have you given her her first sitting?'

'Dear sir,' cried Agnes, half laughing, 'I can only hope it will also be the last! She is the strangest person I ever saw or heard of; indeed, they are *both* so unlike rational / creatures, that I think it hardly safe to be in a room with them!'

She then described the extraordinary mutations of countenance her model had undergone, the fantastic language and behaviour of her companion, and the utter impossibility of working from such a subject.

Her auditor smiled at this recital; but, indulgent as he usually was to all her wishes, exhorted her on the present occasion, not to take alarm too soon, but to venture another trial: 'Humours change,' said he, 'and the same caprice that made her frown and smirk, ogle and look stupid to-day, may make her sit quiet, and behave soberly to-morrow. It would have a bad effect were you to give up the undertaking, upon the plea of not being able to execute it, and I should be sorry such a report should get about.'

This was enough to determine Agnes, at all hazards, to persevere in her disagreeable task. She had never opposed his known wishes, or / neglected his advice; and now to begin, on account of these annoying strangers, would have been to put arms in their hands to annoy her still more. All she entreated of her friendly monitor was, that he would endeavour to be present at the next sitting.

'I cannot answer,' replied he, 'for having it in my power. Fear nothing, however, my dear; they will conduct themselves better, I make no doubt; and at all events, you must try and accustom yourself to deal with as many different tempers as faces. The path you are now pursuing is not always strewed with rose leaves, so keep a garden for them in your own good-natured bosom.'

Docile to his bidding, and armed both with forbearance and resolution, Agnes was already seated at her painting-desk, when, the next morning, the two ladies re-appeared. Their demeanour, on entering, was calm and composed; they walked slowly forward, courteously inclining their heads, but nor speaking a word, and being / seated, the original of the intended picture, with an air of profound gravity, fixed herself in an attitude the most formal, drew up her head to the utmost extent of her fair long throat, and turning neither to the right nor left, sat as rigidly immoveable, as a figure of wax. The tall friend, equally solemn, folded her arms over her bosom, and leant back in her chair 'with eyes upraised as one inspired,'[80] appearing to be rapt in deep meditation. Not a syllable was uttered. This was better than the perpetual mobility of the preceding day; but it promised little in favour of the intelligence and expression of the picture; and had they been persons she liked, Agnes would have made an effort to set on foot some general subject of conversation. As it was, she proceeded with her work in silence; caught the shape of the face, the colour of the eyes, the delicate form of the nose, in short, was making a very faithful and dull copy of the dull prototype before her, when, to her dismay, every / time she looked up, her eye was met by a yawn so formidable, that it seemed as if nothing but dislocation could ensue. Amused, though somewhat shocked at the unceremonious procedure, Agnes did her utmost to avoid imitating so dangerous a precedent; but the dead silence of the room, the force of example, and the little pleasure she took in her occupation, overcame her good intentions, and yawn after yawn, half suppressed, but rapidly succeeding each other, made her eyes water so violently, she could no longer see to guide her pencil. But, what became of her, on perceiving, after some time, that these inconvenient symptoms in her employer, were but preliminary to her falling fast asleep! The tall friend carried the matter still further, for in a very little while, she fairly began to snore; whilst the other, losing the power of maintaining her head in its erect position, let it insensibly sink so low upon her chest, that Agnes could no longer see any part of her face except the / tip of her nose, nor, in a very short time, even *that*, for her rich veil falling forward, produced so total an eclipse, it was vain to attempt penetrating through it. The embarrassment of Agnes was truly ludicrous. For some moments she put down her pencil, and to stifle her laughter, buried her face in her handkerchief, then, coughing gently two or three times, in order to wake them, but without success, she took courage to say: 'I beg your pardon, madam, but may I request you to raise your veil?' The lady started, put her hands up as if to comply with this entreaty, and after some delay, threw off, not her veil and bonnet only, but her black ringlets, and jetty eye-brows, and exhibited to the delighted, but almost incredulous girl, the lovely laughing face of Isabel Le Strange! In one and the same instant they sprang towards each other with open arms, and embraced most cordially, Agnes however, half reproachfully, exclaiming: 'Wicked, wicked / Isabel! What a trick have you been playing me! You do not deserve, that I should be so glad to see you!'

'Yes, yes, I do, dear girl! The trick, though an excellent good one, cost me more pains to carry on, than it did you to bear. If you could but imagine the difficulty I had to keep my countenance, when I saw you looking so desperately perplexed, so amazed, so almost scared at my several pieces of mummery, you would rather admire the self-command I have exerted, than harbour any malice against me, poor innocent soul that I am!'

'You are a horrid person, say what you please!' cried Agnes. 'But what has become of your still more horrid companion? your '*shadow lengthened by the setting sun*'?[81]

From behind a lofty screen placed before a window that occasioned an inconvenient cross-light, issued forth at that moment, in full male attire, Monsieur de Verneuil, accompanied by Mr. St. Hubert. /

On this fresh surprise, Agnes, struck speechless, gazed from one to the other, almost suspecting that her eyes played her false; till suddenly recollecting a passage in one of Lady Glenfeld's early letters, received at Florence, she felt assured that in de Verneuil, she beheld the husband of Isabel, and probably the sole companion of her present journey. Finding however, that she continued silent, Isabel archly said: 'What naughty ideas are trotting through your brain, Agnes? Are you not secretly accusing me of all manner of impropriety, in going about the world masquerading with this dangerous cavalier? Are you not afraid of consorting with me, and scandalized at my having dared to profane your sanctuary with my unhallowed presence?'

'Far, far otherwise, my dearest Isabel!' answered Agnes, again embracing her, 'I am on the contrary, enchanted to have the opportunity of wishing you joy, and of offering likewise my / most sincere congratulations to M. de Verneuil.'

This was spoken in French, and with a smile so flattering to de Verneuil's feelings, that he caught her hand, and pressing it to his lips, cried:

'You make me, by your goodness, mademoiselle, ashamed of the mystification in which I have borne so large a share! But here is one,' looking at Mr. St. Hubert, 'not quite exempt from reproach on the same account.'

'Now this I hold to be a most shabby mode of defence,' cried Isabel; 'we owe half the amusement, and all the success of our carnival frolic to the good-humoured participation of Mr. St. Hubert in our folly; and we really must not be ungrateful enough to try to get ourselves out of the scrape at his expense.'

'Is this true, dear sir?' enquired / Agnes. 'Did you know who you were introducing to me, when, with so natural and innocent a look, you talked of the *young French lady*, who wished to sit for her portrait?'

'I should be particularly obliged to you, my dear,' answered Mr. St. Hubert, endeavouring not to laugh, 'if you would have the goodness to forbear asking troublesome questions. Madame de Verneuil's carriage is at the door; go and take a country drive with her. I dare say you will not be sorry to hear all her news; and, in the mean while, her husband and I, will go to the capitol, or wherever else he chooses to accept my services as his *cicerone*.'[82]

'Unfortunately,' said Agnes, 'at two o'clock, a lady is coming for the last time, to sit for her portrait.'

'I have arranged all that,' resumed her kind old friend; 'the lady has been civilly put off, and you are perfectly at liberty: so, go and enjoy your holiday without scruple, / and not with the less zest for having earned it by past application.'

Agnes thankfully accepted the boon he had obtained for her, and calling for Adrienne, hastened to prepare for her projected excursion.

Isabel, new to Rome, applied to her companion, when seated in the carriage, to know whither they should go? She named *Monte Mario*,[83] and orders were given to the servants accordingly.

'And now tell me, dear Isabel,' cried Agnes, 'when did you leave England? and how was my kind Lady Glenfeld when you came away?'

'I shall first dispose of what relates to others,' answered her friend, 'and then give you the heads of my own little history, which I am sure you must be curious to hear, though you are too delicate to ask for it. To begin with Bertha. She was well and serenely happy as when you saw her in France, but likely soon / to have her serenity rather disturbed, though her happiness I trust increased, by the birth either of a son or daughter, whichever it may please the fates to send her. The life of Lord Glenfeld's uncle is gradually wasting away, but without severe suffering, and the probability is he will close his existence under their roof. Bertha is his consolation and delight, and she is grown so fond of him, that I believe she hardly aspires at anything better than continuing to be his nurse till she wants one for herself. You look at me, dear Agnes, as if you thought I was speaking of her admirable conduct with unfeeling levity; but my head is full of other things at present, and I cannot bestow upon the subject any more time. *Bisogna compatirmi,*[84] as you say here in Italy. Well, now to come to what regards myself. You are to know that after mamma had read the very favourable account of de Verneuil, which that best of all human creatures, Walsingham, sent to Bertha, she softened / a little in our favour, more especially as she saw that fretting for a French lover made me grow so ugly that I should probably never get an English one. All the rest of my family, I will do them the justice to say, warmly pleaded my cause from the moment de Verneuil became personally known to them. Lord Glenfeld came to town purposely to try his influence. My eldest brother, Walsingham's particular friend, instigated, perhaps, by him, exerted his utmost eloquence in our behalf: *bref*; mamma's tardy and half-unwilling assent was at length obtained, and you probably suppose I then felt perfectly happy – no such thing! The affair had "*dragged its slow length along*,"[85] so interminably, and, unlike our Bertha, I had been so ill-disciplined to submit to opposition, that during the period of suspense, my health gave way, and when medical advice was called in, it was judged indispensable to send me immediately to a warmer climate. It was a prescription I had not the / least objection to, provided de Verneuil might be the companion of my travels. He was generous enough to accept me without hesitation, regardless of all my hectic symptoms; and as mamma could not accompany me (being full of bustle and business preparatory to the more important nuptials of Louisa and Caroline) the next point was to find some respectable substitute to take care of me during the journey. Had your stupid governess, the worthy Mrs. Dawson, been forthcoming, I should in all likelihood have been committed to her charge; fortunately for me, I was spared the trouble of devising a decent excuse for despatching her home on the first favourable occasion. Nothing could have induced me long to submit to having such a torpedo about me. My luckier stars threw me into the hands of one of the best and cleverest persons, in her condition of life, that ever existed. She is still with me, and is the daughter, dear Agnes, of / two of your earliest friends, Mr. and Mrs. Blake of Meadwell.'

'O tell me,' interrupted Agnes, starting at the sound of these once-familiar names, 'tell me, dear Isabel, are they still living? Where do they reside? What circumstances are they in?'

'They are still at Meadwell, and enjoying ease and competence.'

'But surely they have not been there the whole time I have been absent from England?'

'I believe they have; but their daughter can satisfy your curiosity much better than I can, and she is longing to see you. She knew you even before her parents did, and still calls you *little Miss* Agnes.'

'You amaze me! Where did she know me? I have no recollection of having ever seen her in her father's house.'

'Listen to me, Agnes; I am going to tell / you a fairy tale. There was once upon a time a very, very pretty little girl, living shut up, not in a turret, but in a somewhat dismal nursery at the back of her papa's handsome London residence. This little girl was between three and four years old, and had the misfortune of being motherless. Her only attendant was a young and kind-hearted country damsel, anxious to do well, but knowing so little in what that well ought to consist, that her leading principle was to indulge her young charge in every possible way she could devise. Under this system, the child lived contentedly enough, you may well imagine, and the injustice of being caged up in so extraordinary a manner, never gave her the smallest disturbance. It was not so with her *Bonne*, who regarded the proceeding as a most flagrant abomination. It happened that a sister of the little girl's deceased mother, being compelled to visit London on business, called at her brother-in-law's fine mansion to see her young / niece. She was conducted, flight after flight, up a back staircase, to the very top of the house, and was there shewn into the half-furnished garret inhabited by the object of her search. The indignant aunt shed many tears, partly of anger, partly of sensibility, on beholding for the first time the neglected orphan of a sister she had passionately loved; and then asked the simple maiden in attendance whether this was the accustomed apartment of the child, or one she had merely been put into whilst her own was altering or repairing?

'"Oh no, ma'am," answered Margaret, perfectly ready to pour forth against her master the ire she had long secretly hoarded up; "little miss never has any other room. Her papa has taken a second wife, a very fine lady, with a power of money, who has an only daughter by a former marriage. This daughter is to have all her mamma's fortune when she dies, and is waited upon with as much state as a young princess, whilst no more value is set / upon master's own little girl than if she were the child of a cobbler!" On further inquiry, however, it appeared that the father, though he was weak enough to let his daughter be thus injuriously overlooked, was in fact extremely fond of her, and never omitted seeing her daily, loading her with play-things, and lavishing upon her the tenderest caresses. The mother-in-law sometimes met her in the hall, when her maid took her out or returned with her from walking, and spoke to her with some appearance of good-nature; but she never sent for her, never admitted her to associate with her own little girl, and hardly even to see her. Now, you must know,' continued Isabel, whose nursery tale she saw was listened to with more and more attention, 'you are to know that the good aunt in question was somewhat vindictive as well as affectionate. Her fervent love for her sister, made her consider the conduct of her brother-in-law as criminal, and worthy of all punishment, and / she determined at once to emancipate the child, and to avenge the dishonour done in her person to the memory of her departed mother. She confided her mad purpose to poor Margaret, who at sixteen, ignorant and inconsiderate, saw not the harm of robbing a father of his child because she did not happen entirely to approve his behaviour to her, and with a facility which she has since deeply deplored, consented to all that was required of her. She was first sworn to secrecy, and then instructed in two days' time, to walk forth with the child, as if for the purpose of giving her her accustomed exercise, but in reality to enable the aunt to meet and join them, without again appearing at the house; thus leaving the father completely ignorant that she had ever been within his doors. From the appointed place of rendezvous, they ascended a hack post chaise, and immediately left town. Afterwards, by various conveyances, and a circuitous route, they arrived at the village of Meadwell. This / spot had been recommended by Margaret as being the residence of her parents, and a place where they would never be sought after, since she had been hired in London, and her master knew not of what country she was a native. Here the aunt represented herself as the mother of the little creature she brought with her, and rented a small house, or rather cottage near the Blakes, retaining Margaret as her sole servant; and with such promptitude and secresy had she executed her plan, and with such prudence had all her subsequent measures been taken, that she totally escaped pursuit and even suspicion.'

Isabel stopt a moment, and stole an apprehensive glance at her pale and agitated companion, who still sitting in a listening attitude, and apparently tortured by this interruption, hastily snatched her hand, and in an eager but ill-assured voice, said: – 'Go on – for pity's sake, go on!'

Without any comment, Isabel thus complied: /

'Margaret Blake continued in the service of her new mistress nearly as long as that lady lived. At the period of her death, however, which occurred about three years after her arrival at Meadwell, Margaret was absent. She had been urged, even by her mistress herself, to accept a very lucrative offer of accompanying a lady and her two children abroad. Previously to her departure, Margaret's father and mother had become great favourites with her lady, and so high an opinion had she of their worth and honesty, that she appointed Mr. Blake her executor, leaving him a trifling legacy, and strongly recommending the friendless little girl to his kindness. It was found on opening her will, that the slender property her husband had left her was so secured that no part of it could be alienated from her son. All therefore she was able to bequeath her little niece, was a small sum of ready money, with difficulty hoarded up for that purpose, and a few personal effects, / the amount of which, when sold, Mr. Blake invested for her in a saving's bank. It is supposed, from some words she uttered during her last illness, that she had intended drawing up a full account of the transaction in which she had been concerned, and causing Margaret to sign it as well as herself, in the presence of proper witnesses; but her attack was sudden, and its fatal termination came on too rapidly to give time for the accomplishment of this purpose. A paper indeed was discovered, containing some allusions to the heads of the story, but no names were inserted, and it bore the character rather of a bitter remonstrance, than of an explicit narrative.'

'How true!' interrupted Agnes, as if speaking to herself, 'and yet now, how clear the whole appears!'

'Have you then seen that paper, dear girl?'

'I have.' /

'And – have you no suspicion to whom it relates?'

'Ah, Isabel! I have more than a suspicion – I am now firmly convinced Mr. Wharton was the person she meant to address, and Mr. Wharton, it appears, was my father!' She wept bitterly as she uttered these words, and added with deep feeling: 'Poor, poor, man! If he has erred, has he not also suffered? He loved his child, even she who assisted in bereaving him of her, owns that he loved her. Had he not been so inhumanly wronged – had he not been deprived of a domestic tie so avowedly dear to him, who can tell how different might have been his course of life? Never, never was man more cruelly injured!'

'True, dearest Agnes,' cried Isabel, pressing her hand with a look of interest; 'but remember, that your poor aunt, from being so eccentric, so passionate and flighty, could hardly be considered as of sane intellects, and / was scarcely responsible for her own actions. In her last moments it was apparent that some mystery weighed heavy upon her mind, which the Blakes have since told their daughter, she struggled hard, but in vain, to disclose. They believed it had reference to you, but were under an absolute impossibility of divining in what manner. Margaret had never been absolved from her vow of secrecy, and had left England without daring to infringe the obligation it laid her under. You were therefore sheltered in the house of her parents as the undoubted daughter of her late mistress. But, Agnes, have you no curiosity to learn how Mr. St. Hubert has taken this discovery?'

'Has it, then, been already communicated to him?'

'Yes; and I will tell you in what manner. We arrived at Rome rather early the day before yesterday. Margaret, from having heard me as we approached the great city, repeat your name so continually, and talk so much of / my impatience to meet you, and of the surprise you would be thrown into on seeing me, began asking so many odd questions about you, that I was induced in my turn to question *her*; and thus by degrees I drew from her all the detail I have been giving you. By means of your correspondence with Bertha, I was become perfectly acquainted with Mr. St. Hubert, and was burning with impatience to announce to him what, from his already established partiality for you, I was certain would give him so much delight. I consulted with de Verneuil, and we agreed to invite him to dine with us at our hotel that very day, under the specious pretext of having news to communicate to him relating to a friend for whom he was much interested. Fortunately he was disengaged, and without ceremony accepted our unceremonious invitation. In the course of the evening we prepared him for Margaret's confession, and finally brought her forward to vouch it all in her own person. He heard us / to the end with profound attention, and without once interrupting the deposition: but, when thoroughly convinced, you would indeed have had just cause to triumph, had you seen with what enthusiastic joy he hailed you as his niece – as the daughter of his favourite sister! The excellent and beautiful old man (for he is really the beauty of elderhood) with tears in his eyes, spoke of you in terms of praise which I dare not repeat, assuring us that had you been his own and only child, you could not have held a higher place in his heart; altogether, we thought him the most agreeable companion we had met for a long time.'

'This assurance of his kind and affectionate readiness to acknowledge me,' said Agnes, 'comes most opportunely to lighten the weight at my heart. The remembrance of my poor father's last letter to Lord Glenfeld, in which he mentions me with such generous placability, notwithstanding all the evil I have brought upon him, haunts and afflicts me. I would give / the world to see, and to be reconciled to him!'

These were feeling Isabel could not enter into, but as she was fearful of giving pain, by attempting to combat them, she thought the wisest plan would be to turn the conversation. With the extenuating points in the character of Mr. Wharton she was little acquainted; her general impression of him was, that he had merited his disgrace, and in all respects was an unprincipled and worthless man.

'Your uncle,' resumed she, sliding over the intermediate subject of their dialogue, 'left us, or rather sought to leave us, at an early hour, with the intention of immediately proclaiming to you the discovery of the day. But I had already arranged a little plot in my head, by means of which I meant that you should take leave of your recent profession, with a taste of the plague that might accompany it, not easily to be forgotten! – I unfolded the scheme to my two laughing hearers, and after / some coaxing and praying, engaged Mr. St. Hubert to lend me at least a little indirect assistance, and above all, inviolably to keep my secret. As for Verneuil, he entered heart and soul into the project; and the trick being rather after a French pattern, performed his part in it, you must allow, to admiration. The fact is, his was the leading character, for I was so afraid of laughing, or of being found out by my voice, that I scarcely dared speak at all. But now, dear girl,' continued Isabel, observing that her friend, though she tried to smile, still looked more thoughtful than she wished, 'let me entreat you to shake off this gravity before you again meet your uncle. To see you thus, would be enough to check the overflowing gladness of his heart; and remember also, Agnes, what an ungracious effect it will have, after travelling all the way to Italy in search of an imaginary brother, to accept the proferred kindness of a real uncle with apparent indifference.' /

'This hint,' said Agnes, determined to profit from it, 'is truly friendly, my dearest Isabel, and I thank you for it, with the utmost sincerity.'

'O you do not half know me yet,' laughingly resumed Isabel; – 'I am a great deal wiser, and better, than you suspect! to assert that I equal our nearly faultless Bertha would be presumption; who does? but there is this to be said for me, I might perhaps have been almost as good, had I not been so differently educated. Even yet, I can feel a little for others, though it must be owned, I have been allowed to grow up with ideas of self-importance sadly destructive of genuine benevolence. Sickness and vexation, however, have not been quite thrown away upon me; they have brought me a little to my senses; and as I no longer want to play the beauty, and am persuaded that in my new career, I must depend upon my good behaviour for retaining the heart I have gained, I am not without hopes that you / and Walsingham, Bertha and my really excellent de Verneuil, will, some day or other, make of me a very meritorious personage.'

'By the way, have you heard any thing of poor Walsingham since the death of his fellow traveller?'

Agnes, whose colour had heightened on hearing herself so unexpectedly associated with the subject of this inquiry, answered not without some degree of confusion, in the negative.

Her sly companion was by no means unobservant of the effect she had produced; and willing to prolong the amusement, it afforded her, thus pursued the conversation: 'We saw him in our way through Florence, indeed, he spent nearly a whole day with us, and as I had learnt from Bertha how much he had lived with you, and Mr. St. Hubert during the time you were at that place, I was in momentary expectation of hearing him say something about you: but he never mentioned you, till just before we / parted, when he surprised me not a little by telling me, he had been informed, you were on the point of being married.'

'Married?' repeated the astonished Agnes.

'Yes, married, my good friend! and in confirmation of the report, his informant, whoever he was, had invented an exceedingly plausible story. Mr. Danvers was said to have modelled your bust, in order that your head might be transferred to his Antigone, which, with the whole group, was to be re-sculptured in marble by desire of the nobleman, to whom you are engaged.' –

Provoked as she was, Agnes could not forbear laughing at this absurd fabrication.

'I know not,' she cried, 'who can have had an interest in arranging so ingenious a mosaic, made up as it is of truth and falsehood; but the plain fact is, that Lord Glenfeld wrote to commission Mr. Danvers to send his wife a bust of me; and Mr. St. Hubert, grateful for the patronage Lord Glenfeld had always / extended to his nephew, thought he might take the liberty of substituting a whole length statue for a bust; and desired Mr. Danvers, (with such alterations as were necessary to suit a detached figure) to represent me in the up-looking attitude of Antigone. When finished, it is to be sent, in my name, as a present to our Bertha.'

'Oh, I die to see it! – I dare say it will be the exact image I have always had in my own mind for the figure of Pity!'

'Antigone,' said Agnes, 'is but a personification of Pity,[86] made more intense by filial love.'

'Poor Walsingham!' resumed Isabel, – 'how shamefully I ill-used him; I laughed at his whole story, and at him for believing it?'

'And did you shake his faith in it?'

'Not a whit! he told me that the person who sent the news from Rome, had actually seen the model in Mr. Danvers' *studio*, and had heard from his own lips, that he had begun / a copy of it in marble for an English nobleman. The likeness was said to be so striking that no one who knew you, could fail to recognize it in a moment.'

Agnes was too little pleased with this account to trust herself to make any answer to it: but she most sincerely wished the marble had remained undisturbed in its quarry.

The unsuppressed exultation with which, on their return, the grateful girl was received and embraced by her happy uncle, at the same time that it gladdened her heart, affected her almost to tears: – 'Old bachelor though I am,' cried he, 'who shall ever dare call my gallantry in question? have I not been a miracle of obedience to a lady's wishes? – It was to comply with the entreaties of Madame de Verneuil that for nearly two whole days, I gave up the pleasure of claiming you as my niece? – Of telling you, my dear Agnes, how often I have fervently wished, though I believed hopelessly, that nature had indeed connected us! – I have / watched you, and studied you, and been learning you by heart for above eight months; and if I were not afraid of spoiling you, I should say, that the more I have watched, and the more I have studied, the more thoroughly I have approved and loved you! Come, come – no tears, my good girl; this is to be a day of jubilee. Go and dress yourself; I have invited a chosen few to feast with us on the joyful occasion, and foremost of the number are Monsieur and Madame de Verneuil.'

All past off at the banquet, which was sumptuous, to Mr. St. Hubert's entire satisfaction. He introduced his newly-found niece, by the name of Miss Wharton, to his assembled guests, and placed her at the head of his table. Every body present was in gala costume; and in the evening, innumerable other visitors arrived, and a regular ball took place, that ended not till the night was far advanced.

Agnes thus fêted and honoured, must have / been more than mortal not to have felt elated; and, in fact, so unrepressed was her contentment, that it animated every feature of her face, and gave to her whole aspect a character perfectly new, in the eyes both of her uncle and of Isabel, who neither of them had known her till after her spirits had been subdued by adversity – by the consciousness of being without natural protectors – by the prospect of poverty and dependence, and by the pardonable regret of having, probably for ever, lost her former station in society. How changed, how bright was now the scene before her! She had found in one and the same day, a near and dear kinsman in Mr. St. Hubert, of all men the one she would most have wished to belong to; and in his nephew, the aimable and accomplished Mr. Danvers, who had invariably treated her with so much friendliness, she had discovered, if not a brother, a relation not far removed from a fraternal one, and a cordial participator in her happiness. She had / now, except on account of her father, scarcely a wish ungratified: and even that, she was fortunate enough next day to find in a great measure, anticipated. Mr. St. Hubert, during a long walk he engaged her to take with him after breakfast, told her that through the medium of young Cowley, who he had heard from Madame de Verneuil, was believed to be in correspondence with her father, he hoped to get a letter safely transmitted to him.

'And in that letter, my dear,' continued the benevolent speaker, 'I mean to address him in the character of a brother-in-law, and frankly to make a tender to him of my services. We will not dispute his having done wrong: – we will not pretend to say that he is not justly stigmatized in the opinion of the world, or deservedly amenable to the laws of his country. But from *us*, dear Agnes, he is entitled to much mercy, first as your father, and next, as the patient and unresisting victim of a surrender, honourable in you, but utterly / ruinous to him. From *me*, he merits lenity as having been whilst she lived, the kind and indulgent husband of a sister whose memory will ever be dear to me, and through the influence of whose virtues, had the tie lasted, it is probable the whole tenor of his after-life might have been as honorable as its commencement. Neither in England nor in Paris can he ever, we are well assured, venture to show himself; but if he prefers any other part of Europe to a longer residence in America, he shall be supplied with the means of returning, and of living in comfort and independence. I will settle upon him an annuity, reversible at his death, to my nephew; and whether he comes over, or remains where he is, console yourself, Agnes, with the reflection, that as your father, and as the widower of my sister, he shall always be secured from pecuniary difficulties.'

Agnes had no language to express the profound sense of gratitude and joy with which / her heart was touched on hearing these most generous assurances. Mr. St. Hubert read all that she felt in the eloquent silence of her looks; and satisfied with having made her happy, pressed her hand with a benignant smile, and hastened to talk of other things.

'Yesterday,' said he, 'whilst visiting different galleries with Monsieur de Verneuil, who do you think I met at one of them? Our delightful friend, Miss Temple. She talked of favouring you with a visit; said she had heard much of your talents and success; and most condescendingly promised to omit no opportunity of recommending you amongst her friends. I thanked her with a very grave face, but told her it was much to be regretted you had not been aware of her kind intentions at an earlier period, since nothing would have flattered you more than the honour of her patronage, and the permission of painting from such a model! Unfortunately, I added, you had now renounced the profession.' /

'Oh then, the report of her approaching marriage is true, I find,' cried she.

'Of course; – are not reports always true? But permit me to ask who is the destined bridegroom?'

'Ah, Mr. St. Hubert, you are very sly! – I cannot however, believe that *you* alone are ignorant of what every body else knows; and I take it much amiss that you will not, by a frank confession, entitle yourself to receive my congratulations on the good fortune of your fair *protégée*.'

'O, I accept the congratulations,' cried I, 'on whatever score they may be given! They are always pleasant things, and I know that you are of a disposition to feel particular pleasure in offering them.'

'We then parted,' continued he, 'she laughing at what she called my exemplary discretion; and I heartily glad to escape from her on such easy terms.' /

Agnes willing to avail herself of this opening, was beginning to tell her uncle what had given rise to the rumour, when they were accosted by one of his friends, who continued with them during the rest of their walk, terminating at the hotel where Isabel lodged, and where Agnes had requested to call that she might have an interview with Margaret Blake.

In the unobtrusive and pleasing demeanor of this young woman, Agnes saw a worthy descendant of the well-remembered friends of her childhood. She had however, been separated from Margaret too early to retain any personal recollection of her, though Margaret herself fancied that she should have known her dear Miss Agnes any where. There was much to tell and much to hear on both sides, and their conference had lasted nearly two hours when Madame de Verneuil came in to interrupt it.

'Well, dear Agnes,' cried she, 'have I not / been very forbearing in resigning you so long to this good creature? She deserves it, I allow, and every thing else that I can do to prove my sense of the obligations I owe her. On first leaving

England, I was hardly in a fit state for the journey, and we were forced to stop more than once on the road, in consequence of my weakness. What I should have done without her, and what would have become of my poor frightened de Verneuil, I cannot imagine. She was the support and comfort of us both; and so adroit, so attentive, and so encouraging, that I had more confidence in her good management, and experience in a sick room, than in all the doctors they could bring me. But come – I find that in talking of her merits, I make her blush and look uneasy; so, to avoid saying any more, I shall run away from you, Margaret, and take your dear *little Miss Agnes* with me.'

Mr. St. Hubert, who was still in the drawing-room reading, was now assailed most urgently / by Isabel to induce him as well as Agnes to accompany her and her husband to Naples. She said they were limited as to time, Monsieur de Verneuil having promised his family not to remain in Italy longer than was indispensably necessary for her health.

'And as I am now so much better,' continued she, 'we are bound in honour to keep our word; but first, I must have a peep at Naples, after which I care not how soon we turn our steps homewards – that is Paris-ward, which after all, as a place to live at, I have the bad taste infinitely to prefer to any other.'

'I rejoice to hear it,' said Mr. St. Hubert; 'since you have married *Paris-ward*, it is wise to encourage a partiality to your adopted country. For myself, I have an engagement on my hands here at Rome which I cannot break away from. My nephew is on the point of being married; and as I also, madam, pique myself on honourably maintaining my word, I / must not forfeit that which I have given him of being present at his wedding. As for Agnes, if she *very* much wishes to accompany you, I will not oppose it; but I own she would please me better by staying here another week, and conferring on her cousin the compliment of being bridesmaid to his pretty English betrothed.'

It is needless to say that Agnes instantly declared her resolution of remaining with her uncle; and Isabel, catching at the words *another week*, eagerly said; 'Do you mean, dear sir, that in so short a time, there is any chance of your following us?'

'I do; – it was never my intention to continue here later than till about the end of March.'

'Then, I am perfectly resigned to your bridal plan; the delay is nothing, and I hope I shall hardly feel it.'

The conversation now changed; Monsieur de Verneuil came in from an exploring ramble, / delighted with what he had seen, and with the beauty of the weather; and whilst he and Mr. St. Hubert were engaged in an animated discussion on the subject of some antiquities he had been looking at, Isabel suddenly said: 'Pray, my dear Agnes, do you know a Mrs. William Stratton who is here?'

Agnes answered in the affirmative.

'Have you ever been to any of her parties?'

'I have been to several.'

'Are you going to her this evening?'

'I am invited, but meaning to spend the evening with you, I sent an excuse.'

'Oh the pity! – Had you been going, I would have gone too. I had a letter of introduction to her from a lady in London, who told me that she was here at the pinnacle of all *ton*; visits have been paid and mutually returned by us, and I have now received an invitation from her for to-night to a concert, and I cannot tell what besides. Let me hear a little about her; / we have never met, and I have not the least idea what she is like.'

Mr. St. Hubert catching these last words, anticipated Agnes' answer, – 'She is like,' he said, 'one of the many minor queens of fashion that abound in foreign countries, and do very little honour to their own. The native inhabitants are so much divided in opinion concerning them, that by some they are laughed at, and what is worse, are regarded by others as real specimens of English refinement and elegance. She is a lady who dashes at every thing; – who writes dramas, paints pictures, models busts, composes music, recites her own verses, and sings her own bravuras. Furthermore, she gives balls, concerts, dinners and masquerades; – she is never tired, never quiet, and would think an evening thrown away that was not spent in a crowd.'

'And are any of the Romans such barbarians as to be insensible to all this extraordinary variety of merit?' /

'The Romans have not the least objection to her parties, – for, besides being sure of good refreshments, they often meet with good company, and seldom fail to see or hear something to gratify their sarcastic propensities; but do not imagine that, generally speaking, they are for one moment duped by her pretensions; they would see through them even in a compatriot; how much more in an *ultramontane bel-esprit?*'[87]

'Yet,' said Agnes, 'if a foreigner is unaffected, and shows a disposition to be grateful for civilities received, there are no people kinder than the Romans.'

'I beg, my dear Agnes, you will ascribe to them no particular merit for that!' cried Isabel with vivacity. 'The same may surely be said of the French, and not seldom even of the English, though their greater reserve of character may make their kindness more tardily apparent.'

'Well argued, Isabel!' said her husband, / 'Mr. St. Hubert, I am sure will not hesitate to acknowledge, that in all civilized countries real genius, accompanied by simplicity of manners is an assured immunity from ridicule, whilst the *charlatanerie*[88] of affected pretenders, provokes (and justly) the whole force of its artillery.'

'True; – genius may be cavilled at by envy; but it can with difficulty be rendered ludicrous.'

'There is no degree of malice or detraction,' cried Isabel, 'I would not heroically submit to, for the glory of being envied! But to excite derision, would I think drive me mad!'

'You would not know any thing of the matter, my dear madam; no one laughs at another to his face; and were that even to happen, as excessive vanity is the chief ailment of ridicule, it is also the surest preservative from mortification. A vain man is the most unsuspicious creature in the world, and / will innocently join in the laugh against himself, and then look round to discover the jest.'

'Probably,' said Agnes, 'that is what makes vain people so good humoured.'

'You may be assured it contributes to do so in no small degree. I might not be able to feel much respect or friendship for a vain man, but I would rather have him for an inmate than a very proud one.'[89] /

CHAPTER V.

> 'In winter's tedious nights, sit by the fire
> With good old folks, and let them tell thee tales
> Of woful chances, long ago betid.'[90]

TWO days after this conversation, Monsieur and Madame de Verneuil were to have set out for Naples, and the morning subsequent to their departure had been appointed for the marriage of Mr. Danvers.

But all these plans were necessarily overthrown by the intelligence given to Mr. St. Hubert within two hours of the time when they had been talking these said plans over. He was assured by a friend, on whose information he could depend, that the marriage of / Protestants could not be celebrated at Rome, where the English have no ambassador. It was therefore determined that the whole party should repair to Naples, and Isabel readily consented to defer going till all the others were ready.

Accordingly, they left Rome in strong force, full of happy anticipations; and after a speedy and most prosperous journey, arrived at Naples in as good spirits as when they set out, the lovely season of the year, the softness of the temperature, and the marvellous clearness of the heavens[91] contributing not a little to the general gratification.

'My dear uncle,' said Agnes, looking delightedly around whilst on the road, seated in an open carriage, 'how glad I should be if you would comfort me with the assurance that it is not very unpardonable to prefer the *beautiful* to the *sublime*.[92] To tell you the honest truth, I almost hate the more tremendous features of nature, and find inexpressible pleasure / in surveying scenes of cheerfulness, cultivation and fertility. It is unjust to say that such scenes are deficient in variety. No two landscapes – no two points of view in which the same landscape can be seen, are ever alike; some bend in a river; some new appearance in lights and shadows upon the distant hills; some change at every turn of the road in the disposition of the trees, and a thousand other accidental causes, occasion a perpetual diversity, and are quite sufficient to enchant us without the accompaniment of roaring torrents, unfathomable precipices, threatening avalanches, or any of the other horrors that constitute the bleak, desolate, and terrific characteristics of the sublime.'

'Whilst you are a traveller,' answered Mr. St. Hubert, 'I would advise you to cultivate a taste for *both*, since it is impossible near the Alps and Apennines, to avoid encountering as many horrors as beauties. At the same time, I am ready to acknowledge, that I believe / there is a vast deal of *humbug* in the enthusiasm so often professed on these matters. To a poet's eye, "in a fine phrenzy rolling,"[93] sublimity may indeed be congenial, and in his verse he may give it shape and stamp it with the impress of his own genius, setting every image distinctly before his readers; but that the common run of town-bred travellers should suddenly become such raging admirers of these tremendous scenes, surpasses my powers of belief. I remember once to have heard an Englishwoman in Switzerland describing in rapturous terms to a friend the grandeur of a *catarrh* near Interlacken.[94] Her auditress, with some surprise, repeating the word rather sceptically, the other without hesitation answered: "Yes, my dear, a catarrh; some called it only a waterfall, but I assure you, it was much more, it was a positive catarrh."[95] Imagine, therefore, with what qualifications this person came abroad to fall in love with and to describe fine prospects.' /

All preliminaries being arranged previous to the impending nuptials, the bride and bridegroom with their English friends, proceeded to the British ambassador's whose chaplain was to perform the ceremony.

Agnes, as bridemaid, dressed in spotless white, pleased with the part that had been assigned her, and looking more than usually gay and happy, accompanied the young bride in her uncle's carriage (for since her being publicly acknowledged as his niece he no longer kept his establishment upon so frugal a footing). Next to her sat the brother of the bride, who was to give her away; and the fourth place was occupied by Mr. St. Hubert. His nephew and a friend, followed in another carriage.

Too much engaged in discourse with each other, or in thinking of the approaching solemnity, to attend to anything in the street, Agnes's party drove on without noticing a light open travelling vehicle which stopped at / the entrance of a great hotel at the very instant they were passing it. Mr. St. Hubert, however, less mentally pre-occupied, was not equally unobservant of outward objects, and a quick glance of his eye, shewed him that the newly arrived traveller was Mr. Walsingham. Their looks met, and they both bowed, one with an expression of cordial friendliness, the other with an air of the utmost respect, but with a face paler than it had ever yet appeared.

The marriage ceremony and its attendant felicitations over, the whole party returned to partake of a splendid breakfast at the temporary apartments of Mr. St. Hubert; after which, his new niece and her husband drove off to a villa which the same friend who had accompanied them to church, had lent them near Naples.

As soon as they were gone, Agnes having changed her dress and feeling too unsettled to apply to her usual pursuits at home, took / Adrienne with her and went out for a drive. In the meanwhile, Mr. St. Hubert sallied forth to call upon Mr. Walsingham.

He was in deep mourning, was very thin, and looked depressed almost to sadness, though he strove to welcome his kind visitor with something like a smile.

'I trust,' said Mr. St. Hubert, 'we should have found each other out, independently of the accidental circumstance of our carriages passing at the moment you arrived. Is this your first visit to Naples?

'No, I have been here before, and am now merely passing through in my way to Sicily.'

'But ought you not – excuse me – to be looking after your affairs in England?'

'They are all in so fair a way of being settled for me, that my prolonged absence is perfectly immaterial.' Then, after a short silence, 'I hope,' said he, 'Miss Danvers is well?'

'There is no Miss Danvers now,' smilingly / answered Mr. St. Hubert. 'You must ask after her by a different name.'

'I think,' resumed Walsingham, making an effort to speak with composure, 'I saw her in your carriage when you drove past me this morning.'

'Yes – we were all going to the wedding. Had you arrived a little sooner, we should have endeavoured to prevail upon you to be of the party.'

Walsingham merely inclined his head, and after another interval of silence, said:

'I was aware, as you approached, of the business you were going upon, from hearing one Englishman say to another: "Here comes the bridal party; let us have a look at the beautiful Agnes."'

'They shewed their good taste! She was indeed in extraordinary beauty, and totally threw her poor little companion into the shade.'

'Happiness,' resumed Walsingham, suppressing / a sigh, 'beautifies even beauty itself.'

'Yes; and my good little Agnes is of so social a spirit, that she can be made happy by merely witnessing the happiness of others. The bridegroom's delighted face was of itself enough to cheer us all.'

Walsingham had heard as much as he could bear; the 'bridegroom's delighted face' was more than could be endured, and to change the conversation he asked Mr. St. Hubert whether he had become acquainted with Monsieur and Madame de Verneuil.

'Most intimately; and am charmed with both. They are now at Naples, and I hope you will shortly go to see them. But come, if you have nothing better to do, walk with me to the hotel where I lodge, and I will shew you a portrait of Madame de Verneuil, begun by your friend Agnes. When leisure serves, she may perhaps finish and make you a present of it.' /

'Were I to accept it,' cried Walsingham, faintly smiling, 'should I not incur some risk of having my throat cut by de Verneuil?'

'Why that's true, and it is as well to be prudent. But there can be no danger in going to look at it. If you dislike meeting strangers, I can ensure you from that annoyance; the bridal folks are all gone, and the only person you are likely to see is Miss Wharton.'

'Miss Wharton? – Who is she, sir?'

'A relation of mine who keeps house for me, and is perfectly *sans consequence*.'[96]

Walsingham took up his hat, and without further question, followed his mischievous guide.

Agnes was still absent, and the two gentlemen entered her sitting-room together. Mr. St. Hubert walked straight up to the table at which the day before she had been painting, and opening a drawer, drew forth the promised picture. The astonished Walsingham gazed / at it a moment without speaking, and then laughing in despite of himself, said: 'Oh, *this* I may safely accept, de Verneuil would not refuse it to his most dangerous rival.'

'You are no judge of likenesses, I see, my good friend. We, who are connoisseurs, all thought the sketch – for it is no more – a very exact representation of the original.'

Walsingham shook his head incredulously, and replacing the picture in the drawer, said: 'I have seen other works by Miss Danvers that have enchanted me; but this, I own, is not of the number; neither can I believe it was ever seriously meant for a resemblance of Isabel. Not only the hair and eye-brows are totally different from hers, but it has all the obsolete affectation of a *petite maîtresse* of the time of Louis XV.[97] It would be great charity to show me something else.'

'What – to sweeten your fastidious palate, I suppose? Well, look at that; it is done partly from memory, and partly from a slight pencil drawing sketched at Paris.' /

So saying, Mr. St. Hubert handed to him a miniature of Lady Glenfeld. Walsingham knew it instantly, and was enraptured with it. 'Who would suppose,' cried he, 'that these two pictures could have been done by the same person? This is admirable! It has all the sweetness of Lady Glenfeld's countenance – her candour of expression – her delicacy of features – and without being beautiful, is more engaging than beauty itself. This is a portrait no one acquainted with the original could look at without delight.'

'I am glad,' said Mr. St. Hubert, 'I have put you into better humour with poor Agnes' handiworks. Here are one or two other things might be worth your looking at, but I am afraid of boring you.'

Walsingham was beginning to protest against this unfounded apprehension, but at that moment the door opened, and Agnes, her cheeks bright as health and fresh air could make them, entered the room,[98] humming a favourite / waltz. If *she* started on seeing him, how much greater was *his* amazement at sight of her! Mr. St. Hubert internally enjoyed his perplexity, but taking no notice of it, he calmly and kindly said, addressing Agnes, 'Well dear, have you had a pleasant drive?'

'Am I dreaming!' exclaimed Walsingham, recovering the use of speech, 'Do I really behold, I will not say, Miss Danvers, but my dear Bertha's friend?'

'Her friend I trust for life,' cried Agnes, warmly; 'but why this surprise, Mr. Walsingham? Where could you more naturally expect to find me, than under the protection of Mr. St. Hubert, of my indulgent uncle?'

'Your uncle?'

'Has he told you nothing of the happy change in my affairs?'

'What change? Explain yourself, I conjure you! I can bear suspense no longer; in one word, say, are you *married*?'[99] /

'Not *yet*,' in a suppressed but significant tone, answered Mr. St. Hubert; whilst Agnes, looking down, blushing scarlet deep, yet involuntarily half smiling, stood silent and confused, the image of all that was lovely and irresistible. Walsingham gazed at her with transport, and had he dared, would have poured forth aloud the passionate emotions of his soul, for never had she appeared to him so bewitching. That pale countenance, which but a few moments before had borne traces of so much dejection, was now flushed with new-born hope; his eyes sparkled, and the spirit that lighted them up, seemed to diffuse itself throughout his whole being, to give elasticity to his movements, and a renewal of all its youthful, though long-obscured animation to his character.

Afraid of trusting himself to say too much to Agnes, he now turned to Mr. St. Hubert, who was archly observing him, and said: 'Take your own time, sir, to give me fuller / information; I can live upon what I have already obtained at least a whole day!'

'I don't believe a word of it! You will be asking a hundred questions before the present hour is elapsed! However, I am willing you should immediately know, that I am perfectly innocent of having gone to your hotel with any intention of playing the rogue with you. Your own demeanour during the visit, particularly when Agnes' change of name, and "*the wedding*" were spoken of, threw the temptation in my way, and I had not resolution to withstand it. I beg now to inform you, that this lady was only officiating as bridesmaid at the said wedding, which was that of my nephew, William Danvers; and farther, that I have had the happiness of obtaining the fullest conviction, that she is the daughter of my youngest sister, Mr. Wharton's first wife. If there is any thing more, you might sleep the better for adding to your this day's stock of knowledge, come and dine / here, and we will do our best to content you.'

A look of modest, but frank encouragement from Agnes, confirmed the joy of Walsingham on receiving this invitation, which he accepted with the eagerness of one, who scarcely dared credit the reality of his good fortune, and almost feared it would escape him. For once, he found that appearances might be trusted; and every succeeding hour of that most felicitous day, proved as bright as the hour that had preceded it.

During the continual opportunities (dating from this moment) which he and Agnes had of seeing each other, it may easily be imagined, he neglected not to ask for somewhat more circumstantial information, than he had been able to glean from Mr. St. Hubert's summary mode of treating her affairs. She satisfied his curiosity unhesitatingly, and unconditionally, being too delicate to question him on the subject of his deceased friend, whose fame she / felt, he was as much bound to preserve now she was in her grave as whilst she was still living. Walsingham however, though gratefully sensible of her forbearance, took no advantage of it; but in return for her ready explanation, gave her an explicit history of all that related to his connexion with his unhappy fellow-traveller.

'To enable you to understand what is to follow,' said he, 'I am obliged to go back to the days of my childhood; but do not be alarmed, I have no design to involve you in a tedious recital of my nursery adventures, or school-boy exploits; but it is necessary you should know, that I lost my father, a country gentleman, of moderate fortune, at a very early period of my life, and was left under the guardianship of a mother, still young and handsome, who in a few years married again, and settled in London. Her husband was a merchant, living in splendour, such as is ascribed to the ancient Tyrians, "whose merchants / were princes, and her traffickers were the honourable of the earth."[100] All that luxury could invent, was displayed upon my mother's beautiful person, and in her equipage, furniture, and dwelling. She enjoyed these advantages, alas! with but too high a relish; they chilled her heart towards the offspring of her first marriage; and without knowing why, I found myself slighted, in a degree that was most painful to my feelings, and became still more remarkable after the birth of a daughter, whose entrance into life, was hailed with rejoicings as extraordinary, as if she had been born to a throne. You heard me once, I believe, proclaim my aversion to heiresses. If ever such a sentiment had found its way to my heart, it might perhaps have been justified by what I daily witnessed in my mother's house. The importance attached to every look and movement of my little sister, and the inconceivable bustle that was made about her, were enough to have taught me, not merely to hate / heiresses, but to hate *her*. Such a sentiment never entered my heart. She was one of the few favourites it was impossible to hate; one of the very few, whom nothing could spoil. We loved each other most affectionately, and almost the only pleasurable hours I spent at home, were due to her sweetness and attachment. When scarcely eighteen, she married a gentleman-like, and amiable young man, who was in some sort of partnership with her father. My mother wished for a nobler connexion, and many were ready to indulge her ambition. But Georgiana loved the object of her father's choice, and on this occasion, his will was peremptory, and my mother was compelled to submit. For some years, all things went on prosperously and uniformly; but now comes the trying part of my narration; now begins a tissue of horrors, I can hardly find courage to unfold!'

He got up, and walked a few minutes disorderedly about the room, Agnes looking at him / with tearful compassion; and then, returning to his seat, hastened as rapidly as he could to the termination of his tale.

'Two hours only before I so suddenly left Paris, the post brought me a short, and scarcely legible letter from Georgiana, dated Calais, and containing, as nearly as I can remember, merely these words:

"Come to me, my dearest Gerald; come to me, my kind brother! I am in distress, too great to describe, and have no friend but you, on whose compassion I can throw myself!"

'Shocked and alarmed at this inexplicable and urgent supplication, I lost no time in complying with it, not even permitting myself the delay, of taking leave of Lady Glenfeld. Georgiana was too firmly established in my good opinion, to be suspected of any real act of imprudence injurious to her reputation; but appearances might have been against her; some calumny might have been invented difficult / to disprove: at all events, it was evident, there lurked under the obscurity of her note, a disgraceful mystery, I was in no haste to communicate to any one.

'On arriving at Calais, my worst anticipations (though, I thank Heaven, not of her misconduct), were more than justified. She met me drowned in tears, and I learnt, when she was able to speak, that her father was a bankrupt; that he had escaped from his creditors, and she believed had succeeded in quitting the country; that her husband, involved in the same calamity, though ignorant, till the bubble burst, of the impending insolvency, had likewise been forced to seek security in flight. Every thing they possessed had already been put under sequestration, and it was with difficulty my poor sister had been able to raise a sufficient sum to convey her, with one maid, and her child, out of the kingdom. Anxiety for the safety of her father and her husband, pity for her ruined little / girl, the dread of public scorn, and a thousand mournful forebodings, depriving her of rest, and throwing her into a state of constant nervous irritation, laid the foundation of that insiduous malady, which has since destroyed her. Our mother, happily for herself, as it proved, had died before this degrading reverse overtook her family. Georgiana had formed no plans for herself, but lived from day to day, in the hope of hearing from one or both the fugitives, and of being perhaps, eventually re-united to them. I feared the expectation was delusive, and secretly wished to conduct her to Italy, as well for the benefit of her health, as to remove her further from the danger of hearing contradictory and alarming reports. I was compelled however to wait at Calais, till the burning heat of summer had sufficiently subsided, to enable her to travel; and during that dreary interval, avoiding all society, and scarcely allowing ourselves even to be seen, my only solace, and a gloomy one / it proved, was that of reading the English newspapers in the privacy of my own room, well knowing how likely they were to contain matters, unfit for her inspection. In fact, they abounded with details and animadversions relative to her father's affairs, which it would have been death to her to have seen; the charges against him were so strong, and such allegations of fraud, and even *forgery* were brought forward, that my soul sickened as I read! But what was my consternation, on finding in one of these journals, an announcement, printed (as if in triumph) in large characters, of his detection and seizure, in an obscure hamlet, in North Wales. It had been universally supposed, he had effected his escape to Holland; but some accident or imprudence had detained him on our shore, and finally betrayed his place of concealment. The conjectures, the anticipations, nay, almost the *hopes* expressed, that he would pay, by the forfeit of his life, for the ruin he had / brought upon so many individuals, chilled my blood! I trembled for my poor Georgiana's kind, and guiltless husband, for such I sincerely coincided with her in believing him to be. In the speculations, and hazardous, though hitherto, successful enterprizes of her father, he had never had any direct participation, having done little more than lend his name, and embark his fortune in the concern; and so upright and honourable was his character, that he was probably the very last man, to whom his too-adventurous partner would have laid open the real nature of his proceedings.

'It was difficult constantly to disguise from my sister, the frightful apprehensions I entertained. However, I so far succeeded, that I got her away from Calais, still unsuspicious of her father's detention. She was cruelly tormented by her incessant anxiety, to hear either from him, or from her husband; but when I represented the impossibility of / their knowing where to direct to her, till from their own place of refuge, they could learn through some correspondent in England, what route she intended to take, her impatience was calmed, and she wrote directly to her husband's sister, entreating her to inform the fugitives she was on her way to Italy, and at every considerable town which she named, should enquire for letters the moment she arrived. It was a relief to her to have taken this step; but I dared not suffer her letter to go out of my hands. News had reached me, that her husband, the unfortunate Newhurst had also been traced, and taken into custody at a small sea-port, whilst waiting in disguise for a favourable opportunity of embarking. Both partners were now in confinement, and an accumulation of evidence, or at least accusation, was brought against them, too overwhelming, I feared, to be parried or disproved. Many of the public journals spoke with pity, and a certain degree of consideration / of Newhurst; all were outrageous against his principal, and some implicated the two prisoners in equal guilt. With this weight of disastrous intelligence upon my mind, which it was my sole aim to conceal from Georgiana, I would not for worlds, in traversing France, have passed through Paris, or have associated with any of my countrymen. My precautions were so long successful, that I began to flatter myself I should have time to gradually prepare my sister's mind for what she had to hear; but reluctant to perform my cruel office, and too ready to cling to the persuasion that by delay I gave her a better chance of acquiring the health and strength requisite to support the blow, I weakly deferred the communication till it came upon her, through the medium of accident, with an abruptness so unmitigated, that it seemed doubtful which would first fall a sacrifice, her intellects, or her life.

At *Le Maschere*, a single house, one stage distant from Florence,[101] where we stopt a day / or two on account of a slight indisposition that seized the child, Georgiana entering unexpectedly the room where the little creature was amusing herself under the eye of her maid, saw that the latter had been crying, and at the moment of her appearance, endeavoured to hide a newspaper, which it was evident she had been reading. Suspicion and terror instantly assailed my poor sister, who demanded with unwonted vehemence, a sight of the fatal paper. The maid, trembling in every limb, aware of the consequences that might result from obeying her, yet not knowing how to refuse, sought to run out of the room: but Georgiana, conscious she could not oppose her design by force, knelt at her feet, clung to her knees, and supplicated her with such intense, such agonizing earnestness to yield to her request, that the poor creature, unable, and unaccustomed to resist her, suffered herself, however unwillingly, to be overcome, crying out at the same time: "There is not / a word of truth, ma'am, in what you are going to read. You may depend upon it, it's all a mistake, it's all slander, and it is a thousand pities you should trouble yourself to look at it!"

'Georgiana heard her not, she was devouring the killing lines she had been so importunate to see ... But let me not dwell upon the desperate resolution with which, in despite of the mist gathering over her eyes, in despite of the convulsive sobs that burst from her breaking heart, she was enabled to conclude the horrid perusal, at the close of which, uttering one long, but faint though terrific shriek, she dropt insensible, and apparently lifeless on the floor.'

'Oh, heaven!' exclaimed the pale and awe-struck Agnes, 'what was contained in that dreadful paper?'

'An ample and unpalliated account,' answered Walsingham, in a smothered voice, 'of the public execution of her father! And, / oh, horror of horrors! an appendix to that fearful tale, announcing that her husband, despairing of his own acquittal (though it was believed without reason) had found means to destroy himself in prison!'

A dead silence succeeded these harrowing words; Agnes seemed transformed to stone, she was as colourless, as cold, and as immoveable. Walsingham himself powerfully agitated by the recollections he had been recalling, yet, on witnessing her deep and speechless consternation, felt his heart smite him for having so severely worked upon her compassionate nature. He brought her a glass of water; he spoke to her with the most anxious tenderness; thanked her for the sensibility she manifested for his unfortunate sister, but besought her not to let it overpower her, and shewed so much solicitude for her recovery, that penetrated by his soothing accents, tears came to her relief, and she was soon able to acknowledge his kindness, and to implore / him to continue his affecting narrative. He would, for her sake, have deferred the subject till another day.

'Ah, no,' cried Agnes, 'conclude the sad tale at once, and hereafter, unless you wish to recur to it, never shall it be alluded to again!'

Walsingham thus urged, went on with his narration:

'I had been wandering listlessly about the country, when the scene I have described took place, and at our usual dinner hour, strolled back to the inn, without having the most distant suspicion of the disastrous tidings that awaited me. The people of the house looked dismayed and mysterious; our sitting-room was vacant; the child's temporary nursery contained no one but its little deserted tenant; every thing wore an appearance of discomfort and forlornness. I asked the poor baby where her mamma was? Her mamma, she innocently answered, had fallen down, and nurse was putting her to bed! At that moment, I / caught sight of the crushed newspaper lying on the ground, near the spot where Georgiana had sunk down. You may imagine with what mingled avidity and apprehension, I seized and read it! With this lecture ended every doubt, every shadow of hope. It proved not only that the catastrophe in England was complete, but seemed to presage the destruction of another, a more blameless victim than either that had preceded her. I went with a heavy heart to the door of my sister's room; her maid, on seeing me, waved me back, and cautiously came out on the landing place, to tell me in a low voice, that her mistress, exhausted by a succession of convulsion fits, was beginning to grow a little calmer, and would, she thought, be better if left undisturbed. I agreed with her; but asked how that detestable paper had found its way into the house? She said, a courier with whom she was acquainted, had passed through *le Maschere* that morning with an English family, / and had thrown it to her as he drove by, thinking that news from home would be interesting to her. The unfortunate manner in which she had been surprised whilst reading it, I have already recounted. Who was there to blame? or what blame could have repaired the mischief already effected? The only thing to do, was to provide, through the recommendation of the landlady, some proper attendant in lieu of her accustomed nurse, for the forsaken little girl, and to wait with patience till Georgiana was capable of removing.

'Her first interview with me, was of a character that will not bear to be retraced, yet never can be forgotten. No bursts of intemperate anguish broke from her – no frantic exclamations – no despairing complaints; but a depth of settled sorrow, still, yet incurable; a tender regard for the feelings of others – hopes extinct for herself, but surviving for her child and for me; these were what her generous / nature dictated, and her countenance and language expressed. The unutterable pity which melted my heart on seeing her in such a frame of mind in an hour of such trial, seemed to *age me* all at once, and to throw a weight upon my spirits, which at the moment, I thought no time could ever lighten. Of her assured approach to the refuge of the grave, she spoke with so prepared, I may almost say, so glad an anticipation, that I listened to her at once with grief and veneration. She told me she wished as soon as possible to get on to Florence, convinced from her internal feelings, that either a severe preparatory illness was coming upon her, or that her end was yet nearer than she had foreseen; "and in either case," added she, "it is better for you, dear Gerald, not to remain alone at this solitary place. But promise me, my brother, when we are at Florence, never to name me to a human being. Even if you insist upon calling in a physician, (which for the ease of your / own mind I will not oppose – though what can a physician do for *me?*) let him not know who I am. Speak of me as a sick friend, but say nothing of our relationship; and give me, I conjure you, your solemn word of honour to observe this injunction even till the moment when I am deposited in my final resting-place." I was not just then sufficiently composed to weigh the motives for such a request, and I gave, somewhat rashly, the promise she required. Who that had seen her and known her misfortunes could have found courage for a denial? I have since become convinced that fearing to bring upon me any part of the disgrace attached, as she believed, to the name of her father and her husband, she wished our consanguinity to remain entirely concealed. There was generosity in this idea, but my compliance with what it led her to urge, often exposed me to extreme embarrassment – particularly as related to my intercourse with you and Mr. St. Hubert, the two persons in the / world I most desired to be perfectly open and unreserved with. Bound as I was, you will allow that nothing could absolve me from the necessity of keeping silence. Lady Glenfeld guessed from your letters that I had no intention to entrust you with my sister's history; and she was too truly my friend to betray what she found I sought to conceal. But she spoke of me – did she not, sweet Agnes? with all the kindness that could tend to mitigate the ill-effects that might have been produced by my involuntary want of confidence. I saw the favourable success of her endeavours in your ingenuous face, and how I loved and blessed her for the good she was thus doing me.

'We left *le Maschere,* as my sister had desired, almost immediately, and the illness she had but too truly foreboded, came upon her on the very night after her arrival at Florence. I then thought, so violent was the attack, that nothing could preserve so delicate a frame from sinking under it. She survived it, however, / not indeed to be restored to health, but by more imperceptible degrees to advance step by step to her inevitable fate. The fever, which had never wholly subsided, seemed at intervals, though in fact it undermined her, to animate and give her strength, and then she was capable of conversing with some degree of ease and serenity, but at other times it preyed upon her so fiercely that delirium was the consequence, succeeded by a lassitude and debility so overpowering that for days together she lay speechless, motionless, and scarcely appearing to breathe. In these alternations, or rather, in this progressive state of decline, with some flattering occasional gleams, the winter passed away – a winter long to be remembered by me, as one of the saddest man was ever doomed to spend! With the approach of spring every dangerous symptom was aggravated, and, in short – for why should I torture you by lingering over this most painful period? – the month of March had barely begun, when the gentlest / spirit that ever visited earth fled to a happier home.'

Here was a recital which, even if Agnes had hitherto regarded Walsingham with indifference, was calculated beyond all others to blend her heart with his, and devotedly attach her to him for life. He might have said of her with Othello, she

> 'Bade me if I had a friend who loved her,
> I would but teach him how to tell my story,
> And that would woo her.'[102]

Such, indeed, was not the language of her lips, but it was that of her soft eyes; and Walsingham, penetrated with gratitude, ventured as if a new existence had been opened to his view, to look forward, when assured of her acceptance, to a prospect of happiness. From the depression of spirits he for a while had experienced, he gradually recovered. Nothing could be further from his nature than such depression; but the solitude in which he had / spent so many cheerless months, with the miserable view constantly before him of his sister's sufferings, and slow but sure extinction, sufficiently accounted for the change that had been wrought in him. The influence of diversity of scene, Mr. St Hubert's frank good humour, the beauty of the season and the climate, but above all, the smiles of Agnes, and the certainty of being beloved, 'there where he had garnered up his heart,'[103] soon made of him a new being. Authorized by her, it was not long before he declared himself to her uncle, and solicited his consent to their union. –

'This,' said the smiling old man, 'is precisely what I expected, and to be sincere, precisely what I wished. I have not known you long, it is true, but in some cases it may be allowable to be guided by first impressions, particularly when they are confirmed by the world's fair report. I do not hesitate to say, that I liked your countenance as soon as I saw / it, and I have continued to like it ever since. Agnes, I felt, might have been easily induced to follow the good example; but not being acquainted with the nature of your previous engagements, I gave her no encouragement to talk or to think of you: whether she waited for encouragement is more than I can tell, – I rather believe *not!* – Be that as it may, since she has accepted you, you have my willing and most hearty consent to make her your wife. Happiness is deeply in arrears with her: but her patience, her gentle but noble fortitude, seem now about to reap the reward I have long coveted for them. To a man in love, it is not very necessary to point out the merits of his mistress; I speak not therefore to inform you, but simply to gratify *myself.* The tenderness you now feel for her, I prognosticate will last; she is not one of those awe-inspiring, pattern-women,[104] possessed of every excellence but that of knowing how to be amiable; she is on the contrary, humble minded, but playful, / solicitous to do her duty, but leaving to others the care of their own, she is neither presumptuous, prejudiced, nor dictatorial: and setting aside her higher qualities, she is an uncapricious inmate, an amusing and well-informed companion, and on occasion, one who is as ready to laugh and be nonsensical as if she had never known vexation or inquietude.'

But although so flatteringly ready to entrust to him the happiness of his loved Agnes, Walsingham found that Mr. St. Hubert would by no means consent to let the marriage take place abroad. He said, that with so large a property as Walsingham had now become possessed of, and with the designs he himself entertained in her favour, it was necessary that proper trustees should be appointed – secure settlements drawn up, and all the forms regularly gone through that could render the marriage articles valid and incontestible. Against the idea of receiving with Agnes any addition to the ample fortune he had already / inherited, Walsingham most vehemently exclaimed; but Mr. St. Hubert was not to be dissuaded from his purpose: – 'for two special reasons,' he said, 'I must insist upon being indulged; the first is, my love for Agnes, which makes it indispensable to my comfort to confer upon her every benefit in my power: – the second is, that in what I propose, I am only acting towards you with common justice, and acquitting the debt, contracted by her father during the long period he defrauded you of the income that might have been accumulating for you. Do you think I would suffer my little girl to marry you like a miserable insolvent, reduced to depend upon the bounty of her creditor, not only for past immunity, but for present subsistence?'

Walsingham, though but ill disposed to concur with him, found himself obliged to suppress his dissent, and for the present the matter proceeded no further.

Isabel and Monsieur de Verneuil had hailed / the arrival of their friend Walsingham at Naples with as much delight as if the husband and wife were already tired of each other, and glad of any relief. But it was not so; their affection was undiminished, and promised durability; and their satisfaction was the result of the genuine regard they entertained for him. Of course, Isabel was not slow in perceiving the terms he and Agnes were upon; and she loved both parties so well, and was so convinced of the joy their union would give to Bertha, that she lost no time in writing to her, expressly for the purpose of announcing it.

Towards the end of the letter, speaking of Mr. St. Hubert, she said: –

'The magnificent old man, Walsingham has told de Verneuil, insists upon bestowing on Agnes a marriage portion of twenty thousand pounds. The remainder of his fortune will probably go to his nephew, Mr. Danvers, unless the charming Elder should meet with / any other woman as ready to fall in love with him as I am, and should be induced to marry. During a *tête à tête* conversation I had with him yesterday, relative to the unhappy Georgiana and her connexions, I was amused by one of his characteristic reflexions. "So little can be said," he observed, "to the honour of poor Wharton, that I confess I have no objection to a small family blot on Walsingham's escutcheon, as well as on that of Agnes. It puts them more upon a par; and should they now and then, impelled by human infirmity, yield to the temptation of indulging a little ill-humour, neither party, even in the fullest fervour of their spite, can taunt the other on the subject of their relations.

'Is not this being most comically provident of comfort against future contingencies? I think both Walsingham and Agnes would find it difficult not to laugh if I dared tell them what he said, but it is too tender a point to touch upon with them. /

'We shall be here about a month, and then, before the summer heats begin, we all intend to journey homeward. The temperature hitherto has been, generally speaking, delicious, but not always exempt from piercing winds, which, to my feelings at least are more cutting – more subtile and penetrating than our coldest and roughest English blasts. I have often thought the air here must be filled with little tiny, tiny invisible lancets, not made of highly tempered *steel,* but of highly tempered *ice.* However, by observing the cautions my good Margaret Blake recommends – and she is perfectly acquainted with this climate, and its effects upon foreigners, who like me, are not very strong, I have escaped all mischief, though too often, at the price of many a delightful morning excursion, which I have been obliged to forego. Our social evenings make me rich amends; we always spend them together; and five happier people are not easily to be met with. Italy, and its fine arts, and fine skies, / and fine scenery, is after all, to us northern barbarians, very like the plums and sugar greedily devoured by the grocer's boy the first week of his apprenticeship: they pall upon us,[105] and we are glad to recur to our accustomed food; viz: our green woods and meadows – our well-furnished and ugly houses, and our domestic fire side. No room looks familiar and pleasant in my eyes, that has not the advantage of a chimney; they may say what they please in vindication of that deficiency here; I protest, there are many days when it is more wanted in this country than in ours, and the only reasonable motive that can be assigned for their not having it is, that the hot weather lasts longer than the cold. Meanwhile, in winter (for winter they *have*, and not always of short duration) quantities of poor people are burnt to death by cowering over little earthen fire pots filled with hot cinders, which they carry about by the handle like work baskets wherever they go, and by which / they often set fire to their clothes, when it is next to impossible to save them from destruction. Now it is hardly worth while to risk such a calamity for so small a benefit as that of a tea-cup-full of wood-ashes that neither give light, cheerfulness, nor warmth enough to comfort a patriarchal blue-bottle fly! If I were in a captious humour, I could, in speaking of Italian customs pick sundry other holes in their coat.[106] Their intolerable love of half cooked vegetables; their pillows stuffed with wool instead of feathers, which on waking, make one's head feel bruized, and one's neck dislocated. Of course all this could be easily remedied by persons meaning to stay long enough to make it worth while to take the trouble: but we who are only birds of passage, grumble and submit. In great towns, and first-rate inns, these little grievances are more seldom met with. However, upon the whole, my journey has gratified me extremely; but to be perfectly candid, I must acknowledge, that my acquaintance with the / inhabitants is extremely superficial; I do not speak their language fluently, and have very much confined myself to the society of our countrymen. Agnes has resided much longer amongst them, and appears to me to converse in Italian with all the facility of a native. She can give you whatever details you may desire, and she will do it in the true spirit of justice and gratitude, called forth by the thousand kindnesses she has received.' /

CHAPTER VI.

'How noiseless falls the foot of time,
That only treads on flowers!'

SPENCER.[107]

NEARLY three months after the receipt of the letter inserted in the preceding chapter, Lady Glenfeld wrote thus to her sister, then at Paris:

'Our friends are arrived, dear Isabel, and Agnes is actually under my roof. Lord Glenfeld, with his wonted indulgence, consented to accompany me to town to receive her. She gives an excellent account of you, and says you are not only perfectly well, but in the highest / beauty, and in eminent favour with all your new relations. Of Monsieur de Verneuil, she adds, that he improved upon her every hour, and that he is one of the most honourable and at the same time, agreeable men, she knows. Think you, dearest Isabel, I heard all this with indifference? Ah, no: – my delight at it was as sincere, as my felicitations are cordial. I have only to wish, that you may ere long, give me the additional joy of seeing you in England.

'Mr. St. Hubert and Walsingham are at an hotel, near us, but merely to sleep and dress. They spend the chief part of their time, as you may well imagine, with us. It is truly gratifying to see Walsingham's frank and manly countenance beaming with an expression of such enviable happiness. I have, in former times, often known him gay, but his merriment was too apt to be followed by fits of abstraction and seriousness which proved that all within was not at ease. The fact is, his mother's inexplicable / coldness and neglect, affected him deeply even from his boyhood; and I remember to have heard him more than once assert, that it was to be feared the man who possessed not the qualities that could endear him to his own mother, was born to pass through life unloved by any other woman! Such an impression could not but furnish food to great dejection, relieved at intervals, however, (happily for him), by the buoyant spirits natural to his time of life and original disposition. Agnes' affection has totally dispelled all this melancholy distrust, and such is the effect upon him of the confidence he reposes in her, that he no longer appears the same man; and I must say, to me, who prefer equanimity to the most brilliant flights, he has gained infinitely by the change.

'But of Agnes herself, let me now speak. Beautiful as I always thought her, she has unquestionably improved beyond measure since I saw her about a year ago. Her carriage is / more easy and graceful – her figure more formed – and her countenance with all its native sweetness unimpaired, has acquired a something which, if I can hardly call dignity, I can at least assert, would repress the most distant approach to impertinence, or unauthorized familiarity. Modesty is still its characteristic; but timidity – at least, bashfulness, is gone.

'It would be superfluous to praise Mr. St. Hubert to you, who already know and love him so well; but I must say that he not only fully comes up to, but surpasses the idea I had formed of him. So fine a countenance I never saw: it has every thing in it one could wish; – its acuteness is softened by benevolence – and the frankness it expresses, has nothing blunt or alarming, but is qualified and accompanied by a degree of polish which neither Lord Glenfeld nor I had anticipated, and which has most agreeably surprised us. /

'He showed me this morning, a letter from Mr. Wharton, in answer to the information he had given him respecting Agnes, and in acknowledgment of the kindness with which he had offered to settle upon him an annuity. Nothing can be better expressed than his feelings on both these subjects: – but Mr. Wharton is Mr. Wharton still! – neither demon nor angel, yet a little of both – and as unable to resist temptation where wealth and consequence are in question, as at any period of his life. The substance of what he relates concerning his personal adventures – dressed up as he knows how – reads like the story of a hero of romance. If he is to be believed, everything that has happened to him has been the work of destiny, in whose hands he has been merely a passive instrument. But we know Mr. Wharton, and it is therefore not easy to give implicit credit to such a representation. His statement is, that when he landed in America, he knew but one individual on that vast continent. By that / individual he was received most hospitably and kindly, and through his means, obtained an introduction to various respectable families, and assurances that every exertion should be made to procure for him some honourable employment. Meanwhile welcomed in the best society, and retaining as we all know, a fine person and insinuating address, he succeeded ere long, in rendering himself particularly acceptable to one of the wealthiest residents of the place – a widow – (age, character, and personal appearance, not specified,) whom he persuaded, in short, to marry him. He concludes his narration, extremely cleverly drawn up, with renewed acknowledgments to Mr. St. Hubert for his generous offers: – sends his blessing, his good wishes and his tenderest love to Agnes, – his "charming daughter," – and ends by giving thanks to Providence that the union he had meditated between her and young Cowley, had failed to take place, Harry being, as he confesses, his natural son! Imagine, / only, dear Isabel, what might have been the consequence to these two innocent creatures, of the vices and subterfuges of their father! Agnes thinks not so seriously as I do of the danger she incurred, protesting there never was a moment when she could have been induced to accept him: "As a brother," she adds, "he will be most welcome to me, for I have always had the feeling towards him of a sister; – as a husband, my heart invariably shrunk from him; – I cannot therefore picture to myself, in a very terrific manner, a risk I never ran."

'We all hope, nay, feel nearly assured, that Mr. Wharton, having now the means, will behave liberally towards his son; but perhaps it is hardly to be wished that he should withdraw him from the profession he has been preparing himself for, with such zeal and assiduity. He is said to have talents of the very first order.

'Agnes and he, had their first interview / yesterday; they were together some time, without witnesses; but on coming forth, their looks denoted the most perfect harmony and kindness, with scarcely, even on his part, the least agitation. He was introduced to Mr. St. Hubert, and renewed the slight acquaintance he already had with Walsingham. We detained him the rest of the day, which he spent in good spirits; and went away, I trust, as well satisfied with us, as we were with him.

'Mr. St. Hubert observed to me, that in a few years, when *cette fleur de fatuité*[108] that is now in full blow shall have dropt off, he will be in every respect, a distinguished and superior man: "for luckily," he adds, "his conceit has blossomed early, and the fruit when it ripens, may, and I trust will be, of a healthy, and well-conditioned quality."

'London is now so empty, and even if it were full, Agnes is such a stranger to its inhabitants, that you will be surprised to hear she has found a house to visit at. The house / in question, is that of Madame Morinval, who was formerly, second in command under Madame Leroux, but is now at the head of *l'Etablissement*,[109] and very much in vogue. For myself, I would not employ any one else for my court or gala dresses for the world; and you will easily conceive the pleasure Agnes has, in bespeaking from her, all her wedding paraphanalia. I need not enlarge upon the satisfaction of the worthy woman, on seeing again, and in such prosperous circumstances, the young creature, for whom, nearly eight years ago, she manifested so much interest and affection. It was gratifying to witness their meeting, more especially, as Agnes brought her letters from her son and daughter at Paris, and was able to corroborate, from personal observation, the good account those letters contained, of their health and welfare. By the way, I hear from Adrienne, whom I am never backward in encouraging to talk of her mistress, that during the few days / she lately spent at Paris, she found time, more than once, to go and see the family of the poor printer, Dupuis, with whom she lodged, on escaping from Mr. Wharton's, and whom she has benefitted in the most essential manner. The youngest boy, her little favourite Jeannot, she has apprenticed, at his own ardent desire, to a mathematical instrument maker; she has placed his young sister at a creditable school; has settled on the sickly mother, a small annuity, and to each remaining individual of the honest family (including an aged widow, poorer than themselves, who lodges with them), has presented a certain sum, to lay out in whatever way they preferred.

'After a day spent in such acts, how easy must the pillow feel at night! We leave town, Lord Glenfeld and I, in about a week, and Agnes goes with us. Her uncle and Walsingham, are compelled to remain here some time longer, the latter, to settle his own affairs, relative to the inheritance that has devolved to / him; and the former, to look after the marriage articles of his niece. As soon as possible, they will follow us, and the wedding is to be celebrated in the country, at our parish church. Where they will go afterwards, is not yet decided. Agnes has a great wish to see Meadwell again, and the good Blakes, her early patrons. If there is any house in that neighbourhood which would suit them, I think she will persuade Walsingham, and her uncle (for he is to live with them) to engage it, in preference to a large mansion they neither of them care for, attached to Walsingham's newly acquired property. I am perfectly friendly to this plan, since the distance at which it would place us, with good roads and good horses, would be nothing; and the country is extremely pretty, and Meadwell is a spot, which, from early associations, I should have great pleasure in revisiting.

'Mamma is with Caroline and her husband, in Suffolk. Louisa is gone into Scotland, to / pay a visit to her new relations, and will probably stay there some months. I like these two brothers-in-law very promisingly; that is to say, I anticipate that when I know more of them, I *shall* like them very much.

'Adieu, my dearest Isabel. Tell Monsieur de Verneuil that I shall not like *him* at all, unless he adheres to his promise of bringing you over next spring. Meanwhile, write often; take care of your health; do not suffer Margaret Blake to think of leaving you, and believe me, ever with the warmest affection, your own,

BERTHA GLENFELD.'

END OF VOL. II. /

LONDON:
SCHULZE AND CO., 13, POLAND STREET.

THE ROMANCE OF PRIVATE LIFE.

BY
MISS BURNEY.

IN THREE VOLUMES.

VOL III.

THE HERMITAGE.

LONDON:

HENRY COLBURN, PUBLISHER,

GREAT MARLBOROUGH STREET.
1839. /

LONDON:

SCHULZE AND CO. 13, POLAND STREET. /

THE HERMITAGE.

CHAPTER I.

Don Pedro. In faith, lady, you have a merry heart.
Beatrice. Yea, my Lord, I thank it, poor fool, it keeps on the windy side of care.

SHAKSPEARE.[1]

'MY dear Hugh,' said Mrs. Fitzmaurice, as her husband was quitting the room one morning after breakfast, 'come back a moment; I have a favour to ask of you.'

'What is it? What is it, Bess? I have an appointment with Jervis, and am in a great hurry; don't detain me, for I dare say you / only want to ask some trifle you might just as well order or buy without my interference.'

'No, no; I neither want to buy or to order! I want to ask your leave to invite Ella to accompany us into Shropshire.'[2]

'With all my heart! Ella is a very pleasant girl, and I wish she may be induced to consent: but at such short notice, and at this gay time of the year, I very much doubt it.'

'There is no reason to believe *she* will object; but – mamma – I fear mamma may make some difficulty.'

Mr. Fitzmaurice looked at his wife's ingenuous, but somewhat uneasy countenance, with a half-suppressed smile, and returning to his chair, said:

'What put this scheme into your head, Bess? It seems to have occurred to you very suddenly.'

'True; I had no thoughts of it when I / went to Mrs. Clare's last night; the London season is still at its height, and I concluded, Ella would like to enjoy another month of its gaieties; but the way in which I saw her drawn on to encourage – or, rather, to attract young Sedley....'[3]

'Ah, I thought as much! But, dear Bess, let young Sedley shift for himself. He will either withstand the lures thrown out for him, or submit, with a good grace, to his fate, and turn out a very happy fellow.'

'But, Hugh, it is not creditable to Ella to obtain an offer by such means.'

'Ella knows nothing of the matter; she lets herself be guided by her mother; who, to do her justice, manœuvres, without initiating her daughters into her plans; they are passive tools in her hands, and, in all innocence, are made to decoy men's hearts, as tame birds are trained to decoy their wild brethren. Ella has no more design in her nature than you had; she dances with Sedley, without knowing or / caring how the thing is brought about; she finds herself seated next to him at dinner, and supposes it is by accident, she meets him when riding out, and is glad he should happen to choose the same road, and the same hour, that has been chosen for her. Sedley may sometimes fancy she lends a hand to all these combinations; but as, nevertheless, he still hovers within the sphere of her attractions, the probability is, he will marry her, and to his own surprise, find that he has got a perfectly single-minded, artless, and undiplomatic little wife.'

'Do you mean to say, my dear husband,' cried Mrs. Fitzmaurice, changing colour, 'that *you* were lured on in this way? that the attentions you paid me, were all the result of my mother's covert machinations?'

Fitzmaurice saw with concern, that the soft eyes of his wife were swimming in tears, and that her lips actually quivered as she spoke. He affectionately threw his arm round her / waist, drew her towards him, and kissing her varying cheek, answered in a soothing voice:

'I cannot retract what I have said, dearest Bess, though I have been a brute to hurt your feelings, by speaking so unreservedly. Take comfort, however, in the reflexion, that I always saw you were unconscious of your mother's views. The smiles you bestowed upon me, came direct from your own heart; you acted upon no plan, but you really felt favourably disposed towards me; and seeing that, I forgave the systematic project that had been formed to entice me, and willingly ran my head into a noose, which I have daily and hourly found fresh cause to rejoice in. Were all politic mothers as conscientiously determined to prosecute their designs, without the connivance of their daughters, they might be allowed to scheme on to the end of time, without censure, or ill-consequence. It is only when / they corrupt the genuine simplicity of the poor girls, and make selfish dissemblers of them, that we have real reason to complain.'

'You have consoled me by this good-natured speech,' said the half-smiling wife. 'I was heart-struck by what had first escaped you; but after words of so much kindness, it would only be shewing pique and irritability, to dwell upon the subject any longer. Let us therefore talk again of Ella; must I let her stay in town?'

'I am of the opinion you have no other course to pursue. Mrs. Ormond will think your proposal preposterous, and will scarcely have patience to listen to it. Ella would accompany us willingly enough, if all parties were agreed in desiring that she should; but if her mother objects to it, nay, if she positively forbids it, what can Ella do?'

'Poor girl, nothing! But, Hugh, advise me; do you think it would be right – would / be useful, to give Ella a little hint? in short, to put her somewhat upon her guard against the project that is carrying on?'

'I fear, Bessy, you would be only doing mischief. Ella's conduct, is, at present, thoroughly void of trick and coquetry; but if you put alarming scruples into her head, she will be thrown into the most awkward of all dilemmas. On one side, the fear of displeasing her mother, on the other, the misgivings excited by your suggestions, will destroy that ease, and simplicity of manner, which proves to every impartial observer, that she is wholly undesigning; and from the apprehension of being thought artificial, she will positively assume its appearance.'

'Perhaps you are right, and I therefore will forbear saying anything in allusion to Mr. Sedley; but I cannot, with the same ease, give up the wish of attempting to prevail upon my mother to let Ella go with us.' /

'Well, dear Bess,' said Mr. Fitzmaurice, rising, 'try your influence, and may all success attend you.'

He then left the room, and assured of his sanction, his wife immediately ordered her carriage, and drove to Mrs. Ormond's.

That lady was at home and alone. She received her daughter with her accustomed kindness, and thanked her for coming so early, as she wished very much to have a little private conversation with her. 'So far,' thought Mrs. Fitzmaurice, 'our wishes agree; but how far will their agreement extend?'

'You are to know, my dear,' added the mother, 'that I have some thoughts of asking you to take Ella with you into the country.'

'Indeed!' cried Mrs. Fitzmaurice, struck with the liveliest surprise.

'Yes; I think the life she is now leading might be too much for her were it to continue longer. She is so unaccustomed to these late / hours, and so new to all the dissipation she is engaged in, that it is much better not to extend the trial any further this season. I shall be detained in town myself for at least another month, to sign some law papers, which will not before that time be ready. But if Mr. Fitzmaurice will permit you to take charge of her, I know, my dear Bessy, that Ella could not be in better hands than yours; and I shall not only be perfectly easy about her, but feel particularly obliged to you for accepting the trust.'

Secretly delighted by what she had heard, and beyond measure relieved on finding herself exempted from the necessity of entering upon the embarrassing task she had purposed to undertake, Mrs. Fitzmaurice assured her mother she had no opposition to apprehend from her husband, who, she was convinced, would most readily comply with their wishes.

'Well, my dear, that being the case – and I am inclined to believe you are right, for Ella / seems to be a great favourite with Fitzmaurice – I shall order everything to be prepared for her journey, and you may depend upon it, you shall not have to wait for her an instant. What day do you go?'

'We had appointed Thursday – but if that is too soon –'

'Oh, not at all; this is only Monday. It would be absurd indeed if a girl at Ella's age could not in three days be got ready to travel a hundred miles! But go up to her, my love, and tell her what we have determined upon. You will find her in her little study.'

Mrs. Fitzmaurice, still full of wonder, and hardly believing she had heard aright, ran up stairs, impatient to see what effect her communication would produce upon her sister. As she drew near the tiny apartment, a sound of youthful and sportive laughter greeted her ears, and told her that Ella was not alone. She opened the door, and found the admired, the beautiful, the fashionable Miss Ormond / seated on a foot-stool between two little boys, who were watching the tricks she was causing her poodle to play for their amusement. One of the children had his arm round her neck, whilst hers encircled his waist. The other – a sort of arch looking Robin Goodfellow – was clapping his little hands, and capering with delight at every fresh exhibition of the poodle's genius! A prettier group could not have been imagined.

After watching them some seconds, Mrs. Fitzmaurice advanced, saying with a smile: 'And so these are the pursuits you carry on in your *study*, Ella?'

'And why not, dear Bessy? Is it not quite as well to make a learned dog of poor Zanga, as a learned lady of myself?'

'Perhaps it is. But who are these merry little companions of yours?'

'They are the nephews of Hannah, my maid, to whom I shall now send them.'

She then gave to each a handful of sugar / plums, and a kind kiss on the forehead, and dismissed them.

Crowded rooms and late hours had as yet caused no ravages in Ella's freshness and brilliancy. Many faces might be more regularly handsome, but none more attractive. Its characteristic was freedom from care, openness of heart, and an expression of vivacity that when at all heightened, nearly amounted to joyousness. Yet the same eyes that sparkled with so much glee and animation were capable of indicating the tenderest pity, the most grateful attachment, and the clearest penetration and good sense. It was a face to study, and to find perpetually exciting new impressions. The flexibility of its muscles was such that her very thoughts acted upon them: a gay image betrayed itself by the dimpling though almost imperceptible smiles that played around her mouth; her brow unconsciously revealed the less happy ideas that at intervals crossed her imagination, and this by such slight, yet varied / and intelligible movements, that it was impossible, with any quickness of observation, to mistake the nature of what was passing in her mind. With a countenance so irresistibly prepossessing, was combined a figure that was all ease and symmetry; a hand and arm that might have served as models for a sculptor; an extraordinary quantity of glossy, silken, raven-black hair; and eyes of the deep, dark, yet clear blue of a midnight sky, fringed by the longest and the finest eye-lashes.

The children being gone, and the sisters seated side by side on the sofa, Mrs. Fitzmaurice thus began the conversation:

'I am commissioned by mamma, my dear Ella, to give you a piece of information that may not, perhaps, be very pleasant to you. Mr. Fitzmaurice, however, thinks otherwise; *he* thinks you so extraordinary and so unspoiled a person, that at eighteen, and enjoying all the enchantments of a first spring in London, you / will be content to resign them, and to rusticate with us at Holme Court.'

'Mr. Fitzmaurice is a wizard, and has guessed the truth exactly! But tell me, do you really mean that *mamma* sent you with this information?'

'Yes, dearest; it was she herself who proposed your going with us, sparing me, by so doing, the embarrassment of asking her to permit it, which, to speak the truth, was the chief motive that brought me here so early.'

'Thank you, my kind sister,' said Ella. Then reflecting a few seconds on what she had heard, a comic smile full of meaning, stole over her features; and in a half whisper she murmured to herself: 'How could I be so stupid as not to understand it immediately?'

'Understand what?' enquired Mrs. Fitzmaurice.

'That I am the happiest girl in England, dear Bessy!' and then impelled by the agreeable / train of ideas that had taken possession of her, she started up, and to her own lively singing, began waltzing round the room in a wild fit of spirits that no one could have witnessed without feeling exhilarated. Mrs. Fitzmaurice, though not of a character so animated as her sister, was always willing to participate in the pleasure of others, and sat laughingly contemplating the rapid evolutions of the frolicsome and graceful girl, till almost giddy at the sight, she cried out:

'Enough, enough, Ella! I beseech you do not spin round any longer, but come back to your seat, and let us have a little rational talk.'

Ella, glowing and breathless, complied, and their conversation was renewed with restored composure.

Sportive, and apparently thoughtless as she was, Ella was by no means unobservant or deficient in sagacity. She had been struck, on learning the project traced out by her mother, / with the recollection of a little dialogue she had overheard the night before at Mrs. Clare's ball between Mr. Sedley and a gentleman of his acquaintance who stood near her and Mrs. Ormond in the refreshment room. They were talking of their plans for the summer, and young Sedley, in allusion to his, had said,

'Mine are forced upon me by circumstances, and are anything but agreeable. I am invited into Shropshire by my guardian, to be present at the marriage of his daughter, and shall be obliged to leave town in a few days, and perhaps stay with him for several weeks.'

'But you are out of his hands now; you are no longer a minor.'

'Certainly not: *mais que voulez-vous?*[4] One cannot all at once shake off one's allegiance; and to do the old gentleman justice, he has been an excellent friend to me, and has managed my affairs incomparably.'

'In what part of Shropshire does he reside?' /

'About five or six miles from Ludlow.'

Now Ella, combining this part of their dialogue with what her mother was now negotiating, felt convinced that the reason for sending her to Holme Court, was no other than that of placing her still within reach of Mr. Sedley. The house of Fitzmaurice, she knew was also near Ludlow, and there could be no doubt Mrs. Ormond would take effectual measures to inform young Sedley that Ella was in his neighbourhood. The idea amused her, and she hailed it as the cause of her present agreeable prospects; but young Sedley entered for nothing in her anticipations of felicity. She liked him as an acquaintance; she liked him for the similarity she had discovered between some of his opinions and her own; but as a lover he was utterly indifferent to her. The Shropshire journey, therefore, derived its charms from a source with which Mr. Sedley had not the remotest concern. /

CHAPTER II.

> His life was gentle; and the elements
> So mixed in him, that Nature might stand up
> And say to all the world, this was a man!
>
> SHAKESPEARE.[5]

MRS. Fitzmaurice, when she communicated to her husband the result of her morning's visit, saw, without surprise, but with some perplexity, a broad smile spread itself over his countenance, the counterpart, (though less moderated) of that which had so expressively appeared upon the face of Ella.

'I am surely very dull of apprehension!' cried she. 'I cannot for my life understand what it is that seems so ludicrous both to you / and Ella in my mother's consent, or rather, proposal.'

'Did Ella also laugh when she heard it?'

'Yes; and look just as wicked as you do.'

'O then, she is not quite so simple and unconscious as I had supposed her!'

'Do explain yourself, dear Hugh; what is it you mean?'

'Well, don't be shocked, and I will tell you. Your mother, I am persuaded, acts in consequence of having learnt that Sedley himself is going into Shropshire.'

'Can it be? How did you hear it?'

'He told me so himself at our club this morning.'

'How provoking!'

'Not at all. We shall let every thing take its own course, without forming schemes either to attract or repulse him. When he comes to Holme Court – as most assuredly he / will, let it be at his own suggestion; we need not invite him, unless we have a party, from which, it might appear extraordinary to exclude him. Pursuing this system, his vicinity will no more interfere with our habits, and no more require our attention than that of any other man.'

After a little further discussion, Mrs. Fitzmaurice became convinced her husband was right, and reconciled herself to what at first appeared calculated only to give her vexation.

In various ways, Mr. Fitzmaurice was a superior person, and amply justified the implicit deference with which his wife yielded to his opinions. Not merely was he a man of fashion, fond of, and highly distinguished in society for his talents and taste; he was also a man of letters, and had published several works, some on political subjects, others on matters of general literature, that had acquired him great and deserved reputation. Of a temper, / the most indulgent to every fault, that originated not in real perversity of heart, he was, of all human beings, the easiest to live with, and the least inclined to magnify trifles into importance. No one, however, was safer to consult in cases of difficulty, for his judgment was as sound, as his principles were honourable.

During their journey into the country, he often rallied Ella, on the astonishing philosophy, with which she was resigning the pleasures of London, to ruralize with him and his wife, in a spot, offering so few resources to a fair idol, accustomed, as she had been of late, to clouds of incense, wafted by zealous worshippers. He tried a thousand ways to induce her to confess she was not ignorant of Sedley's intended movements; but in vain. She eluded his attacks with admirable good humour, yet with a dexterity that completely baffled him.

The first week of their residence at Holme / Court, passed without bringing any other visitors than the neighbouring clergyman, his wife, and daughters, and one or two quiet families, accustomed annually to call and welcome the return of Mr. and Mrs. Fitzmaurice into the country. Ella was surprised and disappointed; she had expected something better; but neither her countenance nor manner, betrayed what she felt. Her brother, after three years' absence on the continent, was to have arrived in town, with the friend who had accompanied him, the very day following her departure. She had decided in her own mind, that when he had seen and spent some time with his mother, he would hasten into Shropshire, or, that at all events, his friend would take that route. The established home, the head-quarters of both the young men, when in England, was in the neighbouring county of Worcester. They had been from their boyhood the inmates, and her brother was the declared heir, of Sir Everard Ormond, his / uncle; and she was almost apprehensive of the effect that would be produced by their deferring so long to present themselves to their benefactor. It is true, she could not be quite assured they had not yet appeared; though, as the distance was so trifling between the two houses, she could hardly believe, since there had been no tidings of them at Holme Court, that they had actually arrived at her uncle's. Mrs. Fitzmaurice herself began to wonder at, and blame their delay. She was only the half-sister of young Ormond and Ella; but she could not have loved them more affectionately, had they been the children of the same father; and few circumstances would have caused her greater vexation, than their being guilty of any thing that might be prejudicial to their own interest. What she felt, she openly expressed before her husband and Ella; what the latter felt, she struggled successfully to conceal.

'See how soon,' said Fitzmaurice, in / answer to his wife's lamentations, 'the circle closes when we withdraw our stick from the water! Brothers, lovers, nephews, all dismiss us from their thoughts when out of sight. But have patience, dear Bess; since, if it is supposed you have retired hither "*the world forgetting*," it is only reasonable to expect you should be "*by the world forgot*."[6]

'But how do you think the patience of Sir Everard will hold out? That is of much more consequence than mine!'

'It will come and go, vanish and re-appear fifty times a day. However, when the truant youths at last return, they will probably be let off upon the easy terms of having to listen for ten minutes to a furious declamation, which will end in a cordial forgiveness. Tomorrow, however, I will pay him a visit, and bring you word which way the wind sets. If it blows from a very rough quarter, you may not choose to expose yourself to it; but if it only whiffles about in occasional puffs, interspersed / with sun-shine and calm, I think you had better drive over yourself; especially if you take Ella with you, who, we all know, is nearly as great a favourite as Frederick himself.'

Fitzmaurice had scarcely ceased speaking, when the sound of horses' feet drew their attention to the window, and they all stept forward to see who was approaching. Two young men rode rapidly up to the front entrance, one of whom the Fitzmaurices instantly distinguished to be Mr. Sedley; the other they less easily recognized; he was the quickest in alighting, and they almost immediately lost sight of him under the portico.

Her brother-in-law, ere he turned from the window, snatched a look at Ella, and saw a gleam of rapture flash across her face, that spoke volumes.

'Humph!' ejaculated he mentally, 'Sedley has no reason to despair!'

A short interval sufficed to bring the newcomers / into the apartment. The companion of Mr. Sedley was then found to be Ernest de Gray, the fellow-traveller of Ella's brother, and one of the young men, for whose arrival at Ormond-Hall, Mrs. Fitzmaurice had been so solicitous. He was welcomed by her with great cordiality, and introduced to her husband, who had never before seen him. Then came questions innumerable, respecting Frederick. Where was he? Why had he not also ridden over? How had Sir Everard received him? When had he arrived? &c. To all this, Ernest simply and briefly answered:

'He is still in town. Sir Everard, after reading a letter I brought from him, wrote to give him permission to prolong his stay in London, and seems tolerably reconciled to his delay.'

'But at first, I suppose, he was outrageous!'

'He certainly was not very well pleased.'

'And when did you yourself arrive?' /

'Last night.'

'Did you and Mr. Sedley meet accidentally on your road hither?'

'No, dear Madam, there was no accident in the case. I called upon him at his guardian's this morning, and we agreed to pay our visit here together.'

While putting all these interrogations to the young man, Mrs. Fitzmaurice could not but observe with satisfaction, the wonderful change his person had undergone. On leaving England, which he had done expressly for his health, he was feeble, pale, and emaciated. He now wore a look of vigour and energy, totally foreign to his former appearance. His features, always regular and beautiful, had acquired an air of manliness, an expression of calm, but modest self-possession, that without impairing their general effect, no longer exhibited that over-delicacy, that sensitive diffidence that had attended his earlier years. Encreased in height, but finely proportioned, / his carriage had become firm and easy; his walk elastic, and his whole aspect so different to what it had once been, that it was difficult to conceive how so many threatening symptoms, could, in so short a time, have been overcome.

In favour of the friend who had accompanied him, Mr. Fitzmaurice broke through the rule he had laid down, of never inviting Sedley to prolong or repeat his visits; and cordially pressed both the gentlemen to dine with them; a proposal that was accepted with alacrity.

And how had Ella demeaned herself during this time? In a manner the most singular. She had scarcely spoken a word, and had looked so bewildered, that it was impossible to determine whether she felt displeased or gratified. The truth is, the remarkable difference observable in her former play-mate, Ernest de Gray, completely disconcerted her. The more she looked at him, the more she wondered / how she had been able so immediately to recognize him as he passed the window. The image he had left impressed upon her mind, first of a suffering, but uncomplaining boy, and then, of a gentle, affectionate, but still ailing youth, rendered attaching by the very pity he awakened; this image, still dear to her remembrance, was now to be effaced, and its place supplied by another, that instead of compassion, appeared rather formed to excite respect and deference. It was as if a stranger, with something of the same aspect as her early friend, had assumed his name and station.

But, by degrees, her regret subsided, and she owned to herself that his present appearance was in every respect an improvement; yet, the ease and intimacy, with which she had in former times behaved to him, she felt could subsist no longer; it did not indeed appear as if he himself expected it. He treated her with / attention, with the gentlest good breeding, with a certain degree even of friendship; but without the slightest approach towards familiarity; and no one who had not known how attached they had once been to each other, could, on seeing them at present, have suspected it.

During dinner, it was observed that Mr. Sedley, and it was not his wont, conversed more than any one at table. He was a young man of excellent, plain sense, well-intentioned, and amiable; but he had bestowed little pains upon the cultivation of his abilities, which, though good in themselves, were crushed by a weight of mental indolence, that nothing could surpass or overcome. Yet, whether from joy at again seeing Ella, from satisfaction at the return of his old school-fellow and friend, or from both these causes combined, certain it is, he talked more, and talked better than most of the party would have given him / credit for. Mr. Fitzmaurice's object, however, was to sound the capacity of Ernest. He had been struck by the mild and contemplative character of his countenance, and the little he had heard him utter, was spoken with such simple propriety, his eye was so expressive, and there was, in the inflexions of his voice, something that so irresistibly arrested the attention, that he seized the first favourable opportunity of drawing him out. He questioned him on the subject of foreign literature, and society; and Ernest, who had diligently studied the language, both of Germany and Italy, even before he left England, and had, of course, greatly improved his acquaintance with each in the countries themselves, was well qualified to satisfy his enquiries. Furnished with numerous letters of introduction, he had been admitted, wherever he went, into many of the houses of the most distinguished inhabitants, and had preferred their society to / that (exclusively) of his own countrymen. He had visited with an observant and well-prepared mind, all the principal libraries; had read many of the best authors recommended by men of talents and discernment; and it speedily appeared that he was no less an enthusiast for the fine arts, than an admirer of the historian, and the philosopher. Mr. Fitzmaurice was delighted with him, and it was obvious that Ernest, though the least conceited of human beings, was gratified in the highest degree by the consciousness of being so flatteringly appreciated by one whose opinion was of so much value.

When their horses were brought to the door, and the two gentlemen, by a lovely moonlight, reluctantly took their departure, Mr. Fitzmaurice, on re-entering the drawing-room after seeing them ride off, said:

'Find me, my dear ladies, a pair of young men, worthy, for different merits, to be compared / with our recent guests, and I will give you any reward you may please to ask! Sedley, for genuine good feeling, for native clear-headedness, and unpretending simplicity, is eminently praise-worthy. De Gray is of a higher order. Pray tell me a little more about him. He lives, it seems, at Ormond Hall; but what is his relationship to Sir Everard? What are his prospects? What is his destination?'

'You ask more than either Ella or I can tell you,' answered Mrs. Fitzmaurice; 'we only know that on the death of his mother, who was Lady Ormond's intimate friend, Sir Everard consented to her taking him under her protection; he was then not more than six or seven years old. His father, a staff officer, and a man of family, was poor and improvident, and depending almost entirely upon his pay for subsistence. He died young, and from that time the orphan boy became a fixture at / Ormond Hall, and partook of every advantage of education enjoyed by my brother, and of every indulgence, the large fortune, and the generosity of Sir Everard could bestow. But a dreadful fall which happened to him just as he was entering his tenth year, the ill effects of which it was almost feared he never would recover, threw him into bad health, and made him particularly liable to such excruciating head-aches, that from having been a remarkably active, enterprizing little fellow, he was reduced to lead a life the most sedentary, seldom unattended by pain. The compassion he inspired was general throughout the family; and what, perhaps, encreased it, was his extraordinary and interesting beauty, in despite of all the languor and illness he suffered. Even Sir Everard, rough as he is, and averse to having sick people about him, was touched by the poor boy's sweetness and resignation. He was rarely well enough to accompany / Frederick to school; but when forced to remain at home, a tutor was provided for him; and with all the disadvantages under which he laboured, the progress he made, I have heard, was extraordinary. To complete, as it then appeared, his misfortunes, an apprehension arose, as he approached his twentieth year, that his lungs were attacked; and a temporary residence in a warmer climate, was strenuously recommended, and agreed to without opposition. Frederick, though with less readiness, obtained permission to accompany him; what the journey may have done for *him* we are yet to learn; its consequence to Ernest is, as you see, an entire restoration to health; but I much fear it has not added to my brother's fondness for Ormond Hall.'

'Perhaps not; Ormond Hall, to a young man but little addicted to steady reading, and unprovided with any favourite mental pursuit, / is by no means an attractive residence, its principal recommendation being a magnificent library, the industrious accumulation of former generations. Sir Everard and Lady Ormond are growing old; they exclude general society, and have but few privileged friends remaining with health and spirits sufficient to give animation to the house when they pay their stated visits. Such must have been nearly the case when Frederick went away; and he, no doubt, reflects that the three years of his absence cannot have much improved it. However, he ought to come down at all events; it is a debt of gratitude which he ought to pay, and the sooner the better. Write and tell him so, Ella.'

'Meanwhile, my dear girl,' resumed Mrs. Fitzmaurice, 'what say you to our going there together to-morrow morning?'

'I am perfectly willing. My uncle is always good and kind to me; and Lady Ormond, / with all her oddities, perhaps on their very account, amuses me exceedingly.'

'I own,' said Mrs. Fitzmaurice, 'she does not produce that effect upon me. She rather startles than amuses me; for to tell you the truth, there have been times when I have thought her half crazy, and have felt a little inclined to be afraid of her.'

Ella laughed; 'Afraid of her, poor soul! She never had the wish or the courage to hurt a fly!'

'Her singularities,' observed Mr. Fitzmaurice, 'appear to me to be the effect of great nervousness of absence, of a habit of grotesque gesticulation, and of a mixture the most extraordinary of credulous simplicity, with extensive reading, and ill-digested information.'

'It is more your interest than any body's,' said Ella, 'to defend her sanity; for she professes to look up to you as one of the first of human beings.' /

'She does me great honour! and that opinion of hers, must, I am persuaded, confirm your belief in the soundness of her understanding!' /

CHAPTER III.

> Her discourse is peremptory, her gait ridiculous; and she draweth out the thread of her verbosity finer than the staple of her argument.
>
> SHAKESPEARE.[7]

THE projected visit of the two sisters to Ormond Hall, was punctually put in execution; and though, at first, their reception was somewhat repelling, the half-angry Baronet gradually relented, and changed his dry monosyllables, and forbidding looks, for bantering reproaches, and jocose threatenings.

'A dutiful set of boys and girls I have the felicity to be connected with!' cried he, pinching Ella by the ear. 'A pretty behaved / niece you have been, Mistress Ella, and surprisingly impatient to prove your affection, by coming to see me! And you have a sweet, unencroaching, reasonable, and considerate brother, the easiest in the world to satisfy, and always more ready to think of others than himself! He is not one, who, if you give him an inch, will take an ell! Oh no, it would be heresy to suppose it; I am, on the contrary, in admiration of his marvellous discretion!'

'And I, dear uncle,' said Ella, sitting down on the arm of his easy chair, 'am in admiration of the courage with which you can find in your heart to chide a poor little niece, who, in a burning sun, has come seven miles to see you, and instead of such treatment, expected to be rewarded with a good plate of strawberries.'[8]

The playful smile and accent with which this was spoken, completely mollified all that remained of the old gentleman's ill-humour; / and bidding her ring the bell, and order whatever she chose, he turned to Mrs. Fitzmaurice, and said: 'Now, then, my bonny Bess, since this saucy girl is impracticable, and won't allow me to give her the lecture she deserves, I shall direct all my spite against you, or rather, against your varlet of a husband! Pray, why did he not come with you this morning? Was he afraid, pretty master! of the heat? Or does he, perchance, wait till I pay him the first visit? If he does, give my love to him, and tell him I pay neither first nor second visits to any body; I hate a carriage, and I am too old and too heavy to get on horseback: and unless he chooses to come and live in my gardener's house, in the park, or in one of my nearest farms, he stands a bad chance of being treated with the respect he seems to require. You stare, my dear?

Understand then, that the utmost extent of my excursions is to the dwelling of those personages, / either in my little pony chair, or now and then, on foot.'

'Mr. Fitzmaurice, dear sir,' said his wife, 'will be here, I trust, in a few minutes to answer for himself. He chose to ride, but as he set out after us, and probably comes slow, on account of the heat, we have outstripped him.'

'Well, well, you have given me something like a rational explanation, and I am content. Now, tell me, what think you of Ernest's recovered looks? Does he appear to you the same creature? I should hardly have known him again, but for his voice, and even that has more volume in it than I ever expected his would possess. He is a fine lad, it must be allowed.'

Mrs. Fitzmaurice cordially agreed with him, and having conversed some time on the subject, asked leave to go and pay her respects to Lady Ormond in her dressing-room. – /

'I would not advise you to do any such thing!' cried the Baronet, with a look of mock gravity, 'she knows you are here, take my word for it, and at her own time will appear: but she is up to the eyes in a new work on Diet and Exercise – Temperance and Temperature, and the deuce knows what besides, and to interrupt her, might have almost as dangerous effect upon her health, as a breach against any of the rules she is studying, and – for the present, at least – ready to swear by!'

'But she is already so moderate an eater,' said Mrs. Fitzmaurice, 'that if she still further reduces the quantity, she may do herself harm.'

'Preach to the winds, my bonny Bess, and they will hear you just as soon as she will! she never was talked out of a whim in her life: but luckily for her, one vagary drives out another; and they succeed each other so fast, / that they have no time to do her serious mischief. I know but of one permanent maggot,[9] she ever has had – that of feeding like a sparrow; and she could have hit upon few that I should not have preferred. It has made her so indifferent to what is put upon the table, that she does not know a good dish from a bad one; and if I had not a clever cook, and did not take the trouble daily to look over his bill of fare, and to give him my own directions, I might be set down to such dinners as would not be fit for the pigs!'

Sir Everard had got upon a subject that always irritated him, for, as his personal appearance plainly indicated, eating and drinking were, to him, matters of no trivial importance. He had been heard to say (not in allusion to his wife, indeed, whom in his heart he sincerely valued) that the mistress of a family who after a year's marriage, was incapable of ordering a dinner properly, was a fool not worth keeping under a man's roof! /

Much to the relief of both the sisters, Mr. Fitzmaurice was at length announced, and soon after, Ernest who was out when they arrived, also made his appearance.

A splendid luncheon had by this time been brought up, in which the strawberries asked for by Ella had not been forgotten, but, amidst a variety of other good things, made a conspicuous figure. The party soon assembled round the tempting board,[10] and was engaged in doing ample honour to it, when the lady of the house entered. Tall, thin, and pale – without a single good feature in her face, though without any thing repulsive, she was one of those persons who would have passed unobserved, but for the extreme awkwardness of her movements, her walk, the very form of her limbs, to which no word was so applicable, as that of *ungain*.[11] Ill dressed, not so much from the defective quality or fashion of her clothes, as from the careless way in which they were / put on, she looked as if every thing she wore had been hung upon her by chance. Her cap was awry; her hair, 'a sable silvered,'[12] dangled in lank strings, rather than locks, over her eyes and cheeks, and she came forward holding half open a large octavo volume in one hand, and brandishing in the other a long ivory cutter.

'Ah, there you all are,' cried she, 'and I am glad to see you so employed, though I am much afraid you are eating the very things you ought to avoid. – Good heavens, Ella, don't touch those hard indigestible cherries! nothing in the world is so unwholesome. All stone fruits are pernicious: but white heart cherries are the worst of any; they are absolute poison. I know but one sort of cherry safe to eat, and that is the Kentish: but nobody seems to like it. – My dear Mrs. Fitzmaurice, take some of those raspberries; they are never hurtful; but pray let the strawberries alone. Observe how full of seeds they are; I assure you they are / not safe for a delicate person, and it is a thousand pities they are so much cultivated.[13] Mr. Fitzmaurice, how do you do? I am glad to see you amongst us again. What is there new in the London literary world? – Have you read this work?' striking her ivory knife against the octavo, and telling him its title – 'I assure you it is very clever, and well worth your perusal. It ought, indeed, to be the manual of every head of a family. Ella, my dear, I wish you would oblige me by not eating that cake! It is too rich and too heavy for any stomach but that of an ostrich.'

'Come again in a week, my girl,' whispered Sir Everard, 'and you will find all these prohibitions at an end. For-to day, you must be content to play the part of Sancho Panza, when governor of Barataria.'[14]

Fortunately, Lady Ormond had not appeared till the sisters had taken nearly as much refreshment as they wished, and were well disposed to submit to her restrictions. The whole party / therefore soon arose, and dispersed in various directions around the spacious room. Ella resumed her old station upon her uncle's elbow chair, and amused him with an account of some of the brilliant *fêtes* at which she had assisted when in London. Mrs. Fitzmaurice, extremely fond of green-house plants, went from window to window, to examine those upon the stands: and Lady Ormond, still wielding her formidable cutter, stood apart with Fitzmaurice and Ernest, talking in her usual desultory manner, of authors, ancient and modern – of new discoveries, of artists, of governments but above all, of medecine, as being the subject at that moment uppermost in her mind. In what she said, amidst much that was wild, irrelevant, and positively absurd, there was occasionally considerable acuteness and ability. Fitzmaurice listened to her with the patience of a philosopher who, to attain any expected good, is content to wade through a mass of tediousness; and Earnest, observant / of character, and interested by whatever called forth its peculiarities, remained a nearly silent auditor of what was passing, doing justice alike to the calm forbearance of the gentleman, and the ingenious and original, though often rambling observations of the lady.

In the midst of their colloquy Sir Everard startled all present by abruptly calling out to his wife in a loud voice: 'Jane – Jane, do hear this! – would you believe it? – That old fool, Sir Caleb Hunter, has married again, and taken a gay girl who turns his house out of windows, gives the finest parties in town, and is at the head of the fashion!'

'Well, my dear,' quietly answered his wife, 'how do we know you would not do the same?'

The uncompromising frankness of this reply caused a general laugh. The new turn however, which Sir Everard's interruption had given to her thoughts, drew her towards his chair for the purpose of hearing from Ella / something further of her London engagements. There was no subject she could not, for the moment, take an interest in listening to or discussing; and to judge by the curiosity and attention her looks denoted, it might have been supposed she personally attached as much importance to dress, *ton*, and splendour, as was proved to be otherwise by her whole appearance, and system of life.

Whilst Sir Everard, calling Ella his little 'Morning Post,'[15] was still plying her with fresh questions, and evidently enjoying highly the fashionable gossip she sought to entertain him with, Lady Ormond suddenly cried out:

'Ella, love, you must come and spend a week with us! We shall have the Bloombergs here in a few days, with their eldest daughter, a very excellent girl as any in the world, but rather vacant and futile it must be owned! She will make you a nice companion, however to walk with; and you will keep the house / alive, and give a little zest and flavour to the vapidity of the party.'

Ella laughed at this singular invitation, and was referring by her looks to Mrs. Fitzmaurice for an answer, when Sir Everard, who had not been put into such good humour, for many a long month, hastily took her hand, and kindly said,

'Lady Ormond never made a more judicious proposal! *Do* come to us, my good little girl; it will be charity, for there are few now with your youth and spirits who will throw away their time upon such old drones as we are!'

Ella, affectionately returning his pressure of her hand, readily answered:

'I will come to you, dear uncle, most gladly – unless my churlish sister and her husband forbid it.'

The Fitzmaurices, it will be believed, were far from wishing to oppose such a plan, and it was therefore agreed that on the following / Tuesday, Ella was to return to the Hall for a week.

Soon after, a general stroll in the pleasure grounds was proposed. The sun had gone in, and a light breeze had sprung up that refreshed the air, and rendered walking perfectly practicable.

'We have some improvements to show you,' said Lady Ormond, 'which you know would to us be no improvements at all, if we had not an opportunity of exhibiting them.'

It happened – for neither of them designed it – that during the progress of their walk, Ella and Ernest found themselves insensibly a good deal in advance of the rest of the party. Their conversation, upon the most general and common subjects, had nothing in it to absorb their attention, and the distance to which they had proceeded was the mere effect of being unaccustomed to the slow pace of Sir Everard. Gradually they each became more silent; the spots they passed or were approaching brought / back a thousand recollections, which they neither of them chose to avow, nor yet were able to banish. Here was the picturesque hermitage, within which Ella had so often read aloud to him, whilst he rested his aching head upon the mossy seat that surrounded it. Further on, was the rustic bench on which they had rested and talked, and at length taken leave of each other, the evening before he departed for the continent.[16] There was the little wilderness where she had once found him vainly but courageously struggling with her brother to save from chastisement a favourite but untrained dog, who had interfered by barking with Frederic's sport. The poor animal knew not that he had done wrong, but would infallibly have suffered for his ignorance, had not Ella snatched him up, and ran with him full speed to the house. Though Ormond Hall had never been her established residence, scarcely a year had passed in which she had not spent there with her mother some portion of / the summer. The sight of all these old haunts therefore was connected with so many juvenile remembrances, that it was impossible to behold them with indifference. She made no allusion, however, to what was passing in her mind, but forced herself to assume an air of gaiety, and said:

'In the few words spoken of Miss Bloomberg by my aunt, how inviting a representation was contained of her as my destined associate! I wonder whether, by any possibility, she can prove duller than I have been during this little ramble?'

'Is occasional silence then a proof of dullness?'

'Perhaps you think that after the long flight of eloquence I have been pouring forth to my uncle, some respite might be necessary?'

'On that point,' answered he, earnestly, 'all I can think is, that you are justly entitled to unqualified praise. It was the part of a kind and grateful niece to exert herself, as you / did, for the entertainment of an affectionate uncle, whose age and infirmities now compel him to lead a life so little in conformity with his past habits. I wish I possessed in an equal degree your faculty of amusing him; but I have not your vivacity. However, I take great pride to myself, from observing that he does not listen entirely without interest to some of the details I give him of what fell under my notice abroad; and altogether, I trust he finds me a less unenlivening companion than he had expected.'

'He speaks of you,' resumed Ella, 'with the greatest kindness, and I am sure is much pleased by your return. But, tell me, why does Frederic linger in London? He can plead no business, and mamma herself writes word, that she has urged him to come down, and is anxious to get him away.'

'Be assured,' answered Ernest, 'he will soon arrive; but, at all events, do not make yourself uneasy about him, since he has Sir / Everard's leave to protract his return some time longer.'

'I fear, however, my uncle thinks even more than he expresses on the subject. From what he said when we first came in, there is reason to believe he is very little pleased.'

'Perhaps so; yet remember how indulgent he has always been, and how easily he may be appeased by a few concessions; and rest satisfied, moreover,' added Ernest, half smiling, 'that whilst you are here, Sir Everard will never miss Frederic.'

Finding that the rest of the party did not follow, they now turned back, and found them all still sauntering about the flower garden and the green house.

'I hope, Ernest, you have taken Ella to see my new dairy?' cried Lady Ormond.

'We have not been so far, madam.'

'Well then, I shall have the pleasure of shewing it to her myself the very first day she comes.' /

Then observing a poor lad, with his head tied up, and one eye miserably swelled and discoloured, who was rolling the newly mown turf between the flower beds, she hastened up to him, and asked what was the matter? The clown turned away as if loath to tell, and Ella thought she saw him grin. Lady Ormond, not easily repulsed, followed him; she insisted upon knowing how long he had been in that state, said, that if it was an inflammation of the eye, it should be examined by the family apothecary (which in the country often means surgeon and even physician,) and, meanwhile, advised him to eat very sparingly, and not to drink anything but water. This was too much for the youth's gravity; his wide jaw distended into a broad laugh, and he muttered between his teeth:

'Pity she had not bid me bethink myself of the vartue of water a day sooner.'

'What's that?' cried her Ladyship, 'what's that you say, my boy?' /

Mr. Fitzmaurice, who had distinctly overheard him, now interposed, and good humouredly advising the lad to be, without fresh exhortation, more mindful of the *vartue* of water another time, he drew Lady Ormond away, saying:

'Your Ladyship's charitable anxiety, I suspect may in the present instance, be entirely spared. 'Tis plain to me that the boy's disfigured appearance is the result of some blow or fall suffered during a drinking bout. There was a fair yesterday in your neighborhood, and probably he was one of those who attended it.'

Lady Ormond was indignant, not so much at the lad's having got drunk, as at his having done so before his time.

'Had it been,' she cried, 'his poor old grandfather, now working in our kitchen garden, I should not in the least have objected to it. It has been agreed by all medical writers, that upon elderly people a little occasional excess / acts as a cordial, and rather does them good. But that foolish boy was only putting fire into his own veins! What business has young blood like his with strong and intoxicating liquors? 'Tis a shame! However, I'll have his eye looked at, poor wretch; and I hope the mischance it has met with, will be a warning to him.'

When the Fitzmaurices took leave, and just as the sisters were ascending their carriage, Mr. Sedley rode up. It was natural to suppose he came to visit his friend Ernest, who standing upon the steps until the party drove off, expressed his satisfaction at seeing him, and invited him to alight. But Sedley, it was evident, had no such intention; for as soon as the Fitzmaurices' horses were put in motion, he wheeled his own round, and followed them, waving his hand to his friend, and keeping beside that window of the vehicle at which Ella was seated. Ernest saw the transaction with some surprise; and turning from the door, / walked slowly and thoughtfully to his own room.

Yet, in fact, he might have been prepared for what had passed. One of the earliest communications Sedley had made to him the preceding day, was that of the extreme admiration he had conceived for Ella, and his reasonable hopes that her mother would not be unpropitious to his suit. At the same time, he confessed, that he was withheld from declaring himself, by an unconquerable apprehension of Ella's indifference:

'Her manner towards me,' he added, 'is pleasant and friendly as man could wish; but it is too unembarrassed – too sisterly, if I may say so – to resemble love. I am not without hope, that by quiet assiduities here in the country, where there are so few objects to divide with me her attention, I may be able to make a more serious impression upon her. Be that as it may, I cannot give up the delight of seeing her, as long as there is the faintest / prospect of eventual success – as long, to speak plainly, as I have reason to believe her free from any other attachment.'

Ernest, the unwilling confident of these sentiments, was reduced to hear them in almost unbroken silence. He was in no predicament to enter the lists for himself, and knew too well, that any pretensions he might have ventured to advance, would by Mrs. Ormond have been treated with the utmost scorn. Yet Ella had been dear to him as his own existence from her very childhood; her image had accompanied him abroad – had dwelt undefaced in his heart during the whole of his absence, – and still, at his return, lived there as freshly impressed as on the day of his departure. Painful and difficult was the task he now saw before him. It would be incumbent upon him not only to conceal from her his *own* attachment, but to stand by a passive witness of the efforts made by *another* to attach her. With / what success his courage and self command might bear him through such a trial, he almost dreaded to ask himself. Could he have flown from the dangerous experiment, and once more have renewed his wanderings, how gladly would he that very hour have quitted Ormond Hall!

But something was due from him, nay much, to Sir Everard and his lady. He saw that they regarded him with more than their former affection; that they attached importance to his society, and were revived and animated by his presence. When to this conviction was added the remembrance of so many other benefits – the protection they had afforded his childhood and adolescence – the education they had bestowed upon him, the unfailing compassion his long years of suffering had experienced from them – and the liberality with which they still supported him – he felt that it was impossible, at least till the arrival of Frederic, / to forsake them. Nothing remained then, but to arm himself with resolution to pass through the appointed ordeal without shrinking, and without dishonour. /

CHAPTER IV.

From women's eyes this doctrine is derived;
They are the grounds, the books, the academies,
From whence doth spring the true Promethean fire.
For where is any author in the world,
Teaches such beauty as a woman's eye?

SHAKSPEARE.[17]

MR. SEDLEY had accompanied the carriage nearly two miles, endeavouring to support a conversation which neither of the ladies took much pains to enliven, when Ella, half provoked with him, cried out:

'How shabbily you are behaving, Mr. Sedley, to poor Ernest! You certainly did not ride to Ormond Hall to escort *us* on our road home, but to pay a visit to your friend. Let me advise you not to defer it a moment; for I / see a black and portentous cloud gathering over our heads that threatens us with a deluge. Gallop back, before it pours down.'

'I will,' said he, a little confused, 'I will – but I do not think the weather is so likely to change as you suppose.'

He had scarcely done speaking, when a sudden and loud clap of thunder startled his horse, who rearing and plunging furiously, threw his master – a skilful rider, but at this moment off his guard – against a high bank on the side of the road. The carriage was instantly stopped, and the frightened sisters hastily alighted, and flew to him. He was stunned, and at first unable to speak; but whether materially hurt, neither they nor their servant could tell. Mr. Fitzmaurice was too far in advance to be consulted; and after some deliberation, his wife agreed with Ella that the best plan would be to place him in their carriage, and drive on as quick as possible to the little town of B— which lay in their road, and where surgical / help, if required, might be procured with less delay than by turning back to Ormond Hall. Accordingly, the servant, assisted as well as they were able by the two ladies, removed him to the carriage, placed him as conveniently as was practicable on one of the vacant seats, and the rain now pouring down in torrents, gladly took possession of the other. The unruly horse, it was concluded, would find his own way home. At all events, he must take his chance, for no one could be spared to look after him.

Aware of the urgency of the case, the coachman drove with a rapidity that brought them to the surgeon's door in less than twenty minutes. Sedley was assisted into the house, and immediately blooded. No fracture it was found had been sustained, and he had perfectly recovered his recollection; but the shock had been severe, and the medical man strongly advised his patient to keep exceedingly quiet during the remainder of the day. /

Nothing remained then but to invite him to Holmes Court, an invitation he received with nearly as much shame as gratitude, sensible that it was rather the effect of necessity than of choice, and might be considered as a civility almost forced from Mrs. Fitzmaurice by circumstances. Ella, seeing his modest embarrassment, took compassionate pains to relieve him. She abstained from alluding to his wilful desertion of his friend, and his pertinacity in following her and her sister; attributed all the blame of the disaster to the viciousness of his horse, and affected to believe that no power possessed by man could have restrained so ungovernable an animal. Sedley knew the contrary: but it was more consolatory to hear the horse censured than himself, and in his heart he truly thanked her for so considerately sparing him.

Mr. Fitzmaurice, always hospitably inclined, received him, on hearing what had occurred, in a manner to dissipate entirely all remaining / diffidence. A messenger was immediately despatched to inform the gentleman at whose house he was visiting of the accident that had befallen him, representing it however in terms as little alarming as possible. This precaution taken, the young man was sentenced to go and lie down for an hour or two, with strict injunctions not to make his appearance till summoned to dinner.

When he was gone, Ella, glad to withdraw her thoughts from the frightful scene she had witnessed, seated herself at the piano-forte, and began playing and singing with all her accustomed animation.

'How little,' said Mr. Fitzmaurice, who was in the adjoining library, with his wife, 'how little do romance writers really understand the human heart! Where is the author, who an hour or two after his heroine had seen her lover in danger of breaking his neck, would venture to represent her singing as blithely as a bird? Ella ought, in *etiquette*,[18] to be still / trembling and smelling at her salts. I am scandalized at a proceeding so little in accordance with all rule and precedent!'

'You are mistaken, dear Hugh; Ella is breaking through none of the rules of romance – for she is not in love.'

'I allow there seems at this moment little reason to suppose her so; but Bessy, the case was different yesterday! I saw a flash of joy dart from her eyes, as she descried Sedley from the window, that told a very different tale!'

'Well, time will show. I can believe that she was, to a certain degree, pleased – at least, not *dis*pleased – on seeing Mr. Sedley; but her happy temper and bright countenance, give to her, at almost all times, an air so gay and gladdening, that a very little additional satisfaction makes her appear in a state of absolute rapture.'

'Your mother,' resumed Mr. Fitzmaurice, without answering this speech, 'expresses in her last letter a great wish to know whether / Sedley has been to see us. Now I, who always like, when I can, to pay my court to her, think it would be good policy to write to her this very day, informing her that he is under our roof, giving a pathetic account of his accident, and above all, taking care not to betray to her the abominable insensibility of her warbling daughter. Listen, Bessy, how beautifully she swells upon that note! Let us hope she is practising for the evening!'

When Sedley came down to dinner, at which in addition to himself, were present three or four other gentlemen, scarcely any symptom of indisposition, except a little paleness, appeared upon his countenance. He was congratulated on his amended looks, and fortunate escape; and this led to a series of frightful stories of similar accidents, which had occasioned dislocations or fractures the most horrible – incurable internal hurts – concussions of the brain, or instantaneous death. The ladies cried out for mercy, and implored the guests to change the / conversation. In compliance with their wishes, more agreeable subjects were started; such, for instance, as a little country scandal, probably to make amends to the fair sisters for the unpleasant topic they had at first chosen; then one of the company gave a curious detail of a trial that had, in an extraordinary degree, engaged the public attention during the last county sessions; next came a short discussion on farming; a much longer one on good eating, and towards the end of the repast an animated specimen of party politics.

Dinners, both in town and country, have often been seasoned with worse intellectual condiments![19]

The evening was spent by part of the company at the whist table; by the rest, in listening or appearing to listen, to the musical performance of Mrs. Fitzmaurice and her sister. Some, it is true, thought the opportunity a good one to enjoy an unobserved nap. Sedley to do him justice, was not one of the number. / He knew nothing of music, and cared for it, perhaps, as little; but he loved to look at Ella whilst she sung, and to mark the perfect freedom from affectation and grimace of her beautiful and unruffled features.

The next morning, with an appearance of such confirmed recovery as left him, even in his own opinion, without excuse for prolonging his stay, he was trying to reconcile himself to the necessity of taking leave after breakfast when Mr. de Gray was announced.

The sight, on his first entrance, of him by whom he had been so abruptly deserted the preceding day, seated next to Ella, and taking his early meal with her upon the footing of *un ami de la maison*,[20] startled and even caused him to change colour;[21] but, resuming his outward composure in a moment, he went up to Mrs. Fitzmaurice, and after the usual salutations, said:

'I was deputed hither by Lady Ormond, to enquire how you got home in the storm yesterday; / she was persuaded it must have alarmed you.'

'We *might*, there is no doubt, have justified very amply Lady Ormond's opinion of our cowardice, had time been given us,' answered Mrs. Fitzmaurice, smiling; 'but just as the first peal of thunder reached our ears, a different subject of alarm so wholly engrossed us, that it drove every other from our thoughts.' She then recounted the misadventure of his friend.

'Ah, poor Sedley!' cried Ernest, going round to him, and instantly recovering all his wonted cordiality towards him, 'I am sorry your handsome mare is given to play such tricks. But how are you now?'

'Perfectly well,' answered the other, holding out to him his hand, 'and very much obliged to you, my dear de Gray, for not telling me I deserved worse for behaving so ill to you.'

Ernest, half laughing, accepted the offered / hand, and then began talking of something else. He staid about an hour, and when he departed, Sedley accompanied him.

Of all who had witnessed the entrance of Ernest, Ella alone had observed the momentary change his countenance had undergone; and her flattering heart had whispered to her a hope that his emotion had proceeded from jealousy, and proved that his early affection for her was not extinct. Intoxicated by this idea, the gay spirits it threw her into during the rest of the day, astonished even the Fitzmaurices, well as they were acquainted with the natural hilarity of her disposition. But as the sight of happiness is always, to the good, a source of pleasure, they felt their own animation excited by hers, without knowing or enquiring the cause.

Ella had no plan for the future – no hope that Mrs. Ormond would ever sanction her marriage with Ernest, and not the most distant intention of engaging herself to him without / that sanction. Time, she fancied, might do something for her; and to time she trusted. All she now thought of, was the happiness of again associating with him, of resuming her former station in his heart, and of remaining single for his sake. These were the visionary projects of a girl of eighteen, who, though guided by extreme good sense on all other subjects, was on this a mere child, as unreflecting as she was inexperienced and enthusiastic.

The impending visit to Ormond Hall, which she looked forward to with delight, and Ernest almost with apprehension, changed nothing – when at last it took place – in her sentiments. The continual opportunity they had of being together, unconsciously diminished the reserve almost amounting to formality, with which Ernest had hitherto treated her, and had planned to continue towards her. They sought not to be alone, but enjoyed with ecstacy the pleasure of being under the same roof, of reading, / walking, conversing with each other; and so well did they learn to understand the mute language of the eyes, that without uttering a word, there was scarcely an opinion either entertained, which the other did not intuitively comprehend. Miss Bloomberg, though in reality as dull and insipid as Lady Ormond had described her, was however no incumbrance to them. She was good natured and well mannered, and they never attempted to avoid her, or in any way desired to render her association with them unpleasant to herself.

In the course of their daily rambles, sometimes on horseback, sometimes on foot, it happened one morning, that in passing through a village adjoining Ormond Park, they caught a glimpse at an open window of a small farmhouse, of so beautiful a female face, that Ella involuntarily checked her horse, exclaiming:

'What a lovely creature! Do you know who she is, Ernest?'

'Yes; she is the eldest daughter of Mrs. / Nelson, who nursed me so kindly in my sick boyhood, and who has lately given up her own cottage to come and keep house here for her brother, who, some months ago, lost his wife.'

'But where has this eldest prodigy started from? I have often been to see the mother during my visits at Ormond Hall; but I never knew she had any other daughter than little Anne.'

'The girl you have just seen has been living with her grandmother, near London, and is but recently returned home, in consequence of the death of her old relation. Mrs. Nelson went to town to fetch her, and came back only a few days ago.'

'I should like,' resumed Ella, 'to go into the house and make acquaintance with her. Should you have any objection, Miss Bloomberg?'

'None in the least; on the contrary, it would give me pleasure to see her nearer, for / I think she would make a remarkably pretty miniature.'

Miss Bloomberg's great accomplishment was that of painting miniatures, which she succeeded in making provokingly like, and totally void of grace, spirit, or expression. She had begun one of Ella, which no one in the house, except her own parents, encouraged her to finish; for to all who were in the habit of observing a countenance like Ella's –

> So sweetly mutable, so brightly wild,[22] –

a representation merely conveying an idea of her features, without one spark of their genuine intelligence and expression, was more than could be borne!

'Let her,' said Lady Ormond, 'exercise herself, and welcome, in painting what is called *still life* – stalls of vegetables, baskets of fish, earthen-ware pans, and bright copper kettles – and I dare say she will do them great justice. / But I would not trust anything that had breath in it to her petrifying pencil, unless it were a mole or a dormouse, or her own face, reflected from a looking-glass!'

This was spoken with more severity than Lady Ormond was often tempted to permit herself; the truth is, Ella stood so high in her favour, that Miss Bloomberg's attempt had really offended her, as a proof of intolerable presumption. But to Ella, the inducement, whatever it might be, that disposed her companion so readily to comply with her wish of alighting, was a matter of indifference; her acquiescence was all she wanted, and jumping off her docile pony, she only waited till Ernest had assisted Miss Bloomberg to dismount, and then led the way into the house.

'Mrs. Nelson,' cried she, after the first civilities were over, 'I am not merely come to see you, but to see your newly arrived daughter. This good little Anne,' continued she, taking the younger girl – (a sprightly pretty lass of fourteen) by the hand, 'is an old acquaintance / of mine: but her sister and I are yet strangers to each other, and I am anxious that we should continue so no longer.'

'Thank you, dear lady,' answered the gratified mother, 'I am sure Ruth will be very proud of your notice. Anne, my dear, go and tell her who is here, and desire her to come down.'

'How does she like this sudden removal into the country?' enquired Ella, 'she has been living near London, I am told, almost all her life.'

'Yes, ma'am: but not very gaily. Her poor old grandmother for the last three or four years, hardly ever went out; and during the whole time Ruth was with her she never saw so much of London as during the single fortnight she spent there with me.'

'I hope you went to see your old friend, Harris?'

This was Mrs. Ormond's maid.

'O, yes, ma'am, two or three times; and I saw your mamma too, once, and master / Frederic, who came in whilst she was talking to us. What a fine young gentleman he is grown! and so affable and thoughtful, you would be surprised, ma'am.'

'I am glad to hear it: but pray, in what manner did his great affability appear.'

'Why, I'll tell you, ma'am. One morning, Ruth and I, who were always trotting about, were caught in a hard shower in Regent Street;[23] your brother was buying something at a jeweller's, and seeing us through the windows he was good-natured enough to run out, and make us take shelter in the shop. But that was not all, ma'am; he would not let us walk home, even after the rain was over; but sent for a hackney coach, and went with us himself to Knightsbridge,[24] where my poor old mother-in-law had lived, and where he came in and paid us a long visit;[25] and he was so pleased with the house (which is but a poor little tenement, either) that he was quite surprised, I should think of coming back into the country, / and wanted to persuade me I could not do better than send for Anne, and remain where I was. But, Lord bless me, the house does not belong to us now; and besides, what would my poor brother have done without me? He has enough to do to look after the out-door work of the farm; he can't be left without somebody to mind the dairy, and keep all straight at home.'

Ella was at once surprised and pleased to learn, by this somewhat prolix recital, that her brother had behaved to the good Mrs. Nelson with so much kindness and attention. He was not wont, she remembered in former times to shew great courtesy to persons in her class of life; and the change that appeared to have taken place in him, she had not been prepared to expect. She looked towards Ernest to observe the impression made upon him by the account: but he was examining a print that hung on the other side of the room, and she could not see his face. Before he turned / round, the beautiful Ruth entered, and Ella from that moment forgot every thing else.

Ruth was at this time in her nineteenth year. In height, she was somewhat above the middle standard, but her finely rounded limbs were admirably proportioned, and her figure had all the flexibility that gives grace and ease, whether in action or in repose. Her face partook in nothing but in bloom of the beauty of her native country; its features were cast in the purest Grecian mould. Her dark brown hair, glossy and luxuriant, and her eyes and long eye-lashes, a shade or two of a deeper tint, gave relief to what might else have been thought the too great delicacy of her complexion. The prevailing expression of her countenance, it was difficult to define; there was much modesty in it; there was also a certain elevation of character observable in its serious though mild composure, that under other circumstances would have been called dignity, or might have been construed into / pride. Ella felt that she was not to be addressed with the sort of familiarity that would have been admissible towards any other girl in the same humble rank; there was something about her that called for more observance, that seemed almost to command respect.

After some hesitation in what way to open the conversation, Ella began by saying:

'I am glad, since you are new to the country, that you have been brought hither at so delightful a time of the year. Perhaps you may at first find the change somewhat trying; but at this season, every day will contribute to reconcile you to it more and more.'

'I am already reconciled to it, ma'am,' answered Ruth, in a gentle, but rich and mellow voice, that enchanted Ella almost as much as her beauty; 'it has often been my wish to come back to my early home.'

'But not, I hope, from having been treated otherwise than kindly where you were.' /

'Oh no, ma'am; my grandmother was always indulgent to me; but I had neither lost the recollection of a place in which I had been so happy as a child, nor of my mother.'

'Your recollections,' said Ella, every moment more pleased with her, 'do you credit; and your return, I am sure, will greatly add to the comfort and happiness of Mrs. Nelson.'

This little dialogue was listened to by that good woman with smiles that denoted plainly the maternal and most pardonable pride with which she saw the effect produced upon her visitor by the language and deportment of a daughter in every way so superior to the rest of her kindred. On her part, Ella's increasing surprise, joined to an irresistible feeling of curiosity, induced her at last, but with some diffidence, to say, addressing Ruth:

'Forgive the enquiry, but surely you must have had some other and higher education, than your grandmother alone was capable of giving you? Did she send you to school?' /

Ruth, who could not but be flattered by this question, answered it in the negative, adding, that she had never had any other advantage of education than that she owed to the opportunity she had enjoyed, for several years, of being present at the lessons received by some young ladies, the daughters of her grandmother's former mistress and constant patroness.

'That was something, certainly, for a girl of observation and quick parts; but tell me, who were these young ladies? You probably associated with them at more hours than those of study? Were they persons of distinction – of polished manners?'

'They were the daughters of the Earl of L—, and, as far as I am able to decide, possessed those qualities in perfection. They were still children when I, a child myself, was first taken to their father's house. At that age, difference of rank is little thought of; they soon became intimate with me, and made me their playfellow, engaging my grandmother / to conduct me to them perpetually. By degrees, their governess took me into favour, and admitted me into the school room; in short, till I was nearly sixteen, scarcely a day passed in which I did not spend many hours in their society.'

'Well, did the intercourse then break off?'

Ruth coloured a little, and for the first time looked slightly embarrassed. Her mother came to her relief:

'The truth is, ma'am,' said she, turning to Ella, 'there were sons in the family, and as they were growing up to be young men, my lady, their mother, thought it was as well not to let a girl of Ruth's age be too often thrown in their way.'[26]

Ella could not but be of opinion that 'my lady their mother' had decided very judiciously. She thanked Ruth for having indulged her curiosity; and taking a kind and friendly leave of her and Mrs. Nelson, departed. /

Her conversation, during nearly the whole way home, turned on the subject of the extraordinary young creature they had just quitted. She was most anxious to hear Ernest's opinion of her, and was fully gratified by the prompt and unqualified praise he bestowed upon her.

'Nature,' said he, 'has done everything for her exterior that the most fastidious critic could desire; and the education she has received seems to have done much for her mind and manners; but, Ella, – will she be the happier for these advantages?'

'Why should you doubt it?'

'Because she is too humbly born, and too destitute of fortune to become the object of an honourable attachment to any man above her own class.'

'And you fear that with an equal she is too refined to be happy?'

'Do you not fear it, also?'

'To speak honestly, I do. Poor girl! she is really to be pitied. Would to Heaven we / could make some clumsy, disagreeable, unintelligent heiress, change conditions with her! She seems born to move in the highest sphere;

> "Nothing she does or says,
> But smacks of something greater than herself;
> Too noble for this place."'[27]

Then turning to Miss Bloomberg; 'You are silent, my dear companion,' she cried.

'Are you considering whether this charming girl will really suit you as a model to paint your next miniature from?'

'No; I was not thinking of that at this moment; but now you remind me of it, I am inclined to believe she would answer my purpose extremely well. Her features are quite classical, and would not be difficult to copy by one so much accustomed to draw from busts.'

'And to convert into busts, every breathing subject!' thought Ernest.

The project however never took place. A succession of unsettled weather came on, and / Ruth could neither be sent for to the Hall, nor without the parade of a carriage, visited again at her mother's. To give employment to her industrious young guest, Lady Ormond, who had interdicted the continuation of Ella's portrait, engaged her to make a picture of some stuffed humming birds, skilfully set up in a glass case, and affording, by the brilliancy of their plumage, ample scope for the exertion of her abilities as a colourist. With this occupation she was quite content; and Lady Ormond privately declared, that the eyes of her painted birds looked *almost* as animated as those which were represented by glass beads under the case! /

CHAPTER V.

If then true lovers ever have been cross'd
It stands as an edict in destiny;
Then let us teach our trial patience.
Time may do much.

SHAKSPEARE.[28]

THE intimacy subsisting between Ernest and young Sedley, and the hospitable reception Sir Everard always gave him, were sufficient pretexts and encouragements for rendering his visits both frequent and long. It was soon perceived by the whole party, that Ernest was by no means his principal inducement for coming so often. Sir Everard began to wink, and nod, and look sly whenever he saw him enter, or heard his name mentioned. The Bloombergs wished it had been the fate of / their daughter to attract so rich a prize. The daughter, perfectly at her ease about the matter, felt assured that if *he* did not propose, some other would; and predestined in her own mind to be married, never doubted that when her time came, a husband would as certainly present himself for her, as for her three elder sisters, and five cousins, who had all made good matches.

Lady Ormond was the person who had observed Sedley's assiduities with the most dissatisfaction. She had a little incipient project afloat in her mind, which it annoyed her extremely to perceive might be interfered with. Her wish was, to bring about a union between Ella and Ernest. They were both poor, it is true, and Ella's mother was ambitious; but Lady Ormond reflected that she had brought her husband a large fortune, a considerable part of which had, by settlement, been left at her own disposal to bequeath, if she had no children, to whomsoever she pleased. /

Ella, meanwhile, wholly unsuspicious of her aunt's secret designs, and sometimes shocked at the abrupt and ungracious manner in which she behaved to Mr. Sedley, exerted herself, in mere compassion, to show him more attention than she would otherwise have manifested. She explained to Ernest, with whom she was always as open and confiding as propriety admitted, her reason for thus proceeding; and he tried to think her right: but it was not in human nature to view her complacency towards another – even whilst himself endeavouring to emulate her good example – without some feeling of pain. Sedley, however, thus supported by the only two individuals in the family of any importance to him, disregarded the cold looks of Lady Ormond, and persisted in his visits; aware, indeed, that he made no sensible progress, yet daily less apprehensive of ultimate failure.

The Bloombergs were now on the eve of departure, and consequently, Ella also regarded / the period for which she had been invited, as drawing to a close. The regret which this inspired, since no week of her happy life had ever been *so* happy – was mitigated by reflecting, that when left without any female companion of her own age, when her walks, her rides, and many of her morning hours would necessarily have no other associate than Ernest, it might have become difficult to keep a sufficient guard over herself entirely to avoid betraying the devoted attachment she cherished. Ernest, likewise, from somewhat similar feelings of self-distrust, submitted to their impending separation with firmness, though with sorrow.

But the courage they were so laudably disposed to exert, it soon appeared was not destined, on the present occasion, to be called into action. On the very evening preceding Ella's supposed departure, Frederic Ormond, her brother, suddenly arrived from town. The surprise caused by his unexpected appearance / was so great, that at the first moment it scarcely seemed to leave room for satisfaction. Sir Everard, from what he had written only a very few days before, had concluded his stay in London would have been further prolonged to an almost indefinite extent. The supposition had displeased and hurt him, though he said but little about the matter. His nephew's now unlooked-for apparition was therefore not hailed immediately with very cordial warmth; and except Ella, no one manifested extraordinary pleasure at the sight of him. But she, uninfluenced by the resentment of others, and guided solely by the feelings of her own affectionate heart, flew to him with rapture; embraced him over and over again; and gazing upon him, after a three years' absence, with mingled eagerness and curiosity, exclaiming:

'How you are changed, dear Frederic, in complexion – in height – in figure – in carriage, and how much to your advantage! I should / scarcely have known you had we met at the house of a stranger.'

Then drawing him towards Sir Everard, who though he had put down his cards, still kept his post, somewhat sullenly, at the whist-table, she said:-

'Look at him, dear uncle; is he not come back to us resembling more than ever your fine whole-length picture of my father?'

She had touched the right chord. Sir Everard not only retained a most affectionate remembrance of his deceased brother, but was extremely proud of his portrait, the work of an artist lately become celebrated, whom it was his boast to have been one of the first to patronize and bring into notice. The double allusion she had made produced an evident effect in favour of the new comer.

'Bad boy!' cried he, extending to him his hand, and looking up at him with an almost involuntary smile of approbation; 'I did not mean to have *smoothed my rugged brow*[29] for / this month to come. But that girl neither bears malice herself, nor will let any one else have the comfort of doing so in peace. Come – sit down here, and tell me what has wrought this sudden change in your plans, and procured us the honour of your gracious presence?'

'The wish, my dear uncle, (which I allow, ought to have influenced me sooner) of getting away from London, where I began to find myself bored; and the desire of seeing my friends in Shropshire.'

'Why, what has happened to poor old London that should have rendered it so unpalatable in the brief space, since you last wrote?'

'It is growing insufferably hot, and besides, is now beginning to be almost deserted.'

'Very flattering and sufficient reasons for wakening a desire to see your friends in Shropshire. But, come, my lad, I will taunt you no longer. In my heart, I am right glad to see you; and if I have growled, it was only because you did not come sooner.'

Then, surveying him from head to foot: Ella is right,' added he, 'you are grown a fine, tall, manly-looking fellow, and much / more like your father than I used to think you. What says my lady, his aunt?'

'I say with you, Sir Everard,' answered Lady Ormond, 'that travel seems to have agreed with him perfectly. To be sure, it has not done such wonders for him as for Ernest; but he did not require it; he was always stout and strong. I read to-day, in a volume of modern travels, a sensible and well-written work, that many who go abroad in flourishing health, return home faded and weakened by the climate, whilst others, who go away sick, are sent there too late to receive any benefit from the change. Upon the whole, therefore, we have reason to rejoice that our two young men, he that was well, and he that was an invalid, have both come back so much improved.'

In the now undisguised satisfaction of his heart, Sir Everard not only declared that Ella should remain at the Hall some time longer, but that Mr. and Mrs. Fitzmaurice should come and join the party. He directed Ernest to ride over to Holme Court in the morning with the invitation; and then, extending his civility to his present guests, he pressed them to remain with him another week. They thanked him; but methodical in all their actions, / said it was out of their power; alleging for reason that they had left their own house a month before to pay a certain number of annual visits, which visits being now over, and the time expired which they had dedicated to that purpose, it would cause too great an irregularity in their proceedings if they still deferred their return home.

Sir Everard, who had no other regard for them than that which long habit had established, accepted their excuse without difficulty; and to Lady Ormond their refusal was almost a relief.

Whilst this little interlude was performing, Ella led her brother to the recess of one of the windows, and made him sit down beside her to answer all her questions about her mother.

'When will she leave town, dear Frederic? What are her plans for the summer? Does she come to Holme Court, or will her first visit be to my uncle?'

'My good little sister,' answered Frederic, kissing her fair forehead, 'I never dreamt of making these enquiries; and if my mother herself ever spoke of her plans, I have totally forgotten what she said.'

'Was she looking well, and in good spirits?' /

'As well as women of her age can reasonably be expected to look: but, Ella, let us talk a little of *you*. I hear you make conquests, and are in progress to achieve one, in particular, of real importance. How goes on your affair with young Sedley?'

'As well as an affair without design,' answered she, parodying his recent speech, 'can reasonably be expected to go on!'

'Come, come, you impertinent girl,' cried he, amused by her look of comic gravity, 'be frank with me; is he likely, do you think, soon to declare himself?'

Ella laughingly answered: 'Ask him yourself when you see him;' and rising, she rejoined the rest of the party.

Frederic Ormond, in many respects, resembled his sister; but more in features than in expression. He had an air of high fashion, an address easy and graceful; and manners which, when he pleased, were highly prepossessing. It was to be regretted that with so many advantages the defects of his temper too frequently contributed to deprive him of the power to conciliate general good-will. His heart, however, was not without nobleness and warmth; but so fearfully alloyed by overbearing haughtiness, that few were able to distinguish / between the ore and the dross it contained. Even Ernest, long as he had known him, understood his character but imperfectly. Frederic was rarely confidential with him, rarely disposed to explain what might appear questionable in his conduct; it was as if he had thought himself injured by his companion's not giving instinctively a favourable interpretation to every circumstance, however dubious, in which he was concerned. But what Ernest had seen and casually heard of his dissipated habits abroad, had impressed upon him an opinion of his want of morals, which it was not always in his power to conceal. Frederic tried to persuade himself that he equally despised his approbation and his censure: but it was not so; there was less of contempt than of anger in his feelings; for the esteem of Ernest, could it have been obtained at any less cost than that of a wound to his own pride, would have been of all possessions the most precious in his sight.

Amongst the individuals that were dearest to him in his own family, Sir Everard and Ella held the foremost place, the first, from a deep sense of gratitude for his invariable indulgence, – the second, from observing in her a warmer attachment to himself than in any of / his kindred. With regard to his mother, the injudicious system she pursued with him had alienated much of his affection from her. She saw in him (what no one could deny) many faults; but she saw not that it was worse than useless to attempt to correct them by harsh reproofs and dogmatical advice; it was, in fact, provoking so proud a spirit to rebellion: and whilst much, if not all she wished, might have been won by kindness; her mistaken measures so completely destroyed her influence, that she found herself left to vent her remonstrances 'to the impassive air.'[30] With his half-sister, Mrs. Fitzmaurice, he had had comparatively little intercourse, from the circumstance of there being amongst the relations of her late father, many who were desirous of receiving her whenever her mother and sister were from home; consequently, whilst a girl, her visits at Ormond Hall had been much less frequent than those of Ella. What he knew of her, however, pleased and suited him; she was sweet-tempered and amiable, and with her he felt himself secure from all dictatorial molestation. It gave him, therefore, satisfaction to hear, on the return of Ernest from Holme Court, that both she and her husband had gladly accepted the baronet's invitation, / and meant to be with them that very day to dinner.

'So far, so good,' cried Sir Everard; 'we have secured for ourselves a little set of chosen guests, who will gladly join with us in celebrating Frederic's return. But this is not enough, the tenants and labourers must have their festival. As for our wealthier neighbours I shall not be at the trouble of collecting and pampering a number of people I care nothing about, who want nothing I can give them, and to whom every day in the year is a day of feasting and idleness. To the cottager, rest and a good dinner are a real holiday.'

'Very true, dear uncle,' cried Ella; 'but may I venture to propose a little addition to your scheme?'

'Speak out, my good girl – what is it?'

'Merely this, that you will permit the servants to have a ball, and to invite as many of their friends as will fill the great oak parlour.'

Everybody present agreed in approving this amendment, and the servants' ball was consented to without hesitation.

Pleased with her success, she went herself to / announce the agreeable intelligence in the housekeeper's room.

'Ah, Miss Ella,' cried two or three of the maids, gathering round her, 'we owe this to you! You are always ready to stand our friend. It's a pleasure to see you come to the house, for if ever any particular favour is granted us, it is sure to be when you are here to ask for it.'

Ella did not deny having solicited the ball, but she said her uncle had so readily and cheerfully agreed to it, that they ought to be as much obliged to him as if it had been his own plan.

They all agreed in requesting her to thank him, and then dispersed to communicate the news to their fellow-servants, and to ponder upon the pink or blue cap-ribbon that it would be most becoming to wear on the festive evening.

Faithful to their promise, the Fitzmaurices arrived at the time they had appointed, and were met and welcomed at the hall door by Ernest, and the rejoicing Ella. Frederic appeared not till the family had assembled round the dinner table, having been out the greatest part of the morning, and only returning in time to make a hasty change in his dress. Mr. Fitzmaurice / and he had already a slight knowledge of each other, from having met at Mrs. Ormond's, in town, before Frederic went abroad, and they now renewed their acquaintance with mutual satisfaction. /

CHAPTER VI.

This is the prettiest low-born lass, that ever
Ran on the green-sward: nothing she does, or seems,
But smacks of something greater than herself;
* * Good sooth, she is
The queen of curds and cream.

SHAKSPEARE.[31]

THE tenant's feast, at which Sir Everard shewed himself a moment, accompanied by his nephew, had all the recommendations which good and abundant cheer could give it, in addition to a most hospitable welcome, and full license to be as noisy and jovial as they pleased. Ella was satisfied to hear of this from a distance; but at the opening of the approaching ball, both she and her sister meant to be present in person, as did all the rest of the party, including Mr. Sedley. Accordingly, when the appointed evening came and the company had assembled, and the musicians / taken their stations, Lady Ormond, leaning on the arm of Mr. Fitzmaurice, his wife on that of Sir Everard, and Ella attended by young Sedley, and followed by Frederic and Ernest, entered the spacious and lofty room in which the revels were to be held. In the motley collection of brothers and sisters, cousins and friends drawn together by the invitation of the domestics, many were to be seen who came from a distance of six or seven miles. During a considerable portion of the day Ella had witnessed, from a side window of her dressing-closet, looking towards the courtyard leading to the offices, the arrival of successive parties, in various costumes and various conveyances, which she had not always been able to survey without a smile. Some came on pillions and brought their gala dresses in bandboxes or bundles on their knees, wearing, *ad interim*,[32] their usual attire; others alighted from their chaise-carts half adorned for the evening, and half equipped in the coarse garments suited to their daily occupations. Amongst these were many stout and ruddy maidens, with arms the colour of beef seen through the clear muslin of their sleeves; their thick hair in curl papers and their leather shoes and worsted stockings peeping / from beneath the thin drapery of their gown skirt, and most of them with bright ribbon sashes hanging down to their ankles. In the ball-room, however, their appearance exhibited more consistency. The *papillotes*[33] were discarded, and the hair curled like wire around their plump faces. The feet, either by force or good-will, were enclosed in thin light-coloured shoes; and on the wide massive hands were painfully drawn the inflexible gloves afforded by country shops. Few amongst them were pretty, but many had ingenuous and good countenances, and were, with some exceptions, beyond comparison, superior to the young men. These, in addition to the slouching clumsiness of rustics, had, generally speaking, a heavy dogged look, that gave no very favourable idea of the sweetness of their temper. A few, the sons or foremen of petty tradesmen in the neighbouring town of —, affected smartness and gentility; wore their watches suspended round the neck by chains, brushed up their hair till it stood on end, coaxed their whiskers into tolerable importance, and tightened their waist till it became a matter of some speculation to understand how they could breathe. These were by far the most amusing personages of the assembly, and their evident good opinion of / themselves, rendered them in some measure fair objects of derision; but except Frederic, all were upon their guard, and resolutely banished from their faces every smile or look that might have given offence. Frederic was less scrupulous. His supercilious eye and the sarcastic curl of his lip whilst regarding them, annihilated much of the self-complacency they had enjoyed prior to his entrance: thus poisoning their enjoyment, though adding little to his own.

Ella, who was to open the ball, after having spoken a kind word to all those with whom she was acquainted, gave her hand to Mr. Sedley, who had engaged her immediately on his arrival, and was proceeding to the upper end of the room, when stopped by Lady Ormond:

'Mr. Sedley,' said her Ladyship, 'I hope you will excuse my interference; but this is a ball given entirely on a family occasion for the gratification of our own people; and I am sure they would rather see Sir Everard's niece dance with Mr. de Gray whom they look upon as one of ourselves, than with a gentleman they can only consider as a stranger.'

Poor Sedley, extremely disconcerted, yet endeavouring to hide his confusion under a / laugh, bowed as he resigned the fair hand he had thought secure, and said:

'Thus may disappointment overtake a man between the cup and the lip! Be it, however, as you determine, madam; I trust I shall be more fortunate another time.'

The good humour of this answer did not sufficiently touch Ella, to restrain the lively pleasure with which she heard her aunt's proposal; and the involuntary pressure she gave that lady's hand, betrayed a secret which she had hitherto most successfully concealed. Being led, a willing prize, to the unprepared but delighted Ernest, they were exhorted to take their places without delay.

Sedley, meanwhile, to avoid the appearance of pique, proposed himself to Mrs. Fitzmaurice, and was accepted. Her husband took out one of the least awkward of the country damsels, and the rest of the company followed in pairs, filling the long space from one end of the room to the other, till the crowd became so thick, it was found necessary to divide the dancers into two sets. Frederic took no part in what was going forward; he stood leaning against the wainscot near his uncle, conspicuous from his height, and still wearing the same / look of cold mockery, which had already made so many shrink within themselves. At intervals, he cast an eye upon his watch, as if impatient for the moment when he might with decency depart.

The first dance being over, Sir Everard, though he had been gratified by the sight of so many cheerful faces, began to wish for his accustomed rubber, and to meditate a retreat. Ella perceiving what was passing in his mind, went towards him, and leaning down, said something in a whisper that induced him once more to settle himself in his chair, and smilingly promise that he would abide her pleasure. Just as this little arrangement had been made, Mrs. Fitzmaurice, hastily approached, saying:

'The most beautiful girl I ever saw in my life has just entered the room. Come and look at her, Ella, and tell me whether you know who she is.'

Ella readily guessed, from the epithet 'beautiful,' that it could be no other than Ruth; but she was surprised. It had appeared to her, that a promiscuous crowd, like the present, was so ill fitted to suit the taste of a young creature, who, though in fact of the same degree, soared so immeasurably above all / those who were assembled, that it was out of the question to suppose any thing could induce her to appear as an equal amongst them.

But Ella soon perceived that she had been mistaken; for as she advanced with her sister towards the lower end of the room, she saw Mrs. Nelson and Ruth slowly making their way through the throng, and trying to discover some vacant place along the forms, where they might find room to sit. Ruth was dressed almost with the plainness of a Quaker;[34] she was in mourning, without the slightest ornament; but it is not in language to do justice to the noble simplicity of her demeanour, to the pure lustre of her faultless complexion, nor to the effect produced by the symmetry of her admirable features, and the mingled composure and sweetness of her countenance.

Already a little group of admirers, foremost in the number of which was Mr. Fitzmaurice, hovered around her. He had been one of the first to distinguish her, and now stood at some distance, gazing upon her with the wrapt attention of a *connoisseur* surveying a masterpiece of Grecian sculpture. Young Sedley also was there. But he who distanced every other in the contest to approach her was Frederic, who unceremoniously pushing aside all that impeded / his progress, forced his way up to her, and pointing to a footman who was toiling towards them, with a light chair under each arm, said:

'I have ordered seats for you, and here they are.'

Mrs. Nelson, curtsying, and half ashamed, thanked him in a low voice, whilst Ruth only raised her eyes an instant to his face, and dropped them again in silence.

'Is this fair wonder,' said Mrs. Fitzmaurice to her sister, 'the daughter of our good Mrs. Nelson?'

'Yes,' answered Ella; 'and if Ernest is to be believed, she is as much to be pitied as admired.'

'Pitied! why?'

'For being too handsome and too polished for a village maiden. But let us go nearer, and speak to her.'

They did so; and Ruth, rising from the seat she had just taken possession of, stood up whilst they talked to her, answering their enquiries with modest propriety, and appearing gratified by their notice. Presently Ernest came up to her; and Mr. Fitzmaurice, perceiving that so many of the family were acquainted with her, approached nearer, that he / might be made known to her also, and was instantly followed by young Sedley. At last, Sir Everard and Lady Ormond, finding themselves deserted, came likewise, and were evidently as much struck by her extreme beauty, as any of the party.

They immediately entered into conversation with her, hoped her long residence near London would not make the country appear dull to her, and cordially congratulated Mrs. Nelson on her return. The poor woman, though delighted, was almost oppressed by these public civilities; and seeing the effect they produced upon her neighbours, many of whom were standing around with wondering and not very friendly looks, was relieved when the general observation was called off by the intervention of a new subject of curiosity.

The unexpected sound of a key bugle, blown with great ability, was suddenly heard re-echoing through the stone passage leading to the ball room, and whilst all eyes were turned in that direction, a figure appeared at the door that caused a universal buzz of astonishment. Habited in a splendid Eastern costume, a youth of small stature, delicate features, but dark complexion, was seen slowly advancing through the opening crowd, bearing in one / hand a light furled up banner, in the other, a rich gold and crimson bag. On reaching Sir Everard and Lady Ormond, he reverentially paid his obeisance three times in the oriental fashion, and held forth his gorgeous bag, containing a quantity of printed numbers on detached pieces of card, inviting them by signs to make their own selection. When this had been, with smiles, and many expressions of curiosity, complied with, the mute Asiatic passed on to others of the party; whilst various young assistants, fancifully, but less richly, attired, and also provided with silk bags, went round to offer their contents in different parts of the room to the rest of the company. When all the tickets were disposed of, he that bore the banner prepared to retire. Arrived at the door, he stopped, turned, and during a renewed flourish of the bugle by its invisible performer, dexterously unfurled his small standard, and displayed to view the following doggerel rhymes painted upon it in large characters:

> 'Though I am mute, I am not blind,
> To Fortune's Temple you shall find
> I'm a true guide; then where I lead,
> Arise, and follow me with speed.'

There needed no second invitation. As / many as could push their way through the door-case, poured impetuously into the passage, and rushed after their singular conductor. All present would have imitated their example, but one of the young aides-de-camp called out in a shrill voice:

'Await the return of your friends! There is not room for so many at once.'

A prohibition so express was not to be disregarded; but to these undisciplined rustics, whose imagination was strongly excited by what had passed, and whose impatience to reach the promised temple knew no bounds, it was, for the moment, a severe disappointment.

Meanwhile, those who first attained the goal, after traversing various passages, were introduced into a small room, fitted up with canvass as a tent, and adorned with evergreen boughs and garlands of flowers, amongst which were interspersed a multitude of brilliant little lamps. The *coup-d'œil*[35] was extremely pretty; but what most attracted the attention of the villagers, was the display, in two large booths opposite each other, of almost all the wares usually found at country fairs. For the men, there were coloured handkerchiefs, pocket knives, tobacco-boxes, shaving-glasses, / shirt pins, riding whips, &c. In the women's booths were ribbons of every description, muslin for caps, prints, coloured and framed, work-baskets, silver thimbles, needle-books, scissors, &c. Every lot was numbered, and the person who had drawn its corresponding number in the ball room, was entitled to claim the prize it designated. In each booth was an attendant, ready to receive the tickets as they were given in, and to deliver the prizes.

The first party having retreated in high glee, and loudly extolling the merits of a lottery *without blanks*, was speedily succeeded by a second, and that by a third and fourth, till at length every claimant was satisfied. The dancing was then recommenced; but Ella, declining to stand up again, prevailed upon Sir Everard and his lady, before they went back to the drawing-room, to take a peep at the Temple of Fortune. Ruth and her mother, who had not yet given in their tickets, were invited to accompany them; and the Fitzmaurices, with the three young men and Ella followed.

At the entrance of the tent, they were again saluted by the youthful standard-bearer. /

'Ella,' cried Sir Everard, 'all this fanciful raree-show is of course of your devising. Tell me then, now the surprise is over, who are your actors? This pretty mussulman,[36] for instance, who is he?'

'*He,*' answered Ella, laughing, 'is Mrs. Nelson's youngest daughter, Anne.'

'Is it possible? Well, my lass,' continued the Baronet, patting the tittering girl upon the shoulder, 'you could not have performed your part better, had you lived all your life in the service of a three-tailed Bashaw.'[37]

'But, my dear Ella,' said Lady Ormond, 'allow me to ask why the costume of an Asiatic was chosen for your usher to the Temple of Fortune? Might it not have been better to have caused your little agent to appear as one of the winged genii we read of in the Arabian Nights?'[38]

'Much better, dear aunt; but I had no wings to equip him with, and no time to fabricate any; whilst, on the contrary, the dress you see him, or rather her, wear, is, with very little alteration, precisely the same I had on at Lady C—'s masquerade. My only object was to heighten the amusement of the evening to the country people, and furnish them / with something unusual to stare at; and for that purpose I own it did not seem necessary to study correctness of plan.'

'And did you also, child,' enquired Sir Everard, 'wear that formidable dagger which Anne carries at her girdle?'

'No,' said Ella; 'I was to personify an Eastern lady, whilst Anne was to represent a youth. To complete her costume, therefore, it seemed proper to supply her with arms; and I borrowed from Ernest the dagger his father brought from Egypt.'

'It is a dangerous plaything, my girl,' resumed the Baronet, addressing Anne, 'and the sooner you lay it aside the better. Take it from her, my dear de Gray.'

'Let me look at it, Ernest,' said Frederic; 'I had quite forgotten your having such a weapon.'

Then unsheathing it, and examining its bright blade and keen edge,

'It is indeed a tremendous instrument,' he continued; 'no bone or muscle could withstand it: but I imagine it would inflict a very easy death.'

At these words, Ella, hastily stretching out her hand for it, gave it back to Ernest, exclaiming: /

'My uncle is right: it is no toy to trifle with. Pray put it out of the way, Ernest. After what has been said, it gives me pain to look at it.'

'Then be assured,' said Ernest, with a smile, 'it shall never again offend your sight.'

Lady Ormond, not entirely recovered from her medical mania, now expressed a hope that poor little Anne would be no sufferer by the tawny drug with which her face had been dyed.

'It is the opinion,' said she, 'of several sensible writers, that all mineral, and even many vegetable colours, are extremely pernicious when applied to the skin.'

Ella, assuring her Anne would not be injured by the harmless compound that had been used on the present occasion, they advanced into the interior of the tent. Its light and sparkling effect – and by such simple means – was much commended. Ella said she had met with such cheerful and ready assistants in the accomplishment of her little plan amongst the domestics, that the whole arrangement had been completed without having recourse to any other aid. She then took Sir Everard by the hand, and led him up to the men's booth, / whilst Frederic conducted Lady Ormond to that prepared for the women. Their prizes were immediately produced, and proved to be so valuable, that they almost shrank from the idea of receiving them.

'Why, you silly child!' exclaimed Sir Everard, looking half vexed, 'do you think we wanted such costly nicknacks as these, to convince us of your good will? I could find in my heart to scold you furiously.'

'Here stands the culprit, uncle,' cried Ella, pointing to her brother; 'let all your ire be directed against *him*. I am innocence itself!'

The objects in question were a gold snuffbox, of the most beautiful form and workmanship; and a lady's writing stand,[39] of singular elegance, furnished with every accessory that ingenuity could invent; seals set in gold of all dimensions and design, penknives, weights to keep down papers, of the greatest variety of fantastical shapes; pencils and metal pens in ornamented cases; in short, the whole train of superfluities which to genius are unnecessary, to dullness of no advantage. They had been brought by Frederic from abroad as presents to Sir Everard and his aunt, but with some other of his effects, not having arrived at the / Hall till two or three days later than himself, Ella, who had seen them in his room on the morning of the ball, had entreated he would allow her to include them amongst the prizes of her lottery.

'With all my heart,' said he, 'if you can ensure their finding their right destination. I have no inclination to let them become the property of any of the interesting personages with whose company we are this evening to be honoured.'

His sister explained to him the plan upon which the prizes were to be distributed, and promised that those intended for her uncle and aunt should fall into no other hands. He then yielded to her request without further difficulty.

On hearing from whom the elegant offerings proceeded, Sir Everard and his lady became more reconciled to their value, remembering, that what in Ella would have been an act of ostentation, or a childish extravagance, was but a *souvenir d'amitié*[40] in her brother, which the income they so liberally supplied him with enabled him perfectly to afford. They therefore accepted his gift not only without scruple, but with manifest pleasure. The remaining prizes, without much regard to form and order, / were rather dispensed, as inclination dictated, than as chance had seemed to appoint.

Mrs. Fitzmaurice had gained a neat little spinning wheel, which she made Ruth's mother exchange with her for a quantity of useless cherry-coloured ribbon. Ruth's ticket brought her a morocco purse and some other trifle, which Mr. Fitzmaurice insisted upon her giving up to him for a morocco pocket-book and silver pencil case. The young men dared not venture to make such transfers; they accepted their prizes, whatever they might be; and Sir Everard, summoning them to accompany him into the drawing-room, Mrs. Nelson and 'the fair Maid of Ormond Green,'[41] as he chose to denominate her, took their leave, and returned to the ball-room.

Whilst seating himself at the whist-table, the Baronet, whose mind still dwelt upon the occurrences of the evening, asked Ella where she had picked up her clever performer upon the bugle horn?

'It was Mrs. Nelson's nephew,' answered she, 'the young carpenter, Philip, who undertook the service for me. There is scarcely any thing he has not a smattering knowledge of, / and amongst his various acquirements is that of blowing the bugle.'

Satisfied with this answer, he questioned her no more during several deals; but then, though in a less direct manner, reverting to the lottery,

'Ella, my girl,' cried he, 'I seem to be in a lucky vein this evening; I have already won the first rubber, and seem to be in a fair way of winning the second. You shall go halves with me, if I continue equally successful.'

'Thank you, dear uncle,' cried Ella, gaily; 'I am quite resigned to whatever you are pleased to decree.'

'Poor child!' resumed he, 'you must have ruined yourself in furnishing out those two booths.'

'Oh, if that is your reason, uncle, for making me a partaker of your winnings, I am obliged, in common honesty, to decline the obligation. I was so largely assisted by my sister, that my share of the expense was next to nothing.'

'But why did you not apply to *me?* In my own house it was but fair to let me be my own paymaster.' /

'Had Ella done so,' observed Mr. Fitzmaurice, 'what would have become of the little surprise she meditated to give you? – Half her pleasure depended upon that.'

'And, after all, dear Sir,' she resumed, 'I was obliged almost to betray myself, to prevent your hurrying away before the lottery began.'

'You betrayed nothing, child. How could I suspect what was to happen by your whispering to me a request to stay ten minutes longer for "a particular reason"? Those were words that assuredly told but little. They had the effect, however, of making a good obedient boy of me, though I own I was getting almost as weary as Frederic, and that is saying a good deal, – is it not, Fred?'

To this no answer was given, for Frederic was not in the room; and Sir Everard concluded he was gone off to bed in disgust: but on being enquired for when wine and biscuits were brought in, great was the Baronet's surprise to hear that Mr. Ormond was still in the ball room, and had been dancing!

'Humph!' ejaculated he, as soon as the servants were withdrawn, 'it appears that master Frederic can be more tolerant of unpolished company than I had suspected! It is / wonderful what the contemplation of a pretty face can do! Well, the case is common enough; and luckily the beautiful Ruth has a prudent circumspect mother, who will know how to take care of her.'

This little soliloquy was heard in silence; no one present wished to cast censure upon Frederic; yet it was difficult to approve his subjecting Ruth, by such ill-judged attentions, to the invidious remarks of those very people whose vanity he had wounded not an hour before, and whose resentment would now find such willing vent in sneers and inuendoes mischievous to her good repute. Still more difficult was it to forbear wondering, that a man so morbidly fastidious should thus unresistingly yield to the fascinations of low-born beauty, should overcome his feelings of disdain for her fellows so far as to mingle in their pastime, take hands with them, and voluntarily put himself upon their level.

Ella saw nothing in all this but matter for mirth. No picture could be more amusing to her imagination than that of her stately brother dancing amongst the spruce apprentices, and lumpy clowns his eye had lately measured with so much scorn. Mrs. Fitzmaurice, more easily alarmed, was filled with doubts and misgivings / as to the effect upon Ruth's peace of mind, of these extraordinary distinctions from a young man so elevated by station, by personal appearance, and above all, by manners so superior to those with whom the poor girl was ever likely to hold intercourse. She communicated her apprehensions to her husband:

'Bah, bah!' exclaimed he, 'Frederic is a thousand times more in danger than Ruth! If he can with impunity expose himself to gaze on the attractions of that loveliest "mortal creature of earth's mould,"[42] he is indeed a hero! She is a thing to look at only on Sundays and holidays. I never saw a being who came up so truly to my ideas of real beauty; and I tell you, Bess, it is not merely the beauty of outward form, – there is *mind* in her face. The deep serenity of her superb eye, announces thought and discernment. She is not to be caught by a few honeyed phrases; and I again repeat, Frederic incurs a million times greater risk from her, than she does from him.'

'This is poor consolation, Hugh.'

''Tis the best I can give you. You were anxious for the safety of Ruth, and I tell you she is in no peril. As for your brother, the / worst that can happen to him is a temporary heart ache, which change of scene will cure, and which, for the time, will do him the essential good of humbling the loftiness that has hitherto made him look down with so little tolerance on his inferiors.'

Happy would Ernest have been could he have viewed the case in a similar light; but this was not in his power. From what he deemed himself justified in believing to be Frederic's principles, no woman peculiarly distinguished by him could be exempt from danger; least of all, one in the subordinate rank of Ruth; and his apprehensions for her were proportioned to the just sense he had of her rare endowments, and the grateful regard he entertained for her mother. To parley with Frederic he knew would be vain; but some good might perhaps be effected by gently cautioning Mrs. Nelson. It was neither his design nor his wish to represent Frederic unfavourably to her; but it might be possible to accomplish his aim without resorting to such invidious means; and he determined to make the experiment. /

CHAPTER VII.

If I'm traduced by tongues, that neither know
My faculties nor person; let me say,
'Tis but the common fate.

SHAKSPEARE.[43]

FOR some time subsequent to the ball but little change occurred in the posture of affairs at Sir Everard's. Sedley persevered in his visits, and Lady Ormond persevered in her frigid manner of receiving him. By degrees, however, this treatment began to make a more painful impression upon him; for he perceived that Ella relaxed considerably in her endeavours to compensate to him, as heretofore, for her aunt's ungraciousness. The truth is, seeing her sister, Mr. Fitzmaurice, and the Baronet always well disposed to be courteous to him, she felt that he was no longer dependent upon her for support, and left him to their care, giving herself / no greater trouble about him than about any other occasional visitor who came to the house.

Ernest was less remiss, and continued to show him all his usual friendliness and attention: nor in so doing was there, it must be owned, any extraordinary merit. He could not but be perfectly aware that Sedley's chance of succeeding was every day becoming less; – and they are few who cannot soar to such a pitch of virtue as to treat with kindness a rival they do not fear. But the kindness of Ernest was not enough; it could, indeed, do little towards alleviating the hourly increasing distrust and anxiety which preyed upon Sedley's mind. His countenance lost entirely its customary expression, and became as absent and thoughtful as it had hitherto been careless and contented. Ella saw it, and saw it with concern; but she justly reflected, that any effort on her part to dispel his dejection, would be but giving a temporary renewal and encouragement to his hopes, in order again to crush them. Whilst she regarded him only as one of her mother's objects of speculation – as a *bon parti* she was to try and secure – yet observed not anything serious in his own views, she flattered herself there subsisted between / them a sort of tacit understanding, that permitted their manifesting the utmost friendliness towards each other, without being participators in Mrs. Ormond's designs. It was now apparent those designs corresponded but too well with his own wishes; and Ella therefore determined upon availing herself of her mother's absence, to put a complete end to every expectation he might have formed. Aided by his unpresuming character, her task was less difficult than, with a more confident man, she would have found it. He yielded, though with deep regret, to what seemed to be her irrevocable, though unavowed decision, and became almost a stranger at Ormond Hall.

The secret satisfaction she derived from this circumstance, received its first check from observing in the looks and in the few words that passed between her brother and Ernest a marked coldness that indicated either an actual or an impending breach. She sought in vain to obtain from either an explanation of these angry appearances; they were impenetrable. Frederic affected to laugh at what he called her true feminine sagacity in 'finding out meanings never meant;'[44] and Ernest, more gently, assured her the symptoms she had remarked were but temporary clouds, that would soon / pass away, and be succeeded by fairer weather. Still she was not exempt from anxiety, and waited in vain from day to day for the commencement of that reconciliation he had seemed to foretell. It made no progress. The countenance of Frederic continued to denote that he was deeply offended; and whilst at times, defiance and disdain flashed from his eyes, at others, they expressed a vague inquietude – a lurking suspicion, that often gave him an air of irritation and restlessness agreeing ill with the arrogant assumption of superiority he sought to maintain.

Ernest, firm and unembarrassed, neither retorted scorn with scorn, nor blenched beneath the hostile glances that were directed against him; yet he was not at ease, and showed in a thousand ways that the dissension subsisting between them, gave him pain, and weighed upon his spirits.

The Fitzmaurices, after a visit of ten days, were compelled, by the expected arrival of some friends at their own house, to announce their departure. Ella was half reluctant to accompany them. True, the same want of a female companion, which had made her, some time before, scrupulous of remaining exposed to be too much with Ernest, still existed; / but this might be obviated, she found, by encouraging the daughter of the neighbouring clergyman to come frequently to the house; and as she was in much favour with her uncle and aunt, no objections were anticipated. By staying, she knew also that she should be giving them pleasure; but her chief inducement, was the hope of allaying by her presence, perhaps by her good offices, the angry feelings subsisting between the two young men.

When, therefore, on the day preceding the departure of Mrs. Fitzmaurice, Sir Everard and Lady Ormond expressed their regret at losing both sisters at once, and though, doubtful of success, pressed Ella still to remain, she hesitated not, but rejoiced their hearts by her consent; and her brother-in-law, who partly suspected her motive, (for the appearances that had so forcibly struck her had not escaped his discernment,) sincerely approved her resolution.

Once more, then, established at Ormond Hall, and provided, in Miss Kirby, with an amiable and well-educated associate, Ella pursued her accustomed rides and walks, and her favourite in-door occupations with all her wonted spirit and diligence. And not to Ernest only was her protracted visit a source of delight; / Frederic was also gratified by it. Her vivacity supplied the place of his own, and relieved him from the necessity, during meals, of keeping up the conversation. At other periods of the day he was seldom at home, or if it happened otherwise, it was generally at a late hour in the evening, when, to avoid remarks on his silence, he either played at chess with his sister, or took a seat at his uncle's whist table.

One morning, on the arrival, during breakfast, of the newspapers and letters, Sir Everard whilst distributing the latter according to their directions, said to his nephew:

'Here's one for you, Fred, from your mother; tell us what she says about coming into the country.'

Frederic put the letter calmly down, and went on with his breakfast, only saying,

'Are there any more for me, Sir?'

'No,' answered the Baronet.

'And, upon my word,' cried Ella, a little impatiently, 'you hardly deserve *that!* Why don't you read what my mother says, Frederic? She has not written for some time, and I am anxious to hear what she is doing.'

Frederic, half jestingly, held out to her the letter with one hand, whilst with the other he leisurely stirred his tea, saying: /

'If it will amuse you very much, you may read it for me.'

She was almost tempted to take him at his word, but recollecting there might be things in it meant for no eye but his, she gently pushed back his hand, and said,

'Ah, Frederic, you would not have ventured upon such an offer, had you thought me capable of accepting it!'

'I assure you,' cried he, laughing, 'I did not hold it forth as a trial of your virtue, – though,' he whisperingly added, 'I shrewdly suspect I shall find it a heavy trial of my own patience!'

'Why do you think so?'

'Because the good lady has a passion for writing such interminable lectures, it hardly ever happens I am able to get through them.'

'Well, but try this once, my dear Frederic; there can be nothing to lecture you about now you are leading such a quiet life in the country.'

Having finished his breakfast, he at length consented to satisfy her wishes, and breaking the seal of his letter, began languidly to peruse it. But he had not proceeded through many lines before the blood rushed impetuously to / his face, and crimsoned his very forehead. His brow became contracted, and his lips firmly compressed together, evinced the strongest internal agitation. Ella, who was the only one observing him, dared ask no questions; but she silently and with some alarm, sat gazing at him, till he suddenly started up, and prepared to leave the room. No longer able to controul her apprehensions, she followed him, and passing her arm through his, said in an under voice, full of kindness and concern:

'Have you received any bad news, my dearest brother?'

'No, Ella,' answered he, sternly, 'but *good* news! It is always good, when we have an enemy – a diabolical enemy – to be made aware of it!' And as he spoke he darted a look of fury towards the unconscious Ernest, who was running his eye over one of the newspapers, and precipitately quitted the room.

Ella stood still as if petrified; pale and shocked, she scarcely believed she had heard aright. That Ernest could merit such an accusation she deemed utterly impossible; but that it should have been called forth by the perusal of a letter from her mother, was so extraordinary, so incomprehensible, that no suggestion offered itself to her mind capable of / accounting for it. Ernest had always been treated and spoken of by Mrs. Ormond with distinguished regard; she could not, therefore, have written anything concerning him with feelings of malevolence; and yet, what but some heavy charge against him could so vehemently have exasperated Frederic? Perhaps her mother had been misled by some calumnious report, or still more probable, some ambiguous expression of hers had been misinterpreted, a circumstance but too likely to happen in the present irascible state of Frederic's mind. At all events Ella, after a few moments' consideration, felt persuaded that the kindest and most friendly thing she could do, would be to afford Ernest, by a hint of what was passing, a speedy opportunity of vindicating himself both to her brother, and through him to Mrs. Ormond. Yet, she dreaded to instigate him to seek an immediate interview with Frederic, since, whilst his anger lasted, the insulting language he might use it would, perhaps, not be in man to avoid resenting. With all the prudence, therefore, which her age and inexperience qualified her to exert, she finally came to the resolution of endeavouring to keep the two young men as much apart as possible till the first animosity of Frederic / should subside; and then cautiously to prepare Ernest to enter on his own justification. To retard an evil is to the young, almost equivalent to escaping from it; and Ella, after fixing upon this plan, became comparatively composed.

It was now the beginning of August; the weather was sultry and oppressive, and morning excursions were given up. Miss Kirby, however, failed not to come as usual, content to spend her time with Ella, whether in active or sedentary pursuits. Lady Ormond, was shut up for the morning in her own apartment. She had just received, with other new publications, the latest numbers of the Edinburgh and Quarterly Reviews;[45] knowing which, the whole family was prepared, for some days to come, to hear her, with the most comic vacillation, turn from whiggism to toryism, from the strongest party-spirit on one side, to *as* strong a party-spirit on the other, according as the various articles came under her inspection. The fact is, whatever she last read drove out the remembrance of what she had read before; and with a *bonhommie*[46] and unconsciousness almost incredible, she was in matters of literature a perfect Zimri: 'Everything by turns, and nothing long.'[47] /

The two young ladies, with somewhat more consistency of plan, had lately undertaken the perusal of a select number of the British poets, alternately relieving each other in the office of reader; and whilst one was thus engaged, her companion worked or drew. Ernest sometimes joined them, and the book was then put into his hands, an arrangement they were always most ready to adopt, since he read remarkably well. The room they sat in was cool and quiet, and communicating with that which Sir Everard always occupied till dinner-time, Ella could in a moment, if wanted, fly to him, tell him the day of the month, if he was writing; find the second volume of the book he was reading, or perform for him any of the little services she delighted to render him, and he never thought so well executed by anybody else. On the present occasion, then, Ernest was invited to accompany them to their retreat, and as usual, to be their lecturer. The book was Cowper's Task,[48] to which they continued listening with unabated pleasure till Miss Kirby reluctantly announced that she could stay no longer, having promised her father to return early in order to transcribe his sermon for the next day. The excuse was not to be combated; Ella thanked her for the / time she had bestowed upon her, and suffered her to go without opposition. Ernest volunteered to accompany her to the rectory gate.

Soon after their departure, observing that a slight shower had fallen which had refreshed the air, Ella resolved to take a little stroll. As she ascended the stairs for her bonnet, she met Ernest coming hastily down.

'How soon you are returned!' cried she, with some surprise.

'The reason is,' answered he, 'that we met Mr. Kirby, who took charge of his daughter himself; and I then made my bow.'

'And where now are you going?' resumed Ella, anxious that he should not, for the present, throw himself in the way of Frederic.

'I can scarcely stay to tell you,' said he; 'Philip Nelson has been putting some additional shelves in my book-closet, and has done it so awkwardly, that he must come and take them down again. I saw him a few moments since, preparing to return home, and I am anxious to stop him.'

Re-assured by this answer, she good-humouredly nodded, and passed on.

After having visited the green-house and / flower-garden, she was induced to direct her steps towards a spot in the pleasure-grounds where her uncle had permitted her to order the erection of a rustic seat. To do this, it was necessary to pass the hermitage, in approaching which, she thought she could distinguish loud voices from within, voices too well known to her to be mistaken. Had then her brother and Ernest at this inauspicious moment encountered each other? In great apprehension that it might be so, she hurried forward, bent at all events upon interrupting their unfriendly conference. The door of the little edifice was partly open, and had she pleased, she might distinctly have overheard their conversation without being perceived; but this was a meanness that did not even enter her imagination; and without pausing an instant, she suddenly stood before them.

Frederic was half reclined upon the mossy seat that ran round the building; he looked fatigued and heated, but less intemperate and violent than his sister had expected, although manifest signs of splenetic impatience still lowered on his brow. Ernest, more agitated than Ella had ever seen him, was pacing rapidly backwards and forwards within the narrow enclosure, a deep glow burning upon / his cheek – his eyes flashing fire – his arms folded tightly over his heaving breast, and his whole appearance indicating an intensity of emotion it was with difficulty he could control. It seemed as if the two young men had changed characters: Frederic was to a certain degree calm and collected; Ernest evidently boiling with indignation, and in a state of the strongest excitement; as the one had taken fire, the other seemed to have cooled.

'Ella, Ella,' exclaimed he, stopping short on seeing her enter, 'why do you come here? Leave us, I entreat.'

'No, no, Ella,' cried her brother with a laugh of bitter sarcasm, 'stay where you are, unless you can prevail upon this agreeable gentleman to go away with you. I came here, weary and heated, after a long ride, for quiet and rest. Mr. de Gray chose suddenly to favour me with a visit; a visit, which, whatever *he* may think, I am of opinion has lasted quite long enough. I now, therefore, request him to terminate it, and leave me to the comfort of reading myself to sleep. A tiresome book may have that good effect – a tiresome talker keeps one awake to no purpose.'

Ella making an effort to smile, though much / more disposed to cry, now said: 'You are very impertinent, my dear brother. If I were Ernest, I would leave you to dose away your ill-humour, and bestow all my attention upon your better-bred sister. What say you, Ernest? Will you be my escort to my aunt's dairy?'

'Yes – yes,' he hurriedly answered, struggling to recover his self-command, 'but walk on a little way first, and I will follow you.'

'Better go with her at once,' said Frederic, after a desperate yawn.

'Ella will forgive me; I have but one – one word more to say to you, and then I am at her command. Ella, will you not grant me this little delay?'

Judging from her brother's indolent composure, which, however provoking, did not appear to be assumed, that there was no immediate danger in leaving them together, Ella in answer to the request of Ernest, said: –

'I suppose I must comply; but come as soon as you can, for the weather looks threatening, and I fear we shall have another shower.'

She then quitted them, and sauntering slowly / forward, meditated with no little concern on all she had heard and seen. For the first time in her life, she had beheld Ernest rather as an object of fear than of love! She then recalled to mind, with astonishment, the severe and even awful resentment his countenance had expressed. It was impossible, however, to judge how far the goading spirit of Frederic might wilfully have conduced to rouse and urge this vehement irritation. And after all, were not the passionate feelings manifested by Ernest, of a more generous character than the caustic insolence of her brother? Yet, to former specimens of the same spirit, how long, and with what admirable forbearance, had Ernest submitted! There must, assuredly, at the present moment have been provocation given of a far more serious nature; some attack upon his character, – some charge of dishonour; on those points alone could he have been so keenly susceptible; sneers and attempted ridicule would have fallen harmless. /

CHAPTER VIII.

Is whispering nothing?
Is leaning cheek to cheek? skulking in corners?
Is this nothing? Why, then the world, and all that's in't
Is nothing.

SHAKESPEARE.[49]

THESE and similar reflections brought her, ere she was aware, to the entrance of the dairy. She was surprised, and somewhat uneasy that Ernest had not overtaken her, since leisurely as she had walked, it would have cost him so little exertion. It was possible that pre-occupied by other thoughts, he had taken a different and more circuitous path; trusting this was the case, and still hoping he would soon appear, she accepted the dairy-woman's invitation, and went into her cool parlour to rest herself. Whilst thus at the good gossip's mercy, she was compelled to listen to a succession of strictures and anecdotes on the subject / of the neighbouring villagers, that for scandal and invidiousness, could not have been excelled by a whole conclave of aged country-town spinsters, long practised in the art of defamation. Amongst the rest, she failed not to bring forward the names of Mrs. Nelson and Ruth, saying slyly: –

'They two be no fools, Miss Ella, whatever else they may be! My belief is, the best thing we can all do, is to see, and hear, and say nothing. Who knows what Mrs. Ruth may come to be?'

'I hope,' said Ella, 'she may come to be the wife of some deserving man, who will treat her kindly, and have the means of maintaining her with comfort.'

'Ah, Miss, that's not what they, (I mean both mother and daughter) are fishing for; they look for grander prey, I can tell you, though, may be, near as the thing *consarns* you, you know less about it than any of us.'

'Concerns *me*, Mrs. Roy! what can you mean?'

'I mean as I says, Miss Ella; but perhaps it would not become me to speak more plainer. I might affront you, my dear young lady, and I am sure I would not wilfully do that for the world. All I shall say is, there be strange doings going on at John Nelson's farm.' /

'But of what kind, Mrs. Roy?' enquired Ella, impelled in despight of herself, by 'such ambiguous givings out,'[50] to feel a certain degree of curiosity; 'pray explain yourself. I promise not to be affronted, whatever you tell me.'

The notable dame, who desired no better than to be a little urged, now readily, and with more explicitness proceeded to substantiate her charges.

'Why you know, Miss Ella,' said she, 'you have two fine young gentlemen at the Hall – your brother and Mr. Ernest. Now, if you'll believe me, that cunning mother Nelson and her upstart daughter have an eye, as sure as you are born, upon one or other of them for a husband for Mrs. Ruth.'

'Nonsense, Mrs. Roy!' interrupted the half laughing Ella. 'How can you encourage yourself to believe anything so absurd?'

'Well, well, it may be nonsense to suppose that either of them will take her for a wife; but, then, she will let herself be taken for something worse! Miss Ella, I tell you no story when I say, there is not a day passes that Mr. Frederick does not spend hours and hours at the farm. I have seen him, with my own eyes, go in and come out; I have seen / him walking with her in the orchard with his arm round her waist. I have seen him sitting in the arbour, holding her hand.'

Interrupting her once more, Ella hastily said:

'But have you ever seen Mr. de Gray doing any of these things?'

'I have seen him in very earnest talk with her sometimes, and looking very sweet upon her, I assure you; but he does not go there quite so often as your brother; though I dare say, if it was not that he can so seldom avoid meeting him, he would be as much at the house as Mr. Frederick.'

Ella was utterly confounded! Amidst all the variety of assertions that could have been imagined respecting Ernest, this was the very last that would have occurred to her. Did the animosity then that now subsisted between him and Frederic, originate in jealousy? She could not – she would not believe it! Ernest – the very soul of honour – the grateful and affectionate foster-child of Mrs. Nelson – the undeclared though not undetected lover of Ella herself – it was next to impossible that what was reported of him could be true. To this persuasion Ella clung, and it enabled her to sigh from off her heart a weight of misery, that for some minutes had almost crushed it. /

But of Frederick, alas! what was she to think? Was *he* deliberately planning the seduction of that modest, beautiful, interesting Ruth? And was her poor mother so blind as not to perceive the danger of her child? Had she no charitable friend to warn her? She was upright and full of good intentions; but she was uninformed, and not endowed with much natural sagacity. A mind so constituted was peculiarly liable to be deceived; in addition to which was the danger of being misled by her too great confidence in the honour and integrity of one whom, like Frederic, she had known from a child, and would think it almost a sin to distrust.

Ella ruminated in silence on all this; and then, partly provoked, partly alarmed at Ernest's delay in joining her, she arose to return home, with the fixed determination of going herself the following morning to Nelson's farm, and endeavouring to investigate the real state of the affair.

Her mind occupied with this design, and the manner in which it would be best to effect it, she observed not, till she had proceeded some way from the dairy, that it was beginning to rain; yet, rather than turn back, and listen involuntarily to any more of Mrs. Roy's disagreeablè / communications, she preferred hurrying on, in the hope of reaching some place of shelter before the shower had increased sufficiently to penetrate the trees bordering, from space to space, the path she was pursuing. As she ran rather than walked, anxious not to cause alarm by arriving very wet at the house, she heard the sound of a horse's feet at a distance; and, as well as she could see through the misty atmosphere, ascertained that the animal belonged to Ernest, who was himself riding him at full speed in a direction totally opposite to the one she was pursuing.

'Now really, Ernest,' she internally cried, 'this is very unhandsome! What is become of your promise to join me at the dairy-house? and how is it, that instead of walking to overtake or to meet me, you have gone home for your horse, and are galloping away contrary? Poor fellow,' she added, softening towards him, 'perhaps he was reluctant to let me see the traces of passion his recent conference with Frederic may have left upon his brow. In that case, I forgive him; for it would be truly painful to me to witness on his countenance an expression so foreign to that I have always been accustomed to observe in it.'

She had stopped unconsciously whilst thus / soliloquizing, and given the rain, which was beginning to come down very fast, time to soak through her walking garments. The sight, therefore, of the hermitage at a short distance, was gladly welcomed by her, and she sprang towards it with all the haste in her power.

The air was now become so thick and gloomy, that the little building, in which the light was at all times much subdued, scarcely could be measured by the eye; and it was not till Ella had stood several minutes shaking her cloak, and wiping with a handkerchief the rain drops from her hat, that she perceived she was not alone, but descried a human figure stretched upon the same mossy seat on which she had, not long before, seen her brother. She knew at once that it was him; and quietly approaching the spot where he lay, she leant forward to imprint a kiss upon his forehead, curious to ascertain whether he was really asleep, or only feigning to be so, in order to prevent her questioning him as to what had passed between himself and Ernest.

There was, in the feel to her lips of his smooth white forehead, a something that made her start. Warm as was the weather, it seemed as if the object she had touched was unnaturally chill; and she raised her head, almost / shuddering, to contemplate him more intently. As well as she could distinguish, his countenance was deadly pale, but calm, unruffled, and handsome as ever, yet either he was in a swoon, or sleeping so profoundly, that it appeared more like the effect of some strong narcotic, than the natural repose of a healthy man. An open book had fallen from his hold, his shirt collar was open, and his neckcloth lay beside him, evidently thrown off with a view to coolness.

Ella, perplexed and uneasy, gently sought to rouse him by taking hold of his hand, and distinctly but calmly, pronouncing his name. No effect resulted from these attempts; and becoming seriously alarmed, she took courage to feel for the beating of his heart. Its pulsation seemed to have entirely stopped; and aghast at the discovery, what was her additional horror when, on withdrawing her hand, she beheld it dyed in blood, and felt the warm stream dropping from her fingers upon her garments!

A piercing shriek escaped her, at the same moment that a vivid flash of lightning revealed to her the *Egyptian dagger*, worn by Anne Nelson on the evening of the tenants' ball. It lay at some distance in a corner of the building, / where, but for the intense glare of the lightning playing upon its brilliant handle, she might long have failed to detect it. The direction in which it had been thrown was such as to render it almost impossible that Frederic could have cast it there himself; yet that the fearful deed had been effected by that tremendous weapon, though not by his own hand, Ella when she desperately forced herself to examine it nearer, could have no doubt; for its blade was reeking with fresh blood! The shock was too much for her; with one heart-broken exclamation of 'Oh, Ernest!' she sank senseless on the floor.

Nor was it very wonderful that the name she had pronounced should have been the first to suggest itself to her mind. The dagger belonged to de Gray, who she believed had never exposed it to view after the caution given him by Sir Everard; it could not, therefore, have been used by any one but himself. Then the quarrel that had so lately occurred between him and her brother; the extraordinary, the unprecedented rage his countenance had exhibited when she beheld him last; and, finally, his sudden and rapid flight – all darted through her mind in an instant, and left her the most hopeless and miserable of human / beings; – left her mourning profoundly the loss of a beloved brother, and half annihilated by the conviction that Ernest had been his assassin!

The storm was abating, though it had not entirely subsided, when Ella's maid, provided with a large cloak and umbrella, after looking for her mistress in the flower garden, and through the pleasure grounds nearest the house, sought for her at last in the hermitage. The sight that there presented itself almost bereft her of her reason. A stream of blood proceeding from her brother's couch, had reached the unfortunate Ella, and rendered her the most ghastly and terrific object. She was motionless and wholly insensible, and for many minutes her trembling and terror-struck attendant believed her to be dead; and, with glaring eyes, bent over her, and saw nothing but the supposed corpse of her lovely and beloved young lady.

But when, at length, she descried the body of Frederick, and witnessed the state which *he* also was in, her agony of horror knew no bounds. Scream after scream burst from her, and, flying from the building, she ran like one distracted to call together any of the labourers, or gardener's people, who might chance to be / within hearing. Her appalling cries soon drew a number of such persons around her, all eagerly enquiring what was the matter, and surveying her pallid face with mixed astonishment and affright. When made aware, by being conducted to the hermitage, of the real state of the case, the consternation, the dismay with which they were seized, it would be impossible to describe. Some appeared absolutely petrified by what they saw; others became nearly outrageous; some poured forth the deepest execrations against the unknown assassin, others vented their feelings in wild exclamations and conjectures, and many gazed at the mournful spectacle with heartfelt but silent sorrow.

The first individual to suggest any rational mode of proceeding was one of the under gardeners, who said, that to avoid giving Sir Everard a sudden shock, which might be fatal to him, it would be advisable to convey Miss Ormond to the Hall by the back way, and to go with as few attendants, and with as little bustle as possible. Ella accordingly was raised, and when carried into the open air, gradually recovered her consciousness. The first use she made of it was, to entreat that her supporters would set her down, and allow her, / for one single moment, to re-enter the hermitage alone.

She spoke faintly, and almost inaudibly; but such was the intense interest she excited, that her request was immediately understood and immediately complied with. It was for the purpose of securing de Gray's dagger from discovery that she compelled herself to revisit a scene fraught with such horror! Criminal and for ever lost to her as he was, she could not bear that he should stand forth to the world in the light of a detected murderer. The poniard, she had every reason to believe, was the only evidence that could be brought against him; and that she determined to secrete till some opportunity should occur of making away with it. Having, though with a shudder, snatched it up, and found its scabbard, she concealed them beneath her dress; and once more approaching her unfortunate brother, knelt down beside him. Awed by the reflection, that she now beheld in him only the mortal remains of one whose soul had returned to the God who gave it, she reverently applied her lips to his lifeless hand, and burst into a paroxysm of tears, that probably contributed to preserve her senses from wandering, though they could not ward off the illness with which / she was threatened, or remove the anguish already preying upon her heart.

On rejoining the persons waiting for her without, she, with thanks and in accents of kindness, dismissed all but Hannah her maid, and a youth she had been in the habit of employing when she wanted to be rowed in the little pleasure boat floating on a narrow trout stream that ran through the grounds. For some part of the way home, her path skirted this well known stream; and whilst Hannah and the lad lingered a moment to observe the state of the boat after the heavy rain that had fallen, she contrived, unobserved by either, to cast from her into the water the dagger it was of such consequence to get rid of. This done, she became more composed, and began to feel the propriety of sending for Mr. Fitzmaurice, the only friend within reach to whom the difficult and most painful task could be confided of preparing poor Sir Everard and Lady Ormond for the calamitous tidings that awaited them. Standing still, therefore, and summoning all her firmness, she said to the youth who attended her:

'Woodhatch, you must make all the haste in your power to Mr. Fitzmaurice's. The groom at the Hall will, if you tell him I desire / it, lend you a swift horse. You know the way; go as quick as you can – tell them, at Holme Court,' she faulteringly added, 'what you have seen, and entreat Mr. Fitzmaurice to come to me without a moment's delay. Say nothing concerning your errand to my uncle's people, lest any unguarded report should be suddenly carried to him. And now, my good lad, lose no time, but be gone instantly.'

The youth, without uttering a word, darted forward with the speed of thought, and was out of sight ere she could have said, 'He's gone!'

Relieved at least from one anxiety by having thus despatched him, she slowly pursued the same path he was so rapidly flying over; and as she crept along, leaning upon her compassionate Hannah, silent tears coursed each other down her cheeks, and her face indicated such unutterable woe, that no one could have contemplated it without the deepest commiseration.

To escape remarks on her blood-stained garments, in case of meeting any one, Hannah had thrown over her passive mistress the cloak with which she had set out in search of her when the rain first began. They consequently / reached the Hall without attracting any particular notice; and Ella, impatient to throw off her tell-tale apparel, readily assented to the maid's proposal of undressing, and lying down in a wrapper upon the bed.

'And now, Hannah,' said the wretched girl, 'leave me for awhile; I need to be alone. But go to my dear uncle, and tell him I am come in wet and tired, and wish to obtain a little rest. Caution all the head servants, who alone have access to him, to leave the dreadful task to Mr. Fitzmaurice of gradually preparing him to learn our misery. Put all those hideous things,' pointing to the clothes she had taken off, 'out of sight, and do not come in again till I ring, or till Mr. Fitzmaurice is arrived.'

When left in solitude, Ella's first act was to throw herself on her knees, and address the most fervent supplications to Heaven for submission to its decrees; for pardon to the guilty Ernest on his expiating, as far as in him lay, the tremendousness of his sin by a life of heartfelt sorrow and repentance. She prayed for ability to endure the agony inflicted by the consciousness of his culpability; implored pity for the poor old Baronet, bereft so suddenly of his adopted son; and ardently petitioned for power to be to him a comforter and a support. / Such supplications could not but in a measure tend to calm her. She arose, threw herself once more on the bed, and with clasped hands and tearful eyes, lay mournfully meditating on the dreadful events of the morning.

Meanwhile the dinner hour – an hour to which Sir Everard always attached considerable importance – was fast approaching; and as he sat, dressed and ready for the expected summons, alone in the drawing-room, he grew impatient for the entrance of the rest of the family. Surprised and somewhat displeased at being so long left by himself, he rang, and on the entrance of the domestic, (his own valet as well as butler) he peevishly said:

'Are neither of the young gentlemen come in yet, Andrews?'

'No, Sir.'

'Very extraordinary! Why it only wants five minutes to six! I consented to dine an hour later than I like, in order to please Frederic. But my belief is, that at whatever time we are to be served, he would always be behind-hand. Have you heard from Hannah how her young lady is?'

'Hannah was ordered, Sir, not to go in till she was rung for; and Miss Ormond has not yet touched her bell.' /

'So! it appears, then, that Lady Ormond and I shall have to dine by ourselves. Well, be it so; I shall not wait for any of them.'

Whilst this little dialogue was passing, Mr. Fitzmaurice galloped up to the house. Sir Everard heard his approach; and not being so placed as to see from the window who it was, concluded that either Frederic or de Gray had arrived.

'Oh, here comes one of the truants,' cried he, 'and I suppose the other is not far behind. Now then, Andrews, go and tell the cook to send up dinner directly.'

To comply with this command, Andrews was quitting the room, when a second horseman was heard riding towards the house; upon which Sir Everard, much pleased, cried out:

'Aye, aye, I said so; here comes the other tardy boy. Well, I hope they will not be very long at their *toilet;* for if they are, they stand a chance of having their soup abominably cold.'

Perfectly convinced that the two young men were returned, the Baronet, without further parley, suffered Andrews to retire.

It was with deep reluctance, however, that / Mr. Fitzmaurice, after a delay, in the apartment of the heart-broken Ella, that could be extended no further, at length compelled himself to obey the repeated messages that were sent to him, by his aged and unsuspecting host.

When he appeared before him, the pallor of his countenance, the involuntary tremour of his voice, the strangeness altogether of his terror-struck look startled Sir Everard so much, that changing colour, he hastily exclaimed:

'Heaven and earth, Fitzmaurice! what has happened? You have been with Ella; – is she ill? Did any accident befall her when she was out? Speak! for mercy sake, speak!'

'No accident has befallen Ella, my dear Sir Everard,' answered Fitzmaurice, hesitatingly, 'but —'

'But what?' interrupted the Baronet.

'Evil, irreparable evil has overtaken one who was most dear to her. She has been subjected to a dreadful trial – that of beholding the still warm and bleeding, though lifeless body of the victim!'

'Bleeding body! – lifeless victim! – What on earth are you talking about? When could the poor child see any such fearful object? Not in my grounds, surely?' /

'I grieve to say, Sir Everard, it *was* in your grounds; I grieve to add, that you must prepare your mind to hear of a calamity the greatest perhaps that could have fallen upon you.'

Sir Everard, trembling and turning very pale, collected himself a few moments, and then, in a low, husky, inward voice, with difficulty was able to articulate the name of *Frederic!*

Mr. Fitzmaurice sighed heavily, and cast down his eyes in silence.

The unhappy old man gave a violent start, and then sat motionless and heart-struck. Yet, the impression made upon his mind was less dreadful, perhaps, than the reality. He felt persuaded his nephew had fallen in a duel, though who his adversary had been he could by no means surmise. But that in open day – in grounds so continually traversed by labourers, servants, and even villagers, a murder so daring could have been perpetrated, never entered his imagination.

Fitzmaurice took no pains to set him right. It was sufficient for the present that he should be apprized of the young man's death; there was no necessity for adding to the horror of the intelligence. /

Anxious to return to Ella, anxious to spare Sir Everard the misery of having to give any orders respecting the immediate disposal of the body, he was glad to see Lady Ormond enter the room, as it afforded him an opportunity of quitting it himself. Hitherto the remains of the slaughtered youth had been left undisturbed in the hermitage, watched by his own valet, dispatched thither by Andrews. An inquest was to be held either late that night or early the following morning. The chief person to be examined, properly speaking, was Ella. She was in no condition, however, to attend on any such occasion. Attacked by fever and even in danger of delirium, it would at once have been cruel, and probably useless, to have inflicted upon her such a task. Hannah, therefore, and the persons whom her screams had brought to the hermitage were alone called upon. Nothing transpired, after the strictest examination, at all elucidative of the mysterious manner by which the young man had come by his death. No strangers had been seen about the grounds, no weapon had been detected by which the wound could have been given; it ended, in short, in a strong suspicion on the part of the coroner and many of his people that the unhappy Frederic had been / his own executioner. The only circumstance that made against this supposition was the disappearance of the instrument by which the blow had been struck. It was possible, however, some of them thought, that the deceased might have committed the deed before he entered the hermitage; in which case, it would have been easy for him to have thrown away the knife or dagger of which he had made such fatal use. Fitzmaurice himself was not entirely without an apprehension that this might really have occurred, for Ella would sooner have died than have dropt the slightest word that could have implicated de Gray.

Meanwhile, what had become of de Gray? He had returned to the Hall shortly after the arrival of Mr. Fitzmaurice, and shut himself in his own room. The fact is, that at the distance of about a mile from the house, that gentleman, who was riding extremely fast, had overtaken him, and to account for the extravagant speed he was exerting, as well as to prepare him for the appalling news that must too soon reach him, had slackened his career to communicate as gently as he could, the occurrence of the morning, as it had been detailed to himself by young Woodhatch. Never was consternation more strikingly displayed than / that with which Ernest listened to this recital; it absolutely drew groans from him, and such was its effect, that he seemed at one time on the point of falling from his horse. When the tremendous narrative came to that part which described poor Ella as having entered the hermitage alone, and been the first to discover the mangled state of her brother, he could suppress his agitation no longer, but covering his face with his hands, cried out: – 'Oh, Mr. Fitzmaurice, say no more, I implore you! I cannot – cannot bear it!'

A profound silence had succeeded this vehement entreaty, and at the end of a few seconds, Fitzmaurice had put spurs to his horse, and galloped forward in advance of his horror-struck companion.

When they met again it was in the presence of the sorrowing baronet and his lady. Ernest thought it due to them to make an effort – if not to console, at least to show them that he sympathized in their feelings. He, therefore, compelled himself, though almost tottering under his own weight, and pale even to ghastliness, to enter the library, and there he found Fitzmaurice.

Lady Ormond, the instant her young *protégé* appeared, rushed forward, and throwing her / arms around him, rested her head upon his shoulder and wept bitterly. Neither she nor Sir Everard spoke, but the latter, his face wet with tears, made a friendly sign to him; and then turning towards Fitzmaurice, who had previously been talking of Ella, listened intently to hear what further he had to say concerning her.

'I can but repeat, my dear sir,' resumed that gentleman, 'that it would be too much for her were she immediately to see either you or Lady Ormond. The harrowing spectacle she has beheld, has wrung her heart to agony, and shaken her nerves to pieces; it will require time to restore her to anything like serenity. But she is young; she is anxious to resign herself to the will of heaven, and to spare her friends the misery of seeing her present sufferings. All-healing time, we may hope, will do much for her. Meanwhile, we must for the present allow her to indulge her feelings in solitude.'

In speaking thus, Mr. Fitzmaurice, as far as his knowledge of the case extended, expressed his real sentiments. But the matter was more serious than he suspected. Ella was threatened with a dangerous illness, which every moment seemed to be gaining ground; and / before morning, so alarming were the symptoms, that Mr. Watts, the medical man of the family, who spent part of the night by her bedside, sent off as soon as it was light for further advice. The malady was long, and its result frequently dubious; but throughout its whole course she never for a moment fell into a state of raving and incoherency. Often speechless, and reduced to the feebleness of an infant, she uniformly preserved her consciousness; and during the many many lingering hours that infirmity condemned her not only to spend in bed, but to lie in the same posture, incapable of turning herself, her senses continued unimpaired, and were employed in silent prayer. Mrs. Ormond, though a woman of the world, and too prone to imagine that such wisdom as she practised was compatible with the innocence enjoined by holy writ, was in principle, at least, a Christian; and her precepts, refined and purified by passing into the ingenuous minds of her daughters, had made of both the sincerest and most humble believers. The leading supplications poor Ella now addressed to heaven, were first, that whilst her illness lasted, she might still be preserved from delirium; and this prayer was the effect of consideration for the safety of Ernest, whom she / dreaded to betray should her mind begin to wander. Her next, and most earnest aspiration, was a repetition of the one she had offered up so fervently before – it was for the criminal himself; that he might, by timely and deep repentance, obtain the remission of his guilt. For herself, she again implored strength to combat against despondency, and to submit unmurmuringly to the early destruction of all her temporal hopes. Such petitions could not be wholly fruitless; and that they were in some degree effectual, was proved by the sweetness and gratitude with which she accepted the services of those who attended her; by the affectionate looks she cast upon Mrs. Fitzmaurice, who the moment she heard of her illness, quitted everything to establish herself by her bed-side; and by the perfect resignation with which she bore the tedious nights of sleeplessness and fever she was doomed to pass.

In the course of a few days, another well-known face appeared beside the pillow of the youthful sufferer. Mrs. Ormond, apprized with all due caution by her son-in-law of the recent tragedy, and of the indisposition of her youngest daughter, hastened down to Ormond Hall in a frame of mind impossible to describe. Horror at the fate of her son was undoubtedly / a predominant feeling in her breast, but she almost hated herself for its not being accompanied with more tenderness; she shuddered – but her tears were few; and though fully sensible that it was a catastrophe most deplorable, she experienced more real grief on learning the illness of Ella than all the frightful visions of murder attending the violent death of Frederic were able to call forth. Such were the consequences of having too early given up her son into other hands, and at once weaned him, as it were, from his home and from her heart. By so doing, she had, indeed, secured him a rich inheritance; but the acquisition was made at the expense to both of the natural affection which depends not merely on the links of kindred, but on habit and familiar intercourse to maintain its warmth. As he grew up, she observed that he manifested a self-consequence and a spirit of independence, her own proud temper could not tolerate. Whenever they were inmates, their dissensions, even during his boyhood, were frequent, and occasionally violent. But these unfortunate misunderstandings might have ceased and been forgotten, had she on his return from the continent, adopted with him a gentler mode of conduct. He came back well disposed to treat her with / deference and regard; but she chilled him by exacting too much; wearied him by her ceaseless murmurs at his disrespectful neglect of her advice; mortified him by treating his opinions with contempt: and enraged him by censuring all his pursuits. As if jealous of the prosperity to which she had herself contributed, she made his exaltation above his sisters a subject of reproach, and went so far as to qualify him with the epithets of upstart and *parvenu*. He was too like herself to be patient of such language, and they soon became more alienated than ever. The time, however, was now come, when Mrs. Ormond bitterly repented the harshness she had shewn. Her last letter to him, in particular, weighed heavy on her mind. It had originated in certain communications addressed to her by an anonymous correspondent, and was full of acrimony and the severest reprehension. By calculating dates, it appeared certain that her child – her only son – had received this galling letter on the very day, and but a few hours before he had ceased to exist. With what feelings towards his mother had he spent those final hours? Oh, could she have foreseen his coming fate, how different would have been her language! Vain wish, and wholly ineffectual / to banish the regret she was doomed to carry to the grave.

It might, perhaps, be allowed, in mitigation of her conduct to her son, that the disposition of her daughters, so eminently differing from his, had taught her to be fastidious, and accustomed her to too high a standard of filial merit. Their docility, their affectionate solicitude to please her, and the gratitude they evinced for every indulgence she granted them, rendered the contrast between Frederic and his sisters painfully striking. Their mother, justly sensible of their value, was warmly attached to both; but Ella, in an especial manner, had from her very infancy, been the chosen darling of her affection. There was a charm in the gentle but fearless hilarity of her character, that was irresistible; and to a parent often accused of austerity, no gratification could exceed that of seeing her child so perfectly at her ease, and so unfeignedly happy in her presence. Ella had never known what it was to check a laugh or disguise a feeling of pleasure when under her mother's eye; and her obedience had always had the merit of being the free-will offering of her heart. Add to this, the pride Mrs. Ormond took in her talents and beauty, and the high hopes she / entertained of their effect upon the world, and it will not be matter of wonder that her partiality exceeded what might have been expected from a woman who had always made it her boast that she never suffered her feelings to outrun her prudence.

She had now to undergo a heavy trial. For more than six weeks the fate of this beloved girl hung suspended between life and death. Whether from inability or disinclination, she rarely spoke; but her eyes, though dimmed by sorrow and sickness, expressed kindness and love whenever her mother or Mrs. Fitzmaurice approached her; and when able to stretch forth her wasted and almost transparent hand, it was to invite one of theirs, which she would hold with fondness, or press, as if for relief, against her burning forehead. The poor old Baronet and Lady Ormond, during this melancholy period, found their best support in Mr. Fitzmaurice, who as well as his wife, had once more taken up his abode at the Hall, where his presence could never have been more eminently useful. Ernest, it is true, was under their roof; but he could make no exertion for the alleviation of their sadness; his own was almost greater than he could bear. The perilous state of Ella, joined to the recent / calamity on which his mind perpetually dwelt, made him solicitous to shun observation, and to wander, day after day, in the most unfrequented spots he could find. The only thing he sought with real interest in the house, was an opportunity of questioning Hannah on the subject of her mistress's health; all else appeared to have become indifferent to him. Other calamities, full as grievous as those of his own family, had come to his knowledge, though hitherto not generally spoken of at the Hall, since it was believed that they bore but too much connexion with the death of Frederic. The beautiful Ruth was no more! She was accused of having procured her own destruction by taking poison, and her broken-hearted mother, ill in bed, was not expected long to survive her. Could misery well go further? and could Ernest, in addition to what he felt for himself and his friends at home, be otherwise than profoundly affected by these new disasters? He tried repeatedly to gain access to poor Mrs. Nelson, but was always unsuccessful. Excuse of various kinds were made to colour the refusals to admit him; and at last, apprehensive that his efforts, if persevered in, would give pain, he discontinued them and resumed his customary lonely wanderings. /

CHAPTER IX.

Take her
This virgin by the hand, and call her wife,
Endowed with all my fortunes; requite me thus,
And make me happy.

MASSINGER.[51]

WITH the slow but progressive advance towards convalescence of poor Ella, began one of her most difficult trials. She had hitherto been able to bear no other fatigue than that of being conveyed, for an hour at a time, from her bed to the sofa. But the moment was approaching when she would probably be removed, during a part of the day, into the adjoining dressing room; and then she well knew her uncle, Lady Ormond, and Mr. Fitzmaurice would be solicitous to see her, and with them would undoubtedly come – Ernest! How should she find courage to endure his sight? The very idea of looking at, of hearing / him, of being compelled to speak to him, had such an effect upon her, that whenever she dwelt upon it, symptoms of returning fever betrayed themselves, and fresh fears took possession of her mother and sister.

At length, the safe and simple expedient suggested itself, of entreating them to tell Ernest, in her name, that with his sight would be associated so many overpowering recollections, that till she had recovered more strength it would be better they should not meet. It was a message no one was surprised at. Seen so continually together – their age the same – their footing in the family so nearly equal, that it was difficult to distinguish the appointed heir from the young *protégé*, – Frederic and Ernest might have been considered as brothers; and, as Ella had justly observed, it was impossible to behold the one without recurring mentally to the other. Ernest himself was sensible of this truth, and submitted with a sigh to his exclusion.

Time passed on, and Ella's indefatigable nurses had the consolation of seeing their cares productive, under Providence, of all the benefit they could rationally hope for. She gradually regained the power of moving from one room to another unassisted; she could occasionally / employ herself in some slight needle-work; and, for a short interval, she could bear to let Mrs. Ormond or her sister read aloud to her a few pages of some religious book. But if she attempted to peruse the volume herself, her thoughts wandered, and with fixed eyes she continued regarding the same place, without turning the leaf, or seeing a letter that was before her. Conversation, of a regular or protracted kind, she was equally powerless to support.

But, alas! her own dreary reflections she could at all times pursue. They carried her back incessantly to the last frightfully eventful morning of poor Frederic's life. She saw again in imagination the enraged look he directed towards Ernest on leaving the breakfast room after reading his mother's letter. She remembered having, later in the day, encountered Ernest descending from his own apartment in pursuit, as he said, of Philip Nelson. Was not that the fatal moment when he had gone to arm himself with the murderous dagger? Probably he knew that Frederic was in the little edifice; perhaps their quarrel had already begun, and Ernest, insulted and vilified, had in the frenzy of revenge been stimulated to wash out the offence in the offender's / blood! Merciful heaven! where could Ernest – the just, the temperate, the humane Ernest – where could he have learnt so execrable a lesson? Oh, who might after this deem himself secure in his own virtue? Had it been foretold to this unhappy young man, that he should one day perpetrate such an atrocity, would he not have exclaimed with Hazael, 'Is thy servant a dog, that he should do this thing?'[52]

That he was now dejected, altered, continually seeking to be alone, she had on divers occasions, gathered from the conversation of her mother and sister. Ah, could he be otherwise? It was impossible his heart could at once have become so callous, that every feeling of compunction should be dead within him. Yet it was strange that after such a deed he could bear to dwell amidst the friends of his victim – could bear to haunt the scenes polluted with his own guilt. She wondered more and more as she meditated upon it, that having so suddenly disappeared when the blow had been struck, he had ever found courage to return. All spoke of him with pity and kindness, attributing his depression to regret at the loss of Frederic. But who pitied him like Ella? Who shed in secret such bitter tears, / or poured forth to heaven such fervent intercessions for him, as the suffering Ella?

Of real pity, it may be said as of mercy: – it is twice blessed;[53] it blesseth its possessor, and it blesseth all who live within the influence of the tempers it has chastened. Never was this truth more fully illustrated than in the case of Ella. Contrary to all expectation, the illness and sorrow she had been so little disciplined to endure, rather softened than irritated her; and when all the native gaiety of her character was gone, her continual endeavours to lighten the anxiety of others, and to be as little burthensome as possible to those around her, rendered her dearer to their hearts, than she had ever been during her brightest and most sunny hours.

The Fitzmaurices, when all apprehensions for her life were at an end, allowed themselves occasionally to go home for a week or two, resigning her to the care of her assiduous mother. After a while, Ella with the secret purpose of relieving Mrs. Ormond from such constant attendance, expressed a wish to see Miss Kirby again. She was immediately invited, and came with all her former alacrity; but when she beheld the dreadful ravages made by disease on her so lately sparkling and happy / friend – her colourless and wan countenance – her attenuated form – and heard the faint accents of a voice heretofore so gladdening and so mirthful, she could not wholly suppress her tears. Ella perceived them, and as she sat beside her, kindly wiped them away, asking at the same time after her father, and trying to avert her attention from the change in herself, that so much affected her. After a short struggle, Maria Kirby recovered more composure, and the rest of the visit passed without any outward demonstration of emotion.

The society of this excellent girl was a real blessing to the slowly convalescent Ella. She came almost daily, exacting no exertion, ready to converse or read when her friend seemed to wish it, or to sit silently at work, without betraying weariness or discontent. From time to time, they raised their heads, and looked at each other with an affectionate half smile, and then resumed, the one her quiet feminine occupation, the other, her reclining attitude and mournful musings. To add to her merits, Maria never brought with her any startling or unpleasant news. She had no passion for causing a stare; and Ella remained in complete ignorance as well of the death of the lovely Ruth, as of all the other village histories. /

Mrs. Ormond, perceiving that her daughter had now a companion to whose gentleness and discretion she might at intervals safely confide her, often left them together, and once more began to direct her attention to matters which for awhile had lost their importance. Her beloved Ella appearing no longer on the immediate road to join her sister angels in heaven, the provident parent conceived it was time to renew the consideration of her interests on earth.

More than three months had elapsed since the death of Frederic; and, by certain hints thrown out unguardedly by Lady Ormond, his mother understood that Sir Everard was meditating a new disposition of his property highly advantageous to Ella, though subject to some condition she (Mrs. Ormond) was most anxious to be made clearly acquainted with. She beat about the bush a long time, in hopes of prevailing upon her sister-in-law to be more explicit, but without success. Lady Ormond, though too apt to say more than she intended, in moments of abstraction, could become cautious when she perceived that advantage was meant to be taken of her imprudence; and it was not without considerable self applause she retired from the conference, assured of having baffled Mrs. / Ormond's curiosity. She had not, however, succeeded in suppressing the workings of that lady's imagination, who soon persuaded herself that the whole mystery was this:

Sir Everard, according to her opinion, after leaving the bulk of his fortune to go with his title to his now nearest of male kin, George Arundel, a young man already in great affluence, had bequeathed to Ella a considerable legacy. Certain speculations, resulting from this idea, were immediately set afloat in her active mind: community of interest might bring the parties acquainted – they might become attached. Arundel was well born; his connexions were all people of distinction, and he held precisely the sort of rank in society it was her wish to see Ella shine in. True, report stated him to be penurious and narrow-minded. She was sorry for it; but, after all, these were defects from which a wife might suffer less than from heedless prodigality; and there might be exaggeration in the case; for it often happened that men of large fortune were expected to do so much, it was no easy matter to satisfy the avidity of their claimants by any thing short of boundless extravagance. She was firmly convinced, therefore, that Arundel might be well worth captivating; and should / her conjectures as to the contents of Sir Everard's Will prove just, she saw not why the experiment should not be tried, – nor why it should fail.

Ernest, meanwhile, to the satisfaction of all who interested themselves about him, gradually shook off a portion of the gloom that had oppressed him, and spent at least some part of his evenings in the general sitting room. Becoming at the same time extremely impatient to be admitted to see Ella, who had received every individual of the family except himself, he ventured to apply to Mrs. Ormond; representing to her, that though he had hitherto submitted unmurmuringly to the prohibition, he now feared that every day which was added to his banishment would add to the pain and difficulty it would cost Ella to revoke her sentence. He, therefore, besought her mother to intercede for him, in order that the term of his exclusion should be extended no farther.

Mrs. Ormond assured him he might rely upon her good offices; but did not disguise from him that she had little hope of immediate success. Ella, she added, was so shattered, that the slightest emotion overcame her, brought on sleepless nights, and again quickened her pulse to an alarming degree. As a / proof of this, she told him, that her daughter having a few days before, whilst passing the dressing room window, perceived him at a distance in the park, was seized with a tremour so violent, that it was with difficulty she was preserved from falling, and supported in safety to the nearest chair.

'But this,' said Ernest, with a look of consternation, 'is horror and aversion!'

'By no means,' answered Mrs. Ormond; 'it is the effect, rather, of an unfortunate, though natural association of ideas, that inseparably connects with your sight the remembrance of poor Frederic. The ravages caused by an illness wholly to be attributed to the shock of his death, have affected her spirits and nerves as much as her person, and deprived her, for a time, of the strength of mind necessary to combat against such impressions. But, be assured, they will ere long abate. Meanwhile, have patience, and make every possible allowance for her, not only as a mourner, but as a being newly rescued from the grave. When I see a fit moment to speak for you, I will not neglect it. All must depend, however, upon the progress of her health.'

A few days after this little dialogue, Mrs. / Ormond, in pursuance of her promise, ventured in reality to sound the sentiments of her daughter.

'My dearest Ella,' said she, 'do you not begin to feel a little wish to breathe the outward air? Could you not bear a short drive in my carriage?'

Ella said she had never thought of it.

'True, my love, because till very lately you have been too ill to make the attempt; but I think you might now be benefitted by it; and in this quiet part of the world you are secure from meeting any troublesome idlers, who might wish to stop you, and make you talk. None but old friends could come in your way.'

Ella perfectly understood her; and becoming, if possible, still paler than before, after a moment's pause, she faulteringly said:

'My dearest mother, if it will not be a disappointment to *you*, I must own, that to *me* it would be infinitely pleasanter to remain quietly in my own room.'

'Then be it so, my Ella. My disappointment can be no other than that of finding you still too weak to undertake any exertion.'

And there the matter rested.

When Mrs. Ormond made a faithful report / to Ernest of what had passed, he instantly said:

'If, as seems too probable, I am the unfortunate cause of the imprisonment to which she condemns herself, it shall immediately terminate. I will pay a visit to my friend Sedley, in Dorsetshire; and Ella, when I am gone, may be induced to try the efficacy of air and exercise. She can never regain strength whilst persisting in her present plan.'

This considerate proposal was faintly, and for form sake, opposed a moment, but finally accepted; and at dinner the same day he announced his intended absence to Sir Everard and Lady Ormond.

'You are very right, my dear lad,' cried Sir Everard. 'Were I as young as you are, I would remove from hence to-morrow. This house is no longer the same to me; it has become the very head-quarters of gloom and depression. If poor Ella could bear the journey, and the season were less advanced, I would go to my snug old castle in Wales, and settle there perhaps for the rest of my days. I have not been near it these ten years; but, should I live till spring, I may still put my plan in execution.' /

This however was a project never doomed to be realized.

After the departure of Ernest, Mrs. Ormond succeeded in prevailing upon Ella to let herself be driven out almost every day; and it was soon apparent that she derived considerable advantage from the experiment. Still, her mother felt persuaded that she would never again be her former self. Those laughing eyes, full of sport – that beautiful mouth, almost as expressive in its silence as in its speech – the enlivening and sweet-toned voice – all were changed; and it appeared as if, even when restored to bodily health, the character of her mind would be so different, it was impossible her countenance could ever resume its early animation.

'She will still be beautiful,' thought Mrs. Ormond; 'but it will be the beauty of a "pensive nun."[54] As I look at her at this moment, I could almost fancy a smile on that once gay countenance would astonish and startle me. Poor Ella! Is this sadness, are these broken spirits to accompany thee through life? At nineteen years of age, to bid adieu to all the joys of youth – if such must be the case – is a harder lot than I had believed thee destined to experience.' /

On returning home from one of these drives, about ten days subsequent to the departure of Ernest, Mrs. Ormond, having accompanied Ella to her apartment, and seen her seated at her early dinner, was repairing to her own room, when she was met by her maid, with the alarming information that Sir Everard had been found in his chair in a sort of fainting fit, and was now in bed, and extremely unwell.

She hastened instantly to him. He knew her, and endeavoured to speak; but his voice was scarcely audible, and his articulation much affected. Mr. Watts and a regular physician had been sent for, and were impatiently expected. Lady Ormond, stationed by his bedside, sat watching his countenance with acute anxiety.

The struggle lasted three days, and on the morning of the fourth, all was over; – the liberal, kind hearted, honourable old man had breathed his last. At a late hour the preceding evening, recovering for a short time the power of making himself understood, he expressed to Mrs. Ormond a wish to see Ella. Hitherto, she had, in consideration of her health, been held in ignorance of his situation; but on hearing him make such a declaration, her / mother hesitated not to go to her, and acquaint her gradually and considerately with the truth. Extremely shocked, and deeply afflicted, Ella seemed in a moment to recover all her lost energy. She scarcely waited to hear the conclusion of Mrs. Ormond's recital, before she hurried to the sick room with a speed of which she knew not herself that she could have been capable.

On entering, her uncle was the only object she saw – the havoc which the approach of death had made in his countenance, the only circumstance that arrested her sorrowing attention. Drowned in tears, she received the hand he feebly offered her, on her knees; and kissing it with mingled reverence and love, continued to hold and tenderly to press it amidst sighs and sobs she vainly strove to repress. He spoke a few fond words to her, and making signs to those who stood near her, to raise her, she suddenly felt, while leaning forward to embrace him, that he was endeavouring to join her hand to that of some one placed on the other side of the bed; at the same time, she heard him, with difficulty, murmur forth:

'May ye be happy! heaven bless ye both!'

Darting forward, at these words, a quick / and penetrating glance, she found herself opposite Ernest de Gray – felt her hand locked in his, and saw him with moistened eyes, fixedly regarding her.

Tenderness for her uncle restrained, even at that painful moment, the scream that was bursting from her, but with a thrill of terror, she snatched away the hand a murderer's touch contaminated, and sunk upon the bed in a state of insensibility.

She was instantly removed, and the poor Baronet's last hours were not distressed by the consciousness of her indisposition.

Ernest had arrived during the interval of Mrs. Ormond's absence in her daughter's room. By some accident, the messenger who had been dispatched to him the preceding day had been detained on the road, and thus had prevented his reaching Ormond Hall till he feared it would be almost too late, notwithstanding the speed with which he travelled to see his benevolent protector still alive, or at least still in possession of his senses; but Sir Everard had recognized him instantly, and bestowed upon him a look expressive of all his wonted regard. He had done more; he had apparently sought to testify that a union between him and the niece he so fondly loved, / was the latest wish of his heart. But Ella – the once affectionate and confiding Ella – she on whose permanent kindness he had placed such implicit dependence – how deplorably must she have changed ere the mere sight of him could seem sufficient to half kill her! With what scarcely concealed antipathy had she shrunk from him; – what mingled anguish and dismay had been visible in the transient look she had directed towards him! Could such manifestations be the mere result, as Mrs. Ormond had assured him, of an *unfortunate association of ideas?* It seemed to him that they derived their origin from some latent cause of a far deeper and more insurmountable nature: – but this was no time to devote himself to intense meditation on the subject. He endeavoured to confine his attention as much as possible to Sir Everard; sought to support Lady Ormond, whose affliction was most sincere; and throughout the melancholy night, seized with avidity the slightest opportunity of rendering his presence useful or consolatory.

On her part, Mrs. Ormond, whose quick ear had caught the purport of the Baronet's last words, and seen their accompanying action, had been thrown into the utmost perplexity. She was wholly unable to comprehend his inducement / for uniting the young people in the same blessing, and still less for joining their hands as if to consecrate their solemn betrothment; she turned the matter over in her thoughts in every possible way, and ended by concluding that Sir Everard, though apparently conscious of what he was doing, had in reality been acting under the influence of some confusion of ideas amounting almost to delirium. How else account for the singularity of a proceeding that devoted Ella, with all her personal attractions, her accomplishments, her birth, and her thousand agreeable qualities, to an obscure youth, who well-born and amiable as he was, had neither patrimony, family interest, nor defined station in society?

This persuasion continued to possess her, till – the sad scene being closed, and the kind old Baronet gone for ever – his last Will and Testament, bearing a very recent date, was produced and read. Therein it was found, that Ella was provisionally appointed to succeed her brother in all the advantages that had been intended for him, exclusive of Sir Everard's title, which would necessarily descend to his nearest male relation. If at the Testator's demise, Ella still remained unmarried, she was / required to give her hand to Ernest de Gray, on his consenting to take the name of Ormond. If she declined the union, she was to forfeit to him half the inheritance. Two executors were appointed, one of whom was Mr. Fitzmaurice. There were various minor clauses in the document, but bearing no relation to either of the above parties; amongst the rest appeared a grateful remembrance of the faithful services of several of the old domestics. Lady Ormond was spoken of in terms honourable to herself as well as to the Testator; but in consideration of her own already ample property, and the disinterestedness with which she had declined receiving any addition to it, the only bequest assigned to her were a few pictures she had a particular value for; and the privilege, during life, of residing, at her choice, either at Ormond Hall, or at the mansion in Wales.

Nothing had ever filled Mrs. Ormond with greater astonishment than the contents of this, to her, most unexpected, and to say the truth, unpalatable Will! That so noble a property should be clogged by a condition, which she believed even to Ella herself could be so little acceptable, vexed her to the very soul. With such an accession of fortune, to what might not her daughter have aspired? But by marrying / Ernest, though she might live in affluence, what new dignity would she obtain? how would the sphere of her connexions be enlarged, or her consequence increased? It was giving her the means of attaining the highest distinctions that society could bestow, and forbidding her to use them. Without being assured of the fact, Mrs. Ormond strongly suspected her sister-in-law of being the prime mover of these testamentary dispositions, and she was perfectly right. After the death of Frederic, when her Ladyship began to reflect on the necessity there was for a new arrangement of Sir Everard's affairs, she frankly told him that she had reason to believe a very lively and mutual attachment subsisted between Ella and Ernest; they had not, indeed, made her their confidant, having rather betrayed than avowed their affection; yet she thought her observations might be depended upon. Being warmly interested for them, her first idea had been to improve the circumstances of Ernest by assuring to him the possession of whatever property she had at her own disposal.

'Even this,' she added, 'would not have made him a despicable suitor, though I never felt quite secure that it would satisfy the ambitious / aims of Mrs. Ormond. It was all, however, whilst our poor nephew lived, that could be done; and I tried to flatter myself that to contribute to the happiness of her child, my sister-in-law might be induced to abate something from her lofty pretensions.'

Her Ladyship then proceeded to represent that since they had had the misfortune to lose their dear Frederic, there remained no one, save Ella, who had any claim to become his substitute, or who in fact required it. Mr. Arundel had already more wealth than he had heart to make a meritorious use of. 'Let, then, the fortune be so disposed of, that Mrs. Ormond should have no excuse for rejecting Ernest; let Ella be constituted her uncle's heiress, but not without some strong stipulation in favour of the young man, lest the very circumstance of Ella's nomination should furnish her mother with an additional reason for elevating her views above his reach. By making him,' concluded Lady Ormond, 'joint heir with Ella, you will benefit the two in one; and be assured, that rather than suffer her daughter to lose a moiety, or even any part of the inheritance, Mrs. Ormond, as soon as she is apprized of your determination, will be the first to urge on the marriage.' /

These arguments, as has been shewn, had their full effect, and the Will was duly drawn up, signed, and sealed in the spirit they had awakened. /

CHAPTER X.

E l'aspettar del male è mal peggiore
Forse che non parrebbe il mal presente.

Ciò detto tace, e la risposta attende
Con atto che 'n silenzio ha voce e preghi.

TASSO, GERUSALEMME.[55]

THE double shock Ella had suffered from the death of her uncle, and the interview for which she was so unprepared with Ernest, threw her back, and for many weeks not only suspended all improvement in her health, but tended materially to its detriment. In this interval, Mrs. Ormond had leisure to school herself into greater tolerance of the *malencontreux* Will. To like it was impossible; but she had too much sense to persist in fretting at an irremediable evil; and by way of dissipating her chagrin, she devoted much time and thought to the most favourable means of getting / Ernest elected a member of the legislature. Some such promotion she deemed indispensable to his success in society; for as a mere private individual, enriched by the caprice of an old man to whom he bore not the remotest affinity – decorated by no title – distinguished by no military achievements – holding no rank as a diplomatist – unknown at the bar, and even in the world of letters – it was impossible to introduce him, with credit to herself, in her own circle. She gravely consulted Mr. Fitzmaurice on the subject, who far from answering her with corresponding gravity, treated the whole business as a jest.

'It is unlucky,' said he, 'that this project of yours should be rendered somewhat less practicable than might be wished, by the late barbarous suppression of so many rotten boroughs. They were commodious things; and in this case, for instance, would have been inappreciable. What other method remains of getting Ernest made M.P. I do not immediately perceive. But have patience, dear madam, perhaps some ten years hence, he may find constituents amongst those who are now to become his tenants; and if he behaves well, that is, spends his money freely amongst the / tradesmen at Ludlow, and above all, pays his bills without complaining of imposition, who knows whether *they* also will not become his friends, and lend him their "most sweet voices"?'[56]

Mrs. Ormond, though trying to smile, was turning away half angrily, when her son-in-law detained her by the following consolatory prediction:

'But it is probable that you will soon find it is only throwing away time to meditate further on the measures to be pursued for Ernest's aggrandizement, since, of what consequence can it be to you how obscurely he vegetates, if Ella eventually refuses to marry him?'

'Refuses to marry him?' repeated Mrs. Ormond, amazed.

'Even so. I was completely mistaken, it appears, when I told Bessy, some months ago, that her sister was attached to young Sedley; she has clearly convinced us of the contrary. Perhaps my present observations are equally unfounded; for, with all humility, I confess myself not very skilful in reading ladies' hearts; but my impression is, that far from being disposed to unite herself to him, the very sound of his name – every word, in short, that recalls / him to her mind is painful and distressing to her.'

Mrs. Ormond, by repeating the same arguments she had on a former occasion made use of to Ernest himself, attempted to account for these symptoms; but Mr. Fitzmaurice was far from feeling convinced of his error, though to avoid molesting her, he forbore to pursue the subject.

What he had said, however, joined to her own recollections, fermented by no means feebly in Mrs. Ormond's mind.

'It would be truly singular,' she mentally cried, 'were I to find myself compelled, by the force of circumstances, to plead with Ella the cause of Ernest de Gray! But, thanks to poor Sir Everard's ill-advised Will, such must, in fact, be the case, if she proves really inclined to reject him; for I cannot let her sacrifice to an overstrained sensibility for her brother so large a portion of the fortune conditionally bequeathed to her. She has ever shewn herself, till lately, perfectly well-disposed towards him as an early companion and playmate; and though the sentiments she entertained for him partook in no degree of love, they were sufficiently friendly to afford her every chance of happiness as his wife. Taking / then all these circumstances into consideration, I shall hold myself fully justified, when her health permits it, in representing to her plainly and firmly, my opinion of the conduct she ought to pursue.'

With this resolution *in petto*, Mrs. Ormond, unused to opposition from her female children, and probably not better disposed to bear it from them than from her son, suffered the affair for the present to lie dormant.

In the meantime, Ella affected in various ways by the momentary glimpse she had had of Ernest; 'hating the crime, yet pitying the criminal,'[57] dwelt incessantly on the remembrance of the mingled sorrow and tenderness his countenance had expressed, on his tremulous pressure of her hand, and on the deep sigh he had drawn when she so abruptly tore it from him; these meditations, in short, led to the discovery that she had not only from a principle of humanity, of Christian charity forgiven and prayed for him, but that she actually still loved him! There was something in the detection of these latent sentiments that filled her with self-abhorrence; she regarded them as manifestations of a heart utterly devoid of all sense of decency – of all natural feeling; they made her shudder at her own depravity. / 'What! *a murderer* – the murderer of my brother! Is it possible I can be so abandoned by heaven as still to cherish an affection for him? I am a monster, unworthy to see the light! In my own defence what have I to plead save the memory of his former seeming virtues? Virtues how frail, since unequal to arm him against the suggestions of wounded pride and gloomy revenge!' To these terrible reflections succeeded at intervals, since her transient interview with him, others that threw a gleam of doubt on the reality of his guilt.

'Standing beside the bed of death,' cried she, 'beholding me for the first time since the fatal act, could his looks have exhibited a sorrow so gentle, so unagitated by conscious criminality, had he really been the wretch, "defiled with blood,"[58] that circumstances have compelled me to believe him?' Oh, what consolation there was in resting her mind, for however brief a space, on even the shadow of an uncertainty! Never did human being, labouring unjustly under the darkest accusation, sigh more ardently for exculpation than Ella now sighed for the power of convincing herself that she had wronged him.

When the testamentary dispositions of her / uncle were made known to her, they produced a mixed effect of gratitude, sadness, and disinterested pleasure. It was grievous to think that a liberality meant to remove every impediment to her union with Ernest should by his own act be rendered so wholly unavailing; for where was the inducement that could now have influenced her to marry him? At the same time, it was gratifying to know that even when rejected, his participation in the inheritance would leave him an independent and comparatively affluent man.

But this was not, it will easily be believed, the view of the case taken by Mrs. Ormond and she availed herself of the earliest opening Ella's returning strength rendered it safe to make use of, in order to come to an explicit understanding with her.

'My dear Ella,' she began, 'I have ever believed you superior to affectation or caprice. Whence come it, then, that the early regard we have all seen you manifest for Ernest de Gray, and which we believed him so justly to merit, seems now converted into indifference – or worse – into averseness? What has he done to forfeit your good opinion? You are silent. Am I then to suppose the change originates in your own fickleness? Or has it been / brought on by the reluctance you felt, after the catastrophe of your poor brother, to see again his companion and friend? This might be allowed for, my dear child, during the first paroxysm of your grief; but you now are naturally becoming calmer; your health, I bless heaven, is improving, and it begins to be time to exert your reason, and to struggle against a weakness which by many persons will be construed into a desire of appearing singular. Why should you permit yourself to be so much more unwilling to renew your intercourse with Ernest than with any of us? Were we not all connected with the lamented Frederic? Yet you shrink not – happily – from *our* society. Be consistent, then, dear girl, and whilst you receive the rest of the family, banish not the individual who has most earnestly supplicated for admission.'

To this remonstrance, the severest that had ever been addressed to her, Ella listened dissolved in tears. At the question, 'What has he done to forfeit your good opinion?' her heart died within her, – she shivered and gasped for breath; but what could she say?

The predicament in which she was placed admitted of no explanation of the past, of no compromise for the future. She must run all / hazards, incur, since unavoidable, the displeasure of her mother – abide its consequences – endure the general blame of her family – and what was harder still, combat against her own feelings; but every evil was preferable to that of pretending to be on terms of friendship with Ernest de Gray. Mrs. Ormond, irritated by her silence, persevered in her admonitions till she saw by Ella's change of countenance that she was in danger of fainting. Somewhat softened, she then arose, kissed her, called her a naughty child, rang the bell for Hannah, and left her to her care.

A few days after this – conversation it could not be called – but monologue, Ella, much to her own relief, was removed to Holme Court. Lady Ormond, notwithstanding that it was now mid-winter, had determined on a journey into Wales, to examine the mansion Sir Everard had left her the option of residing in if she preferred it to Ormond Hall. Ernest, unhappy where he was, asked permission to accompany her, a request she gladly complied with. The two carriages set off on the same day, one for Wales, the other for Holme Court; but Ella, before she went, saw only her aunt. Ernest had entirely desisted from making any application to be received; and / nothing could be further from her intention than to hold out to him the slightest encouragement to break through the tacit plan of avoidance he seemed to have adopted.

On quitting Ormond Hall, a place she had so much loved, such was the painful impression made upon her mind by the events which had occurred there, that she felt as if emancipated from imprisonment; and, in truth, it was so; for with the renewed ability of venturing out, the dread of seeing again any of the spots which might recall the past, was so forcibly connected, that except in a carriage, she had never gained courage to venture beyond the threshold. At Holme Court she was haunted by none of the same recollections; there she had never seen Frederic at all, and Ernest but as an occasional, though always welcome visitor; there no accents of contention, no looks of hostility, no sights of blood, had ever encountered her; and unfavourable as the season now was for being much out of doors, she found relief in wandering about the grounds, and, as she gathered strength, in extending her walks, accompanied by Hannah, to a greater distance. Bodily fatigue, in some cases, is mental rest; and Ella found no method so effectual of procuring the blessing of tranquil / sleep at night, as that of wearying herself by these long rambles during the day. In other respects her mode of life was similar to that of the rest of the family. All being in such deep and recent mourning, few if any visitors were admitted; the mornings were spent as each individual liked best; and in the evening the little circle assembled near the drawing-room fire, and no one being much disposed for conversation, their spirits being still much depressed, Mrs. Ormond read aloud, occasionally relieved by Mr. Fitzmaurice or his wife. As for Ella, the sound of her voice was become of such rare occurrence, that it seemed to surprise even herself when it struck upon her ear, and others turned round if she spoke, as though doubting whether it were *her* they had heard.

Thus passed weeks and even months, during which she entered beneath no roof save that of the poor cottagers to whom she carried relief, or that of the village church. The first time she was allowed to brave the cold of the latter building, and to attend divine service, no words can do justice to the indescribable emotion she experienced when the minister in reciting the commandments, solemnly pronounced, '*Thou shalt do no murder.*'[59] It was as if the dagger that had slain her / brother, had pierced her own heart. Had a supernatural voice from heaven uttered the awful prohibition, it could not have thundered in her ears with more terrifying energy. Never had the crime of Ernest struck her in so tremendous a light, never had she trembled with such agony for his eternal welfare! Still prostrate on her knees long after the rest of the congregation had risen, she heard not, knew not what was passing around; the cry of her heart was: 'Forgive him, oh, merciful heaven! forgive, forgive him!' and as these reiterated though silent aspirations burst from her, a flood of tears poured from her eyes. Mrs. Fitzmaurice, fortunately was her only companion in the pew. She was far from surmising the cause of her present agitation, but she saw that it shook her as though she had been in the crisis of a fever. She abstained for a considerable time from interfering with her emotion; but apprehensive at length that its further indulgence would be hurtful to her, she gently touched her on the shoulder, whispering: 'Compose yourself, my Ella.' The exhausted girl started, drew a heavy sigh, hastily wiped her streaming eyes, and gathering her thick black veil round her face, slowly arose and resumed her seat. For many succeeding days / Mrs. Fitzmaurice observed in her a sadness more affecting than any she had yet witnessed. Her heart it was evident had received a new blow; her eyes almost continually swam in tears, and unknown to herself, her respiration was broken by short convulsive sighs, that told a tale of mental suffering, her sympathizing and affectionate sister, heard not without the most tender compassion.

Mrs. Ormond, however, though so devoted, so assiduous during the height of her daughter's illness, was now becoming impatient of the continuance of her dejection. Already mortified by the uncertainty she was held in as to the final decision Ella would come to respecting Ernest, and vexed at the inroads such obstinate sorrow would make upon her beauty, perhaps even upon her constitution, she abated much of her usual kindness towards her, and partly from policy, partly from real displeasure, maintained a coldness of demeanour whenever they were together, ill-calculated to produce the effect of reviving the poor mourner's spirits, but eminently well adapted to add to her distress.

Such was the state of affairs at Holme Court, when a letter reached Ella – a letter from a quarter of all others the least expected, / from Ernest de Gray. It were superfluous to describe the feelings with which she received it, the mingled anguish and complacency with which she gazed at the well-known characters, the curiosity combined with fear with which she sought to anticipate its purport – these must be left to the imagination. On gaining courage, in the privacy of her own apartment, to break the seal, her heart sunk whilst perusing the following cold and brief address, the production, evidently, of an offended spirit: –

'Pardon me for intruding upon you the sight of my hand-writing; what I have to say shall be comprised in as few words as possible: but these words it is necessary should be spoken.

'Lady Ormond is on the point of leaving Wales to establish herself again at Ormond Hall. Whether, according to her desire, I shall accompany her depends upon *you*. I will not most assuredly, seek to abridge the distance that now separates us, if it is still your intention to persevere in the system of avoidance you pursued when I was last in Shropshire. Better ten million of times be at the furthest antipodes from each other, than / in a nominal vicinity, productive only of such bitter mortification and regret!

'Let me entreat that as a guide by which to regulate my proceedings, you will bestow upon me – were it only one line – an answer to this.

'Farewell – heaven preserve and bless you.[60]

'Ernest de Gray.'

What a letter to have been written by the companion of her childhood – the friend of her youth – the chosen of her heart! And yet, proudly indignant as it proved him to be, Ella saw that it admitted of many palliations. Unaccused, unconvicted, he had been treated by her as a culprit; he had for months resided under the same roof with her, and been interdicted her presence; her dying uncle had joined their hands and united them in the same blessing, yet she had, without any reason assigned, treated him with a harshness the most revolting. Was it not natural he should resent it? Had he not a right, unless his offence was charged upon him, to be considered as an innocent man? With all the inherent candour of her disposition, Ella meditated intently on what was due to justice; she put herself in Ernest's place, and acknowledged / that under the same circumstances she should feel as he did. Setting aside, therefore, as much as it was in her power, all passion and prejudice, she came after a night's deliberation, to the resolution of writing to him in these terms: –

'I am become fully sensible that an explanation is due to you, and I will prepare myself to enter upon it. I could give you no stronger proof of my wish to act with equity, since the revelation I engage to make, will be to us both almost too dreadful to be borne!

'Having such an interview and such a task in prospect, the anxiety I shall suffer till you arrive will rob my nights of rest, and my days of every moment's peace. Hasten your journey, therefore, as much as it may be in your power.

'Adieu. May the blessing you have called down upon me, return seven-fold into your own bosom!

'Ella Ormond.'

From the moment she had dispatched this letter, the important consequences that might ensue from it, were never absent from her thoughts. She spent the interval between its / departure and the impending meeting in literally *preparing herself*, as she had said, for the conference. She apprized her mother of the visit she expected, and besought her to let it take place, without witnesses, in her dressing-room. No request could more have propitiated Mrs. Ormond, who assented to it most gladly.

The critical moment at length drew near. She heard from Hannah, whilst undressing at night, that Lady Ormond had arrived at the Hall late that evening. Intelligence such as this, it may well be supposed, drove all possibility of sleep from her eyes. Hour after hour she lay considering and reconsidering the mode in which she should receive him – the words in which she should clothe her fearful meaning – the most allowable way in which she might seek to soften to him the shock of what he was about to hear; these and a thousand other ruminations engrossed her mind throughout the wakeful night, the first that, spent without rest, she had ever found too short.

It was yet early the following morning, when she heard the voice of Mrs. Ormond on the stairs, her steps and those also of some other person approaching the door. With just / strength to raise it to her lips, she hastily drank a glass of water, made signs to Hannah to close the window curtain and retire; and then threw herself back upon the sofa, awaiting with a palpitating heart the dreaded moment when the door should open.

It speedily arrived; and once more she and Ernest were in presence of each other. Mrs. Ormond brought him up to the sofa, uttered two or three short sentences, which were unanswered and unheeded, and stole quietly out of the room.

A dead silence succeeded her departure. Ella, who had not yet dared to raise her eyes, tried to recal the resolutions she had formed – tried to speak – tried to look at him; but her courage failing, the first sound that broke the solemn silence, was that of her deep and heart-bursting sobs.

In a tone serious and impressive – a tone that penetrated to her soul – Ernest now said:

'Why is this, Ella? Why have you permitted this interview, if it thus demolishes you?'

His voice, startling to her as was its first sound, yet had the effect of soothing her, by the memory it revived of so many happy hours. / The tears she had shed had lightened the oppression of her heart; and struggling successfully to obtain more composure, she was at last enabled to address him:

'Ernest,' she said, tremulously, 'sit by me. You have much, alas! to hear, and I have promised you the most unreserved explanation. For that purpose, it is necessary that you should know the origin of the sorrow that for the last six months has preyed incessantly upon my mind, and at one period brought me to the very brink of the grave. The subject is one that cannot be more harrowing to you than it is to me; for believe me, Ernest, it was neither indifference, displeasure, nor caprice that induced me so long to estrange myself from you. The interest and affection I have felt for you from a child, I will not hesitate to confess, I have never been able to withdraw from you.'

An acknowledgment such as this, made at any other moment, and under any other circumstances, could not fail to have transported him; but uttered by those blanched and quivering lips, accompanied by looks expressive of so much woe, and hints so alarming of what was yet to be communicated, it lost all power of inspiring joy, and he could only say: /

'With what delight should I hear these words, but for the apprehension of that which is to follow them!'

'You are right, Ernest; they are words, which however true, however sincerely spoken, will be completely neutralized by what remains to be said. But I spoke them to give you the consolation of knowing, that even whilst accusing you, I am exempt from all feeling of enmity towards you, – that I pity, have forgiven, and am still your friend; though you have placed a barrier between us that can never be surmounted.'

'What barrier, sweet Ella? Tell me without shrinking; you have prepared me for every thing.'

By slow degrees, often gasping for breath, pausing continually for courage to go on, Ella at length made known to him the full extent of her suspicions. She retraced to him all the circumstances that had preceded her brother's assassination; she reminded him of the previous discord that had so evidently subsisted between himself and Frederic; she recalled to his recollection the then apparently insignificant incident of having met him so hastily descending from his own room a short time before the catastrophe; of the loud accents of / contention that had drawn her into the hermitage; of the fierce and unusual indications of passion his own looks and manner had betrayed; of the engagement he had made to follow her to the dairy, and of its subsequent failure; and lastly – in a low, inward, and scarcely audible voice, accompanied by a thrill of uncontrollable horror, she with difficulty murmured:

'Ernest, I was the first who found him – wounded – lifeless – weltering in his blood, – and *your* dagger lying beside him!'

The ghastly scene, as if still present to her view, worked so powerfully on her imagination, that pressing her throbbing temples with her hands, she dropped her head upon the table before her, and groaned aloud.

Ernest had listened to her, from the moment she began speaking, with intense interest, and with every variety of emotion her discourse was calculated to excite. Sometimes his face was only expressive of concern for the agitation he saw her suffer; sometimes it denoted extreme surprise; and, at others, a train of painful retrospections clouded his brow, that threw an air of solemn thoughtfulness over his whole countenance. But, at the mention of the *dagger*, every faculty appeared paralyzed; his arms fell powerless by his side; his eyes became fixed and almost vacant; / and though his colourless lips moved, the keenest ear could not have detected any sound issuing from them. Thus he sat, for many minutes; at length, slowly raising his hand, and passing it two or three times across his eyes, he got up, and without speaking, moved with hesitating steps towards the door. Ere he reached it, Ella, uncovering her wan face, looked after him, and clasping her hands with indescribable anguish, cried out:

'Oh, Ernest, have pity upon me! Go not without breathing one word in your defence! Alas, alas! I now feel that there has always lingered a ray of hope that you might have some proof to bring forward of your innocence. But this silence kills me! it seems to set a seal upon your guilt; it bereaves me of my only remaining consolation – that of still daring to doubt; for let me acknowledge, that now I have seen you, your single asseveration would suffice to absolve you, if not to my judgment, at least to my heart. It would give me something to exist upon; it would excuse me in my own eyes, and persuade me that I might still cherish you in secret without sin!'

'Generous – excellent Ella!' exclaimed Ernest, deeply touched by the tenderness of these expressions, 'how shall I thank you for such / exquisite kindness?

how shall I find words to tell you with what veneration I regard the merciful quality you possess of knowing how to separate the sinner from the sin? Grieved am I to say, that whether innocent or guilty, we must inevitably part! I have no possible means of disproving the charge you have so reluctantly brought against me; and since that is the case, I would not – were you even capable of consenting to it – for all that the united world could offer me, connect your fate with mine! To you, lenient and compassionate as you are, I fearlessly entrust the further keeping of this horrible secret. As you have hitherto guarded me from infamy, so I beseech you, still to confine your suspicions to your own bosom: it will be a proof of mercy you never shall have cause to repent.'

'Sooner would I die than breathe a syllable that could injure you! But it is terrible – oh how terrible, to be left in this uncertainty! Ernest, I ask no longer for *proofs;* give me but your bare word – pronounce but this short sentence: "I am innocent," and you restore me to peace – you bestow upon me new life – you enable me, even were we never to meet again, once more to value existence, and to put faith in human goodness.' /

To this energetic supplication, Ernest was about to reply, when Mr. Fitzmaurice, ignorant that he was in the house, and having a letter on business to show Ella, unexpectedly entered the room. He, of course, on beholding the young visitor, determined to abridge his stay; but Ernest, as if anxious to terminate the conference, made some excuse for accompanying him when he went down stairs; and, shortly after, mounting his horse, rode back to Ormond Hall.

Ella, on hearing the sound of his horse's feet, repaired to the window, and through the tears that half blinded her, stood watching him till in the distance he was lost to her sight. So confused were all her thoughts, so perplexing was the incertitude in which she remained, that it was long before she became sufficiently collected to ask herself what impression the recent conference had left upon her mind. It was one that was far from being reassuring. The reserve so pertinaciously maintained by Ernest could not but be regarded as fearfully ominous; yet, when her spirits became calmer, she found that the mere circumstance of having overcome the shock of first seeing him had removed a heavy weight from her heart, and, that his composed demeanour, his guarded but feeling language, had also, though / she knew not why, contributed materially to diminish the terror of the interview, and to soften the recollections of the past.

Mrs. Ormond, when her daughter joined the family, perceiving in her no increase of dejection, but rather an appearance of improved tranquillity, was satisfied that all would end well; asked no questions, made no allusions to the visit of the morning, but secretly congratulated herself on the approaching termination of what she concluded to have been a mere lovers' quarrel. /

CHAPTER XI.

> Caquet bon bec de jaser au plus dru,
> Sur ceci, sur cela, sur tout,
> Disant le bien, le mal, allant de place en place.

La Fontaine.[61]

The ice being now broken, as Mrs. Ormond expressed it, and remembering *que ce n'est que le premier pas qui coute*,[62] she was in constant expectation of seeing Ernest again at Holme Court. But when a fortnight elapsed, and then three weeks, without any tidings of him, her surprise was extreme. Ella herself was not entirely exempt from sharing in the same feeling. If he came not, she thought he might have written; he might have afforded them some indication by which to judge of his future intentions: a silence and an avoidance so absolute were incomprehensible, and condemned her to a state of suspense / she found it difficult to bear without murmuring.

An explanation, however, came but too soon. Mrs. Fitzmaurice was commissioned one morning to announce to her sister, with all possible gentleness and caution, that her husband had just received a letter from Ernest, dated London, containing the astounding information, that he was on the eve of setting out for the continent; that he renounced all pretension to Miss Ormond's hand, and had caused a document to be drawn up and properly authenticated, by which he made a resignation in full of every claim he had been invested with by Sir Everard's Will, surrendering the whole, now and in perpetuity, to his niece.

This was indeed a blow! It struck Ella to the heart; for whether regarded as an indirect avowal of conscious guilt, or merely as an indication of his hopelessness to prove his innocence, it equally tended to part them; and what to her was an additionally afflicting consideration, it impoverished whilst it made an exile of him. Personal mortification she experienced none; this was not a line of conduct, she well knew, prompted by indifference or aversion, though whence exactly it originated, it was impossible to decide. At all events, it manifested a disinterestedness / of character, which, whilst deeply lamenting its effects, she could not but warmly admire.

Mrs. Ormond, on first being made acquainted with the purport of his letter, was highly indignant at his having presumed to anticipate a rejection that ought only to have proceeded from Ella herself. Further reflection calmed her displeasure. She had never cordially approved the match, though the forfeiture that would have been incurred by opposing it, had extorted from her a consent resulting rather from motives of policy than inclination. This new state of the affair reanimated her slumbering ambition; and seeing in Ella the sole and undisputed heiress of Sir Everard, the hopes she cherished of her future elevation knew no limits.

Meanwhile Lady Ormond grievously annoyed at the perverse turn her efforts for the advantage of her young favourites had taken, and blaming both, but chiefly Ella, for their failure, sedulously avoided having any communication with the family at Holme Court, and invited a distant relation to come and alleviate to her the solicitude of Ormond Hall. Like her sister-in-law, she attributed the division of the lovers to a quarrel; and never having been able to draw from Ernest any explanation of its origin and progress, she concluded / that it had entirely resulted from Ella's long and obstinate estrangement from him, and the not unnatural resentment with which it had inspired him. When therefore his present determination was announced to her, she combated it 'more in sorrow than in anger;'[63] furnished him with a letter of credit on her banker, and strenuously exhorted him not to prolong his stay abroad beyond the period necessary to enable him to overcome his ill-requited attachment.

It was about this time that Ella first heard of the violent death of the young creature she had so much admired – the unfortunate Ruth Nelson. The distance between Ormond Hall and Holme's Court being but a few miles, many of the villagers around the latter place had seen her, and knew her family. By some of these she was informed, that the poor mother, after a long and dangerous illness, had quitted the country with her surviving daughter, and was gone, it was supposed, to reside near London. Her brother had given up his farm, and accompanied by his son Philip, the young carpenter, had also left the neighbourhood. Not one of the race remained in Shropshire, and since their departure, no tidings had been heard of them.

Ella was inexpressibly shocked, and deeply grieved by this melancholy account. It seemed / to her but too evident that there was a fatal connexion between the death of Frederic, and that of the rash and despairing Ruth. She had undoubtedly loved him. Ella remembered the torrent of information to that effect which had been poured upon her by the gossipping and invidious Mrs. Roy. It now appeared there was unfortunately too much warrant for what had been said, although she could not persuade herself even yet to give entire credit to the dame's assertions respecting Ernest. Whatever might have been his provocation to commit the deed of which she was compelled to think him guilty, her mind never rested long upon the supposition of its being jealousy. She might, however be wrong; and if she was – if a vehement passion for Ruth, and hatred of Frederic, as his favoured rival, had led to the crime – how fearfully had he been punished by the self-inflicted death of his mistress! What an aggravation of his remorse must it be, to reflect that the blood with which he had loaded his conscience had been spilt in vain!

Whilst Ella dwelt involuntarily and almost perpetually on these painful reflections, Mrs. Ormond, heartily weary of the sameness and retirement of Holme Court, was disposing herself to return to her own house in Wiltshire. When she communicated this intention to Mr. and Mrs. / Fitzmaurice, she added that it was her design to pay one or two visits on the road, which visits, as Ella was still in such a depressed state of spirits, it might be better not to make her undertake.

'I shall, therefore,' she continued, 'if you are willing to let her remain with you, leave her here a little longer. Your quiet mode of life exactly suits her; and it is to be hoped, that as the spring advances she may recover somewhat more cheerfulness; but, to tell you the truth, I do not expect she will ever again be what she was. However,' she added, with an expressive look, 'the fortune she now possesses will I trust make up for any abatement in her personal attractions; and she is still quite handsome enough to form an excellent *mariage de convenance*.'[64]

'Such as, I presume,' said Mr. Fitzmaurice, looking as serious and as innocent as he could, 'you are now meditating to negotiate for her. May I venture to enquire who is the favoured individual?'

'Nonsense! you may assume as sly an air as you please; but, I assure you, I have no negotiations of the kind you mean in view. I alluded merely to what *may* be hereafter.'

'No doubt, no doubt, dear madam, that was all! Let me only put in a good word for young / Sedley. He may not be quite so clever as our perverse friend, Ernest; but at all events he merits, I should think, quite as much favour, though untitled, as the new Baronet, Sir George Arundel. What is your opinion, my dear madam? Are we of the same mind?'

Mrs. Ormond, at these words, both felt and looked exceedingly conscious. She wondered how Fitzmaurice had obtained such insight into her as yet incipient views; for the truth is, she really had pondered on the practicability of effecting an union between her daughter and Arundel. Once before, the idea had occurred to her; but subsequent circumstances had laid it at rest. Of late, it had revived; and her son-in-law, who knew her well, judging from the coldness with which she had recently spoken of Sedley, hesitated not to believe that she was looking forward to Arundel, as the richer man, and now a titled one, to supply his place.

When, in answer to Fitzmaurice, she found it necessary to speak, what she said was so vague, and appeared uttered in such a spirit of raillery, that it would have baffled any man of less penetration. Upon him it had no effect; he had studied her character too long; and no words in which she could have disclaimed his insinuation would have gained with him the smallest credit. /

Mutually distrustful, they parted with little regret; and Ella remained once more the sole guest at Holme Court, where many weeks elapsed without producing the slightest variation in her mode of living. She regretted sincerely the thorough estrangement from the warm-hearted Lady Ormond which had taken place; but had not courage to seek her at the hall, and in scenes fraught with such terrible recollections. Mr. Fitzmaurice, however, called there repeatedly; he was a great favourite with the solitary widow, and therefore ventured, ere long, to avail himself of her good graces, in order to obtain for his wife the same privilege. They were both kindly received, and Ella was affectionately enquired for.

'I do not expect,' she added, 'to see her here at present; but tell her, I still have the truest regard for her, and whenever her health and spirits enable her to make the exertion, shall be sincerely glad to welcome her.'

Mrs. Fitzmaurice promised safely to deliver this friendly message, and then permitted herself to ask whether her aunt had heard lately from Mr. de Gray?

'Ah, poor de Gray! it must be allowed, my dear Mrs. Fitzmaurice, that your sister has dealt rather hardly with him. When she heard of his intention to go abroad, I wonder she could have / the heart to keep up the quarrel – whatever it was about, – that induced him to go. Take my word for it, she has done it at the expense of her own happiness, and merely because her pride stood in the way of a reconciliation. She loved him, that I am very sure of, and I have no doubt loves him still. How it will all end, I cannot pretend to foresee; but my firm belief is, she never will accept any body else.'

Before Mrs. Fitzmaurice, who felt much puzzled how to answer this speech, had time to speak, the room door was opened, and Miss Flemming, the relation Lady Ormond had invited to become her companion, made her appearance. She was a personage no longer young, but still active, and full as lively as at any period of her life nature had ever intended her to be. Well mannered and gentle, with some remains of a pretty face, and a person always neatly attired, she could cast no disgrace upon her more prosperous connexions, and was always kindly treated when she went to see them, provided she did not stay too long. Her list of nephews and nieces, brothers and brothers' wives, sisters and sisters' husbands, was interminable;[65] and her great delight was to talk of them, even to those who had never heard of their existence. She would ring the changes for a whole morning upon her 'dear / nephew Tom,' her 'pretty niece Louisa,' her 'funny brother-in-law Frank,' her 'clever sister Sophia,' &c.

Fortunately, Lady Ormond had the convenient faculty of abstracting her attention from every thing that wearied her, and, consequently, heard not one word of all this unmeaning chatter. Miss Flemming therefore sat at her work-table, maundering uninterruptedly her endless enumeration of family merits, making purses for some, work-bags for others, needle-books for the children, and socks of knitted lambs-wool for the elders. She had one favourite seat in whatever room she occupied, and generally one odd volume of plays or tales lying beside her work-box, into which, for about a quarter of an hour before dinner, she would occasionally look. But it was no unusual thing for the volume to fall out of her hands, as sitting bolt upright, its perusal gradually drew her to sleep. On a Sunday, she always appeared with a number of little hymn-books, and religious essays, neatly bound, the gift of a 'dear niece,' or 'kind sister;' and these, week after week, she would alternately turn over, with a firm persuasion she was doing right; and as soon as the clock announced the hour to be half-past nine, gather them together, light her candle, bid her associates good night, and retire to bed. /

'She is as harmless,' Lady Ormond was wont to say, 'as the white china cat she brought me lately from Worcester. I cannot love her, but I can look at her with a certain degree of complacency, from the consciousness that she is well-principled, is no backbiter, does not speak loud enough to force my attention to the nothings she utters, and has a good natured though insipid countenance. After all, insipidity, if unaccompanied by discontent, is less fatiguing to live with than perpetual brilliancy. Give me anything but dogmatism, conceit, or ill-humour.'

Such as she was, Mr. and Mrs. Fitzmaurice were introduced to her, and showed her all manner of courtesy. They declared it would give them great pleasure to do the honours of Holme Court to her, and invited her to dinner on the following day.

'We have one or two other friends coming,' added Mrs. Fitzmaurice, 'and I think if you will join our little party, you will like them. I fear my aunt could not be induced to leave home.'

'No indeed, my dear,' said that lady; 'but I strongly recommend Miss Flemming's accepting your invitation. She has been leading a very dull life here, and a little change will do her good.'

'Oh, my dear madam,' cried Miss Flemming, / 'I never found it dull, I assure you, and I can't think of leaving you alone.'

'Yes, yes, you can – at least, you must try; so, Mrs. Fitzmaurice, just tell us at what hour you dine, and my good friend here, who I know loves to be as punctual as the clock, shall be with you before the cook has quite done pouring the soup into the tureen.'

Miss Flemming simpered, the Fitzmaurices named the hour at which they hoped to see her, and soon after took their leave.

Ella, when made acquainted with what had passed, was pleased to find that Lady Ormond had spoken of her with kindness.

'She was always so indulgent and good to me,' said the grateful girl, 'that I could not but love her; and to know that I had permanently lost her favour, would have given me very severe affliction. What sort of person, my dear Bessy, is her Miss Flemming?'

'The least disagreeable of any professed companion I ever met with. She is civil, without being fawning, and really has the manners of a person accustomed to good company.'

'Very true,' said Mr. Fitzmaurice; 'but, between ourselves, I suspect she is desperately silly. "There is no speculation in those eyes"[66] of hers; / and her simper, if I were to watch it, would provoke me beyond bearing.'

'Then do not watch it, dear Sir,' cried Ella; 'if she suits my aunt, and has no prominent defects, we ought to be contented.'

On the morrow, when the few guests the Fitzmaurices had invited were all collected, Miss Flemming among the rest, Ella, to comply with the wishes of her sister, showed herself for the first time since her illness, (when the family was not alone,) in the drawing-room. The cause of her long seclusion was too well understood to bear being alluded to; but those who had previously known her, expressed the pleasure it gave them to see her, with perhaps more warmth than they intended, though not in a manner that could really distress her. Miss Flemming was the only one in the course of the day who, without meaning it, said any thing to awaken unpleasant recollections. She told Ella, whilst sitting beside her after dinner in the drawing room, that she had the pleasure of being acquainted with some friends of hers, who had been visiting at Ormond Hall a little before the death of poor dear Sir Everard.

'I allude,' continued she, 'to the charming family of Bloomberg. What delightful people they are – the daughter especially. She talked to / me a great deal about you, Miss Ormond, and the pleasant rides and walks you used to take together. She put me continually in mind of my dear niece, Lucy, though, I must own, she is not quite so pretty. Perhaps Lucy's sister, Margaret, is rather more like her; but, I should say, that neither of them are quite so pale, nor quite so short. She does not sing, which they, dear girls, do most beautifully; but she seems fond of music, and told me she should like very much to hear any of my nieces, if she should happen some day to meet with them. She draws very well, I fancy; but I am no judge, though I take much pleasure in looking at such things. She showed me a picture she had taken of you, Miss Ormond; but if you will believe me, I am so stupid, that now I see you, I can't persuade myself to think it was very like. I suppose, however, it might; for her mamma said it was the very image of you. And now I remember, the hair was the same colour, and that little mole on your chin was exactly in the same place.'

Ella, who began to think it would be right to say something, now informed the good-natured small-talker to whom she was forced to attend, that the miniature she spoke of had never been entirely finished.

'Oh then, I suppose that is the reason I / cannot recollect its being quite like you. Miss Bloomberg is so clever, that I am sure she would not have failed in catching the resemblance, if she had had time to finish the picture. There was a young person, she told me, in the neighbourhood of the Hall, quite a cottager, who was so beautiful, that she always regretted not being able to get at her, as she wished of all things to paint her portrait. I asked Lady Ormond to procure me an opportunity of beholding this surprising creature; but she shocked me by saying the poor girl is dead. I dare say, Miss Ormond, *you* have often seen her.'

'Not often – but I never can forget her;' and as Ella uttered this short sentence, a shiver ran through her frame, and she spoke in a tone of such solemnity, with lips so white and quivering, and eyes swimming in tears so ready to overflow, that even the unobservant Miss Flemming was struck by her manner, and heaving a deep sigh, exclaimed:

'Ah, poor thing! I do not wonder you should be affected by her early death. It is very sad to think that one so lovely and so young should have been snatched away so unexpectedly. But you know, my dear Miss Ormond, it was the will of Providence. She was probably removed for her own good – taken from the evil to come / – appointed to die before she had committed any great sin; and is now, we may suppose, happier than this world could ever have made her.'

Ella was almost overcome. Such a speech made in relation to the wretched suicide was dreadful! Had she not been assured that an abrupt flight from the room would have astonished all present, and drawn upon Miss Flemming the most eager enquiries as to the subject of conversation which could have produced such an effect, she would have taken immediate refuge in her own chamber. But in so doing, the probability was, that the horrible catastrophe of Ruth would have been related at full length, with whatever accessory details could have accompanied it: and thus Miss Flemming with her want of tact would, on every possible occasion, have harrowed her by making the painful affair a matter of conversation. Rather than *that* should be the case, she compelled herself to get up deliberately, and, though shaking with emotion, to bring from a distant part of the room a small portfolio of coloured engravings representing the costumes of different countries; this she placed on the table near which her unconscious tormentor was sitting; and having opened it, invited her, in a voice as steady as she could command, to come and look at it. She readily complied, and thanking Miss Ormond / a thousand times for the trouble she was taking on her account, and finding in almost every fresh plate some point of resemblance between either the figure, the dress, or the attitude of the personages displayed, and the different individuals of the beloved family ever prominent in her mind.

'Dear, how very droll!' she cried, on looking at a Neapolitan fruitwoman, 'this puts me quite in mind of my niece, Matilda. She wears earrings as like these as possible; and I have often seen her in a dress of the same colour as this woman's petticoat. But is it not a pity they should wear their clothes so exceedingly short? O here is a Polish officer; I declare he is the very image of Lewis, my youngest brother, only not so handsome. His boots are very like those of Lewis, and the hair upon his upper lip (moustaches I believe they are called) is quite the same.' Then turning over the leaf, 'Well,' she cried, 'this is really comical! Here is a young French lady in the very attitude I have so often seen my dear Amelia sitting in; and this child, standing upon one foot and resting the other upon the bar of her mother's chair, is as like my darling little Caroline as if it had been done for her. I recollect seeing her stand in this way continually, and I have often been afraid it might hurt her shape, which was the prettiest and the most graceful / that was ever seen. But I dare say it won't, for none of our family were ever awry.'

Thus she ran on, till the gentlemen came up from the dining parlour much to the relief of Ella's feelings, though somewhat to the annoyance of her ears; but she infinitely preferred this unmeaning chit-chat to the trying topic the good lady had before chosen.

After this day, Mrs. Fitzmaurice, partly to please her aunt, who was gratified when any attentions were shown her companion, and partly from motives of good nature, frequently invited Miss Flemming, who leading so retired a life at Ormond Hall, thought it delightful to drive a few miles to Holme Court; and if the evening was bad, thought it still more delightful to stay and sleep there. Mr. Fitzmaurice, by degrees, got exceedingly sociable with her, and laughed and talked nonsense with her to her heart's content. Without meaning to flirt as it is called, she bridled, and smirked, and affected now and then to turn aside her head, as if she suspected he was going to touch upon some subject that might shock her delicacy. She felt not that he was good-humouredly quizzing her; and when he reproached her for never having married, her cry would be – 'Oh Mr. Fitzmaurice, how can you talk so?' whilst in spite of herself, a titter might / be faintly heard ere she had time to put up her handkerchief to silence it.

'Why, my dear lady, what can be more natural than that I should talk so? Do I not hear you every day and every hour referring with unwearied delight to the perfections of your multiplicity of nephews and nieces? It is not one or two that you select to introduce to our notice, and to bestow your valuable commendations upon. To do you justice, you have no spirit of favouritism. Now, with such rare impartiality of disposition, what an excellent mother you would have made! Little Billy would never have been more favoured than little Johnny; nor would little Lizzy have been more indulged than little Sophy: they would all have been caressed and admired alike. Is it not then a sin and a shame to have devoted the capacity of lavishing all this indiscriminate love on the offspring of others, instead of bestowing it on your own?'

'Upon my word, Mr. Fitzmaurice,' cried the worthy spinster, looking really a little abashed, 'you are too bad! I never heard any one run on so in my life. My brother Sam, indeed, has sometimes joked me about marrying; but he is a sailor, and says anything that comes into his head.'

'By what you tell me, Miss Flemming, I am / sure he is a sensible fellow. He sees the error you have fallen into, and no doubt is far from thinking it too late to repair it. I could myself, for instance, recommend to you the most eligible partner.'

'Now pray, Mr. Fitzmaurice,' interrupted the lady, her colour considerably heightened, 'pray do not talk in this queer way any longer. I declare I have not the smallest wish to know who the gentleman is; and if he were to propose to me to-morrow, ten to one but I should refuse him.'

'No, no, you could not be so hard-hearted. On the contrary, come and dine with us on Thursday, and you shall make acquaintance with him.'

'I tell you again, Sir, I have no desire to make his acquaintance; and, as for coming on Thursday upon *his* account, be assured it is the last thing I should ever think of. But Mrs. Fitzmaurice has already been so good as to engage me for that day, and I have no notion of breaking my promise because this gentleman – whoever he is – has also been invited. It can be nothing to me.'

'Well, well, we shall see; don't be too sure of your own invulnerability.'

Then turning to Ella, who sat reading at one of the windows, he advised her to join him in a / stroll before dinner, and left Miss Flemming to gather from his wife, as cunningly as she was able, some information respecting their intended guest.

Mrs. Fitzmaurice, laughing, and much amused at the dialogue that had been passing, was forced to confess that she had not the slightest idea who the personage was to whom her husband had alluded.

'I did not know,' she added, 'that any one but our good and agreeable vicar and his wife were expected, with perhaps one or two of their family. But if other company should be coming, it may make the party more lively.'

Meanwhile, Ella, who in a slight degree felt her curiosity also awakened, interrogated her brother-in-law, and begged to hear whether the whole of what he had been saying was uttered as a hoax, or whether there really was any meaning in it?

'A great deal of meaning, I promise you, my dear Ella. Did you ever see squire Roberts – our jolly, foolish, good-natured, ruddy-faced neighbour?'

'Yes, I think I have.'

'Well then, he is the Cœlebs I purpose introducing to our Cœlibia.[67] Of course, I have no expectation that a wedding will ensue from their meeting at my table; but it will be amusing to / watch her look of mingled consciousness and prudery, contrasted with his air of open undesigning empty-headedness. He sometimes aims at being facetious, and as his jokes are quite good enough to please her, the perplexity she will be thrown into by her inclination to laugh, and her fear of being suspected by us of aiming to pay court to him, will afford me, at least, no little entertainment. At all events, whenever she begins boring us on the subject of any of her dear nieces and nephews, I shall have a fair excuse for telling her that I will listen to no family praises from her that do not relate to some child or children of her own.'

'But you will break her heart if you deprive her entirely of the privilege of talking of these beloved relations.'

'I only mean to deprive her of the liberty of exercising that privilege when I am present. She may find many good tolerant souls who may not object to listen to her; but I fairly acknowledge that, with regard to myself, she has entirely worn out my patience, and I am determined, if possible, to turn her ceaseless current of tinkling vapidity into some other channel.'

'What will you gain by that? Is not one tiresome subject as fatiguing as another? It is / not in the nature of things that poor Miss Flemming should ever converse sensibly or amusingly.'[68]

'Very true; but the annoyance of silliness is somewhat mitigated by being varied; and as we have encouraged her intimacy, and shall, probably henceforth see a good deal of her, it is but an act of self-defence to debar her from the constant use of the same weapons. For the next few weeks, I mean to talk to her of matrimony; after that, Bessy may assail her on the price of muslins and ribbons; then, if you can muster spirits for it, you may question her respecting the wonderful new sights she beheld when last in London, which sights, though she has occasionally touched upon them, she has by no means exhausted the pleasure of describing. Thus, you perceive, I have devised certain changes to lighten the tediousness of her prattle, by which we may all be benefitted.' /

CHAPTER XII.

You bear a gentle mind, and woman's heart;
Good sooth, I would not be a wooer in your way,
For all your blushing comes to.

SHAKESPEARE.[69]

THE appointed dinner party met on the specified Thursday, and Mr. and Mrs. Fitzmaurice did the honours of their house with their accustomed hospitality and good breeding. The vicar, Mr. Orme, was accompanied only by his son and eldest daughter; the youngest, a lovely girl of fifteen, had caught a severe cold, and her mother sent an apology, being unwilling to leave her. Squire Roberts, having no wife, nor even sister, of course came alone; but good and somewhat noisy spirits supplied, both to himself and others, the place of any associate; for he always laughed, and was loud enough to do duty for two, at least. When Mr. Fitzmaurice introduced him to Miss / Flemming, which he did, directing towards her a very significant look, to the usual form on such occasions, he added these words:

'I beg particularly, my dear Madam, to recommend this good friend of ours to your acquaintance. You will find him, at all times, a most animated and jocose companion; he will also soon discover that he has met in you with a particularly lively and amusing person; and I foretell that you will suit each other exactly. Here, Mr. Roberts, take this vacant chair, next to our kind guest, and do your best to entertain her.'

Mr. Roberts, of course, did as he was bid, and with a loud but not very intellectual laugh, flung himself into the seat recommended to him.

Meanwhile, Miss Flemming, the veriest prude in existence, had been thrown into the utmost embarrassment by what had passed – looking fifty different ways, now to the right, then to the left – sometimes up, and sometimes down – straight-forward, or at an acute angle upwards, or an obtuse one downwards – all ways, in short, except in the plain direction of Mr. Roberts' broad good-humoured face: – in fact, seeing nothing. For his part, he never dreamed of her being distressed by such awkward feelings, nor ever observed whether she turned her eyes towards him, or had any eyes / at all. As soon as Fitzmaurice left him, he began his appointed task of being entertaining.

'I hope, ma'am,' said he, 'you like our county. We natives are proud of it, and with good reason; for only think what a number of useful, and as one may say, valuable productions, it abounds with. There is our wool – I suppose there are no such fleeces in any part of England, Ireland, or Scotland to boot. Then we are famous for brawn, ma'am; and there's our Shrewsbury cakes,'[70] he added, with a laugh that rung through the room: 'they are not to be despised, I can tell you! I am sure, if it was not for spoiling the good dinner I know Mrs. Fitzmaurice will give us, I could wish for one at this moment!' here another laugh, that threatened never to come to an end. 'But really,' added he, recovering the power of speech, 'if I talk of these cakes any longer, I shall make myself so hungry, that I shall be tempted to begin gnawing my gloves – ha, ha, ha, ha!'

This last joke almost overcame the shyness of Miss Flemming, who had much difficulty to forbear joining in his mirth; a gentle titter, indeed, she found it impossible to suppress, but nothing beyond that had she courage to permit herself.

'Our county,' pursued Roberts, 'has another / great advantage – the number of excellent fishing streams it contains. You are to know, ma'am, that though in general I am a mighty stirring body, I can sit whole hours, almost whole days, fishing. It's very odd, one's taking a fancy of that sort. It seems but stupid work to a mere looker-on; and you know the old joke, ma'am, about an angling-rod – that it is "a long stick, with a worm at one end, and a fool at the other!"[71] How I used to laugh at that saying! But somehow, when I left off being quite so fond of hunting and shooting, and all that, I felt dull for want of some out-of-door amusement; and so I thought I would try fishing, and it has answered very well indeed; for I now like it quite as well as I used to do the more robust sports I formerly delighted in; not that I have entirely given them up either. I am still ready enough to go out on a fine morning with the hounds, or my pointers. But I do not quite relish sallying forth in disagreeable weather; in short, ma'am, I am rather less young, and a good deal less harum-scarum, helter-skelter than I used to be. Ha, ha, ha, ha!'

Miss Flemming's faintly responsive *tee-hee* had scarcely ceased, when dinner was announced, and her chatty neighbour started up to offer her his arm. She accepted it of course; but cast a somewhat / conscious glance towards Mr. Fitzmaurice, as he looked back a moment whilst conducting Miss Orme, and was relieved by perceiving there was no smile upon his face. At table Squire Roberts occupied a seat next her; and so obedient was he to the charge he had received, that he spoke to no one else, determined to acquit himself handsomely of the office entrusted to him of amusing her.

From time to time she still directed a rather suspicious look towards her host; but observing nothing to alarm her in the expression of his countenance, she gradually shook off much of her bashfulness, and not only listened and smirked, but actually tried to take her fair share of the talk. Here she was foiled. The worthy Squire, having once got the lead, could by no means prevail upon himself to give up the reins. It was seldom he met with so passive an auditor as Miss Flemming had hitherto proved; and to renounce the enjoyment of holding forth uninterruptedly to a civil dumby,[72] was more than he had fortitude to resolve upon. Certain it is, that his loss was not great, since, if he *had* allowed her to finish any of the speeches she began, it would have been merely to hear how much he reminded her of one or other of her brothers, or of her sister's husband, / or of her eldest nephew Frank. These were unknown personages the Squire had no desire to become better acquainted with; so he went on, copiously pouring forth his harmless common-places, interspersed, ever and anon, with what to him appeared jocularity, for 'gentle dullness ever loves a joke.'[73] Reduced therefore to enact the mere part of a listener, Miss Flemming did the best she could for herself; she determined to be patient; and her constitutional good temper enabled her to put her resolution into practice.

The consequence was, that the Squire, after the ladies retired, held forth warmly in praise of the meek victim of his loquacity. He had not, he said, met with so pleasing a woman for many a long day. She was just what a female ought to be – quiet, civil, and attentive.

'I like her prodigiously,' added he, 'and had I met with such a person earlier in life, there is no knowing what I might have been tempted to do with my liberty!'

This was spoken with one of his most tremendous bursts of hilarity, which was followed up by a chuckle that every gentleman at the table found irresistible. Mr. Orme was the first to recover his gravity.

'Why,' said he, 'talk of what *might* have been, / Mr. Roberts, rather than of what *may* be? It is never too late to repair an omission. If this lady has all the good qualities you are of opinion would have contributed formerly to your happiness, is it not reasonable to suppose they might contribute to it now?'

'O hang it, vicar! – the time is past for any change in my habits. I am a determined old bachelor, you may rest assured. Why, I could no more, at my time of day, alter my mode of living, and become a *lady's man*,[74] than I could fly.'

'Well,' said Mr. Fitzmaurice, looking very innocent, 'you know your own feelings best, Squire; and I should be sorry to encourage you to think seriously on the subject, being persuaded, in my own mind, that Miss Flemming has not the slightest wish to change her condition. But that need not hinder your taking pleasure in her society; and as she is very often at this house, and you are so near a neighbour, you may, by stepping in when so inclined, meet with her very frequently.'

The sly master of the house, after speaking thus, changed the subject. The fact is, he had no design to say or do anything towards promoting the union the vicar had suggested. His sole object was to promote a temporary jest. /

The evening was spent very much as the former part of the day had been. Messrs. Orme, father and son, kept up a brisk conversation with their host, on a variety of topics, whilst Ella sat quietly at her work, and Mrs. Fitzmaurice and Miss Orme occasionally chimed in with them, or played and sung in parts, content to amuse themselves, without exacting constant attention from others. Not so Squire Roberts; he never gave up his post next to the devoted Miss Flemming, nor ever discontinued his fancied endeavours to *entertain* her.

When at length he and the Ormes departed, Mr. Fitzmaurice could not forbear, as she sipped her wine and water, and ate a biscuit, complimenting Miss Flemming, who was to remain with them that night, on the conquest she had made.

'I never saw our worthy friend, the Squire,' said he, 'so caught by any lady as he has been to-day by you. I hope the partiality has been mutual. Tell me, Miss Flemming, how did you like him? Is he not very chatty and gay?'

'Yes, indeed, very; only I feel a little tired.'

'Ah, bah! you say that, my dear madam, to disguise the favourable impression he made upon you. I am sure you could not fail to like him.' /

'Well, perhaps I did; but for all that I could not help continually thinking of Ormond Hall, and the unwelcome guest who has arrived there.'

'What guest?' cried Ella, breaking through her now too frequent fits of silence.

'Why, a little before the carriage was announced, in which I was to come here, who do you think drove up to the house?'

'Oh, tell me – tell me quickly!' cried Ella, gasping for breath, and for an instant imagining it was Ernest de Gray.

'Well then – it was the new Baronet, Sir George Arundel.'

'Sir George Arundel?' they all repeated.

'Yes, it was, indeed. I never shall forget the look of astonishment Lady Ormond cast towards him when the servant announced his name, and he advanced to pay his respects to her.'

'On what pretence did he say he called?'

'He seemed a little confused when he first entered; but, recovering his composure, he told her Ladyship, that having occasion to pass within a few miles of her place on his way to some friend's house in Denbighshire, he could not refuse himself the pleasure of paying her a short visit, and claiming her hospitality for the night.'

'Cool!' observed Mr. Fitzmaurice. /

'Had my aunt ever seen him before?' enquired Ella.

'Yes, I believe so; but not for several years.'

'And as being the immediate successor to my uncle's title, I am sure,' cried Mrs. Fitzmaurice, 'she must now have seen him with very little pleasure. Pray, what sort of looking man is he, Miss Flemming?'

'He is tall and slim, with a dark complexion, and a quantity of black hair standing on end on his head, and shading his cheeks and upper lip.'

'Has he good manners?'

'He bows well and speaks gently, though not with an agreeable voice. I should say, if it was not for the sort of hoarseness he seems afflicted with, that he is not very unlike my dear military nephew, Tom; only Tom has finer teeth, and has the clearest voice possible.'

Here Mr. Fitzmaurice, wincing at this recurrence to 'dear nephews,' hastened to give another direction to her thoughts.

'As you do not appear, dear madam, to have taken any great fancy to him, you had better remain with us to-morrow. I should not be at all surprised, if you do, that you might have another opportunity of seeing Mr. Roberts. He has forgotten his stick, I perceive, in the hall; and there / can hardly be a doubt he will call for it in the course of the morning.'

'I assure you, Mr. Fitzmaurice, that would be no inducement to me to stay. The gentleman is very well; I am far from saying otherwise; but to own the truth, he is such a prodigious talker, that he quite wears one's spirits. Besides I should not, if I wished it, escape seeing Sir George Arundel by staying here longer; for I heard him say, when Lady Ormond mentioned my being engaged to dine at Holme Court, that he purposed calling upon the family there, before he left the neighbourhood.'

'The family is infinitely obliged to him!' said Mr. Fitzmaurice, drily.

'His thinking of coming is very odd,' observed his wife. 'We none of us know him except by report; and what we have heard can have given us no desire to make his acquaintance.'

Ella, meanwhile, lighted her bed-room candle, and not being in any degree interested about the gentleman, bade the party good night, and retired.

Mr. Fitzmaurice, however, detected, or fancied he detected, the hand of Mrs. Ormond in all this. He was convinced it was her wish to encourage the Baronet to pretend to her daughter; and / hesitated not to believe that his visit to Lady Ormond had been suggested by her, and that she had also put it into his head to introduce himself as a family connexion, to the Fitzmaurices. Where she had met with him, after her departure from their house, he could not exactly tell; but reflecting, that, as well as herself, the Baronet resided in Wiltshire, it was not difficult to suppose she might have met with him at some of the houses in the neighbourhood; or, enterprising and persevering as she was, it might easily be believed she had herself invited him to her own dwelling at Greenford Lodge.

'*C'est une maîtresse femme!*'[75] thought Mr. Fitzmaurice. 'She will leave no stone unturned to effect a favourite object. I would that the one she has now in view were as unexceptionable as young Sedley! I fear Ella will have much annoyance to endure on account of this amiable prototype of our "dear military nephew, Tom."'

The morning came, and shortly after breakfast, Lady Ormond's carriage called for Miss Flemming. As the vehicle drove off, Ella, attended by Hannah, set forth on one of her accustomed walks to visit some of the cottages in the neighbouring village. Their inhabitants knew and loved her, and she now seldom felt so happy as when administering to their comfort, either by / listening to and soothing them, whilst communicating a tale of sorrow, or distributing amongst them money or clothing. She had not hastened from home to avoid Sir George, for the fact is, she had forgotten that he was expected. On her return, therefore, to Holme Court, she heard he was in the drawing room without any emotion; and having taken off her walking things, waited not to be enquired for, but unhesitatingly made her appearance.

It was the first time Sir George had seen her for several years; and having heard how dangerously ill she had been, he was agreeably surprised to behold her looking so well. Her walk had given bloom to her cheeks, and that bloom lent a brilliancy to her eyes they had almost ceased to possess.[76]

'I am charmed,' cried he, hastily approaching her, 'to find you have so perfectly shaken off all appearance of ill health. The accounts that had reached me of your very severe indisposition had not prepared me to see you thus blooming and animated. I cannot tell you the pleasure it gives me to be so pleasantly undeceived.'

To this Ella made some slight answer, and sitting down near the table, drew forward her work box, and sought for some employment.

Mr. Fitzmaurice was expecting every moment / to hear him say something about her mother; but whether that lady had cautioned the Baronet not to bring forward her name, or whether influenced by the consciousness that he might perhaps betray he was acting under her influence, certain it is, she was never mentioned. The subjects that were discussed were all of a general nature, except what related to his visit at Ormond Hall, which to the surprise of the whole party, he said he had obtained Lady Ormond's permission to extend to another day or two.

'The weather is so fine,' continued he, 'and the little I have seen of the park and the surrounding country appears so beautiful, that I am loth to quit the neighbourhood, without becoming better acquainted with it.'

There was a pause, during which Mr. Fitzmaurice could not help thinking, that had such a speech been made by any body else, he should naturally have given the speaker an invitation either for that day or the next; but, suspecting the Baronet's views, he was by no means inclined to lend them any assistance, and though feeling awkward, he remained silent.

It soon appeared that Sir George had no intention of waiting for encouragement. Beginning to apprehend his visit might be thought to have lasted long enough, he rose to depart, and ere he / turned from Mrs. Fitzmaurice, after bidding her good morning, added:

'If you are disengaged to-morrow, my dear madam, and will permit me the honour of dining with you, I shall hold myself very fortunate.'

Mrs. Fitzmaurice could only say that she should be extremely happy to see him; her husband murmured something to the same purpose, and the smiling Baronet bowed himself out.

Left to themselves, the trio gazed at each other some moments in silent wonder, and then with one accord – for even Ella could not withstand the impulse, gave way to a hearty laugh.

'The good gentleman,' cried Fitzmaurice, 'will never lose anything for want of courage to ask for it. His installing himself so unceremoniously at Ormond Hall – nay his going there unasked at all – and his self-bestowed invitation hither for to-morrow, are two instances of easy assurance that cannot easily be matched.'

'Shall we ask any body to meet him?' said Mrs. Fitzmaurice.

'No, no; I want to find out what metal there is in him. There may be some stirling ore; but I am much mistaken if there is not also a good deal of alloy in his composition.'

'I never heard any other harm of him,' said Ella, 'than that he is rather penurious. But / what have we to do with that? We want nothing from him, nor can he have the smallest design to obtain anything from us.'

'Perhaps you may be mistaken, my dear little Ella; but time will show.' /

CHAPTER XIII.

Un homme de moyen âge,
En tirant sur le grison,
Jugea qu'il était saison
De songer au mariage.

Fureur d'accumuler, monstre de qui les yeux
Regarde comme un point tous les bienfaits des dieux;
L'homme sourd à ma voix
Ne dira-t-il jamais: C'est assez, jouissons?

LA FONTAINE.[77]

WITH the same composed aspect and manner he had exhibited the preceding day, Sir George again made his appearance at Holme Court, on the day following. Again he addressed Ella with marked courtesy, but there were no compliments paid on this occasion to her brilliant bloom, the truth being, that her complexion, when not animated by air and recent exercise, had never regained its natural hue since her illness, but was, generally speaking, as pale as monumental marble. Still the Baronet thought her very handsome, and moreover, he knew her to be very rich.

Throughout the repast he supported his share in the conversation with propriety and good / sense, though neither with originality nor spirit.

'He is,' said Mr. Fitzmaurice, when he was gone, 'a good average specimen of a creditable talker. For one who soars above him, you will meet with twenty on the same level, or even a little below him. If I could help it, I would as rarely associate with such persons as I would compel myself to read a merely rational, matter-of-fact book. They teach us nothing, are too good to be laughed at, and too insipid to be laughed with.'

There was but one thing in his guest that struck Mr. Fitzmaurice as being singular – the extraordinary solicitude he showed when the ladies left them after dinner, to learn all the particulars of the death of the unfortunate Frederic Ormond. It did not appear that he had ever seen much of him; nor did he profess to have entertained any peculiar regard for him; yet he was indefatigable in his enquiries, and often assumed, whilst listening to the answers he received, a look so portentous, that his companion knew not how to interpret it.

An explanation was soon obtained. Miss Flemming, the first time she came to Holme Court after the termination of the Baronet's visit to her patroness, was full of news, which in no / slight degree she was anxious to communicate.

'Oh, Mr. Fitzmaurice,' she began, 'you will be shocked to hear what a disturbance and confusion that terrible Sir George Arundel has occasioned at Ormond Hall! You know how fond dear Lady Ormond is of Mr. de Gray; – well, would you believe it, the Baronet has had the cruelty to tell her he is convinced that poor young man was the murderer of her nephew Frederic!'

Mrs. Fitzmaurice gave a violent start; her husband smiled contemptuously, and Ella fortunately was not present.

'Pray, Miss Flemming, on what foundation did Sir George say his conviction rested?' enquired Fitzmaurice.

'Why, I will tell you. He has been exceedingly curious, you must know, on this frightful subject from the very first day of his arrival. However, he did not attack Lady Ormond then, but before he went to bed, he sent for Andrews, the late poor dear Sir Everard's valet, and examined him closely in his own room. Andrews could tell nothing but what we all know; but he pumped out of him the names of those who had entered the hermitage when the murder was first discovered, and the two next days made it his principal business to find them out, and to cross-question / them as if they had been at the bar of the Old Bailey. Only one person was found who could give him the least information. This was a woman who weeds the gravel walks, and sweeps up the leaves. She happened to be so employed at the back of the hermitage the day the poor youth was killed, and accidentally mentioning the circumstance, Sir George never rested till he drew from her an account of her having heard high words between Mr. Frederic and Mr. Ernest, and having afterwards seen the latter rush towards the Hall, and in a little while, gallop full speed out of the park. She soon after left the spot, and went to pursue her work in another place.'

'And is this all on which the Baronet reposes his atrocious charge?'

'Not quite. He applied to the stable people, to know what Mr. de Gray had said, and how he had looked when he reached the Hall and ordered his horse. But nobody had seen him; he had saddled the animal himself and ridden away whilst the grooms and servants were at dinner. Still unsatisfied, Sir George entered almost every cottage or hut on the premises, and in the village; but heard nothing worth his trouble till he stopt at the dairy, and entered into conversation with Mrs. Roy. From her he gathered as much gossip / as he could desire. She brought up the name of the beautiful Ruth Nelson; told how fond Mr. Frederic Ormond had been of her; blamed her mother for allowing his constant visits; and insisted upon it, that both mother and daughter were designing artful people. She then mentioned Mr. de Gray, and said that he also went to see Ruth as often as he could without running the risk of meeting Mr. Ormond. In short, they were both in love with her, she averred; and on that circumstance Sir George built his accusation. He positively affirmed that jealousy had been Mr. de Gray's inducement to destroy his rival; and recapitulated, in my presence, all that he had been labouring to pick up against the good and amiable young man Lady Ormond has so long had such a high opinion of. The quarrel in the hermitage, overheard by Martha Long, the sweeper, who he declares has since owned that the name of Ruth Nelson once or twice reached her ears; the precipitation with which de Gray had fled from the building, saddled his horse, and galloped out of the way the whole morning; the court he could not forbear paying to Ruth Nelson at the very time he was fully aware that Mr. Ormond admired her; the fear he had of detection whilst lurking after her; and last of all, his persevering residence abroad, constituted, Sir George / said, a train of circumstantial evidence, that left not in *his* mind, at least, the smallest doubt of his guilt; and would go far, he was very certain, towards condemning him in any court where the crime could be tried.'

'And how did my aunt bear all this calumny?' cried the indignant Mrs. Fitzmaurice.

'Bessy,' said her husband, very gravely, 'it *is* calumny, and we shall ever consider it as such; but it is calumny to blast a man's reputation with general hearers, and will do Ernest irreparable injury. I grieve at it, for his sake – for Lady Ormond's – for our own.'

'Oh, as for Lady Ormond,' cried Miss Flemming, 'she does not believe a word of it! In my life I never saw her so angry as she was with Sir George for giving a moment's credit to such horrid things. She positively dismissed him from the house, telling him he never could repair the mischief his vile slanders might occasion, and heartily regretting having permitted him, even for a moment, to enter her doors.'

'And what said he to these severe reproaches?' inquired Mrs. Fitzmaurice.

'He assured her Ladyship he was only actuated by a love of justice. He had heard, he said, before he came, that many had been surprised at the tenor of Sir Everard's Will. Mr. / de Gray was very generally believed to have played an exceedingly subtle, underhand part; and though, certainly, no one accused him of being accessory to Frederic Ormond's death, that event was everywhere pronounced – and even with sneers – remarkably *fortunate* for the young gentleman appointed to marry the Baronet's heiress, and to adopt the family name. To say the truth, this disposition of his property was deemed rather unfair to the Testator's real kinsmen, who, however distantly related, had indisputably stronger claims to be considered than a youth wholly unconnected either by blood or marriage with any of the Ormond race.'

'Did my aunt make any remark upon this statement?'

'She merely said that Mr. de Gray having lost all chance of enjoying any participation in the fortune by renouncing the hand of Miss Ormond, the sneers at his *good luck* might henceforth cease.'

'Well! Did he say any more?'

'He expressed great surprise that her Ladyship's blind partiality to Mr. de Gray, prevented her seeing that his renunciation of Miss Ormond's hand, originated in the fear of being prosecuted by Sir Everard's relations for having used undue influence over him at the time his / extraordinary Testament was drawn up. It was known to have been dictated, signed and sealed a very few days before his decease, when, in all probability, his faculties were impaired, or at least no longer so clear as they were previous to the shock of his nephew's murder. The complaints made of the injustice of the Will, had, in all likelihood, come to Mr. de Gray's knowledge, and thence the apparent disinterestedness with which he had surrendered the ill-acquired benefit he had hoped to derive from Sir Everard's infatuation.'

'Is it not obvious from all this,' said Fitzmaurice, 'that Sir George's enmity against de Gray is the effect of avarice – disappointed avarice? When first he heard of young Ormond's decease, he doubtless flattered himself that with Sir Everard's title, whenever its possessor dropt, he should likewise inherit the major part of his fortune. A handsome legacy would possibly be awarded to Ella; she was well known to have been a favorite; but that was all. Now that he finds it rests with de Gray to break through his determination of giving up her hand, the Baronet's dread that the young man may change his purpose, and eventually profit by the testament intended to promote his advantage, engenders all the malice he so unscrupulously displays. A / more dangerous foe poor Ernest could not have encountered. He will move heaven and earth, I fear, to ruin his character, and whenever he returns to this country, I should not be at all surprised were a prosecution to await him!'

Mrs. Fitzmaurice gazed at her husband with consternation; whilst Miss Flemming raised her hands and eyes in speechless dismay.

'I exhort you both,' resumed their companion, 'to forbear saying one word to Ella on the painful subject; unless she should ever be compelled to associate with this odious man again, she had better know nothing of the matter. Here she comes; let us change the conversation.'

The unsuspicious girl, addressing Miss Flemming with her accustomed kindness and civility, inquired, with a half smile, how long Sir George Arundel had favoured her aunt with his company?

'He went away the day before yesterday.'

'And had he made any progress in her good graces before his departure?'

'Not much.'

Ella said no more. She felt that he would have gained but little ground, by a longer intercourse with herself, and could not be much surprised at his failing to please her aunt. /

Whilst these animadversions on what had so recently passed at Ormond Hall, were occurring in the family of Mr. Fitzmaurice, Sir George during a long confidential interview with Mrs. Ormond, gave her a circumstantial account of the researches he had instituted in that neighbourhood respecting the untimely death of her son; entered into a full detail of all the petty proofs he had been able to collect against de Gray, and then dwelt with the bitterest resentment on what he termed the insulting contradiction his statement had met with from Lady Ormond, and the angry terms on which she had suffered him to leave her house.

The Baronet's wily auditress listened to him with profound attention, though with as little credulity as Lady Ormond herself. She never for a moment attached the slightest belief to the guilt attributed to Ernest, nor was she wicked enough to gratify Sir George by professing on that point to think as he did, but taking a middle course, she joined with him in inveighing against her sister-in-law's infatuation in favour of de Gray – blamed her vehemence – accused her of inhospitality – and then gradually drew from him a statement of the impression the sight of Ella had made upon his feelings. This was so favourable, that she determined immediately to send / for her home. After the quarrel that had occurred at Ormond Hall, she was very sure the Baronet stood no chance of being received there again; and she well knew the Fitzmaurices would encourage no visits from one who had offended their aunt. The only way therefore of bringing Sir George and Ella into communication, was by letting him see her at Greenford Lodge, where he had long had reason given him to feel secure of a welcome reception, and where with perfect ease to himself he might ride over from his own place two or three times in a week.

The regret of the Fitzmaurices on parting with their dejected but uncomplaining young guest was as affectionate as sincere. In the mind of Mr. Fitzmaurice, indeed, something more than regret took place; he feared for Ella's peace, and foresaw with great concern the vexations she would probably have to undergo from her mother's machinations. It was plain to him that she was recalled purposely to be thrown in Arundel's way, and what would be her dismay when she made the discovery, it gave him pain to anticipate. After long hesitation he resolved the evening before she left Holme Court to arm her against any effort that might be made to propitiate her in behalf of the Baronet, by acquainting / her with the malicious imputations he had openly brought against de Gray, and the mean toil he had undergone to make himself master of every shadow of proof in support of his uncalled for investigation.

It would be impossible to describe the secret terror, the ill-suppressed anguish of the pitiable girl whilst listening to this communication. The danger to Ernest which she had once feared, but of late had thought blown over, seemed about to overtake him; the various indications of his criminality which she herself had been staggered by, were now brought together – were become, in all probability, the talk of the neighbourhood, and (exclusive of the fatal *dagger*) sufficed to awaken distrust in all who heard them. In speechless sorrow she hung her head, dropt into a chair, and burying her face in her handkerchief, wept some of the bitterest tears she had shed since the first shock of the tremendous event had overtaken her. Fitzmaurice, still unsuspicious of her attachment to Ernest, attributed the grief he saw her suffer to the recollection of her brother's hapless fate: and being too considerate to attempt offering her consolation by common-place arguments, he merely pressed her hand, and gently quitted the room. When left alone: 'He is lost!' she internally exclaimed, 'his fair fame is / sullied for ever, perhaps destroyed! The tale of infamy will spread, and even should his innocence hereafter be proved, the few who will know and acknowledge the fallacy of the charge, will be out-numbered by those whom its refutation will never reach!'

Worlds would she have given to possess the means of getting a letter conveyed to him, but she had not the most distant idea where to direct to him; and she had heard from Miss Flemming, that even Lady Ormond was at present ignorant in what part of the continent he was travelling. A full and explicit statement of the reports which had got into circulation respecting him, and the horrid conclusions drawn from them, she thought might have produced the good effect of inducing him to bring forward evidences of his guiltlessness before a knowledge of the accusation had become quite general. One person alone occurred to her who was likely to be acquainted with his address; this was Mr. Sedley. He was to have accompanied Ernest abroad, but had been prevented by the illness of a near relation: she had reason, however, to believe the friends corresponded, and if such was the case, a letter might be safely forwarded to Ernest wherever he should be.

Prompt in executing every innocent purpose, she sat down to her arduous task that very night, / after Mr. and Mrs. Fitzmaurice had retired to rest. Having recapitulated the alarming rumours that were getting afloat, she urged in language more forcible than she had ever thought herself capable of employing, the indispensable necessity of producing without delay an ample contradiction of the criminality for which he stood impeached in the public estimation. This letter, written with the dispatch of an energetic mind, and the warmth of a kind heart, she inclosed in another addressed to Mr. Sedley informing him that it was of the utmost consequence he should send it off the instant it reached his hands. Having concluded her melancholy employment:

'Alas! I can do no more,' she mentally cried; 'and who can tell whether this feeble effort will produce any beneficial result? Yet, to avoid public opprobrium, Ernest may still, I trust, be worked upon to stand forward in his own defence. True, he resisted the urgent supplications I once before addressed to him, but rather than incur universal disgrace, and the never-ending hatred of his fellow men, he will surely, surely set at naught the scruples – from whatever cause originating – that have hitherto sealed his lips.'

Thus communing with herself, the anxious Ella retired to bed, where for many hours she was kept waking by the appalling images her / fancy called up; and even after sleep had closed her tearful eyes, the dreams by which she was haunted, brought before her in such vivid characters, scenes of judicial investigation, of convicted guilt, of all men's unpitying abhorrence, of condemnation, and of Death! that the hideous picture awoke her in an agony of horror; and she preferred, early as it was – day only beginning to break – rising from her bed, putting on a wrapping gown, and seeking relief from such thoughts in any sort of occupation that presented itself.

As she pursued her journey the next day towards Wiltshire, the prospect of soon seeing Sir George Arundel, and of being compelled to tolerate him, was indescribably vexatious to her. He might have been induced to act as he had done by a real belief in the turpitude of de Gray; but even supposing him influenced by no unworthy motive, there was something so heartless in the manner he had chosen to verify his suspicions, that she knew not how to forgive him. The public and extensive inquiries he had instituted amongst persons of the humblest description and of all ages and sexes at Ormond Hall, were at once inhuman, and as far as related to Lady Ormond and the other friends of Ernest, in the highest degree indelicate. At all events, the Baronet's / plea of being actuated by the mere love of justice, weighed but little with the unhappy Ella, who thought that mercy far surpassed justice, especially where justice was uncalled for, and mercy was only required to be silent.

Her reception at home was nearly as cordial as in times past. Mrs. Ormond was pleased by her speedy obedience to her commands, and not altogether dissatisfied by her looks. She was pale indeed, and thinner than formerly: but the first might be occasioned by the fatigue of the journey, and the other, there was reason to hope, time and her native air would remedy.

Nothing was said, no allusion made throughout the evening to any thing that could molest her, or recal unpleasant thoughts. Mrs. Ormond was in unusual spirits, at least she exerted herself to appear so, and when that was the case, had the faculty of rendering herself peculiarly entertaining; and Ella, who loved her, and was gratified by the kindness with which her arrival had been hailed, listened to her anecdotes with complacency, and for a while was beguiled into forgetfulness of her deep seated grief.

Several days passed, during which no Sir George Arundel appeared. None except a few intimate neighbours shewed themselves; and whatever Mrs. Ormond might do, her daughter / could not but rejoice at his delaying so long to favour them with his company. The first tidings she heard of him were from Hannah, her maid; who coming up one morning after breakfast to Ella's dressing-room, told her the Baronet was below, adding: – 'I hate the sight of him, ma'am. He has defamed poor Mr. de Gray so shockingly, that there is not a creature in this county, nor in Shropshire either, where he is not spoken of with disrespect.'

'I know, Hannah,' said her mistress, trying to look calm, 'I know that Sir George thinks very unfavourably of Mr. de Gray; but tell me, is his opinion generally followed? Are all those who have heard him disposed to believe what he has asserted?'

'I am afraid they are, ma'am. He has brought forward such a heap of little circumstances against him, that the men below, as well as everywhere else, when the matter is talked of, declare they amount to almost positive evidence. I have fought many a battle for him, but they only tell me I speak in his defence because I like him, and wish to find him innocent, not because I have any thing really to say in his defence. And when I hear that, ma'am, what can I do?'

'Nothing, my good girl,' answered Ella, with / a sigh, 'nothing more than still to wish him well, and still to hope that his fame may, ere long, be cleared.'

'I am sure I *do* hope it, with all my heart and soul. And, ma'am, I must, if you please, tell you something that has taught me to like young Mr. Sedley very much indeed. It is reported that he met Sir George somewhere, and heard him speaking of his friend, Mr. de Gray in so abusive a manner, that he warmly took his part, and they had a violent quarrel about it.

'Thank heaven,' thought Ella, 'there is still one generous spirit in the world reluctant to admit his unproved guilt!'

When obliged to obey her mother's summons to the drawing-room, she had so far fortified herself against the danger of betraying any strong emotion, that instead of shrinking at the sight of Arundel, averting her eyes from him, or tremulously answering his address, she regarded him with a fixed and steady look, not wholly exempt from severity, and spoke with a tranquil coldness that threw him to a distance from whence he was not able to return the whole day. Mrs. Ormond, though highly displeased, could take hold of nothing on which to found a complaint. Ella was guilty / of no ill-breeding; she appeared not to shun their visitor; it was rather he who shunned her. That she laid him under great restraint was unquestionable; he ventured not in her presence to touch upon what – before her return – he had openly, and even whilst the servants had been in the room, descanted upon; that is, the turpitude of de Gray, and the advantage to the community of bringing so heinous an offender to justice. Deprived of the theme which of late had been uppermost in his mind, he lost his accustomed flow of conversation, was absent and even embarrassed; and though Mrs. Ormond urged him to stay dinner, he declined the invitation, and departed.

'Sir George seems out of spirits to-day,' said that lady when he was gone.

'Yes, I think he does,' answered her daughter.

Mrs. Ormond looked hard at her, as if to detect what meaning was couched under those words; but Ella's countenance indicated nothing that she could interpret. It was grave and calm, and expressed no more than a mere assent to her mother's remark. How to understand, therefore, the reserve of the Baronet, and the chilling politeness of her daughter, she / was totally at a loss. It was probable, indeed, she might have heard of the attack he had made upon the reputation of Ernest; but Mrs. Ormond had not the most distant suspicion that Ernest held any distinguished place in her heart. On the contrary; the reluctance she had shewn to see him after the death of her brother, to admit him as a suitor when it was known that the Will of Sir Everard had appointed him to be her husband, and finally the apparent composure with which she had borne his departure for the continent, all contributed to convince Mrs. Ormond that she hardly entertained for him a sentiment so favourable even as indifference. Then why should the charges promulgated by Sir George, excite in her sufficient displeasure to estrange him entirely from her good graces? He had informed Mrs. Ormond that Ella, when he last saw her at Holme Court, had been perfectly courteous, and spoke of her frequently in terms that proved him by no means inclined to despair of winning her regard. The conduct of both parties which she had just witnessed, certainly held out no prospect of the realization of these hopes; and the inexplicable silence of her daughter, condemned her to a state of perplexity extremely irksome to / her feelings. There seemed not any thing immediately to be done, however; and Mrs. Ormond, well aware of the danger of precipitation, and accustomed to prosecute her purposes with quiet perseverance, left to time and circumstances, judiciously managed, the accomplishment of her wishes. /

CHAPTER XIV.

Question him as you list, you naught shall learn; –
Leave all to th' unsparing mower, scythe-bearing
Time, who, with wings out-spread, flies over this
Round earth, disclosing many a deed, 'twere
Happier for the doer had still lain
Buried to eternity.

NOT SO OLD AS IT SEEMS, – A TRAGI-COMEDY.[78]

A WEEK had passed and no second visit had been paid by Sir George. At the expiration of that time, tidings reached the two ladies at Greenford Lodge – so Mrs. Ormond's place was called – that a duel had occurred between the Baronet and Mr. Sedley, the former of whom was slightly, the latter severely wounded. Ella was sitting with her mother when the news arrived, and dropping the pencil with which she had been drawing: 'Oh, poor Sedley!' she exclaimed, 'how I grieve at this intelligence!'

'Indeed, so do I,' said Mrs. Ormond, / 'but do you not feel some concern also for our neighbour, though his injury may be less?'

'None upon earth!' answered Ella, with unwonted earnestness. 'He has brought this evil upon himself. How could he ever imagine that the friend of Ernest de Gray could endure, unmoved to hear him publicly and even exultingly vilified in the barbarous manner Sir George has practised?'

'But you cannot be sure, my dear,' said Mrs. Ormond, startled at the warmth with which Ella had spoken, 'you cannot be sure that this duel has been fought on de Gray's account?'

'Certainly not *sure*; but I heard some days ago that Mr. Sedley and the Baronet had had a quarrel on the subject, and it is therefore, natural to conclude their duel may have originated from the same cause.'

'Very true, my love; but I did not suppose anything could have induced you to take so warm an interest in what relates to young Sedley. Tell me honestly, are you attached to him?'

'Not in the least, my dear mamma, as a lover; but very much so as the friend of an injured man.'

'Then you are at present entirely "fancy free"?'[79] /

'At all events, dear mamma, I am not only at present determined against marrying, but I know that my ever marrying at all, is the most improbable thing in the world.'

Mrs. Ormond smiled incredulously, but prosecuted the subject no further. A man on horseback was dispatched to Arundel House, to make inquiries after the wounded Baronet, and Ella repaired to her dressing-room to write to Mr. Fitzmaurice.

The dangerous state in which young Sedley was known to be lying, as well as the extraordinary cause of the combat, rendered it a matter of such public notoriety, that not only the newspapers were full of it, but both in town and country, scarcely anything else was talked of. A week had not elapsed after the event, when Ernest, who had read an account of the whole affair in a foreign paper, set out the instant post horses could be procured on his return to England, and in an incredibly short time found himself seated at his friend's bedside, watching over him as if he had been a brother. To the warm-hearted young man, who had given so unequivocal a proof of the sincerity of his regard, it may well be imagined the sight of de Gray was most consolatory and delightful. The married sister at whose house in London he was staying, welcomed / the new comer with nearly equal satisfaction. She had imbibed none of the prejudices against him which were now almost universally prevalent. Her brother's affection for him would have been enough to secure her good opinion, even if she had not herself known him many years, and always entertained a cordial esteem for him. Here, therefore, he remained, conferring and receiving benefit, reading to or conversing with the invalid as his strength seemed best able to bear, but sedulously avoiding any mention of Sir George Arundel, or of what had given rise to the duel. Sedley, though longing to receive from his friend's own lips an explicit account of the dreadful catastrophe of Frederic Ormond, was withheld by feelings of delicacy, from leading to a topic he saw de Gray was desirous to avoid. Thus during his whole convalescence, which was not perfected under six weeks, he had the forbearance to abstain from seeking to gratify a curiosity it was as impossible he should not secretly feel, as it was that Ernest should not be aware of what was passing in his mind. A slight degree of constraint was occasionally experienced by both parties, in consequence of this systematic reserve, but nothing resulted from it prejudicial to their friendship; and when Sedley's re-establishment was sufficiently confirmed, they parted / with the warmest sentiments of mutual gratitude and affection.

It was de Gray's purpose, previously to his departure once more for the continent, to pay a short visit to Lady Ormond. Her invariable kindness, and unshaken trust in his uprightness, demanded from him this proof of respect, and called for his most heart-felt acknowledgements.

As he approached the Hall, his thoughts engrossed by many a mournful recollection – the images of Frederic – of Sir Everard – and, above all, of Ella, presenting themselves alternately to his mind, he was painfully struck by the expression of countenance of almost every man he met. Labourers going back to their work after their early dinner – cottagers' wives standing at their doors, boys playing by the road side, all of them people he had known and been accustomed to be greeted by with smiling heartiness, either turned away their heads, or 'eyed him askance,'[80] some with apparent fear, others with a scowl testifying mingled rage and aversion.

'Sir George's design is answered!' thought he, throwing himself back in the carriage. 'He has made me detestable enough in the eyes of my fellow creatures to satisfy his utmost rancour!'

A deep sigh followed this reflection, and forbearing / to gaze from the window any more, the carriage speedily stopped, and he found himself at the portico of Ormond Hall.

Here he met from the domestics with a somewhat improved reception; yet even in them he saw not the warmth and frankness of manner with which, from a boy, they had been wont to welcome him after every little absence from home. Andrews, the good old butler, was the only one in whose countenance he could perceive no change. The rest looked as if the villainous rumours spread abroad had produced effects upon their minds hardly perceptible even to themselves, yet of a nature, in no small degree, injurious to him, – partaking at once of suspicion and dislike.

Proceeding silently past them, with feelings the most dejected, he followed Andrews to the library where Lady Ormond was sitting, attended by her faithful companion, Miss Flemming. The instant he was announced, the former uttered an exclamation of joyful surprise, and starting up, sprang forward, with unalterable kindness, to embrace him.

'My dear Ernest! – my poor boy!' she cried, 'how glad I am to see you! There are demons at work trying to blast your character. But now you are here, you must stand up in your own / defence, and retort upon those who seek to injure you by the disgrace they are endeavouring to affix upon your name. Your friend, Sedley, has behaved nobly. I hear you have been attending upon him during his late sufferings. You have done right, my dear boy. Such a friend is not to be neglected; for you have now, I grieve to say, but few of the same sort remaining.'

'Have I *any*, dear Madam?' said the unfortunate young man, forcing a faint smile.

'Yes, Ernest: Miss Flemming tells me, that the Fitzmaurices have never failed to support you whenever they have heard you attacked. Our good clergyman, Mr. Kirby, and his daughter have always warmly defended you. Thus, you see that two of the most respectable families in the neighbourhood do you ample justice;

and as to the others, and the credulous country people, their opinions are not worth regarding, being the result of that ignorant love of the horrible, which the vulgar – high as well as low – invariably exhibit.'

'My dear Lady Ormond,' said de Gray, despondingly, 'unless the real perpetrator of the hideous deed should hereafter be detected, I see not how my innocence can ever be proved. I can bring forward no witnesses in my own behalf; I am supposed to be the last who conversed with poor / Frederic in the hermitage that fatal morning; I was seen to quit it in haste and agitation, after having been heard speaking with extraordinary vehemence and anger; and then observed galloping furiously from the park. None of these things, my kind and dear friend, can be denied; and did they amount to evidence against me sufficiently strong to call for the forfeit of my life, I could only resign myself to the severity of the law, I will not say without lamentation, but certainly – without resistance.'

Terrified by this unexpected statement, Lady Ormond, after a few moments' silence, eagerly said:

'Ernest, you shall not remain in England another day! Sir George Arundel is now perfectly recovered, and is the very man to bring you before a court of justice, and to urge in your accusation the precise circumstances you have been recapitulating. Since such are the facts he would have to relate, and such your utter incapacity to account for or discredit them, who knows what the consequences of a trial might be? I cannot bear to reflect upon it! Oh no – in this country you shall not remain, I am determined. It contains but few you have any reason to regret, and those few would rather a million times / submit to be separated from you, than have you residing here, if not as a culprit upon trial for your life, at least as a suspected felon, shunned and hated by all who encounter you! My poor boy! – to think that it should come to this! – that one whose innocence I would stake my existence upon, should thus be driven from his country by the mere force of untoward appearances! It is most lamentable!'

De Gray now informed her, that previously to his coming it had been his full intention, as soon as he had seen her, to hasten back to the continent.

'I might, it is true,' he added, 'challenge Sir George, and in my own person seek vengeance for his aspersions: but we live not in times when right and wrong can be proved by the ordeal of success in single combat. Were I to wound him as desperately as poor Sedley has been wounded, it would only add to my misery – it would neither clear me in the opinion of others, nor afford any gratification to a spirit of vengeance which I do not feel.'

Miss Flemming, who for some time had been sitting by, weeping plentifully at the hard measure dealt to the favourite of her patroness, now exclaimed: /

'Ah, Mr. de Gray, you are too good! – too placable towards that abominable man! What business is it of his to step forth with all these surmises – to blacken you in all companies – to go about acting the part of an inquisitor, questioning and cross-questioning every servant, labourer, woman, and child around the place? I am sure I wish with all my heart my brother, Sam, had him for only one day on board his ship!'

'Come now, my good Flemming,' interrupted Lady Ormond, 'do not begin talking nonsense either about your brother Sam, or any other brother, sister, cousin, nephew, or niece you have the happiness to possess! The present is no subject that will bear to be mixed up with such inapplicable absurdity. You know, that on common occasions, I let you go on to your heart's content; but I cannot endure it now.'

Poor Miss Flemming, to whom this was the first lecture her patroness had ever addressed, looked exceedingly foolish; but with all humility, closed her lips, without attempting the slightest vindication of herself.

Meanwhile, de Gray, who had scarcely heard a word of what was passing, but had for some / seconds been rapt in thought, now addressing himself again to Lady Ormond, said:

'Since you assure me that at Holme Court I still have friends, it would give me great satisfaction to call there before I leave the neighbourhood. Do you, my dear madam, see any objection to my doing so?'

'I will be very honest with you, my poor boy! Yes, I *do* see objections to it. You cannot go there without meeting many of the peasantry, both men and women; and the truth is, the pains which have been taken to exasperate them against you have been so successful, that there is every reason to fear you might be insulted in the grossest manner. Instead, therefore, of going yourself to Holme Court, let me write a line to Fitzmaurice, inviting him hither. When his visit has been paid, and it is beginning to get dark, you shall have post horses put to your carriage, and set off for the nearest port.'

With an air more of sadness than surprise, after what he had already witnessed, Ernest acquiesced in silence to this proposal, and the note was immediately written and despatched.

Scarcely had it been gone five minutes, when Mr. Roberts was announced. He had of late been re-admitted to the privilege of visiting at / the Hall, which he had enjoyed in the life-time of Sir Everard – a privilege which, as an idle man, he was far from undervaluing or neglecting. On his first entrance, his ruddy countenance exhibited all its accustomed laughing good humour; but when his eyes rested upon Ernest, the change was instantaneous; it was as if a Gorgon's head had suddenly appeared before him;[81] his colour almost forsook him, his mouth contracted, his brows elevated themselves half way up his forehead, and losing all presence of mind, he ejaculated in a tone of horror:

'Lord bless me! who could have thought of meeting *him*!'

'Mr. Roberts,' said Lady Ormond, very angrily, '*you* might have thought of it, had you given yourself time to think at all! You cannot be ignorant that Mr.

de Gray has always been deemed by me an injured man; you cannot be ignorant that I have known and loved him from a child. You must be equally well aware, that not even by the mother and sister of the murdered Frederic has this young man ever been accused or suspected.'

'Say no more, dearest madam,' interrupted Ernest, shocked at an assertion he knew too well poor Ella could so easily have disproved, 'say no more, I implore you! Mr. Roberts does but / partake with others of the strong feeling existing against me, and that he has so openly given expression to it, is owing to his having been taken by surprise. I will now go into the next room to write a letter, and leave him to pay his visit without further molestation.'

Accordingly, Ernest quitted the library, and Mr. Roberts remained to confront the united displeasure, as testified by their looks, of the two ladies. Could he have escaped without further parley, he would instantly and most gladly have made his bow; but he had not courage for so decided a measure; and comfortless as he felt whilst staying, he was too awkward to know how to depart. Lady Ormond saw, and enjoyed his confusion. Good-natured as she usually was, she yet determined not to lend him the assistance of being the first to break through the awful silence. Miss Flemming displayed a caricature imitation of her patroness's example, heaving deep sighs, shaking her head, and pathetically moving her hands up and down upon her lap. The poor man looked first at one lady, and then at the other; the countenances of both continued inflexible; and not knowing what else to do, he at length compelled himself to stammer out:

'I am sure I am very sorry – I would not for the world, ma'am – indeed I had no intention – I / would not, on any account, ma'am, have given you offence. – I was taken unawares, you see –'

Lady Ormond began to soften a little. 'Mr. Roberts,' said she, 'I know you were, and I know that you are a kind-hearted man, who would never have adopted these horrid prejudices against a youth you have so long been acquainted with, had they not been so industriously propagated in all directions, that there is scarcely an individual in the county – perhaps throughout the kingdom – who does not in some degree participate in your feelings.'

'Well, ma'am, what you say is very true. I certainly, of my own accord, should never have thought anything disadvantageous of Mr. de Gray, who, as you observe, has been so long known to me, had the cry of the county been less violent against him. But you can have no idea, ma'am, of the ill-will with which he is every where spoken of! And it was but this very morning, as I passed through Ludlow, that I heard a knot of men swearing that if he ever showed his face in this part of the world again, they would be the first to drag him before a magistrate, and to make a public declaration of every suspicion they entertain against him. Now I know very well, ma'am, that unless some responsible person steps forward / as his prosecutor, the virulence and denunciations of a clamourous crowd are not likely to do him much harm. Still, they show what the spirit of the people is respecting him; and I will confess, left upon my mind an impression I was unable to conceal when I so unexpectedly beheld him standing before me in this room. Should a trial ever come on, and should Mr. de Gray be successful in proving his innocence, nobody will rejoice more than I shall. And now, ladies, hoping for your forgiveness of what has passed, I will wish you good morning, and do myself the pleasure of calling again, when your time and thoughts are less painfully occupied.'

He then departed, and Lady Ormond, always considerate and candid when leisure was afforded her for reflection, observed, as soon as he was gone, that though he had shown himself too prone to be influenced by the insinuations of others, he was exempt from malice, and she really believed would be highly gratified were Ernest's reputation cleared.

Instead of the anticipated visit from Mr. Fitzmaurice, the messenger sent to Holme Court brought back a note from him. It ran thus:

'My dear Lady Ormond,

'You tell me it is the intention of de Gray to / leave the Hall this evening. I beg you will endeavour to prevent his doing so till I have seen him. I may have that to communicate which will render his delay highly expedient. I have no hope of being with you till late, being detained by indispensable business.

'Ever yours, dear Madam,

'Most truly.

'HUGH FITZMAURICE.'

'Holme Court.
Tuesday.'

On reading this note Lady Ormond turned pale. 'Fitzmaurice is a magistrate,' cried she, 'is it possible that any of these wretched creatures have actually been to him to make depositions against Ernest? And if they have, is there no probability of their coming hither to apprehend him?'

'Oh no, no, dear Lady Ormond!' cried Miss Flemming, whose feelings being less interested, for once saw things more rationally than her friend, – 'Were there the smallest danger of that, would Mr. Fitzmaurice wish him to defer his journey? On the contrary, he would be the first to urge his setting out instantly.'

'I believe you are right, Flemming; but this has been a trying morning; and firm and strong / as are my nerves in general, I own they are now a little shaken. But ring the bell for luncheon, my good friend, whilst I go and see what poor Ernest is about.' /

CHAPTER XV.

> The pangs at this sad heart, of deep remorse –
> A true, tho' tardy, sense of justice, and
> A spirit even yet, capable of
> Gratitude and love, have hither brought me.
> Do with me what is fit, I'm come to pay
> The forfeit of my crime.
>
> NOT SO OLD AS IT SEEMS, – A TRAGI COMEDY.[82]

ABOUT half an hour previous to the reception of Lady Ormond's note, Mr. Fitzmaurice, in his capacity of magistrate, had been enquired for by a young man, decently habited, tall, meagre, and incessantly harassed by an ominous short cough, who, with an air of settled melancholy, a sunken chest, a hollow eye, but full of the fiery lustre brought on by fever, and a bright hectic spot on each cheek, betrayed, by every possible symptom, the fearful ravages which confirmed disease was making on his constitution.

Mr. Fitzmaurice, hearing he came upon business, and pitying his blighted youth, encouraged him to sit down. /

'I thank you, Sir,' said the poor man in a feeble, husky tone; 'I thank you for the permission. I have much to tell, and am so short-breathed and weak, that I could hardly get through my task were I to stand.'

Some refreshment was then offered him before he began; but he declined everything except a draught of fresh spring water, begging, when it was brought, that the decanter and glass might be left upon the table.

After these preliminaries, a tale was poured into Mr. Fitzmaurice's ear that rivetted his whole attention. It appeared that the man with whom he was conversing, was not wholly unknown to him, though mental suffering, combined with bodily, had so altered him, that he no longer seemed the same being. The substance of what he related was as follows:

He was the nephew, he said, of Mrs. Nelson, who had lived many years at Ormond Hall as the nurse of Mr. de Gray. His father was one of Sir Everard's tenants, and cultivated a small farm on his estate. 'He bestowed upon me,' continued the young man, 'a better education than lads in my station usually receive;

but he could not afford to do more for me afterwards than bind me apprentice to a carpenter. I was fond of reading, however, and kept up, by that means, what little / knowledge I had acquired. Lady Ormond countenanced and encouraged me, and often lent me useful books. The neighbours all showed me marked good will, and welcomed me cordially to their houses whenever I had leisure to enjoy a little recreation. When the apprenticeship ceased, I resided entirely with my father, who was indulgent and kind. I had as much employment as served to maintain me, and in short, till the death of my mother led the most enviable and happy life.'

Here the speaker paused; his features became agitated – he breathed short, and pressed his hand upon his heart, as if to still its accelerated pulsations. Mr. Fitzmaurice waited patiently till he was able to resume his narrative; and, after a brief interval, he went on to say, that on the decease of his mother, Mrs. Nelson was solicited by his father to give up her own housekeeping, in order to take charge of the domestic management of his farm. She brought with her at first only one daughter – the youngest; but before long, she went up to London to fetch home the eldest.

'Oh, Sir,' exclaimed the tremulous young man, once more breaking through the thread of his narration, 'how shall I find words to describe the violence – the madness of the love I conceived for that beautiful creature! She had not been / under the roof with us a week before I made known to her the ardent passion she had inspired. She rejected my suit, Sir, but not with pride and arrogance, though with great firmness, and a sort of mild dignity, that ought to have put an end to my pleadings. I soon suspected she had some other attachment, and watched her narrowly. My distrust, Sir, was but too well founded! She loved, and, to all appearance, was adored by – by no less a person than Sir Everard's heir – by young Mr. Ormond!

'The jealous rage this discovery filled me with – the burning hatred it awakened in my breast against him – I have not language to express! His views in courting her I believed to be most infamous; and my father, who soon discerned what was passing, entertained the same opinion, and spoke on the subject, more than once, with much force and freedom to my aunt. It was all in vain: Mrs. Nelson was so infatuated in favour of the high-born wooer – so confident in his honour, and in her daughter's discretion, that nothing could convince her of the danger of letting their intercourse go on. I grew more and more alarmed, and not knowing what other step to take, wrote, in a disguised hand, an anonymous letter to Mr. Ormond's mother, informed her of / what was taking place, and put it into the post at Ludlow.

'Meanwhile, Mr. de Gray, who had repeatedly met the unfortunate Ruth and her lover walking about the lanes in our neighbourhood, and had also seen the latter at our house almost every time he came there himself, remonstrated with my aunt on the impropriety of encouraging these perpetual interviews, and warned her to place no reliance on the expectation she cherished of seeing her daughter married to Mr. Ormond; it was a mere delusion, he told her. Frederic might admire Ruth for a season; he might even be honourable enough to take no advantage of the dangerous confidence that was placed in him; but that he would ever become the husband of one who (though so beautiful, so superior in manners and acquirements to all others of her own class,) was still so far beneath him, according to the opinion of the world, was not to be thought of. My father chimed in with Mr. de Gray, confirming and sanctioning every word he uttered; and you may well believe, Sir, that in my heart so did I, although I took no share in the conversation.

'For a day or two, Mrs. Nelson, who was fond of Mr. de Gray, and looked up to him with a certain degree of respect, endeavoured to be / guided by his counsels, prohibited the habitual walks of her daughter, and looked coolly upon Mr. Ormond whenever he called. He saw that something unusual had occurred – this sudden change of conduct, he was sure, could not have been effected without interference from some quarter or other; and, determined to know the truth, he never rested till he had drawn from the weak woman a full avowal of all that had been said during Mr. de Gray's last visit. His indignation was excessive, and vented itself in language that convinced me he would not easily pardon what he termed his companion's mean and unmanly spirit of detraction. I early found that my anticipation was just, for being at that time frequently employed at the Hall, I often had opportunities of seeing the two gentlemen together, when they either met and parted without speaking, or when Mr. Ormond addressed to the other such sneering and sarcastic observations, that it was with evident effort Mr. de Gray commanded his own resentment.

'I approach now, Sir, the tremendous moment of that mysterious act which I sought this interview purposely to disclose. You may wonder at my calmness: it is the effect of fixed despair – of hatred of existence, and of a determination no longer to allow an innocent man to / suffer in my stead. Mr. de Gray, Sir, is that injured man: – the murder of which he is accused was committed by me!'

Notwithstanding the calmness which the self-denounced criminal professed to feel, it was evident as he uttered the last sentence, that every fibre in his frame quivered with agony. Mr. Fitzmaurice was himself shaken by such mixed emotions – joy at the exculpation of Ernest – and commiseration for the unhacknied sinner before him, that he was compelled to have recourse to the water on the table, of which he swallowed a large draught before the sickening horror he experienced enabled him to speak.

'Unhappy man!' he then said, 'was it mere jealousy that prompted the terrible deed? or had you any additional cause of hostility against your victim?'

'I *had*, Sir! A cause, which even yet, I cannot reflect upon without sensations of renewed – of still unsatisfied revenge and abhorrence! Ruth – the chaste, the beautiful, the guileless and beloved Ruth, had fallen a prey to the villain's seductive arts! My father made the discovery, by overhearing some part of a conversation carried on in the arbour of our garden, between her and her betrayer. He darted forward and suddenly / confronted them, reproached Mr. Ormond to his face for the infamy he had brought upon the miserable girl and her whole family, and called down upon his head the bitterest maledictions. My aunt, hearing the loud and furious accents of his voice, rushed from the house in alarm to ascertain the cause. Scarcely crediting what she was told, yet afraid to express her doubts, she could only interpose her own person between Mr. Ormond and her exasperated brother, who increasing in violence every minute, was with difficulty withheld from yielding to the impulse that tempted him to manifest his sense of injury by blows! Happily for herself, the disgraced Ruth had fallen into a state of complete insensibility, from which she was only recovered to give way to the most frightful desperation, and at intervals, to suffer from convulsive fits so violent, it was scarcely possible to retain her upon her seat. Mr. Ormond, I was assured by my weeping aunt, had shewn the strongest remorse, and the utmost tenderness and compassion for her sufferings. I hope it was so; fiend, indeed must he have been could he have contemplated unmoved the havoc he had occasioned. But however that may have been, when I came home, and heard from my father the particulars I have been relating, I shudder at the remembrance of / the frenzied, the deadly craving for revenge they awakened in my breast. My exasperated father was scarcely less transported by passion than myself; in short, we strengthened each other in our vindictive feelings, and continued nearly through the night, talking over the several methods that occurred to us of bringing our enemy to punishment. You may imagine, then, sir, the disposition of mind I was in, on repairing the next morning by appointment to Ormond Hall. Mr. de Gray had engaged me to put up some book-shelves for him, and though but ill able to execute the undertaking with my accustomed exactness, I had accomplished it, and was just leaving the room when my eye rested upon an unsheathed dagger lying amongst a variety of other curiosities on the table. I had seen it before, on the night of the ball given by Sir Everard to the servants; I had heard his nephew observe, as he attentively surveyed it, that the death it would infallibly inflict by a single blow, would at least be an easy one.

'"The experiment shall be tried!" murmured I, with ferocious determination, "I have no wish to condemn thee to a prolonged agony. Thy life is doomed, but it shall be taken without butchery." Thus resolved, I seized the dagger, sheathed it, and deposited it within the bosom of my coat. / After that, I descended without meeting any one, and walked across the park towards our farm.

As I proceeded, deeply meditating upon the revengeful design I had formed, I saw Mr. Ormond at some distance rapidly advancing along the very path I was pursuing. I wanted boldness to assault him in open day, and slunk behind a clump of trees till he should have passed; but instead of walking on in the direction of the Hall, he turned into the hermitage. A few seconds after I likewise beheld Mr. de Gray approaching, though from an opposite quarter. I had no reason to shun him; yet such was my consciousness of the savage thoughts engrossing my mind, that I feared lest some indication of them might be perceptible in my face, and therefore wished to avoid his scrutiny. Accordingly, I waited to observe which way he meant to go, before I issued forth from concealment. He, also, I soon saw, entered the hermitage, and I was on the point of quitting my retreat and pursuing my way to the farm, when after two or three loud speeches uttered alternately by both, I was rooted to the spot on hearing Mr. de Gray exclaim: – "Frederic, this accusation is a mere pretence; you know me too well to believe I could be capable of the meanness of writing anonymous letters; but the fact is, you want by an attack / which you know must annoy me, to silence me on a subject much nearer your own heart; yet, why do I say *heart?* you can have none, or it must be of the blackest dye, to have permitted you to wrong the unfortunate Ruth in so irreparable a manner!"

'"I congratulate you, sir" answered Mr. Ormond, in a tone of mockery, "on the despatch with which your passion for prying into affairs that do not concern you, is sure to be rewarded. Have you been laudably employed this morning in listening to the conversation that has been passing at the farm? I should think that must have been the case, since I only returned from thence five minutes ago, and had not the pleasure of seeing you whilst there."

'"What possible purpose," resumed Mr. de Gray, extremely irritated, "can you expect to answer by all this insolent ribaldry. Will it make less the amount of your guilt? Will it silence the complaints of Ruth's family? Will it pacify the upbraiding of your own conscience, if you have one?"

'"Perhaps not," interrupted the other; "but I will tell you, my good fellow, what this flippancy of mine really may effect; it may, when made known to my uncle, in addition to the naughtiness I have perpetrated at the farm, induce / him to take you into greater favour than ever, to contrast your conduct with mine, and if he cannot give you his title, at least to bestow upon you a handsome share of his unentailed property. Now what is the use of watching me so indefatigably if you keep all your discoveries to yourself? Communicate them to Sir Everard and the ladies, and my life for it, you come into a large slice of my aunt's fortune as well as her husband's."

'"Frederic," cried Mr. de Gray, exasperated beyond all measure, "I could not have believed you to have been so vile a miscreant! To hear you alluding with such callous derision to the misery you have occasioned at the farm, is worse even than to hear you attempt to defend it. I care nothing for the paltry insinuations you have thrown out against me; you put no confidence in them, or if you do, your opinion is of no value to me now. All I wish is —"

'"Come, come, sir," interrupted Mr. Ormond, "enough of all this! Remember that you are the last man to whom I am responsible, and the very last from whom I am inclined to endure foul language, or to listen to a sermon. Be so good, therefore, as to leave me."

'Before this could be answered, they were joined by Miss Ormond, who took some pains to / induce Mr. de Gray to accompany her on a walk, being, I am well convinced, anxious to terminate a conference which she could not but perceive was of no amicable nature. She was unsuccessful, and left the place alone though with the hope that Mr. de Gray would soon follow her. When she was gone, her brother put the finishing stroke to his previous insulting arrogance, by contemptuously declaring his conviction that Mr. de Gray was seeking, in a clandestine manner, to ingratiate himself in his sister's favour. Every other charge had been borne without shrinking, but this last was more than human nature, could tolerate. It drove Mr. de Gray with looks almost frantic, from the hermitage; and in a shorter space of time than I could have supposed possible, he had repaired to the house, had mounted his horse, and was seen again, impetuously riding towards one of the park gates. Mr. Ormond had saluted his exit from the little building, by a scornful laugh; after which all was profoundly quiet. I might then have quitted my place of concealment; but one of the women employed in sweeping the pleasure-grounds was at work very near me; and I had no wish she should know I had been performing the part of an eaves-dropper. Having waited till she had removed to some distance, I stole forth, more inveterate / against Mr. Ormond than ever, in consequence of the infamous share he had so lately borne in the dialogue I had overheard. A diabolical impulse tempted me, before I departed, to cast one glance into the interior of the hermitage, the entrance to which remained half open. To my inexpressible surprise, considering what must have been the excited state of his mind but a few minutes previously, Mr. Ormond I saw had dropped into a calm slumber. I softly approached him....Oh, sir, – oh, Mr. Fitzmaurice, spare me the dreadful task of giving a detail of the sanguinary act that followed! It was an act, which when committed, I could not for an instant bear to contemplate. With its perpetration, all my ferocity subsided, and like another Cain, I felt as if every man who beheld me must read the story of my transgression written upon my burning brow.[83] I threw from me the murderous weapon, which by a single blow had so unerringly satiated my revenge, and fled. Not a human being met me by the way; it was an hour when most of the labourers were dispersed at their several places of employment, and the servants at Sir Everard's were at dinner. The park was, therefore, deserted, and I reached our farm without encountering the slightest observation. But on throwing open the door, leading into a kind of / hall usually occupied by the family, I was struck with consternation at the sight of Mr. de Gray, conversing earnestly with my father. I would have retreated; they had seen me, however, and probably from my looks prognosticating something extraordinary, anxiously called me back. I refused to return, till my father pursued me, and seizing my arm drew me forward, demanding to know in heaven's name, what was the matter? Grown desperate, I then exclaimed: – "I am a man of blood! – I am an assassin! – You should fly me, for I am the outcast of earth and heaven!" Saying this, I staggered towards a chair, and sinking into it, buried my face in my hands and groaned aloud.

'"Philip, Philip!" cried my poor agitated father, "what are you saying? Of whose blood do you speak? Tell me the meaning of this wild language!"

'"It can have no meaning," cried Mr. de Gray, "do not alarm yourself, Mr. Nelson; – Philip is incapable of the crime of which he accuses himself! Something has shaken and disturbed him, and when he recovers his composure, he will tell us what it was."

'"Is this true, my son? Is it indeed as Mr. de Gray supposes?"

'"Oh father! why do you thus urge me? / Why do you compel me to tell you what will nearly kill you when you hear it? I have stabbed our enemy to the heart! He that injured us, can never injure us more!" My father clenched his hands, and cast up his eyes with looks of consternation and despair; whilst Mr. de Gray, beginning to comprehend the purport of my words, grasping my arm, in an accent of horror, cried: –

'"I adjure you, Philip, to speak out! What enemy – wretched man! what enemy do you mean?"

'"I mean Frederic Ormond! the destroyer of poor Ruth; I have murdered him! he now lies a corpse in the Hermitage."

'A loud and piercing shriek from the landing-place of the stairs above us, at that moment reached our ears, and caused me to pause, and look around, trembling and aghast. Immediately after, my aunt stood before us. Never shall I forget the expression of her countenance. She had been up the whole night, watching over her miserable daughter; her dress was disordered, her eyes swollen, her complexion pale as death, in addition to which, the look of woe impressed upon her face, was such as to be almost torturing to behold. She came up to me, at first with sternness and hatred in her aspect; but gradually / softened, and ended by throwing herself upon my neck, and weeping piteously, saying in broken accents: "O what hast thou done, unhappy boy! Thou hast taken a life for which thou must forfeit thy own! We shall lose thee; – my Ruth will die of hopeless sorrow – and thou – O heaven! – thou wilt perish by the sentence of the law!"

'"What talk you of the law, and of his perishing?" cried my father, as if awakening from a trance, "has he done any thing more than justice may acquit him for? He has taken our vengeance into his own hands, vengeance for such deep, deep wrongs as can never be repaired; if, in so doing, he has been guilty, *I* am the person to suffer! I confirmed him in his revengeful feelings, I almost instigated him to punish, at any risk, the heartless betrayer of my brother's daughter. If the law condemns the act, let it condemn us both."

'"Mr. Nelson, hear me," said Mr. de Gray, much affected at my aunt's profound distress, as well as by the self-sacrifice my father's paternal feelings led him to determine upon. "I grieve to witness the tribulation you are all undergoing; I grieve also, let me add, at the catastrophe of Sir Everard's nephew, and I am truly concerned to have been present at the time, when the perpetrator of the deed, made an avowal of his crime. But for / your sake, Mr. Nelson – for that of my unfortunate nurse – for that, even, of Philip himself, who, if time is granted him, may live to repent, I solemnly promise never to reveal the name of the culprit, never to make known one syllable of what I have this day heard. Had Philip been less agitated, less unguarded, I need not have become acquainted with the appalling secret; but, though he has betrayed himself, I will take no advantage of his imprudence. Nothing can now restore his victim to life, and I cannot hold myself bound to denounce to no purpose, an occurrence I hardly blame, more than I pity. Should there ever be a false accusation brought against any other person, I then shall be obliged to acknowledge the truth; but except on such an occasion, my inviolable secrecy may be relied upon. And now tell me," added he, observing that my father and aunt were preparing to overwhelm him with thanks and benedictions he was desirous to avoid, "have any of you seen Mr. Kirby this morning?"

'"I have, sir," said my father. "I met him whilst he was out walking, and to own the truth, would gladly have avoided him; but he was too near me for that, and as he immediately spoke, I was forced to stop."

'"Well, what passed? Did he hear from you any thing relating to Ruth?" /

'"He did, indeed sir; my countenance betrayed to him that all was not as it should be; he fancied there was illness amongst us, and with his usual kindness, inquired anxiously after every individual of the family. When he named the ill-fated Ruth, he saw such confusion in my looks, that he began to suspect something worse than a common indisposition, and expressed so much interest for us, and questioned me so closely, that I could not withstand his benevolent urgency."

'Here he was impatiently interrupted by my aunt, who, in great alarm, cried out; "Oh, brother! You surely did not communicate to him my child's disgrace!"

'"My dear nurse," said Mr. de Gray, soothingly, "supposing he *did*, to whom could he have confided the afflicting truth with more security of receiving good counsel, and unfeigned commiseration?"

'"But what security have we that he will not betray us?"

'"Do not call it *betraying* to consult with a friend of long standing, and whom he knows to be warmly attached to you, upon the best means of hushing up the disastrous affair, and of withdrawing Ruth from the observations of the neighbourhood. It was with this intention that, sending / his daughter forward, after having met me returning with her from the hall to his house, he revealed to me the sad particulars he had gleaned from Mr. Nelson, and asked whether it was not my opinion as well as his own, that Ruth should be immediately sent from home? Shocked as I was by what he had told me, I recovered sufficient composure to say, I perfectly agreed with him. We then parted, he went back to the parsonage, and I soon afterwards, repaired to the hermitage to pour forth – I cannot deny – some portion of my just indignation upon Frederic Ormond."

'But let me,' concluded young Nelson, 'cut short what remains to be told of this wretched history. When Mr. de Gray quitted us, my father exhorted me to return to London without delay; there was no knowing, he said, what poor Ruth, might, in a moment of distraction, should she learn the death of Mr. Ormond, be driven to say, especially if her mother were imprudent enough (which was not wholly impossible) to throw out any hint of my having given the fatal wound. I saw the reasonableness of this representation, yet, was unwilling, on many accounts, to go. However, my father eventually prevailed, and I departed, leaving him to account for my sudden disappearance by telling the neighbours, / that I had been sent for to assist a relation, who was a builder, in completing a heavy piece of carpenter's work, which he had contracted to get finished by a given time. There was some truth in this statement, the artificer in question having repeatedly urged me to become one of his workmen, and renewed the application very recently. Much to my father's relief, no suspicion whatever was excited by my removal. The mysterious affair of the murder, continued to be as impenetrable as ever; a thousand wild conjectures were afloat, but not one that approached the reality. Meanwhile, the unhappy Ruth, through the indiscretion of a female servant, became acquainted with the frightful end of her betrayer. Already disordered both in mind and body – feverish, sleepless, and during several preceding days, resolute to reject almost entirely every species of nourishment, the tidings were too much for her; her intellects were overthrown, and availing herself of a moment when she was left unguarded, she put a period to her existence. Shortly after this awful termination of the tragedy in which I had borne so prominent a part, my father wrote me word that as soon as my aunt was sufficiently recovered from the shock (which had thrown her on a sick bed) of her daughter's decease, it was his intention to give up his farm, and establish / himself with her and her surviving girl, Anne, in the neighbourhood of London, where, perhaps, he might obtain employment under some agriculturist. His accustomed residence had become hateful to him, and yet more so to my broken-hearted aunt. Their scheme therefore was put in execution with as few unnecessary delays as possible; but, sir, change of place did as little towards contributing to their peace of mind, as it had done towards the recovery of mine. My father perpetually accused himself of having incited me to take Mr. Ormond's life, my aunt was full of self-reproach for having permitted, nay encouraged the dangerous intercourse between Ruth and her treacherous lover; and I, with the consciousness of blood-guiltiness weighing heavy on my soul, knew not one moment's real tranquillity. Had it not been for the apprehension of adding to my poor father's misery, I should long ago, have surrendered myself to justice. That father, Mr. Fitzmaurice, now lies in his grave; I saw his remains consigned to their last resting-place, and solemnly vowed, as I stood, during the funeral service, beside his coffin, to expiate my guilt, as far as such an act *could* expiate it, by a voluntary immolation of myself to the laws of my country. Since I reached this neighbourhood, I have learnt with what inveterate / malignity Sir George Arundel has been blackening the character of Mr. de Gray, and endeavouring to affix upon him the execrable charge of having murdered the nephew of his benefactor, with the hope of succeeding to his property. Such intelligence, of course, could only give additional strength to my determination of avowing myself the real criminal. Receive therefore, sir, my deposition, and act upon it, as the laws may require.'

It was not without sorrow that Mr. Fitzmaurice found himself under the necessity of complying with the unfortunate young man's wishes. Proper measures were taken to give authenticity to his confession; a warrant was made out for his apprehension, and that very day he submitted, with the most unaffected resignation, to be conveyed to the nearest prison, there to await his trial at the approaching assizes. /

CHAPTER XVI.

What tho' the offer's clogg'd
With a condition that somewhat mars
Its worth, since made by one who to it ties
Himself? Yet, would'st not thou be happier
Good, simple soul, to change a solitary
Home, a straightened income in thy wane of
Life, for ease and affluence?

NOT SO OLD AS IT SEEMS, – A TRAGI-COMEDY.[84]

IT was about four and twenty hours after the momentous avowal just recorded, that a chaise, and four post horses were seen, dashing furiously up the drive leading to the front entrance of Mrs. Ormond's house in Wiltshire. It was a bright, sunny evening early in May; Ella was reading at an open window in the drawing-room; her mother sat at work not far distant, and Sir George Arundel, who had dined with them, and was the only guest they had had, was walking up and down the apartment, with what has long been voted so unpardonably detestable, creaking shoes; now and then stopping to speak to, or listen to Mrs. / Ormond, and at intervals endeavouring (though with but momentary success,) to engage the attention of her daughter. The sound of the chaise, its rapid advance, and the unusual hour of its coming, awoke in her far more interest than any thing the baronet could suggest, and she waited impatiently till a servant should inform them who the vehicle had brought.

'I should not be much surprised,' said Sir George in a low voice to Mrs. Ormond, 'if this were a messenger bringing intelligence that Ernest de Gray has been committed and taken from Ormond Hall, to the county jail. I have had information given me, that it was his design on leaving London, to pay Lady Ormond a visit, and I think the number of those, who in that neighbourhood, believed in his guilt, was quite sufficient to lead to his being taken into custody.'

Mrs. Ormond perceiving Ella's eye directed towards her, affected not to hear the Baronet very distinctly, and made no answer to what he said. Presently an unwonted sort of bustle in the house, and an indistinct murmur of voices, reached their ears, and before they could ring the bell to ask what was the matter, the drawing-room door flew open, and Ernest de Gray himself appeared, and / with glowing cheeks and radiant looks, advanced hastily towards the lady of the house.

Struck dumb at sight of so unexpected an apparition, the work she had been employed in, dropt from her hand, and she could only gaze at him with expanded eyes, and varying complexion; whilst Sir George, actually staggering from excess of amazement, caught hold of the back of the nearest chair, and stood open-mouthed, yet silent, staring as though a rattle-snake had fascinated him, at the daring intruder. Ella started from her seat, as he entered, with a half-suppressed cry of pleasure; for instant conviction that he was come to proclaim his innocence, took possession of her mind on perceiving him, and, as with out-stretched hand she greeted him, every feature, glowed with pure and unalloyed delight.

'This is like yourself, dear Ella,' cried de Gray, seizing joyfully the proferred hand. 'You wait not for legal confirmation of my guiltlessness; the mere fact of being here, after all the atrocities of which I have been accused, has cleared me at once in your generous mind. Others there are, however,' added he, looking significantly at the Baronet, 'who may require stronger proof that I am neither a fraudulent legacy hunter, nor a / murderer. For such persons,' he continued, producing a large sheet of folded paper, evidently engrossed in a law-hand, 'for such persons, I have been provided with a document, by which it is thought that even the most reluctant to credit my justification, cannot fail to be convinced. Read it, Sir George; it is an attested copy of the voluntary confession made by the self-condemned and pitiable culprit, whose name is affixed to it, in the presence of Mr. Fitzmaurice and another magistrate. It will account for my having hitherto borne so passively the vile and wicked calumnies, that have been with such industry circulated respecting me.' Then, turning to Mrs. Ormond, de Gray entreated her and Ella, to accompany him into an adjoining room, whilst Sir George was engaged in perusing the important paper; 'I shall there,' he added, 'be enabled, without disturbing his attention, to give you an abridged account of its interesting contents. I am sure you must both feel anxious – painfully anxious, to learn some of the particulars connected with the calamitous transaction of last August. It is a subject I grieve to revive; but circumstances render my doing so indispensable: and after this afflicting detail has once been given, no future allusion to it shall ever escape me.'

Having thus prepared them, he proceeded as / briefly as was consistent with clearness, to recapitulate the narrative Philip Nelson had communicated to Mr. Fitzmaurice. The effect produced by the anonymous letter the former acknowledged having addressed to Mrs. Ormond respecting the conduct of her son in regard to the hapless Ruth, struck that lady forcibly. She had always regretted the angry reproaches it had drawn from her, and now lamented still more deeply, the unmerited attack it had brought upon de Gray as Frederic's supposed accuser, and the quarrel it had occasioned. To Ella the incident she was most impatient to hear explained, related to the mystery of her having found Ernest's dagger in the hermitage, moist with blood. Though neither doubt nor suspicion now found place in her mind; yet, the singularity of the fact excited sufficient curiosity to render her desirous of having it satisfied. De Gray made the truth fully known to her; and, she then communicated to him the precaution she had taken (before her return from the hermitage to the house) of casting the destructive weapon into the water.

'To that considerate measure,' cried he, 'I perhaps am indebted for not having been arrested as soon as I returned to England, and subjected to a trial which might have proved immediately fatal to me. When in addition to the accumulated / circumstantial evidence, which it was supposed might be brought against me, this occurrence of a dagger known to be mine, covered with blood, and found at such a critical moment in the hermitage, must have decided my fate.'

'But would it not have been self-murder,' said Ella, 'to have persisted to the last in concealing the name of the real criminal?'

'I am not casuist enough to determine,' answered de Gray; 'I only know, that I should have been guilty of perjury had I betrayed Philip Nelson, after the solemn promise I had given him, never to reveal his secret.'

'Thank heaven,' resumed Ella, clasping her hands, and looking upwards, 'thank heaven you have been spared so dreadful a trial! Mamma,' continued she, seeing her mother looking at her with some surprise, in consequence of being wholly unprepared for these demonstrations of interest in behalf of de Gray, 'mamma, it is time you should read my heart; and even in the presence of Ernest, I will not scruple to tell you, that what you mistook, during my illness and slow recovery, for indifference or averseness, was in fact too intense a degree of anxiety respecting him. Hovering between the fear, nay, almost the belief of his being guilty, and the faint hope of his proving blameless, I knew not how to / regulate my behaviour towards him so as to ward off mistrust from others, neither could I well bear, so soon after the calamity we had experienced, the sight of one whose presence would so forcibly have recalled to my mind the image of his lost companion. But, my dear mother,' added she, a lively blush tinging her pale cheek, 'I have long been most affectionately attached to this much-wronged friend, and it has required no small degree of self-command to conceal it from you.'

Whilst Ernest gratefully pressed to his lips the hand of the ingenuous girl, her mother, forcing a smile, said:

'But why, my dear Ella, exert any self-command about the matter? Why seek to conceal from me your real feelings at all?'

'Because, had I owned my regard, at the time you were pleading for him, I must also, as a reason for refusing to admit him, have confessed the suspicions, reluctantly as I entertained them, which his conduct had given rise to.'

Mrs. Ormond now saw that nothing could be done: Sir George Arundel must be given up, and Ernest de Gray accepted. Personally, she certainly preferred the latter; but when fortune, high connexion, and the advantage – paltry as it was – of being a Baronet's lady, were taken into / consideration, she could not but feel mortified at the loss to her daughter of distinctions she was herself weak enough to value so much beyond their worth. However, as it was always her endeavour to 'assume a virtue if she had it not,'[85] she determined to avoid betraying her vexation; to put the best face upon the matter, rather than incur the risk, by seeking to prevent the marriage, of coming to an open breach with her favourite child, and to show herself as cordially disposed towards Ernest as it was in her power to make her countenance appear.

The trio still remained together, still continued pouring enquiries upon de Gray, and commenting upon his answers; and though it was now nearly dark, neither remembered to call for lights, nor bestowed a thought upon the gentleman in the next room. Such at least was the case with respect to Ella and Ernest. Mrs. Ormond's memory, doubtless, was not so remiss; but it was irksome to her to have any immediate communication with him, and always glad to put off the evil day, she deliberately resolved to forget his vicinity, as long as circumstances would allow. At last a servant entered, bringing back to Ernest the paper he had left with Sir George, and delivering to his mistress a message from the Baronet, purporting that an appointment at home / compelled him to depart rather hastily, as he found he had already outstaid his time, and had not a moment to spare for taking leave.

'Is he gone, then?' said Ella.

'Yes, ma'am; he only gave me the packet and message after he had mounted his horse, and then rode off.'

'It is singular,' cried Ernest, when the servant retired, his colour rising, 'that he should go without expressing any opinion of the document he had been perusing.'

'You unconscionable person!' said Ella, half laughing. 'How could he have expressed his opinion more intelligibly than by riding away in a huff? Had he been happy enough to detect any flaw in the testimony you had put into his hands, can you suppose he would not have been the readiest of the ready to seek an interview with us before he left the house?'

'True, dearest Ella, but can you blame me for wishing that he had, when returning the paper, given me some assurance of his intention to contradict, as publicly as he had disseminated, the assertion of my guilt?'

'No, no, I do not blame you,' resumed Ella, in the same playful humour; 'but let it be a comfort to you to know, that if he does *not* do you the justice you require, I myself will prosecute / him for defamation; and when the damages are paid, you shall have leave to light as large a bonfire before his house as they will amount to. Now is not this a very equitable decision? and a great deal better than working yourself up into an honourable fury, and insisting upon making the baffled detractor fight a second duel?'

'A great deal better, Ella. Assure yourself, however, that it never was my intention to challenge him. Poor Sedley has done as much for me in that way as can contribute to redeem my reputation; and I must say, that I think it will be far more firmly established by legal evidence, than by all the duels that could be fought.'

It was fortunate that neither the Ormonds, nor in fact, Ernest himself, expected much from the Baronet's candour, generosity, or that 'love of justice,' of which he had once boasted himself susceptible. The only reparation he ever made for the aspersions he had uttered, was that of abstaining, for the rest of his life, from visiting any of the family.

During the interval that elapsed between the apprehension and the trial of Philip Nelson, his consumptive symptoms increased upon him so fast, that he died in prison. As his guilt could not have been disproved, and the law must have sentenced him to a public execution, those who / took an interest in him could not but rejoice that he was spared the shame of such an end. His worthy rector, Mr. Kirby, visited him continually, and described him as being in a state of mind the most sincerely penitent, humble, and submissive. The bereaved mother of the once beautiful Ruth, now deprived also of a nephew she had dearly loved, and of her brother, survived not long the destruction of her family. She left her surviving daughter to the care of her only remaining relation, a farmer's wife in Wales, and breathed her last a few months after the decease of young Nelson.

At the expiration of a twelvemonth from the time of Frederic Ormond's tragical end, Ella and de Gray proceeded from Ormond Hall to the parish church, and were united by Mr. Kirby in the presence of a numerous assemblage of as cordial and zealous friends as ever young people were blessed with. At the head of these stood Lady Ormond, with nothing, as she truly averred, to regret, but that Sir Everard had not lived to witness so auspicious a day. Miss Flemming was, of course, present, and when the ceremony was over, and the party returned to the Hall, would have dwelt with delight on the supposed resemblance she had all at once discovered between half a dozen of her own nephews and nieces and the handsome bride and bridegroom. / But luckily for the company, and even for herself – since Mr. Fitzmaurice would have been sure to arrest the flow of her eloquence – Mr. Roberts took possession of her, and claimed her whole attention whilst relating the success of his last fishing day, and describing the superior quality of his new artificial flies. Wearied, but patient, she suffered herself to be monopolized, partly as a proof that both she and Lady Ormond had forgiven what had passed the day he unexpectedly met Mr. de Gray at the Hall; and partly from a constitutional good nature, that rendered her incapable of hurting the feelings of another by any appearance of slight, or any voluntary exhibition of annoyance.

Such was her forbearance, and such the effect of a disposition of so much mildness and suavity upon the Squire, that after taking a few days to ponder on the subject, and to work himself up to a suitable pitch of courage for undertaking so rash a measure, he actually wrote a proposal to her in due form, laying himself, his fortune – in short, all his worldly possessions, including, of course, dogs, horses, fishing-tackle, and sporting apparatus of every description – at her feet.

The offer, (whether or not the first of its kind, she best knew,) perplexed her extremely. She dearly loved Lady Ormond; yet there was much / to tempt a spinster with a narrow income, in the prospect of becoming mistress of an affluent establishment, and wife to a man who, though tedious, was otherwise unexceptionable, as far as good conduct, good humour, and, she believed, good principles went. Besides it was something to wipe off the disgrace of Old Maid-ism; and many a Miss Flemming, although happy in that state, when no chance appears of altering it, is but too ready when the long despaired of power of doing so is put into her hands, to exchange it for that of a marriage far more unpromising than the one now in question. At all events, the worthy soul could come to no decision without consulting her honoured patroness. Accordingly, with a tear in her eye, a simper upon her lips, and a flush upon her cheeks, she repaired to the library, and holding forth the important missive, said with a nervous tremour, that gave to her voice almost the tone of a criminal:

'Will you, dear madam, if you are not too busy, just run your eye over this letter? It has put me into such a flutter! I am sure, I should sooner have expected anything in the world than an application of this kind.'

'Why, my good Flemming,' cried Lady Ormond, half laughing, and holding the letter in one hand, whilst stirring the fire (it was a wet, / chilly day in September) with the other, 'one would almost think, by the agitation you are in, that it was a declaration of love.'

Poor Miss Flemming blushed scarlet, but turning aside her head, unable to repress an involuntary giggle, she made no answer, leaving her kind hostess to peruse the letter, and most anxious to hear her comments.

An unconscious smile stole over her Ladyship's features as she proceeded, but having reached the bottom of the page, and seen there the writer's signature at full length, she paused a moment, and then said:

'Well, my dear Flemming, I suppose you wish to hear my opinion of this proposal? In the first place, I think it a very handsome one. It breathes a spirit of unquestionable regard and manly sincerity; and with such a man, you might be reasonably happy. But before you answer him, let me warn you, my good friend, both for his sake and your own, not to contract such an engagement from the apprehension of ever finding yourself in reduced circumstances. Whilst I live, my heart and my house will always be open to you; and at my death, you will find yourself competently provided for. I wish not to tie you down, however, to be my constant companion. Whether you stay with me or not, you shall from / this moment be made perfectly independent; and all I regret is, that I did not make the arrangement sooner. Do not consider what I now say as a bribe to you to refuse

Mr. Roberts. On the contrary, I should be happy to see you bestow your hand upon him, could I be persuaded that you accepted him from no mere motive of pecuniary prudence. Marry him or not as you please. But whatever your determination may be, you shall be made, exclusive of what he may do for you, entirely free from controul, and put in assured possession of such an income as would make you easy for life, even were you living solely at your own expense.'

This speech which was uttered by Lady Ormond whilst still holding the poker, unknown to herself, and flourishing it vigorously about in the eagerness of discourse, had the effect of touching the affectionate heart of Miss Flemming so deeply as to draw a shower of unfeignedly grateful tears from her eyes. The conclusion of the business was, that her liberal-minded hostess sent her to her own room to compose herself; and when there, the first thing, after drying her eyes, that she did, was to write the humblest acknowledgments for his good opinion to her unexpected suitor, with a rejection worded so gently, that the fear of offending him was perceptible in every sentence. /

Much relieved by having accomplished this task, she yet, from motives of delicacy, said nothing to Lady Ormond till questioned, dreading to have it thought that she was in any hurry to induce her to fulfil the promised dispositions in her favour of which she had spoken. The matter being once clearly understood, her Ladyship without delay forwarded directions to her agent to take the necessary measures for immediately transferring to Miss Flemming the property she meant to secure to her. Had she chosen it, this transfer would have put her in actual possession of a sufficient revenue to enable her to set up her tent wherever she pleased. But her honest attachment forbade the admission of any such wish. The sense of independence made no other difference in her conduct and feelings, than that of increasing, if possible, her deference and humility. To love her benefactress better, was scarcely in her power. The augmented regard was all on Lady Ormond's side, who experienced in its full extent how true it is, that those we serve are precisely the persons whom those very services teach us to hold dearer than we ever did before.

For some time after his marriage, Ernest de Gray knew but one draw-back to his perfect felicity. Happy the man of whom that can be said! He felt that it would be a subject of severe regret / and mortification to his generous friend and defender Sedley. That *he* for whom that youth had so fearlessly ventured his life – whom he had, though untrusted, confided in as an innocent man, when every voice was raised in his accusation – that *he* should have stepped in between him and the woman he loved, could not but be a most trying occurrence. All that Ernest could do to break the shock, was to write to him the day before the ceremony, not as if to qualify the act, or to offer any vindication of himself for having determined upon it, but simply to inform him, earlier than he would learn it from the public papers, that such a match was about to take place. He added nothing further, called for no congratulations, (which to have done would, in fact, have been insulting) but wound up with warm and cordial thanks for the noble reliance he had placed in him, and hearty wishes for his entire restoration to health.

No answer was received to this unwelcome letter, nor any tidings heard to set de Gray's mind at ease, till he learnt by accident, and with great joy, of the revival of Sedley's anxiety to travel, and of his departure to visit the East, with an accomplished and experienced friend, who had already traversed several of the regions in that part of the globe. /

Ella and de Gray, though not constant residents at Ormond Hall, spent much of their time there, to the infinite delight of its warm-hearted mistress. They ever were welcome guests, also, at Holme Court; and though occasionally they resorted to London during the gay season of the year, they eventually rented a beautiful place at no great distance either from the Hall or from the Fitzmaurices, and made it their head-quarters as long as Lady Ormond lived.

Mrs. Ormond's was not a happy old age. Her children, indeed, behaved affectionately and most attentively to her. But the marriage of Ella had disappointed her most ambitious views, and soured her temper. She was rich, but solitary, since, with an extensive acquaintance, many of whom were individuals full of genius and eminently agreeable, she had not one select and real friend. She had lived *in* the world and *for* the world; and her reward was, that when her spirits and her strength began to fail, she was neglected; and being unable to bear the fatigue of giving splendid parties, was hardly known to be still in existence.

Her daughters, at length, became her only visitors; yet even their presence and unwearied kindness could not make her forget her son – her harshly treated son – nor erase from her mind the / fear that it was owing to her ill-timed severity, during his boyhood, she had failed to gain his confidence and to acquire sufficient influence over him to counteract the evil propensities which led to his contracting such vicious habits, and becoming so deplorably unprincipled. She never mentioned him; but he was seldom absent from her thoughts; and her unnatural conduct, bringing its own punishment, awakened in her the keenest self-reproach, and, let it be hoped, the most sincere and effectual repentance.

THE END

LONDON:
SCHULZE AND CO., 13, POLAND STREET.

ENDNOTES

Volume I

1. *O night ... Michael Drayton*: SHB divides her narrative into chapters, each headed by a well-chosen epigraph. Her half-sister Frances Burney had given her well-meaning advice on how to find appropriate texts. 'If you have not heard of or tried the plan I will tell you a short cut to getting mottos – Beg – Borrow – or the other thing Dr Johnsons Dictionary –' (*JL*, vol. 12, p. 962), to which SHB responded: 'dear Johnny – His Dictionary, – Shakespear's Plays – & my own old Common-Place books, give me the fairest chance of hitting upon *apropos* bits' (*Letters*, p. 426).

   The first epigraph is taken from a poem by Elizabethan poet Michael Drayton (1563–1631) added to the sonnet sequence that first appeared in 1594 as *Ideas Mirrour*, published under the shortened title *Idea* in subsequent editions; the major revisions (of 1599, 1600, 1602, 1605, 1619) reflect the growth and development of the poet's style and techniques. This poem was the only new sonnet added to the 1602 edition as 'Sonnet 41'; in later revisions its position was changed to thirty-seventh. The lines (in the last revised edition of 1619) differ somewhat from those quoted by Burney,

   O, Thou that art so courteous else to all!
   Why should'st thou, Night, abuse me onely thus,
   That ev'ry Creature to his kind do'st call,
   And yet 'tis thou do'st onely sever us?

   Charles Burney owned a copy of Drayton's works (*Catalogue*, p. 27).

2. *Cheltenham Theatre*: A temporary playhouse in Cheltenham, associated with the famous actor John Kemble (1757–1823) and his sister Sarah Siddons (1755–1831), was replaced in 1805 by 'an exceedingly neat and commodious little Theatre' built by J. Watson in which 'nearly all the distinguished actors' of the day appeared. It was destroyed by fire in 1839, the year this work was published (H. Davies, *The Stranger's Guide through Cheltenham*, 3rd edn (Cheltenham: H. Davies, [1842]), p. 121).

   For the opening setting, SHB chooses a place she knew well, having visited the spa in 1838 after a long illness: 'I thought myself strong enough to try the waters, & found they agreed with me perfectly'. Thereafter, she would make an 'annual visit' until 1841, when she moved there permanently and spent her remaining days there. The lively atmosphere was invigorating to an invalid: 'I like the morning Band at the Monpelier Spa, and the morning exhibitions, and Concerts, & all the Cockney doings'. From the windows of her boarding-house on the Promenade, she enjoyed watching, 'the folks, pedestrians, equestrians, carriageites &c' (*Letters*, pp. 419, 445–6, nn. 4–6).

3. *blonde lace*: Blonde lace, first made in 1745, was produced from unbleached silk, with two threads twisted and formed into hexagonal meshes. The colour was that of the raw silk (*OED*).
4. 'Quel chien d'homme!': 'What a detestable man!'
5. *She looked without seeing ... whence they came*: The authenticity of SHB's portrayal of the bewilderment and homesickness of a child travelling abroad may owe something to personal experience; at the age of nine she was sent away to Switzerland for a few years to further her education. All her life she seems to have retained memories of this formative experience, as well as a fluency in French (*Letters*, p. 10, n. 8).
6. *Well do'st thou hide ... Dryden*: The first part of the epigraph is taken from the translation by John Dryden (1631–1700) of the 'The First book of Homer's Ilias', included in the *Fables* of 1700. The first line has been rendered slightly inaccurately: 'But well thou do'st, to hide from common sight' in the original (ll. 745–6).
7. *I do not think so fair ... Shakspeare*: The second part of the epigraph quotes Shakespeare, who accounts for almost half the novel's epigraphs and was easily SHB's favourite author, whose plays she read, quoted and saw performed throughout her life and urged others to read as the basis of a good literary education (*Letters*, p. 142). She may have inherited the enthusiasm from her father, whose eagerness to acquire the latest edition and whose absorption while perusing it may be reflected in a comic scene in one of her novels (see *Traits of Nature*, 5 vols (London: Henry Colburn, 1812), vol. 1, pp. 10–29). Charles Burney owned no fewer than seven editions of Shakespeare and bequeathed one to SHB in his will, a conveniently portable one with small print, edited by his friend Edmond Malone (1741–1812) whose first edition of *The Plays and Poems of William Shakespeare* was published in 10 volumes in 1790. The text of SHB's quotations has been checked against Malone's text, although line-numbers have been keyed to the Oxford for convenience (*Catalogue*, pp. 50–1; Scholes, vol. 2, p. 265).

   The lines quoted here are from *Cymbeline* (1610), I.i.23–5. The original differs slightly; the second line has 'and such stuff within' instead of 'Such foul stuff within' and the passage ends with 'he' rather than 'him'.
8. *village of Meadwell, about five miles beyond Gloucester*: Meadwell is fictional; Gloucester is located about 100 miles west of London.
9. *the 'small still voice,' the voice of conscience*: The phrase has biblical and Shakespearian resonance: the 'still small voice' (that comes after the fire in 1 Kings 19:11–12) is connected with conscience in Cardinal Wolsey's 'still and quiet conscience' after his fall from power in *All is True (Henry VIII)* (1613), III.ii.381, first acted in 1613 and now believed to be a collaborative effort of Shakespeare and John Fletcher (1579–1625). Thomas Gray (1716–71) connected the 'still small voice' to 'Gratitude' in his *Ode for Music* (1769), l. 64.
10. *My friends ... Cowper*: from 'Verses, Supposed to be written by Alexander Selkirk, during his Solitary Abode in the Island of Juan Fernandez', published in *Poems* (1782) by William Cowper (1731–1800). The poem begins with the well-known lines, 'I am Monarch of all I survey'; the second quatrain of the fifth verse is quoted here. Cowper was one of SHB's favourite poets; she was still reciting lines from his *Poems* forty years after it had been published (see *Letters*, p. 241).
11. *Bury Street, St. James's*: Another familiar setting, Bury Street, running off Jermyn Street just south of Piccadilly, was around the corner from where SHB's uncle the agriculturist Arthur Young (1741–1820) lodged when he stayed in London. The street was built

on land owned by Henry Jermyn, Earl of St Albans (1605–84) in the 1670s and 1680s, and probably named after Bury St Edmunds where his country house was located, as was (some time later) the farm of Arthur Young (B. Weinreb and C. Hibbert (eds), *The London Encyclopedia* (Bethesda, MD: Adler & Adler, 1986), p. 109).

12. plumassier: one who trades or works in ornamental feathers.
13. chère épouse: dear wife.
14. demoiselle de boutique: shop assistant.
15. *the tender salute of her husband*: a kiss, by way of salutation, an expression used through the nineteenth century. The *OED* cites an example from Frances Burney's diary in 1782.
16. 'Mais qui est cette pauvre petite?': 'But who is this poor little girl?'
17. 'Laisse-la venir ... tout cela tantôt': 'Let her come, my friend. I will explain it all to you later.'
18. bienheureux événement: happy event.
19. savoir faire: The French phrase for an instinctive knowledge of the right course of action had just recently been absorbed into English; the first instance cited in the *OED* is from a Walter Scott novel of 1815.
20. air triste: a sad, dejected look.
21. protégée: a female protégé, i.e. someone who receives the protection or patronage of another; the first instance given in the *OED* is taken from Frances Burney's novel *Cecilia* in 1782.
22. 'Comme elle est jolie!': 'How pretty she is!'
23. *large grey parrot*: A large grey parrot features in SHB's letters as well, connected to the boarding-house in Bath in which she was living in 1839. It is associated, as it is in this tale, with a depressing scene: 'nothing to look at but blackened stone buildings containing lodgers, the gayest amongst which was a grey parrot, who now and then whistled, but still oftener screamed. How I bore the thing so long, I am now surprised' she wrote in the winter of 1842 (*Letters*, p. 452).
24. *'Vilaine Cendrillon ... mon bouillon'*: The doggerel rhyme could be translated as, 'Naughty Cinderella, Quick, quick, bring my soup'.
25. 'Tais-toi, impertinent!': 'Shush, you impertinent!'
26. *'Tis vilain bird*: 'Tis a naughty bird.
27. *'Va t'en vite ... à ton donjon'*: An idiomatic translation to the doggerel rhyme might be, 'Hurry up, you old fright, Hurry to your dungeon'.
28. *Green Park*: Located just west of Bury Street, Green Park is a green oasis of fifty-three acres bounded by Piccadilly and Constitution Hill. Enclosed by Henry VIII and made into a Royal Park by Charles II, it was remodelled by John Nash and re-opened in 1826.
29. *acquiring a better carriage ... with more* aplomb. 'Carriage' is being used in the sense of posture, the way she carried herself; 'aplomb', a word that had only recently been absorbed into English from the French, meant assurance, confidence, self-possession.
30. *There's nothing that I ... Have a Wife*: The lines are taken from the opening act of the play, *Rule a Wife and have a Wife*, written by John Fletcher and first performed at court in 1624 (I.vi.12–14). A witty comedy depicting the battle of the sexes, its popularity continued well into the nineteenth century.
31. *you have* two *Christian names; Agnes and Lucy*: The two Christian names given to the heroine have religious connotations suggesting her angelic nature: Agnes, the name of the saint for young maidens, also evokes the *Agnus Dei* or 'Lamb of God', while the name Lucy is also that of a virgin martyr and resembles the Latin word *lux* for light. SHB here

plays with the angelic connotations of the name Agnes long before Dickens exploited them more fully.

32. Soubrette: young servant-girl or maid.
33. bien douce est bien raisonnable: very sweet and very reasonable.
34. le moins du monde: in the least.
35. on ne peut pas ... un peu abbatue: as gentle as could be although still a bit downcast.
36. *a small* Camera Oscura: In Latin meaning dark chamber, the camera obscura was an optical device in which light admitted through a hole at one end of a darkened chamber or box projects an image of external objects on a flat surface. The phenomenon, known in ancient times and described by Leonardo da Vinci, was developed by Johann Kepler; by the eighteenth century, portable models were used by artists. The photographic camera was invented when the hole was covered by a double convex lens and paper or glass placed at the focus of the lens (*OED*). The present-day word 'camera' is a shortened form of the term.
37. *Blenheim spaniel*: One of many varieties of the breed of spaniel, this one is named for Blenheim Palace, the palatial mansion of John Churchill, first Duke of Marlborough (1650–1722), named after his famous victory in 1704, and built by Sir John Vanbrugh (1664–1726) and Nicholas Hawksmoor (*c.* 1662–1736) near Woodstock, Oxfordshire. The Blenheim spaniel, a type of the toy spaniel favoured by King Charles, is distinguished by its colouring.
38. en robe de chambre: in a dressing-gown or robe.
39. *one of Berquin's many beautiful tales*: Arnaud Berquin (1747–91), the first French author to specialize in writing for children, was best known for his *l'Ami des Enfans* in 12 volumes (Paris, 1782–3), for which the Académie Française granted him a prize and which was often reprinted throughout the nineteenth century.
40. *de Vere*: The connotations of the surname 'de Vere' are suggestive: the 'de' signifies noble descent; 'vere', the feminine form of the Latin adjective 'verus' means 'true'. In French (in which SHB was fluent), the word for 'truth' is 'la vérité'; thus the surname 'de Vere' seems a fitting one for the heroine, signifying her incorruptible integrity, 'of truth'.
41. *a canter in the Bois de Boulogne*: a park and pleasure-ground since the seventeenth century on the western edge of Paris. The vestige of an ancient forest, the Bois de Boulogne extends over more than 2,000 acres, interlaced with promenades and bridle paths.
42. sang-froid: In French literally 'cold blood', meaning coolness, composure, indifference, the word had migrated into English almost a hundred years earlier (*OED*).
43. *she possessed a vigour of understanding ... rarely to be met with*: Agnes's characteristics as a heroine come close to those paragons of virtue mocked by Jane Austen in *Northanger Abbey* (1818). Naturally beautiful and socially poised, Agnes enjoys gardening and fancy-work, makes friends with living creatures, and shows aptitude in every branch of learning (music, drawing, languages and even weightier subjects), all conspicuously lacking in Catherine Morland. Less conventional is the emphasis given here, in rolling Johnsonian phrases, to her intellectual accomplishments: strength and independence of mind and moral judgement.
44. *no creature 'of earth's mould'*: a line spoken by Comus (l. 244) in *A Mask Presented at Ludlow Castle* (1637) (frequently called *Comus*) by John Milton (1608–74). The same passage is quoted at greater length below (see note 42 to Volume III). SHB classed Milton among the classics that she liked to reread when she could get hold of nothing new, and quoted his works frequently in her letters (see e.g. *Letters*, pp. 58, 400).

45. *He's sick with self-love … SHAKESPEARE*: The epigraph conflates two passages from Shakespeare's *Twelfth Night, or What You Will* (1601), a speech in which Olivia accuses Malvolio directly, 'O, you are sick of self-love', (I.v.86) and a later scene in which Maria denounces the absent Malvolio as a puritan hypocrite (II.iii.144–6). (The original has 'the best' instead of 'for well'.) Shakespeare's play may have inspired one of SHB's tales, *The Shipwreck*, published in 1815 (imprint date 1816) as the first volume of *Tales of Fancy*, which features a heroine shipwrecked on an island who dons male attire to keep company with the hero.
46. *the annual journeys you have been obliged to make to Nice*: The south of France with its warm climate was recommended for invalids; SHB's niece and nephew, who were both consumptive, had been ordered to the 'vine countries' (*Letters*, pp. 263, 285, n. 5, p. 288, n. 1).
47. mauvaise honte: extreme diffidence, excessive self-consciousness.
48. tirade: A long and vehement speech, the term had come into English from the French early in the nineteenth century (*OED*).
49. *'the sublime and beautiful'*: The aesthetic treatise *A Philosophical Enquiry into the Origin of our Ideas of the Sublime and Beautiful* (1757) by Edmund Burke (1729–97), in which he discussed the characteristics of and distinctions between the two terms, was influential well into the nineteenth century.
50. *tear a passion to rags*: In Shakespeare's play *Hamlet, Prince of Denmark* (1600–1), Hamlet instructs the players not to 'tear a passion to tatters, to very rags' (III.ii.10).
51. *Spa*: A town located 22 miles south-east of Liège in present-day Belgium, which became so famous for its mineral springs that the name 'spa' was adopted as a generic term.
52 *'once a pliant hour'*: a quote from a line in Shakespeare's play, *Othello, the Moor of Venice* (1603–4), I.i.150, in which he describes his courtship of Desdemona. Shakespeare's dramatization of jealousy aroused by evil seems to resonate through Burney's tale.
53. *Never had the young man received such a lesson … feelings of a lover*: Perhaps an echo, of which there are many in SHB's writing, of Jane Austen, and especially *Pride and Prejudice*, 3 vols (London: T. Egerton, 1813), her 'prime favorite of all modern Novels', which she claimed to have read as many times 'as bumper toasts are given – *three times three*!' (*Letters*, pp. 201, 420).

    The proposal scene here in which Agnes asserts her 'independence' and Harry, who 'had not harboured the slightest apprehension of failure' (p. 43), demands to know the reason for 'this extraordinary refusal' which has the effect of increasing his love, is similar to the first proposal scene in *Pride and Prejudice* in which Darcy is 'properly humbled' by Elizabeth and his reformation is begun (vol. 2, pp. 188–94; vol. 3, p. 369).
54. *she attained her eighteenth year*: The same grandiose phrase was ridiculed by John Wilson Croker (*c.* 1780–1857) in his review of the *Memoirs of Doctor Burney … By his Daughter, Madame d'Arblay*, 3 vols (1832), 'She relates … that when she *attained* her *fifteenth* year (that is, we presume, when she had accomplished her *fourteenth*)', *Quarterly Review*, 49 (1833), pp. 97–125, on p. 108.
55. *Antigone … the ill-fated Œdipus*: In the cycle of legends concerning the royal house of Thebes (dramatized in three plays by Sophocles), Antigone, the devoted younger daughter of Oedipus, accompanies and cares for her self-blinded father as he wanders in suffering exile (after he has fulfilled the oracular prediction that he would kill his father and marry his mother). In sculpture and art, she is represented as a type of filial devotion.

    SHB was familiar with classical and neo-classical sculpture such as the one described, having lived in 1821–2 in a house owned by William Hamilton (1777–1859), private secretary to Lord Elgin, who had filled his house with casts taken from the Parthenon frieze, and 'busts and statues' of Antonio Canova (1757–1822). Canova's work was much admired in Rome by English travellers who then commissioned works to send back to England. See *Letters*, pp. 235–8.

56. *in 'her mind's eye'*: from *Hamlet*, a play quoted frequently throughout the novel; Hamlet claims that he sees his father: 'In my mind's eye, Horatio' (I.ii.184).
57. poste-restante: From the French, literally, 'post which remains', the direction 'poste restante' on a letter indicates that it is to be held at the post office until called for, an option useful for travellers. SHB had used the service herself when she was in Italy. The system had its flaws, however; her mail was sometimes opened and read by someone with a similar name, and she in turn complained of receiving letters intended for her namesake, written in German (*Letters*, pp. 315, 317, n. 21).
58. *Rue de Colombier, No. 29, Paris*: La Rue du Vieux-Colombier still exists in Paris in the sixth arrondissement, just south of the Boulevard Saint-Germain, but the numbers stop at 25.
59. *Every man has not a soul of crystal ... Beaumont and Fletcher*: The epigraph is taken from *Philaster* (1610), the first major success of the collaborative team of Francis Beaumont (1584–1616) and John Fletcher (1579–1625). Subtitled *Love Lies a Bleeding*, it has been compared to *Hamlet* and is credited with inaugurating the vogue for romantic tragi-comedy that lasted through the century. In the original, it is the 'actions' not the 'thoughts' of 'Every man in this age' that are read through (I.i.249–52).
60. *Mrs. Le Strange*: It is curious that SHB chooses for her characters the unusual name of a well-known Jacobite family who had been close to the Burneys. Isabella Strange (1719–1806) was a woman of 'most powerful understanding' and 'wit' (Charles Burney, 'Memoirs', cited in *JL*, vol.1, p. 142, n. 13). Her daughter Isabel would have been 80 in 1839.
61. *a Woolwich cadet*: A town on the south bank of the Thames about 10 miles south-east of the City of London, Woolwich had been the site since Tudor times of a naval dockyard and later an arsenal in which, in 1721, a Royal Military Academy was founded. The cadets lived in barracks and attended lectures in a magnificent building built by Sir John Vanbrugh. In 1808, the Academy moved south to Woolwich Common where many famous soldiers received their training. See Weinreb and Hibbert (eds), *The London Encyclopedia*, p. 166.
62. *As guests in a country house ... showed but little want of feeling*: The passage is reminiscent of the scene in Austen's *Pride and Prejudice* which attempts to define the truly accomplished woman: she must have 'a thorough knowledge of music, singing, drawing, dancing, and the modern languages, to deserve the word'. Three of the four attributes described in that passage are given here and in the same order. The final qualification, the 'certain something in her air ... the tone of her voice, her address and expressions' (vol. 1, p. 39), is not unlike the 'lively' conversation 'good sense' and 'feeling' shown by the daughters of the Le Strange family that rounds off the description. On the connection between Austen and SHB, see further L. J. Clark, 'Jane Austen and Sarah Harriet Burney', *Persuasions*, 17 (1995), pp. 16–25, and 'A Contemporary's View of Jane Austen', *Notes and Queries*, 241 (1996), pp. 418–20.
63. *the one 'dim star' in this resplendent constellation*: The companion star to a brighter one is often eclipsed; the luminosity of a star also depends on the heat of its surface and its size and distance from the earth. The figurative potential of the phrase has been exploited by writers such as Virgil, Scott and Byron.

64. *Report has been a little premature ... confirmation of the rumour*: Several strands of Austen's *Pride and Prejudice* are evoked in this exchange of correspondence. The letter of congratulation from an aunt on a surprising conquest of an eminently eligible though seemingly superior suitor that arrives somewhat prematurely brings to mind the exchange between Mrs Gardiner and Elizabeth over her engagement to Darcy (see vol. 3, chs 10 and 18). The phrase 'a report so universally prevalent amongst our English friends' recalls Mr Collins's less favourable missive on the same subject (ch. 15), and the palpable insincerity of the aunt's professions and slighting opinion of her niece ('Pray how has she grown up in point of looks?)' brings to mind Lady Catherine de Bourgh's insulting views. The emphasis on 'the approaching marriage of *one* of your daughters' evokes the plight of the Bennets with their five daughters to match with husbands; in SHB's tale, the Le Stranges have four.
65. *the difference between English and French people of* ton: 'The fashion, the vogue, the mode' and by transference, fashionable society. The word was introduced into English in the eighteenth century; one of the first uses cited in the *OED* comes from Frances Burney's first novel *Evelina* (1778) and it was a concept that continued to fascinate her throughout her literary career. The attitude of SHB was typically more sceptical and scathing; she tends to use the word in a tone of disapproval, as in the phrase 'completely thoughtless, dashing women of ton' (*Letters*, p. 278).
66. *St. Cecilia*: The virginal and martyred saint is the patroness of music; her feast day on 22 November has inspired many odes (by poets such as Dryden and Pope), often set to music (by composers such as Purcell and Handel). SHB's father Charles Burney set to music an *Ode on St. Cecilia's Day* that was performed to a large audience at Ranelagh in 1759 (see Scholes, vol. 1, pp. 95–6).
67. *'Three Graces'*: in Greek mythology, the three daughters of Zeus: Aglaia (Splendour), Euphrosyne (Mirth) and Thalia (Good Cheer) who preside over banquets and other social occasions, bringing festive joy. A favourite subject of classical and neo-classical artists, they are usually depicted as a trio of lovely maidens dancing in a circle, the personification of grace, beauty and charm. They were represented in a well-known sculpture by Canova commissioned by the sixth Duke of Bedford in 1814 and brought over to England on completion.
68. *She is not fair ... Beaumont and Fletcher*: The epigraph quotes a collaboration of Beaumont and Fletcher, *A King, and No King*, written for the King's Company and first performed at Christmas 1611, a tragi-comedy that evokes tyranny and incest but ends happily. A ten-volume edition of their plays published in 1750 was in Charles Burney's library; the lines I.i.157–60 describe the beauteous princess, supposed sister of the King, saved from incest by the unexpected discovery that he is, in fact, a usurper of the throne.
69. *I resolved to reduce her to obedience by a* coup de main: In French, the literal meaning is a knock or blow of the hand, but the expression was reintroduced into English in the eighteenth century with a figurative sense, the first instance cited in the *OED* being from a letter of Frances Burney in 1793. Here it might also be used to mean a successful move or strategy.
70. *I will resign what I usurp ... Shakespeare*: Though attributed here to Shakespeare, the epigraph is actually an amalgamation, the first two lines being a quotation from the *Beggars' Bush*, a play first performed in 1622, which appears to be a collaborative effort of three playwrights: Beaumont, Fletcher and Philip Massinger (1583–1640). In the original text, 'held' is replaced by 'forced' (I.ii.117–18). The last two lines are found in Shakespeare's *Twelfth Night* (I.v.13–4) with 'but all' rather than 'than all' in the original. The middle line occurs in neither play, but serves to bridge the two passages.

71. *an excursion to St. Cloud*: a town about 6 miles south-west of the centre of Paris in which was located the Château de Saint-Cloud. Constructed in 1572, it was acquired by Marie Antoinette in 1785; the property was nationalized in 1793 and witnessed the proclamation of Napoleon as Emperor in 1804. Built on a hill overlooking the river Seine, Paris and the Bois de Boulogne, the park features a tiered Grand Cascade designed in the seventeenth century.
72. *called us* fair damsels: A high-flown and archaic word for a young unmarried woman taken from the romance seems a fitting choice for a pompous hypocrite to make while pursuing these young women with unwanted attentions.
73. *Vulgarity ... has never yet been defined*: The meaning of vulgarity as 'the quality of being vulgar, unrefined, or coarse' (*OED*) is not unclear, though the application of it at any given moment or in any given society will always be relative (often to the speaker).
74. *'pleasing, anxious'*: line 86 from the much-quoted poem by Thomas Gray (1716–71), *Elegy Written in a Country Churchyard*, first printed by Dodsley in 1751.
75. jour de fête: festive day, holiday.
76. fiacre: a small four-wheeled carriage for hire; a French cab (in English a hackney-coach) (*OED*).
77. *two or three* rouleaux: 'A number of gold coins made up into a cylindrical packet' between twenty and fifty or more (*OED*).
78. *So prayed the maid ... Ogle's Chaucer*: *The Canterbury Tales of Chaucer, Modernis'd by Several Hands*, 3 vols (London: J. and R. Tonson, 1741) was assembled by George Ogle (1704–46), who never completed his plan of modernizing all of Chaucer's work. SHB quotes from 'Constantia: or the Man of Law's Tale', modernized by Mr Brooke, the third line altered somewhat from the original, 'To ev'ry Peril Arm'd, and Pain resign'd' (vol. 2, p. 141).
79. *'The die is cast!'*: a choice of action which is irrevocable, from which there is no turning back. The proverb was supposedly quoted by Julius Caesar (*c.* 102–44 BC) when he crossed the Rubicon in 49 BC. Among other sources, the story was given in Plutarch's *Lives*, which SHB mentions reading in 1835 (*Letters*, pp. 392, 396). Shakespeare later uses a variant of it in *Richard III* (1592–3), 'I have set my life upon a cast / And I will stand the hazard of the die' (V.vii.9–10).
80. *That bonnet is only fit for a quaker*: a bonnet of the type characteristically worn by members of the Society of Friends, having a projecting poke or brim. The word 'Quaker' (originally used as a derogatory term) refers to members of the religious movement founded by George Fox in 1648–50 that emphasized the direct relationship of an individual with God and rejected prescribed forms of worship (*OED*). During a Quaker meeting, those attending would sit in silence until moved by the Spirit and might tremble or 'quake' with emotion, hence the name.
81. *to exhibit myself with you at* Long-Champs: a grassy plain located at the south-west corner of the Bois de Boulogne, once the site of an abbey.
82. Melpomene: one of the nine Muses, daughters of Zeus and Mnemosyne (according to most accounts) who preside over the arts and other intellectual endeavours. Melpomene came to be regarded as the muse of tragedy and is usually represented holding a tragic mask as well as a dagger or club.
83. *disguised in the mask of Pope's Goddess of Dullness*: The Goddess of Dulness presides in *The Dunciad*, the literary satire by Alexander Pope (1688–1744) first published in 1728 and subsequently revised (with an expanded edition in 1729; the *New Dunciad* in 1742 and *The Dunciad in Four Books* in 1743).

84. *hautbois*: the French or archaic spelling for the double-reed high-pitched wind instrument (now usually spelled 'oboe') *(OED)*.
85. *'Ah, oui, mademoiselle ... C'est ma mère'*: 'Oh, yes, mademoiselle, willingly' ... 'She is my mother'.
86. *'Ah, qu'oui, mademoiselle ... la peine d'entrer'*: 'Oh yes, mademoiselle. Everything is ready; please come in.'
87. *'Voilà un commencement ... Et belle comme le jour!'*: 'Now there's a start ... that bodes very well. How gentle and kind she is, this dear young lady. And beautiful as the morning star!'
88. commissionnaire: errand-boy or messenger, one entrusted with small commissions.
89. *a* pièce de vingt francs!: a coin of twenty francs. A silver coin representing a monetary unit of the decimal system after 1795, the franc would be worth about 9*d.* or 10*d.* in 1839 (*OED*).
90. traiteur's: in France, the keeper of an eating-house who could supply or send out meals to order; later a caterer (*OED*; *Larousse*).
91. *to earn a few* sous: a few cents, a few pennies, small coins.
92. *quire*: 'Twenty-four (formerly sometimes twenty-five) sheets of writing-paper' (*OED*). The flight of Agnes to humbler lodgings where her first act is to keep open her lifeline of epistolary correspondence is reminiscent of other heroines, such as Richardson's Clarissa.
93. Dimanche: Sunday
94. *what the French call* un air éveillé: i.e. he was a bright, alert, quick-witted lad.
95. *I've made some trial ... Beaumont and Fletcher*: The epigraph is taken from a play written solely by Fletcher and not, in fact, in collaboration with Beaumont (who had by then died); first licensed under the name *The Wandering Lovers* in December 1623, it is assumed to be the play called *The Lovers' Progress* in the 1647 folio (*ODNB*). The six lines quoted here are part of a dialogue in IV.iv: the first three (ll. 71–3) and the last two (ll. 75–7) are spoken by Lidian, disguised as a hermit, in response to the noble Lisander's question in the middle line (l. 74).
96. *He put Agnes' letter into his master's hand, and quitted the room*: The scene which follows bears an eerie resemblance to the most dramatic moment of SHB's own life, when, as a young woman, she suddenly absconded from her home, leaving behind all her things and a note to her father to explain her actions. The vividly imagined scenario of the impact on the household created by Agnes's departure is convincing in its details, and resonates with sympathy for the deserted (though guilty) father. See further, *Letters*, pp. xxxvi–xl).
97. Tragic Muse: Melpomene; see note 82 above.
98. *Neuilly*: Once a village west of Paris bordering the Bois de Boulogne (about 4 miles from the city centre), Neuilly-sur-Seine was a wealthy enclave.
99. espièglerie: a prank or roguish trick, mischievousness. Although introduced into English in the nineteenth century, it seemed to be viewed as rather un-English behaviour, the product of a foreign education (see *OED*).
100. 'Que voulez-vous!': 'What do you expect?' The expression is frequently used by the English to characterize a French speaker; the first citation given in the *OED* is from 1830, in a letter of Claire Clairmont's to Mary Shelley.
101. fracas: 'A disturbance, noisy quarrel, "row" or uproar' (*OED*).
102. *Je trouve en elle ... Voltaire's Nanine*, Comédie: From the comedy inspired by Richardson's novel *Pamela*, *Nanine, ou L'Homme sans Préjugé* (1749), by François-Marie-Arouet, known as Voltaire (1694–1778), whose works were considered by Charles Burney 'unfit

for the perusal of Females' (Scholes, vol. 2, p. 268), but were nevertheless enjoyed by SHB. The passage cited here is the Count's speech in I.ii.69–76, with the first three lines quoted somewhat inaccurately, and the fifth and sixth transposed. The original starts out, 'Je veux, madame, une femme indulgente, / Dont la beauté douce et compatissante, / A mes défauts facile à se plier' (*Nanine*, in *The Complete Works of Voltaire*, ed. M. de Labriolle and C. Duckworth (Oxford: Voltaire Foundation, 1994), vol. 31B.

My own translation of the passage here would read:

I find in her an indulgent woman
Sweet-tempered and tender-hearted,
Who bends easily to my desires,
Is pleased to reconcile with me,
To govern me, without being tyrannical,
To correct me, without taking a caustic tone,
And in my heart to penetrate little by little,
Like a soft day in delicate eyes.

103. femme de chambre: lady's maid or chamber-maid.
104. badinage: light banter, used here in the sense of frivolity or playfulness.
105. petite poste: district post office.
106. incroyable: incredible, unbelievable.
107. *Many persons in your place would be wretched*: Many a heroine in Agnes's place was indeed 'wretched'; closest to home, Cecilia, the dispossessed heroine of Frances Burney's play *The Witlings*, written in 1778–80, is full of self-pity: 'Is then every Evil included in poverty? ... Are Contempt, Insult, and Treachery it's necessary attendants?' (V.i.187–9). Although there is no evidence that SHB had read this play (which was never performed in Burney's lifetime), Cecilia's misfortunes were amplified and extended in Frances Burney's second novel *Cecilia* (1782), in which an heiress contrives to lose her fortune, as in this tale does Agnes.
108. *'Montez, montez, monsieur, c'est ici'*: 'Come on up, come on up, sir, it is here'.
109. *'On vous demande, mademoiselle, ouvrez s'il vous plait'*: 'Somebody is asking for you, mademoiselle, open the door, please'.
110. *'Je demande bien pardon à la chère demoiselle'*: 'I humbly beg the dear young lady's pardon'.
111. *'Tout ce que vous dites ... vous éclairera'*: 'All that you say, sir, is perhaps well and good, but accomplishes nothing! Won't you please come down, and Madame Bernard will light you out.'

Volume II

1. *I do partly think ... Measure for Measure*: The lines are Isabella's, pleading to the Duke to show mercy to Angelo in Shakespeare's *Measure for Measure* (1603), V.i.442–4.
2. '*Et elle ne me connaitrait pas ... si elle me connait!*' 'And she wouldn't know me, *me*, really? ... Go to, my dear, you don't know what you are saying. I am going to knock at her door, and you will see whether or not she knows me!'
3. *their master in laying by for what is called "a rainy day"*: The wisdom to lay by something for a rainy day, i.e. to save something against evil times, was proverbial.
4. *With her no earthly thing is ever right ... Dodsley's Collection*: Robert Dodsley (1704–64), the footman-turned-writer, bookseller and friend of Pope who published Samuel Johnson's *Dictionary* and other important works. His *A Collection of Poems. By*

Several Hands was a major contribution that 'set the canon for mid-eighteenth century poetry' (*ODNB*). Three volumes appeared in 1748, to which a fourth volume was added in 1755 and the last two (making six in all) in 1758. The poem 'The Duty of Employing one's Self: An Epistle', by Edward Rolle, appears on pp. 64–7 of the 1758 edition, which is the same edition quoted in a letter of SHB's of 1832 (*Letters*, p. 368). The lines (30–2) have been feminized here to fit the context ('them' and 'their' changed to 'her' and 'she') and another slight word alteration has been made ('can' replaces the 'could' of the original).

5. *"Here is my throne; bid kings come bow to it!"*: Constance, referring to her 'sorrows' in *King John* (1596), II.i.74. Though rarely staged now, Shakespeare's play was popular in the nineteenth century, with successful actors taking the lead roles: SHB saw a strongly-cast production at Covent Garden in 1810 with Sarah Siddons as Constance, John Philip Kemble playing King John and Charles Kemble as Philip the Bastard. The performance of Mrs Siddons made such an impression on her that when she returned home, she made a sketch of the actress's face in the scene immediately following the line quoted here (*Letters*, p. 116).
6. There needs no ghost to tell us this!: from Horatio's words to Hamlet in I.v.129 after their encounter with the ghost. SHB quotes frequently from this play, especially from the atmospheric opening scenes. What Horatio actually says is, 'There needs no ghost, my lord, come from the grave To tell us this'.
7. diligence: a public stage-coach in Europe. It was large (some could hold up to thirty passengers) and fast (covering up to one hundred miles a day) but very bumpy on the uneven French roads until the late eighteenth century when they were hung on springs. SHB's uncle Arthur Young, who had travelled in France before the Revolution, considered them 'detestable ... Overcrowded, badly sprung and fond of starting in the small hours of the morning' (A. Young, *Travels in France in 1787–1789* (London, 1889), cited in C. Hibbert, *The Grand Tour* (London: Weidenfeld & Nicolson, 1969), p. 35). Another feature would be the indiscriminate intermingling with the other passengers for the duration of the trip.
8. *travelling with a swiss* voiturier: the driver of a carriage or coach. SHB recommends a Swiss driver and the method of conveyance she herself used to travel from London to Lausanne in 1829. The advantages were that the driver was 'decent' and 'respectable' and looked after everything; the fare of £18 had included all meals and accommodation along the road (see *Letters*, p. 468).
9. *We have yielded ... as no other people* would *have yielded*: Possibly a verbal echo of Mr Knightley's address to Emma in Jane Austen's novel *Emma*, 3 vols (London: John Murray, 1816): 'I have blamed you, and lectured you, and you have borne it as no other woman in England would have borne it' (vol. 3, p. 430).
10. *"the horrors of the last"*: Referring to the coming Day of Judgement or the fear of dying, the most famous coinage of this phrase may be that of Samuel Johnson (1709–84) in the final number of *The Idler*, 103, issued on Saturday, 5 April 1760, in which he writes of the 'secret horrour of the last'. In some, though not all, editions, the number is titled with the phrase, 'Horrour of the Last'.
11. mon possible: my best, my utmost. A similar phrase was used in English in the nineteenth century, 'to do one's possible', which is now rare and obsolete.
12. *'the great globe itself'*: a phrase from Prospero's speech in Shakespeare's *The Tempest* (1611), IV.i.153.

13. *'Have you read Foresyth?'*: The *Remarks on Antiquities, Arts, and Letters, during an Excursion in Italy* (London, 1813) was written on the basis of an eighteen-month tour of Italy in 1802–3 by school-master Joseph Forsyth (1763–1815), who was arrested in France on his way home when war was renewed. A learned and observant man, Forsyth wrote his work during a period of imprisonment (1803–14) in an effort to secure his release. He died soon after his return from forced exile; his book meanwhile went into several editions and was 'widely regarded as one of the better written and more useful books on Italy'; a fourth edition was published at London in 1835 (*ODNB*).
14. *take care of that pretty Leghorn*: a bonnet made with 'straw plaiting ... from a particular kind of wheat imported from Leghorn' (*OED*). SHB had known the coastal town of Livorno during her stay in Italy from 1829 to 1833.
15. *the coarsest Dunstable in England*: i.e. a plain straw bonnet. The name of a town in Bedfordshire, Dunstable can be used as an adjective to mean 'plain, downright'; it also refers to 'a kind of straw plait made at Dunstable or to the method of plaiting it' (*OED*).
16. effusion de coeur: outpouring of emotion.
17. *a premature old maid in the worst sense of the term*: Somewhat surprisingly, spinsters do not fare well in SHB's fiction, which adopts the conventionally satiric treatment of them. Her letters express self-consciousness about her own role as spinster and show full recognition of the characteristics traditionally assigned to it, 'to be very cross, ugly, spiteful &c'. She is scathing about the 'old Maids' she is condemned to associate with, who 'when not touchy, and ill-tempered ... are not seldom eminently trivial, inquisitive, and empty-headed' (*Letters*, pp. 43, 464). For a fuller treatment of the subject, see L. J. Clark, 'From the Margins to the Centre: The Spinster as Author, Narrator and Actor', *Burney Journal*, 6 (2003), pp. 36–54.
18. hors de combat: out of the fight, sidelined, eliminated.
19. salon: a large apartment, serving as the principal reception room for guests.
20. *ask why he does not use a trumpet?*: A straight or convoluted tube by means of which persons somewhat deaf could hear more distinctly (*OED*), it figures large in the journals of Frances Burney, who found the use made of it by bluestocking Elizabeth Vesey (*c.* 1715–91) irresistibly comic; Sir Joshua Reynolds (1723–92) also made use of one in later life. SHB complained of increasing deafness as she grew older, and used a trumpet herself in her last year (*Letters*, pp. 445, 447, 481, 483).
21. *her faults then are more of temper than of heart*: a conventional dichotomy used memorably about the death of SHB's own mother by Frances Burney, who remarked, 'Her Temper alone was in fault, not her heart or intentions. But for that impracticable Temper, I should always have loved her as I did at the first'; she goes on to relate the prayer she said over the coffin in the presence of her half-sister SHB (*JL*, vol. 12, p. 783).
22. *"sweet are the uses of adversity", says my dear Shakespear*: Duke Senior speaks these words in *As You Like It* (1599–1600), II.i.12. The words 'my dear Shakespear' echo expressions in SHB's *Letters* (see e.g. pp. 230, 387). His plays evidently had a profound impact on her: Shakespearian motifs abound in her fiction and even the basic plot and structure her novels owe something to the Bard.
23. passe pour cela: pass it over; overlook it; let it pass.
24. *to translate a Frenchman's idiom*, take a walk on horseback: Actually, a literal translation of the correct phrase in French, *faire une promenade à cheval* would be 'to make' (rather than 'take') 'a walk on horseback'.
25. *James' Powders*: The famous medicine patented by Dr Robert James (1705–76) in 1747 as a remedy against fevers, the powder contained phosphate of lime and oxide of anti-

mony. Besides inducing perspiration, they also had a purgative and (in large doses) an emetic effect (*ODNB*). The Burneys were great believers in their efficacy, Frances Burney dosing her son with them throughout his childhood and still praising their virtues decades later (*JL*, vol. 1, p. 68, n. 2; vol. 11, pp. 479–80; vol. 12, p. 633). The powders had their detractors in their day and some believed that they played a role in bringing on King George III's 'madness', a view that has been confirmed since by research which suggests that the arsenic contained in the antimony may have triggered the porphyria from which he suffered. See further I. MacAlpine and R. Hunter, *George III and the Mad-Business* (London: Allen Lane and Penguin, 1969).

26. strolling *over the world*: 'Strolling' is a word often associated with vagabonds, players, minstrels or other itinerants. A woman travelling alone by vetturino might be seen in this light, as Burney herself learned on her own solo trip from an awkward encounter with a friend of her brother's who seemed to consider her mode of travel somewhat disreputable. It is significant that she had 'not the courage' to travel home the same way, which she referred to as 'vagabonding' (*Letters*, p. 294, n. 2, pp. 351, 368, 470, n. 1).
27. guinguette: A cabaret or popular nightspot in the suburbs, often in the open air; a place fitted up for drinking, eating and dancing (*Larousse*). Such a venue would have been rather low class and therefore unsuitable. A similar concern runs through Frances Burney's novels, which often focus on the embarrassment suffered by the heroine when forced to associate (and be associated) with those of a lower class.
28. *'a sable silvered'*: from Horatio's description of the ghost in *Hamlet*, I.ii.241.
29. *ape the importance of a* Grand Seigneur: a great noble, a high and mighty lord. To 'ape the importance of a Grand Seigneur' would be to put on airs. The word was adopted into English but is now obsolete (*OED*).
30. *She named one of the most eminent in Paris*: SHB's heroines often share their author's affinity for drawing, 'an old mania' at which she sometimes 'fagged as hard as if fagging for bread'. In Florence in 1830, she engaged a drawing master and confessed: 'I have repeatedly drawn from seven o'clock with only brief intervals of rest for meals, till six or seven in the evening'. Her portfolio of drawings made in Italy was mentioned as a personal bequest in her will (*Letters*, pp. 304, 485–6).
31. mal aria: in Italian, literally, bad air. It was thought that the atmosphere in the marshy countryside around Rome was unhealthy at certain times of the year, giving rise to a feverish disease.
32. *of* bringing an old house about my ears: a proverbial expression, now obsolete, meaning to get oneself into trouble.
33. coupé: a closed four-wheeled carriage with two seats inside and a seat outside for the driver, or (as in this case) the front compartment of the diligence with one seat next to the driver (*OED*).
34. *to kill her patient with kindness*: The words recall Petruccio's plan to 'kill a wife with kindness', in Shakespeare's *The Taming of the Shrew* (1590–1), IV.i.194.
35. *O Italy! ... Elegy, by Mrs. West*: The lines (81–4) from *An Elegy on the Death of the Right Honourable Edmund Burke* (1797), by Jane (née Iliffe) West (1758–1852), are quoted slightly inaccurately. The original lines are written in the past tense; it was 'warmth' not 'fire' that Prometheus stole from Jove; and the 'lovely magic wand' of the last line is of lowlier manufacture, 'And bolder Painting snatch'd his plastic Wand'.
36. *They were approaching the Simplon*: The famous pass through the Alps near the Swiss-Italian border, the Simplon features in many travellers' accounts (including Burney's own); among the more famous was that of William Wordsworth (1770–1850), who

hiked through it in 1790. Travel was made somewhat easier after 1807 when Napoleon built a carriage-road, although it could still be dangerous when the road was washed out and travellers had to clamber up narrow paths and over raging streams on planks made of tree trunks (see S. Foster, *Across New Worlds: Nineteenth-Century Women Travellers and their Writings* (New York and London: Harvester Wheatsheaf, 1990), p. 45). The crossing of the Alps was often an emotional experience heightened by the 'strange magnificence of the scene' (F.Trollope, *A Visit to Italy*, 2 vols (1842), cited in Foster, *Across New Worlds*, p. 51).

37. *Baveno ... view of Lago Maggiore*: Many travellers in the nineteenth century were also 'enchanted' with the 'Lake District' in northern Italy. Baveno has mountain views as well as a promenade along the lakeshore. Lago Maggiore, the second-largest lake in Italy, is about 50 miles beyond the Simplon Pass and belongs to both Switzerland and Italy. A glacier lake, its mild climate in both summer and winter allows Mediterranean and exotic plants to flourish.
38. *so much has of late years been written ... add any thing new to the picture*: The passage echoes one in SHB's letters. On completing the writing of *The Renunciation* in Italy in 1832, she announced that it had, 'a little in it, but not much, about Italy, become now rather a hackeneyed subject' (*Letters*, p. 375). Travel books on France and Italy were already considered a 'stale commodity' when her father published the account of his musical travels in 1771 (see note 42 below), for which reason he suppressed all the non-musical narrative or observations (*Critical Review*, 32 (1771), p. 143, cited in R. Lonsdale, *Dr. Charles Burney: A Literary Biography* (Oxford: Clarendon Press, 1965), p. 98). 'In 1820 there were thirteen new travel books on Italy and in the 1840s they continued to appear at the rate of four a year' (Foster, *Across New Worlds*, p. 29).
39. *domestic habits ... in a loose wrapping gown*: in her night-gown. The 'domestic habits' of Italian family life echo passages in SHB's letters from Florence describing the home of two elderly women with whom she lodged (1831–3). One of them, she writes, 'spends the remainder of her time ... lounging upon a sofa, without a cap ... without other garments than a gown & shift!' (*Letters*, p. 350).
40. eau sucrée: water with sugar in it.
41. tisane: an infusion of tea or herbs, often with medicinal properties.
42. *'land of music'*: The view of Italy as the 'land of music' was generally held; it was certainly the opinion of SHB's father Charles Burney, who wrote in 1770 that 'the Italians at present surpass the rest of Europe in no one art so much as in their Music' (cited in Scholes, vol. 1, p. 150). On the basis of that belief, he embarked on a tour to gather musical materials later published as *The Present State of Music in France and Italy* (1771). On his travels, he noted that music permeated every level of Italian society and declared in his introduction that 'music still *lives* in Italy' (2nd edn (London, 1773), pp. 2, 400; Scholes, vol. 1, pp. 163, 168).
43. *the harsh, discordant ... Italian ladies she conversed with*: Compare: 'Indeed I can find but one fault with the few Italian ladies I have been introduced to, – they have the harshest and loudest voices in the world' (*Letters*, p. 349).
44. *two or three Italian friends ... give an idea that they are quarrelling*: Compare, 'On entering a room, it is difficult not to believe, if there are four or five ladies present, that they are quarrelling; they really bawl and scream –' (*Letters*, p. 349).
45. *on a superficial view ... kindness of disposition*: Compare, 'You, who only saw these people when they stood upon their pps, & their qqs with the *Signorine Inglese*, and received you

only as visitors, can have not the remotest conception of what they are when at home' (*Letters*, p. 381).

46. *less newspaper* éclat: less publicity, less exposure.
47. *she was not merely styled* la bella, *but* la bellissima Inglese: The adjective meaning 'beautiful' in Italian was not enough; the superlative form, 'the most beautiful', had to be used.
48. conversazione: an evening assembly for conversation, socializing and amusement often described by travellers to Italy in the eighteenth century. SHB attended several during her years in Florence which were held by her two hostesses: 'they invariably have one, two, or three friends dropping in without form of an evening' (*Letters*, pp. 326, 327, n. 16, pp. 350, 367). Introduced into England, they were called an 'at home' or private assembly; Frances Burney was one of the first people cited in the *OED* to use the Italian term.
49. *ortolans*: a European bird, a 'migratory bunting' that frequented gardens (hence the name); it had brown feathers, 'a yellow throat and a grey or (in the male) olive-green head' and was widely regarded as a culinary delicacy (*OED*).
50. *the so justly celebrated gallery, and the Palazzo Pitti*: The Gallerie degli Uffizi (constructed 1560–74), one of the great art museums of Italy, and, across the river, the Palazzo Pitti, a fifteenth-century palace whose magnificent collection was begun by the Medici family in the seventeenth century, and was opened regularly to the public in 1828. SHB was living near them for several months in 1830, during which time she visited the gallery 'two or three times a week' and described the Pitti as an 'inexhaustible resource' (*Letters*, p. 304; see C. Pescio, *Complete Guide for Visiting the Uffizi* (Firenze: Il Turismo, 1979) and *Complete Guide for Visiting Pitti Palace* (Firenze: Il Turismo, 1981).
51. *the beautiful statues of Niobe and her children*: In Greek mythology, Niobe, the Queen of Thebes, proud of her many fine children (seven boys and seven girls), boasted that she was superior to Latona, the mother of Apollo and Artemis, who then felled the children with arrows as punishment. Niobe, frozen in grief, was turned into a stone that weeps incessantly.

    In the Uffizi Gallery in Florence is the group of statues of Niobe and her children; found in a vineyard in 1583 and brought to Florence in 1775, they have stood in the same hall since 1780 (Sala di Niobe). Roman copies of Greek originals dating from the early fourth century BC, they originally adorned the Temple of Apollo in Rome (see Pescio, *Complete Guide for Visiting the Uffizi*, p. 133).
52. *Venus de' Medici*: The beautiful marble sculpture of Aphrodite emerging from the sea has been attributed to Cleomenes (in the first century BC), who was copying the original in bronze, executed by Praxiteles in the fourth century BC. The most famous statue in the Uffizi, to which it was brought in 1717, it stood as the high point of the Grand Tour and was one of SHB's favourite sights in Florence (Pescio, *Complete Guide for visiting the Uffizi*, p. 67; *Letters*, pp. 320, 321, n. 2).
53. *muddy canals, (represented by Canaletti as being so translucent)*: The Venetian Antonio Canale (1697–1768), usually called Canaletto, whose highly finished canvases of city views were favoured by English travellers looking for souvenirs to take back from the Grand Tour. The canals were frequently the subject of his paintings in which the buildings and figures were meticulously rendered, often using a camera obscura. SHB did not visit Venice, but Charles Burney had expressed disappointment on his first view of the city, which did not match his expectations raised by Canaletto's paintings (Scholes, vol. 1, p. 167).
54. *Goldoni's Memoirs*: The *Mémoires* of Venetian playwright Carlo Goldoni (1707–93) had been published fifty years earlier, at Paris in 1787. A translation by John Black was

printed by SHB's own publisher Henry Colburn in London in 1814. After a successful career writing for the stage in Venice (1748–62), marred latterly by rivalry with Carlo Gozzi (1720–1806), Goldoni left in 1761 for Paris where he remained for the rest of his life; his later plays and memoirs are written in French. SHB had heard some of his light comedies recited in Florence and attended the Teatro Goldoni located there; her father had owned several editions of Goldoni's plays (*Letters*, pp. 328, 349; *Catalogue*, p. 22).

55. *"amongst all those potent grave, and reverend Signors"*: taken from Othello's speech in I.iii of Shakespeare's play (l. 76), evidently a favourite with SHB, who cites this same scene three times in the course of this work.
56. *our memorable inn at Dole*: Located about 230 miles south-west of Paris on the road to Lausanne (which is about 100 miles further on), Dole was at the meeting-place of several roads in Roman times. It has a Gothic church dating from the sixteenth century, a college (formerly Jesuit), and a fifteenth-century tower.
57. Cospetto!: An Italian exclamation, the equivalent of 'Good gracious!' or 'Oh my goodness!' SHB had learned it from her Italian tutor, Gaetano Polidori (1764–1853) (grandfather to the Rossettis), from whom she took lessons in 1805, and began using it in her letters not long thereafter (see *Letters*, pp. 66, 68, n. 27, p. 118).
58. *Erase the written troubles of the brain*: from Macbeth's speech to the Doctor (V.iii.44) in Shakespeare's play (1606); the original line has 'Raze out' rather than 'erase'.
59. chefs-d'œuvre: masterpieces.
60. *green-stall*: a shop or stall selling 'greens' or vegetables (*OED*).
61. Poste Restante: see note 57 to Volume I.
62. *"Love will hope where reason would despair"*: The 'Epigram' is that of George Lyttelton, first Baron Lyttelton (1709–73):

    None without Hope e'er lov'd the brightest Fair,
    But Love can hope where Reason would despair.

    This version was printed anonymously in Robert Dodsley's *A Collection of Poems. By Several Hands* (see note 4 above). In the 1748 edition of 3 volumes it appeared on p. 61 of vol. 2. (For this identification, I am grateful to Stewart Cooke.) The authorship was made clear, however, when it was included in the posthumously published edition of *Poems by the Right Honourable the Late Lord Lyttelton* printed at Glasgow by Andrew Foulis in 1773 (on p. 60), and it also appeared in a more extensive posthumous collection of his works printed in London by J. Dodsley in 1774, *The Works of George Lord Lyttelton* (p. 623). It was later reprinted in various collections of poems or epigrams.
63. *thinks it a great event ... in their way to the nearest town*: Perhaps another echo of Austen's *Pride and Prejudice* in which Lady Catherine and her daughter 'stopping in a low phaeton at the garden gate' created such a stir that Elizabeth believed 'that the pigs were got into the garden' (vol. 2, p. 158) or when Mr Collins watches out of the window to see Miss De Bourgh's carriage pass by which he 'never failed coming to inform them of, though it happened almost every day' (p. 168).
64. *"these little things please little men"*: from Oliver Goldsmith's (*c.* 1728–74) *The Traveller, or a Prospect of Society*, published in December 1764. Line 42 actually reads, 'These little things are great to little man' in the first edition (though some later editions read 'men').
65. maussade: dull, cheerless, depressing.
66. *Bertha ... expert in most of the pastimes usual amongst boys*: The desirability of a girl being liberated from the constraints of female education and treated equally with her brothers is a message that appears elsewhere in SHB's fiction. See, for example, *Traits of Nature*,

where the pernicious system of favouring boys results in creating an incipient 'tyrant' in the nursery (vol. 1, p. 41).

67. tableau de genre: a genre painting or subject picture, i.e. a style of art in which scenes and subjects of ordinary life are depicted.
68. *Perugia*: a city in the region of Umbria in central Italy, near the Tiber River. Among other attractions, it boasts one of the finest town halls in Italy, a cathedral, a medieval fountain and many fine churches. An artistic centre of note, there are fine frescoes in several of the buildings.
69. *'round unvarnished tale'*: Othello's words from I.iii.90.
70. pris son parti: taken her decision.
71. *Let us about it ... Shakespear*: The first two lines of the epigraph quote the words of Sir Hugh Evans in Shakespeare's *The Merry Wives of Windsor* (1597–8), IV.iv.79. Falstaff's buffooneries in this play were quoted by the Burneys as a family catchphrase (*Letters*, pp. 463, 465, n. 3). The next three lines are spoken by Proteus to Silvia in Shakespeare's early play *The Two Gentlemen of Verona* (V.iv.23–5); 'crave' is actually 'beg' in the original.
72. beau ideal: ideal of beauty or 'the highest conceivable type of excellence' that fulfils one's ideal (*OED*). It was a concept under discussion in the nineteenth century.
73. *"wreathed smiles"*: a phrase from one of the companion poems of John Milton, 'L'Allegro', l. 28; 'Il Ponseroso' will be quoted later on. Both were published in his *Minor Poems* (1645).
74. *Give sorrow words ... bids it break*: The words are Malcolm's, urging Macduff to give vent to his grief over his grievous loss of kin in Shakespeare's *Macbeth* (IV.iii.210–11).
75. une écriture superbe: a superb handwriting, i.e. in a beautiful hand.
76. minauderies: affectations, coquetries.
77. rouge: A fine red powder used as a cosmetic to heighten artificially the colour of lips and cheeks. The first citation in the *OED* (to replace the English word 'paint') comes from Lord Chesterfield in 1753.
78. *an accent so provincial ... banks of the Garonne*: The Garonne, a large river in south-west France flows from the Spanish Pyrenees into the Atlantic Ocean. The visitor was apparently speaking with a country accent from the southern provinces of France.
79. *"cupid's bow"*: In Roman mythology, Cupid is the son of Venus and Mercury, identified with the Greek Eros. The god of love, he is usually pictured as a beautiful young boy armed with a bow and arrows. 'Cupid's bow' was a familiar image by this time; the shape of the double-curved bow was likened to the outline of a shapely mouth, though (in print, at least) not until after this date. See *OED*.
80. *'with eyes upraised as one inspired'*: The reference is to William Collins's 'The Passions. An Ode for Music' (l. 57), first published in his *Odes on Several Descriptive and Allegoric Subjects* in December 1746 (imprint date 1747). It was later set to music by Dr William Hayes (*c.* 1708–77) and performed at Oxford in 1750; Hayes was professor of music at the university who directed the performance of the anthem which earned Charles Burney a Doctorate of Music in 1769 (see Scholes, vol. 1, pp. 142–5).
81. 'shadow lengthened by the setting sun': from Alexander Pope's *Windsor Forest* (1713), l. 194. Pope, one of SHB's favourite authors, is quoted frequently in her letters.
82. cicerone: a guide who shows and explains the antiquities of a place to strangers. The term was originally applied to learned Italian antiquarians whose services were sought by visitors, but the term was adopted into English in the eighteenth century and came to be applied more generally to mean 'guide' (*OED*). During her time in Rome, the diarist

and friend of Wordsworth Henry Crabb Robinson (1775–1867) had acted as *cicerone* to SHB and introduced her to the antiquities of Rome.

83. Monte Mario: the highest hill in Rome, 139 metres high, which offered views over the countryside.
84. Bisogna compatirmi: Pity me, my plight.
85. "dragged its slow length along": from the well-known line in Pope's *An Essay on Criticism* (1711) describing the alexandrine, 'That like a wounded Snake, drags its slow length along' (l. 357). The same line, curiously enough, was quoted in a letter of SHB's in 1836 to describe her reading of *The Renunciation* to an audience of friends in Italy, and how she found that the interest dissipated as the work progressed (and the tale 'dragged'), hence her reluctance to publish it without arduous 'remodelling' (*Letters*, p. 409). It is unknown if this revision ever took place.
86. *Antigone ... personification of Pity*: see note 55 to Volume I.
87. ultramontane bel-esprit: an intellectual who adheres to the doctrine of absolute supremacy of the Pope, here used more broadly to imply reactionary politics and a vitiated wit.
88. charlatanerie: A similar word in English (since the seventeenth century), spelled charlatanery, means quackery, imposture, an 'action which bespeaks a charlatan' (*OED*).
89. *as excessive vanity is the chief ailment of ridicule ... a very proud one*: This conversation linking vanity to ridicule and distinguishing between vanity and pride surely owes something to the famous dialogue between Darcy and Elizabeth on the subject in *Pride and Prejudice* (see vol. 1, ch. 11).
90. *'In winter's tedious nights ... long ago betid'*: The words are those of the titular hero of Shakespeare's play *Richard II* (1595), bidding farewell to his Queen in V.i.40–2.
91. *arrived at Naples ... clearness of the heavens*: The description of the journey from Rome to Naples resembles the accounts received by SHB from Henry Crabb Robinson, who travelled there after parting from her in Rome and noted the 'delightful' journey, favoured by 'the very best of weather', appreciated the 'fine colours' and clear air on the Pontine Marshes and enthused over the 'glorious view of the city & bay' of Naples (H. C. Robinson, Travel Journals, 13–15 March 1830, cited in *Letters*, p. 302, n. 6). The letter he sent to SHB on the occasion was so vividly detailed that she claimed that she could follow him 'step by step' and promised to take his letter as a guide to any future trip to Naples (*Letters*, p. 303).
92. *to prefer the* beautiful *to the* sublime: see note 49 to Volume 1.
93. *To a poet's eye, "in a fine phrenzy rolling"*: The poet is likened to the madman and the lover by virtue of the strength of his imagination by Theseus in Shakespeare's *A Midsummer Night's Dream* (1595), V.i.12.
94. *Interlacken*: Situated between two lakes, Thoune and Brienz in central Switzerland, Interlaken was a popular destination for nineteenth-century travellers for its magnificent Alpine views. It has a Gothic church, an Augustine abbey and an eighteenth-century château.
95. *some called it only a waterfall ... it was a positive catarrh*: The joke arises from the confusion of vocabulary: *la cataracte* in French (*la cateratta* in Italian) denotes the English 'cataract' or waterfall of considerable size, whereas 'catarrh' in English (or *le catarrhe* and *il catarro*) refers to the discharge from nose or eyes that accompanies a cold or an inflammation of the mucus membrane (*OED*).
96. sans consequence: without importance.
97. petite maitresse *of the time of Louis XV*: an elegant or fashionable woman of the time of Louis XV (1710–74), King of France, whose dissolute life was mirrored in the decadence of the French court and the administrative disorder of his reign.

98. *Agnes, her cheeks bright as health and fresh air could make them, entered the room*: The passage recalls Austen's *Persuasion*, 2 vols (London: John Murray, 1818) and Anne Elliot's heightened complexion when she climbs the steps from the beach at Lyme with 'the bloom and freshness of youth restored by the fine wind' (vol. 1, p. 104). A similar passage occurs in SHB's letters, when she writes of two attractive young visitors 'looking fresh, and rosy, and just as people ought to look newly come out of the Spring air' (*Letters*, p. 201).
99. *are you* married?: possibly an echo of the Duke's questioning of Mariana in the trial scene of *Measure for Measure* V.i.170.
100. *ancient Tyrians ... the honourable of the earth*: inhabitants of the ancient Phoenician city of Tyre (founded *c.* 2700 BC), a prosperous centre of trade whose luxury and corruption were proverbial. The verse is taken from Isaiah 23:8.
101. *At* Le Maschere ... *one stage distant from Florence*: Le Maschere, a small place twenty miles north of Florence by the shortest road, is almost an hour's drive today.
102. *'Bade me if I had a friend ... would woo her'*: Othello describing the hint from Desdemona which emboldened him to woo her (I.iii.163–5). Perhaps SHB had recently reread or seen the play, which is quoted no fewer than five times in *The Renunciation*.
103. *'there where he had garnered up his heart'*: the words of Othello bewailing the supposed betrayal of his love by Desdemona, 'there where I have garnered up my heart' (IV.ii.59).
104. *she is not one of those awe-inspiring, pattern-women*: The adjectival use of pattern for what serves as a model, frequently applied to a person (as in 'pattern-girl') is now rare (*OED*). The phrase 'pattern-man' was used in Maria Edgeworth, *Tales of Fashionable Life* (1812), which SHB had read (*Letters*, p. 141).
105. *Italy ... they pall upon us*: Many remarks about Italy in the novel echo passages in SHB's letters, which seem to have functioned somewhat as a writer's notebook. The very same image in almost the same words is used in a letter of February 1831: 'Italy is to me like the plums in a Grocer's shop to a new 'prentice boy; – it is very irresistable at first, but palls after a while' (*Letters*, p. 339).
106. *pick sundry other holes in their coat*: to find fault with or grounds for blame. The same phrase is used by SHB in a letter from Rome (*Letters*, p. 296).
107. *How noiseless falls the foot of time ... Spencer*: The lines are by William Robert Spencer (1770–1834), with whose family SHB had become acquainted in 1815 (*Letters*, p. 189). The passage is found in his verses dedicated 'To the Lady Anne Hamilton' in *Poems* (1811), ll. 3–4. Popular in London society, Spencer also knew the Crewe family well enough to dedicate a poem to Elizabeth Emma Crewe (later Cunliffe) (*c.* 1781–1850), a stylish socialite with whom SHB would come to have close dealings as governess to the Crewe heiresses (1822–9).
108. cette fleur de fatuité: the bloom of self-conceit or self-complacency.
109. l'Etablissement: establishment, business.

Volume III

1. Don Pedro. *In faith, lady ... Shakspeare*: an exchange between Beatrice and Don Pedro in Shakespeare's *Much Ado About Nothing* (1598), II.i.293–5. SHB sympathized with the feisty heroine of this play, whose words she quoted elsewhere, 'O that I were a man!' (*Letters*, p. 309).

2. *into Shropshire*: For the setting of her last tale, SHB turns to her roots, the country around Shrewsbury (the county town of Shropshire, the West Midlands county on the Welsh border), where her father Charles Burney had grown up.
3. *young Sedley*: There is some similarity between the names chosen by SHB for her characters and those used by her half-sister Frances Burney in her novels: the heroine 'Ella' recalls the pseudonym 'Ellis' of *The Wanderer*; the would-be suitor, young 'Sedley' brings to mind 'Sir Sedley Clarendel', SHB's favourite character in *Camilla* (*Letters*, p. 17), which also features a kindly uncle, 'Sir Hugh', not unlike 'Hugh Fitzmaurice' here. Though less close, the hero Ernest has some assonance with Edgar of *Camilla*.
4. mais que voulez-vous?: literally 'but what do you want ("me to do")?' or, idiomatically, 'but how can I help it?'
5. *His life was gentle ... SHAKESPEARE*. Antony's requiem over the body of Brutus, slain by his own sword, at the end of Shakespeare's play, *Julius Ceasar* (1599), V.v.72–4.
6. '*the circle closes* ... "by the world forgot"': a quote from Pope's 'Eloisa to Abelard' published in *Works* (1717), l. 267. SHB quotes the same line in her letters to describe a sense of isolation during the lonely winters in Florence and connects it to the same image, that of withdrawing a stick from water (*Letters*, p. 342).
7. *Her discourse is peremptory ... SHAKESPEARE*: Burney has adapted the words of the tiresome Holfornes in Shakespeare's *Love's Labour's Lost* (1594–5) and changed the gender to apply to a female pedant. The epigraph combines various phrases selected from two of his speeches in the opening scene of Act V between the three foolish scholars (ll. 9–14; 16–26). In this novel and elsewhere, Burney's unthinking adoption of the conventionally satiric view of educated women seems somewhat surprising, given her own situation and predilections; it is doubly ironic here to twist these words out of context from a play that depicts women overcoming male resistance and forcing them to surrender to the triumph of love.
8. *who, in a burning sun ... good plate of strawberries*: The 'glaring sun', the crotchety old gentleman and the strawberries bring Austen's *Emma* to mind; all are present at the strawberry-picking excursion at Donwell Abbey (see vol. 3, ch. 6).
9. *maggot*: used in the figurative sense of 'a whimsical, eccentric, strange, or perverse notion or idea', now archaic (*OED*).
10. *The party soon assembled round the tempting board*: An echo, perhaps, of the scene at Pemberley when Elizabeth and the Gardiners are invited to meet Miss Darcy 'and the beautiful pyramids of grapes, nectarines, and peaches, soon collected them round the table' (Austen, *Pride and Prejudice*, vol. 3, p. 268).
11. *her walk ... that of* ungain: In the eighteenth and nineteenth centuries, 'ungain' was used as an adjective meaning awkward, clumsy or ungraceful; evidently, it was a family expression since one of the examples cited in the *OED* comes from a letter of Frances Burney, written in 1776.
12. *'a sable silvered'*: The words from *Hamlet*, I.ii.241, quoted for a second time in the novel (see note 28 to Volume II).
13. *I am much afraid you are eating ... they are so much cultivated*: Lady Everard's solicitude for her guests' health is very similar to the feelings of *Emma*'s Mr Wodehouse, which were 'in sad warfare' over the serving of supper: e.g. 'Miss Bates, let Emma help you to a *little* bit of tart – a *very* little bit. Ours are all apple-tarts. You need not be afraid of unwholesome preserves here. I do not advise the custard' (vol. 1, pp. 24–5). On reading Austen's novel, which afforded her 'much amusement', SHB had been struck with the old

man's 'gentle selfishness', and the character of Sir Everard (as well as his lady) seems to owe something to Mr Wodehouse (*Letters*, pp. 199, 201, citing *Emma*, vol. 1, p. 8).

14. *Sancho Panza, when governor of Barataria*: Sancho Panza, the faithful squire of *Don Quixote* (1605) in the work by Spanish novelist Miguel de Cervantes Saavedra (1547–1616), accompanies Quixote on his travels. The duke who entertains them in the second part of the work (1615) as a practical joke appoints Sancho Panza governor of 'the island of Barataria' where he is prevented by a learned doctor from eating any of the sumptuous food for fear of its harmful effect on his constitution. Hungry and dispirited, Sancho Panza resigns after a few days and returns to his master.
15. *calling Ella his little 'Morning Post'*: A London daily newspaper founded in 1772; in 1795, it was acquired by Daniel Stuart (1766–1846), who increased its circulation tenfold and then sold out at a huge profit. Initially mildly Whig in politics, it attracted writers such as Coleridge, Lamb, Southey and Wordsworth to write for it. By 1830, however, it had gone over wholly to the government side, combining 'political conservatism with social snobbery', a stance which lasted until its demise in 1937 (S. Koss, *The Rise and Fall of the Political Press in Britain* (London: Hamish Hamilton, 1981), p. 42). It was, however, one of the first dailies to print regularly notices of plays, operas and concerts.

    Ella being described as the 'Morning Post' calls to mind passages from SHB's letters in which she describes the art of making small-talk out of the items gleaned from the news to try to entertain her ageing invalid father; later she used the same technique to make conversation and practice Italian with an elderly visitor who came to see her in Florence (see *Letters*, pp. 136–7, 155, 178, 383).
16. *the spots they passed ... before he departed for the continent.* Ella's poignant memories of ramblings round the grounds, the 'picturesque hermitage', 'mossy seat' 'rustic bench' and 'little wilderness' evoke Gothic heroines like Emily St Aubert who loved to 'ramble among the scenes of nature' in a similar landscape; she lingered on 'the wild wood-walks ... wrapt in a melancholy charm'. Emily also had a favourite retreat, the 'little fishing-house ... in a woody glen' in which she first became aware of the hero and which was the site of shared memories (Anne Radcliffe, *The Mysteries of Udolpho*, ed. B. Dobrée (Oxford: Oxford University Press, 1998), p. 6.
17. *From women's eyes this doctrine is derived ... Shakspeare*: from Biron's speech in Shakespeare's *Love's Labour's Lost*, IV.iii. In the First Folio (1623) and editions based upon it (such as the Malone edition that SHB owned), the first three lines are ll. 301–3, the second two occur in ll. 311–12. However, later editors took out some twenty lines in the midst of Biron's speech (including these ones) which are otherwise repeated (with slight variation) later on in the same scene (ll. 349–51).
18. *in* etiquette: prescribed formalities, conventional rules or unwritten code, here used (somewhat ironically) in reference to the prescribed behaviour of a heroine of a romance.
19. *Dinners ... seasoned with worse intellectual condiments*: The conversations at dinner-parties are also the occasion of remark in *Emma*, with the same hint of world-weariness: 'everybody else had something to say; everybody was either surprised, or not surprised, and had some question to ask, or some comfort to offer' (vol. 1, p. 126). The sense of social constraint in a woman's life that is epitomized in Austen when Emma watches the vignettes of village life unfold on the main street and is 'amused enough' (vol. 2, p. 233), is voiced also in SHB's fiction.
20. un ami de la maison: a close or intimate friend of the family.

21. *The sight ... caused him to change colour*: Sedley's accident with his horse and the heroine's compassion during his recovery that is witnessed and misinterpreted by an observing hero all recall a similar mishap with the same results occurring to Sedley's namesake in *Camilla*. It is a familiar motif in SHB's work as well; in both *The Renunciation* and *Country Neighbours* (1820), a period of recuperation in the home of the heroine confirms a young man's ardour. The latter tale is an even more apt comparison to *The Hermitage* in that the heroine both witnesses the accident and feels implicated in it, since it is the young man's desire to be with her that has helped precipitate the crisis.
22. *so sweetly mutable, so brightly wild*: from the 'Elegy on the Death of a Lady' (l. 15) by William Mason (1725–97), published in his *Elegies* in 1763. The original line has 'how' twice instead of 'so'. Mason was a friend of Thomas Gray as well as Charles Burney, with whom he shared musical interests.
23. *Regent Street*: In 1839, Regent Street had only just been constructed; designed in 1811 by the architect John Nash (1752–1835), work began after an act of parliament in 1813 and was completed in the 1820s under the auspices of the Prince Regent, later King George IV (1762–1830). The original purpose was to connect Carleton House, where the Prince resided, with Regent's Park; it developed into a major thoroughfare and focus for fashionable shopping in the West End (*ODNB*, under Nash).
24. *Knightsbridge*: Once a village outside London south of Hyde Park, Knightsbridge in the early nineteenth century was still fairly rural and just starting to be developed; the houses were modest and considered rather shabby.
25. *were caught in a hard shower ... paid us a long visit*: The scene has several literary antecedents: in *Evelina* (1778), a shower of rain drives the heroine and her (vulgar) party into a shop, where they appropriate Lord Orville's carriage to convey them home (vol. 2, ch. 23); earlier, the rakish Sir Clement Willoughby had seen them safe home in a coach with less creditable motives (vol. 2, ch. 15). Frederic's chivalry also brings to mind Robert Martin's solicitude for Harriet Smith when she is caught in a shop by a shower of rain in *Emma* (vol. 2, ch. 3).
26. *not to let a girl of Ruth's age be too often thrown in their way*: Ruth's genteel education above her station combined with her extraordinary beauty, which has the effect of making her attractive to her mistress's sons, recalls the situation of Pamela and Mr B. in Samuel Richardson's novel.
27. *"Nothing she does or says ...Too noble for this place"* King Polixenes's description of the princess Perdita in Shakespeare's *The Winter's Tale* (1609), IV.iv.157–8; the passage will be quoted at greater length in the epigraph for Chapter VI (p. 265 below).
28. *If then true lovers ever have been cross'd ... SHAKSPEARE*: The first three lines are taken from Hermione's remarks in the opening scene of *A Midsummer Night's Dream* (1595), I.i.150–2. The fourth line added at the end does not occur in the original.
29. smoothed my rugged brow: a line from Milton's 'Il Ponseroso' (1645), 'Smoothing the rugged brow of Night', (l. 58).
30. *'to the impassive air'*: The line 'To visitation of the impassive air' appears in a translation of the *Divina Commedia* of Dante Alighieri (1265–1321) by the Revd Henry Francis Cary (1772–1844), Assistant Librarian of the British Museum. His translation, entitled *The Vision; or, Hell, Purgatory, and Paradise, of Dante Alighieri*, was published in 1814, with a second edition in 1819 and a third not long before his death in 1844. SHB was so impressed by this work that she wrote to a friend not long before her own death to ask him to purchase a copy for her, printed with the 'Italian on one side, & English on the other' (*Letters*, p. 457). Cary's translation remained standard into the twentieth century

(*ODNB*). The line, cited from the revised edition of 1844 is found in 'Purgatory', Canto 28, l. 110, on p. 302.

31. *This is the prettiest low-born lass ... Shakspeare*: words from IV.iv of Shakespeare's *The Winter's Tale* (1609), referring to the princess Perdita who has been raised incognita as a shepherdess. The first three lines are those of Polixenes, King of Bohemia (ll. 156–8); the next two form part of his servant Camillo's reply (ll. 160–1). The theme of hidden identity and the plot, in which a seemingly low-born lass (whose true gentility is evident) eventually succeeds to her true patrimony and takes her rightful place in society, actually seem more relevant to the first tale of *The Romance of Private Life* than this one.
32. ad interim: from the Latin, meaning 'during the intervening time', 'meanwhile' (*OED*).
33. papillotes: curl-papers; a papillote is 'a small triangular piece of paper used to enclose and hold in place damp hair which has been wound into a curl' (*OED*). A term borrowed from the French, it was used in English from the mid-eighteenth century on.
34. *dressed almost with the plainness of a Quaker*: Members of the Society of Friends emphasized simplicity of life and dressed plainly. See note 80 to Volume I.
35. coup-d'œil: a view or vista, visual effect; also spectacle or panorama. A citation for the latter meaning in *Larousse* comes from Mme de Sévigné, one of SHB's favourite French authors.
36. *mussulman*: the archaic spelling of Muslim.
37. *in the service of a three-tailed Bashaw*: The earlier form of the Turkish title *pasha*, a 'three-tailed bashaw' would be of high rank ('as indicated by the number of horse-tails borne on his standard') (*OED*).
38. *winged genii we read of in the Arabian Nights*: *Les Mille et Une Nuit* created a sensation when it was published in Paris in 12 volumes between 1704 and 1717, translated by orientalist and scholar Antoine Galland. *One Thousand and One Nights* (also known inaccurately as *The Arabian Nights*) contained stories collected over thousands of years, originating in several countries in the ancient Arab world. The first six volumes were translated into English in 1707 by an unknown translator (referred to as 'the Grub Street Translator') as the *Arabian Nights Entertainment*, and this had run through almost twenty editions by 1800. There were other translations of the French edition available in English, like that of Edward Forster published in 5 volumes in 1802 with twenty-four engravings by Robert Smirke. But with the growing interest in orientalism, two new translations directly from the Arabic were currently being published: one by an administrator in India, Henry Whitelock Torrens (1806–52), who brought out volume 1 of *The Book of the Thousand Nights and One Night* in 1838; the other by orientalist Edward William Lane (1801–76), which was in process (*The Thousand and One Nights*, 3 vols, 1839–41). Lane's copious notes, based on extensive travel and research in Egypt, were popular enough to be published on their own; his work remained the leading translation for decades, and was still being reprinted fifty years later.
39. *a lady's writing stand*: a repository for writing materials and letters as well as for writing on; a portable box or case with a sloping surface (*OED*). SHB herself was enthusiastic when presented with such a gift by her brother: 'Judge of little Scribble's rapture!' (*Letters*, p. 14).
40. souvenir d'amitié: a token, momento or keepsake of friendship. Frederic, as the heir presumptive to his uncle's estate, was evidently granted a generous income from it and so was much richer than his sister.
41. *'the fair Maid of Ormond Green'*: Fair maids connected with place names occur in many a title, including a ballad by John Gay, *Molly Mogg, or, The Fair Maid of the Inn* (1726);

a play by Thomas Heywood, *The Fair Maid of the West* (first acted in 1617); and a novel by Sir Walter Scott, *The Fair Maid of Perth* (1828), but perhaps there is no direct literary antecedent. Whatever the origin, the effect of the remark is to cast the fair Ruth in the light of a heroine of a folk-tale, ballad or romance.

42. *"mortal creature of earth's mould"*: Milton's Comus asks 'Can any mortal mixture of Earth's mould / Breathe such Divine enchanting ravishment?' (ll. 244–5). (See also note 44 to Volume I.) The word 'creature' was later juxtaposed with Milton's phrase 'earth's mould' (as it is here by SHB) in a poem by Thomas Moore (1779–1852), *The Loves of the Angels* (1823), 'To living creature of earth's mould', l. 291.
43. *If I'm traduced by tongues ... SHAKESPEARE*: The words are those of Cardinal Wolsey in I.ii.72–6 in *All is True (Henry VIII)* (see note 9 to Volume I). In the original, the 'tongues' are described as 'ignorant'; it is 'the fate of place' rather than 'the common fate' and the phrase 'yet will be / The chronicles of my doing', preceding the words, 'let me say' has been left out here.
44. *'finding out meanings never meant'*: The phrase occurs in a sermon by Vicesimus Knox (1752–1821), 'On the Duties of the Preacher and the Hearer' published in his *Christian Philosophy*, 2 vols (London, 1795), vol. 2, p. 478, which went through several editions in his lifetime, and was also collected into his posthumously published *Works*, 7 vols (1824). Probably part of her 'Sunday reading' of sermons and devotional material, the identical passage is quoted in a letter in 1828 and in another of her novels (*Letters*, pp. 150, 273).
45. *the Edinburgh and Quarterly Reviews*: the influential and rival quarterlies. The *Edinburgh Review*, started in 1802, was given a strong Whig cast by its first editor, Francis Jeffrey (1773–1850), whereas the *Quarterly Review*, begun in 1809 as an antidote and published by John Murray (1778–1843), had a decidedly Tory bent. John Wilson Croker wrote for the latter; he is remembered for his scathing attack on John Keats's *Endymion*, as well as his intemperate reviews of the works of Frances Burney. The Burneys themselves favoured the more literary *Monthly Review* founded by Ralph Griffiths (*c.* 1720–1803). Charles Burney wrote for it and at least one of his daughters contributed to the reviews; a finely bound copy of the complete run was found in his library when he died (*Catalogue*, p. 37).
46. bonhommie: simplicity, guilelessness, simple good-heartedness.
47. *a perfect Zimri: 'Everything by turns, and nothing long'*: Zimri, named after biblical figures, is a character in John Dryden's famous satirical poem *Absalom and Achitophel* (1681), apparently modelled on George Villiers, second Duke of Buckingham (1628–87): 'A man so various, that he seem'd to be / Not one, but all Mankinds Epitome' (ll. 545–6). The phrase quoted here is from line 548, which starts with 'Was'. *Zimri* had other Burney associations, as the title of an oratorio written in 1780 by Charles Burney's friend Dr John Hawkesworth (*c.* 1720–73) and set to music by the blind organist John Stanley (1712–86), whose appointment as Master of the King's Band in 1779 had dashed Charles Burney's hopes for the same position (Scholes, vol. 1, p. 323).
48. *Cowper's Task*: The well-known poem by William Cowper, *The Task* (1785), was a favourite of SHB's; she continued to quote it in her letters fifty years after it was published (see *Letters*, pp. 182, 196, 401).
49. *Is whispering nothing? ... SHAKESPEARE*: the words are those of the jealous King Leontes in *The Winter's Tale* (1609) when he begins to suspect the fidelity of his wife. The epigraph selects just a few phrases scattered throughout his speech in I.ii.286–98.

50. *'such ambiguous givings out'*: Hamlet to Horatio in alerting him to his future strange behaviour (I.v.179).
51. *Take her / This virgin by the hand ... MASSINGER*: from *The Fatal Dowry. A Tragedy*, first acted in 1616 or 1617, of playwright Philip Massinger (1583–1640) in collaboration with Nathan Field (1587–*c.* 1619). Massinger included it in the collection of his plays printed in 1632 and it later inspired Nicholas Rowe's *The Fair Penitent* (1703). The words of the epigraph are spoken by Rochfort giving away his daughter to Charalois (II.ii.301–4). SHB leaves out the words 'bless me so' before 'Requite me thus' and the original reads 'happier' not 'happy'. The phrase 'take this virgin by the hand' seems to have passed into the language and, curiously enough, was quoted by SHB's uncle Arthur Young in a treatise on politics.
52. *'Is thy servant a dog, that he should do this thing?'*: Hazael responds in these words to the prophet Elijah who has foretold the evils that Hazael will perpetrate on the children of Israel, slaughtering men, women and children. Despite Hazael's denial, the prophet's predictions would eventually come to pass (2 Kings 8:13).
53. *Of real pity ... it is twice blessed*: probably a reference to the famous description of mercy in Shakespeare's *The Merchant of Venice* (1596–7): 'It is twice blest: It blesseth him that gives, and him that takes' (IV.i.183–4).
54. *"pensive nun"*: a phrase from Milton's 'Il Ponseroso', l. 31.
55. *E l'aspettar ... TASSO, GERUSALEMME*: The epigraph is taken from the epic of Italian poet Torquato Tasso (1544–95), *Gerusalemme liberata* (1580), concerning the First Crusade and the capture of the holy city. The first two lines quoted are those of Canto I, stanza 82, ll. 649–50; the last two appear in Canto IV, stanza 65, ll. 513–14. SHB had encountered Tasso's poetry with her Italian tutor in 1805 when she spoke of her enjoyment of *Aminta* (1573) (*Letters*, p. 66). Later, she spent the long, lonely winters in Florence (between 1830 and 1833) reading the Italian classics.

    The English version below is taken from the popular translation by John Hoole, *Jerusalem Delivered*, 3rd edn, 2 vols (London, 1767), a copy of which was owned by Charles Burney (*Catalogue*, p. 52):

    More dreadful to their anxious mind appears
    The distant prospect, and augments their fears:
    ...
    At this unwelcome speech the damsel turn'd
    Her eyes awhile to earth, and silent mourn'd;
56. "*most sweet voices*": words used by the titular hero of Shakespeare's *The Tragedy of Coriolanus* (1608) to describe the citizens' voices raised in his support (II.iii.112).
57. *'hating the crime, yet pitying the criminal'*: An idea originating with Seneca (*c.* 4 BC–AD 65), Stoic philosopher and dramatist; his essay 'Of Anger' appears in a work owned by Charles Burney (*Catalogue*, p. 51), *Seneca's Morals by way of Abstract*, edited by Sir Roger l'Estrange, the twelfth edition of which was published in London in 1722. Seneca suggests that, in sentencing a criminal, a dignified judge 'condemns the Vice, not the Man; and looks upon the Wickedness without Anger' (p. 307). His views were influential on St Augustine (AD 354–430), who Christianized the thought; the paradoxical ideal of forgiveness, 'hating the sin yet loving the sinner', was frequently expounded in devotional literature throughout the period. An adaptation of Seneca's thought was eloquently expressed by Pierre Corneille in (1606–84) in *Le Cid* (1637) in which Chimène faces a moral dilemma: 'Et que puis-je esperer qu'un tourment eternel / Si je poursuis un crime aimant le criminel?' The last line could be translated idiomatically as 'If I hate the crime,

but love the criminal' which is close to SHB's formulation. This sympathy was famously denounced by Samuel Johnson in *The Rambler*, 60 (13 October 1750), citing the remarks of another, 'Let me remember ... when I find myself inclined to pity a criminal, that there is likewise a pity due to the country'.

58. *"defiled with blood"*: a biblical phrase, it occurs in Isaiah 59:3: 'For your hands are defiled with blood, and your fingers with iniquity'.
59. 'Thou shalt do no murder': from the Ten Commandments given by God to Moses on Mount Sinai (Exodus 20:3–17). The sixth of these 'Thou shalt not kill' is pronounced in the thirteenth verse.
60. *Pardon me for intruding ... heaven preserve and bless you*: Ernest's letter starts and ends in much the same way as Darcy's letter in *Pride and Prejudice*: 'You must therefore, pardon the freedom with which I demand your attention ... I will only add, God bless you' (vol. 2, pp. 195–203).
61. *Caquet bon bec ... La Fontaine*: from one of the Fables of Jean de la Fontaine (1621–95), 'L'Aigle et la Pie' or 'The Eagle and the Magpie', Fable xi in Book XII, published in 1694. The twelfth line, first half of the thirteenth and fourteenth and last part of the seventeenth lines are put together here to form the epigraph. A versified translation of the lines selected reads:

    At once Miss Chatterbox began to gabble
    At such a rate ... with [her] miscellaneous babble ...
    By [hopping] round from spot to spot.
    La Fontaine's Fables, trans. E. Marsh (London: William Heinemann, 1933), p. 44.

62. que ce n'est que le premier pas qui coute: translated idiomatically, 'that the first step is the hardest'. The famous 'bon mot' of Marie née de Vichy-Chamrond, the Marquise du Deffand (1697–1780), on the legendary walk of the decapitated St Denis. SHB quotes the same witticism in her letters in which she also mentions the *Letters of the Marquise du Deffand to the Hon. Horace Walpole* (1810) which includes the anecdote (*Letters*, pp. 149, 375, and nn.).
63. *'more in sorrow than in anger'*: Horatio's words on describing the countenance of the Ghost in *Hamlet*, I.ii.228–9.
64. mariage de convenance: 'A marriage arranged or contracted from motives of convenience, mutual advantage, or expediency' as opposed to a marriage of inclination or a love-match (*OED*).
65. *Her list of nephews and nieces ... was interminable*: The hint for this character may have come from a fellow inmate of SHB's boarding-house in Bath, described in similar terms in her letters: 'Miss Purefoy, a merry Irish girl, with a large Bath acquaintance ... who is out almost every night amongst cousins, and aunts, and Mrs This or Miss That "The sweetest creatures in the world"' (*Letters*, pp. 387–8).
66. *"There is no speculation in those eyes"*: the line in which Macbeth addresses Banquo's ghost, in *Macbeth*, III.iv.93, begins, 'Thou hast' rather than 'There is'.
67. *he is the Cœlebs I purpose introducing to our Cœlibia*: evoking the novel by Hannah More (1745–1833), *Coelebs in Search of a Wife* (1809), the remark implies that both parties are seeking a mate and may find it in each other.
68. *It is not in the nature of things ... converse sensibly or amusingly*: In her persistent silliness, Miss Flemming seems to owe something to Austen's Miss Bates, who would find it hard to restrict herself to saying only three dull things at a time (*Emma*, vol. 3, p. 370).
69. *You bear a gentle mind, and woman's heart ... Shakespeare*: Another epigraph taken from Shakespeare's and Fletcher's *Henry VIII*, this one is constructed from several

speeches in II.iii. The Old Lady tells Anne Boleyn that she has 'a woman's heart' (l. 28); the 'sooth' is also hers (l. 30), as are the next two lines quoted here (though she actually says 'a young Count' not 'wooer' in ll. 41–2) but the words 'You bear a gentle mind' are spoken by the Lord Chamberlain (l. 57).

70. *Shrewsbury cakes*: Named for the county town of Shropshire, a Shrewsbury cake (a compound of butter, sugar, eggs and flour) was a flat round biscuit-like cake, noted for its crispness (*OED*). Congreve had used its well-known properties as a metaphor in *The Way of the World* (1690): 'as short as a Shrewsbury cake' (III.i.532).
71. *you know the old joke ... a fool at the other!*: A joke often attributed to Samuel Johnson although it has not been traced to his writings or recorded sayings. The earliest known attribution to Johnson was by Lt-Col. Peter Hawker (1786–1853), a keen sportsman who published *Instructions to Young Sportsmen*, a popular book which first appeared in 1814 and had gone through several editions by 1839. He cites the remark as an instance of Johnson's 'contempt' for fishing (5th edn (London, 1826), p. 172). The same witticism has also been quoted as Jonathan Swift's, for instance in the *Monthly Review*, 46 (1805), p. 443 (in a review of 'The Angler; a Didactic Poem', by Charles Clifford). An earlier reference than both of these is that of Sir Thomas Frankland, *Cautions to Young Sportsmen* (1800), who retails the joke but attributes it simply to 'some ... wag friends' (2nd edn (London, 1801), p. 10). (For this information, I am indebted to the general editor of the Boswell Project, Gordon Turnbull.)
72. *civil dumby*: a variant spelling for 'dummy', a dumb person or a deaf-mute that later acquired a pejorative connotation.
73. *'gentle dullness ever loves a joke'*: a quote from Pope's *Dunciad*, Book II, l. 34.
74. lady's man: a man who pays court to the ladies; the term was used in the late eighteenth century and gradually replaced the word 'gallant' over the next hundred years (*OED*).
75. 'C'est une maîtresse femme!': a capable and managing woman; it could also imply one who is domineering and strong-willed (*OED*).
76. *Her walk had given bloom to her cheeks ... they had almost ceased to possess*: Anne Elliot's walk on the beach in *Persuasion* also restored 'the bloom and freshness of youth' to her complexion and brightened the 'animation of eye'; the restoration of her pretty looks attracts an unworthy cousin whom she resists in favour of her soul-mate, a young man she has known and loved in her younger years. The situational resemblances here to Austen's novel are strong; this particular scene has already been evoked elsewhere in this work (though not in this tale; see note 98 to Volume II).
77. *Un homme de moyen âge ... La Fontaine*: The epigraph splices together two fables of La Fontaine, whose poetic adaptations of the form helped start a vogue in England. Here, the first four lines of 'L'Homme Entre Deux Ages, et Ses Deux Maitresses', Book I (1668), Fable xvii, are juxtaposed with the opening of 'Le Loup et le Chasseur', Book VIII (1678), Fable xxvii, ll. 1–2, 5–6. In Marsh's translation (see note 61 above), 'The Middle-Aged Man and his Two Mistresses' (p. 24) opens:

    A Man in middle life
    Noticed his hair was greying:
    'Twas time, beyond gainsaying,
    He thought about a wife.

    The lines selected from 'The Wolf and the Sportsman' (p. 281) have been translated (with some liberties) into English verse as:

    Thou Fiend accurst, insensate Greed of Gain,
    T'whom all Heav'n's bounty seems but little worth,

> …
> Man heeds not me …
> Who bid him pause t'enjoy what he has won.

78. *Question him as you list* … A TRAGI-COMEDY. The source of these verses has not been found and it seems possible (an idea first suggested by Carolyn D. Williams of the University of Reading) that SHB wrote them herself. There are several points that could support this thesis. First, there is the style, which does not match that of any known writer of tragi-comedies nor inspire confidence in the play that would result (nor the likelihood of its being staged). Second, there is the peculiar aptness of the epigraph to the narrative, a fit which seems almost tailor-made, unlike many of the others. Even more revealing is the fact that three lengthy epigraphs in a row purport to be from the same source, which is unusual and departs from the author's practice up until now; each motto has heretofore been carefully constructed from snippets of lines and even phrases chosen from various sources. The pressure of trying to bring the narrative to an end and the need to find apt quotations whose supply may have dried up might suggest this creative option as a possible solution.

    An alternative is that SHB may herself have written a tragedy in verse (she did write poetry; see *Letters*, pp. 487–8) and drew from an unknown work of hers in manuscript which has not survived. For both hypotheses, the title 'Not so Old as it Seems' ('A Tragi-comedy' implying an earlier period) would then be a sort of private joke.
79. *"fancy free"*: the words of Oberon in *A Midsummer Night's Dream*, II.i.164: 'In maiden meditation, fancy-free'.
80. *'eyed him askance'*: Another Miltonic echo, this time from *Paradise Lost* (1667); citing from the revised and expanded edition of 1674, the phrase comes in Book IV, l. 504, 'Ey'd them askance'.
81. *it was if a Gorgon's head had suddenly appeared before him*: In Greek mythology, the Gorgon were monstrous creatures. The three sisters (of whom the best known is Medusa) had bodies covered with scales, hands of brass, teeth like tusks and hair entwined with snakes; their appearance was enough to turn all who gazed on them into stone.
82. *The pangs at this sad heart … A TRAGI COMEDY*: see note 78 above.
83. *like another Cain … upon my burning brow*: In the biblical story, after Cain had murdered his brother Abel, the Lord decreed that he should be 'a fugitive and a vagabond' on the earth but set a mark upon him, 'lest any finding him should kill him' and earn vengeance sevenfold (Genesis 4:8–15).
84. *What tho' the offer's clogg'd … A TRAGI-COMEDY*: see note 78 above.
85. *'assume a virtue if she had it not'*: Hamlet's bitter words to Queen Gertrude in III.iv.151. Hamlet, of course, used the pronoun 'you' rather than 'she'.

SILENT CORRECTIONS

Substantive Corrections

5 Before long] Before lon
17 insolences.] insolenccs.
32 attempts should] attempts shonld
45 had volunteered] had voluntered
54 almost quarrelled] almost quarelled
54 deficiencies,] deficiences,
76 with the kindest] with the kindnest
104 the slightest] the slighest
114 accompanied by] accompained by
115 what had occurred] what had occured
125 those who have] those who who have
131 what you were] what you where
134 adored him for] adored him him for
139 retained a beautiful] retained a beauful
147 she found] she fonnd
151 his behaviour] his behavour
161 loud voices] loud voice
163 did not immediately] did not immemediately
166 of my behaviour] of my behavour
166 might betray the] might betra they
191 wherever] whereever
198 he had begun] he had began
217 neither presumptuous,] neither presumptious,
223 upon the satisfaction] upon the astisfaction
228 'I am of the opinion] 'I am opinion
235 '*by the world forgot*'] '*by the world forget.*'
253 any objection, Miss] any objection, Mis
255 remain where] remain were
270 unsheathing] unsheating
286 deadly pale] dealdy pale,
289 she was rung for] she was rang for
299 raised their heads] raised their head
310 recall the past,] recal the past,

315 thrill of uncontrollable] thrill of uncontrolable
327 I would not be a wooer] I would not be a woer
329 you are of opinion] your are of opinion
331 standing on end] standing an end

Corrections to Punctuation

40 I expected.'] I expected.
48 her country.] her country.'
59 more; and] more; 'and
62 Mrs. Marchmont during] 'Mrs. Marchmont during
64 helpless state?"'] helpless state?'
64 poor man, and] poor man,and
74 smiling. 'But] smiling. But
75 Young ladies,' she] Young ladies, 'she
88 enquired Agnes.] enquired Agnes,
100 shoulders. 'Young] shoulders. Young
108 unmolested? Write to] unmolested? 'Write to
141 young gallant?'] young gallant?
143 (though no chicken!)] (though no chicken !)
144 tolerable order;] tolerable order,
145 this place?'] this place?
145 do not know,'] do not know;'
146 in their boxes.'] in their boxes.
150 in England, then?] in England, then?'
163 Mr. St. Hubert, 'neither] Mr. St. Hubert,' neither
163 friends in Florence?'] friends in Florence!'
170 high degree of civilization] highdegreeofcivilization
187 "cupid's bow"?] "cupid's bow?"
190 *the setting sun*'?] *the setting sun*?'
193 '"Oh no, ma'am,'] 'Oh no, ma'am,'
193 Now, you must know,'] 'Now, you must know,'
218 upon with them.] upon with them,
235 'Humph!' ejaculated he] 'Humph! ejaculated he
238 said Mrs. Fitzmaurice,] said Mrs. Fitzmaurice,'
244 and kindly said,] and kindly said
252 undergone;] undergone ;
257 "Nothing she does] Nothing she does
257 for this place."'] for this place.'
262 cried he, amused] cried he,' amused
266 the sweetness] thesweetness
267 pure lustre] purelustre
272 "a particular reason"?] "a particular reason?"
275 she felt] shefelt
277 the conversation] theconversation
285 Poor fellow,' she] 'Poor fellow,' she
292 wet with tears,] wet with tears;
305 By making him,'] 'By making him,'

307 “most sweet voices”?’] “most sweet voices?”’
325 Mr. Fitzmaurice’] Mr. Fitzmaurice
335 originality nor spirit.] originality nor spirit.’
346 thing in the world.’] thing in the world,’
356 the next morning] the nextmorning
360 Mr. de Gray, much] Mr. de Gray,much

Hyphenated Forms at Line-ends

This table is a list of hyphenated forms that in the original text broke over the line, but which do not do so in this edition. Given below is the form chosen in this edition and the original break. Note that the ‘/’ symbol indicates a line break, and not necessarily a page break (though both may be true, in some cases).

5 experiencing whenever] experiencing when-/ever
6 turned-up nose] turned-/up nose
7 maid, who whatever] maid, who what-/ever
10 right-minded people.] right-/minded people.
11 his pocket-book] his pocket-/book
14 tax upon her good-nature] tax upon her good-/nature
17 canaries, goldfinches] canaries, gold-/finches
19 more long-sighted] more long-/sighted
25 adjoining bed-chamber] adjoining bed-/chamber
29 dressing-room, bed-chamber] dressing-/room, bed-chamber
41 was overcome] was over-/come
41 only a twelve-month] only a twelve-/month
42 enlarge her understanding] enlarge her under-/standing
43 somewhat] some-/what
53 remarkable for self-possession] remarkable for self-/possession
54 they were whenever] they were when-/ever
55 was overlooked] was over-/looked
59 the sister-in-law, it must] the sister-/in-law, it must
64 the small picture-room] the small picture-/room
64 portable fire-engines,] portable fire-/engines,
65 important undertaking,] important under-/taking,
79 the half-smiling] the half-/smiling
86 how her good-nature] how her good-/nature
94 hard-earned] hard-/earned
95 bricklayer’s] brick-/layer’s
101 young Frenchman] young French-/man
108 steps homewards] steps home-/wards
109 hereafter] here-/after
113 peut-être] peut-/être
121 petty shop-keepers] petty shop-/keepers
130 gentleman-like address] gentleman-/like address
131 resumed her Ladyship] resumed her Lady-/ship
131 selfish outcries] selfish out-/cries

134 finely-shaped] finely-/shaped
138 female fellow-travellers] female fellow-/travellers
144 head-dress] head-/dress
149 baiting-place] baiting-/place
151 good-humour] good-/humour
153 outline, at length] out-/line, at length
154 friends and well-wishers] friends and well-/wishers
160 for form-sake] for form-/sake
161 magnificent drawing-room] magnificent drawing-/room
161 ill-pronounced] ill-/pronounced
162 son-in-law] son-in-/law
163 boarding-house] boarding-/house
167 newly-acquired] newly-/acquired
169 gloomy forebodings] gloomy fore-/bodings
173 over-matches] over-/matches
173 womanhood] woman-/hood
180 and well-born] and well-/born
186 *well-spelt*] *well-/spelt*
186 undertook] under-/took
189 overcame her good] over-/came her good
190 cross-light] cross-/light
190 speechless] speech-/less
191 wherever] where-/ever
206 bride and bridegroom] bride and bride-/groom
209 new-born hope] new-/born hope
218 a little ill-humour] a little ill-/humour
228 good-natured speech] good-/natured speech
231 raven-/black hair] raven-/black hair
235 bring the newcomers] bring the new-/comers
237 native clear-headedness] native clear-/headedness
253 a small farmhouse] a small farm-/house,
260 whist-table] whist-/table
262 overbearing haughtiness] over-/bearing haughtiness
265 towards the courtyard] towards the court-/yard
268 heard re-echoing] heard re-/echoing
269 shaving-glasses] shaving-glasses,
269 needle-books] needle-/books
279 till dinner-time] till dinner-/time
283 country-town] country-/town
285 walking to overtake] walking to over-/take
286 one heart-broken] one heart-/broken
291 of his horror-struck] of his horror-/struck
292 by her bedside] by her bed-/side
294 her broken-hearted] her broken-/hearted
300 and narrow-minded] and narrow-/minded
302 by his bedside] by his bed-/side
308 companion and playmate] companion and play-/mate
311 drawing-room fire] drawing-/room fire

313 in her dressing-room] in her dressing-/room
314 heart-bursting sobs] heart-/bursting sobs
321 half-past nine] half-/past nine
321 she is well-principled] she is well-/principled
325 interrogated her brother-in-law] interrogated her brother-/in-law
327 straight-forward, or at] straight-/forward, or at
328 difficulty to forbear] difficulty to for-/bear
335 matter-of-fact book.] matter-/of-fact book.
336 to cross-question] to cross-/question
339 in that neighbourhood] in that neighbour-/hood
342 had been uppermost] had been upper-/most
346 man on horseback] man on horse-/back
359 from the landing-place] from the landing-/place
362 my broken-hearted aunt] my broken-/hearted aunt
367 bride and bridegroom] bride and bride-/groom

For Product Safety Concerns and Information please contact our EU
representative GPSR@taylorandfrancis.com
Taylor & Francis Verlag GmbH, Kaufingerstraße 24, 80331 München, Germany

www.ingramcontent.com/pod-product-compliance
Lightning Source LLC
Chambersburg PA
CBHW070931100726
47908CB00001B/175

* 9 7 8 1 1 3 8 2 3 5 9 5 3 *